PLAYER MANAGER

PLAYER MANAGER

TED STEEL

Podium

To my beautiful wife, Loretta.
Watching you try to explain the concept of this book to your dad
will always remain one of the highlights of my life.

Cover design by Damonza

ISBN: 978-1-0394-3839-2

Published in 2023 by Podium Publishing, ULC
www.podiumaudio.com

Podium

PLAYER
MANAGER

PRE-SEASON

A MATTER OF LIFE AND DEATH

"Football's not a matter of life and death.
It's much more important than that." —Bill Shankly

I locked my front door and waved at the surveillance camera across the road. It had been installed when the police suspected a former tenant of selling speed. I guess they were right, because there were a couple of bullet holes in the brickwork. I lived there now, and I didn't deal, but the camera stayed, as did the holes.

I set off with a click of my earbuds, trying to unpause a podcast: *Softly Spoken Soccer.* The play button was stuck. It took three tries to get it to obey me. Flea market crap.

Don't worry if you don't follow all the jargon that follows. The incomprehensibility is the point.

Podcaster 1: *What Zinchenko offers is more than just a flat 3 or a wing back. He can invert, he's quality in the half-spaces. I'd feel fine with him as a 6, he's so press-resistant, or even as a left 8.*

Podcaster 2: *That's right. He has good comps with half the team. He's going to be the technical leader, mark my words.*

Podcaster 1: *His pass maps show his range and verticality on the ball and his heat maps show his workrate. He's a pressing machine. Last season, we had our fingers crossed that Tierney wouldn't get injured. But Zinchenko beats him on almost all metrics.*

Podcaster 2: *Tierney can't invert.*

I clicked pause, shaking my head. I understood *most* of what they were saying. I'd been kicking balls before I could even toddle, and I'd watched thousands of games. But in the last couple of years, the level of technical analysis had gone wild. Even normal fans were talking about abstract topics like xG (expected goals), bickering about whether Big Chances Created was really a better "metric" than assists, and were WhatsApping spidergraphs of a transfer target's "defensive actions."

It was all a bit much.

I wouldn't say the data and analysis was sucking all the fun out of the game, but it was a long way from the stories I grew up on. Arsenal once signed a player called John Jensen because he scored a wondergoal to win Euro '92. He then played ninety-nine times for Arsenal, scoring exactly once. Not quite the free-scoring midfielder they'd seen on TV. Or take the case of Ali Dia—a player no better than you or me—who played half an hour of Premier League football after pranking his way into the Southampton team. These stories wouldn't happen today; the spidergraph would show that John Jensen was no goal threat, and that Ali Dia had literally zero to offer.

So yeah, football seemed to be getting a bit like a giant database where every data point for every player was known.

And don't get me started on tactics. I'd watch a match and then hear people talk about incredible tactical tweaks that the managers had made. Um, excuse me? When was that? I just couldn't see it! Sometimes I'd pause a match and see that both sets of players were in very precise formations. But I couldn't do anything with that info. I mean, sometimes, the worst teams looked exactly the same in the freeze-frames as the best teams.

I didn't get it.

But what was I supposed to do instead? Become a politics fan? Join a book club? There are no book clubs in my part of Manchester. It's what's known locally as "rough."

Talking of which . . .

I was passing through this little park. Sometimes I avoided it because it was always full of bored teens looking for trouble, but recently I'd been trying to make myself go there. Why should I be afraid? I mean, I *was* afraid, but I wanted to be less afraid. Know what I mean?

Anyway, the teenagers mostly played football or basketball or listened to their shitty music. I felt their eyes on me sometimes, wondering if it'd be fun to mug me. Or maybe that was just in my imagination.

Maybe not, because today something was different. The kids had put down some jumpers and bags to make goalposts, and they were sort of milling around like there was a game going on. But there wasn't a game going on, and that was bad news for the poor, innocent fish-out-of-water guy who just happened to enter their park at the wrong time.

Strange thing was, the fish out of water wasn't me.

There was a very tall, very thin man pushing a bike. He was wearing a black suit, his socks were too long, and he had a real old-fashioned hat on. A few of the teens were moving towards him. They blocked his path, and one took hold of the handlebars. This was going to get messy.

I caught up with them in a few strides.

"Jack!" I said, as though delighted to see an old friend. "What are you doing here? I thought you were on holiday."

The old man scanned me—his eyes were wrinkled but there was a quick mind in there—and grinned. "Sigmund!" he said. "Ah, well, the voyage was cancelled. How've you been?"

I took the handlebars from a slightly confused teen, and started pushing. He offered no resistance. "Fine, fine. Remember you told me about that book? *Foucault's Pendulum*? Absolute piece of shit. Now, be serious. You didn't actually like that. You didn't *actually* read it."

We were walking away, and the kids were letting us. Suddenly, a ball fell from a tree, followed by a kid. And the match resumed.

We kept talking shit until we left the park. "I'm going to ASDA," I said. "What about you?"

"That's a supermarket, is it? Yes, I can go there with you."

I checked his hands to see if they were shaking. He seemed completely unaffected by the incident. Me? My heart was pumping. Veins full of adrenaline. Perhaps he wasn't as smart as I'd thought. Perhaps he was, in fact, too stupid to realise he had just been in danger. As I thought that, he looked at me with an amused twinkle in his eye. "Thank you for helping me. That was very . . . kind of you."

I don't know why, but I felt a chill down my spine. Just for a second, it seemed like the oldster was disappointed. That he'd wanted to get beaten up! The moment passed; I mean, the whole notion was absurd. "Yeah, no problem. My real name's Max, by the way."

I looked down at the bike I was pushing. It was extremely heavy. Weird shape. It took me a while to work out what was bothering me about it, but it boiled down to one thing—there were no plastic parts. Drawing my attention was a gleaming copper bell. I resisted a childish urge to ring it.

"Sigmund suits you better."

"Those kids are going to be calling me Sigmund all the time now. It's no way to reward me!"

He shot me another look. Did I detect a smirk? An eyebrow trembling with amusement? "You were much closer with your guess. I'm Nick." We shook hands. "Do you like soccer, Max?"

"Yep."

"I saw the way you changed when that ball fell from the tree. You reminded me of a dog. You wanted to run and catch it."

I laughed. "I suppose. I do have a weird fantasy every time I walk past a game like that, that they'll shout 'hey, do you want to play?' and I answer, 'who, me?' and then slip into midfield and sort of get all Barenboim."

"Barenboim is a famous soccer player?"

"No, he's a conductor."

"Ah! I see. Yes, I see. Would you like to be a famous player, then? Or a famous conductor?"

I considered that. The shop was just ahead. About three minutes walk. Here was this old man I'd never see again. Why shouldn't I tell him what was really on my mind? "Not a conductor, no. And I don't need to be famous. Player? Maybe. Probably not. I'm not that good, not even close, and I'm not that competitive. I want to win but not like those elite guys. But you know what I've been thinking recently? These top managers like Guardiola and Klopp. They just see football in a totally different way to me. Like literally, we're watching two different things. It's kind of amazing. I think I'd like to be able to see the game the way they do."

As if responding to the same signal, we stopped walking at the exact same second. He gave me another odd look, then a crooked smile. "That's very self-aware of you. Very interesting. I've never heard that before. It's been a long time since I heard *anything* like that."

His intensity was starting to creep me out, but we started walking again and I had to balance the bike, so I didn't have time to dwell on it.

Nick lowered his head while thinking and then said, "Would you sell your soul to be a top football manager?"

I laughed. This guy was nuts. "No. What? It's just weird that I've got this hobby and spend so much time on it, and I'm really not making any progress. I'm falling behind, in fact. But it doesn't matter. It's not important."

He nodded. "I think my use of language has created a little gap between us. I'm not from this country, you know."

I wouldn't have guessed. He had zero accent. Maybe he was one of those Polish plumbers who'd come over.

"I think what I'm trying to say is . . ." He took out an absolutely beautiful pocket watch and stared at it. He adjusted the crown, smiled, then dipped it back into his jacket, chain and all. "I have it. Would you *wish* to see football the way those people see it?"

"Sure," I said.

"Say it in a complete sentence."

More than happy to help a foreigner improve his English, I said, "I wish I could see football like a top manager sees it."

"Good. Now ring the bell three times."

The guy was bonkers! But we were mere steps from the entrance now. I reached over and rang the bell. Bring! Bring! Bring!

"Superb," he said. "Yes, that's most excellent." He chuckled. It didn't sound right, coming from that face. But his face now was different to when I first met him just minutes before. Wasn't it? More angular? Fewer liver spots? Whatever it was, he was now handsome. Devilishly handsome.

He reached into his pocket and pulled out a wallet. "You are purchasing some needful things, are you? Would you mind buying some headache tablets?"

He took the bike from me. I frowned. "You're going to wait here? I mean, I won't be that long, but . . ."

"Take as long as you want. Voila." He handed me a hundred pound note. I didn't think we had those anymore, but on closer inspection it was Scottish. Who knows what they get up to north of the border.

"Oh," I said. I could already imagine the stress of trying to use this at the checkout. In theory it was legal tender across the UK. But in practice . . . Whatever. I took it and went inside.

The paracetamol was less than a pound, so I bought it with my own money, along with some toilet roll, a Pot Noodle, milk, and milk chocolate Hobnobs. When I returned to give him his tablets and his weird money, the guy had vanished.

ASDA has a security guard. He told me the old man had ridden away as soon as I'd gone inside. Fucking mad old coot.

I made my way home through the park. I should have gone around it. I didn't want to see those kids for a few days. I wanted them to forget we'd ever interacted.

But I was feeling a bit odd. Not sick or anything, just weird. Like my nerves were too long for my skin. My hands felt swollen and heavy. My throat was dry. Nothing serious. Just weird. Just a bit off.

Fortunately, the game was in full flow so the lads wouldn't have any need to harass me. I kept my head down as I went past. But then a movement twenty yards away caught my eye, a guy doing a dribble past his opponent. I couldn't help but look at it.

What I saw made me throw my hands in front of my face. I stepped backwards, away from the danger. I stumbled, and kept stumbling until my foot caught on a tree root. I fell. The kids laughed their heads off, but I remained still.

My breaths were coming thick and fast. I closed my eyes, counted to ten, and opened them again. When I looked at the tree, everything was normal. There was nothing wrong with my eyes. I turned, gingerly, to my left and saw a bin. All good. But when I lifted my head up and looked at the kids, the bizarre addition to my vision was still there.

Numbers.

I looked away—just a normal day in red-brick Manchester. I looked back at the kids.

Numbers.

Take the one nearest to me—still laughing, by the way. He was wearing a Man City kit, which marked him out as a grade A idiot of the highest order. When I let my eyes settle on him, numbers appeared above his head. They were laid out like a database, though many of the cells were empty.

STEVEN McGOUGH		
Born 4.4.2005	(Age 17)	English/Irish
Acceleration 5		
		Stamina 1
	Heading 4	Strength 2
		Tackling 4
	Jumping 2	
Bravery 11		Technique 1
	Pace 5	preferred foot R
	Passing 1	
Dribbling 2		
Defender (Centre)		

Staring at any of the other players had the same effect. It was terrifying. I lay back down and put my hands over my face.

Eventually, one of the kids came over and asked if I was all right. I said I wasn't. He offered to call me an "ambo." I said I'd just take it easy and make my way home in a bit. He said that wasn't an option, because I was ruining the game by dying next to the pitch. He grabbed my arm, pulled me up, and helped me walk home.

I don't remember saying anything. I have a vague memory of the guy being chatty. Trying to keep me from going unconscious or whatever. Then I have a really specific memory of him saying, "Mate, you've got bullet holes in your house."

"That was my ex-wife," I said.

He snorted. "All right, Sigfried. I've took you home like a bodyguard. You gonna give me half those Hobnobs?"

It was like he was at the top of a well, and I was stuck down at the bottom. He seemed distant. Echoey. "Sorry," I said. "I need them."

"So I don't get nothing? Man. Mum always says no good deed goes unpunished." He gave me an uncertain look. "Serious, though. I could call someone."

"Ugh," I said, and closed the door on him. I stumbled to the kitchen and took two paracetamol. I didn't even try to go upstairs.

DEVILISHLY SOGGY

I work in a call centre doing customer service. I make 350 pounds a week, and spend 200 just on rent. My house is a narrow shithole in a place with such a violent history that the BBC refers to it as "the notorious Moss Side area of Manchester." You know, when they're announcing a shooting or whatever. It's pretty much the only area where I can afford to rent a house on my own.

I overslept, but when I finally did wake up, I felt fine. Not groggy, no hangover.

I decided to turn up for work after lunch. My boss asked me why I was late, and I blagged it. "I told you I'd be at the doctor, remember?"

She didn't remember, but I was the employee with the best stats, and call centres are all about stats. Also, I didn't usually take the piss. When I called in sick, I was sick. When I said I was late because the bus crashed, I showed her a selfie of me and the bus deep in conversation with a lamppost. She pursed her lips and suggested that maybe next time I could put my doctor's appointment in writing. *Absolutely, my dear,* I thought. *Next time I have an out-of-body experience, I'll let you know in advance.*

I stayed late to make up the hours and also because, for once, the job felt good. It was normal, you know? Our customers always had the same problems, so most of the time the work was pretty mindless. Solve the problem, end the call. Solve the problem, end the call. My stats were great.

I left work feeling better. Whatever had happened the night before hadn't happened since. I'd gone past thousands and thousands of people and not seen any numbers. I'd even seen a group of lads in their kit on the way to have a kickabout. Nothing.

I was looking forward to getting home, making a tea, and dunking those chocolate Hobnobs until they got devilishly soggy. I hopped onto the bus, went upstairs, and peered out of the window. Curry place, second-hand shop, terraced houses. Red bricks, modern Tescos, student flats. The same things I'd been seeing day in, day out since I left 6th form. The big park.

Wait, what? I stormed downstairs, but too late. I'd fallen asleep or something and missed my stop. I wasn't, like, in South Manchester or anything, but it was still annoying. I could get a bus back a couple of stops or walk a little extra. It was a nice evening. Easy decision.

Platt Fields is pretty famous in Manchester. It's a huge park named after Platt Lane, a nearby road. It's not that far from Maine Road, where Manchester City's ground used to be. If you haven't heard of Manchester City, they're quite well known in the area. There's a decent sports complex on Platt Lane that City's academy used to use.

My feet were operating with a mind of their own. I was halfway through Platt Fields, heading towards Platt Lane where I knew there'd be some football going on. I grunted and turned myself north, to where my house was. But then again, I couldn't avoid football for the rest of my life, could I? If I saw a football match and there were no numbers, then last night had simply been a hallucination.

I turned again, and ambled towards the all-weather football pitches. I heard a referee's whistle, and all the hairs on my neck stood on end. I took a deep breath, and walked faster. *Let's get this over with . . .*

CONRAD ETUHU		
Born 28.9.1999	(Age 23)	Nigerian/English
Acceleration 4		
		Stamina 1
	Heading 2	Strength 2
		Tackling 2
	Jumping 5	
Bravery 7		Technique 1
	Pace 4	preferred foot R
	Passing 1	
Dribbling 1		
Midfielder (Right)		

I stood, stock still, on the sideline, trying not to have a complete freakout. The numbers hovered over every player. It was like one of those augmented reality apps that took what your phone's camera was seeing and added monsters or balloons or whatever. In this case it was showing me the attributes of people playing football. Including their names, nationalities, and birthdays! What the actual fuck?

The longer I stayed there watching the game, the more I calmed down. Yes, this was insane. Yes, this was an identity thief's dream come true. And yes, maybe that crazy old guy had used advanced hypnosis techniques on me. After all, he did look a bit like Derren Brown. Maybe he'd injected me with nanobots that were hijacking my brain. Or potentially, that Scottish money carried a curse. Like an actual curse. Isn't that what *Macbeth* is about? Witches and curses and everything?

But . . .

But it wasn't hurting me. I looked around, and nobody was re-acting to me at all. If my eyes were turning pure black or some oth-er weird side effect every time I "scanned" a player, surely someone would have asked me to stop.

So . . . I could see the attributes of these football players.

So what?

I did a very slow 360, taking in the scene around me before focus-ing on the football again. Basically, everything else was normal. Total-ly normal. Yes, I'd see a jogger and rate her looks out of 10. But I didn't actually *see* the number. I was just being a superficial, misogynist pig. That wasn't new. And there were some guys playing rugby on the next pitch. That didn't trigger any pop-ups. No weird visions from rugby.

So I focused on Conrad Etuhu again and compared him to what I remembered of Steven McGough, the boy from the park the day be-fore. Steven had acceleration and pace 5, while Conrad had 4s for both. And yes, Steven might have seemed a little faster. But maybe the other players were just slower? Or the game wasn't as serious? Were these numbers absolute or relative to the particular match I was watching?

Both had 1s for passing and technique. I kept my eye on Conrad, and honestly, he didn't seem that bad to me. Certainly not 1 out of 10 bad. But it wasn't out of 10, was it? Steven had bravery 11, and a couple of the other players I was watching had scores of over 10. So it was . . . out of 100? That seemed ludicrous. But then again, the whole thing was ludicrous.

So where had these numbers come from? Nick, the old Pole with the Scottish money? But he thought a famous composer was a star player. He didn't know the first thing about football.

All I could do was keep watching and see if maybe the numbers changed during the game or something like that. They didn't.

But when the match ended, something did change. Instead of seeing the attributes of the players, there was a little tiny envelope icon in the bottom-right corner of my vision. It didn't stop me from seeing anything in the "real" world, and it was transparent unless I stared at it. I mean, it wouldn't have caused me to crash my car or anything like that. And it didn't take me long to work out how to "tap" on it and open the message. Pretty much, I just had to will it to open.

When I read the text, I knew that I was in for a hell of a ride.

SUPER SCOUT

Congratulations! You have completed the tutorial. You have gained reputation. You may now see your experience points. You may now spend your experience points.

Your Reputation in England: Unknown

Your World Reputation: Unknown

XP: 23

New Achievements: Scouting 1; Slummin' It
Perks Unlocked: Player Profile 2; Attributes 1; 4-4-2; Super Scout

I stood there staring at this message for so long that when I came back to my senses, I was surprised to see that another match had started on the pitch in front of me. I've completed the tutorial, have I? I had a LOT to say about that, but no one to say it to. Nick would get an earful the next time I saw him. Three questions to start with: 1) Why wasn't I told there was a tutorial? 2) How did I finish said tutorial? 3) What the fuck have you done to me you absolute DICK?

So what was different now that I'd completed the tutorial? I scanned the new players and didn't see anything different. There was one real speed merchant who had acceleration 11 and pace 10, and one Mediterranean-looking guy who had the highest technique score I'd seen: 8. The players were different, of course, but I wasn't different.

I tried to "open" the message again, but it had gone. But I wanted to re-read what it said! I tried "clicking" the corner of my vision where the envelope icon had been, and a new "screen" appeared in my vision. Now this one *would* cause me to crash my car! In a panic, I looked away. It vanished. I checked out my feet, the sky, the corner flags. All good. Breathe in for three seconds, breathe out for four. I let my eyes unfocus and tried to bring the new screen back.

On the left were some tabs. One said "Max Best" and tapping that gave me three options: Personal Profile (where I could see my experience points and achievements), News, and Retire. The last one seemed very ominous. Below "Max Best" were three more boxes, but they were blank.

Top and centre of the new screen was the title "Max Best News." Below those words lay a kind of Twitter feed. The latest post said, "Perk Unlocked: Super Scout." Around the tweets were different kinds of filters, including ones like Contracts and Media, Transfers, and Records. Clicking on these filters proved as easy as reading my messages; I just had to think it. Of course, I had no news about contracts, transfers, or records, so the filters were useless. For now.

I clicked on the news item that said "Perk Unlocked: Super Scout," and found that it contained a description. A *brief* description.

Buying the Super Scout perk adds CA and PA data to player profiles.

Cost: 10,000 XP

UNIQUE SPECIAL OFFER: Buy before August 1 and pay only 1,000 XP!

Great. Love getting a deal. Now I just needed to know what CA and PA meant. I tried clicking on those terms, but nothing happened.

Anyway, it wasn't urgent, because I didn't have 1,000 XP. I had 23. No . . . 24.

Now that was a head-scratcher. I'd earned one experience point recently, but had absolutely no idea how.

Moving onto my previous news items, I found explanations for my achievements. Scouting 1 was awarded because I'd examined the profiles of ten players. I had been awarded 1 XP for that as part of the 23 from the tutorial. But awarded by whom? By God? By Nick? By the Football Association?

Slummin' It also gave me 1 XP. It came because I'd spent more than half of my time watching non-league matches.

O-kay . . . So some XP came from hitting targets. If this curse followed video game rules, maybe there would be a list of achievements that I could aim towards completing. I glanced at my XP. Still 24. Hadn't earned any for a couple of minutes. I didn't know how much I should care about XP, but I already knew that I'd at least try to get 1,000 to unlock the CA/PA perk, if only to find out what CA/PA meant.

Speaking of perks, I investigated the other ones that were available to buy. Player Profile 2 would cost 100 XP and would unlock a tab called History. Attributes 1 would let me see another player attribute, at a cost of 315 XP.

Finally, I could buy 4-4-2 for 50 XP. This was considered so obvious by the . . . interface designers? . . . that there wasn't even an attempt at explanation. 4-4-2 is a way to set up a football team. Pretty much the most basic formation, especially popular with amateur teams. So if I bought this, what would I, personally, get?

With a sigh, I closed all the screens. Bonkers. Bizarre. Pointless.

I ambled over to the half-way line and asked how long was left. The manager of the red team looked at his watch and said, "About ten minutes."

"Thanks."

I decided I'd watch those ten minutes and, at half-time, I'd go home and try to put my thoughts in order. There had to be a meaning behind all this, right? What was the point of me being able to see numbers reflecting someone's pace? The only thing I could think was that if I watched enough football, I might find someone fast enough to qualify for the Olympics. But what good would that do me?

The half-time whistle blew, and I started making my way home. I thought about buying a wrap from the little stand they had next to the indoor complex. I checked my pockets. I still had the hundred pounds that Nick had given me, but there was more chance of me playing for Manchester United than this little stall giving me change for a hundred. A Scottish hundred no less. I counted the rest of my cash. I could just about wrangle a chicken wrap with no drink. If only my bank balance went up like my XP did.

The thought made me freeze. I opened what I was coming to think of as my personal profile, and found that I now had 34 XP.

Wait wait wait. I had 24, and then I watched about ten minutes of football. Could it be that simple?

I bought the cheapest wrap—God I wished I had another pound for some onions—and went to watch the second half. These games had forty-minute halves, and sure enough, at the final whistle, I'd earned another 40 XP.

Well, well, well.

With 74 XP in the bank, I had a choice. I could buy 4-4-2 right away, or keep saving up. What I really wanted was to buy the Super Scout perk. But I also wanted to find out what all this was about. Like, what was the point of it all? It seemed obvious that buying something would give me a big clue.

So, I moved away from the pitch, sat on a bench, and bought 4-4-2. It was easy enough. A matter of clicking and confirming.

And . . . absolutely nothing happened. I clicked around through all my screens, menus, and subtabs, and just couldn't find anything different, except that I'd lost 50 XP.

Ah well. If I earned 1 XP per minute, the mistake had cost me fifty minutes, basically. I just had to watch more football.

There were no more games going on outside, but there was one in the sports hall. I went and sat in the little stand and did some maths on my phone. To get 1,000 XP I'd need to watch about eleven games. There were eleven days left in July, not counting today. I could easily do it if I simply had to be near some football matches.

Doing the maths, and thinking about when and where I could reliably find games to watch, took me about five minutes. But in that time I'd only added 2 XP. That was worrying. If I earned less and less XP per minute, then things would get very tedious, very quickly, and I wouldn't come close to having 1,000 by the end of the month.

One of the players caught my eye. It was seven-a-side and one team had two female players. The one I was interested in didn't have good attributes, at least not in a footballing sense. I allowed myself to stare discreetly at her for five minutes, and another check showed me that I'd earned 5 XP.

Time for another experiment. I watched the game, allowing myself to get distracted, looking at what the other spectators were doing, checking my phone. Guess what? After ten minutes of that, I'd earned 3 XP. Then I set a timer for six minutes and watched the game carefully until it beeped, and boom—6 XP in the bank. Clearly there was something about how intently I watched the matches that factored into how much experience it was giving me. That made sense.

A vast, stadium-shaking yawn oozed out of me. I'd learned enough for one day.

A GAME IS A GAME

Thursday. Day one of eleven. Finished work at five. Home for an early dinner, then down to Platt Fields to watch as much footy as possible. Bagged 70 XP, bringing my total to 110. There were more games going on but I was desperately thirsty, and there was a live match on TV. I wanted to watch it to check if watching from my sofa gave me XP. That would allow me to grind, big time.

It turns out that watching on a screen didn't give me any XP, and I didn't see any attributes for the players. Just to check, I found some old matches on YouTube, and they also had zero effect. I would have to physically turn up if I wanted to progress, whatever that meant in this context.

Talking of context, I did a cheeky incognito search for phrases like "augmented reality but in my head" and "I'm seeing things" and "are Scottish curses real?" Nothing. I searched for CA PA and got a bunch of pages about Corrective and Preventive Action. I tried CA PA football and found links to varsity teams in California. One Reddit thread seemed promising, but when I clicked on it, the whole screen was distorted like the code had failed, and it gave me a headache. Long story short, I got absolutely nowhere and had to accept terms of service and accept cookies every time I clicked absolutely anything so I gave up.

Friday. Day two of eleven. Quick detour after work. Mission: buy a flask. You're supposed to put them in the dishwasher before you use them, but I had no time for luxuries like common sense. I wanted to grind through to 1,000 XP to secure Super Scout ASAP. And grinding meant bringing things with me that would let me stay out longer: hot tea, cash for an onionless chicken wrap, a couple of apples for afters, and a library book to read while the teams were warming up. Lovely. My investment paid off with 80 XP, and I could have had more; there were games going on till it got dark, and even then some continued under floodlights.

Day three of eleven. I thought Saturday would have been a bumper day with many back-to-back matches to watch, but it wasn't that straight-forward. In the morning, I found some casual games in the park, three on four, that kind of thing, but they didn't give me XP. Too small? Not serious enough?

As for the lack of bigger games, perhaps the weather was too good and people were barbecuing or shopping or going to the pub. Mean-while, hardcore football fans were on their way to watch the Saturday fixtures. The Premier League clubs were mostly jet-setting around the world. United were in Thailand or Australia. Spurs were in Korea. A quick search told me that the biggest professional game going on near me was a friendly between Altrincham (fifth highest professional league) and Stockport County (fourth highest). It would cost twenty quid for a ticket, plus a burger and a drink, plus parking. Forty or fifty quid all-in, plus tons of general hassle. Worth it? Not really. A game is a game, right? I didn't see why I should start breaking the bank when I could get XP for free if I looked hard enough.

I expected to be able to watch at least two games the following day, plus at least one every evening after work. I was on track to hit my target. There was no point getting an ulcer about it and ending up in the hospital.

So I decided it was as good a time as any to go . . . to the hospital. Plot twist!

Actually, no. It's more of a care home. My mum's in one. She isn't well, and she's not going to get any better.

I got in the car and drove, but I drove the long way, the way that took me past Hough End playing fields with its countless foot-ball pitches. It seemed that there were no games going on, but to the side, tucked in behind some trees, is a little facility used by the police for God-knows-what. Probably some kind of leisure centre. Diversity training that they all take VERY seriously, I'm sure. It doesn't matter and you don't care, but guess what they've got? A football pitch. And there was a little game on!

I parked and jogged in. No one stopped me. The game was eight-a-side, and, moronically, they were playing the full length of the pitch. The game was garbage. There was too much space. The players couldn't pass the ball, so it constantly went out for a throw-in or goal-kick. The worst players tried to do the most difficult things, while the best players played neat, simple passes, and their reward was seeing less of the ball than their shit teammates. Keeping my attention focused on this travesty of an excuse for sport was hard. Really hard. I *earned* those XP. I was up to 250, a quarter of the way there!

A few hours after I set off, I arrived at the care home and found they'd moved all the patients around again. I stopped a nurse to complain about it. Surely it's important for these patients to build a routine? To be in familiar places? She was sympathetic but said, for once the home was blameless. My mother had *insisted* on moving. That was very strange. Very unlike her. Almost impossibly out of character. Her catchphrase was, "Don't make a fuss."

I found her and settled in for a session of what I call "being there." We'd never had long chats even when she was healthy, and these days her moments of lucidity don't coincide with my visits. The doctors encourage me to keep trying, though, and the nurses assure me she benefits from me being there.

"Max," she said, shocking me by recognising me straight away. She was in her favourite chair watching telly. She gave me a level stare. "You must see Anna. Go and see Anna immediately."

"Anna? Who's that? Why are you in this room? The last one had a better view."

"Anna is next door. She's my friend, and I want to be next to her."

I was torn. Mum was awake and herself, and it seemed insane to leave when she was like this. It was increasingly rare. On the other hand, me staying would merely agitate her. I decided to leave the room, but slowly.

Mum was having none of it. "Be off with you. I'm watching *Love Island*." I got to the door and hesitated for just a moment. "To the left," she barked.

There was nothing for it. I turned left and went to see this Anna person. I knocked, heard a loud, clear "enter," and swung the door open. Three steps into the room, the same voice told me to stop. It came from a medical bed in the centre of the room. Anna was clearly much sicker *physically* than my mum. Much older, too; Mum was too young to be in a place like this. At first glance, Anna was a generic old woman. White hair and that.

"Solly," she said. A mutt raised its head and looked at me. He looked like he'd have preferred to stay in his little dog bed, but he dutifully got up and approached me, giving me a wary sniff before starting to growl. The growl grew into a tiny bark. Solly was trying to moderate his volume. Good dog! "Solly doesn't approve of you."

"Then he's an impeccable judge of character."

Anna didn't laugh. "Who *are* you?"

"I'm Mary's son, Max. I hear you're friends now."

"Thick as thieves. Solly adores her."

I spared a bit more of my mental run-time to look at her. The wrinkles around the nose, the shape of the lips. She had a powerful aura. One of those women with too much energy who are always thundering around the garden or organising fetes, if fetes still exist. "You've got an accent there."

"Polish."

Another one. "Do you know a guy called Nick?"

"All the residents here are women. Perhaps you mean one of the locums?"

"No. Don't worry about it."

"You don't seem concerned about Solly's low opinion of you."

"That's because he is a dog. And hardly a thoroughbred."

"You confuse him with a horse. You *should* be concerned. Solly is a *very* spiritual animal. He has seen many things and he *sees* many things. He is *never* wrong."

She was speaking in a tone I couldn't quite put my finger on at the time, but in the car later it came to me: medium, spiritualist. Crystals, oversized bracelets, and all that. I just didn't care in the slightest and wanted to get out of there as fast as possible without doing anything unforgivably rude. "If Solly comes in here with me, he can watch the end of *Love Island*."

"Oh, that." She scrunched up her nose. By now I'd locked her face into my facial recognition software. The nose, in particular, was quite distinctive. "Your mother has wonderful latent spiritual gifts. She has real talent for the occult. We spend many evenings stargazing, explor-ing the tarot, discussing the mysteries of the universe." She made an unconscious lip-smacking gesture like you might see a horse do. "But she loves those lowest common denominator shows. The lower the better." She sighed.

I was almost out of the room when I turned back. "By the way," I said. "Mum's looking much better, and it seems you're a big reason for that. So, thanks. Bye. And bye, Solly."

That really should have been a meeting so trivial and inane as to never warrant another mention, another microsecond of thought.

But as you'll see, it was a pretty big deal.

And not the way you'd think.

HOOFING AT RANDOM

Day four of eleven. I got up early and drove to Hough End. It wasn't *that* far to walk, but it was a little bit *too* far in case I was stupidly early. But even when I got there at 9 a.m., there were people milling around getting the pitches set up, tying nets to the goalposts, setting up corner flags, and rummaging inside a huge bag of shirts and shorts. The rituals of Sunday League football.

I went to ask a manager-looking guy what time the games were kicking off. There were some at ten, he said, but after that he didn't know. I popped home for a nice cuppa, and was back at 9:50. I watched the game as closely as possible. These were proper forty-five-minute halves, so I came out with almost 80 XP. I did lose concentration a few times, but we can gloss over that. No one concentrates on anything one hundred percent of the time. Also, the quality was abysmal. One of the worst games you've ever seen. Just loads of men with low attributes running around shouting and trying to run off their hangovers.

Mercifully, that game ended. Another team was hanging around the side of the pitch waiting to use it. Their game would start at 12:15, they told me, but the genius of going to Hough End was that there were so many games happening that I didn't need to take a break. I shuffled across to another pitch and watched part of that, then went back to the pitch where I'd started. Doing that meant I could watch games pretty much non-stop from 10 a.m. until the final whistle on the final game at 2:30.

In total, I got 225 XP. It could have been more, but the more I tried to power through, the more tired and distracted I got. Still, good haul. Really good haul, bringing me to 475 XP. Nearly halfway there, with a week to go.

The next few nights were a slog. The poor quality was starting to get to me, as was the sameness of all the players. There wasn't one guy with good attributes.

Monday was all right, because the game I ended up watching was pretty good. Both teams had enough half-decent players to make every attack seem dangerous, and it seemed like both teams were trying to do tactics, though I couldn't tell you what. It was pretty easy to concentrate during that one. Tuesday I couldn't find a good game and ended up frustrated and going home early. On Wednesday there was a pretty huge thunderstorm, and no games were played.

Which left me slightly stressed, because I was on 560 out of one thousand with only four days left. The last day was a Sunday, so I assumed Hough End would be rammed with Sunday League games again. But what if the weather was bad? If I missed this deadline, the chance of me ever watching enough abysmal football to get ten thousand XP (to buy Super Scout full-price) was zero. Less than zero.

I spent much of Thursday wondering why I was putting myself through this. Most of the matches were beyond dull and veering into something like torture. When a player blonked the ball at the goal and it flew so close to the sun that it nearly hit Icarus, I had to watch that player half-heartedly jog towards the ball, get it, come back to the pitch, and throw it to the goalkeeper. That's what I was doing with my life, because if I didn't pay attention I wouldn't get XP. When there was an injury and all the players ran to the side of the pitch to drink blue Powerade, I couldn't have a little potter around or check my phone. I had to stare at the injured player or the referee or the stationary ball.

And why? What would I get?

I didn't know. But I knew I'd already come this far. Surely I could summon up a little more effort, a handful of evenings.

Thursday night, I dragged myself to Platt Lane and watched parts of two games. One hundred twenty XP and a nice chat with the chicken wrap guy who I was getting to know a bit now that I was a regular customer.

I went into the sports hall to watch some more, and there was a bit of an upsetting incident.

Both teams were very snide and aggressive. The game reminded me of a simmering pot. It seemed like it would come to the boil at any moment, but it never quite got there.

One team had a player running around windmilling his elbows. If you believe inbreeding causes facial defects like eyes being too close together, then this guy was your poster boy. I knew his name from the curse, but let's call him Pitbull. The profile page told me that Pitbull was a defender, but he was playing up front. I scanned the rest of his team, and they could have reorganised more efficiently. But then again, I was pretty sure the attributes I could see were based on full-size matches. After all, you didn't really have left-backs or defensive midfielders in these smaller games. So maybe the position attribute didn't matter in a game like this. Right? Or should players with defensive characteristics play in defence no matter how big the game was?

By now, you might have guessed what happened. Pitbull felt me staring at him. When his team conceded a last-minute equaliser, after having been in the lead for most of the game, he blew his top, and I was first in line for his wrath.

With his eyes so close together, his forehead looked massive. I was sure his primary form of communication was via the medium of headbutting.

"What you looking at?"

I'm looking at your genetically malformed face, mate. "What?"

"Said, what you looking at?"

"Oh," I said, leaning back. I had been angled forward, watching the game so intently I strained my neck. I rubbed it while twisting. "I was trying to work out why you don't play at the back."

"You what?"

"Aren't you a defender?"

"No. I'm a striker. Top scorer."

I massaged the little muscle above my collarbone. This was worrying. If I couldn't trust the position attribute then I couldn't trust anything. Which would render the whole thing futile. Which meant if Polish Nick had done this to me, the whole thing was a prank. "Oh."

Pitbull, to his huge credit, saw my confusion and calmed all the way down. He even showed a little empathy. "I used to play centre-back at school. Were you at Ducie?"

"No. Maybe I saw you once, though." I was about to make some suggestions about how they could reorganise their team but decided to beat a hasty retreat while my nose was still in one piece.

Day nine of eleven. Friday was brutally hot. A game started, but at half-time both teams agreed to quit. There were games in the sports hall, but I was a bit wary of going in and having another confrontation. Especially because the heat was making me fractious. Every little thing was driving me insane. Bus taking too long at one stop? Holy fuck, sort it out! Shop out of cheddar? Who do I have to murder to fix your supply chain, mate?

I had a little chat with Emre, the chicken wrap guy, hoping to vent my frustration a bit, but he said it wasn't even that hot. That wound me up, because it was the hottest day in recorded history. Sure, maybe it's technically hotter in Turkey sometimes, but Turkey has a fuck-ing OCEAN and air conditioning and buildings with those Byzantine protection wall decorations that sort of keep the heat out somehow.

"There's aircon in the hall," he said.

"They aren't always that keen on me watching," I said, casting a forlorn glance at the building.

He went quiet at that. Stopped fiddling with things on his little stand. He was weighing up what to say to me and how to say it when he glanced over my shoulder and called to someone. "Beth. Got a sec?" I turned to see a woman striding past, about twenty, wearing a track-suit and carrying indoor trainers with little rubber grips on them. She was attractive enough, but she had those eyebrow things. Sort of looks like they've been shaved off then drawn back on in marker pen? I don't know if that's what happens, and I don't want to know.

"Sup Emre?"

"My best customer here wants to watch a game, but he's shy."

"And you want me to take care of him?"

"Yes, please. But don't get him wet, and don't feed him after midnight."

She looked me up and down and flicked her head towards the hall. "Come on, then." I nodded thanks at Emre and tagged along with the woman. I thought I should make polite small talk, but she didn't need any prompting; she had things she wanted to say. "It's the first game of the season. We play seven-a-side, rolling subs. This lot are dirty, but we'll beat them. Been working on me fitness over the summer. Every time I thought about skiving and going on the razz, I thought of Chloe Kelly, how hard it's been for her. If she can come back from an ACL, I can do a few shuttle runs in the morning. God, I hope we win."

Her way of talking was disconcerting. Surely she'd just expressed confidence they'd win the game. Had I missed something? "We?"

"Duh. England?"

She thought she was playing for England? What? "What?"

"The final! Are you—oh." I knew that look she was giving me. It wasn't the first time I'd seen it from someone who'd just met me.

I tried to smile to show her the incandescent intelligence that burned within me. "This is the first game of the season, you said. But now you're saying it's the final. You'll forgive me for being confused."

She pulled a face. "This isn't—I'm talking about England. England versus Germany. Euro 22." It was obvious that I didn't know what she was talking about. Her mad eyebrows shot up with surprise. "Women's football," she said, but her good humour had left. To her, I was one of those trolls who always banged on about women's football being slow and the goalkeepers being shit.

I showed her my palms. "I come in peace, sister. Hashtag not all men."

"That's not a very good hashtag."

I grimaced. "Isn't it? Sorry. I don't do social media. I've only heard about it second-hand. Got the wrong end of the stick maybe."

She looked at me much like Solly the dog had, but she came to a different conclusion. Or just gave me the benefit of the doubt. "England are in the final of the Euros. Playing Germany. It's huge. The whole country is talking about it. You literally must have heard about it."

I had heard some podcasts talking about something with women, but that's what the skip forward button is for. Now I wondered what I'd been missing, tried to fill in the blanks. My imagination ran wild. All the way back to 1966 in the World Cup. The men's World Cup. "England versus Germany in the final? That's pretty . . . epic."

She smiled. "At Wembley."

"You're fucking kidding."

She liked that, for some reason. "No."

"Women's football at Wembley. The Wembley? Ninety thousand-seat stadium Wembley? The literal home of football?"

"Yep."

My mind started racing. So there was a game on Sunday night. If I was still short on XP after the Sunday morning games, or if they were cancelled because of bad weather, maybe I could get down to London and watch this women's football thing. If I got XP for watching un-coordinated male players hoof the ball at random all over Manchester, surely I'd get XP for watching the highest level of women's football. The curse would have to be very misogynist to give me credit only for watching men, or mostly-male teams. How long would it take to drive to London? Three hours, was it? Four? If the kickoff was at 7 p.m., I could watch a few hours of Hough End magic in the morning and still be at Wembley with hours to spare.

Beth was watching me go through these calculations. "What are you doing?"

I was close to blushing. "Just wondering if I could watch an early match here in Manchester and still make it to the game."

"To the final? Are you crazy? It's sold out."

"Ninety thousand tickets for women's football sold out?" I was in-credulous, which was a bad vibe. But my surprise wasn't really along the lines of "but the games are shit." It was more like, "but when did this get so popular?" I had just enough intelligence to realise I'd offended Beth in the microseconds before she made certain I *knew* she was un-happy by turning away and leaving. I would likely never see her again, but I didn't want to end on a low note. I chased after her and said, "Sor-ry, sorry. I'm not trying to be a dick." She stopped and turned. "I'm just blown away. Honest. You've got to admit that's mind-blowing."

She briefly looked furious, but it passed. "Barcelona had over ninety thousand twice in one month."

"Fucking hell."

She gave me another long look. It felt long anyway. "How old are you?"

"Twenty-two."

"And you don't do social media?"

"I had Facebook but I deleted it."

"You've got TikTok though."

"I don't." At that, she seemed to lose interest in me. She looked at her watch and started striding towards the sports hall. I tried to keep pace but fell behind. She was nearly at the doors. I had to yell, "Can I still watch?"

"It's a free country." The doors slammed behind her.

Not exactly a heartfelt invitation. But I took it. In that brief mo-ment, I wanted the XP more than I feared what lay inside.

WEIRDLY EXCITING

What lay inside was an echoey sports hall, nicely cool, with a bunch of women warming up in front of exactly one spectator: me.

I didn't have long to wait for kickoff. The wall clock started counting down from twenty-five minutes, so twenty-five minutes each way, quick half-time orange and biccy.

The game was enthusiastic but short on quality. I wouldn't say it in front of Beth, but the goalkeepers were really bad. One thing in the game's favour was a general feeling of positivity. Just a lack of snide challenges, much less cheating, much more encouragement. And one thing is for certain: the time absolutely flew by. I had no problem keeping my attention on the game, and yes, I got 1 XP per minute, just like normal.

Beth (known to most of her side as "Beff") was the best player, and she had the highest stamina, so in the last ten minutes, she dominated and scored two goals to put the game to bed. It finished 11–7.

Her team was ecstatic, and after a few high-fives and hugs, they shook hands with the other team and went to their side of the pitch where all their kit bags were. Stupidly, I had hung around, thinking about certain things I'd noticed in the game. Too late, I tried to slip away. Beth bounded up to me before I could escape and dragged me towards her teammates. They were quite international, probably some kind of university team. Beth was high on victory and the bursts of speed her extra training had allowed her. "So, what did you think?"

"I enjoyed it. Can I come next week too?"

The rest of her team made cooing noises like I was flirting. Beth said, "First you have to prove you were really watching." Her teammates ate up this twist in the tale. They had front-row seats to an exclusive one-off *Love Island* special.

I said, "What do you mean?"

"Are you some rando perv who wants to look at our legs or what? Were you watching the game, or were you watching us?"

I got it. And I smiled. I'd never been able to say this before in my entire life, but right at that moment, I was uniquely qualified to comment on their footballing ability. Completely detached from their appearance. What I knew about them from their player profiles was totally objective. I was pretty sure it was, anyway. "Well, the first thing I noticed was that Nobuko is left-footed but only uses her right."

The team's general level of fun and jolliness didn't change right away, but Nobuko looked crushed and the rest caught on. "How do you know my name?"

I'd only gone and put my foot in it FOUR SECONDS into the conversation. Why do I think of myself as smart when I'm so consistently stupid? "I heard someone say it during the match."

"They all call me Nobby."

"Yeah, but a Japanese woman called Nobby is obviously going to be Nobuko."

They relaxed a bit but not so much Nobuko, who wasn't convinced it *was* obvious. But she didn't want to make a scene, and she had other fish to fry. "How do you know about my foot?"

That was easier. I mean, there's no way to know someone's left-handed just by looking at a photo, but it's much easier if you see them do something that shows their dominant hand, such as playing tennis. So it was a breeze to bullshit my way out of that one. "Just a sense from the way you move. Your balance. There's nothing wrong with the way you kick the ball, but it didn't seem totally right. I had this feeling that . . ." Nobuko was staring at a spot on the floor. "Well, anyway. Look, Beth, guys, I keep annoying everyone by accident. I should just go."

There was uproar. No! Not annoying. Don't go. Nobuko was shaking her head slightly, and she waited for a lull. "My family is extremely traditional. To write left-handed in Japanese is very hard. They didn't force me to be right-handed like in the old days, but they encouraged me. And I was happy to try. Why not? Easier to fit in. So now . . . yes. He's right. I am shocked. I never knew it was so obvious."

She was close to tears. This was brutal. I hated that I had done this. But on the other hand, it was weirdly exciting. One significant piece of evidence that the player profiles were real! Though now I had a so-cial issue to deal with. "It's not SO obvious. Honestly. You could ask a hundred people to comment on you as a footballer, and I'd be the only one to say it. Seriously."

"He's right, Nobby," said Beth. "You can't tell."

"Okay, I'm going. It was fun. Thanks." They tried to stop me leaving and invited me to join them in the pub. I held firm. Plus, I had very little money left. "Same time next week? Or did I fail the test?"

Beth walked outside with me. She said she didn't know what time they'd be playing, but she could text me. There was something going on. Was she into me? It felt like a blatant lie to get my number.

I took her phone and started typing it in, but paused. "This is just for the football."

"Right."

"I'm serious." I typed in my number and saved it.

She took her phone back without looking at it. "What about me?"

"What?" I was worried she was going to get all intense. Was it too late to snatch her phone out of her hand?

"You saw Nobby was left-footed somehow. What about me?"

Ah. That was easy. "You should play in defence. Bye."

As I walked away, she looked down at her phone. "Bye . . . Max what? Oh, he's left a fake name. Fucking hell."

Saturday was the day before the deadline, and I didn't quite get to 1,000 XP. Still, I thought my overall plan was pretty sound. After brek, I went to the police facility, and kept going back every half hour or so in between drives to the shops. Once, I even went to the library in Withington where I spent some time looking up my curse on a computer that couldn't be traced back to me. "Slummin' It non-league achievement," "CA meaning football," "What's it called when you see things NOT schizophrenic," "Does doctor patient confidentiality apply in England?"

No help. No evidence that anyone else had this problem. And in the case of looking up CA, a splitting headache and another corrupted website.

Anyway, one time I drove to the police and saw a game on. This time I was mentally prepared in case anyone came to challenge me. My plan was to say I had come to watch my friend Niall Stephens, one of the names I'd seen the last time I was there. This Stephens guy had a habit of shooting from the halfway line no matter the state of the game, to the growing apoplexy of his teammates. I felt like most of the regulars would know him. And if there was a second game, I'd refer them to one of the players from this current game I was watching. "Oh," they'd say, sympathetically. "He was here earlier."

The game was bad again, but this time I focused on one attribute: tackling. I took the players with the highest and lowest scores—there were many that had a one, so I focused on a guy playing in midfield who had more chance of being involved in tackle situations—and kept an eye on them through the game. I tried to keep a tally. The guy with the "good" tackling attribute did slide in and win a couple of tackles, but so did the rubbish one. The "good" one looked slightly more convincing to my naked eye, but the point of watching them was to see how their performance related to these numbers, not to put my own interpretation on it. In the end, there just wasn't enough data from one tiny, amateur game. Maybe I'd invest some cash in going to see a professional game and see what came out of that. I still had that Scottish money, after all. But there was absolutely no chance of me going out of my way to watch god-awful amateur games or overpriced professional ones if I bought Super Scout and found it was as useless as 4-4-2. If it was another bust, then this journey was over.

After the football, I went to get petrol—catastrophically expensive—and bought *Hot Goss*, a trashy celebrity news magazine. I drove to the care home and read some articles about *Love Island* to my mum. Halfway through, Anna, looking much improved, came in, sat by Mum's bed, and wheezed, listened, and asked me to read their horoscopes. I did, but grew frustrated by the sheer stupidity of the thing so offered her a choice between another article on *Love Island* or a story about a woman who'd fallen in love with a murderer. She chose the latter.

The forecast for Sunday morning was 50% chance of thunderstorms. I only needed 110 more points. Just a game and a bit! If the storms didn't hit until lunchtime, I'd make it.

The first game kicked off under dark grey clouds. I was so distracted by them, I didn't get full XP. Stupid. At full-time, I moved over to another pitch where they'd kicked off twenty minutes late. I guessed the players would try to finish their game even if there was a fair bit of rain, but that maybe the matches scheduled for later would be cancelled. Of course, in the event of an actual storm, it was game over for the day's schedule and game over for Project Super Scout. It was frustrating; I knew I needed one more set of matches to kick off. Just one more!

The skies darkened. There was lightning in the distance, though I couldn't hear the thunder. Every minute counted. I had to pay attention. I tried to imagine my eyes being pulled open like I was being *forced* to watch the games.

Goals flew in on all the pitches around me. One–nil over here. Four–two over there. But the only number I cared about crept up slower than me climbing up a stepladder.

I had 950 XP.

I had 975 XP.

984.

98 . . . 5.

Then, disaster. Huge cracks in the sky, like ship masts splitting in half, condemning all who sail in it to drown. And drown we did.

Hundreds of men gathered their most vital possessions and ran for what little shelter there was. I let four complete strangers into my car—it stank of mud and sweat for days after.

Stuck on 985 XP! Stranded! Shipwrecked! At first I was depressed. To come so close and fail by fifteen minutes. Pure torment! But the good-natured banter of the guys distracted me, especially when the conversation turned to women's football. Three of the four guys had been watching the Euros—reluctantly at first, "there was nothing else on"—but with growing interest. When the discussion moved away from the general ("But aren't the goalkeepers shit?") to the specific ("She's got to pick Russo to start ahead of White" and "Bright won't be able to stop Alex Popp; England are in for a rude awakening."), I knew I'd missed out on something big. A shared, collective experience. A national carnival.

Again, my thoughts turned to making a mad dash down to London to see if I could get a ticket. Maybe I could pay someone to let me watch the first fifteen minutes.

Petrol: half a tank each way, a hundred pounds there and back. Ticket from a tout: several hundred quid. Sandwich and a bottled water in London: an arm and a leg. Parking: a kidney.

I rubbed my face hard and decided to give it up as a bad job and let my life return to normal. Maybe I'd go and watch the girls play football every Friday night, without creeping them out in future, and upgrade my skills over the years (or until I was cured). Basically, treat my condition as a mild curiosity and not let it change how I lived.

I turned to the guy in the passenger seat. I knew his name but had learned my lesson about revealing too much. "If you've got all your kit I can drop you home."

There was a silence that stretched into the back of the car. I turned and saw them all looking at me like I was a deep-sea fish with seven heads and hooks for teeth. In the few seconds before someone spoke, I tried to retrieve the conversation I'd tuned out. They had been talking about tactics and players from their game. What?

"Take me home?" the guy said. "We've got the whole second half to play."

"There's a huge storm!" I said.

"It'll be gone in a couple of minutes," said one guy in the back.

"The pitch!" I said, thinking about how waterlogged it would be.

They didn't seem to care. "As long as the ref sticks around, it's game on. Not letting a bit of rain ruin our season."

A bit of rain! I couldn't believe my ears. There had been about a metre of rain in the last five minutes. At one point I'd checked the water level outside the car to see if we'd start floating off.

They continued talking about the game, getting more and more animated when discussing which opposing players were giving them the most shit and what to do about it.

They were going to keep playing! These absolute morons! These absolutely beautiful absolute morons!

I could have kissed them.

Deliriously happy, I blurted out, "You should target Matty Smith! He's actually a striker and he's got no stamina. Make him sprint a couple of times and he's toast."

The passenger seat guy said, carefully, like he was talking to a mentally challenged person, "Which one is Matty Smith?"

I dialled my excitement down by about ten percent. "He's the left-back. He's wearing number twelve."

The guys looked at each other. Finally, the oldest one nodded. "We can move Arkhy out there, have him run at him."

I should have quit while I was ahead, but my mouth had a mind of its own. "Hit your goal kicks over there, too. The guy can't jump, and he can't head it."

There was another silence. The oldest guy gave me a hard look. "Do you watch a lot of them?"

He meant their opponents. "No," I said. "Never seen them before. I'm just . . . I'm sort of training to be a scout, is all. I've been at City's academy a lot." This was stretching the meaning of the words way *way* past breaking point. Platt Lane hadn't been City's academy for years, and even the vaguest follow-up question about what exactly I was *doing* at the "academy" would mean a lot of cringeworthy backpedalling.

Another silence, this one much deeper than the last. It wasn't merely suspicion and anxiety; we realised the storm had passed and the worst of the rain had gone. The next sounds were those of car doors opening and slamming. The lads did a little jog towards their pitch, but the oldest one turned and said, "Target the full-back, yeah?"

"Yeah."

He nodded and jogged off. I followed, ruining my trainers in the thick Manchester mud, and watched the older guy giving instructions to his team. I noticed he was wearing Man City shinpads.

They followed my advice and scored two goals in fifteen minutes.

As the second goal was being damply celebrated, I bought Super Scout and my life changed.

Permanently.

SEASON 2022-23

1

HYPOTHESIS

Something was different. Now, in addition to seeing heading, jumping, pace, passing, and so on, I could also see a player's CA and PA.

How did I celebrate this life-changing event? Not even with a shrug. What did I do with this glorious new superpower? I took a trainer off and poured out a litre of water and mud.

With a series of sighs and bone-cold shivers, I wandered from pitch to pitch. Three games had resumed after the storm, and one was waiting for a batch of lads to come back from a nearby caff. Almost every player had a CA of 1 and a PA of 1. A few had 2 or 3. One guy had a PA of 4. I watched him for a while, but he seemed no different from anyone else.

My menus, tabs, and screens were all otherwise the same. Still no help section. No glossary. No list of achievements I could unlock. Certainly no explanation of CA and PA.

I stuck around for the last game to resume, but when it did, enlightenment didn't follow.

So I'd achieved my goal. Whoop-de-doo.

I went home and had a long shower, then went to devour articles about Euro 22 until the match started at 5 p.m. From what I read, England had scored a lot of goals and been playing sensational football until their knockout game against Spain, who had outplayed them and were horribly unlucky to lose. Germany would be a test on another level. They were as technical as Spain but had Alex Popp up front. The papers talked about her like she was The Terminator. In the clips I saw, there would be a thicket of defenders and then this tall, powerful woman would scatter them like bowling pins and smash the ball into the net. How could you stop that? With a harpoon, maybe. Or better, an ion cannon.

Near kick-off, Beth texted me:

u watchin?

It had been quite a long time since a woman had texted me, so I can't say I wasn't flattered. Which is a roundabout way of saying I was flattered.

Me: The thing about Etruscan furniture on BBC 2? Yeah. Who knew earthenware was so interesting?

Her: u gonna make me use full sntncs?

Me: Are you trying to write syntax?

Her: sen-ten-ces. there's nowt on BBC 2 about pots. why u so weird?

That caught my attention. I hadn't mentioned pots. She'd read "earthenware" and thought of pots. And she was at university. Why was she pretending to be illiterate?

Me: I've been reading up on women's footy, and it says until recently England had a man in charge. Former Man United player, too. I'd feel a lot more confident if he was still around.

Her: i no ur winding me up. Wont work. im buzzin

She was right that I was teasing her. The male former player (the lesser Neville) had been something of a disaster and the current manager was considered a legit tactical genius. But you can't out-tactic an actual Terminator.

Me: If I was trying to wind you up I'd tell you I'd placed a 500 quid bet on Germany to win with Popp to score first.

Her: u wasted ur £££. Popp's out.

It seemed like she was winding ME up, because I'd seen Popp's name on the team sheet. But I double checked, and the news had broken that Germany's star player had injured herself in the warm-up. Horrible luck.

Me: Wow. So England have this in the bag, right?

Her: do not ginx this

Me: I promise never to ginx anything. lol

Her, two minutes later: jinx

The final kicked off, and right away, Germany had a player clean through on goal. A decent shot, well-saved by Mary Earps. Earps projected an air of supreme confidence, as did the German goalie. And why not? They were professional athletes playing for big clubs. It wasn't like the old days.

The game was fascinating and tense. England looked nervous; Germany seemed destined to win. I felt there were several shifts in the tactics from both managers. Germany were dominating the ball, but England were trying to absorb the pressure, let the Germans move up the pitch, then break on the counterattack.

Counterattack! CA! Could that be the meaning? A player's ability to counterattack?

Which would make PA . . . I tried to think of football words beginning with "p." At the top of the list was "pressing," which was the ability to close down and put pressure on an opponent, and maybe take the ball from them or force them into a mistake. Modern pressing had been perfected in Germany and was taken to an extreme by teams like Liverpool. So . . . Counter Attack and Pressing Ability?

That would probably match up with modern football theory and make CA and PA two of the attributes pro players would need to succeed. Interesting.

Again, I thought about going to watch a professional game to test this hypothesis. With my Scottish money, I could afford one Premier League game. Team loyalties aside, which team would be best to watch? Man City? Well, those players would have high PA but City usually had seventy percent possession and didn't spend a lot of time on the counterattack. Liverpool? High PA and CA, probably. Would that be statistically interesting? Would it tell me anything if *all* the numbers were high? It depended on who they were playing. The best choice to learn a lot in one match was Man United. Under a previous manager, they'd played a very effective counterattacking style, and I expected some of their players would have high CA scores. Meanwhile, the most recent managers had tried and failed to get them to press in a modern style, so I could expect the players to have lowish PA—if my theory was right. I started to guess at the CA and PA of certain players. Marcus Rashford, God love him, would be near the max in CA and abysmally low in PA.

Testing would have to wait until I could get into a stadium.

Back on the TV, England scored a phenomenal goal, a cheeky lob in the final in front of ninety thousand fans and millions on TV. Staggering, really. Germany increased the pressure, equalised, and from that moment there would only be one winner. But England stuck at it, hung in there, and won in extra time with a scrappy goal from Chloe Kelly.

I could see why Beth found her an inspiration. They looked similar, and Kelly played for Man City. Kelly was a proper Mancunian from top to bottom (suspicious tan, bleach blonde hair, gobby), and here she was scoring the winner in a massive, massive game. I wondered what part of Manchester she'd grown up in. I was astonished to read on Wikipedia that she was from London. No wonder people complain every high street looks the same.

Emotions were high as England celebrated. For many of the players it had been a long journey to get to this point. Paying for their own kit, training in squalor, their achievements met with total indifference. And now they were the biggest show in town. It was quite emotional. Chloe Kelly was interviewed by the BBC but when she heard her favourite song being played, she ran off mid-interview, microphone and all, to sing with her teammates. Hilarious. My first thought was that she could win Sports Personality of the Year and, with the right sponsorships, she could make a ton of money. A ton.

About ten minutes after the match ended, I realised I was absolutely drained. It wasn't just the rollercoaster and the palpable emotion of the final; I'd been thinking about football almost nonstop since I'd met Nick. First, I needed an early night, and then I needed a total break.

I dobbed a blob of toothpaste onto my brush and stuck it into my mouth. My phone buzzed. It was Beth. The phrasing made me spit toothpaste onto the mirror.

u cummin to celebrate?

2

WOMEN ARE
FROM VENUS

The Premier League was nearly back. This coming weekend, in fact. Arsenal were playing Crystal Palace in the first game . . . oh. On Friday night. I had sort of promised Beth I'd be at the sports hall to watch her. A bit annoying to miss the big match, but then again, I needed to see footballers in the flesh.

So to speak.

I stayed home after work on Monday and used Tuesday to visit Mum. Wednesday, I wandered around Platt Lane and Platt Fields scanning players to see if there were any interesting CA or PA numbers. There weren't. I did, however, get 5 bonus XP for scouting my five hundredth player.

That brought me up to 21 XP. In the "shop," I currently had access to Player Profile 2, which promised to unlock a tab called History. That was selling for 100 XP. Attributes 1 would add another data point to a player's profile, but that was retailing at 315 XP. At some point, the option to buy "4-4-2 diamond" appeared, for 100 XP. I wouldn't buy any more formations, because they seemed to be useless. If it was the only thing left to buy, then maybe. Maybe I would be forced to buy them to unlock other options. In the meantime, given a choice, my preference was to see more attributes, but I wouldn't pull the trigger on that even when I had saved enough XP. You know, in case another special offer turned up. I love getting a deal.

With no time pressure, I felt chill enough to go "gamespotting" on Thursday as well. I was hoping all this watching, all this time, all this *work*, would lead to something. I couldn't imagine what exactly. But there had to be something, right?

Right?

The only thing I could think of was that seeing all these numbers could help me win at Fantasy Football. I'd have to go and watch every team in the Premier League, and, as far as I knew, you didn't get money for winning. But I signed up and selected a team, just in case.

But that got me thinking—you could win money *betting* on football. This curse might give me an unfair advantage. Something to think about.

Friday evening was another sweltering one, and I was happy for the air con. It was all a bit awkward with Beth though. She told me the wrong kick-off time to get me there half an hour early, and I spent the whole 30 minutes in terror that she might start talking about her feelings or worse, *our* feelings. I kept the conversation on safe topics, like what happens next for women's football, whether Haaland would be a success at Man City, and if they turned *Foucalt's Pendulum* into a musical, which band or artist should write the songs? Okay, maybe not the last one. I was becoming something of an expert in *Love Island* from reading the articles to my mum and Anna, and that helped me eat through the minutes.

When the opposition turned up, I nearly broke my forehead in half from frowning.

Beth noticed and laughed at me. "What?"

I tried to speak, but was mostly just splurting out noises. "They're . . . little people?"

Another laugh. "They're Manchester City's under-sixteens."

That explained the spotless laser blue kits, the very serious-looking coaches, and the many bags of equipment. "Under-sixteens? That one looks about ten." Until they started kicking balls around, I wouldn't know their actual ages.

"So? These are some of the best kids in the country. They'll crush us. They always do."

"Why are they playing *you*?"

"There aren't tons of girls playing football. They pretty much take games wherever they can. And they support this league. It's one of the oldest women's leagues in Manchester."

"So you're a charity case. I knew it."

That got me a smack on the arm.

When the warm-up started, a lot of things happened at once. I could finally see Beth's CA (1) and PA (6). Hers was the highest PA I'd seen yet, and it kind of made sense, because her main strength was running around harassing her opponents. But she only held the record for highest PA for the eight microseconds it took my eye to glance at the nearest Man City toddler.

SARAH GREENE		
Born 4.10.2007	(Age 14)	English
Acceleration 6		
		Stamina 4
	Heading 1	Strength 3
		Tackling 1
	Jumping 3	
Bravery 3		Technique 13
	Pace 4	preferred foot R
	Passing 9	
Dribbling 12		
CA 12	PA 167	
Midfielder (Centre, Right)		

Holy Moses! PA 167? So it's not out of 20, then? Just that attribute, or all of them? She wasn't the only one of the newborns with a high PA. The entire squad ranged from 33 to 169. Meanwhile, none had a CA higher than fifteen.

This wasn't what I'd been expecting, and it wasn't the only baffling thing. Sarah Greene had higher speed attributes than Conrad Etuhu, and higher strength too. But it stood to reason that Etuhu could have picked her up one-handed while the reverse was *not* true. The girl was a bag of bones. So I was back to distrusting the numbers . . .

. . . And it took me a minute to realise that Beth was trying to introduce me to their new teammate. Lula was from Mexico and was studying surface engineering. It came to me that although I knew a fair amount about Beth, I didn't know what she was doing at uni. There was no time—the game kicked off.

Again, it was seven-a-side, rolling subs, twenty-five-minute halves. But this time, the shape of the game was radically different. It was unlike any amateur game I'd ever seen, which is probably because one side would grow up to be professionals and had pro coaches. The City kids would pass the ball left and right, left and right, and when pressed, would play it back to the keeper, who would hang onto it for a few seconds longer than I thought was right. Someone, usually Beth, would sprint at her. In response, the keeper would pass it to one of the two options on the sidelines, and City would quickly play it forward with Beth out of position. When a good chance came along, they'd shoot, and if nothing came up, they'd play a safe pass and keep possession. After three minutes they'd scored a goal, and Beth's team had barely touched the ball.

It was . . . clinical.

I watched a few more minutes, and the score moved to 2–0. Something on the other touchline caught my eye. The City manager, a woman with the drab shoulder-length hair of a business studies teacher, did a little high-five with her assistant.

And that's when it clicked. This whole gameplan was a trap. A sneaky, insidious, Venus Fly Trap trap.

A couple of years before, Arsenal had a Spanish manager who tried to change the way they played. Instead of booting the ball down the pitch, the goalkeeper would always pass the ball to a nearby defender; the opposition would swarm all over the Arsenal defence, and they'd inevitably buckle. But once, and I remember it clearly, Arsenal got it to work. As the opposition tried to blitz them, they fizzed the ball all around the pitch, dragging the other team out of position one by one, then hammered a beautiful goal down their now-defenceless throats. That was the model, the platonic ideal of that tactic. It seemed like a high-risk move to me, borderline foolish, and indeed, the manager was later sacked. But seeing it here, played out by these little girls against these university students, it felt like bringing a gun to a knife-fight. In fact, Beth's team were so unprepared, it was like bringing a gun to a marrow growing contest.

And that was all fine and good, but they didn't need to high-five about it. They didn't need to plaster their faces with smug grins.

My blood was boiling.

3

THE MAN

"Sophia," I said, "sub for Beth."

The substitute blinked. "Beth doesn't come off. She's the fittest."

"Do it now. I need to talk to her."

Sophia called Beth and did a complicated hand wave that Beth didn't understand. She came over to the side to ask what it meant. I took her by the wrist and coaxed her off the pitch. Sophia jogged on.

"What the fuck?" said Beth.

There was no time for social niceties. "Stop pressing the fucking keeper! You're killing us."

"The fuck?"

"They're waiting for you to storm up there like a headless chicken, so they can hit us on the break."

"Us?"

"Do you want to win or not?" Me, Beth, us, our desires and fears, they slipped away. For the first time, I was communicating with her honestly. She snapped into some kind of game state and started paying proper attention. I repeated myself for clarity. "Don't press the goalie. Pick a defender, and press her instead. Got it?"

"Right."

"Sub on."

At the next break, Beth replaced Nobby.

"What is going on?" she said.

"Nobby, are we cool?"

"What?"

"Are you mad at me for saying you're left-footed?"

"No. It was a shock. We're cool."

"Move to left midfield and track Greene. Number five. If she tries to pass you on your left, block her. If she cuts back inside or passes back, let her."

"Uh, okay."

"I want to see what happens when we dam up their attacks."

"Dam?"

"Like on a river. To block the water. They've been practising all these set moves, but can they play creatively?"

"Yes, definitely. They're really good."

I shook my head. "Let them prove it."

The game started to take on a new shape. City's moves broke down, and they'd go back to the keeper to restart. Once, Beth charged at her, but I literally screamed with frustration, and she back-pedalled into a more useful position. Another time, she pressed a defender and nabbed the ball, but shot just over. Against last week's opponents she'd have backed herself to dribble closer to the goal, but against this lot she had so little of the ball she couldn't remain calm when she did have it.

Every time there was a substitution—the women seemed to have their own way of knowing when to change and who would replace whom—I gave an instruction to the player who came off. Weirdly, they all tried their best to do what I said.

I did have a moment of hesitation with Lula. Her face screwed up when I told her what I thought she should do. I thought she was going to tell me off for mansplaining or whatever, but I was way off the mark. She shook her head. "My coaches. They all say the same thing. I travel eight thousand kilometres, and it's the same history."

"Same story," I said, vaguely. It was still 2–0 and approaching half-time. During the break there would be some kind of reckoning. Probably the best thing to do would be to get ahead of the recriminations. Apologise to the ladies and explain that I'd become sucked into the emotion of the game—that I was just here to watch and not boss them around. But I glanced over at City's coaches, and they looked worried. They were talking to each other with hands covering their mouths, so I couldn't fucking lip read. They were worried, and I'd done that to them! I felt an inexplicable surge of violent pride.

Fuck mansplaining. I wanted to win.

Half-time was only five minutes long, so we had a lot to get through. The ladies had put in a hell of a shift already (meanwhile the little brats on the other team had barely had to run and were fresh as daisies), and four collapsed to the floor while the others sat on the plastic seats and put their heads between their legs. I was about to start reorganising them when the referee came over.

She was wearing all-black and she looked about sixteen years old. She had the team sheets in her hand. "Excuse me," she said. "Are you the manager for this team?"

"No," I said.

"It looks like you're managing them."

"So?" said Beth, slightly too aggressively.

"So you didn't write his name on the team sheet. You have to write your manager's name up here." She tapped an empty spot.

"We said he's not our manager."

"Fine. Then he can't manage you."

I pointed across the great divide. "Did they complain?"

The referee didn't understand me at first. "City? No, they didn't *complain*. They don't have to. You didn't fill in the paperwork."

"I'm their personal chef, and we're talking about nutrition."

The ref gave me a look. "I can hear what you're saying. It's obviously managing."

"Look," I said, trying to be reasonable. "I'm just giving advice. If the City coaches don't like it, I'll stop. If they're okay with it, what's the harm?"

"The harm is that you didn't file the paperwork," sighed the ref. "But I'll talk to them, I suppose." She wandered away.

"Right ladies, I'm about to get kicked out. Here's what I think, take it or leave it." I looked around, pointing to the women in turn. "Jane, keeper. Don't need a coaching badge for that one. Beth and Nobby, you stay at the back. Don't go forward. Beth? No go. You're Millie Bright now. You're John Terry. You're . . ."

"Yeah, I got it. I'm in defence."

"Lula, you're up front. You guys," I indicated the other four. "You're the midfield. You've got to press and harry."

"Hurry?"

"Harry. Snap at their heels. Rottweilers. Don't let them go forward. They're very happy to turn back. Give them the option to go back, and they'll take it. There's four of you for three slots, so run hard, and sub often. Yeah?"

There was some nodding at that. "We're losing, though," said Beth. "I mean, losing 2–0 isn't that bad. Much better than what we normally do. But . . . I mean, if we just sit back and defend, how are we going to score?"

I didn't exactly have a master plan for that. Seeing the attributes of the players and their preferred positions could help me set up the team—maybe—but the other team were much better in every way AND the players were mostly where they were supposed to be. "If you're happy losing 2–0 that means they'll be unhappy winning 2–0. Yeah? If you keep it tight, they'll start taking more risks late in the game. Or am I way off? Seriously, tell me if I'm way off."

Beth was nodding. "No, yeah, that sounds about right. So we keep things tight, frustrate them, and look for chances in the last five or ten minutes. Ladies?"

The response was some mild whoops and handclaps that shouldn't have got my blood flowing, but holy fuck, they did.

I glanced up and saw the referee talking to City's head coach. The ref kept pointing to the empty line on the team sheet. The manager snapped at her and turned back to her team talk. The ref looked at her watch and wandered out into the middle. She dropped the match ball onto the centre spot and blew her whistle.

Relief! The Man was letting me manage. Which was funny, because The Man wasn't a man and I wasn't a manager.

4

THE WEAKEST LINK

The second half started, and things went great. The reshaped team looked as solid as a rock. City passed, passed, passed. Sideways, sideways, back. Side, side, back. When they did try to burst forward, Beth would knock the ball out, or Nobby would delay the attacker long enough for one of the midfield terriers to get back and support. Then City would reset, and let us get our breath back.

Every tackle, every block, every interception was treated like a goal, and I could feel the team starting to really believe in themselves. This, I thought, was probably the first time they'd all been in the right positions. They could *feel* its rightness!

Five minutes passed, and my pulse was sky high. City's manager was growing more frustrated on her touchline. She gave instructions to a batch of kids and did a big swap—four replacing four. The new lot lined up with two at the back—the only logical number, really—but they hugged the sidelines as though one was a left-back and the other a right-back. Lula stayed in the centre, unmarked; she'd be one-on-one with the goalie if we ever got the chance to pass to her. City's manager had balls, that was for sure. I kept an eye on this tactic, because it didn't feel right. It had the vibe of another trap. Sure enough, I noticed that one of the defenders would sprint down the line trying to cause an overload. I told Lula to drop into the space the overloader left. There was one big ricochet, and the ball blooped into the air, almost exactly to where Lula was. If she could control it, she'd be through on goal! But the loop was too slow, and City got back to cover. Moving her out there had been the right move though, because after another mass substitution, City reverted to having two central defenders.

The clock kept ticking. Ten minutes gone. Fifteen left. City should have just passed the ball around and taken the win. But I imagined this manager bumping into City's manager, Pep Guardiola, and him asking how the team got on last night and her saying "we won 2–0" and his fixed smile causing her utter shame. I suppose that's why they kept winning, because they always wanted more. Well, my plan was to use that admirable tendency against them, and, in my humble opinion, it was working like a charm. The City coaches were getting stressed, and the kids were starting to get nervous, starting to make sloppy passes.

During a tiny break in play, I called Lula, Sophia, and Freyja over. "Next time they play the ball back to the keeper, you three blitz her. Go from different angles."

"Fucking hell, Max," said Sophia. "You told us not to do that."

"A hundred times," confirmed Freyja.

"And now they don't expect it," I said. They went off and formed a quick huddle. Later, I learned they were deciding on a word that Freyja would shout to trigger the press.

The match kicked off, and City passed it round a bit. One of the midfielders got stuck and turned and lazily dabbed a pass back towards the keeper. Almost before she'd made contact with the ball, Freyja shouted "Black Friday!" and the three women sprinted at the goalie. Who, naturally, as I would have done, panicked. She had enough presence of mind to clear the ball, but only to one of our midfielders, Bella, who played it forward to where we now had three attackers versus the keeper. City's defenders raced back, there was a bit of pinball, and after a couple of scuffs and near-misses, the ball dribbled over the line.

The referee blew her whistle, and I was convinced she'd disallow the goal for unsportsmanlike conduct; you're really not supposed to recreate *Braveheart* when playing association football. But she pointed to the centre spot, and the scoreboard updated.

It was now 2–1.

I didn't cheer. I didn't let my energy leave me; I needed it. I wrapped it around myself like a cloak of fury. City's manager wasn't smirking now. Her players looked terrified. It was such a *rush*.

My team ran over for quick instructions: "Keep it tight. Let the pressure build."

Beth reached her hand out, and the others put theirs on top. I added mine to the pile, and all the hands were taken away with a quick cry of "team!"

Wow. Goosebumps.

The next few minutes, the tension kept building. When was the last time anyone had run these City girls close? Their nerves were fraying. One or two of their subs looked legit terrified. It was awesome. We were the underdogs and had nothing to lose. City were supposed to be a superpower. If we scored again, it would be humiliating. There were more blocks, we tracked our runners. When City played a 1–2 to get in behind, someone was there to cover.

Meanwhile, the next phase of my tactical battle with City's manager arrived. She changed something, but I couldn't work out what it was. The flow of the game was suddenly all one-way. City were getting closer and closer to our goal. I couldn't see what had changed, so I couldn't react.

There wasn't much time. City were starting to get shots away. Jane saved two easy daisycutters, but another try smashed against the post, and one missed by so little I thought it must have actually been a goal that passed through a hole in the side of the net.

It was at the kickoff that I saw what was happening. One of City's three midfielders was pushing forward to support their striker. That meant Beth and Nobby had two people to worry about. City, meanwhile, were now outnumbered in midfield. It didn't matter to them, though; they still had complete control. If anything, their midfielders were happy to have more space to work in. All I could think to do was to ask Freyja to drop into defence. It shored things up slightly, but it was like putting a plaster on a crack in a dam.

There were seven minutes left, and I didn't have any tools to change anything. We were clinging on, hoping for a lucky break.

Weirdly, our break came from the City manager. She hadn't made a mistake the whole match. Apart from being a smug cow, she'd taken risks and mostly tried to be proactive. But now she brought on a new player. Everyone in their bloated squad had been on and off the pitch except this one. She was called Carmen, and she was barely fourteen. She had the worst attributes of all the players, and the lowest CA and PA. She really seemed out of place. Literally, her preferred position was striker but she was being used in defence. I couldn't believe my eyes!

All we had to do was pressure her, and she'd give the ball away. If we did it at the right time, we'd get a goal out of it for sure.

"What are you grinning about?" It was Sophia.

I was about to tell her my plan. Put pressure on the fourteen-year-old until she cracks like an egg! Make omelette out of her mistakes! Then rub her face in it. HahahahahHAHA! I took a mental step back. A bunch of enthusiastic twenty-year-olds were playing a bunch of talented fifteen-year-olds in seven-a-side indoor footy, and I was treating it like I was Napoleon marching across Europe just because the other manager expressed satisfaction that her tactics had worked out well. Meanwhile, my idea of managing was to crush some little girl who must have known she was the weak link on a good team. What the actual fuck was wrong with me? My bloodlust drained away. Sophia was giving me that look I knew oh so well. "Ah . . . just thinking of a joke." And that was that. I kept my dark thoughts to myself.

Beth, Nobby, and Freyja proved an effective wall, but once City's players realised we had stopped trying to score, they swarmed forward, and finally scored a third goal with under a minute left on the clock.

Three–one. City seemed happy with that, and the match ended with smiles all round.

I sort of sat there in a daze. Pretty tired, actually. Mentally fatigued, like I'd been playing angry chess. City's manager came up to me. I stood abruptly, ready to apologise.

"Hi," she said, holding out a hand. "I'm Sandra. I haven't seen you before."

"Max," I said, still wary of a telling-off.

"That was fun! You gave us all kinds of problems. Great work-out. The girls will be delighted."

"Will they? They don't look very delighted."

"Fine. I'll be delighted on their behalf!" She laughed. She'd been pretty hard-faced during the game, but the game was over, wasn't it? I tried to lighten up too.

"Those kids are great," I said. "So talented. But why don't you let Sarah dribble?" I'd said a name I shouldn't know again! So stupid! "And that other one. Number 8 there."

"We try to avoid dribbling in these games. It winds people up. Leads to injuries. You've seen us play before, then? That's how you knew how to play against us."

"Oh, right, yeah." Part of me wanted to say that I'd worked it out on my own, wanted to show off, but this was better. I wasn't keen to draw attention to my affliction.

"Bye, Max. See you around. Next time we won't go easy on you!" She laughed again.

Next time? No way. There were other ways to spend a Friday night. With a start, I checked my phone. I was missing the Arsenal game! If I ran home, I could catch the last half hour. Beth spotted me. She grabbed my phone and slipped it into her bag. "No way. You're not running off. We have a lot to talk about." She looked around. The whole team had gathered. "Pub," she said.

"Pub," came the reply.

"Wait," I said. I had a little envelope in my vision. I opened it and read my news. I had a new achievement: coaching my first game. That came with 1 XP as a bonus. But I'd gone from having 74 XP at the start of the game to having 165 now. That was . . . far more than I should have had. The game had only been fifty minutes long! I'd earned double XP. Was it because City's players were so good? Was it because I'd been so invested in the game? The only way to find out was to "manage" the team again. Next week, the opponents would be the usual garbage. But that was fine. It was more data. More answers. As long as these ladies let me be their manager one more time. I had to make sure that happened.

"Max!" said Beth. How long had I been staring into space?

"Pub," I said, putting my arm around her. "Definitely pub."

5

FANTASY FOOTBALL

My mum sent me a link. That in itself was odd; it hadn't happened for two years. Most of the time, she couldn't remember her passwords.

The link was to a Facebook quiz. Absolute trash, designed to harvest your data, not something I'd normally even click on. But for once I started going through it, and, to my surprise, it was quite interesting. It was a series of choices: painting A and painting B side by side, and you had to guess which was made by a human and which was by AI. I sort of expected there would be a catch, and the AI would have created all of them. But I never got to the end.

It was question four that got me. Image A was a red train on a track in the countryside. But it was just the engine, with no carriages behind. There was something about the image that unnerved me. I closed the tab within microseconds of seeing it, but the memory of it haunted me for days.

I spent Saturday nursing a hangover, and Sunday was ruined when Man United lost, meekly, at home against Brighton. I took Monday evening off to binge-watch sitcoms and carried that over into Tuesday. I think the curse didn't like that I wasn't obsessing over football nonstop, because the monthly special deal appeared on Wednesday morning.

UNIQUE SPECIAL OFFER

New perk available until the end of August: Fantasy Football.

Cost: 2,000 XP (MEGA VALUE)

Effects: The Fantasy Football perk gives three new abilities:

1) Bench Boost. Your substitutes will play better in one game of your choice per season.

2) Triple Captain. Your captain's influence attribute will be tripled for one game of your choice per season.

3) Free Hit. Increase the chance of a penalty, free kick, or corner resulting in a goal by ten percent. One use per game.

This was weird for many, many reasons, but let's focus on two. First, the new abilities were named after "jokers" you could play in the Premier League's official Fantasy Football game. The effects were different though; the curse had simply taken the names and tweaked them.

Second, it struck me that the curse was treating me like I was in charge of a football team. Who else could pick a team's captain or choose the substitutes?

And that assumption was ludicrous. I was as close to managing a team as I was to landing a date with Margot Robbie. I literally knew no one in the football industry. Even the idea of going to a Sunday League team and offering to manage them was insane. People have been put in asylums for less.

I realised that one of the attributes I couldn't see was influence. I spent a few minutes wondering what the effect of that would be. Inspirational players like Roy Keane and Patrick Viera would have high influence, right? Did it lift the other players? Did influence only matter if that player was selected as captain? Or would Keane still propel his team forward if he was in the team but not the captain?

Anyway, all of these questions were irrelevant. I'd struggled to get 1,000 XP in July, and more than a week into August, I only had 165. If I spent every waking moment driving around Manchester looking for games to watch, sure, I could get to 2,000. But nah.

That said, I was interested in going to see a professional match, just to nail down what CA and PA meant. So I spent Wednesday evening on my laptop looking for a game in the Greater Manchester area, as soon as possible. My preference was, naturally, United. First, because that's my team; second, because I know their players so well; and third, because seeing those players in person would give me some very definite results about the whole attributes thing. For example, Ronaldo might be the best header of a ball in the history of the game. If his heading was rated at twenty, that would give me a definitive boundary. If it was rated at, I don't know, forty-four, then maybe scores were out of fifty. Similarly, Rashford had to be close to the max in acceleration and pace. Eriksen would be near the top in passing. And so on.

But their next home games were against Liverpool and Arsenal—good luck finding a ticket for those—followed by Leeds, Newcastle, and Tottenham. All big games. Maybe there would be a chance to get a ticket to the Leeds game, but even if that was possible, it would be six weeks away. Annoying. I posted on a forum that I'd love a ticket to the Liverpool game, but I doubted anything would come of it.

I skipped City—I didn't intend to give them any of my cash, ever—and went down the leagues. In a way, there was too much choice. Wigan versus Bristol City in the Championship? How about Bolton versus Salford City in the EFL Cup? I was strangely drawn to Preston versus Watford. Watford had recently been in the Premier League, so I assumed they still had some decent players. They also had a guy called Rey Manaj, who they had bought from, get this, Barcelona. Surely, he'd be interesting? The only question was whether I could wait that long. The match was a couple of weeks away.

I picked up some XP on Thursday night and talked to Emre, the guy who sold wraps and kebabs at Platt Lane, about British footballers who ended up in Turkey. He had amazing stories about Graeme Souness's time as manager of Galatasaray. But the main focus of the week was Friday night and my second time managing Beth's team. We filled in the paperwork correctly, I gave the players instructions, and they carried them out. There was nothing much to do, no star players to defend against, no particular weakness to exploit. The other team were awful at everything, equally.

After five minutes I checked, and, lo and behold, I'd earned ten XP. So I was getting 2 XP per minute for managing compared to just 1 for watching. And the quality of the opposition didn't matter, because this rabble were miles behind the girls from City. And clearly the intensity of my managing didn't matter either, because after setting them up, I was extremely passive.

With all the players in the right positions and with a simple game plan, we crushed them. The final score was 8–0. I was 100 XP richer, but I just felt . . . dissatisfied. There was no challenge to it. Beth and the girls were very happy though and dragged me to the pub again. This time, I didn't go home with Beth. I didn't see the point in managing them again. I told her, in front of the rest of the team, that in the morning I had to go and see my sick mum in the hospice. There was no way Beth could fight back without seeming like a selfish B.

XP balance: 365

I did go and see Mum, but not in the morning. That's when the care home smells the worst. After lunch is good, because the mood is high and everyone's sleepy. And if the sun's out you can have a nice cup of tea in the grounds, which are not Versailles but are still nicer than the dark, damp, narrow streets and alleys of Moss Side.

We ended up playing cards. The four of us: me, Mum, Anna, and Solly. The dog didn't get dealt a hand; he just lay on Mum's feet. Sometimes he'd get up, turn around, and resettle.

It was all very chill and felt like something we'd been doing our whole lives. Frankly, Mum was being cured by Anna. That was the only way to think about it. Instead of slipping further into her disease every time I saw her, she was moving away from it. Normally, you'd use words like "struggle" or "fight," but it wasn't like that. She was just getting better. Even her dexterity was better; she could deal the cards, albeit slowly.

We were playing with matchsticks as our stake, and I was losing, badly. Once I was down to my last five matches, I gave Anna a sly look. She was cheating. She saw me looking and shook her head left and right about half an inch. Then she did an almost invisible nod towards Mum, and I was supposed to understand something from that.

As revenge, I turned the discussion to *Love Island*. Anna glared at me. Even Solly lifted his head and gave me a disdainful look. I leaned back and stuck a matchstick in my lips. Winner.

"How are United doing?" Mum asked.

"Not great," I said. "Lost the first match of the season. They looked good in preseason though. I think the new manager will do well."

"That's good," said Mum. "I'm sure they'll win the next one."

Which just proved that if Anna was right, and Mum had some psychic abilities, it did NOT extend to predicting sports results. Because United were about to get absolutely annihilated. And that would be my ticket—literally—to everything that would follow.

6

CATACLYSM

Football glossary: *Hat trick. Three goals in one match. "He scored a first-half hat trick."*

Shambolic. Humiliating. Debacle. Shocking. Hilarious. These were the words being tossed around after just thirty minutes of Manchester United's 4–0 defeat to Brentford. United's goalkeeper, David de Gea, the highest-paid Spanish footballer in the world, with wages of twenty million pounds a year, allowed a one-mile-per-hour shot to dribble through his hands. And that was only the start of the cataclysm.

Brentford's wage bill was one-tenth of United's, and their starting eleven cost a combined forty-five and a half million pounds. Five of United's players cost more than that *on their own*, including Lisandro Martinez, a new signing considered (by everyone outside of Old Trafford) too short to play centre-back in the Premier League. He was awful, frequently bullied, and unable to cope with Brentford's fast, powerful forwards or their clever set pieces. He looked like the little girl City had sent on near the end of our match, too small, not talented enough, and an obvious weak link. Unlike me, Brentford had no qualms about exploiting it.

Brentford's players looked hungrier and more determined, and the stats proved it. As a team they ran fourteen km (eight point seven miles) more than United.

United were trying to pass the ball short from the goalkeeper to attract the Brentford players, just like Man City's girls had done against Beth's team. Except where the fifteen-year-old girls were using it to trick their much older opponents, United were using it to bring pressure on themselves so they could implode further.

After the fourth goal, when United continued to play in the limp, lethargic, almost suicidal way they had started the game, I joined in the fun and started laughing. Imagine being paid that much money and caring that little. It was hard to know who to be mad at. From the players, anyway. The vampiric ownership was a different matter. But let's start with David De Gea. It would take me FIFTEEN YEARS to earn what he took home in ONE WEEK.

And he didn't give a shit. Neither did any of the others.

It was abject, shameful, pitiful, and United rightly finished the weekend at the bottom of the League.

Soon after, my inbox was flooded—a slight exaggeration—with offers of tickets to the next game from disgusted, furious supporters. I snapped one up and drove to the guy's house to get it before he changed his mind. Sixty pounds. Not cheap, and I had to listen to a ten-minute rant about how shit all the players were. True. But I had a ticket.

I didn't really want to watch United get pissed on by their old rivals, Liverpool, one of the three best teams in the world. But at least I personally would get something out of it. Most likely I'd be the only United fan in the stadium who could say that. One way or another, I'd learn more about this curse. One way or another, I'd get some definitive answers.

Although I was looking forward to the match in a fatalistic kind of way, football wasn't currently my favourite thing in the world. When I thought about it, my mind always turned to the stupendous amounts of money being squandered. United would hire a manager, spend two hundred million pounds buying him the players he wanted, then sack him and start the process again with a new guy who didn't rate the old players. So the players bought in the previous cycle, and the one before that, were on the bench or in the reserves earning unthinkable wages, their short careers going nowhere.

As a United fan, in the old days, even when they were having a bad run, you could expect them to go and buy someone else's best player and solve the problem that way. When Leeds won the league, United bought Eric Cantona from them. Leeds stopped winning; United shot into the distance. Years later, Newcastle started to challenge United, so United bought Andy Cole, Newcastle's star striker. United won the treble. Some time after that, United came second on goal difference, so they bought Robin Van Persie from Arsenal, and he scored a ton as United cruised to the title. Ah, the good old days. I wish I'd seen them.

But now, the rampant spending was fuelling the problem, not fixing it. They bought Pogba but didn't know what to do with him. They bought Di Maria and had no place for him in the team. They bought Ronaldo, and the team became hashtag content for his Instagram feed.

Millions and millions of pounds flying out of the club, left, right, and centre. A torrent of cash and incompetence. Hilarious to fans of other teams, fair enough, but for someone making 1,400 pounds a month, it was all hard to take.

And that's partly why instead of watching Chelsea versus Spurs, or going to Hough End to get XP, I went to the care home. Mum and Anna were watching *Flog It!,* a TV show where people bring antiques to be valued. (*What price for Ronaldo?*) I drew up a chair and sat next to them in depressed silence. Solly the Psychic Dog took pity on me and sat on my feet.

"You're sad," declared Anna. "You should take him for a walk."

"That's what I'd do if *he* was sad," I said.

"It works both ways," she said. "His leash is on the side table."

We trudged the streets. I was in some sort of delayed shock from the match. *Four–nil!* This was probably how they felt in Rome when they heard Hannibal had wiped out the Legions. Just loads of people walking around not saying anything, not believing their own reality, not knowing where they were.

Solly knew where he was, and he started pulling me towards a big park. There, we wandered from tree to tree and bush to bush. He seemed to be having a great time. His jolly little tail wag, the hot sunshine, and the cool shade started to cheer me up. I started to think about more optimistic topics than Man United's future: global heating, rampant inflation, the imminent collapse of liberal democracy.

A woman with a dog of her own stopped for an encounter. "Oh, he's so cute! What's his name?"

It took me a second to snap back into my body. The woman had bent and was giving Solly an aggressive cheek rub. "Solly."

"What is he?"

"A Tennessee Subcritical," I said. Solly and the other dog were sniffing each other very intently. It was pretty graphic. Shouldn't be allowed in public.

The dog owner frowned, but then looked up at me like I was George Clooney, big eyes open wide, enjoying being teased. "There's no such thing."

"I don't know what he is. He's from another one of the patients. I'm just walking him."

She laughed. "I knew it. Hot guy with a cute dog, round here of all places. Of course you're sick. Irreversibly damaged, no doubt. How long have you got left to live?"

"About three nights."

"Is there no cure?"

I was thinking of something funny to say. Some witty comeback. But why? I was already in. "Let's drop him off, and then you can invite me to your place."

Solly helped me take my mind off things, it's fair to say. I took him for a "walk" the next night too, with similar results. Solly was a total assist machine. I thought about going for the hat trick, but putting it like that made it seem tawdry, so I skipped a day. The day after was Thursday, and, while walking him, a total cutie pie started chatting me up. But Solly didn't like her. He kept trying to hide behind me, doing tiny whines and all those things dogs do when they're scared.

You're probably thinking I ignored him and took a shot at an open goal.

No chance. I don't believe in the paranormal, except Scottish curses, but I'm not a complete idiot. At least I hope not. I let the woman down gently and found a stick to throw for the dog. The smooth-brained idiot loved it.

As a side note, I went past the little park near my house a few times and finally saw the kid who'd helped me get home. He was mid-game and didn't notice me. I did a little shop at the big ASDA, and, on the way back, I waved him over.

"Mate," I said, trying to press a pack of Hobnobs into his hands. "Thanks for helping me home that time. I was pretty out of it."

"Say that again."

"But I should have given you the biscuits."

"Nah, man. I was joking." He tried to push the Hobnobs back into my plastic bag.

"Nah, you could have left me there on the ground and that. I'm just saying thanks."

He took the pack, just to shut me up. "Aight, sorted." He looked at the game that was continuing without him. He was itching to get back to it.

"One thing, though. I have a kind of half-memory of something you said. I've been wracking my brains trying to work it out."

"What's that?"

"It was . . . it was something about 'good deeds' but there was 'punished' as well. It made no sense."

He sort of sneered at me, but then he remembered. He clicked his tongue. "No good deed goes unpunished, man. You never heard that?"

"I don't think so. What's it mean?"

"Means you do something good, you get banged. So why bovver?"

I rubbed the side of my head. I could have popped a balloon with all the static. "That's not how it goes, is it? You helped me out, you got a pack of Hobnobs. That's like one pound fifty of top quality choc."

The kid said "tsk" and started to walk away. "I dunno man. I leave the philosophising to the taxi drivers."

In other words: don't think too much.

The strange thing was, I took his advice. He was an ugly street kid, one I used to avoid like the plague, but here he was pouring out single-malt shots of wisdom. I had a *real* special power, and its name was Solly. I stopped trying to understand my new augmented reality. I stopped worrying about the curse and what it all meant. My attention shifted back towards the stats that mattered, the stats that would get me paid. The call centre. Helping real people with real problems. Making my boss happy. Making sure my name was mentioned at promotion time. Maybe not this year, but the year after.

I decided to leave the exploring to the explorers and the data analysis to the podcast nerds.

I slept like a baby for a few nights. Life was tolerable.

But then it was Monday, August 22, the day Manchester United played Liverpool. And that's when I knew my days in the call centre were numbered. Because what I saw that evening was fundamental to everything that followed.

7

REVELATIONS

Manchester United have won England's top league twenty times. Liverpool have won it nineteen times. They are two of the biggest, most famous teams in the world. The rivalry between the clubs and fans is white hot.

I hadn't been to a match, concert, or even a movie for years, since before the pandemic. Approaching Old Trafford was like heading towards the biggest petri dish in the north of England. Seventy-six thousand people in one space. What would I catch? I had to push such thoughts away.

The closer you get to the stadium, the more people you see, and the more you hear.

In Firswood, a handful of United fans were hanging around a car checking their phones for the team news. Another clutch hung outside The Quadrant pub. Drinking. A few laughs. On Warwick Road, a trickle of people unhurriedly walked towards the giant stadium, then a stream, then a river. And outside one corner of the ground, was the Liverpool lot. Singing, chanting, taking selfies and TikToks. Enemies. Just a hint of menace. Things were calm now, but they might not stay that way. It's called an undercurrent because you can't see it.

Inside, I found my seat and heard some familiar chants and many, many new ones. New players, new songs. New times, new anthems. The away end was noisy, as it always was. Mocking us. Gloating.

As the match kicked off, an enormous roar made the hairs on my neck stand up.

Old Trafford is an all-seater stadium, which means you're supposed to sit down the whole game. The club sometimes gets into trouble with the local authorities because fans stand up too much. I wasn't helping. I was up and down like a pogo stick.

First, there was the speed and quality of the match. The intensity was typified by Lisandro Martinez, the short defender who had been bullied in the last game. Today, he was a different beast, thundering around the pitch like a Spartan warrior, making challenges, winning headers, and celebrating routine blocks and clearances like they were pivotal moments. The home fans loved it; the stadium was rocking. He was voted man of the match. What a turnaround!

LISANDRO MARTINEZ		
Born 18.1.1998	(Age 23)	Argentinian
Acceleration 11		
		Stamina 14
	Heading 14	Strength 14
		Tackling 14
	Jumping 13	
Bravery 15		Technique 15
	Pace 10	preferred foot L
	Passing 15	
Dribbling 12		
CA 173	PA 182	
Defender (Centre, Left); Defensive Mid		

In addition to the rough and tumble ebb and flow of a high-stakes, high-intensity Premier League game, one made even more vitriolic by the United fans protesting against the clueless owners, I was constantly being bombarded with revelations. Sometimes I'd stand up, amazed at a new discovery, only to realise that I was the only guy in the whole block on my feet at that moment. People must have thought I was a total nutjob. But I didn't care.

Revelations:

1. Attributes were out of 20. I saw this in the warm-up. Ronaldo had heading 20 and jumping 20. End of discussion.

2. Attributes almost certainly went up and down during a career. Young Ronaldo had been lightning fast, but now he had one of

the lowest pace/acceleration scores on either team. Fair enough. The guy was nearly forty. But he could still leap like he was on a trampoline.

3. Some of the attributes were surprising, but most weren't. As an example, Fred (United's preposterously-named Brazilian midfielder) had higher pace than Marcus Rashford, who I would have bet was the fastest player in the whole league. Not so, it seemed. Fred came on for the last twenty minutes, and he did seem fast. Faster than he looked on TV, certainly. Not surprising was the fact that Rashford's dribbling was eleven. Not even in the same league as the best dribblers on the pitch: Liverpool's Mo Salah (twenty) and Luis Diaz (eighteen).

4. Attributes weren't everything. Virgil van Dijk, who had been flawless for about four years, had a shockingly bad game despite having sky-high numbers. Ditto Salah, who was muted, though he scored a goal like he always does against United.

5. This one blew my mind. During one brief break in play, I checked my XP and had so many I thought I'd misremembered what I'd started with. But no, I was just earning XP at a staggering rate. I did a test and found I was getting 7 XP per minute. I'd made another false assumption: a game is not a game. This game was worth seven Sunday League ones. I mean, it made sense—I was watching elite players with elite managers in a top stadium—but it really came out of the blue. As a bonus, there were two minutes of injury time in the first half and six in the second half. Sunday League refs never played injury time. They wanted to get home. So I went from 365 XP to 1,051. Hitting two thousand by the end of the month suddenly seemed possible. One more Premier League match plus a few evenings at Platt Lane. Easy!

6. CA and PA probably had an upper limit of 200.

7. CA and PA definitely didn't mean counterattacking and pressing. I was dead wrong about those. It was obvious pretty quickly. Players I knew to be shit at pressing had high PA, and players who didn't seem especially good at counterattacks had high CA. So what, then? Well, I'm no statistician, but one thing jumped out at

me; nobody had a CA higher than their PA. Or to put it another way, everyone's CA was lower than their PA.

A few examples:

Player	CA	PA
Ronaldo	182	200
Salah	189	193
Alexander-Arnold	187	192
Sancho	173	186
Heaton	130	150
Garnacho	90	173

A very quick discussion of these players. Apologies if you've worked it all out already. Feel free to skip a couple of paragraphs. Ronaldo is considered, along with Messi, to be one of the two best players of all time. Personally, I don't see how you can ignore Maradona. Or Pele. Or Cruyff. But anyway, Ronaldo is right up there. That's why I thought 200 would be the boundary for PA, whatever it meant.

Salah played for Liverpool, which meant I couldn't actually like him. But he was certainly one of the best in the world. Ditto Alexander-Arnold, a frightening attacking right-back whose weakness was defending. Any thoughts I had that the left column might have meant defensive skill while the right meant attacking was quickly dispelled when I saw his numbers.

Sancho was a weird one. He was a slight, frail-looking technician. He often had games where he didn't do anything substantial, but here, he dribbled through the Liverpool defence and calmly took his time to slot the ball into the corner. He was obviously *great*, but was he *good*?

Heaton was United's reserve goalkeeper. That his numbers were so much lower than the others made a lot of sense. He was a perfectly good Championship player. The Championship is the level below the Premier League. He'd been brought in to be the backup to the backup, but today he was on United's bench, because their *actual* second-choice keeper had thrown his toys out of the pram and would surely leave the club soon.

Then there was Alejandro Garnacho, an eighteen-year-old substitute. I'd seen him in a couple of preseason games; he was lightning fast and seemed unfazed by being on the same pitch as world famous players. Good prospect.

I felt like I was close to understanding these numbers. It didn't seem that hard. But for the last twenty minutes of the match, the tension was so unbearable—United's brittle defence clinging on to a lead against a brilliant attack—that I couldn't do anything other than focus on the game before me. When the final whistle blew, and United had the three points in the bag, I literally sagged with relief while strangers all around hugged each other, spread the world's happiest germs, and chanted against the ownership and for the players. It was barely-contained mayhem.

During the walk to my car, I decided to go all out to buy Fantasy Football. That meant using the leftovers from my Scottish money plus blowing up my meagre savings. But it made sense. It felt right. I didn't have much of a clue what CA was, but I had a strong suspicion PA was the key to everything.

At home, I checked the upcoming Premier League fixtures with a growing sense of dread. United didn't have a home match for the rest of the month. It seemed pretty clear that I would have to go and watch Man City if I wanted to buy the perk.

I shuddered as I typed, for the first time in my life, "Manchester City" into a search bar, and nearly gagged when I clicked through and saw that awful, awful light blue banner on my screen.

There was one thing I didn't need to worry about, at least. I knew there would be plenty of tickets available.

8

RAFFI BROWN

Solly didn't get a walk that week; I was racking up XP. I still didn't quite know what was happening to me, but I finally had a sense that it would lead to something good.

City were playing Crystal Palace on Saturday, the 27th. I had four evenings before then, plus the Sunday League bonanza the day after, then three days after that. So hitting 2,000 XP by the month's end seemed easy. The only real issue was the cost. I'd spent more than one hundred pounds on tickets to two games. That was unsustainable.

Anyway, I had a genius idea that I tested on the Tuesday before the City game. I drove to the Powerleague five-a-side pitches in Ardwick. Ardwick always seems so far from Moss Side, but when I looked on the map it was just a few miles away. My perceptions of distances were still firmly fixed in the public transport phase of my life; I'd only had a car for a year.

What I was hoping for was a continual stream of weekday matches to watch, just like Hough End on Sundays. If I got XP for the organised league matches at Powerleague, I could score a lot of XP in one evening. If I also got XP for the "friendly" games there, then I was quids in. Yes, it would probably only be 1 XP per minute, but it would be free.

I got there at quarter past six, and there were two games going on. I asked a goalkeeper if he minded me watching, and he said no. I think he liked having an audience. He put a bit of needless flash into his saves. It didn't take long to learn that I was getting XP. I set a twenty-minute timer, and when it went off I took a ten-minute break. Then I went back to whichever game was going on, and there were more and more through the evening, peaking between eight and nine thirty. I'd stuck 120 XP in my pocket by nine thirty, and was just about to call it a night when I thought I'd just watch one minute of the nine thirty kickoffs to help me unlock the scouting X players achievements.

And that's when I saw him.

RAFFI BROWN		
Born 8.8.2001	(Age 21)	English
Acceleration 7		
		Stamina 4
	Heading 8	Strength 4
		Tackling 3
	Jumping 7	
Bravery 6		Technique 8
	Pace 10	preferred foot B
	Passing 12	
Dribbling 7		
CA 2	PA 139	
Midfielder (Centre)		

PA 139! That was almost as much as Tom Heaton, a Manchester United player. Preferred foot: B. Clearly that was B for Both. Perfectly two-footed. Very rare, very valuable. His attributes were not over-whelming, but I had a sense that there was something special about him. I stuck around to watch, intrigued.

He was strangely ugly. I keep reading that beauty is related to sym-metry, and seeing Raffi Brown was the first time I thought the theory might have legs, because this kid was lopsided. His mouth looked like it had been drawn by a primary school kid; it sloped down to the right slightly. His eyes also had slightly odd slopes, like the same primary schooler had rearranged herself, or moved the paper she was drawing on. His nose stuck out to the left; his eyebrows were different lengths; his ears didn't match. If all this makes him sound like Quasimodo, dial that image much further back towards normal human. He wasn't gro-tesque. He was just slightly off in every way. Including how he sort of lumbered around the pitch.

But then he got the ball, and I actually gasped. Suddenly, he was totally transformed. He had the balance of a ballet dancer and the power of an Olympic sprinter. He shrugged off a challenge, feinted to pass with his right, dragged the ball back onto his left, and played a pass through to the striker. The whole thing took maybe 0.7 seconds. Do you believe in love at first sight? You should.

Entranced, enchanted, I stayed to watch this guy, my pulse racing every time he got the ball. And every time he got the ball, he did something. A delightful, cushioned one-touch pass. A shot that made the goalkeeper dive the wrong way. How? A spin under pressure, seeing there was no pass on, and a calm turn to play the ball back to his keeper. So simple, so obvious, and something that so few amateur players would do. Then, there was his defensive work. He tracked his runners, made interceptions, was always somewhere useful, always having an impact on the game. The other team kicked him, tried to rile him up, but he was like a zen master. He finished the half unruffled, and, as far as I could see, with one hundred percent pass accuracy.

At half-time, I asked the goalkeeper for the name of the team, then went to reception pretending I was one of their players and wasn't sure what time the game was next week. She told me.

I waited at a bus stop trying to process what I'd just seen, and only at the last second did I stop myself from getting on a bus. I had *driven* there! I got in my car and waited until I was a bit more clear-headed, then drove home at about three miles an hour while my brain kept accelerating.

What had I just witnessed?

I went to the Powerleague on Wednesday and Thursday evenings too and took Friday off.

XP balance: 1,431

Saturday was the City game, and I wasn't looking forward to it. I dreaded seeing all the City players with much higher numbers than the United ones.

But what I saw was a fucking fantastic match, a proper classic. Crystal Palace scored two goals before half-time. I tried not to celebrate the Palace goals. I was in the home section. This was the kind of match City sometimes struggled with. Teams who had fast players could hurt them on the break; I didn't need to be a tactical genius to know that. And that's what happened. Palace absorbed City's anaemic pressure (no shots in the first half) and used fast counterattacks to create chances. Boom. New season, same as the old season.

But one thing had changed for City this year. In addition to having about thirty world-class midfielders to choose from, they also had new signing Erling Haaland, a freak of nature who looked and moved like a Viking marauder. Roared on by an electrified, frenzied crowd, he scored a dramatic second-half hat trick to secure the win for his new team.

ERLING HAALAND		
Born 21.7.2000	(Age 22)	Norwegian
Acceleration 18		
		Stamina 16
	Heading 16	Strength 19
		Tackling 8
	Jumping 15	
Bravery 18		Technique 14
	Pace 18	preferred foot L
	Passing 12	
Dribbling 13		
CA 189	PA 197	
Striker		

Amazing numbers.

Elsewhere, United beat Southampton 1–0, while Liverpool blew away the cobwebs, winning a record 9–0. (By the way, in the real Fantasy Football game I had used my Triple Captain on Mo Salah, and he was the only Liverpool player not to score or assist! Despite my new powers, I was shockingly bad at the game.) Those big teams *should* be winning most weeks, given how much money they spent. But as United had proven, sometimes spending money didn't guarantee success.

Talking of spending, how much had Haaland cost? If I remembered correctly, not that much. I thought I remembered seeing sums like fifty-one million pounds being mentioned, but this was one of the hottest players in world football. United had signed the short defender for more, and had just bought Casemiro, a thirty-year-old midfielder who never scored, for even more.

After the game, while I waited for the majority of fans to leave, I did a quick online search. And yes, the transfer fee paid to Haaland's previous club, Borussia Dortmund, was "only" fifty-one million. But City also had to pay Haaland's agent a staggering thirty-four million. Thirty-four million quid for the easiest bit of work any human has ever done!

Imagine the phone call.

"Hello, is that Manchester City?"

"Yes."

"Do you want to buy Erling Haaland?"

"Yes."

"Great, I'll send over the paperwork."

Amazing.

As we say in England, it's nice work if you can get it.

I did that thing again where I stood up like I'd seen a goal.

Nice work if you can get it . . . agent fees . . . nice work if you can get it . . . thirty-four million pounds . . . nice work if you can get it . . . *how can you get it?*

A picture flashed across my mind: a player standing with one foot on a ball, looking at me with his arms crossed, an amused smile playing across his crooked lips.

Raffi Brown.

9

A PROMISE TO MYSELF

Becoming an agent—it made so much sense. Agents were everywhere these days. Casual fans knew some of them by their first name: Mino, Kia, Jorge. They had more power than some managers. Imagine being a middleman in modern football. Making ten percent of a few transfers here and there and I'd be spending my evenings frolicking on an inflatable unicorn in my personal swimming pool.

The daydreams came thick and fast . . .

I'd been so distracted by the whole "finally a potential use for this curse" thing that I didn't notice I'd passed 2,000 XP. My balance was 2,081.

But I didn't buy the Fantasy Football perk right away. I wanted to think things through.

Fantasy Football, along with most of the other perks and screens, was aimed at, as far as I could tell, football managers. It was geared towards contracts, transfers, formations. But I was never going to be a manager. Why should I buy a perk to boost my team's in-game performance? I would never *have* a team.

Literally, the only reason to buy it was because it was on special offer. Actually, it was slightly more than that. Super Scout had been on special offer, discounted from ten thousand to 1,000 XP. But Fantasy Football was listed as 2,000 XP and had no normal price. So it wasn't merely on discount; it was something that might never be available again.

What else should I spend my XP on?

Probably the Attributes 1 perk, and then Attributes 2, and so on. Why? Because knowing more about individual players would give me a genuine edge, be it in terms of betting or scouting. Did I have what it took to be an agent? Why not? Find a player, get him a club, take ten percent. How hard could it be?

But Attributes 1, 2, etc, would always be available to buy, right? That's how it seemed. And if they suddenly stopped being available, if the curse stopped playing by its own rules, then fuck it. I'd smash retire and hope that got rid of the whole mess. I wouldn't have to waste my time and money on this whole "live football" thing anymore. It wasn't totally rational, but I was leaning towards buying the Fantasy Football perk, then grinding to unlock more Attributes. All with a view to scouting Raffi Brown and riding that pony all the way to Obscene Wealth City. I decided to sleep on it.

I bought Fantasy Football. Why? Because that's what I'd been saving up for. I felt like I had to follow through with my promise to myself. You can't move the goalposts halfway through a game, right? Maybe there would be a time to use it in the next forty years of my life. If I lived that long, and if future scientists found a way to play football on a desert world where grass was extinct, I could be the manager of Atreides Town or Stillsuit City.

Was the heat getting to me? You decide.

Now, though, with Fantasy Football in the bag, I had a new target: unlocking the Attributes perks to learn more about players I saw. I only needed 219 XP to get the first one. I could do that in two evenings at Powerleague, but I didn't want to be hanging around those pitches 24/7 in case they decided I was a weirdo and kicked me out. I needed to mix things up a bit.

Going to another Premier League match was out of the question for a couple of months. I was flat broke after the two I'd attended, and that included the help of the Scottish money. So if, as I expected, the next special offer cost 3,000 XP, then it could go jump off a cliff.

Anyway, I realised that I had one place where I could use my shiny new perk while gaining XP: the North Manchester Women's Indoor Limited Invitational League. Also known as "the league Beth played in."

The only catch was that it meant reconnecting with Beth. Potentially tricky. Could I get Solly to do some of the work for me? I decided to man up for once.

With a sigh, I dialled Beth, made small talk, and invited myself to be their team's manager again. There was a long silence—too long to be believable—before Beth said she'd think about it. I tried to pretend to be worried, like I understood her predicament. But I knew that if she didn't say "no" right away, she'd eventually cave. She liked winning and she liked me.

So those were my Friday nights sorted. I planned to save Bench Boost and Triple Captain for the next game against Man City under-sixteens. But the Free Hit I could try every game. That actually sounded fun. The only problem was there weren't a lot of free kicks or penalties in that league. Something to worry about later though.

So Friday was women's night. Sunday was Hough End and maybe some police. Mondays I'd probably take off. Tuesdays were Power-league and perving over Raffi Brown. Wednesdays, whatever. Thursdays, probably Platt Lane. Saturdays I'd probably take it easy, but I did want to find someplace with regular games just in case I needed XP fast. Maybe I could try one of the lower division teams like Altrincham. I doubted I'd get 7 XP per minute, but you never knew. Failing that, there were other Powerleagues in Manchester. I'd just have to drive a bit further.

All in all, I was in a good location to grind for XP if that's what I needed to do.

XP balance: 181

I spent Monday evening at the Powerleague in Ardwick. I know, I know. I said I wouldn't go there all the time but I'd come up with a good plan. I went in full kit. I had the black United kit from the 90s and wore full shin pads and everything. Proper John Terry stuff. (John Terry didn't play in a final but changed out of his suit into his team's kit for the trophy presentation, earning him the eternal nickname Full-Kit Wanker.)

Being in a full kit made it seem like I was simply early for my team's game, and helped me blend in. Plus, and I'm getting proper Agatha Christie here, being in a kit made people look at the kit and not at me. I still didn't want to push my luck, but going two nights in a row was doable as long as I changed my "costume."

The great thing about these Powerleague places, apart from the *really* nice artificial pitches, was the bar. I didn't drink more than a half a pint when I was driving, but I enjoyed being in the bar area with loads of people around me chatting about footy. It was a pretty good-natured vibe, lots of banter and LOLs, which was kind of hilarious when you had seen the people raging like fucking *orcs* on the pitch not twenty minutes before.

Anyway, one team must have been from Christie's Hospital or something, because there was this gaggle of nurses at a table drinking girly drinks while a related group of doctors/male nurses/cancer patients were at the next table drinking big beers.

Seeing the nurses made me realise that I hadn't done any searches on my condition recently. Had I just accepted that I saw numbers every time I was at a football match? Was I really okay with that?

Although I was hoping to become an agent and make shitloads of money, I did want to know if I was cracking up or not. It didn't help that my mum had a brain illness. So, I saw this as an opportunity to get some advice, face to face, from healthcare professionals I would never see again.

I approached the table. There were four nurses—God I hoped they were nurses, or I was about to humiliate myself—of varying levels of hotness. There was a quiet one on the left that I thought was a mega-babe. The others were plainer, and one in particular was a gobby B. Almost as soon as I spoke, I knew I'd made a mistake. But I tried to plough through. If they had an answer for me, it'd be worth whatever sticks and stones they threw.

"Hello, ladies," I said.

"Here we go," said the gobby one. Even though I made eye contact with anyone but her, she did all the talking. "Can't even drink in peace."

"Right. Sorry to disturb you. I'm trying to remember the name of this book."

"You need a librarian, mate."

"It's a medical thing. I've heard about it in TV shows or podcasts. It's like . . . a dictionary of medical problems. It's like, if a problem isn't in that book then it's not considered a real problem. Do you know what I'm talking about?"

"Talking a lot of shite if you ask me."

Okay. Total bomb. "Right, thanks for your time anyway."

I retreated to my little table and scratched my head. I knew that such a book existed, but searching for phrases like "medical dictionary" led, obviously, to medical dictionaries. What I wanted was something a bit higher level. The thing proper doctors used. Would it be helpful for me? I didn't know, because I couldn't remember its name. Even if I had a copy in front of me, what would I do? Skim from start to finish looking for keywords like "Polish cyclist," "identity theft enabler," or "what's the difference between pace and acceleration?"

I was staring at a TV screen, not really paying attention while sipping my drink. A dude was suddenly in front of me. He didn't look scary.

"Mate," he said, placing his beer on my table. My table!

"Yeah?"

"You were asking about medical books."

I glanced over at the table of nurses. The cute one quickly looked away. "Oh, yeah."

"Why?"

"I've got a medical problem, and I want to look it up."

"That's what the internet is for."

This guy was starting to piss me off. The scene was over. Why couldn't he leave me alone? I said, "There's a book that has a list of every disease, and if it's not in that book it's not a real disease. I saw the nurses and thought they'd know the name. Is that all right? Are you going to fucking glass me for asking a question?"

The guy picked up his beer and backed away. Too fucking right. My fists were clenched into tiny ping pong balls with gigantic knuckles.

As he settled back at his table and started talking quickly to his mates, I unclenched and wondered how much shit I was in. A quick knifing out in the car park? Fuck. What if they knew my car and firebombed it? Even worse, this was where Raffi Brown, my one true love, played. What if I got banned from coming?

And more importantly, why had I lost my shit so suddenly? If anyone had wound me up, it was the gobby woman. Why had I taken it out on the dude? I shook my head a few times, pissed at myself. I drained my little beer and half of my lukewarm coke. I wanted to be out of there ASAP. Ideally, with all the blood still in my skin. I stared at the wall, wondering about all this while pondering the best way to leave. Pick up my stuff in one quick, violent motion like I was a proper lunatic, not to be messed with? Or leave sheepishly, like I knew I'd been a dick?

I was suddenly aware that the guy who'd spoken to me was back, and he was right next to me. Holy fuck!

"Is it this?" he said.

He was indicating something in his hand, but I couldn't understand what I was seeing, because by context and by the curious leaps of my imagination, what was in his hand should have been a switchblade or maybe a machete. At least a steak knife from the kitchen. But actually, it was his phone. I tried hard to focus on it. Then it clicked, and I grabbed it from him.

The DSM-5: The Encyclopedia of Mental Disorders

The DSM-5, the Diagnostic and Statistical Manual of Mental Disorders, Fifth Edition is a tome on mental illness published by the American Psychiatric Association (APA). It has almost unanimous acceptance as the authority on mental health disorders. The DSM-5 contains broad categories of mental illness and, within those categories, all known mental disorders and their symptoms (List of Mental Illnesses). Mental health doctors and other professionals use the DSM-5 to help people pinpoint and understand their mental health problems so that they may overcome them. The information contained in the publication is so thorough and extensive that the DSM-5 is sometimes thought of as the encyclopedia of mental disorders.

"Holy shit," I said. "This is it! Yes!"

"It's American," he said. "That's why you couldn't find it."

"I listen to loads of American podcasts," I said. "I must have heard about it on one of those. Oh God, this is great. Let me just email myself that name. Oh, man. Thanks!"

"No worries."

"And listen, I was out of order before. I'm really sorry."

"Don't mention it."

"No, I will mention it. I don't know why, but I'm wound up tighter than a jack-in-a-box."

"I did kind of notice. But you United fans are all like that." My jaw dropped. How the hell did he know which team I supported? He pointed to my top. "Um . . . the kit?"

"Oh," I said, cringing at my stupidity.

"I shouldn't say this," he said. "But you should buy that book. Find out which one you've got." He laughed—not unfriendly, good banter—and walked off, returning in triumph to his table. I got busy looking up this mental disorders book. It sounded like exactly what I needed.

10

TRANSFER DEADLINE DAY

"FIFA report shows football agents earn £430.8m in latest male player transfer window." —BBC Headline

Transfer deadline day is one of the highlights of the sporting calendar. For those unfamiliar with the matter, football players can't just quit their jobs and get a new one. It's not like they work in a call centre.

Imagine a world where HSBC wanted me to work in their customer retention department. In this world, they are desperate for me, so desperate they are willing to pay my employer 25 million pounds to approve my switch. The rumours of this switch, or "transfer," are broadcast on Sky Sports, Sky News, Sky Sports News, Sky Call Centre News, and Sky Call Centre News HD, nonstop. Because, get this, there's a deadline. At 11 p.m. all transfers stop for five months. You need to get the right staff in the door or suffer the consequences for almost half a year. What stakes! What drama!

Once the fee is agreed (25 million pounds sounds about right, given my stats), HSBC offer me a contract. I'd sign, or not, and Sky Sports would discuss what it meant, in-depth, while waiting for news of Janet Clarke's move from HMRC National Insurance Specialists to Shell's Greenwashing Complaint Line.

With all the analysis, overblown graphics, speculation, and repetition of very few actual facts, transfer deadline day has the same kind of vibe as an election night. In fact, the two things have lots in common: the short-term futures of some venerable institutions are decided, it all seems very important, the dust settles, then you get ready to do it all again.

I tended to be only moderately interested in transfers. If team A bought a player from team B, then team B would have to replace him with someone from team C. Who would probably buy someone out-of-favour from team A. It was just a big merry-go-round. No one cared when call centre workers moved from job to job. What was so fun about football transfers? I liked managers who would take players, work with them, improve them, and build a team that way. A crafts-man, not a trader. But there weren't too many managers like that in the Premier League. The cost of failure was too high. Short-term results were ALL that mattered.

Still, this time transfer day had me glued to my phone (as much as possible during work, then completely after). I was so engrossed in tracking and digesting all the news that I forgot to eat until my stomach started complaining.

Manchester United bought Antony from Ajax, for one hundred million euros, and sold a young prospect for fifteen million pounds. The Antony deal was bonkers, totally desperate. He'd been available for fifty million not long ago. The consensus was that he was a good player but not a one-hundred-million-euro one. The player wanted to go to Manchester. He'd missed Ajax's last game. Instead of playing, he posted a photo of himself and his agent watching . . . Man United. Message received.

Chelsea bought a player from Leicester for seventy million. Leicester replaced him with a guy for thirty million. Nottingham Forest bought more players, which seemed insane to me because they'd already signed twenty guys over the summer. *Guys, you're only allowed eleven in the team! Someone tell them!*

So deadline day itself wasn't earth-shattering, but when the deadline passed, people started announcing truly spectacular numbers.

The twenty Premier League clubs had spent 1.91 BILLION pounds over the summer. Italian teams had splashed out about 650 million. France, Spain, and Germany were all in the four hundred to five hundred million pound range.

The lesson: football clubs were desperately looking for talented players and would pay huge amounts for them. Would go into debt for them. In the case of Barcelona, would literally mortgage their future for them (Barcelona, already in debt, had sold a bunch of assets to buy shiny new players like Lewandowski and Rafinha).

Maybe Barcelona's gamble would pay off, maybe it wouldn't. It didn't matter to me. I needed to find some talent, so I could get some skin in this game. If I could find the next Antony, my cut of his transfer bonuses and salary would mean I'd never have to answer a phone again.

As if to make sure I was hearing the message of the universe, FIFA released a report saying that agents had been paid 430 million pounds over the summer.

In the Premier League, the big result was United beating Arsenal 3–1 with United scoring ruthless counterattack goals and Antony scoring on his debut. Good, but to my naked eye, Arsenal were much the better team.

Meanwhile the media was raging about the video assistant referees (VAR) who ruined four or five of the weekend's matches with their fussy, nitpicky, and sometimes blatantly wrong interventions. I didn't mind VAR in principle, but there was no question the way it was being used was ruining the emotion and the spectacle of the Premier League. Don't celebrate a goal in case the VAR finds a toenail offside. Let's all sit around for four minutes watching the referee watch a pitchside monitor. It was incredibly dumb. Left unchecked, I saw a future in which the sport became less and less popular.

Which meant less and less money.

The gravy train wasn't leaving the station, but the gravy would never again be this rich, this thick, this delicious.

If I wanted some of that gravy, I had to grind.

I settled into my schedule, but without the days off. I was quite motivated to collect XP, even if it was slightly depressing to know that I could get seven times the amount if I had the cash.

But I didn't. So.

On Tuesday, I avoided the Ardwick Powerleague because of the incident with the nurses. Seemed sensible to let memories of that evening fade, even though nothing really happened. That meant missing Raffi's next match, but I was sure I'd find him again. I only needed 34 more XP to unlock Attributes 1, and I was very interested to rescout him with my new knowledge. If I was being serious about this agent thing, though, it meant being careful. Careful to the point of secrecy. Certainly careful enough not to get marked out as a troublemaker. So, I went to Platt Lane, picked up the XP I needed, and bought Attributes 1.

A generic player profile popped into my vision. It displayed the attributes I knew, such as acceleration, in the standard database format I'd gotten so used to, while a flashing block jumped from unnamed cell to unnamed cell. Some sort of random number-generator thing, like those seen on crappy TV game shows. I couldn't be *sure,* because it all happened fairly quickly and was quite unexpected, but I thought I counted thirty-one attributes in total.

At the end of the little cell dance, I was rewarded—and I think that is the perfect word—with "finishing."

The hardest thing to do in football is score a goal. It's a low-scoring sport. A player who can score goals is worth his weight in gold. Or in the case of Erling Haaland, ten times his weight in gold. I wasn't sure what the missing attributes on a player profile were, but finishing was surely the best I could possibly have unlocked. As an agent, I'd rather find a top striker than a top defender. Did agents get a cut of a player's goal bonus? Well, I'd be the one writing the contract, wouldn't I?

I scanned the players in the match I was watching with a big, cheesy smile on my face. James Wedge, finishing two. Okay! Good to know. Information is power!

I had a little daydream about finishing and what I'd see if I could rescout Ronaldo, Salah, and Haaland. It was mad to think I'd seen three of the world's most elite goalscorers in just two games in Manchester. Would they all have finishing twenty?

I guessed Ronaldo would have twenty. His problem wasn't scoring goals, but getting into position to have a shot. Normally, when he was in a dangerous place, the pass from his United teammate was dogshit. Certainly, if his finishing was less than twenty, then that was simply a function of his age. The guy had scored eight hundred goals, for God's sake.

Salah? Let's try nineteen. He was lethal with his left foot and could craft a shot out of nowhere. His stats, though, despite being in a team that was attacking most of the time, were nowhere near Ronaldo's, Benzema's, or Lewandowski's. And I'd rather have Ronaldo's weaker foot than Salah's.

Haaland seemed to score a hat trick every week, but when you watched him, he missed a lot of chances too. I'd put him at eighteen, but wouldn't have been surprised if he was even lower. Or maybe he was twenty, and the missed chances were just statistical noise.

My grin came back. I didn't have to wonder or think or make assumptions. I only had to get back into a stadium with these guys. Then I'd know, definitively, for sure. Objective truth. It's a hell of a drug.

So this was all very tremendous, but I was already thinking of the next steps. There was good news and bad news. The good news was that Attributes 2 was available, as I'd assumed. The bad news was that it was much more expensive, 630 XP. Double! If it kept doubling every time, the last one would cost more XP than grains of sand in the universe. Something like that, right? I didn't feel the need to worry about that just at the moment. Take it one game at a time, baby.

I had also unlocked some other perks I could buy.

There was one called Playdar. It promised to direct me to the player with the most talent within a certain radius. On the one hand, sort of useless, since I was already getting tons of information about players. On the other hand, if I was at Hough End or Hackney Marshes, it would lead me to the best player, and I wouldn't have to waste time on the other games. It was expensive—8,000 XP—which suggested the curse thought it was a valuable thing to have.

Match Stats 1 was available for 315 XP. No explanation was provided.

Player Comparison would allow me to nominate two players, and see how they fared side-by-side. 630 XP. That'd be a timesaver down the line, but right then I had no need for it. I could see Ronaldo's profile any time I wanted just by thinking about it. In theory, I could write down his stats, then call up what I'd seen of Salah, and write them next to Ronaldo's. Buying the comparison tool was a quality of life upgrade that I didn't need.

And, of course, I still had access to 4-4-2 diamond, which would lie on the shelf, unwanted and gathering dust, until the end of time.

On Wednesday, I decided to scout a bit further out and drove to the Powerleague in Stockport. It was basically straight, turn right, straight. But the previous sentence tells you nothing about the traffic, the constant stops for traffic lights, the feeling of rage that was venting out of every car. Especially mine.

It took over an hour and cost me quite a bit in petrol. I'd have to be very, very careful with my spending. I knew I was living very slightly outside my means, and I presently had no means of increasing my means.

So, I was slightly grumpy and fractious when I got there. Fortunately, no one paid me any attention. I wasn't wearing a sports kit, because it was my first time there, so no danger of me being kicked out for being a creep. I was dressed in my most formal call centre outfit, which helped with what came next.

11

BARRETT GRAVES

It was probably just that I was feeling grumpier than normal, but the Powerleague matches were highly irritating. Sloppy passes, failed 1-2s, shots blooted so high they went over the twenty-metre netting that surrounded the tiny pitches.

I wanted to grind. I wanted to get on the football agent gravy train. Why did these guys make it so hard for me?

After half an hour of head-in-hands frustration, I'd earned about 8 XP. I decided to take a break.

In the bar, I drank deeply from the hot news of the day, the sacking of Thomas Tuchel.

Tuchel had taken over a shambolic—and expensively assembled—Chelsea team halfway through a season and instantly transformed them. And when I say instantly, I mean instantly. Like a fucking wizard. They played, if memory serves, two days after he took over, and suddenly they had a totally different tactical plan. For a start, they HAD a plan. And even with my level-zero tactical brain, I could see that they were set up in such a way that every player always had a triangle of teammates to pass to, they were suddenly level nine thousand in press-resistance, and they outplayed Man City, Liverpool, and anyone else who made the mistake of getting in their way.

Fast forward a couple of months, and they were the Champions League winners. The best team in Europe. Wow. Astonishing.

Then Chelsea was forcibly sold because, well, because of that whole "Are We the Baddies?" situation. And the new owners spent in the region of three hundred million pounds buying players Tuchel wanted. But while on this spending spree, they were starting to realise that Tuchel wasn't their dream manager. The rumours were, and this was like reading those *Love Island* gossip articles, that Tuchel didn't reply to their WhatsApps fast enough, and his messy divorce was making him surly and difficult. On the other side of the coin, Tuchel lost faith when the owners suggested they play a 4-4-3 formation. Certainly, this suggestion was within the laws of the game, but even hipster teams tended to employ a goalkeeper. A "claim they deny!" said every single article on the subject, which meant it definitely happened.

Anyway, it was all very soap opera, and I almost couldn't get enough of it. But after reading my sixth article saying the same things, I put my phone away and tried to think about the story from a more strategic viewpoint.

Three hundred million buying specific players for a specific manager, then immediately firing him and getting someone new. Insanity! The owners were burning money on an industrial scale.

What about the Chelsea players? Some players would win, some would lose. The latter would be sold at a loss, replaced by expensive newcomers.

The fans? Most were stupefied by the sacking and its timing.

But one small group was popping open the champagne: agents. They made money coming and going. Three cheers for irrational owners!

I felt refreshed and went to check out the next round of matches.

One profile stood out like a sober person at a northern wedding, made all the more interesting because it was attached to the least interesting player on that particular pitch.

BARRETT GRAVES		
Born 13.1.1999	(Age 23)	English
Acceleration 3		
		Stamina 3
	Heading 6	Strength 6
		Tackling 3
	Jumping 5	
Bravery 4		Technique 4
	Pace 3	preferred foot R
	Passing 4	
Dribbling 2		
Finishing 16		
CA 1	PA 58	
Striker		

Now this was interesting. Quite a little conundrum. Based on the evidence of my eyes, Barrett Graves here was fairly poor at football, and his attributes weren't impressive. But, and this was a Jennifer Lopez-sized but, he had great finishing and relatively high PA. The value of finishing was obvious. But what was PA, exactly?

I'd been pondering that question obsessively and finally thought I'd had a eureka moment. The problem was that I'd acquired it at the same time as CA, making them seem like connected attributes. Attacking and defending. Pressing and counterattacking. Yin and yang. But what if they weren't connected? If I ignored CA and only looked at PA, surely it was obvious what it meant? Something like "Playing Aptitude." Basically, a single number that showed how talented a player was. Some kind of fundamental assessment of quality, like the score out of 100 you get on the FIFA video games.

How PA related to attributes like pace, or how it related to a player's match performance, I had no idea. But I knew it was the one number to rule them all.

At least, I thought I knew.

Now, Barrett Graves—thin with brown, curly hair—had a PA of 58, so he wasn't going to be playing in the Premier League any time soon. But surely there was a spot for him lower down the football pyramid? Especially with that finishing. Right? If he turned out to be good enough to earn five hundred pounds a week, that was fifty a week for yours truly. Enough to get me into every United and City game to turbocharge my XP growth. Enough to afford onions in my wraps. I started salivating, and had to tell myself to get a grip. Onions were a long way in the distance.

I watched the rest of his game, picking up full XP now that I was concentrating properly. Then, when his team were picking their bags up from behind the goal, I moved towards the gate.

"Barrett, right? Can I have a quick word?"

I'd done the "showing I knew someone's name" thing again. Again! The suit helped. Obviously, if I was intelligent enough to know how to buy a suit, I was intelligent enough to find out his name. "Everyone calls me Ziggy."

"Does that mean I have to as well?" This got a laugh, but as I tried to memorise his nickname a strange thing happened. His player profile opened, and the name section changed to say "Ziggy." Mentally tapping on it flipped the cell around so I could see his real name. Cool.

"What can I do for you? I was just going to have a shower."

"Yeah, of course. I have a shower once a week, even if I don't really need it. How can I say this? Um . . . I'm a scout. An agent. Have you *got* representation?"

"Representation? You mean . . . ? No. Is this a wind-up?"

"No. Look, I'm going to hang around the bar for a bit. I'd love to talk to you. No pressure." I could afford to be chill with Ziggy. It was a lot like flirting with a woman you weren't *that* into; there was no real consequence to messing it up. I doubted I'd be this zen when it came to seducing Raffi Brown.

Ziggy looked around at his teammates. Had they set up this prank? But they weren't laughing. I knew what their expressions meant. Why would anyone be interested in Ziggy instead of them? Ziggy was *shit*. "Er . . . maybe some other time. Have you got a card?"

Ooh. Problem. Of course a proper agent would have a business card. "Nope. Waste of paper. I also don't have a 4x4 or a private jet. I also don't smother baby seagulls in crude oil."

One of his mates chipped in. "You've got an iPhone."

"This one is made of *recycled* blood diamonds, all right? Look, Ziggy, it's like this. I want to talk to you about you. About you playing football. As a career. It'll take, like, one minute. I'll wait in the bar."

He nodded, confusion playing all over his face, then trudged off like he'd heard bad news.

The guy who had accused me of owning an iPhone came up to me. "What's the scam, mate?"

I wasn't worried about this guy's opinion of me. "You don't think Ziggers can make it as a pro?"

"No chance. He's bang average at *this* level. Stockport five-a-sides. Professional? Do me a favour. So what's the play? Nigerian 404? Catfish? Tech support?"

I laughed. "Tell you what. Let's make a bet. When Ziggo scores his first professional goal, you give me a hundred quid. And if he doesn't . . ." I looked around the pitches: referees whistling to signal the start of the next round of matches; the warm air starting to cool, so that some players wore t-shirts under their tops; floodlights coming on, though they weren't needed yet; men shouting. "Pass it! To feet! One two! Get back!"

"Yeah, what?"

I'd lost my train of thought. "What? Oh. Well, if he doesn't, it's not too bad here, is it? This is my level. Bang average, like you said. But he's not. He's got something. If I were him, I'd want to give it a go." I lost confidence in what I was saying after I'd finished saying it. *Would* I want to give it a go? Would I want to be a mediocre player? A top, top player, sure, no doubt. Fame, fortune, world travel. Meeting actresses and models. Playing in front of fifty thousand adoring fans every week. But a player at the level Barrett might reach? A lot of hard graft, a lot of hard men trying to take my place in the team or trying to kick me off the pitch. A handful of fans jeering when I hit a corner straight behind for a goal kick. Every witticism echoing around half-empty concrete stands. Every complaint from my manager audible to everyone in the stadium. Every opposition boot containing the potential kinetic impact that would shatter my shin into ten thousand pieces. A good match, one where I wasn't crippled for life, ending with a muddy trudge inside for a cold shower and cleaning my own boots. For five hundred pounds a week?

Not sure that was for me.

Not sure at all.

Whether the guy had tried talking to me since I'd gone into my reverie, I would never know. He'd vanished. I went into the bar and waited.

"Ziggy, I'm glad you came."

"Hugh told me to hear you out."

"Hugh is a scholar and a gentleman. Why are you called Ziggy?"

He looked down. "I look like someone from *The Wire*."

I nodded. I hadn't seen it, but some people talked about it like it was the TV equivalent of a sauna with Charlize Theron. "I'm Max. People call me Max because I don't look like someone from *The Wire*. Ziggy. I'll cut to the chase. I've seen something in the way you play. I've watched countless matches and scouted almost a thousand players in the last few months. Not many have what it takes to be a pro. I really think you could make it. I'm not saying it would be easy. It would be a lot of work for both of us. It might not lead anywhere. Are you interested? Should I pursue it?"

He did that thing where he looked sad with his soft, brown eyes. I wondered how he got on with women. I bet there were plenty who lapped up this "limpid pools of dreamy introspection" thing. "Interested in what, exactly? Like . . . what team? What level?"

I pursed my lips. What level was exactly the right question. I had a choice, to keep bullshitting like I was a top agent or to be honest. "Ziggy, let's be real. I'm spending Wednesday evening checking out players in Powerleague. I'm not expecting to find the next Neymar."

"Right."

"And honestly, I mostly watch the Premier League. So I need to do some research, have a look at the lower leagues, and see where you might fit in." He didn't seem happy that I didn't think he was the next world football superstar, but his posture didn't change. It didn't seem like he was about to leave. So I pressed on. "Have you heard about Preston?"

"No, what?"

"Their last five games were nil-nil, nil-nil, nil-nil, one-nil, and nil-nil. Seems to me they might be interested in a striker."

He gave me a blank look. "I'm not a striker."

"Jesus Christ, Ziggy. Of course you are." It hadn't occurred to me that he wouldn't know his own skills!

"I didn't score any goals today. What makes you think . . .? This is weird." He started to get up.

"All right, look. Don't throw the baby out with the bathwater. I don't need to see you dribble past twenty players and score an overhead kick, do I? If I'm wrong, I'm wrong, but guess what? I'm not wrong. No way. You're a goalscorer. I'm willing to bet my time and money on it. Here's my plan. I'm going to watch Preston. And Altrincham. And whoever else. And when I find the right club for you, I'm going to get you a trial. As a striker. We might have to go a division or two lower just to get you started, because you're pretty old to be getting your first gig. But whoever it is, you're going to play well and score goals. And they're going to sell you to Preston. And you're going to score fifteen goals a season and live happily ever after." I was getting hyper as my flight of fancy took off, more so because I was imagining ten percent of Ziggy's joy being sliced off and deposited into my personal bank account.

He stared down at the sticky floor. Finally, he said, "I doubt it."

I extended my arms. "I just need your phone number. If I get you a trial, you sign a contract making me your agent. If the trial goes nowhere, you don't pay a penny. If I can't find you a club, I'll let you know. And then you'll know."

"Then I'll know?"

"Haven't you always wondered if you were secretly good enough? That maybe you could make it?"

He glanced up at me, looked away, then locked his eyes onto mine again. Almost inaudibly, he whispered, "Yeah." Intensity. Secret reserves of self-belief. The little shit! He was a lady-killer, all right. Note to self: don't leave Ziggy alone in a room with a girl you are serious about.

I unlocked my phone, opened the contacts, and pushed it towards him. "Put your number in." He started typing. Slowly. I think he was feeling the weight of the phone to see if he could detect if he was being scammed. But I was already thinking of the future. "Try and get fitter. High intensity thingies. You know what I mean. Shuttles. And do some pilates or whatever. Can you practise jumping? That's weird, isn't it? I shouldn't have said that. Fuck it, practice jumping. I need people to think you might be a threat from set pieces. And tell these five-a-side fucks you need to play up front from now on. Your agent said."

He handed me my phone back. I felt him checking out my vibe: my confidence (unearned), my suit (not really that good, but in the land of leisurewear, the off-the-peg suit is king), and my smile (genuine). His mirror neurons fired, and there was a brief moment where he let his guard down. A tiny smile colonised his face. "My agent," he said.

"My client," I said, raising my fist in his direction.

We bumped.

My client, I thought to myself on the drive home. The traffic was no better. Every light was against me. Who gave a shit? Not me.

I had a client.

12

NETWORK

Football news was coming thick and fast. There was almost too much to keep abreast of.

First, the women's transfer record was broken. Barcelona bought a player from Man City. Excited, I clicked on the "breaking news" and found the fee was 350,000 pounds. In the men's game that would buy you . . . what? A League Two left-back?

Of course it was good that the amount of money in women's football was growing, but the fee was a disappointment. If I found a good female player, I wouldn't be able to start shopping for a penthouse in Beetham Tower.

Next, the baton of Premier League "crisis club" had been passed on. At the start of the season, Man United had been a laughing stock. Then it was Chelsea, then Aston Villa, Leicester, and now it was Liverpool. They lost 4–1 to Napoli, but the worst thing wasn't the result, it was their lethargic performance. People were saying their outstanding manager, Jurgen Klopp, was under pressure. Madness! They had been close to winning all four trophies a few months ago! Who could they get who was better? But then again, he'd been at Liverpool for seven years. Maybe the players were sick of his methods. Maybe all that frantic running had exhausted them. I saw one forum comment suggesting that Klopp's teams always imploded after seven years. The user described it as "Klopp's seven-year hex." Was that just a whimsical turn of phrase, or had Klopp once met an elderly Polish man?

I didn't think Liverpool would continue playing badly, but if Liverpool wanted to weaken themselves by firing Klopp, let them. Changing managers meant changing players, which meant more fees for agents. Agents like me. Because I was an agent now. I allowed myself a smug smile.

I went to my laptop and typed "how to be an agent." Not long after, I changed the search to include the word "football." I didn't want to work for the FBI.

There weren't any in-depth resources, but basically being an agent boiled down to three steps:

- Get a client
- Deal with contracts
- Network

Yeah, yeah, yeah. Glad I clicked through all your pop-ups to get to those pearls of wisdom.

The contract stuff would be simple at first, then get tricky when dealing with superstar players. Ziggy was never going to be a superstar. No worries there, and by the time I had to worry about image rights and cross-border taxation treaties and so on, I'd have enough cash to pay someone competent to do it for me.

So all I needed in the short-term was to network. Get Ziggy in front of some managers. Get him a trial.

This thought led to a crisis of confidence. Ziggy was twenty-three. Most people in football would simply say he's too old. Ziggy had very little experience. He wasn't even playing eleven-a-side football.

I went for a walk, imagining the conversations I'd have. For some reason my brain decided to torture me with visions of Jose Mourinho, the dour, abrasive, formerly-successful Portuguese manager. His face didn't change as I tried to explain my inexplicable faith in Ziggy. His face didn't change as I admitted that yes, he's old, slow, can't last ninety minutes, and even his friends don't think of him as a striker. Jose sighed and shook his head. "And ju say I must call heem *Ziggy*?" Cold sweat trickled down my spine.

I was in the car, straight after work, driving to Broadhurst Park.

I'd decided that a phone call wasn't going to get me anywhere. I needed to see people face-to-face to have any chance of anything happening. There are millions of football clubs in or near Greater Manchester, but somehow they were all a bit further than I had realised. Chester FC was one hour and twenty minutes. Chorley was an hour. Stalybridge Celtic was forty-five minutes. If I was going to go and hassle someone until they gave my player a chance, it would ideally be just a little bit closer.

So I kept looking down the pyramid until I found a team that fit the bill: FC United of Manchester.

These guys used to be Manchester United fans but they'd "quit" in disgust when United was sold to some vulture capitalists, and they'd created their own club so they could get back to enjoying football. They wanted to feel like fans, not customers.

After some early successes (two promotions, maybe more), they'd kind of fallen off the media's radar. I suppose the club found a level that their fan base could sustain, and stability wasn't interesting to the world's journalists. So what level had they settled into? I'll tell you. Let me take a deep breath before I write this . . . okay. FC United were competing in the Northern Premier League Premier. That's right, *two* premiers in one name. The winners of this league would go into the National League North, and the winners of that league would go into the National League, and that led to England's fourth tier, the aptly named League Two.

It was all hilariously stupid.

Anyway, if Ziggy couldn't make it in the Northern Premier League Premier, England's seventh highest league, he wasn't going to make it anywhere. (Except, perhaps, the Northern Premier League West, which was the division below, the eighth tier. But I didn't think I would make a living as an agent working so far away from the big money.)

So I rocked up just before 6 p.m. and found—to my relief—that there was some activity. A few people carrying black bin bags out of one of the turnstiles, lights on in the stadium, some tinny music.

I walked right through and into the stand. My footsteps echoed. In a horror movie the scenario would have been creepy, but to me it was almost magical. The stadium was tiny, but it was a stadium. There were concrete stairs and signs (Left: Lightbowne Road End; Right: S4–S2). There were long men's toilets and short women's ones. There was a place to sell beer and pies. Red, white, and black backdrops, witty banners, hyper-local sponsorships. It stank of football.

And I just wandered right on through onto the side of the pitch. There were a handful of people walking up and down the terraces, noting seats that were broken, sweeping up crisp packets, chiselling off bits of chewing gum.

There was an older guy with grey hair. With that chin and that nose, he could have been an eighteenth-century prime minister, but he was here scrubbing the dugouts. The juxtaposition between the nobility of his profile and the mundanity of his current task was striking. After watching for a while, I felt . . . how can I explain it? I felt motivated to help.

"Excuse me," I called out. "Can I grab you some rubber gloves? You shouldn't do that in your bare hands."

He turned and gave me a quick appraisal. I had the vague sense that I'd passed muster. "Rubber gloves? What do you think we are, The Ritz?"

I laughed. "Come on, there's twenty p in the budget for some handwear."

"There isn't."

He was being playful, enjoying a little bit of banter. Even if our exchange lacked the heat of James Bond flirting with Vesper Lynd, it beat a lonely silence. But if FC United couldn't afford basic equipment, they couldn't afford my player either. I lost a bit of confidence. "Jesus. At least let me change the water."

"Works for me."

"Where's the nearest hot tap?"

"The bog. Tap's cold, mind you, but the water's warm. Until October, anyway."

"October?"

The guy stopped scrubbing and gave me a longer look. "Energy crisis. Cost of living crisis. Don't you read the paper?"

He was referring to the coming spike in electricity and gas prices. That's gas in the British sense, which refers to a gas. Not gas in the American sense, which refers to a liquid. "Well, yeah. I heard about it. I live alone. I plan to wear a jumper over Christmas."

He snorted. "Make that two jumpers, and make it from October to April, and you may just survive. But, since you're offering . . ." He sat down in the manager's chair while I picked up his bucket of dirty water and took it to the toilet.

The cost of living crisis. Right. That wasn't good news, was it? But if my house got too cold, I could go and stay with Beth. Or one of the dog owners. It wasn't a big deal.

I arrived back at the dugout, and the guy was nowhere to be seen. I shrugged, picked up his sponge, and got to work. He came back five minutes later.

"You're a grafter."

"Not really. Just didn't want this hot water to go to waste."

I kept scrubbing the plastic protection behind the seats, but after ten seconds or so I started to get a weird vibe. I paused and looked around the stadium. The music was off. Half the people had gone. All that was left were a few people in the North Stand, a couple of groundsmen poking the pitch with big forks, and the grey-haired man. He was standing with his back to one end of the dugout. He looked absolutely destroyed. Finally, he glanced over at me and did that British thing where you sort of stand up straight, ignore your inner turmoil, and pretend everything's okay. "You're not one of the volunteers. Who are you?"

"I'm Max. I'm a scout. An agent. I've found a player and want to talk to someone about him."

"You need Neil. But he's not here."

"No, I know. I mean, I didn't *know*. I didn't think he'd be here on a Thursday. Thing is, I'm going to come four times a week until someone gives my guy a chance. I'm going to annoy the hell out of you until you grow to love me."

The grey guy's demeanour changed just for a second. "I like that." He shrunk into himself again. "It'll have to wait, though."

I placed the sponge back into the bucket and looked at my hands. Even after a short exposure, the harsh chemicals had given me some angry blotches. "My guy isn't getting any younger. All I'm asking is a chance. A trial. Maybe a couple of sessions with the first team. The reserves, even! He just needs . . . I don't know. But he'll score you goals. I guarantee it."

"Max, Max." He put his hands up. "This isn't the time. Football's not happening right now." I looked around. The place was deserted. The fork guys were disappearing into some crevice on the far side of the pitch. Every single other person had left. What was happening? Zombie apocalypse? The Russian twat lost the rest of his goddamned mind?

"What?" I whispered. "What is it?"

"Her Majesty the Queen," he said, looking up at the floodlights, "is dead."

13

GOD SAVE THE KING

I'm ashamed to say that my reaction to the Queen's death was selfish, petty, and unbecoming of a loyal subject of the crown.

Basically, my thoughts went like this:

The Queen is dead. All the football will be cancelled. I won't be able to get any XP. I won't be able to find a club for Ziggy. I'll be stuck in a call centre for the rest of my life.

Crazy, of course, and irrational, but the grey-haired man was watching my face, watching me get more and more upset.

And he respected me for it.

Because he thought that I, like the other seventy million Brits, was having a real, honest-to-goodness emotion about the passing of this woman who had been in our lives for ninety-six years! Seventy as our monarch. Our head of state. Our commander-in-chief. Our North, our South, our East and West. Our working week and our Sunday rest.

He started speaking in a dreamy voice. I'm not sure he was actually talking to me. "Think about everything that's changed in your life. Planes and phones. Fashion and music. She's been there, through it all. Constant. Constant as the North Star. It's always been her face on the currency. Her voice at Christmas. When we won the World Cup in '66, she gave us the trophy. Imagine that. Twenty years before I had a microwave. Bobby Moore wiped his hand on the velvet before he shook hers. Men had class then."

The guy was about to burst into tears, and I wanted to hug him. But then I remembered we were both English, and if we hugged in public we'd lose our passports. I tried to speak, but my voice came out rough and I had to clear my throat. Which wasn't planned, but again, it ended up making me seem like a real person instead of one who merely had a frog in his throat. "And here I am trying to pimp my player out. I'm really sorry. I didn't know." I let the silence stretch out. "I'll be off. Will you be all right?"

"What's that?" He was looking up at the floodlights again, like they were shooting stars he could wish upon. "Yeah, yeah. I'll be off, too. My phone's going a mile a minute." He pulled it out of his pocket, glanced at the lock screen, then let it fall back. He briefly snapped out of his grief state. "Tell you what, give me your number. I'll talk to Neil about your player."

Sociopath though I am, this repulsed me. I hadn't actually pursued my plan once I'd heard the news. I'd just had a few stray thoughts. "No, no," I said. "I couldn't."

"Come on," he said. "Spit it out."

I told him my number while he fumbled with his phone. It kept vibrating while he was entering the numbers. No chance he typed it correctly, but I didn't care. We shook hands and I . . . well, the best word for it is I fled.

The announcements started to come thick and fast:

Friday's big match in the Welsh league, Flint Town United against Aberystwyth Town, was postponed.

For the weekend, Spurs versus Man City was postponed, along with every other game in England. Ditto the Scottish league and non-league football. Even kid's games were called off. I mean, nine-year-old kids weren't allowed to play.

Football was in mourning.

So it was weird then, to see every other sport, from minor ones like cricket and golf to big deals like dog frisbee and extreme ironing, go ahead. Those sports seemed to want to keep calm and carry on in the best British tradition, to gather their fans into one space so that they could honour the Queen collectively. Football, though, the working man's game, wasn't trusted. The brutish, boorish fans would make a right mess, wouldn't they?

Long story short, no, they wouldn't. They would have behaved impeccably. But we'll never know, because they weren't given the chance.

It's possible I was more annoyed than the average person because of my personal stake in the situation. I understood that the Football

Association was in a no-win situation and if the Premier League games had gone ahead, the *Daily Mail* (Britain's bestselling newspaper, which had been pro-Nazi in the 1930s) would have gone to town. They never missed an opportunity to punch down. So fine, cancel the Premier League. Cancel the top four divisions, if you feel you have to. But why the *eff* couldn't Beth play on Friday night?

Beth: FRI GAME IS CANX SMH

Me: Wow bonkers. wt actual f

Some women in a sports hall, cooperating, competing, bonding as a team, keeping fit. Was that disrespectful? Was it disrespectful to play football but respectful to play cricket?

Beth: You can't buy condoms from the machine in Spoon's because the queen died

Beth: The supermarket turned off the beeps at the checkout because the queen died

Beth: Crossfit done a special gym routine with a minute silence after every rep

Beth: THIS COUNTRY IS LOSING IT'S MIND

Me: *its

Beth: NOT NOW MAX

Me: You need a comma in there

I thought Beth would text me back and invite me round to burn off her surplus energy. But my grammar policing must have annoyed her a bit too much. She didn't write back.

So I ended up utterly wasting Friday and spending Saturday pottering around my house, thinking about the growing void in my life. It became pretty clear that the following weekend's games would be postponed as well, because of the Queen's funeral. In principle, that sounded right to me; if you were going to postpone one round of games, that was the one to choose. The mistake was postponing *this* weekend's.

And it wasn't just losing two weeks of games. There was also going to be another long break while the national teams played some meaningless friendlies. A break followed by a break. Ugh.

I was starting to have bleak thoughts and wanted a distraction. I tried to watch something light on TV or check the sports news, but it was futile. It was wall-to-wall Queen. I mean, staggering levels of coverage. Beyond saturation. Beyond North Korea. Two hundred channels all showing the same thing; every section of the BBC's website had the same coverage. It was almost comical, except the BBC cancelled comedy shows for a week "as a tribute."

It was all starting to drive me bonkers, and when I read that the Met Office wouldn't be doing weather forecasts during the period of mourning, I very nearly dropkicked my fridge. I had to get out of this insane echo chamber. I considered humiliating myself by turning up at Beth's place. I thought about driving to the care home to borrow Solly. I instinctively knew that both ideas were terrible, and was saved on Saturday at 3 p.m., the time English matches traditionally kicked off, when an envelope appeared in the bottom right corner of my vision.

It was the message announcing the monthly perk.

Respectful Special Offer

New perk available to buy during the reign of Charles III: God Save the King

Cost: 3,000 XP (Debt financing available)

Effects: Nominate a "King" and channel one of his notable attributes into a player of your choosing. One use per season.

Kings: John Charles (STR; HD). Carlos Valderrama (FL; CRE). Michel Platini (PAS; SET). Denis Law (OFF; FIN).

Once again, the curse was giving me more questions than answers. Every answer led to eighteen questions! It was maddening.

But man, I was glad of the distraction. Glad to dive into these rabbit holes. Glad to enjoy the challenge of deciphering this perk.

I tried to be methodical. The first thing to note was that this perk would be available to buy for a while. But not forever. King Charles, or Prince Charles as I would probably always think of him, was seventy-three years old. He was probably good for another twenty years, right? But he could get sick, and English kings sometimes abdicated (normally to marry Americans). Basically, if I definitely wanted this perk, I shouldn't hang around for too long. Its availability was uncertain.

The next thing was the cost. It was a lot, and if the deadline had been the end of September, I wouldn't have even thought twice about going for it. I couldn't have gotten so much XP even if I'd quit my job to watch footy full-time. But there was this "debt financing" thing. If my suspicions were correct, the curse was going to allow me to buy this perk and then work off the XP cost afterwards. Thinking that almost made me buy it immediately. And that's why I don't have a credit card, because the whole financial and retail system is designed to make me buy things I can't afford.

And besides, I had a better plan.

I would save up, buy October's special offer, if there was one, and THEN buy this one, going into debt. This plan felt good. It felt right. I wouldn't be able to buy the November perk (I'd still be paying off my debt then), but I'd be fine with that. With any luck, I'd be able to afford the Christmas one, so I'd go into 2023 with five perks in the can: Super Scout, Fantasy Football, God Save the King, plus ones from October and December. Probably a Halloween one and a Jesus one. Awesome plan. Five stars.

Next, I took a long, hard look at the wording of the effect. I actually wrote it on a piece of paper, so my mind couldn't trick me. *I mean, couldn't trick itself. I mean, what?* I took a break, having a cup of tea and a Hobnob, but not *enjoying* either out of respect for the Queen.

14

THE HALF-TURN

Refreshed, I took another look at the text.

Effects: Nominate a "King" and channel one of his notable attributes (permanent +1) into a player of your choosing. One use per season.

Kings: John Charles (STR; HD). Carlos Valderrama (FL; CRE). Michel Platini (PAS; SET). Denis Law (OFF; FIN).

It seemed to suggest that I'd be able to boost one attribute on one player, once per season. Now, if I was Alex Ferguson in charge of the glorious Man United team of the 1990s, this would be pretty trivial. Every player certainly had fifteen plus in all their key attributes. Sure, taking a player from nineteen to twenty might lead to one goal or one save that was decisive in one particular game. So sure, for a top manager it was worth 3,000 XP if you didn't have anything better to buy. But for me, a sort-of agent with a sort-of client, the upside to owning this perk was immense. A small improvement in a client's skills might be the difference between him impressing in a trial or not. It might be the difference between him getting a pro contract or not. The difference between me working in a call centre forever. Or not.

So the kings, then. I'd heard all the names, of course, but wasn't really familiar with what they'd done in their careers. The first two were on the list because they were called Charles. Like the new King of England. The others? It took me a minute to understand it, but we'll get to that.

John Charles, according to Wikipedia, was a Welsh player who'd gone to play in Italy in an era when British players rarely did that. He could play equally well as a defender or a striker. "World class in two very different positions." Impressive. Wish I'd seen him. From his bio, I guessed that STR;HD would be strength and heading. If I discovered a fifteen-year-old Lionel Messi clone—a tiny, frail genius—maybe I'd give him one point in strength every year for five years so that he could compete in pro football. Maybe. On most players, though, increasing their strength or heading seemed like a waste. Maybe waste was the wrong word. How about, *an indulgence.*

Carlos Valderrama was a Colombian midfielder with giant, mesmerising hair. I watched a YouTube compilation of his best moments, but the quality of the video was trash. I guess they didn't have HD back then. Or more than eight pixels. Still, from the way the camera panned dramatically from left to right, I was able to conclude that he was incredible at passing the ball. FL;CRE had me slightly stumped though. Flair and creativity, perhaps, but I wouldn't have bet my phone on it. Probably not attributes that would make me rich. In fact, many modern coaches disliked "flair players." They wanted automatons to carry out their instructions exactly. Or so it seemed to me.

Michel Platini wasn't called Charles, but his nickname was Le Roi, *The King.* His Wikipedia page was half barely believable evidence of his sublime talent, half crime novel. The least said about that the better. But PAS;SET was undoubtedly passing and set pieces. Could be handy. Take an outstanding player and make him better at free kicks and penalties? Ka-ching!

But let's be honest, I knew I wanted FIN as soon as I saw it. Denis Law was one of Man United's holy trinity—a pretty blasphemous nickname for the three players who share a statue outside Old Trafford: Denis Law, George Best (the most famous number seven of them all, no relation), and Bobby Charlton. Law was a striker, a pure goal scorer. His nickname, you might have guessed, was "The King," and by choosing him as *my* king, I'd be able to increase Ziggy's finishing from 16 to 17. (I had no clue what OFF meant. Offence? Offside avoidance? I spent no more than four seconds thinking about it.)

I spent a few hours daydreaming about Ziggy turning up to his trial with finishing seventeen. Oh, how different it would be to someone with a mere sixteen! I pitied the old, feeble sixteen FIN Ziggy, who could barely hit a cow with a banjo. The new seventeen FIN Ziggy? Well, you could point to any blade of grass behind the goal, and he'd kick a ball straight at it.

But of course, all this was a month away, if I followed my plan and had some luck. In the meantime, I needed to grind—when the Football Association *permitted* me—and grind hard.

The best way was to get to a Premier League match. For that, I needed money. Problem: I had none. Solution: an inventory of my house to see what I could flog.

My haul was feeble. I'd put a few things on my kitchen table. Things I could do without. Things that might fetch a few bob.

The first group included a tennis racquet, a decent one, a gift from a relative when I'd played at school. I checked online, and it seemed like it might fetch twenty or thirty quid. I had my Playstation 3 and some games. Twenty quid. Twenty-five maybe? There was my TI-83 scientific calculator. Some football boots and shinpads, decent ones Mum had got me for Christmas. I wouldn't sell those. I took them off the table. The rest was a bunch of random odds and ends. All fairly feeble. It was very possible I would spend so long trying to sell this junk that it'd be more profitable to walk around town picking up dropped coins.

There was a second section: things I wanted to keep but would sell if a bit of cash was the difference between becoming an agent or not. I had a Nutribullet blender. Great for turning cheap fruit and veg into premium-feeling smoothies. A taste of the Californian sunshine in those long, grim northern evenings.

My laptop and phone could both, in theory, be downgraded. Maybe I'd get a hundred quid in the process. It'd be such a hassle though. Hours of backing up files, of setting things up how I liked them. It would be an ordeal. And the mental anguish from having a computer that booted up in three minutes instead of thirty seconds wasn't worth it, was it? If that hundred pounds turned into a million, then yeah, it would be worth it. But man, it was hard to imagine deliberately making my life *worse*.

Then there was my car. It made no sense to simply sell it. I needed to be able to drive around to scout players, to watch games, to network. Downgrading? Sure. But to what? A skateboard? Just to cover my bases, I went on some websites to get an idea of what I might be able to sell it for. The consensus was about nine hundred pounds. And then what? Buy something for five hundred that would be so unreliable I'd miss important meetings?

This whole line of thinking was obviously a false economy. I had to be rational. And I had to think about my mental health.

I owned this pile of junk and fifty pounds of Premium Bonds. That, plus what I could spare from my salary, was my budget.

I sighed. I knew it wouldn't be enough.

Unknown number: Hi this is Neil. Can u bring ur lad down tmrw. 10:15 Broadhurst. Cheers.

I picked Ziggy up, and we drove towards FC United's stadium. As soon as I'd gotten the text from Neil, all my frustrations about the lack of football had evaporated. I was on Cloud Nine. I was an *agent* bringing my *client* to a *trial*.

FEAR ME, MORTALS, THE TIME OF MAX IS NIGH

Most of you are smarter than me, or at least have more common sense. But certainly you've worked out that my plan to find a club close to where I lived was flawed. Ziggy lived in Stockport and didn't have a car, so I had to go and pick him up and then drive all the way back to where I started—and then some. It would have been quicker to pick him up and drive to Birmingham.

That's not true, but under normal circumstances my stupidity would have been frustrating. If I wasn't so excited, that is.

Ziggy was nervous. He wanted to know what was going on. But I didn't have much to tell him. FC United's match had been postponed, so they were doing a special training session instead. If that session looked like a match, that was an illusion. It was definitely not a match. It was a training session that bore only the vaguest relationship to a match. Right? Ziggy wanted to know if he was going to play or just watch. I didn't know. I'd told him to bring his boots and gear and to eat as though he was going to play. He told me he hadn't slept because he was so nervous. I laughed. I'd slept great then woke up early like it was Christmas.

Ziggy kept asking stupid questions like "but what's happening" and "am I going to wake up with no kidneys" and trying to hide behind his eyelids, so I told him to grab my phone and find "American Girl" by Tom Petty. It came out of the car's stereo. I turned it up and sang the words I knew, which were the first two lines and the chorus. I did a lot of slapping the steering wheel and grinning at female pedestrians. Some colour returned to Ziggy's face. He looked a bit less seasick. Music. It's powerful sometimes. He didn't even like the song. Note to self: find out what music your clients are into.

"Whoo! Right, let's talk about FC United. Football Club United of Manchester. Remember, it was founded by fans of Man United who didn't like the way the club was going. Seems to be a good vibe, friendly but serious. This is a little training sesh they've organised in lieu of their scheduled match. You're here to make up the numbers. Maybe you'll have to be a linesman or put out some cones. Which you'll do with a big friendly smile on your face. *I'm Ziggy and I love doing unpaid work!* Yeah? But there's bound to be a little match, and I reckon they'll let you join in for a few minutes because . . . well, it doesn't matter why. Whatever happens, just go with it. What else? The manager's called Neil. This isn't Real Madrid, but it's a step up from five-a-side against roofers and bakers. Most of these lads have been in your shoes. If they give you shit, they're just testing you, right? Just seeing if you can hack it. Being slagged off is good news, because it means they're interested in you. Smile through anything that isn't well-meaning advice. Do you know what I mean?"

"Yeah. I'm the new kid. First day at school. Don't worry."

"When the game starts, just score goals. After your tenth goal you can try some passes if you want."

He laughed, a warm, genuine, head-forced-back laugh. "Tenth goal. You're mental." He shook his head and looked out. We were getting close. He'd never been to this part of the city. "I can't believe this is happening."

"Barrett," I said, with much less manic energy in my voice. "There are ninety-two teams in the top four divisions. There are hundreds of semi-pro ones. Yeah? FC United is just one option. You might be nervous, you might mess it up. You might trip up over your feet and get subbed off after sixty seconds. Who cares? Who gives a shit? Get it out of your system. We'll have a laugh later. You can meet my wingman, and we'll go get some phone numbers. No big deal. Next week we'll try Stockport Chavs, or whatever team you've got down there. But if things *do* go all right, will you do me one favour?"

"What's that?"

"Will you enjoy it?" I dipped into my grab bag of random football vocabulary. "After today, it's all going to be eating mung beans for breakfast and eighty-eight grams of chicken for lunch. It's going to be murderball and slideshows about moving into the half-spaces on the half-turn. After today, it's all business. Today, though . . . it's the last time you get to just be you. Today, it's still an adventure."

He grinned at me. The colour had returned to his face. "You're really fucking earning your fees, Max Best." He shook his head a few times. "Ten goals. Fun. Adventure. I can do that. There's one thing you should know, though."

Worrying. "Oh?"

He turned and gave me his eyes full-beam. Whites all around. "I'm *great* on the half-turn."

The sexy beast! It would have been even hotter if I knew what it meant.

15

SOME SPECIAL STUFF

We pulled into the car park. The club's own car park, not the one for the fans. The first time I'd felt like a VIP since a friend and I were both in an accident and *I* got the cute nurse.

Ziggy opened the door to get out, but I grabbed his arm to make him stay put.

"Ziggy. Barrett. Mate." I thought about how best to say this. I'd wanted to get a contract sorted out before any trials happened, but events had moved too fast. "We haven't signed anything. You can just walk in and take it from here if you want and cut me out. There's nothing I'd be able to do about it."

"Nah, Max. I'm in. I'm on the Max train."

"I'd feel better if you shook on it."

He gave me a disbelieving look. "We could spit on our palms too."

"Gross. Just shake three times and on the third go, we'll both say 'ten percent.'"

"That's not a thing. You're weird sometimes."

Someone collected Ziggy and brought him to the bowels of the stadium. There was nothing for me to do but potter around the empty stands and hope for the best.

Whatever happened from here was out of my hands.

While I waited, someone in a black tracksuit started putting cones out on one half of the pitch. So it was going to be a fitness session then. Ugh. Why did they need Ziggy?

The players emerged from the tunnel. Ten were wearing FC United's home kit of red, black, and white. Another ten were in all-white. Two goalies were off to the side doing their own thing. That seemed positive. It hinted that there would be a game later, and everyone would play. Including Ziggy. There were no subs. He was there, in white, wearing the number three. That didn't necessarily mean anything, but in the old days, the left-back wore the number three. I'd have felt a lot better if Ziggy was wearing nine or ten. Or even seven, my personal shirt number of choice.

The manager, Neil, had a whistle and was prowling around. He and his fellow coaches were wearing black tracksuits. Every time he whistled, the players would sprint, or jump, or sprint backwards, or do push ups. I was exhausted just from watching. And it went on for ages. More than long enough for me to scout all the players. Their profiles appeared even though they weren't working with the ball. I wasn't, however, getting XP. Fair enough. It was just training. Hopefully, I'd get some when they started the game.

I pottered over until I was within spitting distance of Neil and was about to say his name when a coach appeared in front of me. Blocking me.

"Need something?" he said in a Scouse accent. Liverpool! Somehow they'd infiltrated this Manchester stronghold. Sound the alarms!

His name was floating above his head, along with a lot of question marks in a grid. I hadn't seen these at the Premier League games, but I'd been pretty far from the coaching areas and those guys hadn't actually been *coaching* at the time. Jackie, for such was his name, had a shaved head that tapered far too much. He had sly eyes and his resting face was a knowing smirk. If he came to fix something in your house, he wouldn't steal *all* the coins from your little change bowl but would take just enough so that you'd always wonder: did he . . . ?

"Quick chat with Mister Neil, if that's okay with you, *Jackie*."

Me knowing his name put him off his stride a bit. Deflated him. But that serial killer glint came back into his eyes, and he opened his mouth to snap something back at me.

Neil intervened. "You're Max, yeah?" He strode with purpose and shook my hand. "Nice to meet you. Thanks for lending us your player."

I made sure to turn slightly away from Jackie, even though the composition of the scene didn't really lend itself to that. "Ziggy and I are both delighted. Can I just say something, though?"

"To a fellow Monarchist, absolutely."

Right. So the whole "they think I'm distraught that the Queen died" thing turned out to be important. Mental note added. "Ziggy isn't at the physical level of everyone else. You know he's just playing part time and that?"

Neil nodded. "We asked if he wanted us to go easy on him. He said no."

"Well, he's a fucking idiot," I said. Jackie smirked at that. Neil gave me a blank look. I continued. "He wants to impress. He doesn't look like it, but he's a fighter. If you tell him to keep running, he'll keep running. Until he can't. He's an idiot."

"You wouldn't do that, eh?" said Jackie.

"No," I said. "I wouldn't." I fucking hated this guy!

Neil did a little face scrunch that showed he'd understood me and turned away. He blew his whistle, and everyone switched what they were doing. Neil talked to a coach—another bald guy but a much friendlier one—who ambled over to Ziggy and pulled him out of the session. He made Ziggy do some stretching, which I thought was a very sensitive way to handle it. It wasn't saying, "mate you can't hack this." It was more like "mate we've got some special stuff for you to do." I approved.

We finally got to the match. A coach was clearing up the cones while Neil had the first team in a huddle, giving them some instructions. The white team were just milling around, kicking a ball to each other. Ziggy was standing in the left-back position. I groaned. He looked absolutely drained from all the running, and now he'd humiliate himself in his big game. He had zero attributes that would help him play in the defence. I mean, his all-round play was weak at the best of times. He had one skill, scoring goals.

I rubbed my hands through my hair, gave it a good rummage. Should I go and intervene? My instinct said no. I'd already interrupted the training session once. Agents weren't really invited to training, and if I annoyed people too much, I wouldn't be invited back, period.

I decided to suck it up. Maybe Ziggy would get lucky, and a ball would drop to him that he could smack in from long range. Could he score long-range goals?

I stopped fussing with my hair. I'd realised something.

I'd never seen Ziggy score a goal.

This was absolutely crazy to me. I mean, I'd taken the finishing attribute as gospel and worked pretty hard (and shamelessly) to get him into this trial based on it. Based on this number in my imagination.

Based on nothing.

I took a seat in the stands and tried to make myself small. To blend in. Because I suddenly knew this whole thing was about to blow up in my face.

Sure enough, Ziggy was abysmal. By far the worst player on the pitch. When the centre-back or goalkeeper passed it to him, he took a touch and looked around to see who to pass to. But this took him so long that an opponent would be bearing down on him. Ziggy would play a panicked pass almost at random, kick the ball out of play, or—twice—lose the ball to the red team's winger.

I slid down into my seat even further. I didn't turn to the dugout, but I could feel Jackie smirking at me. Somehow, he was smirking at me in a Liverpool accent, which made it three times as painful.

There was more bad news. I wasn't even getting XP. This was the first eleven-a-side match where I wasn't being credited with experience. I started to think about why that was, but I quickly stopped. I didn't care. I just wanted the match to be over, so I could escape. This was hell.

But then five minutes passed without Ziggy's incompetence further staining the very concept of football. And I dared to scan the players a bit more seriously.

The first thing I noticed was that my client—my soon-to-be-former client once I told him that handshake agreements don't count—had changed. His CA had moved from 1 to 2. I didn't need to go hunting for that information, because the new number was written in green. CA 2. Wow. C for Confidence? He didn't look more confident. He looked like a bomb squad guy on his first day.

Could "A" stand for acclaim? Surely not. Ziggy wasn't covering himself in glory here, and the curse had already used the word "reputation." I doubted it would have scores for both reputation and acclaim. They meant the same thing, didn't they?

Huh.

Next, I focused on the red team, which was basically FC United's first eleven. Their attributes varied wildly, as usual, but overall they weren't impressive. Ziggy was worse than all of them, but it was probably unfair of me to say he was by far the worst player. Maybe he was just unfit and nervous. Still, I would have swapped pretty much anyone else's profile for Ziggy's, providing I could keep his finishing.

The red team's average PA was around 35. Ziggy's was 58, so he should have been one of the better players on the pitch. The white team, made up of reserves and youth team players, it seemed, averaged around thirty. That average was quite distorted by one guy, Callum Gribbin. His PA was 144. He had great technique, passing, and his pace was decent. What was he doing here in seventh tier football, and not even in the first team? I had a quick look on my phone and couldn't find the answer. He'd played for Manchester United's youth team, where he had been compared to Ryan Giggs. Fucking high praise! He'd also represented England under-sixteens and under-seventeens. I didn't get it. Were people just misreading his talent? Was it that simple?

No. Because PA *didn't* mean talent. Ziggy and Gribbin had high PA but were, in different ways, not playing to that level. I was back to square one.

By now, I had calmed all the way down. Even if the Ziggy experiment was imploding, I was here learning about how football clubs operated and testing my assumptions about PA. And I didn't have to buy a ticket. So, all in all, the day was going to be a win. It was also going to be a humiliating slog, but I decided I could take a few slings and arrows.

"That's it, Ziggy!" someone shouted.

I looked over, and from the aftermath it seemed like my boy had gone up for a defensive header and won it, knocking it safely out for a throw-in. Good stuff! I checked his profile, and his CA hadn't moved, which gave me even less confidence in my "confidence" hypothesis.

But it gave *me* the confidence to start shuffling myself along the seats, towards the dugouts. I wanted to see if I could overhear what they were saying, if anything, about Ziggy.

Just as I got into position, Neil blew for half-time. At least, I assumed there would be a second half, because the white team didn't make their way back to the changing room. I looked at my phone. They'd been playing for thirty minutes. Why not forty-five? I shrugged. They probably knew what they were doing.

As the whistle blew, the whole staff stormed onto the left side of the pitch to debrief the red team.

Which, for some reason, I took as a cue to lose my tiny little mind.

16

PEP TALKS

I pottered over towards Ziggy; I guessed he could use a bit of a pep talk. (Pep talks are named after the Man City manager, Pep Guardiola, who latches onto his players like a squid and shakes them violently while chattering at a thousand miles a minute.)

But on the way, the friendly bald coach drifted away from the huddle to grab a little basket of energy drinks. I took my chance.

"Nigel," I said, because it seemed pretty normal that I'd know the names of these guys. Sure, they weren't Royal Family famous, but here in this stadium they were the big dogs. "I'm Max. Ziggy's agent. Can I ask a tiny question?"

He clearly had much better things to do but was such a friendly dude he couldn't turn me down. "Sure."

"Callum Gribbin. Call me crazy, but he's by far the best player here. He should be pissing all over this match. But he's played, like, one league game in two seasons."

"Your question is . . . why that?"

"Yeah."

He looked over at the white team's half of the pitch, where most of the players were sitting or passing a ball to each other while having a chat. Gribbin was on his feet, juggling a ball with ludicrous ease, his expression one of blissful emptiness. "It's a shame," he said. "Can't tell you what happened. He's got the world at his feet. He doesn't want it. It happens. As a coach there's one thing you hate. Wasted potential." He shook his head and walked off, the drinks clanking in their little basket.

Wasted potential!

Of course. SO STUPID.

Potential.

The word scrambled my head.

I knew, for sure, completely, absolutely, without a shadow of a doubt, what PA was. It was potential . . . attributes. Potential . . . ability. Potential . . . acumen. Whatever the "A" was, PA meant talent. Ronaldo: 200. Gribbin: 144. Ziggy: 58.

Ronaldo, presumably, had extracted every ounce of his talent. Five times Ballon d'Or winner. Five Champions League medals. Eight hundred career goals. Had he been born with PA 200, or could you work at it somehow? No! No tangents. I needed to start from the bottom before working up to other questions. This was important.

So, Gribbin. PA 144. Compared to everyone else here, he had what podcasters liked to call a "high ceiling." Not enough to play in the Premier League, based on what I'd seen so far, but the level below that surely? So why hadn't he made it? Lots of reasons. Injury. Lack of motivation. Bad friends, unsupportive family. Yeah, I supposed it would be pretty common to get nowhere near your potential. That . . . that was worrying. But then again, there was still time. He was only twenty-three. Maybe something would click, and he'd never look back.

And then Ziggy. Potentially one of the best players for FC United. But he'd never had any training. No one had ever noticed him. Why should they? His talent was virtually invisible. Even I had never seen him do anything of note. His YouTube highlights reel would be one routine defensive header.

So I'd found a player that no one else would spot. That was my unfair advantage. My edge. There had to be ten thousand guys like him in England. Maybe ten thousand in Manchester alone. If I signed ten thousand and nine thousand didn't get anywhere near their potential, I'd still be as rich as Yorkshire gravy.

So PA was talent. It was clear then that CA was an expression of talent. C. Current. Current ability and potential ability. The obvious correctness of this fact gave me full-body goosebumps.

Ronaldo had CA 182. That . . . that made sense. His career was waning; he looked slower and older in every match, having defied time for so long. That kid Garnacho I'd seen, he had CA 90, well on his way to reaching his potential of 173.

How long would it take Garnacho to hit his ceiling? Most players peaked at twenty-seven or twenty-eight years old. Was it connected to age?

Ziggy had moved from CA 1 to CA 2. Maybe he'd add a point every time he played a match with these semi-pro guys?

No, that made no sense. Garnacho had only played a few minutes of professional football. He didn't have ninety CA from *playing*. There had to be a way to progress without featuring in the starting eleven. There had to be a way to get close enough to the first team that you'd be able to compete for a spot.

I wasn't getting XP watching this game, so Ziggy wasn't getting CA points from playing in it. Probably, anyway. I'd been wrong before. The whole thing was just guesswork.

One thing was obvious, though. I needed to keep Ziggy in this environment as long as possible. I needed to make sure he got a second date.

I'd been standing there in the centre circle for ages. I snapped out of it and looked around like I'd just woken from a winter nap. I checked my chin for drool, but I was dry. The whole thought process must have taken seconds. I wandered towards Neil, but, once again, the world's greatest ever villain blocked my path.

Jackie was doing a pep talk, talking to most of the first team, excitedly waving his arms around and doing little tippy tappy dances. He kept turning sideways. He was trying to illustrate some point, and, when I got within range, he decided to use me as a prop.

"Secret Agent, you be a defender here." He manhandled me into position and then started miming that I was a defender and he, just in front of me, was receiving the ball from a teammate. "So like this, here, I'm square, yeah? Too square." Square is football-speak for horizontal. "Play a square pass" means pass at a right angle to the direction of attack, i.e., sideways. "So then Secret Agent here, he holds me up, I have to turn, and that extra move gives the defence time to get set. Yeah? So now," he said, resetting so that instead of facing his own goal (being square), he turned his body about thirty degrees off. "Half-turn. I do the same, but quicker. No time for dem to get set." Dem is Scouse for them. In this case he meant the defence. "Int that right, Secret Agent?"

I was unimpressed. "What's the difference though, really? The first pass is just as easy as the second."

"Easy, he says." Jackie was delighted. He hadn't set this trap but I'd fallen into it anyway. He called out three names, two to be defenders and one to be a winger. "Right, now there's Andy and Eddie at the back. You're going to get the ball and pass through them into Sandro's path. You said it was easy, remember."

I noticed that half the white team had wandered over to watch the performance. Ziggy was at the back, looking terrified.

"Piece of piss," I said. There was general approval from the players. I was there in my call centre suit, wearing nice-ish shoes. I hadn't kicked a ball for three years. It was clear I would mess it up, but they approved of my bravado.

"Set up," said Jackie.

Nigel, the friendly bald coach, stood a few yards in front of me, a ball at his feet. Jackie was right behind me, his hand on my lower back. Fifteen yards further back, the two defenders were standing with a five-yard gap between them. Sandro was on the right of that line, waiting to sprint forward and collect my pass. The way he was bouncing, he looked like an NFL wide receiver before the snap. I think that was his way of taking the piss out of me.

"Nigel," I said. "Let me have a couple of touches." I thought this would lead to an outburst of mocking, but it didn't. The group seemed to approve. Jackie took his hand away. Of course I'd want to get a feel of the ball. Pro move. Nigel passed it to me, and I touched it back. He passed it again, and I stunned it, rolled it around, and kicked it back. "All right."

"You ready?" said Jackie.

Something in his voice made me turn and look at him. "Are you going to boot me up the arse?"

"Me? Never." That grin. What a prick.

I turned and waited for Nigel to pass to me. When he did, I felt Jackie sort of lunge at me, but as I'd expected, it was just a fake. Just to psyche me out. You'd have to be legit psychotic to tackle an amateur in a suit, so I had mentally discounted Jackie and focused on the ball.

I touched it square, exactly where Jackie had said was "wrong." I planted my left foot just beside it, and allowed my weight to shift through my body, almost as though I was falling, to the right. At the last second, I clipped the ball with my right foot. I pushed through the contact to make sure the ball would fizz through the gap between the defenders. But I put some backspin on it, so it would start to slow before getting to the penalty area, and so that if the goalie rushed out to clear the ball, he wouldn't be able to use his hands.

"Sandro," I yelled. "What the fuck!"

The lazy shit had just stood there.

He looked stunned. "Sorry, man. I thought you wouldn't do it."

"Making me look like a twat," I complained.

"Good lesson," said Neil. "Always make your runs." Neil didn't say much, but when he did, the lads listened.

Attention naturally turned back to Jackie. "Not bad," he said. He'd lost, but he didn't seem unhappy about it.

I'd fallen into some sort of trance—I wasn't really aware of what was going on. I should have been thinking about Ziggy and his needs, but I just wanted to learn about this half-turn shit. "So," I said, thoughtfully, "What's the benefit of the other way?"

Jackie looked at me like I might have been trying to undermine him, and, if it had just been the two of us, he might have reacted differently. But he was at work, and he was a professional. He looked around—the whole squad was watching. Teaching me was as good as teaching them. "Get back in position. Right, now, not so square. So when Nige passes, take a touch, and then freeze. Yeah?"

Nigel—Nige, I suppose—rolled another ball to me. I had reverted to standing square. "Oh, fuck. I forgot the first bit." I kicked it back to him.

There was some friendly laughter. Nige rolled the ball again, but this time I'd sort of pre-turned. I touched the ball and stopped.

"What do you see?" said Jackie.

I shifted my weight like I was going to play the pass, then eased back. I looked around. "Yeah. It's a bit faster, so they have less time to react. But so does Sandro."

"That's why we practise it. To get in sync."

I nodded. I scanned the pitch again, imagining if this was a real game. It was actually thrilling, kicking a ball on a nice pitch in a real stadium. It was so . . . so serious. Not many people get to play football where the pros play. I got back inside my head just in time. "I suppose from this position I could hit a pass to the left, as well."

"That's it. It's more dynamic. More proactive. You take control of the pitch. You're on the front foot; they're on the back."

"All that from one little half-turn?"

"Yep. Details add up. Don't they, lads?" He was beaming now. Delighted. I could almost see his brain whirring: let's get noobs in more often. They're a great teaching tool. "Want to try?"

"Yeah." We got into position, but then I looked at Sandro. "Mate. You going to run this time?"

He made a noise and gestured at me.

Nigel rolled the ball, and from the new starting position I took a touch, looked at where I wanted to play the pass, and hit it straight at the left-sided defender.

"Fuck!" I shouted.

"I knew it!" shouted Sandro, who got jeered.

Jackie slapped me on the shoulder. "It happens. You're programmed to hit that line." He drew a virtual line where my first pass had gone. "When you change your starting position, you've got to change your mechanics. That's why we practise."

"Speaking of," said Neil, and everyone took that to mean what it meant: time for the second half.

I wanted time to think about what I'd just learned, but that would have to wait. I jogged towards Neil and, for the first time, Jackie didn't block me. "Neil, do Matlock Town play a striker at left-back?" Matlock were FC United's next opponents.

He looked amused. He knew where this was going. "You want your lad up front? I know. But this is a sesh for the first team. We don't have time to sort that lot out as well."

"Yeah, I get that. So let me do it."

Jackie had stayed within earshot. "Here we go. He's an agent, he's a silky-smooth playmaker. And he's a master tactician an all. Tommy Tactics."

Neil grinned. "Maybe he is, though."

I held my hands up. "I've been watching them," I said, nodding towards the whites. "And with those players they should be set up in a 5-3-2. And you know who plays 5-3-2? Matlock Town." This last part was pure bullshit. Until I'd checked the fixtures that morning I had literally never heard of Matlock. I mean, there was an American TV show with that name. That was the extent of my knowledge. "I'll set them up in thirty seconds."

Neil gave me a curious glance. "Go on, then."

I zoomed off before he could change his mind. I wasn't going to stay for thirty seconds. The way I saw it, Neil had put me in charge of the whites, so I had half an hour to do something with a team of semi-pros. I was moving up in the world! And Ziggy was moving up the pitch, where he would finally get his shot at immortality.

17

GAFFER

"Whites, to me." The players started drifting in my direction. It seemed like a weird thing to call them, as half the team weren't white. They gathered around, except the goalie, who was over on his own doing weird goalkeeper things. I waved at him to come in. To the others, I said, "I'm Max. My friends call me Secret Agent. You can call me gaffer."

"Gaffer?" said Ziggy.

"Yeah, I'm your new manager. First things first, we need a team name."

"How about, 'FC United Reserves Plus This Guy.'" Suggested one wag, pointing to Ziggy like he was something he'd found by the side of the road.

I gave the guy a look. In my imagination it was, "Jose Mourinho giving you the evil eye," but it was probably "call centre guy on his first day as deputy team leader." I swept my finger around the semi-circle. "You were shit in the first half, but you're going to crush the second. So from now on, you're AFC Phoenix. Right? Now, I want you to play 5-3-2." I held my left hand up, fingers and thumb splayed. I went from left to right, tapping a digit as I spoke a name. "Baz at left-back, Adam, Clive, Gronk, Sam." I switched to holding up three fingers. "In the middle, Paul, Luke, Fash." I pointed to the last two. "Callum and Ziggy up top." Every single player, including Ziggy, gave me the same look. A look which I will now try to describe.

Imagine, if you can, you are a six-year-old boy, and it's your first day at school. You don't care much for maths or English, but you know that after the first break there will be P.E. But when the bell goes, and you rush to the grass, you are pulled away and told that you will be playing rounders with the girls while every other boy gets to play footy.

That was the face they were giving me. Scrunched up confusion and disappointment, and several other expressions I couldn't put my finger on.

Oh, boy.

Big Nev, the goalie, finally made it to the huddle, just as Neil blew the whistle. Nev gave me a dirty look and started trudging back to his goal. The teams hadn't switched ends for some reason. With a shrug, I wandered off to the far side of the pitch, standing opposite Neil and his gaggle of coaches.

"That's it, Phoenix!" I roared, clapping my hands furiously. "Big energy!"

What happened next was one of the most infuriating moments of my whole life. I mean, no joke, I nearly spontaneously combusted. I nearly went full supernova.

The fuckers had totally ignored me and lined up in a 4-4-2 with Ziggy at left back!

I was so shocked and so angry that I did nothing for several seconds. My heart didn't beat, my blood didn't pump. I mean, seriously, the only movement in my whole body was my eyes expanding two inches outside their sockets and contracting, a movement that repeated again and again like in a cartoon.

When I finally regained control of my motor functions, I was just about to extend my arms and summon down the *thunder of the gods* when a tiny, quiet little voice somewhere inside my head whispered to me, *"Can I just say something?"* I knew that voice. It is the voice I use when a woman is crying because of me.

(None of this happened, you understand. I don't hear voices. I'm being whimsical to try to convey how I felt.)

Before blowing my top, I tried to follow the instinct that had warned me not to go full tonto.

I *was* the manager, Neil had said. Even if I had chosen to over-interpret what Neil actually said, Ziggy, at least, would have gone to play where I told him even if the other ten ignored me.

So what the eff was going on?

I took a deep breath and watched the game unfold. When my heart rate dropped under three hundred bpm, I was able to think a little more clearly. I called up my menus and found the whole interface was different. On the left was a column. On the top of this column it said,

"31." Below this it said, "FC United Tactics," and below that it said, "AFC Phoenix Tactics."

But the majority of the screen was taken up by a big rectangle. At the top of this were the words "FC United 3 - AFC Phoenix 0."

Just under that were four tabs: Match Overview, Match Stats, Action Zones, Match Report.

The last three were inaccessible.

Under that section was a list of the goalscorers and what times their goals had been scored.

And then there was a big flashing box of text, white on red.

Murray tries to pass to Smith, but the pass is too strong.

Then it changed to black on white:

Gribbin picks up the loose ball and dribbles forward.

The text box vanished, then reappeared a tantalising moment later.

But he loses the ball.

My head snapped to the right and, indeed, the ball had squirted away off the pitch, and Gribbin was the nearest of my players to it.

Fucking weird stuff, man.

I shook my head. If it was still bothering me later I could do some tai chi or go for a run. But for now, I had limited time to work this shit out. It was pretty likely I'd never get this chance again.

I clicked on "FC United Tactics" and saw the team's lineup, plus a formation graphic on the right. According to the heading and the little icons, which contained each player's shirt number, they were playing 4-3-3 with the left-back pushing far up the pitch and the right-back staying back. I hadn't noticed that with my naked eye. Interesting.

I clicked on a player's name and his profile popped up. Awesome. It meant as long as someone was on the pitch, I didn't have to waste calories turning my head towards him to see his profile.

I switched to "AFC Phoenix Tactics."

It was set to 4-4-2, and Ziggy was at left-back.

Ahhhhhhhhhh.

I closed the screens and went for a little walk up and down the touchline with a wry smile on my face. A couple of things had become clear.

1) Buying 4-4-2 hadn't been a waste. Although if I hadn't bought it, what formation would the team be using right now? I suppose I'd never know.

2) The players had been giving me that strange look, because what I was telling them and what the curse was telling them I wanted them to do was different.

Now that was an interesting question. Was the curse controlling the players? Or was it just bypassing the need for me to verbalise what I wanted? Meh. Leave the philosophising to the taxi drivers.

Anyway, I remembered there was a perk I could buy called "Match Stats 1." That, obviously, would unlock the second tab. I was very interested to see what it'd show, but I wouldn't be in control of any more teams for a while, so there was no point buying it. I had to stick to the plan. Becoming an agent!

Although . . . this management thing was getting more and more attractive by the second.

So I tried to go to the place where I bought the perks, but I was stuck in the match screen. Ah, well. It was probably for the best.

I brought the tactics screen back up and dragged Ziggy up into attack. Nothing happened. I tried swapping him with the left-mid, number eleven. Both icons snapped into their new places. It was still 4-4-2, but now the number three was in the left-mid slot and the number eleven was at left-back.

At first, nothing changed on the pitch, but as the players moved around, Ziggy sort of drifted forwards and the other guy drifted backwards. And they stayed there. I had moved Ziggy closer to his destiny! Whoo!

Neither guy looked over at me or gave any indication that anything weird had happened.

I gave myself thirty seconds to think things through. My players really would have been better in a 5-3-2. Well, why not just change the formation? In my tactics screen there was an option to do just that. I clicked on it, tapped it, mentally savaged it, but it wouldn't budge.

That's because you've only bought 4-4-2, you prick.

Ugh. Well, I could at least squash this eleven into a more optimal version of 4-4-2, with a couple of square pegs in round holes. I had two right-backs, so one went into right midfield, and my best right-mid had to go in the centre. I didn't have a left-mid, but I had a left-footed central midfielder. I put him as left-mid. It'd have to do.

I mentally reassigned the players a couple at a time, so that there wasn't absolute mayhem. When I was satisfied that the players were more or less where they needed to be, the number on the top-left of the "Match Overview" changed to thirty-four. The number of minutes played!

This was all ludicrously easy.

I watched the match play out for a couple more minutes, and my lads felt a lot more solid. Most importantly, Ziggy was up front, ready to pounce. Ready to score a goal and blow everyone's minds with the coolness and precision of his finishing. Ready to fire me into a future filled with home saunas, infinity pools, and a different yoga instructor every day of the week!

I went for a little walk again, to let off some steam. I wasn't thinking clearly! Or maybe I was thinking too clearly, but about the wrong things.

Once I'd got a bit of a grip, I went back into the tactics page to see what I could tinker with.

In a way, there wasn't much, but there was enough. For the team, I could set a passing culture: short, mixed, long, or direct. I could set the level of tackling aggression: easy, medium, hard. (Medium and hard were visible but not currently selectable.) I could also select: pressing or not, offside trap or not, counter attack or not, or instruct everyone to get behind the ball, i.e., defend for their lives.

I could also tweak those settings on an individual basis. So I could have most of the team play short passing, but set my right-back to fire long balls to the left. Um . . . okay.

And I could instruct a player to man-mark someone on the other team. My guy would try to follow the other guy around the pitch, sticking to him like a barnacle, trying to stop him from being involved.

I left most of the settings alone, because I didn't *totally* understand what they would do. I mean, I understood what they'd do on their own, but what would the second-order effects be? If I had someone man-marking an opposition player, wouldn't that mess up the shape of my team? It was safer to leave most things as they were.

But there were two options I selected right away.

First, there was one called "playmaker." Seemed clear what that meant, the team would play through one guy. Like a quarterback in the NFL. When I clicked on that, it gave me a list of every player in the team. I chose Gribbin, and that was done. Next, I put Ziggy as the penalty taker. I doubted Neil would give us a pen, but you never knew. Scoring a goal against a real goalkeeper, even if it was a penalty in a glorified training session, would surely do Ziggy the world of good. And if he missed? Well, I'd murder him and bury him under my patio. No harm done.

Satisfied, I closed everything and turned my attention to the actual game. It continued in its usual patterns for a while, but then I realised something had shifted. I opened the FC United tactics page, but there was nothing different there. I watched the patterns of play a little more, and, while I'd learned to doubt what my naked eye told me, I was pretty sure I knew what was happening.

My boy Gribbin was running the game. And it wasn't just that he was dominating. The kid was taking the actual piss.

18

PLAYING GOD

FC United	3	AFC Phoenix	2
	Second	Half	
Smalls	6	Gribbin	38, 41
Wooley	11		
Da Costa	20		

Ziggy challenges for a high ball.

Murray wins the header.

Smith can't control the ball.

Gribbin starts a dribble.

He moves past Smith.

He moves past Wooley.

He shapes to shoot. Murray slides in to block.

Gribbin pulls the ball onto his left foot and moves forward.

He's one on one with the goalkeeper.

He launches a thunderbolt! Right at the top corner!

But it's saved! Fantastic reflexes by Gordon.

Ziggy can't reach the rebound.

And it's cleared.

Playing God. It's a phrase you normally hear related to doctors. They have one organ and two patients who need it. That's a horrible choice to have to make, but having the power of life and death over someone is godlike indeed.

But here I was playing God in a unique and uniquely satisfying way. I just had to think it, and a grown man would jog over to the other side of the pitch. I just had to think it, and my minions would suddenly start launching long balls towards the opponent's goal, like the agricultural hard-men teams of the 1980s.

Long ball was associated with Wimbledon (the football team, not the other thing). The Crazy Gang. Vinnie Jones before he went to Hollywood. The plan was simple: stonk the ball far away from your goal and towards the other team's goal. Try to "win the second ball," meaning pounce on any rebounds or deflections. If the chaos didn't lead to a shot on target, no problem. Just kick the shit out of the other team as they daintily passed their way back up the pitch. And then hit repeat.

Long ball was primitive football mostly consigned to the dregs of history. Why was long ball even an option in 2022?

I put my hand under my chin to stop from laughing out loud—a bit of prehistoric football actually sounded fun. I ordered the players to kick the ball long. Forget all this modern rondo guff. Tactics? No, thanks. Let's knock it. Get rid. Go deep. "Second ball!" I shouted. I was just about able to keep a straight face.

My guys, regardless of their position, attributes, or the game state, began boofing the ball high, high and long, like they were NFL punters and every down was fourth down.

I let the bombardment continue for a couple of minutes, then changed the passing style back to mixed. The change hadn't led to any shots on goal, and we hadn't really won any second balls. But it had been effective, in a way. FC United had not been expecting the sudden change of tempo, and they were now much less organised. Their tactics screen hadn't changed, but on the pitch they looked a bit ragged. A bit disjointed compared to how they'd started.

This time I couldn't keep the grin off my face. This was so much fun!

Gribbin had been quiet during the long ball minutes. That wasn't his kind of football. But now he was back to being the main man, our conduit. He was zipping around, playing sensible passes, threatening to dribble, probing, keeping the defence on edge.

We got a corner, and, as always, a button appeared in my vision, offering me the chance to play my "free hit" and boost the chance of the situation leading to a goal by ten percent. I'd been saving it in case we got a penalty, but time was running out. I tapped the button; it shimmered into nothingness, an oddly satisfying effect. Gribbin went over to take the corner—I'd realised I could designate him as the set piece taker for everything while keeping Ziggy on penalties—and he held both hands up. Loads of pro players did that. I wasn't sure if it just meant "get ready" or if it indicated where he was going to hit the cross.

He leaned away from the ball as he struck it. It curved slightly, but mostly went as fast as an arrow onto a tall defender's head. A Phoenix defender!

Gribbin takes the corner.

Whipped in with great pace.

Onto the head of Mendonca!

It's a great header!

But it hits the bar!

It rebounds to safety!

So if I hadn't played the free hit, the header would have gone over the bar. Or an FC United player would have got their head to the ball before my guy. Interesting. But corners were generally a low-probability chance, right? Teams scored maybe one in twenty? I'd need to check the data. But I was pretty sure a penalty led to a goal eighty times out of one hundred. The free hit perk would take that to ninety times. That was certainly the best bang for my buck.

But then again, in how many matches did you get a penalty? Mostly you didn't get one, right? I'd have to check that, too.

Um, Max. You're not a football manager. Calm down.

Neil blew his whistle and called his team over for an impromptu meeting. My guys coalesced into three little groups, talking excitedly. I wasn't sure if the main topic of conversation would be me or Gribbin. Another person was moving, crossing the pitch in his tracksuit, heading right for me, as menacing as Darth Vader.

It was Jackie, probably coming to fire me as manager.

He nodded at me. "Tommy Tactics."

"Coach Carter," I said, referencing a Samuel L. Jackson movie.

He stood next to me for a bit, quietly looking at the pitch.

"The away team's dugout is next to ours," he said. "You don't have to stand here like a leper." So he wasn't here to fire me! That was a relief.

"Sunday League habits," I said. "Also, I don't want you hearing my instructions."

"Right, yeah. How's your 5-3-2 going?"

"Pretty good, I'd say."

He forced a smile, then said, "What I'm saying is that you've got four at the back. 5-3-2, famously, has five at the back. See what I'm saying?"

I pretended to be unbothered, which wasn't that hard. "Gribbin is part of the five. He's playing as a sweeper-striker. Free role."

He frowned. Ignored my bullshit. He had something else on his mind. "Gribbin. Yeah. About that. What did you say to him?"

"Say?"

"He never plays like this."

I shrugged. "I told him that we've got a new king and a new prime minister. I told him the country's going to shit, and we all need to pull together. Every one of us. Give it our best, every day, and maybe we can make a go of this little nation of ours."

Jackie laughed, but he was annoyed at himself for laughing. "Seriously, though. The season hasn't started well. If we could get him playing like this, we'd be top of the league."

I didn't really know why Gribbin was playing so well. "I just put him up front and set him . . . made him our playmaker. He's the best player on either team. I dunno. That's it. No magic."

He looked thoughtful. Rubbed his cheek. "All right." He stood there for a while. "Why've you got Smokes at left-back?"

The guy at left-back wasn't called Smokes, so I guessed that was his nickname. "Benson? He can play left or right. Um . . . I don't understand the question."

Jackie gave me a much longer, harder look. "He's never played left-back in his life."

I pointed. "There he is. Doing just fine, I'd say. Hasn't given Sandro a kick."

Another long, hard look. "Your lad isn't going to make it." He meant Ziggy.

"He is."

He shook his head. "He's not. He doesn't have what it takes. He's a nice lad, but he's not got it. You, though."

"Me?"

"Why don't you come down to the next session? Bring your boots. We could use a silky-smooth playmaker. You've got potential."

Potential. The word of the day. "Jackie. I mean, thanks, first of all. Really. But . . . how can I say this?" I held my palm out, hoping the right words would fall onto it. They didn't. "You're wrong. I'm no player. And Ziggy? He's mint. He just needs a coach . . . ." I shot Jackie with twin finger guns and raised my eyebrows.

Charisma check: failed. Jackie shook his head again. "There's no point. We're a football club, not the boy scouts."

And, still shaking his head, he wandered off.

But his path back across the pitch took him close-ish to where Ziggy was bent over, hands on his knees, trying to conserve energy.

I was too far to hear anything, but I saw what happened.

Jackie sort of paused and sagged. Then he raised his head to the sky as if to say "why is this happening to me?" Finally, he shook his bad mood off, got Ziggy's attention, and started giving him instructions. Jackie was holding up two fingers on one hand and one finger on the other, and was waving them around a lot. Ziggy was nodding, paying close attention.

I looked over and saw that Neil had finished saying what he needed to say. He was about to blow his whistle when he saw Jackie. Neil waited a few more seconds, then blew.

It looks like FC United will take a more cautious approach.

I opened the FC United tactics page and saw that Neil had, indeed, tweaked the team. Now they were lining up in a 4-1-4-1. So that was a standard flat back four, with four in midfield exactly the same as Phoenix. But they had a guy in between those two lines. A defensive midfielder. I clicked on him and saw his individual instructions. He'd been set to man-mark Gribbin.

I felt a surge of adrenaline. Neil had been forced to react to my tactics! A real, proper manager! On the back foot, because of little old me!

Almost instantly, I was in my tactics screen, moving Gribbin to the right side of midfield. The defensive midfielder would follow him all the way over there, right? Which would mean FC United would have two defensive players in one zone, leaving a big gap in the middle of the park, and our whole defence would only have to worry about one striker. I could seize control of the midfield AND get two of our defenders to push forward. Yee-haaww!

But I paused.

I wasn't here to earn a "Tommy Tactics" achievement.

I wasn't here to win the match.

It did me no good to show Neil up. If his changes nullified Gribbin, then fine. Good for Neil. Good for FC United.

So I didn't move Gribbin. I left things as they were.

But things weren't as they were.

Something *had* changed. On the pitch, Ziggy's default position had changed. He was almost man-marking one of the two centre-backs he was up against. Had I clicked on something by mistake? No. There was nothing in my tactics page to indicate why he was doing it differently. He'd taken it upon himself.

Frowning, I scanned Ziggy's profile.

The answer was there in green. His CA had increased to three.

19

DEMBA BA

After the match, I hung around the stands for a while, but with the stadium eerily deserted I decamped to the car. For a while, I thought maybe Ziggy had found his own way home. It took so long that I started to get a bad feeling. A premonition of doom. But he eventually emerged and we set off home. He suggested we stop off somewhere to get some food—his treat—so I headed towards Didsbury Village, where the women were two percent hotter than average.

It was a quiet journey. Ziggy was exhausted and introspective, and I was happy to concentrate on my driving. At red lights, I thought about the achievements I'd gotten. At full time, I'd been able to exit the match screen. There were messages waiting for me.

New Achievements: Movin' On Up 1; Free Spirit 1; Coaching 1; They've Rebadged It You Fool; Tommy Tactics 1; Tommy Tactics 2; Tinkerman 1; It's the Taking Part That Counts

I was getting better at reading the messages while driving safely, plus, as a driver, I always erred on the side of caution. (First, because I'd been in one crash already and didn't care to repeat the experience. Second, because if my car got damaged it was going to stay damaged.)

So by the time we got to Didsbury, and started driving around its side streets looking for a place to park, I'd learned what these achievements had been awarded for.

Movin' On Up 1 was because I'd managed at a new high level, going from an amateur team to a semi-pro one. That was interesting; if I was the Man City manager and got a job at Man United, would the curse think that was an upward move? The achievement would tell me. And ditto going from one of the big Premier League teams to Bayern Munich. The biggest team in Germany, sure, but the league was a step down in terms of finance and worldwide popularity. And what about the England national team job? Was that the pinnacle? For an English guy, I mean.

Free Spirit 1 came from setting Gribbin as my playmaker. I supposed if I used playmakers in five games, or ten, I'd get the second ranking.

Coaching 1 was simply for being a manager, i.e., the guy in charge of a team. I'd been the coach for Beth and the women, but this award, like a few others, was only for eleven-a-side matches.

They've Rebadged It You Fool was because I'd changed my team's name.

The Tommy Tactics ones were a bit annoying, because in the descriptions it said, "formerly Tactics Mastery 1." So the curse had heard Jackie call me Tommy Tactics, a totally made-up phrase designed to provoke me, and decided to take it and use it. Anyway, I got the first one when I made my initial team tweak (moving Ziggy to left-mid) and the second when I'd gone long-ball for a couple of minutes.

Oh, and Tinkerman was awarded because I made so many changes in such a short time, and "Taking Part That Counts" was because my team had lost.

A bit harsh. We'd won the half that I had managed.

These achievements were all very interesting and sort of a fun way of reminding myself what I'd done to earn them (not that I needed reminding. The moments were circling through my memory like dishes on a sushi conveyor belt). They all came with a reward of one experience point, except for Tactics 2, which came with 2 XP, and Taking Part, which earned me zero.

In other words, achievements were almost worthless.

But I didn't dismiss them, not completely. There was something strange about the whole achievements thing. I had a suspicion that they might prove useful, somewhere down the line. They weren't a good source of XP, but if there were some that were easy to get, then I'd go for it. For example, if I was a real manager, I would set someone as a playmaker every match, even if it was just for thirty seconds. I'd collect the Free Spirit achievements without risking anything. But I wouldn't actively seek out the Tinkerman ones, since that could destabilise my teams.

And for the hundredth time I reminded myself that I was not a football manager . . .

Ziggy went to the counter to buy "some scran." Scran is Manchester-speak for food. My job was to find a table.

It was a cute little deli, somehow set further back from the main road than the other shops and restaurants nearby, giving it a tucked in feel. Good feng shui. It was overpriced, but it was a great place to bring a date. It was busy, and I was forced to ask to join the end of a six-seater table. It seemed like the two women in the middle seats didn't know the ones at the end, so we weren't crashing anyone's party.

I sat and gathered my thoughts. Exhaustion was creeping down my forehead towards my eyes, like a dribble of soothing Botox. But then something in my brain went "twang," and I let out a little noise. I was worried I'd get a massive headache, but rubbing the area sort of pushed the problem away. Weird.

Ziggy came over and pushed a cheesecake and a cup of tea to my side of the table. He had a little salad and a big sandwich. Looked nice. He tucked in, and I let him take a few bites undisturbed. He needed it.

After a few bites, he closed his eyes. What a time it was to be alive, but to munch on a roast beef sandwich was very heaven!

He leaned towards me and spoke softly. "Are you disappointed?"

"What?"

"I didn't score."

"So? We talked about this. It's a process. And by the end you were really starting to look the part. We'll get you a few more trials and, I don't know, maybe some private coaching or something? Pay that Jackie guy to give you some one-on-one time." I was almost certain that Jackie had directly added one point to my boy's CA just from a brief bit of hand-waving. Ten more sessions like that . . . Ziggy had taken a big mouthful, so he couldn't speak. But there was kind of a mad, panicked bulge to his eyes. I continued. "You think he's too Scouse? Well, he is, but he's a great coach. I've decided that I love him." Ziggy relaxed a bit but still looked vaguely worried. I was reminded that I barely knew the guy. In the car, I had resolved to remedy that. "All right, I need to get to know you a bit more. Rapid fire questions. Ready? I'm driving you to a match. I need to put on some hype music. Get your blood pumping. What's the song? Song or band."

He finished chewing with a distant look, then nodded. "Watashi Kojo."

"Er . . . gesundheit."

He grinned. "No, it's a guy. A musician. He's on TikTok."

"Oh."

"He does EDM, but with an African flavour. It's awesome. You should listen."

"I will do that as soon as I get home," I lied. I coughed. "K. Who do you support?"

"City."

This was going terribly. But whatever. I didn't need to marry the guy. "Favourite player?"

"David Silva." Tiny little midfield wizard. I didn't like that answer, but we'll get to that.

"What's your favourite football chant?" Ziggy did something strange at this point. He sort of bowed his head a fraction, but in doing so, lost thirty percent of his body mass. "What?" I said. My mind was racing. Had the word *chant* triggered him? Had his father been murdered by a Gregorian choir?

He jabbed his head to his right, my left. With a sheepish grin, he said, "They're laughing at us."

Very, very slowly, I turned to look at the woman who was next to Ziggy. She had long straight hair that fell into expensive-looking curls at the ends, wide Julia Roberts lips, big black eyes. Not my type. It was *highly* obvious she was Ziggy's type. He'd gone full puppy dog. "Is everything okay?" I asked her.

She tried to button up her smile, but that just made it pop out even harder. She giggled, then made a big effort to stop. "Sorry. It's just you said you wanted to get to know him and then only asked questions about football. You're such *boys*." She had a Geordie accent. Geordies are people from Newcastle. It's not the sexiest accent in the world, but it's also weirdly exotic. You don't hear it that often.

"Yes," I said, nodding slowly. "We *are* boys," I said, my voice full of encouragement. "That's very good." Ziggy had de-shrunk but seemed reluctant to eat his sandwich now that there was an audience. Fucking hell. "Okay, onto the next round of questions, Barrett," I said. Using his real name got his attention. "Do you prefer Proust or Wittgenstein?"

He froze, just for a microsecond, but said, "Proust."

"Sun Tzu or Clausewitz?"

"Oh, Clausewitz," he said, with a kind of relieved laugh. He'd caught on fast!

But then the woman next to me joined in. As she spoke, I turned my head and got a proper look at her for the first time. Blonde, cute, steady eyes, a slightly off-centre nose which I, personally, was into, a seemingly great body. But mostly it was her lips; they seemed ready to curl into a little smile like she was seeing straight through your little plans and schemes. She, like her friend, had a Newcastle accent. "What's your favourite painting by Clausewitz, Barrett?"

Busted.

Ziggy pretended to chew a few times, to buy himself time to think. But it was futile. "Just the famous one, probably."

"Which one is that?"

"The one with the . . . ah . . . fish?"

Blondie's lips curled, just a fraction. It was delicious. Talking of which, I still hadn't touched my cheesecake.

"Okay, you win," I said, chunking off the end of the triangle. "We shall now retreat from the battlefield and talk about football. Like the boys we are." I plopped the cake into my mouth, and man, it was incredible. Soft, creamy, smooth. The base was solid, but crumbly. I nodded a few times. Overpriced? No way. It was a moment of luxury. Worth every penny. Especially when it was Ziggy's pennies. I pointed my spoon at him. "Right. Let's plan. We need to get you playing eleven-a-side." My voice trailed off, though, because the woman had put her hand on my arm. I stared at it, dumbly.

"What's your name?"

"Max."

"I'm Emma. I have a complaint." She took her hand away.

"Oh?"

"You asked him about his favourite chant."

We both looked at Ziggy. He shrunk. Spoke softly. "I don't really have one?" No surprise. City fans sang "Blue Moon" all the time. That was their entire repertoire. Abysmal.

Emma said, "What about you, Max?"

"Man United have good ones. I thought they were the best but it's probably Newcastle."

"We're from Newcastle!" said the other one.

"He knows," said Emma. "He's just trying to flirt."

"I don't *try* to flirt," I said. "I flirt. But really. Newcastle have the two best chants ever. A few years ago, they signed a player called Demba Ba. I'd never heard the name Demba. Then they signed another one. I think he was called Demba Cisse. So the fans started singing, 'Demba one, Demba two, we've got more Dembas than you!'"

Emma wasn't as impressed as she should have been. "Okay."

"Then they got a player called Habib Beye."

"Hab . . ."

"Habib. Beye. Now, I'm going to do the chant, and you're going to say Habib Beye. You ready?" She was. "Sunday, Monday," I said, then pointed at her.

She looked uncertain. "Habib Beye?"

"Tuesday, Wednesday," I said.

"Habib Beye?"

"Thursday, Friday."

"Habib Beye."

"Saturday, what a day." Now Emma's friend and Ziggy joined in. Not super loud like in a movie. But they joined in. "Been working all week for you!"

Emma laughed, but didn't really know why.

"Okay," I said. "I want to talk about sports with my buddy now. Is that all right?"

"No," she said. "Explain it to me."

"The chant? It's the theme song from *Happy Days*."

"No," she said, pouting deliciously. Oh my God, this woman! "Explain sports."

Crazy. Emma was sexy, intelligent, and didn't live within hundreds of miles of me. An absolutely stellar combination. But I didn't feel like "explaining sports" to her. I'd already lost focus on Ziggy during the training session. I wasn't going to make the same mistake twice in one day. I was about to refuse when some impulse made me look at him. He was glaring at me with prisoner-of-war eyes, huge, trying to convey reams of text with every blink. What? I kept watching. He darted his eyes towards the woman next to him. Trying to say something. "Barrett, would you mind if I talked to Emma for a bit?"

His eyeballs lost their manic energy. Relief. I'd done the right thing. He gave Emma's friend a cautious smile. "I don't mind if . . ."

"Gemma."

"If Gemma doesn't mind."

"Gemma," said Gemma, "doesn't mind."

20

EXPERTISE, ATHLETICISM, MOMENTS OF SURPRISE

I leaned a little closer to Emma, and Emma leaned a little closer to me. "Emma and Gemma. Are you serious?"

"Honest."

"What are you doing in Manchester?"

"We were on a training course. Booked the Airbnb a bit longer to have a little weekend."

"Do you like it?"

"Yeah. It's like Newcastle but bigger. Great shops. Are you going to eat that cheesecake?"

I pushed the plate in front of her and offered her the spoon. "Do you want a clean one?"

She made far too much contact with my hand as she took the spoon from me. She popped it in her lips and dragged it. "It's clean now," she said. Flecks of the cake remained on her lips for all of three seconds, before vanishing into her mouth. I was getting really turned on.

"This was all a scam to get our friends talking, wasn't it?" I said.

"No," she said. "I've always wanted to ask someone with a brain what football is all about. What you see in it."

"There are brains in Newcastle."

"But I live there. I don't want to be that girl that men explain football to. And I'll never see you again, so I thought, now's my chance."

I'll never see you again. That sounded familiar. That was what I did.

Fine. Let's explain why I like football. Totally normal conversation. "All right. Sport. I was watching *Taskmaster,* and they had a challenge where they had to invent a sport. A comedian and a brainiac. The brainiac asked the comedian to distil the essence of sport into a few words. She used that word, distil. So the guy, Alan Davies, he goes, expertise, athleticism, moments of surprise. By the way, I think that's *exceptional* coming up with it so fast. I'm in awe of that. So. Expertise and athleticism. That's sport as a proxy for war."

"War?"

"Instead of men running around stabbing each other, you play football. Win or lose, you're alive. Great. Let's do that instead."

"There's still war though."

I didn't mean to be rude, but I ignored her point. I was getting into the flow. "In the old days you'd train to kill, now you train to play a killer pass. It has the same social effect. Sport is brilliant." I sipped my tea. "Expertise, athleticism, moments of surprise. Honestly, that's good enough for me. I'm into that. But there's more."

"There is?"

"The Premier League. Massively popular. Watched worldwide. There are twenty teams. Half the players have played for multiple teams. Half the managers have managed other teams. Sometimes those relationships end well, sometimes they don't. So you get returning heroes, or heroes turned villain. Pantomime villain, real villain. Sometimes the stadium becomes a hate-filled cauldron."

"Charming."

"Then you've got Manchester versus Liverpool. Not just the clubs, the cities. North London versus South London. Which is the best team in the midlands? So what've we got? Individuals with shifting allegiances. Clubs with grudges and rivalries. You know what that is? That's *Game of Thrones*."

"Come on."

"It's *Game of Thrones* with a ball. And then."

"Then?"

"Then you've got Man United. That's the old money. Man City. That's the new money. Flashing their cash around, buying up all the land, buying all the best players. Rubbing everyone's nose in it. Then along come Newcastle! Your lot. Richer than every other team in the world combined!"

"That can't be right."

"I promise you it is. It's not even close. So what's that? Money versus money? It's *Dallas*."

"The city?"

"The TV show. The soap opera. Today's *Dallas* is probably *Succession*, but I haven't watched it. Whatever. The Premier League is the world's most popular soap opera."

She was doing the thing with her lips that suggested she thought I was talking total bullshit, but she was enjoying it anyway. "You're saying football is a soap for boys. There are women's teams now, you know."

"You don't have to tell me that. I manage one of them."

"You do?" said Ziggy. I don't think his chat with Gemma had petered out. I think my enthusiasm had just been a little too infectious, and they'd stopped to listen.

"Ugh, yeah, just a bit. So it's a soap opera for men *and* women, and it's more than that."

"Oh, yes?" said Emma, amused.

"It's Shakespeare," I said, earnest.

"Okay, I didn't expect that."

"It's Shakespeare," I repeated. "It's Greek tragedy. You work and toil, but then the referee makes a bad decision, and boom, your season is over. Referees are like the gods; sometimes they just send a player off or disallow a goal. Just to test the hero. Just to be a dick. You finish bottom of the league? You're out, mate! Exiled. You have to play far from the money and the fame. Like in Sunderland or somewhere. Or what about a superstar player? He moves from one team to their bitter rivals. He makes more money there, wins more trophies. But now he can never go back to where he was most loved. And there are cruel fates. England prepare for years, puts together a team that can win the World Cup, but just before the tournament, their star striker Harry Kane breaks his foot."

"What!" shouted Ziggy. "Kane's injured?"

I laughed. "No."

"Oh, thank fuck. Jesus. You gave me a heart attack."

"See?" I said to Emma. "Every season is the hero's journey. Triumphs and disasters. Highs and lows. And there's a climax. Someone wins the league. Someone wins the cup. It might not be the team you want . . ."

"It normally is, though," said Ziggy, the City fan. *Enjoy it while it lasts, bro!*

"But it's satisfying that it ends decisively. Every season is a book. Every match is a chapter. It's stories all the way through."

Emma looked at me. She wasn't doing anything sardonic with her mouth. She loaded some cheesecake, but used it to point at me, almost accusing. "You're a romantic."

What a strange way to put it. I didn't feel like a very romantic person. Not in the flowers and fireplaces kind of sense. "Football is romantic. Romance is about hope. The club we were at today. It's a long way from United and City and Newcastle. But it's part of the same pyramid. Any club can move up the pyramid, and up, and up, and be on a par with the big boys. You don't get that in every sport. In football you can be the tiniest little mouse and dream of becoming the mightiest elephant."

"A small mouse would turn into a big mouse," said Gemma, contributing to the conversation wonderfully.

"And the FA Cup," said Ziggy. I was glad to see he was on my side, that he got my point.

"Yes! The FA Cup. More or less every team in the country plays in it. A teeny tiny village team can win a few matches and be playing against United at Old Trafford. Sometimes, really quite small teams get close to the final. One day, a tiny team could even win it. So every year there's hope."

Gemma piped up again. "Romance is getting married on a sandy beach."

I shook my head. "No. Romance is sending a text and not knowing if she'll reply. The agony of worrying if you've messed everything up. Winning the cup isn't romantic. Romantic is being one-nil up after eighty minutes. That last ten minutes where you are put through the wringer. Not knowing how it's going to go. Getting married? You've made it then. There's nothing to worry about. Nothing to . . . to . . ."

Ziggy said, "To yearn for."

I beamed at him. "Exactly."

Emma had a ball of cheesecake in her mouth. "So that's why you like football."

"Yes," said Ziggy.

"No," I said. "There are hundreds more things. I could honestly go on about it for hours. Even Ziggy would get sick of me."

"Who's Ziggy?"

"That's his stage name," I said, which was the cue for Ziggy to start talking about himself. Some light boasting.

But Emma had other ideas. "Just tell me one more thing. Come on, I'll buy you another tea."

"Thanks, no. I feel a bit weird. I'll go soon." I did, indeed, feel weird. Fragments of memories from the match were crowding my head. I was still getting little spikes of pain, and when I rubbed the area, it felt warm.

"Just one."

Well, maybe I could kill two birds with one stone. I sighed. "I think football tells you something about someone's character."

"How?"

"When I went to watch Barrett the first time, there was this guy on his team." I tried to remember the name. "Er . . . Graham. I don't know him, I don't know the first thing about him, but I'd be willing to bet his job is super boring."

"He's a plasterer," said Ziggy.

"Right. Good job, good money. Monotonous, though, innit? So when he plays football, his creative side comes out. Leaks out! It's tragic because his body won't let him do what he hopes it will do. But he never stops trying. Back-heels, spins, nutmegs. Zero percent success rate. But his brain demands he try."

"Holy shit, that's exactly what he's like."

"I'm not saying this is an exact science, Ziggy. It's just a theory. Take someone who cheats at golf. Would you do business with them? I mean, your instinct is no, but why not? Are they likely to cheat in business if they cheat in golf? Is cheating in golf a different sort of character flaw to cheating in footy? I have no idea. I just enjoy speculating. It's interesting to me. And you know what's absolutely fascinating?" I asked Emma.

"What?"

"Ziggy. He *fascinates* me. He's an introvert. He's supportive, tries to make his teammates look good. Will probably pass instead of shooting. Will play left-back instead of striker because that's what he's asked to do. Introvert. But his best skill is the most extroverted thing a player can do, scoring a goal. Scoring a goal makes you the centre of attention. You make the game stop—literally stop! People write your name down in the history books, call it out to the whole stadium. So that's fascinating to me. An introvert doing an extrovert job. And when I asked who his favourite player is—which you ladies found so ludicrous—he said it was David Silva, a creative midfielder. A little tiny invisible genius who made everyone else look good. You'd expect a goalscorer to talk about goalscorers. But he didn't. So what does that mean? Maybe nothing. But maybe he secretly wants to be the sociable introvert who plays the pass, but his team needs him to be the selfish extrovert who scores the goal. So who is he? Is he Barrett? Or is he Ziggy?"

As I finished speaking, I was aware that things had changed around the table. The mood, or whatever. But I couldn't spare any mental run-time to it. Another sharp pang of pain attacked the centre of my skull.

Ziggy was saying something. For the first time since the women had laughed at us, he was giving me his full attention. "What?" I said. "Sorry, I just had a headache."

"You were saying about my next steps," he said. "Talking about finding another trial and that."

"Yeah, I'll do it tomorrow. I feel . . ."

"No," he said. "I mean, there's no need. They asked me to come back."

"Who?"

"FC United," he said. He looked worried, which might have been for several reasons. Mostly the fact that they'd gone behind my back. Should I be worried about that? Probably. Probably, definitely.

"Oh," I said.

"If you don't want me to . . ."

Another, smaller, but not much less painful pang struck me just then. "Jesus, Ziggy, of course I want you to." Slightly calmer, I added, "You're going to smash it. That's what I've been telling you. You'll be their star striker before Christmas."

"Star striker?" Gemma demanded Ziggy tell her all about it. I mentally retreated from that part of the conversation. There was a big silence on my side of the table. Like I'd ruined things with Emma somehow. *Things?* What things? Why did I think like that?

There was still some cheesecake left. I took it and ate the rest, in case my headache was from low blood sugar or something.

Finally, she said, "Thanks. That was really . . . educational."

"Polite," I mumbled.

"No," she said, grabbing my arm and instantly letting go. "Really. But . . . are you okay?"

"Weird headache," I said. "I'll go take a couple of pills and hope-fully sleep it off."

"Oh," she said. Slight hint of disappointment?

"Do you have a spare room?" I said.

"In the Airbnb?" She gave me a dubious look. So she hadn't been flirting after all.

"In Newcastle."

"Oh. No. Why?"

I rubbed my lips to clear off the last bits of cake. "I'm a football agent. I need to find players. Why not Newcastle? It's a real hotbed of talent."

"Is it? Are you good at spotting talent?" Now she was giving flirty vibes again. Choose one!

"Yes. And yes."

She leaned close to me and, in a soft voice, said, "I don't have a spare room but I know where there's a hot bed."

So a pretty good day ended with Ziggy maybe finally scoring (I never asked) and me writhing in bed, sweating . . . alone with a fever and splitting headache. At least I had a solid phone number. Phase two of my scouting empire seemed like it would have an unexpected base: Newcastle. The question was, if I went to stay with Emma, would I get any work done?

21

THIS IS MAX SPEAKING

I woke up feeling great—no trace of the headache—but then realised I had to go to the call centre. Back to reality.

It was brutal. It was torture. I didn't want to be there. I had lost every single shred of appetite for answering phone calls. I didn't give a shit about my stats.

I wanted to move Gribbin to the right-wing. I wanted to switch to a 5-3-2 or overload the midfield. I wanted a five-digit bank balance. I wanted to take Emma to the opera. Well, maybe one of the short ones.

"Hello, this is Max speaking, how can I help you?"

On the football side of my life, I was equal parts happy, excited, and anxious.

Many questions were unanswered, one being, would FC United try to steal my client?

I swallowed such feelings. Marked them as unread. The following Monday would be the Queen's funeral, and that seemed like a good place to stop and rethink everything. Do a bit of strategising. In the meantime, it was back to the grind.

On Monday evening, I drove to Goals Manchester, a Powerleague competitor. Five-a-side pitches, artificial grass. I loved these places. There were quite a few matches going on, but I found it hard to concentrate. I kept wanting to reposition the players or give them instructions. Mark number seven! Play down the left! Basically, I was struggling to get out of the football manager mindset and back into the Super Scout one. I picked up 90 XP.

I also saw a couple of interesting players. Couple of lads with PA 20, could be a backup at FC United. Not really interesting to me with my agent hat on, but I mean, good to know. There was also this older guy with CA 7, PA 50. I had a chat with him, and it turned out he'd been scouted by West Ham when he was a kid and played for a while in a semi-pro league down south. Couple of bad injuries, and now he was just taking it easy.

On Tuesday, I returned to Ardwick's Powerleague to check on Raffi Brown. He was there, all right, as lop-sidedly beautiful as ever. None of his attributes had changed, but now I could see that his finishing was six. A tiny bit of a letdown. He wasn't going to be scoring silly numbers of goals from midfield like Michel Platini. But he was running the game, pulling the strings. I made eye contact with him once, and it was intense. Scary. I think I'd have been calmer having eye sex with Margot Robbie. I nodded slightly, friendly but masculine. He just went about his business.

Later, I got a text from Neil, FC United's manager. It simply said:

5-3-2 my arse.

They'd played Matlock Town who had obviously not played the formation I'd promised. Neil can't have been that unhappy though, because United won 2–1.

XP balance: 268

Wednesday and Thursday went in similar fashion. Just hitting spots I knew to be reliable sources of XP, paying special attention to anyone with PA higher than 1. I was still always trying to do little thought experiments, especially if the games were bad. Like when a pace five player was against a pace eight player, could I see the difference? Yes. And how big did the difference need to be for there to be a clear and obvious tactical benefit? Like, if I had a pacey right-winger, would I play him on the left-wing in order to put him against the opposition's slowest defender? (Sometimes, maybe, but mostly not. But if the pace difference was high enough, then yes. I thought I would.)

There was also stamina. Players with low stamina, which was most of them, faded badly towards the end of games. Players with good stamina, like Beth, could dominate the last ten minutes. These players were unevenly distributed; it wasn't like there were teams of super-fit amateurs winning every game with late comebacks. That'd be interesting though: a team of clumsy marathon runners against a slightly more talented team of, I don't know, bus drivers.

XP balance: 386

On Friday, I snapped at my boss. I'd turned my phone off for a few minutes to get a break. In the past I took my breaks at the end of calls. After I'd solved whatever problem, I'd ask the customer a question about the weather or how their day was going or something bland. I didn't need to think much, and some of the customers enjoyed the little chats.

But I didn't want to do that anymore. As discussed, I'd rather have been watching two forty-year-old men sprint towards a loose ball at the speed of giant turtles, so that I could calculate whether pace two with a one-yard head start was better than pace three. So I just ended the calls and then gave myself a minute or two off the phones.

My boss spotted me staring into space when there were calls in the queue. "Max," she said. "Is your phone off?"

"Yep. I need a break."

"You seem to be taking a lot of these little breaks." Good on her for noticing, I suppose.

"Yep."

"Well, you're not allowed."

I pointed to the stats board. I was in first place, just ahead of the next best employee. I'd been swapping places with her on and off the whole day. Basically, I was doing just enough work to keep up with her, and then I'd pick up the pace in the last half hour of my shift so that I'd finish every day as the top employee, while doing as little work as possible to get there. A season is a marathon, not a sprint. Boss wanted me to go flat-out, 24/7. To squeeze me like a sponge and then chuck me out. I pushed back. "You've seen the stats?"

"Think of the customers, Max. They have to wait. You know what it's like. It's frustrating. And you've got them on hold."

"I think what I'm doing is fine. I'm answering more calls a day than anyone. I need a little time-out sometimes."

"But you're not—"

This was the part where I lost my equilibrium. "They're on hold because you're understaffed. You've been understaffed since the day I started." I had a lot more to say, but my tone had already said it. I cooled all the way down. Switched from direct passing to short. Changed "counterattack" from Yes to No.

She moved closer to me. "Max, you're not allowed to turn your phone off." And then she made a big mistake. She leaned over and pressed the button. The button on my phone. My. Phone. Instantly, a call came down the line.

"Max speaking, how can I help you?"

Boss lady walked away in triumph, but by the end of the day I was in a distant second place in the stats. I wanted to finish third, but I'd built up too much of a lead.

Later, I was looking at Beth's team doing a little warm-up before kick-off in a strange kind of mood. There was the high of knowing I was about to get 2 XP per minute, and knowing I was about to be able to boss people around. To paint one part of the world the colour I wanted.

I knew I was going to quit my job. I couldn't afford to right away; I could very possibly freeze to death if I did. But I had one foot out of the door. But if I was getting out of one job, what was I getting into?

Football. Why would I get into football? Because I had the curse. Because I had the cheat mode. But what if I built a whole career around my screens and my ability to see player profiles, and, after seven years, the curse ended? If I couldn't see the screens, would there be anything left? Did Max Best have what it took?

"Beth," I said. She broke away from the warm-up and jogged over to me. I always worried that she'd be weird or clingy, but she never was. She had her own stuff going on. I felt a tiny surge of affection for her.

"Max."

"When are we playing City?"

"Not next week, the week after."

"Right."

She jogged off again.

"Beth."

She came back. "What."

"Where can I see the league table?"

She raised one of her drawn-on eyebrows at me, but then rummaged in her bag, whipped out her phone, and started double-thumbing it. She handed it to me and jogged off.

Should I go to her WhatsApp and get some hot goss? See who she was sending nudes to? It was briefly tempting. But nah. I pinched the screen to make the page bigger. It was the shitty website of the North Manchester Women's League Indoor Limited Invitational League, and surprise, surprise, it didn't have responsive html tables. Every cell was a mile wide. *How hard could it possibly be to make a nice, clean, online table?* Anyway, City had won every game, and, judging by their goal difference, no game had even been close. Except they'd only beaten us 3–1, so they must have gone goal-crazy in the next match to make up for it.

Looking up and down the table, I was once again aware of my own stupidity. Somehow, after all this time, I didn't know the name of Beth's team. I had always thought of them as just that: Beth's Team. I knew they weren't one of the bottom names, so I made an educated guess that they were the team in third place, Manchester Met Heads. Was that a pun on meat heads or meth heads? The Met part stood for Metropolitan, the name of the second biggest university in Manchester. The team above them had played a game more but were only one point ahead, so there was every chance Beth's team would finish the season in second place. Especially with me in charge.

But that wasn't good enough.

"Beth. Team meeting."

She rolled her eyes, but gathered the ladies.

Now, this was a proper challenge. When I'd managed AFC Phoenix, I'd simply given orders on my screens, and the guys had carried them out. I didn't need to verbalise. I didn't need to explain. But with Beth's team, the Match Overview screen didn't appear. I had to do things the old-fashioned way.

And that was fine by me. I wanted to prove myself.

I looked around at my squad. Keeper: Jane. Defenders: Beth and Nobby. Defensive midfielder: Freyja. Midfield terriers: Sophia, Bella, Bex. Striker: Lula.

"All right, ladies. It's big speech time." I cleared my throat. "Four score and seven days ago, I became your manager."

"Let me stop you right there, Max," said Beth. "We're playing St. Thomas Aquinas. They're shit. We don't need *Braveheart*."

"Fine. Jesus. Listen. These lot are bottom of the league. Next week we're playing the team just below us. Then it's City." I left an ominous pause there. "I want to beat City."

Beth nodded. "That's nice. It's not going to happen. Can we finish our warm-up now?"

"I want to beat City," I said. "If we beat City, I'm going to quit my job." Not totally sure why I said that, but as it bounced its way along my throat and out of my mouth, it felt right.

"What's one thing got to do with the other?" asked Nobby.

"So the way I see it," I said. "We need to treat these two games as training sessions. To practise moves and ideas we can use against City."

"Max," said Beth, exasperated. "When we play them, we're just there to make up the numbers." My head snapped in her direction. Make up the numbers . . . now, *there* was a good idea.

"Beth. We can win. We will win. We must win."

Freyja tilted her head. "You've got a plan, haven't you?"

I grinned. "I may have one or two ideas."

22

INTERESTINGLY UNINTERESTING

Beth wasn't in the mood for my shenanigans. She hadn't played for a while and had a ton of pent-up energy. But she offered a compromise. She told me the team got together to train on Wednesdays, and I could take over the next session and, as she put it, "get all Max."

So the Met Heads played, and won. They had a lovely old time, but I was worried. One of my only advantages against City was the Free Hit perk. But I could only use that if we got a free kick in a dangerous position. That happened a few times against St. Thomas Aquinas, because we were always attacking, but hadn't happened in the first game against City. In fact, almost the entire game had taken place in our half.

How could I get a free kick near the City goal? Or even better, a penalty?

Bella ran past and told me off for biting my nails.

How to get a free kick. Something to think about. Meanwhile, I had other irons in the fire.

I took out my phone and called Ziggy.

On Sunday morning, I popped down to Hough End to see if there were any matches being played. I doubted it, because the Queen's funeral was the following day. To my surprise, there were. It looked like a full schedule.

I drifted around the pitches, picking up XP, scouting some new players and rescouting many more. That latter was interesting for how uninteresting it was. A few players had their stamina in red or green, indicating that they'd changed since I'd last seen them, but it was so . . . unimportant. Some guy's stamina had dropped from 2 to 1. He was getting old? Another guy's had increased from 6 to 7. Training for The Great Northern Run? The other attributes were pretty static. I certainly didn't see any radical changes, but I was only giving the guys quick glances, and I primarily looked at the CA/PA scores. It was possible some interesting data slipped through the cracks. It was also possible I'd one day find myself alone in a lift with Lily James.

What I was really focused on was the touchline. I was looking for a team that didn't have a manager. Manager, in this case, is an *extremely* grand word to describe the role. In my experience, Sunday League teams more or less ran themselves, with one or two alpha/gobby types picking the team and making the substitutions. The "manager" was the guy who washed the kit, filled in the forms, and stood on the touchline shouting encouragement or spewing bile, depending on their character.

There was one team who didn't seem to have a formal manager guy. I watched their match for a while and they were pretty good. Organised and confident. They were winning 3–0 approaching half-time and my impulse was to ask if I could manage the second half.

But 1) why would they want me to? and 2) that didn't really fit with the whole "testing myself" thing I had going on. I glanced over at the other side of the pitch, where the other manager was looking forlorn. Even with the help of the curse, it would be quite a challenge to come back from three down. Taking a good team and making them better was one thing, but taking a shit team and making them winners, that was *epic*.

So I walked all the way around the pitch, past a corner flag, behind the goal, past another corner flag, and back up to the halfway line. The manager guy stood there, along with three substitute players, head down, barely able to watch the action. The subs would sometimes potter off and half-heartedly keep warm. I suppose they knew they wouldn't come on until the second half. It wasn't rolling subs in this league, so once you came off the pitch, you stayed off. The manager's name was above his head, along with a load of question marks, but, for once, I didn't dive in two-footed.

"Hi there," I said. "I'm Max."

"Oh. John."

"What team is this?"

"We're Moss Side Celtic, and they're Wilmslow Mega Titans."

"Wow. That's quite a name." I tapped at my phone until I dug up the league table. "Ouch. Tough season for you guys."

"We've had worse," he said.

"Is that possible?" I said.

"I've seen you around," he said. "You're quite the Sunday League connoisseur."

"I'm insatiable."

"So you've seen worse teams."

"That's true."

"It's a tough league, this one. Loads of teams folded in the pandemic, and the better ones got merged into one division."

We watched the game for a little bit. A Celtic player played a pretty good long pass, but its intended target couldn't quite reach out a leg to control the ball. "Listen," I said. "I've been doing my coaching badges. I'm supposed to do some real-life coaching. You know, it's like for the C badge you need to coach two hundred hours, for B it's five hundred, all that kind of thing. The usual." This was all bullshit that I made up on the spot. I knew there were coaching licences and they were called A, B, C, etc. but if you asked me which was the highest it would have been a guess.

He looked impressed. "Oh, right?"

"Yeah. I know it's a bit weird, but since you're 3–0 down, maybe you wouldn't mind me getting some practice in."

"Take the second half? This is for your badge, is it?"

"This'd be extracurricular. You wouldn't have to sign anything," I said, as though that was the thing he'd be worried about.

One of the subs was nearby. "You're a proper coach, then? You got any experience?"

"I was in charge of FC United Reserves the other day, and we won 2–0."

"Against who?"

I gave him my best cute little grin. "Against FC United."

Reserves beating the first team? He loved that. He was sold. John wasn't quite as keen, and said he'd think about it. Over the next thirty seconds he angled his body away from me, half a degree at a time. I was ninety-nine percent sure he'd turn me down. This was his fiefdom; he was Lord of the Manor. In the past, I'd have scurried away like a crab who'd turned up at a lobster party. But I found I was more and more willing to be humiliated. If you want to learn a skill, embarrassment is the cost of entry.

So I stood there, scanning the players, thinking of what I'd do if I were in charge. Maybe John would let me do the last ten minutes. That'd be all right.

But when the half-time whistle blew, his players came over to the side of the pitch and started fuming at each other. They were getting more and more wound up, pointing, accusing, blaming. Something had gone very wrong with this team, not just today but over weeks or months. The timer on the bomb was ticking down, and there were only seconds left before detonation. And the man holding the blunt pliers was, obviously, John. He wasn't one for confrontation. "Listen up, lads, this here is . . ."

He was putting me in charge! I tried not to look smug. "Max."

"He's a coach, got his badges and that, and he's going to set you up for the second half."

At that pronouncement, there was something like pandemonium. These guys were not happy with John, with me, with each other, with the laws of physics. One word oft repeated was "rando," as in "why are you putting this rando in charge" and "first fucking rando comes along, gets made King, fucks sake." I kept opening and closing my screens, but when John slapped me on the arm and took a step back, it happened. The screen was the Match Overview.

I was in charge; the curse had spoken. I rushed to the tactics screen and started dicking around.

All the bickering, mocking, all the chat of every kind stopped in an instant. After a slight pause, every player's face relaxed. They started sipping their energy drinks, adjusting their shinpads, doing little stretches.

The change in mood was eerie.

"Thanks lads," I said, trying to move on to distract John from the creepy thing he'd just seen. "Second half, 4-4-2 obviously." I was locked into the match screens now, so buying 4-4-2 diamond just to try something different was off the table. As always, I was glad that something was blocking me from mindless splurging. I was planning to spend the following day strategising and whatnot. In the time it had taken me to speak, I'd totally reorganised the team. Still some square pegs in round holes, but it was a decent lineup. At least this time I had two strikers and two lads who could play on the left. "All right. That's it. Have fun out there!"

"What?" said John, stepping forward again. "You're not changing anything?"

Ah. This was a problem. The players—including the substitutes—knew what I wanted. The curse had told them! But this John guy, he wasn't in the loop. As far as the curse was concerned, this guy was now a spectator. So from John's point of view, I'd said hi and then expected the players to know what to do. I needed to say my plans out loud, otherwise John—and everyone who watched me in the future—would know I was using witchcraft and burn me like a well-done steak.

I grinned sheepishly. "That's right. I've got it all up here." I tapped my temple. "Pep's always telling me I need to communicate more. Okay, boys, here's the deal." Over the next two minutes, I "told" the players where they'd play, the overall style I wanted, and mentioned a couple of the individual tactics I wanted them to employ. All for John's benefit, along with tons of hand-slapping, like I was really passionate. How did I keep a straight face? No clue.

Then I said, out loud as an afterthought, that we wouldn't be playing the offside trap.

"Oh, shit, he's a nutjob," mumbled John, but got zero support from the players. Which in itself was odd. Every single team on Hough End was playing the offside trap. Every. Single. One.

The offside rule is the one that causes the most grief to people who don't like football. Instead of trying to explain it, let me describe what the sport would look like if it *didn't* have this rule. That way, you will at least understand why it's needed.

Imagine a bunch of children playing football on the school playground. Let's say there are ten toddlers. If the ball is on the left-hand-side of the pitch, how many kids will be on the left? Obvious answer: ten. As the ball bounces around, the kids are magnetically drawn to it, like a flock of baby ducks following their mother. Fast forward a few years. The kids are now eight years old. Most are still chasing the ball around, but there's one kid with a burgeoning strategic mind. Or he's just a lazy prick. Either way, he doesn't chase the ball; he hangs around the opponent's goal. When the ball comes to him, the little shit thwacks the ball into the empty net and runs around like a hero. This is either 1) low, snide, and despicable or 2) hyper-efficient, depending on your point of view. It's called goalhanging and is generally frowned upon. As a comparison, it's like in an RPG when you amble up to a ninety-nine percent dead boss, stab him in the leg, and take all the credit for the kill. Goalhanging, ladies and gentlemen, is kill stealing.

The solution to goalhanging? The offside rule. Long story over-simplified to the point where it starts to become inaccurate, you can't just hang around waiting to score. You have to let the defenders take a starting position between you and the goal. This is a big advantage to the defender, but the alternative is chaos.

In the first half, Moss Side Celtic had tried to play this offside trap. That meant their defenders would try to stand in a line, and push that line as close to the centre of the pitch as possible. When done correctly, the offside trap forces the other team to drop back, so they can't be ac-cused of goalhanging. It's the difference between having attackers *close* to your goal, or *far away*. If they are far away, it's much harder to score a goal. That's why every single team on the vast playing fields was using the offside trap.

The risk is that when it fails, the other team is going to get a pretty easy path to goal.

And then the offside trap becomes a noose you place around your own neck.

To be good at the offside trap, you need defenders with good posi-tional awareness and a sense of unity. Moss Side Celtic didn't have that, as far as I could tell. So if it wasn't working, why do it?

John had moved away from me, chuntering under his breath, mumbling about randos.

The referee blew his whistle to start the second half. My knowl-edge of football was about to be tested in the ultimate crucible of fire: the Cheshire & Manchester Respect Sunday Invitational League.

23

WILMSLOW MEGA TITANS

Moss Side Celtic	0	Wilmslow Mega Titans	3
	Second	Half	
		Nugent	14
		Collins	19
		Musa	30

The Mega Titans had some flaws:

- They were set up in a standard 4-4-2 but had a defender and a midfielder playing as strikers. Obviously, these were the loudest, bossiest guys who had decided they could best serve the team by scoring all the goals and claiming all the glory. Meanwhile, they had natural strikers playing at right-back and right-mid. In short, their right side was built on sand. I instructed my team to play towards our left so we could attack these out-of-position dudes.
- They only had one sub, but we had three. We had more fresh legs than a French restaurant! If I used them well, we'd be quids in, especially in the last ten minutes.
- They didn't have *me* as manager. Roar! (A moment of fake confidence that I'm sure you'll permit, but seriously, they didn't have a manager of any kind. They'd be much slower responding to my tweaks, if they could respond at all.)

As always with these Sunday League games, the ball started deflecting around like the pitch was a huge pinball machine. I started tweaking everyone's individual passing instructions. Guys with decent passing and technique got to play mixed passes, i.e., they could try long ones when it made sense, while those with low numbers had to keep it short. In the hurly-burly of a match, it's actually not as easy as it looks to play short passes, but the success rate is obviously much, much higher on a five-yard pass than a fifty-yard one. Amazingly, the pinball effect subsided, and we actually kept the ball a little bit. Not like a Premier League team, and far, far even from FC United. But it wasn't that bad! No manager had ever been so pleased by so little!

A quick comment on the players. Everyone on the pitch had CA 1. (Their PA didn't matter for this particular game, but no 1 had a PA higher than 2.) So managing them was all about putting them in the right slots and asking them to do things—or stop doing things—depending on their attributes. Now, this wasn't exactly me testing myself in a curse-free environment but if I (hypothetically) managed these guys every week for a few months, I'd surely get a curse-adjacent idea of their abilities. From that point of view, the curse was just a shortcut.

Was I deluding myself? Hard to say. But yes. I was totally telling myself what I wanted to hear.

That said, the *main* benefit of the curse was seeing CA and PA. Finding new, better players. If I could get a tune out of the players I already had, that would be me and not the curse, right? I could think of myself as a craftsman, as well as a trader. Making soup out of old leather would give me the self-belief to think that I was bringing *some* skills to the kitchen.

The game was going well. Mega Titans started the half confidently, and they were dashing around trying to get the ball off us. But every time we put together three, four, five passes, they wasted more calories chasing us, and they started to sense that something had changed. One change was incredibly obvious. On our side, there was absolutely no bickering of any kind. We weren't exactly three hundred Spartans defending our homeland, but we were all pulling in the same direction. Every player was trying to carry out my instructions to the best of his ability with no thought of status and no word of complaint. Now *that* was one hundred percent the curse.

We got a corner, and I had to decide to play the Free Hit or not. Getting an early goal would hugely change the match dynamic. But I hadn't been idle since the FC United match. I'd done some research and found that, at best, three percent of corners led to a goal. Using the Free Hit on a corner was a waste, an act of desperation. If my tinkering with the team worked, we'd be playing in the opposition half, and would inevitably get free kicks. A penalty, even.

Smith fires in the corner.

But he hits the first defender.

Hmm. That corner had been abysmal. In the FC United game, I'd used Gribbin as my set piece taker, and he'd turned out to have wicked delivery. In *this* game, I had no clue who to use. After some thought, I selected the guy with the highest technique and put him on set pieces. The guy with the highest finishing got penalty-taking duties.

Five minutes passed. Ten. We were in control of the game, and the Mega Titans seemed baffled that we weren't trying for offsides. Their strikers pushed up the pitch, but our defenders simply tracked them. When the Titan strikers got the ball, there were always at least two defenders between them and our goalkeeper. They didn't have much of an idea of what to do. Maybe their strikers would have known, but they were playing out of position.

Talking of which, I made my first substitution. My first real substitution ever!

I had a fast right-winger and put him on the left with instructions to attack, attack, attack. I'd have traded fifty XP for a jet-heeled left-sided player, but I had to use what I had.

Soon, my whiz kid started tormenting the striker who was playing as a defender. To be fair, sometimes my right-footed guy would look extremely uncomfortable on the left side of the pitch, and he did dribble the ball straight out of play a couple of times. But a few other times he sped past the defender and either shot or crossed the ball.

One of these crosses led to:

Wiggins dribbles past Hoolihan.

Wiggins leaves him for dead!

Wiggins is free on the left side.

He tries a cross.

It's blocked!

Wiggins collects the rebound.

He floats it to the far post.

Okoje is there!

GOOOOOOAAAAAALLLLL!

As we celebrated, the Mega Titans huddled together and reshuffled their team. I saw it on the tactics page. They swapped their full-backs around. Is that it? You're not going to fix the real problem with your team? *Well, fuck you guys.*

I told Wiggins to move onto the right, where he would still be against the out-of-position striker, but now Wiggins would be on his favoured side. This was going to be brutal! And I made my other two subs, keeping the energy levels up and replacing a square peg with an oval one. Slightly better. John made some weird noises. Apparently, I'd subbed off a player who threw tantrums if you ever changed him. This time, he was good as gold. Not a peep out of the guy.

We had our first real setback then. We were passing the ball around, moving it over to the left. With a groan, I realised that I'd forgotten to change our pattern of play, and my guys were still under instructions to attack down that side. But the Titans weren't as weak on that side anymore; their new right-back was pretty solid. He cut out one of our attacks and boofed the ball down the pitch where, after a couple of unlucky bounces and one missed header, the defender playing as a striker scored a goal.

We were losing 4–1.

It was my fault. John was whispering—a stage whisper meant to be heard—to the players who had come off the pitch about how stupid it was not to play offside. It didn't bother me. I knew the chain of events. I knew what had really happened. It was interesting that John couldn't see it, though. It was so, so obvious.

I changed our focus so that we'd attack down the right, and we were back off.

Now the action was coming thick and fast, and it was eighty percent in our favour. We had shots, we had half-chances.

Wiggins wasn't running the game like Gribbin had done. If Gribbin had been a puppeteer, masterfully tweaking three strings at a time, then Wiggins was a cheap, radio-controlled car. Much too fast for its own good, but when you lined everything up perfectly it went like the devil.

And we were using him again and again. He had fresh legs. The Titans were starting to run on fumes.

Chance after chance, and then, finally! A goal. AND ANOTHER!

We were 4–3 down but the most comfortable 4–3 of all time. I didn't have to use the tactics board. Things were, finally, optimised. Still, though, I yelled some random football things every now and then. One part "get in you slag" to two parts "Mikey! Watch the underlaps. The underlaps!" It was just theatre. A grand performance, five stars, must see, played for the benefit of one man, John. Fucker didn't even pay for a ticket.

But time was running out. Ten minutes left, and the Titans reorganised their defence again. I left Wiggins on the right; he was having a lovely old time. So there wasn't anything for me to do but watch . . . and hope.

And finally, the moment. Wiggins went zooming after a long pass, and one of the defenders—sick of seeing this happen again and again— lost his shit. He rushed over and hacked the winger down. Penalty!

Now, I knew that Wiggins was never going to catch that ball, and Wiggins knew it. But the referee gave the penalty anyway. Fair enough, I suppose. You can't just go round kicking people.

My striker put the ball on the penalty spot. I slammed the free hit button harder than anyone has ever slapped an invisible button before.

The guy stepped forward . . .

And the fucker hit the post.

The fucker only went and *hit the post*.

With the free hit, that was a ninety percent chance of a goal.

What are the odds of failing a ninety percent shot? It's like, one in a million, right?

I just stood there, quietly fuming, staring at the centre spot so that I'd keep getting XP while I stewed. It wasn't the striker's fault. He was a CA 1 amateur. Nobody had ever taught him how to take a penalty. Maybe he'd never taken one in his life before.

It was ridiculous to be mad at him. But at full-time, when I saw him having a laugh with the other team's goalkeeper, I could have smacked his face all the way off his face.

He wasn't serious. He wasn't committed. If football showed character, then this guy was half-assing life.

It pissed me off.

I thanked John, who I knew was relieved that his team had lost, and wandered off, wondering why I was so upset.

24

MAKING PLANS

"Life is what happens when you're busy making other plans."
—John Lennon

The whole of Monday was dominated by the Queen's funeral. I didn't have to go to work, and this time, it seemed appropriate that the event was being shown on every TV channel. I had to mute the sound, because the audio was so inane. (Example: "And here comes the Prince of Wales, the Duke of Cornwall, and the Duke of Rothesay." And it turns out . . . that's one person!)

But I left the picture on—the pomp and ceremony from a bygone age, ancient uniforms swaddling very modern faces, the leaders from every country on earth—while I thought about what I'd learned, what my current options were, and where I wanted to take my football career.

I took out a piece of paper and tried to organise my thoughts.

Basics.

I'd learned that watching live football earned me XP, and I could use that currency to buy perks that would improve my skills. So far, I'd purchased: Attributes 1; 4-4-2; Super Scout; Fantasy Football.

I'd started the weekend with 386 XP. I got 100 from managing Beth's team, 60 from pottering around Hough End, 80 from my forty minutes of managing Moss Side Celtic, and one from achievements, for a grand total of 627. (The achievements were annoying. The first was called Losing Streak (for losing two matches in a row, zero XP). Next was called **Baggiohno!** (for missing the penalty, zero XP). And I got 1 XP for Sweep the Leg, awarded for pressing an advantage against an enemy weak spot.)

More perks were available to buy, including permanent ones and monthly special offers that would come and go. The benefits seemed to fall into two categories. The curse, as I'd come to think of it, was essentially passive while I was watching (scouting) and terrifyingly active while I was the head coach (managing).

Scouting.

I'd found a couple of players who, with luck, could make it as professionals. One, through a string of coincidences, was currently training with a semi-pro team. With the other, I was waiting until I had my shit together before making first contact. In theory, I could bring these guys to teams and take a cut of their salaries. In theory, there were many more such opportunities. In theory, with seven clients earning five hundred pounds a week, my cut would be three hundred and fifty a week. Enough to replace the income from the call centre and work full-time doing football things.

This could be achieved in a reasonably quick timescale. Within a year, maybe.

Thus it made sense to focus on the scouting aspect of my "career."

Note 1: I knew what some of the missing attributes in my player profiles were, because they'd been mentioned in other perk descriptions. Flair and Creativity (probably), Set Pieces, Influence. Plus something with Offside.

Note 2: Placing players might not be a smooth process. There were indications that FC United were trying to steal my player. It would be good to develop relationships with more clubs. Just in case.

Managing teams.

I'd managed Beth's team in a few matches where they beat teams they would have beaten anyway, and lost to the only good team in their league. I had also led FC United's reserve team to defeat and helped one of the worst teams in Manchester lose.

If that sounds overly self-critical, I felt this kind of reality check was needed. Managing was thrilling, the feeling of power was addictive, and I wanted to do more of it. But it wouldn't pay the bills. There was no question of anyone ever paying me to manage their team.

That said, managing was fun and came with double XP for the same amount of time spent, so it was worth pursuing it. IN MODERATION, MAX.

Health.

It wasn't normal to see things. Several times I'd experienced cracking headaches after intense football-related sessions. I even got headaches when I tried to look up elements of my curse. If it happened more and more often, I would either have to reduce my involvement with the sport or see a professional. The American book of mental disorders was very expensive, double when you included delivery. I was in no position to afford it. Then again, I doubted it would include a section on people who can telepathically control midfielders. Being honest with myself, the only way to stop the curse seemed like the "Retire" option in the menus. I was nowhere near thinking about that.

Perk tier list.

I ranked the perks I had available in order of how much I wanted them and how much they fit my plan.

3 - An Opera with Emma Level

- Match Stats 1 - 100 XP - Good to have. Probably very interesting but can wait.
- 4-4-2 diamond - 100 XP - I wanted it so much! But MAX BEST IS NOT A MANAGER. Write it down 100 times!
- Playdar - 8,000 XP - Talent finder. Possibly really, really useful but shockingly expensive and unknown impact.
- Player Comparison - 630 XP - Quality of life upgrade, can wait.

2 - Laser Tag with Emma Level

- Player Profile 2 - 100 XP - This would unlock a section of a player's profile called History. I actually didn't want that, but it was much more closely aligned with my overall objectives than most of the options. Maybe it would reveal a player's injury record? Tell me if they'd been scouted before? Alert me if they'd tried and failed at a club? For 100 XP it was worth a punt.

1 - Trapped On a Desert Island With Emma But There Are Still Pizzas and Internet There Level

- Attributes 2 - 630 XP - Essential for finding talented players with marketable skills.
- God Save the King - 3,000★ XP - Boosting my clients? Yes, please.

Writing everything down was soothing. I'd been going a bit bonkers wondering if I could stand on my own two feet as a football manager. Why? I mean, why? All I needed to do was seal the deal with Ziggy, find five more players, and get them on basic contracts. Then, once I knew what I was doing, talk to Raffi Brown. Dynamically switching between 4-4-2 and 4-4-2 diamond depending on the game state didn't come into it.

I glanced up at the screen. There were lots of horses and flowery hats. I turned the sound back on. The actual service had to be close now.

So, action plan:

- Keep saving XP until the October special offer came along, then reassess.
- Make contact with more clubs.
- Find more players.

I checked the funeral procession again. There were rows and rows of soldiers. Each one with a slightly different hat and epaulette. That gave me an idea. I needed to go and watch a match in each professional division. That way, I'd know what level of CA and PA my players would need. For example, it seemed like you'd need a CA of 150 to even get on the bench in the Premier League.

I added a bullet point:

- Scout all divisions.

Lost in thought, I stared into an empty mug for a while. Empty? That wouldn't do. I put the kettle on and pottered around the kitchen doing some stretches. When the noise of the boiling water quieted, I realised the people on TV were talking about something other than the Queen. I turned it up while getting the milk out of the fridge.

It was the latest news from the war in Ukraine. Ugh. I muted it again and angrily stirred my tea. War in Europe in 2022! Fucking mental.

I sat back down at the desk and looked at my paper. "Find more players," it said. But where? I'd found a handful of older guys who'd never been discovered by professional clubs. What if I wanted to find a fifteen-year-old? No, I didn't want that. Long-term that would be fine, but I needed cash now. So the *ideal* player would be . . . seventeen or eighteen. Where was the best place to find amazing players who had never been scouted by an English team?

Well, I thought, laughing to myself, anywhere outside England!

And then I dropped my cup, and it smashed into a hundred pieces while the camera zoomed into my face. Enlightenment!

(That's not what really happened. Actually, I just went "huh" and took a sip of tea.)

Here was my breakthrough—refugees! Wiry wingers slightly too young to fight. Little playmaker kids who'd had to flee the invasion. Britain is a warm and generous country, right? We probably took in hundreds of thousands of them. Was it wrong to take advantage of this crisis? Well, is it wrong to find someone, tell them they are special, offer them a job, and make them so rich they can buy a new car every week? I don't know. Leave philosophy to the taxi drivers.

I went to Wikipedia and typed "Alphonso Davies."

Davies was interesting as a player and as a person. As a player, he was nominally a left-back, but in fact his team, Bayern Munich, sometimes just let him run the entire left-hand side of the pitch. In any game he'd be the fastest player, have the most stamina, and be the most skilful. It seemed pretty unfair! As a person, he was born in a refugee camp in Ghana after his parents escaped from Liberia. They moved to Canada, and Davies played for the Canadian national team. It was odd that one of the best players in the world was Canadian. They weren't exactly a football powerhouse. But who knew? Maybe Canada was secretly a football hotbed. Maybe I could meet a Canadian version of Emma who could help me find out.

One website said Alphonso Davies was being paid 103,000 dollars a week. If he kept playing to his current standard, he could triple that with his next contract, especially if he moved to the Premier League.

That was the end of the planning time and the beginning of the daydreaming. What would I buy first, a Porsche or a Rolex? Should my first holiday be a cheap one in Ibiza so I'd know what it was like, or should I skip all that and head straight to the Seychelles?

My attention was drawn to the TV stream on my laptop. The sound was off, and I wanted to turn it back on. But I couldn't move. I was frozen. Charles stood there, looking at his mother's coffin, his eyes red, lips aquiver, expression haunted, and I finally got it. Today wasn't just a technical change in the UK's head of state or a display of Britain's soft power. It was a ritual to mark the biggest change in this or any man's life. Just then, Charles didn't want to be king. He wanted his mum back.

After a few minutes, I folded my piece of paper, tucked it in beside my toaster, picked up my car keys, and drove to the care home.

25

DRILLS

Wednesday was, quietly, invisibly, monumental.

It was the day when I was due to take a training session with Beth's team. But I had a surprise for them. They were in their kit, stretching a calf or a hamstring or slowly turning their neck left and right, keeping one eye on me, waiting for me to get on with my hare-brained scheme. I'd asked Beth to rustle up a couple more players, if poss. She'd come through. As well as the usual mob, there was Eva, a very tall, gangly defender; and Anna, a ginger-haired German winger.

I was flanked by two men.

"All right, Met Heads," I said. "It's speech o'clock. When I first met you—"

"Max," said Beth. "We've got the hall for one hour. Get on with it."

"Fine," I said. "This is Jackie. He's a coach. He's going to do some drills. End of speech."

"Very efficient, Max," said Jackie. "All right—"

"Wait," said Beth. "Who's this guy?"

I followed her finger. "That's Ziggy. I don't know why he's here."

Ziggy looked embarrassed. "I didn't believe it when Max said he was managing a women's team. I thought, I don't know what I thought. But Jackie told me I might as well come and get some extra practice in. If that's okay with you guys."

"Anyone suspicious of Max is a friend of mine," said Beth.

Ziggy unzipped his top, flung it away, and cast off his tracksuit bottoms. Keen!

Jackie started the women off with a light jog. But Ziggy didn't join in. He and Jackie were hovering around me, almost menacingly. Ziggy picked up a plastic bag and handed it to me.

"What's this?" I said, scared to poke my head in.

"Kit," said Jackie. "Get changed."

"Come on, man," I said. "This is for them." I indicated the Met Heads.

"Get changed, Secret Agent," demanded Jackie. "Or I'm leaving. I'm here to satisfy my curiosity."

"You're here because I said I'd pay you a hundred quid," I said. Ziggy's eyes nearly popped out.

"Yeah, which I'll never see."

"You will. Eventually. Once my bonds mature."

"Until then, you're in the session. Hurry up." I didn't really have much of a choice. I slunk away towards the changing rooms. "No, no, no time for that. Do it here."

He wanted me to change in front of the women. Put me in my place? I slipped my shoes off, pulled my trousers down (waiting three seconds so everyone could get an eyeful), then pulled the shorts on. Before taking my jacket off, I rummaged in the bag and pulled out the top they'd brought. It was light blue with a circular club crest and a familiar airline sponsor. "Man City top? Are you fucking insane? There's no way I'm wearing this."

"We knew you'd say that," said Jackie. He unzipped his big sports bag and pulled out a red one. That was more like it. He threw it at me.

I caught it, then immediately dropped it like it was a bag of acid. Gingerly, I picked it up between my thumb and forefinger. "City or Liverpool? Is this your idea of fun?"

"Yeah," said Ziggy, delighted.

"I'd rather play in skins," I said.

"They'd like that, too, I reckon," said Jackie. "Any which way you choose, someone wins." He looked at his watch. "Chop, chop."

I looked at my options. Who did I hate more? With a shudder, I took my jacket and shirt off and pulled on the Liverpool top. At the bottom of the plastic bag was a pair of indoor sports trainers in my size. How had they known?

Jackie brought a whistle to his mouth. He looked me in the eye, blew out a sharp peep, and gave me a little wink. "Line up, ladies!"

The first drill was simple. We formed two lines, facing each other. I was in front of Lula. We just had to pass the ball back and forth. No probs. But I couldn't focus. I was getting tons of information.

First, Beth's CA jumped from 1 to 2. Lula and Freyja's too. That's what I'd been hoping for, but I couldn't have imagined it'd happen so soon!

Next, now that Ziggy was training instead of forcing me into his weird cross-dressing fantasy, I could see his attributes. And they boggled my mind!

BARRETT GRAVES		
Born 13.1.1999	(Age 23)	English
Acceleration 3		
		Stamina 4
	Heading 6	Strength 6
		Tackling 3
	Jumping 6	
Bravery 4		Technique 5
	Pace 3	preferred foot R
	Passing 5	
Dribbling 2		
Finishing 16		
CA 6	PA 58	
Striker		

His CA had soared to 6, his stamina, technique, and passing had all improved by one point. And best of all, his jumping had gone up! Had the absolute madman been bouncing on his bed for hours on end because I told him to?

And he just looked . . . healthier. More confident. More like a footballer. Maybe he'd had a tan sprayed on. Maybe—

"Max!" snapped a voice. Jackie telling me off for not concentrating. But I was *doing* my half of the drill. It was beyond simple. I looked up and down the line of players, and there were a few errant passes. Why couldn't they play a five-yard pass under no pressure?

As I watched, several passing attributes turned green. What the shit?!

Jackie was behind me. He (gently) put his hands on my head and pointed it towards Lula. "Focus."

How can I focus? There's too much going on!

I tried my best, though. I really, really looked at Lula, and I really, really looked at the ball.

The whistle blew. Jackie had seen enough. The next drill was a little more advanced. He had some big lengths of string that he handed out and told us to form them into a circle. "How big?" asked one of the women. "As big as the string," he said, with more patience than the question deserved.

Now each player was standing in a circle of maybe three-metre diameter. Pretty wide. Jackie selected Beth to demonstrate on. He kicked the ball at her—fairly hard—and her job was to control it with one touch such that it would stay in the circle. Beth controlled the first one perfectly. The second, Jackie hit at knee height, and that bounced off Beth and hit the far wall. The third, he chipped up to her chest, she controlled it nicely, and the ball landed at her feet. Not bad!

I was nodding in approval when I saw Beth's technique score increase. It scrambled my brain so much that I didn't hear Jackie's next instruction. Poor Lula had to come over and give me a nudge. She wanted me to kick the ball at her. I tried to copy what Jackie had done, low and hard, at the knee, onto the chest. Lula actually did better than Beth, but her technique didn't increase. That was a disappointment. Could Jackie improve players when he coached them one-on-one? But I couldn't? No, that wasn't it—ladies left and right were getting green technique numbers whether Jackie was watching or not.

Lula called over. "Time to switch."

"No," I said. "You go again."

She shrugged, and I repeated the drill, low, knee, chest. This time, Lula only controlled one out of three, but now her technique score *did* increase! I was happy for her but felt like I understood what was happening even less than before.

Jackie blew his whistle, and everyone looked over at him. "Grab a hoop," he said. We all went to the side of the hall where he'd placed loads of hula hoops. They weren't the ones that were slightly bigger than your hips; they were sort of extra-wide. But still much smaller than the string circles. "Increasing the difficulty, yeah? Put the hoop inside your string. That's your new boundary. Try to keep the ball in there."

Everyone went again, three shots each. I didn't want to improve my technique, so I kept pinging balls at Lula. I took the pace down a bit so that she'd be more able to do it.

Jackie blew the whistle. I looked around. Almost everyone had improved their technique score, and everyone who had PA more than one was now on at least CA 2. In short, they were reaching their potential!

"Very good, very good," Jackie said. "Something you can do on your own to keep your skills sharp. But with all due respect to you ladies, I didn't come here to watch Max Best skive off."

"Huh?" I said.

"You in your circle? Good." He got a ball and was about to kick it to me. Jesus Christ! He had this real bee in his bonnet about how I should do a trial instead of Ziggy. It was irritating. I decided to flunk the test and get him off my back. He hit the first ball, and I crouched and stuck my foot out. The ball bounced off and away. He hit the next one a bit higher. I pretended to bring my thigh towards the ball and use it to deaden the impact, but the ball "accidentally" hit my knee and boinged off. Jackie scrunched up his lips and walked over to me. He didn't stand in front of me like a normal human. He sort of went beside me, barely turned his head, and spoke in a whisper. "I'll take a lot of things, Max. Loose passes, bad shots, bad days at the office. But I won't stand for not trying." We made eye contact. I looked away. "So what's it going to be?"

"I asked you here to coach the girls," I hissed. "It's not about me. You're wasting *time*."

"I'm not doing another thing till you show me what you've got."

"Jesus fucking Christ," I said. Again, I didn't have much choice. To get what I wanted, I had to give him what he wanted. "Fine."

He went back to his spot and got a ball ready. He slapped it at me, extra hard. I let my right foot cushion the impact. It dropped dead. I passed it back to him. He hit it, with curve, towards my left knee. I bent and caught it on my thigh. Passed it back. He hit it with staggering violence right at my throat. I jumped, let the ball impact my chest, and while it popped up above my head, I turned and waited for gravity to take its course. As it landed, I crunched it under my foot.

I turned again and glared at Jackie. "Next drill," I said.

While Jackie and some others put away the hoops and collected the balls, Beth sidled up to me. "Come to the toilet," she said.

"Huh?"

"Toilet. Quick."

I eyed her. "You're horny. Now?"

"That was hot. That was . . . that was like two stags butting against each other."

I shook my head. "Demented."

She nudged me. "And you won."

This was the stupidest thing I'd ever heard, and I made no attempt to hide that fact. "No, Beth," I said. "*He* did."

26

BRAVERY

The next drill was back to the simple passing, which I think was a palette cleanser to help the group forget the "stag rutting." Then Jackie made it more complicated by changing it from two people passing in a line, to four people in a line. One person would pass and then sprint to the other side and be ready to receive the ball. It was tough to control and pass after the sprint. Good drill.

Looking around, I didn't notice anymore increases in the passing attribute. So I went over to Jackie and asked if we could do something with dribbling or finishing.

"You're the boss, boss," he said, changing his plan on the fly.

By the end of the session, Ziggy was still on finishing sixteen. But maybe he'd gone from 16.04 to 16.07. Maybe skill increases took longer the higher they got. He had, however, increased his dribbling, from two to three. Not enough to terrorise a defender, but it was still very pleasing.

And every one of the Met Heads had improved in multiple attributes.

It was a hundred pounds that I didn't have, but it was a hundred pounds well spent.

Everyone helped Jackie gather his equipment and put things away, then went off to have a shower. I was just about to complain that I'd have to go home sweaty when Jackie pulled a towel out of his bag. I snatched it from him and strode away, but after a few paces, I glanced back and he was grinning at me. My traitorous mouth grinned in return. I didn't tell it to do that!

I came out of the shower with lots of thoughts going on. Numbers, attributes, greens, drills, passing, short sprints, circles. Wonderful.

Improving things like passing and technique was not just possible, it was easy.

What about the other attributes?

Bravery. What drill could you run to increase bravery? What effect did bravery have on a football player? Some obvious things came to mind, like a goalkeeper throwing himself at a striker who was sliding towards a loose ball. But I wasn't sure if I wanted my goalkeeper to do that; he could get seriously injured. If we conceded a goal, fine. Just go and score one at the other end. At least our teammate would still have his skull intact.

Acceleration and pace. Get Usain Bolt to take a session. Show people how to explode. How to do those choppy hand movements.

Flair (if flair was an attribute). Probably just a case of making people repeat show-off moves. No-look backheels. Scooped passes. Stepovers. Easy. But if you had limited training time, would you bother with flair?

All this and more was going through my head when I realised absolutely everyone was hovering around the main entrance waiting for me. Huh? As I got to the edge of the group, most of them turned towards me. Maybe it was time for my speech.

I grabbed my jacket lapels and took a breath. "There comes a time in every man's life—"

Beth said, "Oh, finally! Come on."

She slipped her arm through mine. The evening was just turning to chilly. A promise of fog, a silver light diffused, for now, with gold; a golden hint of glorious sun with none of its fierce cruel heat. On such an evening, the football results didn't matter. To experience England like this was to live life as a winner. I sighed with extreme contentment, enjoyed the warmth provided by Beth, and let my brain switch off for a few magical, silver-gold seconds.

The entire mass of people moved together. Many people, many legs, one destination.

"You all right?" I said.

"I'm all right," she said.

Pub. Disease vector. Lots of close contact between men who don't wash their hands. Music played too loud. Sticky floors. On the other hand, beer.

This was some kind of student place, hidden away on a side-street off Oxford Road. We'd colonised an entire quarter, spread out over two tables and two columns. The talk was of football, politics, the royals. *Did you watch the funeral? Who didn't? Did you cry? Me too.*

I was at a table with three virtual strangers. I mean, draw my life as a timeline, and these guys would appear in the final blob you made as you took away the pencil.

Beth was next to me, leaning in. Garrulous, lots of fast, sharp, hard sentences, lots of jokes, good banter, but doing that thing where she tried to hide how smart she was. She mentioned Paris. Ziggy started talking about the city. Beth said, "No, I meant—" but then stopped herself. She meant Paris, the bro from the story of Troy. Later, she dismissed a new TV show as "King Lear with tits." Both times she glanced over at me to see if I'd noticed. Why?

Jackie was a great pub guy, effortlessly charming, effortlessly sharing his thoughts in a melodic wave, rising and falling. Every sentence was a sculpture. But he knew when the jokes needed to stop, and when the time came to say the right thing or make the right noise, he never got it wrong. Some of what he said to me looks harsh written down. You had to be there. You had to hear it.

Ziggy was Ziggy. Quiet, companionable, mostly speaking to help a story progress, to add to a joke, to remind someone what they were saying, or to ask questions.

Me? I was subdued. The company was great. I had lots to say to all of them. But after mindlessly slipping into the situation, I'd woken up with a jolt. I felt like a dog being taken for a drive. *Wait a minute . . . this isn't the way to the park. This is the way to the vet!*

Stress. Stress was in my bloodstream, sucking energy out of my cells to feed itself, to grow stronger. All I could do was sit and marinate in this negativity, feel more stressed at not having seen it coming, dread the moment when I would have to confess.

In the UK it's the custom to buy a round of drinks, i.e., you buy a drink for everyone in the group. Jackie had bought the first round, three beers and a cheeky gin and tonic (which is the same as a gin and tonic, but adding the word cheeky reduces your hangover). According to the invisible, unwritten laws of Pubbery, I was next in line. (Probably followed by Beth, who seemed to have her shit together more than Ziggy.)

I had forgotten this. I hadn't been in a pub with mates for years. When Jackie asked what I wanted to drink, I thought nothing of it. And at first, everything was okay. People took little sips. But then Jackie locked onto the taste of the beer and took a big ol' gulp. As he put the half-empty glass back on the table, I felt like I had one hand locked in handcuffs.

And not in a good way.

More jokes, more laughs, more banter, more swigs. It would soon be time for the second round. Erling Haaland, fifty-one million pounds. Paul Pogba, eighty-nine million pounds. Tottenham's new stadium, one *billion* pounds. A round of drinks, twenty pounds. One of these things is not like the others. One of these things is unaffordable.

Ziggy cracked first. "Max, what's wrong?"

"Huh? What? Nothing. What?"

Beth gave me a little squeeze.

Jackie drained his beer, placed the empty glass on the table, and stared at me with a little smirk. "Your round, Secret Agent."

He knew. Somehow the fucker knew.

I had a choice to make. Get all pissy and defensive, maybe make a scene so that I could storm out with bridges burned but my secret intact.

Or just spit it out. I really, really, didn't want to. But at least it would be out in the open, and they wouldn't put me in this situation again.

How do you increase bravery? Practice.

"Thing is, guys," I said, mostly talking to a beer mat that I was methodically destroying. "I don't have any money." I glanced up at them. Not much reaction. Jackie, in particular, was giving nothing away. "Not to give you my sob story, but I haven't been out since before the pandemic hit. I have just enough income to live alone, eat alone, and be alone. I was miles away after the training, thinking of how to beat City. If I'd realised we were going to the pub, I'd have come up with some excuse."

There was a bit of a silence. Beth looked worried. Ziggy had started destroying a beer mat.

Then Jackie burst out laughing.

I glared at him.

"Mate," he said. "You think you're the only lad short on cash. In this country? With this government? Wind your neck in!" He waved at a barmaid and signalled "same again." "Sorted. Now lighten up, you miserable bastard."

"Max," said Beth. "You're not saying you've got no money? Like, none? But you've still got your job, because you said you'd quit if we beat City."

"I've been spending it going to matches and stuff. Driving Ziggy around and that." I regretted saying that as soon as I said it. Not to protect my image as a top agent or anything. Ziggy knew I wasn't rolling in dough. More because it was unfair to make him feel responsible in any way. He briefly stopped ripping up the beer mat. Jesus, Max.

"Mate!" said Jackie. "I thought you were an agent."

"Well, I am. Sort of. I've got a client, as you know."

He exchanged a significant look with Ziggy, which did not improve my mood. They were hiding something. But then he levelled his attention all the way onto me. "Agents. Scouts. They don't pay to get into games. Jesus, you're not telling me you can't buy me a fucking three pound student beer because you've been paying full whack going to games?"

Um. "What."

He pinched his nose. "Call the club. Tell them you want to come and watch a certain player. They'll leave you tickets at the turnstile or whatever. Fucking hell."

"Why?" said Beth.

Jackie shrugged. "Clubs want to sell their players, don't they? They want good contacts with agents. I dunno, maybe if the ground's full you'll struggle, but how many stadiums are proper sold out every week? Almost none." He laughed again. "Oh, this is delightful. I'm made up about this."

"Will you calm down?" said Beth, hot, defending me.

Jackie leaned forward with a good-natured smile. "I'm just saying that this is the first time I've seen him somewhere he doesn't look like he *owns* the place." He laughed again. "He came to our training—at FC United, that's where I work—and he's poncing about, doing our drills, showing off—"

"What?" said Beth, having totally forgotten the mother lion persona. Jackie had her eating out of his hand. "*What?*"

"Tell her, Ziggy." Jackie leaned back to enjoy the show.

Ziggy's big brown eyes shone. "Well, Jackie was explaining about something, and Max comes along and goes 'oh yeah?' and Jackie goes 'yeah' and Max goes 'seriously?' and Jackie goes 'show us how it's done, then,' so Max does the drill and then goes 'piece of piss!'" He burst into hysterics.

Jackie, highly amused, clarified. "It was even better. He said 'piece of piss' and *then* he did it." He took a swig. "And then he made himself reserve team manager."

Beth nearly spit out her G+T. She had to grab a napkin and try to push some of the booze back inside her. "What!"

"He did well, an' all. That's what's annoying. So Max, you've cheered up a bit?" I had. "Nice of you to join us in the room, yeah?" He took a swig. "Are you happy with the training this evening? Was it what you wanted?"

"Yes," I said. "Delighted." I *was* delighted, but obviously my voice didn't convey that. Jackie shook his head a little. I continued. "Can you come again next week? Er . . . if that's okay with you, Beth."

"Yeah! It was mint. I loved that. We all did." She looked around at her teammates at the nearby tables.

"Maybe," said Jackie. He tapped his beer a few times. "On consideration, my fee has gone up," he said. "What we agreed before, plus you have to wear full Liverpool kit. Top, shorts, socks, Kenny Dalglish shinpads. I'll bring a laminated *'This is Anfield'* sign that you have to kiss before the warm-up."

I groaned.

"And you have to help me with a project."

"Oh? What?"

"You'll find out. In due course. In the fullness of time." He took a swig and changed his mind about the secrecy. "I want help scouting a team. Right up your alley, innit? And one last thing. I want to know what this mania is all about. You want to beat City? Manchester City?"

"We're playing them next Friday. He's fucking crazy," said Beth. "He's off his head."

"You really think you can win, Max?" said Jackie.

"After today, our chances are twenty percent. If you take next week's training, thirty percent. If Beth can convince Eva and Anna to play, too . . . ." I drained the rest of my first beer and felt the fresh coolness of the second one. I was starting to feel the effect. Less strained. More at ease. Warm, physically, mentally, conversationally. "If everything's in place, and Beth lets me try out some tactics this Friday night . . . Thirty. Eight. Percent." I gave these last three words maximum articulation, maximum earnestness, and punctuated them with nods like I was pumping up my own self-belief. *Thirty. Eight. Percent—yes, yes, yes!*

There was a pause while they wondered if I had finally disappeared up my own arse or not.

Ziggy was the first to laugh, but not the last.

I'd intended it to be funny. But I was also utterly, completely not joking.

27

CHAMPION MANAGER

The rest of the evening was a laugh. Totally enjoyable, especially once we started mingling, and I got to know Lula and Freyja a bit better. Seeing a couple of the women leave early to put their kids to bed was an eye-opener. Kids and university? And two evenings a week playing footy? *How to Make Me Feel Like a Sloth*, volume one.

The only really significant thing happened when Ziggy went to the toilet. Actually, he said he was going there, but he somehow ended up merging with one of the groups of ladies standing around a column. I'm pretty sure, but not definite, that I heard him asking what their favourite chant was.

Stealing my material! The dog.

Anyway, while he was gone, I asked Jackie what was going on with Ziggy.

He pretended not to know what I meant and said Ziggy had come to a couple more training sessions. In the first sesh, the one I'd been at, the other lads had liked him. In the second, they started to ask questions. Why is this guy here again? He's shit. He's messing up the drills. In the third, same again.

"Why did you ask him back if he's shit?" said Beth.

Jackie pointed at me.

"What?"

"Max has unshakeable belief in Ziggy. Either he's a lunatic or a genius. At first glance, I would have said Max was a talentless nobody who'd lied about his Monarchist tendencies to get in with some working-class men who should know better." Shit! He knew! "But then I saw him play, and then I saw him organise a team in a minute flat and get a tune out of Frogger that no one has for years."

"Frogger?" I said.

"Gribbin." He enjoyed my blank face, because it let him explain. "Ribbit, Ribbit. Gribbin, Gribbin."

"Oh," I said. "Frogger."

"So what's the harm in letting the kid come to some training sessions? The total destruction of team morale, yeah, sure. But I persuaded Neil to see how it plays out."

"Neil is the manager?" said Beth. "And he lets you do weird little experiments, does he?"

"Yep," said Jackie, with just a hint of smugness, which, if you think about it, is the smuggest you can be. He looked over towards where Ziggy had been. He'd actually gone to the toilet, it seemed. "Max. How good do you think Ziggy can get?"

I wasn't totally sure. But if becoming a Premier League player required a CA of 150—citation needed!—and in the seventh tier, FC United's guys averaged thirty-five to forty . . . . "He can play in the next division up. What's that called, the National League North? Could he make it in the one above that? I *think* so, but more as a goalscoring supersub. A fox in the box for the ends of games. Not sure about as a first-team starter in the fifth tier. I think I'd prefer to see him in the sixth tier banging in fifteen goals a season, and having one legendary year where he scores twenty-five in the league and a hat trick against Nottingham Forest in the FA Cup."

Another tiny silence. I didn't notice these silences happening when other people talked. What was it about me?

Jackie repressed a grin, but his eyebrows gave the game away. He was amused. "Beth, your boyfriend is extremely precise."

Beth leant her head onto my shoulder. "He's not my boyfriend. I just use him for sex."

She couldn't have said anything that sounded sweeter to my ears. I gave her a cuddle-squeeze, checked Ziggy wasn't around, and turned back to Jackie. "So my client. Are you going to give him a contract or what?"

Jackie was still grinning at Beth, but there was some flicker in his expression, and when the moment passed, his grin seemed fake. He looked down at his beer. "Well, Max. If we gave him a contract today, would you see him playing against Warrington? Or the week after against Marine?"

I felt my chin pop backwards like I'd been given a tiny jab. That sort of disbelieving reaction when you're so shocked you need to move your brain away from the conversation for its own safety. "What are you talking about? He's nowhere near ready. But if you keep letting him train he will be. Maybe by January." Three months of training and maybe Ziggy's CA could increase to . . . what? 20? I thought about what that would mean.

"In January, there'll be tons of clubs looking for a striker, even one who can only play thirty minutes a game. We'll definitely get him a club. And they'll be the ones benefiting from your coaching. You should tie him up now. And next season? Boom. Prolific. Get him on an eighteen-month deal, and you'll be laughing."

Jackie was staring at me, expressionless. He'd forgotten to press refresh on his fake smile. "Leave him with us for a couple more weeks," he said, blandly.

Ominous as fuck.

By the end of the evening, I was pretty darn tipsy, so I don't remember some of what happened. I certainly can't explain what happened that Friday.

Housekeeping note: on Thursday I went to Platt Fields to chat with Emre. Since I was falling into debt left, right, and centre, what was a few more pounds? I asked if I could get a wrap and pay him back. He rolled his eyes and was about to refuse when he thought better of it. "No onions," I said. "I don't deserve them yet." Onions are for winners!

So I had a good chat about Fatih Terim, maybe the best ever Turkish football manager. Apparently, there was a Netflix documentary about him, which Emre delighted in spoiling over the course of twenty hilarious, expletive-filled minutes. When I escaped, I picked up 55 XP watching some games.

So, back to Friday. The Met Heads were playing the team below them in the league. I didn't expect it to be much of a challenge. The plan was to get a couple of goals ahead, and then start trying out some tactical plans we could use against City.

But when I got there, Jackie and Ziggy were waiting. Ziggy, obvs, was into one of the team members and was here for his own nefarious reasons. But Jackie? What could he possibly get out of it?

For the first ten minutes, I stood on the sidelines, bossing the women around as I so enjoyed doing. We took a 2–0 lead, but the other team scored right away, so I couldn't start dicking around just yet. Frustrating.

Jackie had seen enough to start quizzing me.

"Why is Beth in defence?"

"Because she's a defender."

Pause.

Jackie: "She's the fittest."

"No she isn't," said Ziggy. In Manchester, fit means sexy.

Jackie: "Do you need a cold shower, Ziggy lad? Max, she's the fittest so you should put her in midfield, and let her do all the pressing."

Me: "We're not going to press City. We're just going to pretend."

"What."

"I'm going to let them have the whole midfield."

"Tommy Tactics has finally lost his marbles."

"I'm going to play 2-2-2 but without the 2."

Jackie laughed and slapped his leg. "I knew it! I knew this was going to be wild."

But the guys turning up to watch me collect 100 XP from the Met Heads wasn't even the weirdest thing that happened that weekend.

The next morning, Beth called me. She never called, always texted. "What?" I said, still groggy from the post-match drinks. Why did people think it was worth giving up their savings to see me drunk?

"It's 9:30. You said to meet you there at 10. I'm just checking you're up."

"I'm up, I'm up. Wait, what?"

Turns out, at some point, I'd drunkenly told Beth about Solly the Psychic dog and that I wanted to "get her tested." She had been keen, because she had always suspected I had invented the story of my mother being in a hospice to get out of dates. When she was telling me all this in the car, I had a vague memory of her complaining that I had been "Dennis Systeming" her. Apparently, in some TV show, a character called Dennis invented a sick relative to manipulate women.

Imagine accusing me of that.

I pulled up to the care home at half ten. Beth tapped one last message on her phone and got out. "It says care home, Max."

"Yep. Does what it says on the tin."

"You've been telling me it's a hospice."

Oh. Right. "Slip of the tongue. Let's get this over with. Chat with Mum first, then dog."

That's when the morning got even more surreal. In the reception area, Jackie and Ziggy were reading celebrity gossip magazines. It was possibly the single most shocking moment of my life, including the time I saw numbers floating above Stephen McGough's head and the day a neighbour came home in his new car, a surplus army tank.

There's no point describing the whole morning, but Ziggy was polite, Jackie was extremely charming, and my mum was enchanted by Beth. We had tea and dry, old-person biscuits, including those ones with the jam hearts. What's the point of them?

The only sour moment came when we'd all just started on our second cup of tea. That was when mum's level of lucidity increased to the point where she realised she had no clue who any of these people were.

"How do you all know Max?"

"Through football," said Beth, whose accent was a little more refined than usual. She was so weird. "He's actually helping us with our team. We're going to play Manchester City next week."

"Oh, he loves his football," said my mum, and there were smiles all round. "He was always in his room, playing the football game. Hours, he'd play it. I could never see the attraction."

This was alarming. While she seemed superficially healthy, suddenly I was forced to reevaluate. Did she look tired around the eyes? Were her hands shaking more?

"What game?" asked Ziggy. I tried to give him a warning look, but he was busy nibbling the edges of his biscuit, trying to eat the maximum amount without getting any jam in him.

"Oh, I never remember the names. He'd play it all day. Carlisle United! I remember that. He was always Carlisle. Said it wasn't a challenge being *Manchester* United."

"Oh," said Ziggy, beaming at her. "Champion Manager!"

"That sounds right," she said.

I couldn't believe my ears. She was delusional. Making up stories. I needed to talk to a doctor about it, but there were all these people here and I couldn't leave them alone with her in case they made it worse. I stood, forcefully, indicating that this conversation was over.

Beth, incredibly, infuriatingly, persisted. "You played Champion Manager, Max? That explains a lot. Why you know tactics and things."

I wandered behind my mum's back and made savage gestures trying to get her to stop. "Ha ha," I said. Then mimed slitting my throat. Why couldn't they just get the message?

Mum chuckled at some fictional memory. She reached her hand over her shoulder, and I was forced to take it. Not that I minded, really, but it limited the body language I could employ. "I remember he cracked the computer, or however you say those computer things. So that he could put himself in the game. Why did it say Max Best scored a goal, I asked him. I'm the Player-Manager, he said! He put himself in the game." She patted my hand a few times. Proud. Proud of this thing that never happened.

Jackie leaned back. "Let me guess. Passing twenty. Technique twenty."

Beth looked as innocent as an angel as she said, "Endurance twenty. Goes all night. I mean, match." Ziggy managed to suppress a huge laugh.

But this wasn't funny. And why were they using a scale out of twenty? That was a weird coincidence. I hated every second of this conversation. I felt like I was being crushed, like the air was being pushed out of my lungs. With one last, huge effort, I smiled and placed Mum's hand back on her lap. "Maybe that's right. But I think that's enough talk about football now. Mum needs her rest. Let's go and see Anna."

With a lot of very confused and bewildered looks, the guys got up, left their barely-touched teas on the side, said bye to my mum, and walked out.

In the corridor, Beth challenged me. "What the fuck, Max!"

I looked around and dragged her through a doorway and into a corridor where we could bicker without disturbing the patients. "What the fuck, Beth! What the fuck, Jackie!"

"What?"

"What was all that shit?"

"Let's try calming all the fucking way down, Maxy boy. Take a breath."

I didn't react well to that at first, but then I supposed he might have a point. I walked away from them, put my hands on my head, and returned. "My mother is very sick, okay? She has mental problems.

What you heard in there was a complete fabrication. A work of fiction. Okay? And you were just encouraging her."

Beth and Jackie exchanged glances. Beth said, "Are you saying you never played Champion Manager?"

"I've never even heard of it. What the fuck is Champion Manager?"

Ziggy was tapping on his phone. Jackie said, "It's the most famous football game. You run a football team. Buy and sell players. Set the tactics. Give the half-time team talk."

I stared at him like he had, I don't know, eight heads. Ziggy pushed his phone towards me. I saw the Google image search results for "champion manager."

The first picture looked like a database. A spreadsheet, maybe. But the cells were all written in something like Korean. Or that kind of space-Asian font you get in cool sci-fi.

Another picture showed a series of blocks with the same font inside. Another one did look vaguely familiar, but again, it was just squiggles and runes and shit.

"This is a game?"

"Wait," said Ziggy. "I can never tell if you're joking. Are you seriously saying you've never heard of Champion Manager?"

I looked at him with a sense of exponentially rising desperation. I felt like I'd be trapped in this conversation for the rest of my life. Just an endless circle of these three telling me I had to know this game—were you supposed to memorise what the squiggles meant?—and me trying to tell them, show them, make them understand.

THAT I HAD NEVER HEARD OF THE FUCKING THING.

"All right," said Jackie. He took the jammy biscuit out of my hand and popped the crushed mess into a nearby bin. "All right. We're sorry we stressed your mum. It must be hard on you."

"Yeah," said Beth, going along to get along. "Soz."

"We were trying to be nice," said Ziggy.

I blinked. "Of course you were," I said. "Of course you were." The crisis was over. I took a deep breath. "Right. Good. So . . ." I slapped my hands together, trying to summon up a cloud of pally positivity. I tried to remember why they were here. Not to talk about impossible, irrational things, that was for sure. "Let's go meet a psychic dog."

28

COMPARE
AND CONTRAST

I'd like to start this chapter by assuring you that my life got back on an even keel, that the next few days were spent calmly grinding for XP, and that nothing else weird happened.

I'd like to tell you that.

But I can't.

The least strange thing was watching Solly interview my guests. Anna was in bed, looking quite weary, but she said she didn't mind a bit of company.

"How do you change him to assessment mode?"

"By asking him, my dear."

I made Beth stand where I had stood the first time I'd been in that room. "Solly. On a scale of one to ten, how good a person is Beth?"

Solly tilted his head at me and pricked his ears. But then he pottered to Beth and gave her a big ol' sniff. He sat down, panted happily, and looked up at her like he was basking in her extraordinary beauty.

"Ten, or close enough," I said. "Jackie. You're up."

With Jackie, Solly was a little more circumspect, walking around and around the Liverpudlian, sniffing all the time, looking uncertainly from Anna to me to Jackie. After ten seconds or so, Jackie said, "Sit! Roll over. Sit." The dog loved being given tasks! "Beg. Shake hands. Good dog! Oh he's a good boy and a sweet boy, yes he is." Solly squirmed on his back while Jackie rubbed his belly.

Solly, ecstatic, looked ready to swap his owner for a younger model, so I put a stop to that whole interaction.

"Ziggy," I said. "Come and be assessed."

Ziggy stood, nervously grinning, one arm rubbing the other. Solly looked up at him with an expression that I could only describe as gormless. And he flopped down onto Ziggy's feet and settled for a nap.

"That's a pass, I'd say," said Anna. But even that little session had taken its toll, so I got the other three out and let her rest.

Sunday morning, instead of going to Hough End, I decided to spread my wings. My route took me down two of Manchester's busiest roads, but since most people were still frying their bacon and opening their tins of breakfast beans, it was, for once, a smooth, quick ride. To Wythenshawe! Home of Manchester Airport, and the biggest council estate in Europe. In short, a poor area with fantastic connections.

Pause for applause.

I know. Clever.

I parked at the Civic Centre and started walking. There were a couple of places I thought refugees might hang out and a bunch of parks. Walking wasn't optimal, but I wasn't in the mood for hyper-efficiency. Walking gave me time to think.

The first refugee shelter place was open. I popped in and couldn't find anyone. Odd. I passed through a park and spotted a couple of football pitches where people were putting up nets. Good! If the morning was a blowout, I could at least pick up some XP.

The second place was more like a food bank, and it was serving cornflakes and milk to a pretty long line of people. Kids, too. *You think you're the only lad short on cash?*

I pushed to the front, which was shocking behaviour, and, even worse, nobody complained. People just looked at me through empty eyes.

"Hey there," I said to the upper-middle-aged woman who was in charge of the cornflakes.

"All right, Chuck? You hungry?"

"Hungry for knowledge," I said.

"It's thirsty for knowledge. Hungry for success," she said.

"Wow. So I'm hungry and thirsty. I never knew."

Not sure why, but this made her laugh. "You want to bend my ear? Go ahead."

"I'm looking for all the Ukrainians," I said.

"They'd be in Ukraine, mostly, I reckon."

"Four million fled," I said, repeating a headline I'd seen that had actually taken my breath away.

"Not to here."

"What do you mean?"

She gave me a sharp look. "You read the papers?"

"Just the headlines. That's enough to put me in a black mood. Try to avoid the whole politics thing, to be honest."

"Why do you want a Ukrainian then?"

"Making a documentary," I said.

She emptied out the last cornflakes and tore open a new box. They were some own-brand stuff, but they looked all right. She passed the box to another volunteer, wiped her hands on her stomach, and gave me her full attention. "We don't like immigrants in this country. We don't want them here. That woman who was Prime Minister, she used to drive a van around London telling immigrants to go home. That woman won a general election. This one now, she wants to put up a wave machine in the English Channel to stop migrants coming across in their poor little boats. Every time a little boat capsizes and the migrants die, they crack open a six-pack of bubbly. The good stuff. That's the country you live in, and you'd know that if you read more than the headlines and the sport."

I . . . I knew she wasn't joking, but she must have misread some article. A wave machine on the English Channel? That was James Bond villain stuff. "Right, okay, but we love Ukraine. We're supporting them."

I'd unleashed something. "Oh, we'll send them guns and bombs and tanks—"

"No tanks," someone in the queue said.

"I'll have yours then," said the person behind.

The volunteer wasn't amused. "But we won't take their women and children, keep them safe. You go home and do a Google about World War II and evacuees and the Blitz. Look at the policies then. Keeping people safe. Look at them now. Compare and contrast."

"Were you a history teacher?"

She lost a bit of her righteous indignation. Looked a bit sheepish. "Thirty years."

I shook my head. "Look," I said. "I don't want to live in ignorance. But be honest. If I read these stories and know what's going on, will anything change?"

"Probably not."

"And how depressed am I going to be?"

"Very."

"That's what I thought."

I thanked her and left the building. I let my feet go wherever they wanted. It had been a pretty upsetting experience. Not just the conversation, but also the line of people waiting for a bowl of cornflakes. And it seemed like my dream Ukrainian powerhouse centre-back wasn't lollygagging around Wythenshawe just waiting for me to turn up. And from what the woman had said, it wasn't like Britain was awash with refugees from other countries either. Maybe I'd stick to five-a-side places and the Sunday Leagues.

As I was pottering around, looking at all the second-hand stores, betting shops, pound shops, and pubs, I saw him.

I saw *him*.

Nick. The guy who'd got me into this whole crazy mess. He was about two hundred metres ahead, turning left behind some buildings.

I exploded into a sprint. I'd always been an average runner, mid-pack, not quite suited to any particular distance. But then again, never before had I been so motivated.

Usain Bolt holds the world record for the fastest two hundred metres of all time—19.19 seconds. I beat his so-called achievement by at least eight. When I turned the corner, I felt a twinge in my side and stopped to catch a bit of breath. But there he was! Up ahead in his old-fashioned suit, his extinct hat, his too-long old man socks. He was turning left again.

I burst forward again, saw him go through a doorway, and followed; he could only have been a sofa's length away!

I hadn't spared much thought to what I'd do when I got hold of him. Punch his teeth out one by one? Ask him who the devil he thought he was? Thank him and ask him for more powers?

But he wasn't there. To the left and right of me were rows and rows of people. I had run halfway along a central aisle. There was no chance he'd slipped into one of the rows. Nick was white but every single person in this room was black. Every eye in the house was trained on me.

My confusion didn't last long. I'd been led here, kited, tricked. For some curse-related reason. I turned and looked up at the pulpit. The pastor, a friendly, serious-looking man in a brown suit, beamed at me. "Come on, then," he said, with a heavy accent.

"What?" I said.

"I asked for a volunteer to draw the winner." He pointed to a little box at the front of the church. "And you stormed in. That's what we like to call an act of divine providence." He grinned at me again. He had great teeth.

"But," I said, spinning around looking for old Nick. He was definitely not there. "But."

The pastor waved at me. "Come on."

I glanced at the front of the church, warily. "You just want me to pick a name? You aren't going to try to baptise me?"

The pastor rocked back, pointed his head to the beams, and laughed hard. "Nobody is going to make you do anything. But I would greatly enjoy watching you pick a name from this box."

That's when I knew what was going to happen. I was going to be forced to pick a certain name. I knew it was going to happen, and I didn't want it to happen. The whole scene made me feel like Nick's puppet. But I almost had no choice in the matter.

I picked up my feet and dragged myself to the front. There was a little box on the table. I was about to stick my hand in when I decided that if I was going to take part in a pantomime, I might as well commit to it. So I went to the other side of the little table and faced the congregation. Rows and rows of churchgoers. One of them, perhaps, with a hidden talent.

I swept my gaze from left to right. Lots of men in suits, women in bright, patterned dresses, tons of children. I looked around to see if I could tell which one it was going to be.

I dropped my hand into the box and let my fingers grip a length of paper. I shoved that one to the side of the box, then fished around the opposite side. I brought my hand out and prepared to announce the winner.

Was this the first time the name had been called out to a big audience? I was sure it wouldn't be the last. If I was right, the name would be screamed by TV commentators, fans, and stadium announcers for years to come. Keeping my voice flat and neutral, I said, "James Yalley."

29

MAX BETH

"Youngster!" said the pastor, full of affection. Was Youngster a nickname or a description?

There was applause and some pleased leg slapping. A couple of "hallelujahs" maybe, but that might have been my atheist brain running riot.

My job was done, but there was no way I was leaving the limelight just yet. When it was a bit quieter, I said, "So, where is he?"

"Youngster, stand up," said the pastor.

Over on the right, a teenage boy in a huge suit. Think three children in an overcoat pretending to be an adult. More applause. He waved at everyone and sat down again.

"What's the prize? Where is it? I'll give it to him."

"The young fellowship have been helping at the food bank. Collecting donations and serving them." I looked in the box, pulled out a few more slips of paper. There were a lot of young people helping their community. "The prize is a new pair of sneakers from the store. We will tell them his size, and they will send the sneakers when they have a suitable pair."

"Right."

He beamed at me. "You do not look impressed."

I must have let my true feelings show, never a good idea. "Look, I don't know. I'm sure it's . . ." James had written his own name on the slip. The trainers were probably those nineteen quid ones from a brand you see on every shelf of the pound shop for a month and then never again. Whatever. James Yalley wanted to be chosen for them. I knew he'd been chosen for something else entirely. But . . . chosen by whom? I took a peek at some of the other names on the slips of paper,

195

just to make sure every one didn't say James Yalley. The pastor cleared his throat. I woke up. "Listen, I've just been to a food bank and it was miserable, so if James is helping out in those places, he's a winner in my book. And this might be weird, but I can offer a better prize. And more immediate."

"Oh?"

"A football training masterclass, this Wednesday evening."

Fish hooked, I spent a couple of days trying to get my shit together. No grinding, just admin. Admin and trying to get ahead of things, trying to anticipate problems before they arose. In the entire scheme of starting a new career, I was doing okay, all things considered. I wasn't to know "inside baseball" details like scouts getting free tickets, so there would be many more embarrassments ahead. But, if possible, I wanted to minimise such events. Thinking about some of the mistakes I'd already made caused my neck to heat up.

Still, it was an incredible moment when I looked at my little collage creation. I'd found this cork pinboard thing in a pound shop, and I'd pinned up the league tables (culled from newspapers left in break rooms at work) from the top seven divisions in English football. I wasn't trying to follow the comings and goings of every team, though that wasn't the worst idea. It was more a sort of single place where I could see all the English clubs that might end up giving me cash, an overview of the entire professional and semi-professional pyramid. Handy if, for some reason, you went so long without hearing the words "Coventry City" that you forgot such a team existed.

Why was this moment incredible? Because Jackie, my fairy godmother, had sprinkled me with his magic dust. Cinderella, you *shall* go to the match! If Man United and City would let me in for free to every game, that would be, like, over 1,200 XP a week! If *any* professional team would let me into *any* game, I could earn, what, 5,000 XP a week? For free?

It was too good to be true. There had to be a catch.

Anyway, for now, the question was where to start. Tiresomely, yawn, apologies, I first considered United. They were nearby, I cared about the results, and I'd get seven times XP. Liverpool? Wearing their top had been like aversion therapy. Now, I didn't close my eyes every time I saw an article about them. And they were near-ish. Everton, too, of course. They were the city of Liverpool's second-biggest team, historically a big club, big stadium, and a full squad of players I'd never scouted. And they had a manager not known for his tactical acumen. Would be interesting to see if I could spot what he was doing wrong!

The rest of the Premier League was a bit too much of a drive. Not a problem in terms of the time and distance, but in terms of petrol. They'd have to wait. Maybe the October perk would be a never-ending petrol tank.

But probably I'd go to a Championship match before my next Premier League one. Going to a game in the second tier would help me build my mental map of the CA levels indigenous to each division. And I had a very, very sneaky suspicion that I might get 6 XP per minute for those games.

Then there was the complete opposite end, the National League North (sixth tier) or the National League (fifth tier).

For me personally, it would be better to start at the higher leagues and make my way down the pyramid. More XP, quicker.

But for Ziggy, I needed to get a clearer picture of the lower leagues and where he might fit in. So that's where I started.

"Bill Brown."

I was on the back foot already, surprised he hadn't said the name of his company (Oldham Athletic) and department (hospitality) like I had to in *my* day job. "Oh hi, Bill. Mr Brown. I'm Max, a Manchester-based scout and agent. I got your number from the website. Hope it's not a bad time. I'm looking to get tickets for the Wrexham game."

"Oh, right?" His tone was casual, friendly disinterest. He was doing something else.

"Yeah." Before dialling, I'd had a choice between "charming noob" and "slick super-agent" and, because I'm vain, decided to try the latter. So I said, "I'm not sure how you guys do it." I'm not sure how *you guys* do it, but I know how *everyone else* does it. Because I'm a pro.

"Just pop down to the main reception half an hour before kick off. I'll see you right." I heard him shuffle around. I guessed he was putting the phone under his chin and getting a pen. I heard him rapidly tapping the pen against a notebook. "You know what? This is actually perfect timing. I've just had a call about someone who can't make the game, so you can have *his* seat. Saves me some work! What's your name again?"

"Max Best."

"Macbeth?" he spluttered.

"No, first name Max. Last name Best. Like George."

"Oh!" He laughed. "Don't be bringing none of your Scottish curses with you, *Max Beth*. What's the line? 'By the pricking of my thumbs, something wicked this way comes.' Are you what's wicked, Max?"

I was a bit unnerved by the mention of Scottish curses, and him calling me *Beth* of all things, so my comeback was twice-fried lame. "The only thing that's wicked are the wicked opportunities I'm going to bring to your club."

"You're not quite at the level of Shakespeare, Max. More second-hand car salesman. I won't hold it against you. 'Fair is foul, and foul is fair.'" Jesus Christ. Was I going to have to read *Macbeth* in order to become a football agent? Give me a break!

"Does that phrase mean it's okay to do whatever it takes to win?"

He paused. "Very revealing you'd come to that conclusion, Max. *Very* suspicious." He laughed. "I'll have to keep my eye on you. By the way, who are you interested in?"

"Excuse me?"

"Why do you want to watch us? Or are you checking out someone at Wrexham?"

"Oh. No one in particular. Just getting an idea of the standard. I have a striker who might suit a club like Oldham. I just want to take a look. Um . . . if that's all right?"

"Sure, sure." He was back to not really listening. "See you on Saturday, Max Beth."

So, no new XP, but another new name in my football contacts list. And free tickets! Or . . . seemingly free. He hadn't actually said, and I'd been too chickenshit to bring it up. Bravery, minus one.

Which takes us to Wednesday and the second training session with Jackie and the Met Heads. Ziggy was there again, as was the guest of honour.

Problem was, I wasn't there.

I was late.

I would enjoy whining about it, but long story short, if you don't own a printer you're going to end up with a USB stick at a public library, which has five employees but only one who can remember the printer password and she's just popped out. My advice is, instead of smashing your head against the nearest wall, just bring a little cosh, and batter yourself with it.

Anyway, with some bizarrely expensive printouts in my premium businessman suitcase (i.e., a hiker's backpack I got on sale), I dashed into the sports hall and was pleased to see the sesh had already started without me. I'd asked Jackie to do anything he could that related to tactical improvements, anything to turn the ladies from individuals into units. Some coaches tie their defenders together with long bits of string so that when one of them moves, they all have to move. Jackie had invented something even simpler than string; there were two at-tackers with a football, passing to each other, getting closer to a group of three players who were holding hands. The goal of the attackers was to pass the ball to each other while going from one side of the hall to the other, while the three blockers tried to get in the way of the passes. Like in netball, the attackers couldn't dribble, so, in theory, the blockers had a chance. In practice, they didn't seem able to coordinate a single line without one person leaving the handhold. It was ludicrous, but they were having a ton of fun, and I suppose they were getting the concept of thinking and moving together as a unit.

I only had time to glance at the drill, before I was assaulted by all the player profiles. There wasn't a lot of green going on, but there was one red number. Bella's passing had dropped to its previous level. News which didn't stress me at all. My working theory was that the attribute numbers were rounded down, so Bella's passing had naturally decayed from 6.0 to 5.99. Thus it showed as five. This drop was actually incredibly helpful to me. I wanted to act on the info right away, but there was so so so much going on and our sixty minutes in the hall were wasting away!

Next, I turned to examine Ziggy. His technique had improved from 5 to 6, and his CA had bumped up two points. He was now CA 8. Still *bad* but . . . starting to get interesting.

But even that wasn't the most important thing.

While Jackie mimed pointing to his wrist, and Beth called out some bit of banter about how I'd be late to my own funeral, I jogged to the side of the room where two teenagers were sitting.

"James," I said. "Sorry I'm late. Why aren't you training?"

James shrugged. He was not very tall, fairly thin, and generally had the build of a middle distance runner. Long distance, maybe. I didn't know.

I didn't watch those events in the Olympics. He was quite a slow talker, very thoughtful and careful. Quite pedantic. "We were not instructed to do anything." He'd had to take a bus from Wythenshawe because there was no way for me to make it from work to his house to the sports hall in time. "We were not sure if perhaps we had arrived at the wrong hall. For the masterclass," he said. His delivery was deadpan, but his eye flicked around the hall. It was like he was saying, "*This* is a masterclass? Mate."

I briefly considered murdering him on the grounds of insolence, but my defence probably wouldn't stand up in court. So I looked at the girl he was with. Girlfriend? Too young. "Who are you, and why are you in my *masterclass*?"

She smiled at me. "I'm Kisi, Mr. Best. We met on Sunday. I'm James's sister."

"We met?"

"I was wearing a lemon and lime kaba."

"Wasn't everyone? Well, it's nice to meet you. James, let's get you in the session."

"Mr. Best, there are not too many players. Perhaps Kisi could be included? In fact, given the makeup of the session, perhaps she should play instead of me."

"The makeup of the session," said Kisi, rolling her eyes. "They aren't wearing makeup."

"Whatever," I said, "Fine. You can play too. Changing rooms are through there."

"Mr. Best," she said. They all called me Mr. Best—all the Ghanaians, regardless of age—despite me saying, "You can call me Max" several hundred times. "This is all I have."

I gave her a quick appraisal. She was wearing denim shorts and a loose t-shirt. One of those pound shop ones that had loads of random English words on that sort of looked like meaningful text but wasn't. In this case, hers read: TRY MY DELICIOUS SALT BEEF NEW YORK BOSTON 1995.

Her trainers were an appalling pink and grey mess, but they looked like they'd do the job.

"Er . . ." I said.

I turned to James. He was a bit more suitably dressed. He was wearing a sports jacket and some long tracksuit bottoms. Black bottoms, black trainers, white socks. "Jesus Christ," I said.

"Please, Mr. Best," he said, giving me a look that should have come from an 80-year-old who had lived through ALL the things and had no time for that sort of language.

"Right, come on, then, I guess." If their clothes wouldn't let them do certain drills, we wouldn't do those drills. No biggie.

"Jackie," I said and gestured I'd like him to pause the sesh. He blew his whistle. The Met Heads+1 pottered over. "All right? This is James and Kisi Yalley." A noise from the siblings made me turn. "What now?"

"It is pronounced Yalley," James said, such that I couldn't hear a difference. "But that is okay. Most people in this country call me Youngster."

"Right," I said, trying to power through. "Youngster and Youngsterer. They're going to help us make up the numbers for the drills I want to do later. In the meantime, Jackie, could we please do a very quick passing sesh?"

He was torn between amusement and confusement (also known as confusion), but started giving instructions. He split the siblings up, which I found interesting. Most people would have made them train together, since they were the newbies, the outsiders, the unknowns.

Beth came up to me. "Max. A word." She tried to pull me away to a corner, but nothing was going to move me away from James Yalley. As soon as the drill started, I'd see his profile, and it was either going to be ones all the way down, a big cosmic joke, or—

"Max."

"What, Beth?"

She hissed at me. "This is our session. You're not in charge here. Bringing a proper coach is one thing, but bringing some randos is bizarre and rude."

I was listening, but not on any kind of emotional level. I did see her point, though. I *had* been rude. It *was* bizarre. "If it goes wrong, I'll make it up to you."

"Max!" she hissed again.

There wasn't time for a University Public Speaking Club debate. I cut to the heart of the matter, as it stood there and then. "Are you going to make me send these kids home, Beth?"

"No, of course not. But—"

"Punch me in the face later, but don't take it out on the kids. They're good kids." I stepped forward. It was about to happen. "Oh, but Beth."

"What?" she said, her cheeks red, back tense.

"I need to borrow fifty quid."

"You little—"

That was when the rest of the players started kicking the ball to each other. And I made a little noise.

"What?" said Beth, anger briefly forgotten. Jackie's head whipped round, and his eyes bored into me.

"What? Nothing," I lied. But I couldn't contain myself. I couldn't stay internal.

Beth moved close to me and whispered. "I've heard you make that noise before, Max, but never in the daytime."

I looked at her and grinned. I looked at the kids and beamed. I looked at Jackie and felt a sudden need to dance. "Singing in the Rain!" "Uptown Funk!" Play what you like. I've got the moves! I did a little shuffle and a little wiggle. "Beth, have you read *Macbeth*? Watch this footwork! *Is this a Jagger I see before me*?" I did another little flourish and pointed one hand at the ceiling.

My pulse was racing, I felt light-headed, I was ready to make some rash decisions. I reached out, took Beth's waist into my arms, and kissed her full on the lips.

30

SHITHOUSERY

Football glossary: *Shithousery. (Previously known as games-manship.) Underhanded conduct aimed at gaining an advantage.*

Can you blame me for dancing?

JAMES YALLEY "YOUNGSTER"		
Born 19.10.2005	(Age 16)	Ghanaian/English
Acceleration 7		
		Stamina 8
	Heading 4	Strength 3
		Tackling 8
	Jumping 4	
Bravery 16		Technique 3
	Pace 8	preferred foot R
	Passing 4	
Dribbling 6		
Finishing 5		
CA 2	PA 181	
Defensive Midfielder, Midfielder (Centre)		

With this kid as a client, I was going to skip years of grinding up the football pyramid and go straight to the Premier League! Straight to the VIP boxes and the meetings with sheiks and "oh, Mr. Best, would you and your client like fifty-yard-line seats at the Superbowl next to Jack Nicholson and Halle Berry?"

PA 181! That was Premier League level, no doubt. And in five seconds of training, he'd increased his CA. This kid was bursting with potential, and it only took the slightest encouragement for it to start leaking out. Don't train him too hard, Jackie! He might pop!

His other attributes were interesting in different ways, but the kid was sixteen, so presumably there would be a lot of development in them. Stamina/tackling/bravery seemed like a good skill set for a defensive midfielder. And DMs were all the rage! Man United had been trying to buy one for years. They'd finally bought Casemiro for silly money, and other teams were looking at West Ham's Declan Rice with talk of a one hundred million pound transfer fee. What's ten percent of one hundred million?

My feet started itching again. They wanted to do a little hop, skip, and jump. All the way to the bank!

I had a mental vision of me depositing ten million pounds in my employee bank account. Then transferring it out the next day while giving my boss's boss the finger.

I exhaled the happiest little breath of my life. The air had gone into a poor person's lungs and come out of a rich man's mouth. A filthy rich man. Premier League rich.

Ahhh.

I was just starting to come back down to earth when another thought struck me. With ten million pounds, I could buy a little semi-pro team and install myself as its manager!

That would be . . . that would be . . .

"Max?"

"Huh?"

Jackie was keen to move on to the next drill. "What's next?"

"Next?" Oh! The masterclass.

"More passing?" he asked.

I blinked and noted that Bella's passing had gone green again. She was back up to 6. Lesson learned.

"How about some quick rondos?" Basically piggy-in-the-middle. Technique work.

"Aight. You getting changed? Kit's here."

"Yep. Just give me a second." I went back into my daydream. It was so warm and cozy in there.

If I owned my own club, I wouldn't need to—*Wait a second!*

My eyes snapped wide open, and I looked at the girl wearing the oddball clothes.

KISI YALLEY		
Born 3.2.2008	(Age 14)	Ghanaian/English
Acceleration 9		
		Stamina 5
	Heading 2	Strength 3
		Tackling 3
	Jumping 3	
Bravery 9		Technique 6
	Pace 9	preferred foot R
	Passing 4	
Dribbling 8		
Finishing 6		
CA 1	PA 143	
Attacking Midfielder (RLC)		

Another one! Speedy little attacking midfielder. Half decent finishing. She was only fourteen; if she kept improving, she would be a very dangerous attacker, comfortable on any side of the pitch. Teams like Liverpool and Man City loved having these mobile attackers who could slot into any gap, left, right, or centre. Sometimes their players would start on the left, play there for twenty minutes, then switch to the right, then go back again. Flexibility was valuable. Maybe that flexibility would make her seem like she had a higher ceiling than she did. Her PA was under 150, but I imagined a lot of managers and coaches would misread her ability, and I was perfectly comfortable ripping Premier League teams off.

"Beth," I said.

"What." She was not sure if she was still mad at me.

"Can we use Kisi on Friday?"

"Jesus, Max."

"What?"

"We're a university team. Everyone in this squad goes to Manchester Met. You're really fucking stupid sometimes." She paused. "And you're a dick."

All right, scratch that then. But still. Another little gem of a player!

I stood there and basked in the fluorescent lighting as the Met Heads and my entire roster of soon-to-be-clients stood in a circle, doing one touch passes to each other while someone in the middle tried to intercept the ball. It was a fairly basic drill, but my body was reacting like I was watching *Mad Max: Fury Road*.

The adrenaline died down a little bit, but I simply stood there, grinning like I was on a class B substance.

"Max. Max? Max. What next, Max?"

I snapped out of it. Jackie was asking me what he wanted, while all the players were looking over, waiting for me to change the drill. "Oh. Right." Well, what we did next depended on how much I cared about beating Man City. A strange thing to wonder, you might think, after I'd mentally built the match up into something of monumental importance.

If you're building a pyramid out of playing cards, it's the only thing in your life. But when the doorbell rings because the pizza has arrived, you forget all about the cards. And when you go back to the pyramid a thousand calories later, do you even remember why you started doing it? Man City under-sixteens? Who cared? It was all about Youngster now. It was all about the Premier League. "Let's just play a little game. Seven-a-side. Have some fun."

A wall of noise met that suggestion. Lula was spluttering, struggling to articulate her displeasure. Eva and Anna, in particular, looked pissed. Beth tried to explain my mistake. "Max, you absolute prick." James and Kisi winced. "You've been going on about beating Man City, beating Man City, beating Man City. We," she said, indicating the Met Heads, "have been coming around to the idea, and now we're all on board. We want to try. We want to go for it. We thought if you believed in us so hard, we'd fucking start believing in ourselves. You fucking mobilised us, and now you're telling us there's no war."

I was astonished. "Beth, you've been calling me a nutjob over this since the first time I mentioned it. None of you have ever said you thought you could win. I thought I was pushing you to do something you don't really want to do."

"Max," said Lula. "We're grown women. We do what we want."

"And what we want," said Bella, "is to beat Man City."

I was pretty sure I heard Beth mumble "prick" again, and that set me off. "Question time, everyone! Who's this an impression of, and who is she talking about? *'He's fucking crazy! He's off his head!'*" Everyone turned to look at Beth. "Why are you only telling me you give a shit now? When I wanted to try some tactics out against Aquinas, you said you'd rather have a laugh." That shut her up. "Just give me a second. Please." I needed to get my head round this new information. I felt a slight tingling of my spider senses. Ziggy was here. Youngster and his sister were here. Jackie, the only coach I knew and my main contact in the world of football, was here. Literally all my eggs were in this basket. I was in danger of smashing the eggs and burning the basket too. I needed to worm my way out of this unpleasantness, and fast.

What was going to happen in the next few days with Youngster? Nothing. It'd take time to find him a club to train with and whatnot. It wasn't urgent. It'd be five years, probably, before he played his first Premier League game. That was a clarifying thought. Five years. A lot could go wrong in that time. He could get a big injury. He could get poached by a rival agent. He could open his Bible one day and hear the voice of God telling him to go and be a missionary in North Korea . . . .

And capriciously changing my goals around Jackie was a bad look. Especially if I wanted FC United to sign Youngster and start his training. Which I probably did. So . . . focus on the City game. Go back to building that pyramid of cards. Beating them would be an achievement. Trying would be fun.

My best move now, I calculated, was showing a little humility. Insincere apologies: one of my superpowers that predated the curse.

I started at the top. "Beth, I'm sorry. For one less thing than you're mad at me for. Beth Heads, if you want to win, let's go for it. The war's back on. James, Kisi, sorry for swearing so much. Let's do a tiny reset, get some water, and meet back here in thirty seconds."

We all sort of deflated a bit, emotionally, and pottered to the various edges of the gym where our bags were. I noticed that Ziggy had latched onto Lula. Oooh, maybe they'd get married and have little striker babies!

Jackie shook his head at me. "Never a fucking dull moment, Max."

"Never a bleeding dull moment. Language."

"Right," he said, eyeing James. "New client?"

"What? How would I know if he was any good after seeing him play, like, six passes?"

"It's just that you were, sort of, dancing. Smooching. You know what it looked like? V-Day." Victory in Europe day, loads of sailors kissing random women in the street. The end of the war. That was it, wasn't it? James Yalley signing for a Premier League team would mark the official end of my war against poverty.

"Jackie," I said, changing the subject. "What's your stance on shit-housery?"

"Okay, Beth Heads, listen up."

"Let me just stop you right there, Max." Beth. Not angry, but forceful. "I know it's just banter, but I don't like it. This isn't my team. It's the university's and it's ours. It belongs to everyone. I just help organise things. Keep things ticking over."

I nodded, tempted to do a little salute. "Okay, soldier, I read you loud and clear. Ten-four. Good copy." She was talking shit, by the way. She was the heart and soul of the team. The only person who didn't see it that way was her. "Okay Met Heads. When I saw you at the first game, you didn't have a sub. Against City last time, you had one. That already made such a difference. So adding Eva and Anna is going to be huge. Thanks, ladies." I rubbed my lip. "The way I see it, City are coached brilliantly, but to a set style of play. In the last match against them, when we gave them the chance to pass sideways or back, and they took it. That's how they're trained. It's second-nature to them. Keep the ball, keep the ball. They've got fantastic dribblers, but they're basically not allowed to do it. They're playing with one hand tied behind their back, but their manager told me that when the kids dribble, other teams start kicking them. Also, if you look at City's men's team, there's very little dribbling. I think that's just the culture of the whole club: Plan A is passing and keeping the ball. Plan B? See Plan A. Jackie?"

"Sounds about right."

"One more thing. Their manager is a risk-taker. I remember watching her and thinking, 'she's got balls.'" Everyone laughed, especially Kisi. "Keep that in mind. So. That's them. What about us? Well, we've got spirit, unity, chuff like that." A few more chuckles. "If we burn calories like there's no tomorrow, we can defend. But we need goals. We need a tactical plan. We need luck." This was something of a key moment. I was going to offer them a way to win, and I wasn't sure I wanted them to go for it. "If we play like we did last time, we've got a twenty percent chance of winning. Throw in an extra five or ten percent because of the subs. Add or subtract twenty percent if you follow my tactical plan."

"Subtract?"

"My plan exists so extremely far past 'genius' that it could, conceivably, be mistaken for madness. Basically, even if we do everything perfectly, we're still the underdogs. There are a couple of things we can do to tip the scales."

Beth sagged. "Why do I get the feeling I'm going to be swearing at you again?"

"Because you have a potty mouth. Beth, listen. I need to know what you're willing to do and what you aren't. My tactical plan depends on it. Okay?" She took a breath in and kept it there, then blew it out. Ready. "Let's start with the worst one," I said. "A little bit of shithousery. A little bit of verbals."

Nobby put her hand up. "What's verbals?"

"It's where you say something to your opponent to wind them up or whatever."

"Oh."

"It's not that kind of league, Max."

"I know, Beth. I know. I'm just suggesting something. And you do it or you don't. Imagine City have taken a shot, and Jane is going behind the goal to get the ball. Hands up if you'd turn to your man and say, 'I like your hair.' No, really. Hands up."

"Why would we?"

"To mess with their head! If they're wondering why you said it, they aren't focused on the game. Your hair looks nice today. Hands up." Beth shrugged and raised her hand. Most of the rest followed. Nobby and Anna were the main holdouts. "Ziggy?"

"What?"

"Would you say it, yes or no?"

"I mean, sure, but what would it achieve?"

"Maybe he'd get mad and punch you, and that'd be a red card."

He thought about it and put his hand up. Kisi copied him, startling her brother.

"Great. Hands down. Same question. Jane's got the ball, and she's fidgeting with her gloves. You turn to your man and say, 'Why does no-one pass to you? Do they not like you?' Hands up."

"Kin hell, Max."

What I was suggesting was a very mild form of what the psychotic Australian cricket team call "mental disintegration." It was more likely to work in games like cricket where there was an extended series of matches between the same two teams. "Come on! Just show me."

This was too much for Kisi, Bella, and Sophia; they joined Nobby and Anna in leaving their hands by their sides. Or in Nobby's case, aggressively folding them.

"Last one. We're winning two-nil. Your man starts dribbling, does a little Maradona run and scores a goal. You wander up to her and say, 'Do that again you'll be going home in a fucking ambulance.' Hands up." Threatening your opponent with actual bodily harm probably sounds demented but is incredibly common in football. A skillful player in a Sunday League game will be punished for every trick or piece of skill. In a way, it's heartwarming that the other team give him a warning first.

At first, no hands went up. I actually felt relieved. Then Youngster put his hand up. "James!" I said, surprised.

"My hand is raised to ask a question. Why would the ambulance take you home? Surely it would take you to the hospital."

"Good point. Everybody write that down. So what I'm getting is that, as a team, your limit is somewhere between ooh nice hair and I'm gonna break your legs you little slag . . . ."

Nobby said, "What are you trying to get at?"

"I'm saying if they start dribbling, they'll win. Hundred percent. There's no way to stop them, you know, without shithousery. So we need to decide how we feel about that. If you're okay with not having a plan, so am I."

Jane was crushing a ball between her palms. She bounced it twice. Goalkeepers love doing that. "They're told not to dribble. They're supposed to pass all the time, right? If we're winning and they panic and start dribbling, then we've won. You know, morally."

A moral victory. That was interesting. I hadn't thought of that. Some bigger kid says he can beat you up with one hand behind his back . . . doesn't expect you to be so tough, so scrappy. Soon as you see him using both fists, you've won. Everyone on the playground says you won. The bully knows you beat him.

"Show of hands," I said. "We go toe-to-toe with them, give it all we've got, and if they start dribbling, that's our victory right there. The rest of the game, we stick six in defence and make the game miserable for everyone."

Every hand went up.

I grinned. It hadn't been smooth sailing, but we'd arrived at a destination we were all pleased with. Even Nobby. Any sensible person would have left it there. Quit while they were ahead.

Beth could read my face better than anyone. "Max. What is it?"

Stick or twist? Let sleeping dogs lie? Stir up the hornet's nest?

"City only beat us by two goals last time. This time should be even closer. So . . . one extra goal could be all the difference. Give me two minutes, and I'll show you something. You'll probably hate it, but let's just throw it up and see where it lands. Yeah?"

"Go on, then," said Beth.

"Jackie. Think you can stop me dribbling past you?"

His eyes lit up. "You're going to take me on?" He unzipped his jacket. "Bring it, Manchester!"

"Ooh, catfight!" said one of the ladies. The atmosphere was much better now that the talk of shithousery was behind us. Little did they know . . .

I grabbed the plastic bag that contained the full Liverpool kit. I turned and pointed to the little room that adjoined the hall. "While I'm putting this eyesore on, everyone pop into the storage room, and bring out six crash mats."

"Crash mats?" said Beth. "What's crash mats got to do with scoring goals?"

31

THE FALSE 9

Football glossary: The False 9: Shirt number nine was histori-cally given to a tall, strong striker who was good at headers. As tactics evolved, the need for this kind of striker diminished, and some managers virtually eliminated the striker position alto-gether. A new position emerged, the False 9. This was normally a midfielder pretending to be a striker, but rarely appearing in attack. Having no direct opponent confuses defenders and leaves them with no specific jobs. These bewildered players end up reverting to a prehistoric mental state, roaming the pitch looking for buffalo, foraging for berries by the corner flag, experimenting with irrigation channels on the edge of the penalty box.

Jackie stood in front of me, acting as the sole defender. Either side of him, the crash mats formed a sort of funnel, starting off nice and wide, tapering to a narrower point behind him.

"Guys," I said, "line up. Watch and learn. I'm going to dribble towards Jackie, take the piss out of him, and then score a goal. Any questions?"

"What are the mats for?"

"Just to give him a chance. Otherwise, I'd zoom around him before he could turn his wheelchair. At his age, he wouldn't be able to stop me." Along with his name, the curse told me Jackie's age. But it didn't tell me his attributes as a player. Even if he was much better than me—virtually certain!—I was pretty sure I'd be able to do what I wanted.

Jackie scoffed. "I'm only twenty-eight, you cheeky little . . ."

I rolled the ball a couple of inches in his direction and fell into a sort of crouch as though I was going to dribble at him. But I immediately stopped and turned to my audience. "Oh, I forgot. Does everyone know what a nutmeg is?"

Jackie laughed, a genuine, big laugh.

Ziggy said, "It's where you kick the ball through your opponent's legs."

"How does it feel to be nutmegged, Ziggy?"

"Not nice. Bit embarrassing."

"How do you think Jackie's going to take it?"

"I reckon now that you've told him what you're planning, he won't let you."

"I don't see how he could possibly stop me," I said, which brought a half-sarcastic oooh from the Met Heads.

I rolled the ball forwards some more. I was running more inelegantly than the most uncoordinated player I'd seen in any Sunday League game. I was pushing the ball forward a bit with my right foot, then shuffling behind it with the rest of my body. I had my head tilted forwards almost ninety degrees, my eyes looking straight down. I mis-kicked the ball and ended up going in a slow circle. Everything was right-sided. Right, right, right. Hey, everyone! I'm right-footed! When I was facing Jackie again, I looked up—BIG movement—and then immediately down at the ball. Jackie wasn't buying that this was how I ran, and he settled into a stance with his weight distributed, on his toes, ready to pounce. My only advantage, really, was that I had the choice to attack down his left or his right.

As I approached him, I decided to go on my left. I'm left-footed, sucka! My whole presence changed—elongated, dynamic, limber—and I threw my left foot towards the ball. I was going to knock it past him. I sensed his eyes widening with surprise, even though he'd been expecting something of the sort. His weight instinctively moved to that side, the better to counter me.

But, surprise, surprise, I had no intention of going to his left. I'm right-footed, yo! Double bluff! I did a stepover, let my leg travel across the ball in a huge, dramatic motion, planted it on the other side, and used it as a pivot to explode to the right. Again, his reaction was automatic. It was virtually impossible not to counter my counter by throwing out a leg. But because his first move had shifted his weight to the other side, this movement was little more than a feeble waft. So far in this particular sequence, I hadn't even touched the ball. But as I pretended to burst past him on the right, I cheekily dabbed it through his legs. I would run around him and tap the ball into the open net.

A humiliating turn of events for the top coach! The ex-professional!

As I passed him, he seemed to flick out a leg and—to put it in appropriate but not quite accurate words—he booted me up the arse.

I tumbled, spun, and landed with a sickening thud on one of the mats. I let out a piercing scream and gripped my shin. "Argh!"

Beth dashed towards me, followed by several others. They crowded me. Did I need medical attention? Was anything broken? Don't move! Don't put pressure on it! Beth used a can of magic spray on me like it was a flamethrower; it cooled and numbed my shin.

"Ziggy," I called out. "Ziggy." He rushed across.

"What, what?"

"Ziggy, if you're the ref, is that a free kick?"

"What? Yes! And a red card." I was strangely pleased to see Ziggy take my side, even if Jackie didn't . . . ah . . . have a leg to stand on. I'd been wondering what would happen if Ziggy had to make a choice, somehow, between Jackie and me. I'd found Ziggy, I'd been his wingman. But Jackie was the guy making him a better player. Jackie knew the door codes to football's inner sanctums; knew the secret handshakes. So yeah, pleasing. "Jesus, Jackie! Mate! You could have broken his leg!"

Jackie hadn't moved to help me. He was watching the scene with no little amusement. If he'd been embarrassed by the nutmeg, he wasn't showing it. "Nah, Ziggy, lad. I couldn't have broken his leg." He grinned. "I didn't even touch him."

On hearing those words, I sprang to my feet. "Feeling much better now. Thanks, Beth. Did I hear someone say free kick?" I jogged to the ball, brought it back, and stopped it dead. I looked from the ball to the goal and back to the ball, which I then gave the biggest thrashing of its life. It flew as true as an exocet rocket, hitting the underside of the crossbar, and thundering down behind the goal line and up into the roof of the net. Very satisfying!

I slapped my palms up and down. Job well done. Here endeth the lesson.

"Wait, wait, wait," said Ziggy, looking at Jackie but pointing at the crash mat. "You didn't foul him? That was a dive?"

"No!" said Jane. "That was a foul. He kicked him! I saw it!"

There was more back and forth like that. I would have liked to bask in the confusion for a while, but time was running out, and we had to get to my big tactics moment. "Ladies and gentlemen," I said, and paused for the rumblings to die down. "Yes, I dived. I would say that Jackie is innocent, but I don't *know* that for sure. He certainly didn't kick me. He was too busy being megged."

Tight-faced grimace from the Liverpudlian.

"Max," said Beth. "Do you want us to cheat? Is that what you're saying?"

"Jackie," I said. "You're the professional. Is executing a triple-axel maximum difficulty spin *cheating*?"

"Yes," he said. "The laws of the game call it simulation. Most people call it diving. It's a yellow card . . . for *you*."

I shook my head. Refs were conned by diving all the time. Even when you were caught diving, you wouldn't always get a yellow card. It was an efficient play. "Is exaggerating contact cheating?"

"No," he said.

"So if Lula has the ball and some little City midget gives her a tap, and she falls to the floor clutching her ankle . . . ?"

"It depends if you want to win at all costs or if you want to be able to sleep at night."

I smiled. "I'm not going to sleep at night if Peter Dinklage has left my ankle black and blue. Listen, everyone. I'm not saying to dive. But I have a feeling if we get a free kick we'll score. Let's say that a psychic dog told me."

Beth interrupted me. "Free kicks in our league are indirect." Meaning you can't score straight from the free kick. Yet another rule designed to make the sport a low-scoring game, you might think. But I'm pretty sure that rule is to stop someone taking an almighty run-up and blasting the ball at the first defender blocking the shot. A ball to the balls hurts, believe me, and the magic spray does diddly squat to help your squatted diddlies.

"So pass, then shoot. Or just smack it at the goal. If the keeper tries to save it, which she will, she'll touch it, and the goal will count. The thing is, everyone, the first goal is huge. It's mega. I don't know a word big enough for this. It's *megahuge*. If City score the first goal, they can pass us to death. Their chances of winning go to seventy percent. If *we* score the first goal, they'll have to take more risks against us, and we'll do them on the counterattack. Score first and our chances of winning are seventy percent. Get a free kick, score a goal, then you can go back to being bionic commandos ignoring every whack to the shins. If letting the referee know you've been kicked is against your religion, that's cool. I've said my piece."

Jackie piped up. "What would *you* do, Max? If you were a Met Head? Would you roll around crying for your mam?"

"If I was a Met Head," I said, "I'd be thinking hmm that cute Max boy is taken, Ziggy is into . . . who he's into. Youngster is too young. Thank God I like older, bald men. I'd also be thinking, I'm ready for my tactics now."

I got them to drag the crash mats back to the storage room while I prepared my little presentation. By the time everyone came back, which wasn't long, I'd gotten out my little A5 notebook and handed Kisi a fistful of colourful marker pens.

I took a black pen out of the mass, turned to a blank sheet, and sketched out the little sports hall. A centre circle, two goals. I drew a circle for the goalkeeper, the two defenders, two midfielders, two strikers. Seven players, seven circles. I looked over at Kisi's hand. She'd reorganised all the pens to be tip-down. "Why've you done that?"

"The ink flows to the bottom, so they're ready to use."

"Did you hear that everyone? Details. Details add up. Don't they, Jackie?"

He replied by giving me a double middle finger.

I took a light purple pen and shaded in my players.

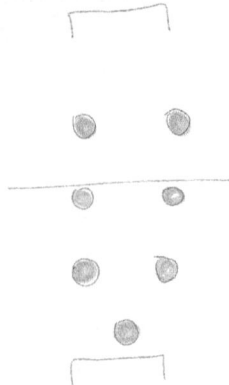

"A lot of teams play like this, whether they realise they're doing it or not. 2-2-2. Last time, City started as 2-3-1, and during the game, we copied them. Eventually, they pushed their third midfielder into attack, which caused us all kinds of problems. But anyway, they're a very midfield-based team. What we did well was to let them pass it. If you run into their traps, you're toast. If you don't do anything stupid, they're actually quite insipid. I went to see the men's team against Crystal Palace, and in the first half they didn't have a single shot."

"We won in the end, though," said Ziggy, showing a hitherto undiscovered death wish.

"Yes, Ziggy, because they are brilliant. I'm just saying their biggest strength can be a weakness. Mindless passing. Robotic football. So, check this out. Kisi, red please."

She handed me what I needed.

I drew two arrows."

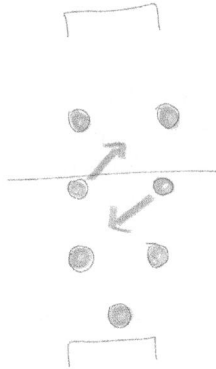

My plan is basically . . . this midfielder attacks, this one defends."

I ripped out the page and handed it to Kisi, who held it up. I turned a new leaf and began drawing a new one. "So what happens if our midfielders don't play in midfield? Beth?"

"Hmm. Not sure. I'm guessing the answer is we lose ten-nil."

"Five points for Hufflepuff! Jackie?"

He peered at my sketch. "You're going to give them the midfield? Completely? They'll overrun you."

"Maybe." I added the final flourishes to my latest drawing. It was, frankly, an instant masterpiece. Destined for the Football Hall of Fame. "You've heard of a False 9. Presenting . . . the world's newest tactical innovation: the false midfield."

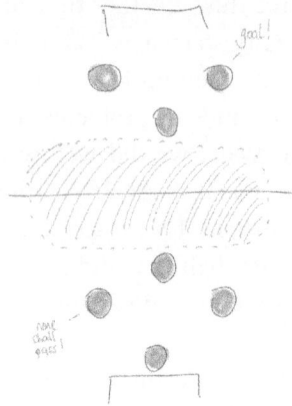

"Three attackers. Three defenders. From 2-2-2 to 3-0-3. What do you think? Anyone? Anyone? Beth, help me out." The mood was relatively skeptical.

"No. You know I'd be in Gryffindor."

Ideally, we'd have had a big ol' chat about all this, but there wasn't enough time. Quicker if I just explained it. They'd have forty-eight hours to digest it before kickoff. Maybe it'd be enough. "We know they love passing sideways. At the start of the match, they'll definitely have one striker. Million percent. We'll have three defenders, so there's no forward passes available. Yes? So they'll just pass from one side to the other for about twenty-five minutes! It'll be awful. I can't wait. Eventually, they'll push a midfielder forward, and then it'll be our three against their two. Okay. We can handle that. Even if they go nuts and push *another* player forward, that's three on three. All you have to do is track them. Stand between your man and the goal. They'll get a few shots away, but they'll be low quality ones."

I took a sip of water. I saw some players staring at my drawing, getting intrigued.

"Right. They miss a shot, they play a loose pass, we get the ball somehow. What do we do? Blast it upfield. To one of our *three* attackers. It will be mayhem. We won't get many attacks in the game, but every time we'll have an overload. We *will* score goals. If we get the first goal . . ." I said, pointing to where I'd been "fouled." "If we get the first goal, that'll just make all these counters even more lethal."

I left a pause for someone to point out the obvious, blatant, fatal flaw in the plan. No one did, so Jackie helped out.

"If you leave the midfield free, City will abandon it too and match you up, and you're back to where you started."

I pointed at him, delighted. "Yes! But look," I said, tapping my first sketch. "We're playing with two midfielders. We're playing 2-2-2!"

Beth threw a water bottle at the floor. "Max! Jesus fuck! You just said we weren't playing midfielders!"

I found her little tantrum quite sexy. Is that weird? "False midfield, Beth. We have to do everything to make it *look* like we have two in midfield. Every goal kick, kick-in, free kick, every break in play, the midfielders are standing in midfield. Yes? But as the play develops, oops! Where did they go?"

Youngster spoke. "It is *Master and Commander*."

"What?"

"It is a maritime movie set in the Napoleonic Wars. The sailors disguise their ship so they can get close to the enemy." He grinned, viciously. It was quite odd coming from that innocent, placid face. "Then they strike!"

I pointed at him. "*Master and Commander*. I'll have to watch that."

"The sound design—" he started, but I gave him permission to shut up.

"Yep, *thanks*."

Jackie nodded. "It might work for a while. You said she's a good manager. She will notice soon enough."

"Or she might not. And so what if she does?" I said. "If we get thirty minutes out of it, we're laughing. Leaves us twenty minutes to hold on. Better than holding on for the entire game!"

Beth picked up her water bottle and checked that nothing had spilled. She eyed me with the tiniest hint of approval. "All right. False midfield. It sounds mental. I'm in. Let's set it up."

32

A TIME OF TRIUMPH

The Met Heads's starting seven set up in the 2-2-2 formation. Jane, Beth and Nobby, Freyja and Sophia, Lula and Bella. On the other team, mimicking City's 2-3-1 formation: Jackie in goal; Eva and Bex in defence; me, James, and Kisi in midfield; Anna up front.

Excitingly, since I was leading this part of the session, I was holding the whistle. My first time as the whistler! (I had brief fantasies of a monthly perk that would let me stop time with a referee's whistle. Max Best, the crime-fighting referee. Tagline: Crime Gets a Red Card. Wow. It writes itself. I'd sell my car to watch *that*.)

We played a semi-serious match for a while, just warming up and getting used to our positions. "Okay, Met Heads," I said, kicking the ball to Jackie, "false midfield, let's give it a whirl."

Jackie took a beat to let everyone get set, then passed to Eva, who passed it to me. I passed to Kisi, who hit it first-touch back to me. I took a couple of strides forward. The nearest Met Head was Sophia. She moved towards me, so, like the City kids would do, I passed backwards to Bex. Sophia followed the ball, but only for a couple of yards. She was now the third attacker and settled into that spot. Meanwhile, my team passed around some more, and the ball came back to me. I was in acres of space. Ahead of me was Anna, surrounded by Met Heads. To the left and right I had the Ghanaians as options. We passed to each other for a while, unopposed. James and Kisi started to drift up the pitch, finally coming into contact with Beth and Nobby. Freyja marked Anna. In a normal game, I'd have dribbled forwards and created an overload, but that wasn't City's plan. Still, at *some* point, a City player in my position would dribble forward even if they were trained not to. We had to give them a reason to obey their coaching. I paused, put my foot on the ball. I wanted to use the whistle but no one was moving, so there was no point. Disappointing. I turned my head and said, "Sophia, if it goes like this with those two midfielders pushing forwards, you can't completely abandon me. Come to harass me until I do something with the ball, then float forward again. Yeah?"

"So I'm a bit more up and down than on the plan?"

"You'll have to use your judgment."

Jackie called out, "When he's passed the ball, stand near him, between him and City's goalkeeper. It'll look like you're marking him, but actually you'll be using him as a springboard to join the attack."

My plan was only a few minutes into the testing phase, and was already being diluted. But this tweak made sense. We couldn't just completely leave one opponent to do whatever she wanted. "Okay, go," I said. Sophia made a show of pressing me, so I turned backwards and looked for a pass. There was none. I blew my whistle. "Guys!" I said, talking to the attackers. "You have to leave me somewhere to go sideways or backwards."

Lula nodded. "So I don't mark my man over here?"

"No. Especially if City's midfielders push on." I turned as I spoke, so everyone could hear. "The key is to let them keep passing harmlessly. If they can't go back, they'll go forward. Which we don't want. Yeah?" I blew my whistle, and the play continued. Lula went goalhanging, leaving a City defender free. I knocked the ball back to her, and the square passing resumed. Defender, midfielder, midfielder, defender. I blew again. "Jackie, does this look like City to you?"

"Yeah," he said.

I nodded. This felt very similar to how the first game had gone once I'd taken control. "Beth, what do you think?"

"Looks right to me."

"Not tempted to come on top of me?"

"Honestly, watching you pass it around is great. Feels like I've got you where I want you. At a safe distance."

"Five points to Hufflepuff," I said before blowing the whistle. My team passed in a couple of squares again.

Time to really test this puppy.

I turned backwards but instantly turned again, threatening to drive forward. Sophia charged at me. I took a single stride forward and shouted, "Anna! Incoming!" I played a smooth diagonal ball to her feet, but, as I'd hoped, Nobby screeched away from her man, and practically hurled herself at the ball. With her right foot, she controlled it, and with her left, mid-tumble, she toe-poked the ball. It flew up the pitch, straight to Lula. Eva and Bex were on their heels, and by the time they got their bodies into motion, Lula had already played a one-touch pass to the left, where Bella had sprinted. Bella faked a shot at goal, drawing Jackie towards his near post. But Bella played an unexpected pass back across the goal, into the path of Sophia, who had burst forward as soon as Nobby had made the interception.

She tapped the ball into the unguarded net.

Holy fucking shit. Holy fucking *shit*! I couldn't have sketched a more perfect demo of how the tactic could work.

I was about to tell Nobby she'd done well, but Beth was way ahead of me, chest bumping her fellow defender. "Fucking yes, Nobby!"

Freyja had picked up some proper Mancunian language and a hint of the accent. Slapping her Japanese teammate on the back of the head, she yelled, "That's fucking class, that, Nobby! Fuckin' mint!"

Nobby nodded, trying to be impassive. But she was very clearly glowing.

The strikers jogged back to their own half, exchanging high fives and sharing a joke.

Jackie fished the ball out of the net and tossed it back to the centre circle. "What are you grinning at, Maxy boy?"

I jabbed a thumb over my shoulder and spoke loud enough for the entire hall to hear. "I don't know, man. I feel like these twats are gonna give City a right hiding." Jackie grinned back at me. I turned to the City fan. "How do you feel about *that*, Ziggy?"

He was smiling along with everyone else. "Don't worry about me, Max. I'm into it."

It would be ludicrous to say that we spent the next fifteen minutes *perfecting* the plan, but we kept working at it, rotating Eva, Bex, and Anna into the first team so they could get somewhat used to the system. We found a couple of issues and ironed out a bit of role confusion.

With a couple of minutes left on the clock, I had an idea. I blew the whistle and said, "I've just thought of something."

Jackie jogged over to me and said, "Don't overdo it. Stop there. Let them digest."

I nodded. Handed him the whistle. "Couple of quick sprints?"

"Go on, then." He indicated that I should join the other players.

"Me? I'm built for pleasure, not for speed."

The next group arrived and kicked us off the pitch. Most of us went for a quick shower. The kids and Jackie waited in the main reception, and, one by one, everyone else joined them. Ziggy was one of the last. Getting himself *nice* and clean! "Ziggy, I've got something for you," I said. "Jackie. Do you want to watch a historic moment in footballing history?"

He narrowed his eyes at me, then glanced at Ziggy. "Sure," he said.

A few of the ladies moved over as well, Lula foremost amongst them.

I pulled out a document and placed it in front of Ziggy, along with a pen. I'd spent quite a while on this, adapting it from something boilerplate I'd found online. "Oh!" he said, sitting down to read it. "Our contract. Right." He glanced up at Jackie and started flicking through the pages.

This was, obviously, a big moment for me. If Jackie was going to steal my client, he'd have to show his hand now. I'd gotten two training sessions out of the guy; I'd seen what a proper coach could do in terms of improving a player. Ziggy was a good lad, and I was still enthusiastic about him. But now I had Youngster. If Ziggy and Jackie wanted to elope to Gretna Green and leave me jilted at the altar, let it happen in front of Lula and the others.

Ziggy skimmed through to the last page. He pointed at the final paragraph. "What's this?"

"If you want to change to a different agent, you have to give me six months' notice or pay that fee. It's just so I can get a mortgage and not have to stress about who's going to betray me. If I lose you, I'll have time to find another client."

He read through the clause again and nodded. It was what I'd said. "Okay," he said, and he picked up the pen.

"Wait!" said Jackie. "Don't sign!"

I knew it.

I knew it.

Jackie, the snake, the despicable coward, the odious gollum, got down on one knee.

What the fuck?

Was he going to *propose* to Ziggy? Had I misread all those glances? They'd spent a lot of time together . . . .

"Okay, perfect," said Jackie. He had his phone out and was pointing it at Ziggy and the contract. "Max, get closer."

Oh.

I stood next to Ziggy, bent down a little bit, and put my hand on his shoulder.

Ziggy signed.

He signed da ting.

Jackie didn't say "smile" as he took the snap.

He didn't have to.

I invited Beth to come with me to take the Ghanaians home. She wasn't keen until I pointed out that once we'd dropped them off, it'd take thirty to forty-five minutes to drive back to her place, and I'd be a captive audience so she could complain about me and delve into all my character defects. "Only forty-five minutes?" she said. "Well, that'll do for the first part of the alphabet."

"A to M?"

"A."

So the four of us drove to Wythenshawe. I asked the teenagers if they'd enjoyed the session. Kisi said yes, she had always wanted to go to the circus. I asked if I was the ringmaster or the clown, and James advised her not to answer. James said he'd liked it, and Jackie certainly was a good coach. And he liked the way I thought about football, even if my venture was, perhaps, foolhardy. Pompous little shit!

Anyway, we talked a bit about football and their studies, and, after a while, the conversation was Beth and Kisi talking about TikTok. "Did you see the one about the hair?" "Do you think Khargol's apology to Nightsexy was sincere?"

That's when I started to tune out.

What was Jackie *up to*? One theory: he'd let me do all the work getting Ziggy a contract, then swoop in and take over as his agent. Sure, I'd get the first six months, but Jackie would get everything after that.

No, that didn't make sense. Jackie could easily have signed Ziggy as an agent, then gotten him a contract at FC United.

It wasn't that.

So what was it?

When we arrived at the kids' house, I invited myself in for tea. Beth was not especially keen, but I whispered that she could add it to her list of complaints. She gave me a dig in the ribs, but that was the end of it. I think she was curious about what I was up to.

Mr. and Mrs. Yalley were home and more than happy to welcome us inside. Their home was small and full of ornaments, plus a lot of textiles on the walls, and a large flag with African colours and a black star in the middle. Mr. Yalley's English wasn't great, so he mostly just sat and beamed at us. Sometimes he'd ask for a particular phrase to be translated. Regardless, both parents were keen to know how the masterclass had gone.

Kisi's chattiness attribute had dropped from twenty to one. Teenagers. Jesus.

"From my point of view," I said, "it went great. Beth was delighted to have your children attend the session. She was, and I hope she's not too embarrassed by this, extremely welcoming and generous." Beth smiled, a perfect smile. She was the ultimate chameleon! Would I pay for this later? It was fifty/fifty if she was feeling annoyed or amused. Probably amused. I was on a roll. I could do no wrong. I jiggled my special dice cup and rolled a double twenty. Let's get these guys signing on the dotted line right now. Forget all this getting-to-know-you shit. "Your children behaved beautifully, of course, not that you doubted it. Anyway, I wanted to pop in quickly and talk to you. James and Kisi are both talented players. As I mentioned, I'm a football agent, and I would like to sign them as clients and try to find suitable teams for them. My rate is ten percent, industry standard. No up-front fees, no hidden fees. Long-term, my role would be to balance your children's financial and footballing needs. Short-term, it's about getting them the training they need to develop their potential." I paused to let that sink in, and for a quick blast of translation. Mr. Yalley looked astonished. I don't know what language he was speaking, but he very clearly asked his wife to repeat what she had said. They had a brief discussion.

Mrs. Yalley said, "They have talent as footballers. Are you sure?"

I frowned. Surely James was the best in his class, at least? I could imagine him not being the stand-out player for his school team, since his role was less eye-catching than the star striker or the tricky winger. But wasn't he the best on his church team or whatever? And I would think that Kisi was taking the piss in almost every game she played. "Yes. Without question. They could both play at a high level."

"My goodness."

I turned to Beth for support, but she was as confused as the parents. She didn't have Super Scout. "Well, look," I said, ploughing forward like the champion I am. "I've got these contracts here. It's standard stuff. If you sign, I can get started on finding clubs."

As soon as I placed the papers on the table, Kisi leapt forward with a pen. "Whoa, Kisi! Your *mother* has to sign. Actually, that's true for both of you, since you're both under eighteen."

James picked up his contract and skimmed through it. He placed it back on the table. "I like playing football with my friends. I am not sure I would like to be a professional footballer. It is a very troubled industry. I will pray on it."

I understood the words he had used, of course. They couldn't be more rudimentary, more single-syllable. But it was the strangest thing. It was like he was speaking the alien sci-fi squiggle language. "Sorry, what?"

"I will pray on it."

"Pray?"

Mrs. Yalley smiled at me. "Do you not pray, Mr. Best?"

"Pray?" I said. "You mean, um . . . *Our father who art in heaven*? That sort of stuff?"

James shook his head. "No, Mr. Best. We are talking about a personal relationship with God."

I found myself staring at a photo. It was, presumably, James as a boy, dressed to the nines in his Sunday best, beaming at the photographer. Great photo, but his eyes had come out red. This kid prayed? Had a personal relationship with God? For half a second I suspected the red contained a hidden camera, and all this was being filmed for a prank show. I shook it off. There was more than one way of living. "Is that you?"

"Yes," his mother said. "James won a prize for memorising scripture."

"I see." I'd messed this up. I hadn't put in the work. It wasn't just that I didn't know how to talk to someone who was *really* religious, it was that I hadn't even known how deep his faith went. If I wanted him as a client, I needed to know what made him tick. It didn't seem to be football, fame, or money, or he'd have leapt at the contract like his sister. Had I blown my one shot at this, or would it be possible to reset and try again? "I have to take Beth home. I'll leave the contracts here, and you can think about the whole thing. But I should come by another time and have a proper talk with you all."

"You could come to the service on Sunday, Mr. Best," said James.

I can't explain it, but when he said that, I knew he wouldn't be signing any contracts, not with me and not with any professional football team. I tried to style it out. "Very kind. I'm not sure you're the right thingy for me. What's it called? Denomination. My family goes to the other church. The one with the ghosts."

Kisi saved me. "What time's the match on Friday, Beth?"

Beth had been quietly following the conversation, and, from her body language, she had sensed the exact moment my time of triumph turned into a day of defeat. "Oh! Er . . . 7 p.m."

"Well, good luck! I hope you win. False midfield!" And she burst out laughing and went up to her room.

We got in my car. I didn't start the engine right away.

"He won't become a footballer because he's a Christian," I said, shaking my head.

"Is that what you heard?" said Beth. I should have asked what she meant by that, but I was in too dark a mood to understand she'd said something significant.

"It's what you get for taking shortcuts," I said. "Should have brought him to a few sessions at FC United. Got him excited. Built up to the idea of him going pro. Made it easy. Natural. Not just plopped a contract on his kitchen table out of nowhere. Jesus." I hid in the steering wheel for a bit, then turned the ignition.

We drove to her house in virtual silence. Me, feeling empty, godless, and poor, staring into an endless abyss (an unusual abyss, for it was littered with pot noodles and cheap, thin, two-ply toilet rolls). Beth, thinking whatever women think when they've seen a man's hopes and dreams crushed right in front of their eyes.

I pulled up outside her place. "Wait here," she told me.

"Uh, what?" I said. Beth was getting out. I leaned towards her side. "Don't you want to invite me in?"

"No sex before a big game, Max. All the top managers agree on that."

"I'm the manager. I can make an exception."

"Nope. Also, I've got an exam tomorrow. Wait there."

So I sat there, holding my steering wheel, feeling pretty miserable actually. Beth was gone for ages. It should have made me feel worse, but it was just more of the same. Somewhere in the world, someone was writing a country and western song about how I'd signed Ziggy but not Youngster. *Ziggy was as quiet as a Graves, but the one Max really wanted was the one that got awayyy . . .*

Tap tap.

I wound the window down. Beth changed her mind?

"Here," she said. She handed me some cash. Two twenties and a ten. "Fifty quid."

"What? Why?"

"You said you needed to borrow fifty quid."

That's right. I said that. "Beth," I said, overcome by emotion. "I just . . ."

"Be off with you," she said. "This is a nice neighbourhood. You're lowering the tone." She turned and sashayed away.

Wednesday had finally come to an end. I had a new client and a real, true friend. But Jesus had stolen my million-pound lottery ticket.

Was that a good day or not?

33

THE BEAUTIFUL GAME

"I dedicate this book to all the people who have made this great game the Beautiful Game." —The autobiography of Pele (who won the World Cup a record three times with Brazil)

The next morning, I felt a little calmer. It was no good catastrophising about Youngster. Maybe my mistakes would mean I'd have to do twice as much work to get him signed. Or maybe there had never been a chance of him becoming a footballer. Either way, I'd do my best to make it happen. Full grind, no shortcuts, no awkward squirming when he mentioned his beliefs.

To that end, I downloaded some Christian podcasts to listen to throughout the day. They used the word "wretch" a lot. And "sinner." I was picking up vocabulary but not really learning what it was all about. There was a Christian bookshop in town, so I popped in after work looking for *Christianity for Dummies* or something of the ilk. I didn't find anything that hit the spot, but they had custom bookmarks for free, and I helped myself to a couple of those.

Later, I went to Platt Fields and had a quick chat with Emre. I asked if he was a Muslim, and he said, "Yes, of course." I asked if he went to the Mosque, and he said, "Yes, of course, every now and then." I asked if he drank beer, and he said, "Yes, of course, religiously."

I laughed and told him I'd signed a client and would be able to pay him back the money I owed him as early as January. He rolled his eyes and offered me another wrap. "I'm ready for my onions," I said, and he was very solemn about how he inserted them. This was a big moment.

"You owe me nine pounds," he said.

"Nasilsin," I said, which was the only Turkish phrase I'd learned.

I pottered off to watch some football. It had been a while since I'd gotten any new XP. Life had been eventful—too eventful maybe—so this was a nice change of pace. Nice, simple, rubbish game of football, 1 XP per minute.

I munched away quite happily.

Emma: Hey, Mister Romance. I need someone to explain football to me. Give me a call if you want to be that man.

This wasn't as out of the blue as it might seem. We'd exchanged a few texts here and there since we'd met. Just simple stuff. Poking the fire. Keeping it on a low heat, ready to drop some, er . . . wood . . . into it. Onto it.

Me: I'm just eating a wrap. Give me ten. But you'll have to call me. I have no minutes.

Emma: Okay.

"Max Best speaking. How may I assist you today?"

"Oh, hello Max Best. This is Emma Weaver. I'm calling in reference to our previous conversation from two and a half weeks ago."

"Whoa!" I said, ending that little role play. "Has it been that long?"

"Eighteen days, in fact," she said. She'd been counting! That cheered me up. "How was your wrap?"

"Too many onions," I said.

"Aw," she said. "At least I know you won't be kissing other girls then."

"Unless they lost their sense of smell to Covid. What are you up to?"

She sat down on something soft. In my imagination it was her bed. "Just cleaning. Tidying. Listening to a football podcast."

Oh! Maybe she was doing her homework to talk to *me* the same way I was listening to Christian ones to talk to Youngster! "Why?"

"Well, that's the thing. Me and the girls are going out with some lads on Saturday. Pub lunch. Pub lunch with the football on. Arsenal against Tottenham Spurs."

With some lads. A tiny pang of jealousy. Just for a microsecond. So brief you would hardly notice it, if you were the type of person not to notice the sudden, fraying hole in your gut. "Right."

"The podcasts are so boring. I was thinking you could give me a few pointers."

"On how to flirt with the lads?"

"I think I've got that covered. Pointers on what to look for in the game." She wanted things to say to the boy she liked. Things that would separate her from the pack of clueless lasses. Ah, well. We'd always have Didsbury.

I had a sudden inspiration. I could use this phone call as practice for my chat with Youngster. Our next conversation was going to be the sales pitch of a lifetime. It'd need charm, enthusiasm, positivity. I needed to pitch with a big smile on my face without worrying about the millions of pounds I'd lose if I said the wrong thing. Not all that different from flirting with a gorgeous blonde. I changed my whole stance. I sort of turned sideways and started using my free arm to make big gestures and put some warmth into my voice. Not too much. Just a little bit more flow, and I'd turn the tap a little more every half a minute or so. "It's gonna be a fascinating game. You're lucky in that respect. What level of complexity do you want?"

"What a question." She sighed and mumbled a few words. If you put a gun to my head and forced me to say what I *think* I heard, then you'd better know that I don't negotiate with terrorists. But I think I heard "imagine" and I think I heard "Manchester." She returned to an audible volume. "Give me the chicken korma version." Mild. Simple.

"Let me think. Small to big. Players. Managers. Fans. Yep, that's good. Good structure."

"You like to structure things?"

I thought about Youngster. Me just crashing forwards without a plan. "If it's important, it's worth planning it."

"You explaining Arsenal to me is important?"

I opened my screens and checked that I was getting XP even though I was on the phone. I was. "Nothing is more important to me. You ready?" She was. So. Arsenal versus Tottenham. "I think I'll start with the fans. Normally I'd start small and get bigger."

"Oh," she said. "Did we start the phone sex already?" Flirting again! What about her Saturday boy?

"You don't want phone sex from me. Last time I tried, her phone melted. So the fans. Both teams are in North London. When the teams are in the same city, the game is called a derby. So this is the North London derby. They'll say it a hundred times on the TV."

"North London derby. Got it. What about in Derby? The city called Derby."

"You're asking if there is a Derby derby? There isn't, but God I wish there was. Let's say that eighty percent of the people in North London support Arsenal or Spurs. By the way, you don't say Tottenham Spurs. It's one or the other."

"Bullet dodged. Thanks."

"So if your side loses, you get mocked for months. At work, in the pub, wherever you go."

"Really?"

"Well, there's only one team in Newcastle, so you might not have seen much of it. If you're in a city with two big teams, it's awful when you lose. Man U are playing City on Sunday and we'll probably lose, and Ziggy is going to be insufferable about it. I might turn my phone off."

"Oh. I see."

She didn't see. She couldn't. Supporting a team isn't logical. I could only begin to hint at the insanity of it all. "It's hard to explain how big a deal the North London derby is. It's really important to them. Let's just say that the night before the game, loads of those fans won't be able to sleep. If you're an Arsenal fan on the *Titanic*, and you've just beaten Tottenham, you're probably pretty chill about dying. Could be worse, you'd say. Could be a Spurs fan."

She laughed. "Jesus."

"Yeah. So historically, Arsenal have been better than Spurs and usually finish above them in the league. The Arsenal fans created a new and unique way to mock their rivals. The day when it's mathematically impossible for Spurs to finish above Arsenal in the league, the Arsenal fans celebrate and call it Saint Totteringham's Day."

"I can't tell if you're joking."

Over on the right side of the pitch, the goalkeeper for the red team took a big goal kick, but hurt himself in the process. Looked like he had tweaked a hamstring. Painful. I thought of what I wanted to say to

Youngster. He'd said something about football being a troubled industry. "Footy is problematic sometimes. It's simultaneously violent and a sort of physical manifestation of the male id. I'm not into that side of it. But it's also a kind of childish playground with mean, stupid, and funny taunts. I'm afraid I kind of love it. Sorry not sorry. Manchester United is shortened to Man U, which becomes manure. Manchester Shitty. Chelsea were Chelski when they had a Russian owner. Stuff like that. Saint Totteringham's Day. I'll text it to you, so you can slip it into the conversation on Saturday."

"Okay."

The red team didn't have any subs, and the goalkeeper could still jog. But he couldn't jump, so his team decided to put someone more agile in goal. The two players began swapping shirts.

"So then the managers. This is really interesting. A real clash of styles. Arsenal have a Spanish manager."

"Uh-huh."

"He's very handsome. You'll like him. Very passionate, well-dressed Spanish guy. Perfect for you. Unless you prefer a very passionate, well-dressed Italian guy. He's the other manager. He's older, though. I'm not sure what your type is."

"You know exactly what my type is."

"Tall. Muscle-bound. Tats. As little neck as possible. Likes to say 'it is what it is' So the Arsenal guy, he's been building this team for three or four years, and now it's *ready*. They want to control the ball and attack, try to score goals. The Beautiful Game. Lots of very attractive passing. Lots of shots. The foreign managers use the word *protagonist*. He wants his team to be the protagonists. If he was a general, he'd be ordering his troops forward. Charge! But orderly. Controlled. Does that make sense?"

"Sort of. Will I see that on the TV?"

Great question. "I think so. It's hard to imagine watching a game if . . . if you don't really watch many games. Do you know what I mean?"

"I do. To be honest, normally it all looks like loads of men running around like headless chickens. And the other manager. He's the opposite, is he?"

I hesitated. First, because the correct answer was probably needlessly complex. But also because the goalkeeper who was now playing in midfield was wincing every time he touched the ball. He should really have left the pitch; he was likely to make his injury much worse. "Well, it's hard to say what's his choice and what isn't. But they have three superstar attackers. The rest of the team is fairly . . . mediocre. That's not the right word . . . . Uninspiring, maybe. Uncreative. Is that a word? Dour. Drab. Spurs are playing with the goalkeeper and seven defensive players, and when they get the ball, they kick it up the pitch and hope their superstars can do something." I realised that what I was describing was not a million miles away from playing a false midfield. Maybe I hadn't invented the concept, after all. "If he was a general, he'd be luring the other army into an ambush. Then he'd unleash the cannons."

"And will I see *that* on the telly?"

"Hmm. If you are fluttering your eyes at some beefcake, and you glance up at the screen, you might see Spurs with the ball in Arsenal's half a lot. But they won't score from those positions. Maybe you should focus on the goals. Watch the replays, and you'll see that the Spurs goals come when they are defending, and they quickly kick the ball up the pitch. There will be, like, two or three white shirts near Arsenal's goal. And when Arsenal score there will be loads of red shirts up there."

"Okay! That's helpful. I think I'm following you. And Arsenal play in red and Spurs play in white. That's good."

Huh. I should have started with that. Red and white. Just like the game I was watching now. "Last thing, and this might be the most interesting one for you." The wounded goalkeeper-turned-midfielder was moving a little more easily now. Maybe he hadn't damaged his hamstring after all.

"Go on."

"The World Cup is soon. You know Brazil is football mad? And to them, the World Cup is like . . . the Olympics plus carnival plus Christmas times a thousand? Well, Brazil have lots of great strikers. Great forward players. And three will be playing in this match. There's a lot of intrigue around that. Of those three, probably only one will be chosen for the Brazil squad. So those three are going to be playing to the max from now till November. Scoring a goal doesn't just mean helping your team win the North London derby. It means you go on the plane to the World Cup, and that other prick doesn't."

"This is the Shakespeare bit."

"Football Shakespeare doesn't always go the way it should, but that's what's been set up in Act I, yes."

"Fun. So Saint Totteringham's Day, sexy Italian, clash of styles, Brazilians. Yes, I think that's perfect. Just the right amount of spice in my korma! I'm excited to watch football! I can't believe it. So listen . . ."

As she spoke, I watched as the not-wounded goalkeeper and an opposing player dashed towards each other, competing for the same ball. The guy in white slid towards it. The goalkeeper-guy lifted his foot to try to block it, but his hamstring popped, and he sort of collapsed into the tackle. Fell right onto the other guy's outstretched lower leg, with both guys going at more or less their top speeds.

It was a sickening collision, but *nobody reacted*. The goalie clambered to his feet, rubbed the back of his leg with a big grimace, and the game continued as normal. But I could see their player profiles. The goalkeeper's acceleration and pace dropped one point. I'd seen this in other matches. Small injuries didn't seem to affect attributes, but something like a six-week layoff (e.g., a torn hamstring) would drop a stat by one point. I felt pretty sure the numbers would go back up in most cases. Once the injury cleared up.

This, though.

This other guy's stats imploded. Acceleration 1, Pace 1, Stamina 1, Jumping 1. Basically, all stats relating to his physical well-being nosedived. I panicked. Had he died? "Holy fuck!" I shouted. I ran onto the pitch, ignored various perplexed and angry cries, and sped to where the guy was. His name was Simon, and the nutjob was trying to stand up. I should have been relieved that he was alive, but I was furious that he was wriggling around. Like a fucking worm! "Stay still you prick!"

"Who the fuck are you?"

"I'm House M.D., mate. I'm Doctor fucking Doolittle. Who gives a shit? Your leg is wrecked!"

"Fuck off. It's fine."

I looked around and didn't see any friendly faces. I'd run onto their pitch and ruined their game. "Who's captain on this team? Tell him to lie down. Jesus fuck." Blood was pounding in my ears. My hands were shaking. I must have hit the screen when I was running over here, because my phone had dialled someone. I hit red and typed 999.

"What's your emergency?"

"Ambulance! Need an ambulance. Platt Fields. The sport centre by Platt Lane."

"What happened?"

"Ah . . . playing football. Guy's broken his leg."

"Are you sure?"

Was I sure? I was the only one who seemed bothered. Even the guy himself didn't think he was hurt. I was—literally—out on a limb. The numbers, though. The curse. "I saw it," I lied. "The bottom of his leg just flopped backwards. It was horrible."

"God," said the dispatcher, under his breath. There was a lot of typing.

I hedged my bets in case I was about to make a complete fool of myself. "The guy is saying he's fine."

"That's the shock. The adrenaline."

"Can we move him?" If we could get him off the pitch, the rest of these pricks could keep playing. The very thought was repulsive. Why was continuing the game even a consideration? This guy would be on crutches for months. Maybe he'd lose his leg. Football? Who cared?

"Better not. We won't be long."

"We'll give him some painkillers or something?"

"Please don't. We'll be there soon. You can cover him with a jacket. Keep him warm."

"Get a jacket!" I yelled. "Keep him warm."

"Can you stay on the line until we get there?"

"Yeah. Sure. Yeah."

"Max? What's happening?"

It was Emre. He'd seen the commotion and had come running. "This guy. Broken leg."

"Shit," he said. He ripped off his jacket, knelt, and gently pushed it under the guy's ankle.

"Wait, is this real?" said some guy.

"He's fine," said someone else. "Piss off the pitch." He moved as though he wanted to haul Simon off the ground.

"Back the fuck away!" said Emre. He wasn't a big guy, but you'd think twice about starting a fight with him. The guy retreated, sullen-faced, bitter. Simon's so-called teammates were staring at me, full of resentment. Some team. This is what I had to sell to James Yalley? This was the Beautiful Game?

Emre seemed to know what he was about. He'd said something once about doing military service. I was glad to have him on the case. "I called an ambo. Can we do anything?"

"This is it. Just wait."

The next ten minutes were awful. There was a lot of muttering from most of the other players. Simon, the injured guy, had started off protesting that he was fine, but had gone quiet. His face was looking clammy. The ambulance turned up, drove all the way onto the pitch. The paramedic bros assessed him and got his leg into a brace. As they lifted him up and into the ambulance, the screams started. His teammates, finally, looked like they gave a shit. A couple tried to talk to me. I brushed past them.

"Emre," I said. "Buy me a beer?"

"Got to get back to work," he said. "Got to keep grinding." He patted me on the back a few times. "Well done," he said, and he jogged back to his stall.

I wandered off in a daze, directionless. I found myself at a chain-link fence, had to retrace my steps. Wherever I turned, there was football. I found a bench and sat, head in hands. I stared at the goalkeeper furthest from the ball. I got XP for that. Whenever the ball came in my direction, I looked away. I didn't want to see anymore player profiles turn red.

XP Balance: 812

Emma: Max. Are you okay? What happened? I heard you shouting.

Emma: Max?

Me: I'm fine. Let's talk tomorrow. I've just seen something really ugly.

34

MANCHESTER CITY UNDER-SIXTEENS

I didn't enjoy work that Friday. I spent the whole day feeling like I'd seen something twisted and grotesque, but I hadn't. Not really. I'd seen some numbers turn red. Simon's leg hadn't actually crumpled. Not visibly, anyway.

But I couldn't shake it off.

I went to the nearest supermarket and looked at their meal deals, but every option turned my stomach. I thought about going home early, but being alone with my thoughts wasn't going to help. After the lunch break, I tried to focus on the customers and their needs. Tried to help some people. Tried to keep them on the line, not to trash my own stats, but to have a constant flow of chat.

I got to the gym early and picked up twenty XP catching the end of the game before ours. It was two of the weaker teams, and both were highly motivated to score a rare win. Every time two players went into a fifty/fifty challenge, I winced. But nothing untoward happened.

The Met Heads came in from the changing rooms and dropped their bags by the side of the pitch. I didn't want to spend more time with them than necessary, so I stayed up in the highest row of seats and tried to look like I hadn't even noticed their arrival. Jackie and Ziggy turned up. Then came Mr. and Mrs. Yalley, and Kisi. But not James. I waved them to sit next to me, and we made small talk for a few minutes.

Then the last person I'd expected to see: Emre. He was clearly looking for me, so I went down to the sidelines. The referee signalled the end of the match I'd been watching. Our game would kick off in ten minutes. Something appeared in my vision. I willed it to become transparent for now.

"Max, mate," said Emre, shaking my hand. Since I'd met him, he'd started to say mate. Not sure why.

"Sup?"

"I wanted to tell you. That guy from last night. It was a bad break. Really bad. But he's gonna be okay. One of the lads came to find me, asked me to thank you. So."

I didn't know how to take the news. I suppose it should have been closure, but I knew it wasn't. "Okay. Thanks. We're about to beat Man City. Beth's team is. You gonna watch?"

He grinned. "Tell me you're gonna beat Besiktas, I'll come for that. But no." He rubbed his jaw. "Gotta keep grinding."

"Nasilsin," I said. He wanted to say something, but, with a shake of the head, he strode off.

Here they came. Manchester City. Speartip of a massive global sporting empire. Billions of pounds of reputation laundering, twenty years of planning, and lo, the culmination. The project, personified. The dreams of a desert nation given tangible form and shape in the lush evening mists of England's green and pleasant land. They came walking out of the changing rooms in their laser blue sweatshirts. Walking. Like the Ireland rugby team walking towards the All-Black haka. Walking subverted into a war dance. Walking as its own challenge. Confident. Calm. Badass. Invincible.

In my head, I'd built them up as enormous creatures. Twice as tall as the Wilmslow Mega Titans. Bayern Munich on stilts. Orc chieftains ruled by a large, floating she-brain.

What I saw was Coach Sandra and the seven dwarves.

I laughed at my own stupidity. These City girls were tiny. Teeny tiny tweenies. They were so young, they had probably all quit TikTok and were onto the new thing, the thing I'd hear about in about sixteen months.

But then they started passing a ball around, and I saw their profiles.

SARAH GREENE		
Born 4.10.2007	(Age 14)	English
Acceleration 6		
		Stamina 4
	Heading 1	Strength 3
		Tackling 2
	Jumping 3	
Bravery 3		Technique 13
	Pace 4	preferred foot R
	Passing 9	
Dribbling 12		
Finishing 4		
CA 14	PA 167	
Midfielder (Centre, Right)		

I'd been so pleased with myself for improving the Met Heads. Beth had gone from CA 1 to CA 3. Lula was on CA 2. As a squad, we'd added some passing, some technique. Gotten a little closer to City. Maybe enough to close the gap with my perks and my mad tactics. But City, the cheats, had been improving, too! Sarah alone had added two points in CA, and almost all her colleagues had done likewise. That was, like, totally not fair, man.

Jackie and the Met Heads wanted to talk to me, but I needed a minute. I went to the toilet and pretended to pee. Actually, I was frantically thinking. What could I do? Could I buy a perk? I didn't get a Match Overview or a tactics screen when managing these seven-a-side games, so the only real option was God Save the King. That was 3,000 XP, but I could go into debt to get it. And then what? Give Beth another point in heading?

Ludicrous.

I washed my hands and went to watch my friends get a fifty-minute lesson in why not to listen to Max Best.

While the Met Heads warmed up, Jackie offered his services as an assistant manager.

"Tommy Tactics and his Scouse Sidekick?" I said.

He wasn't keen on the name. "I was thinking Luke Skywalker and Han Solo, taking down the evil empire. Blasting the Death Star."

"Letting Princess Leia do all the hard work," said Beth, who'd come over to get some water.

"Do we need to get together before kick-off?" I said. In retrospect, I didn't know which one I was asking.

Beth said, "No."

Jackie said, "Yes."

I grinned at them. "I'll go with what Luke Skywalker says."

Beth nodded and went to gather the team. "I'm Han Solo," complained Jackie.

I tsked. "Han Solo is sexy, funny, and charming," I said, extending my arms to show that I was all of those things. "My instinct is to keep it simple for now. What do you think?"

He nodded. "They know what you want. It's just a question of how fast you want them to come out of the blocks."

The team were all in a semicircle. Everyone had come. I'd worried we might lose one to a babysitter crisis. "Ladies," I said. "First things first. Beth is the captain. This is me officially making Beth the captain. Beth? You're the captain. Come here." I'd gotten her a little captain's armband. I wasn't sure how to make sure the perk triggered and was covering all my bases. She wriggled like she was a cat, and I was trying to put a collar on her. "Fuck sake, Beth. This is important." She gave me a weird look and adjusted the armband. It suited her. She knew it. "Right. Let's get off to a solid start. Nothing fancy. Let them get into their passing routines."

Freyja said, "So are we starting with the false midfield?"

"No. Start 2-2-2, and I'll tell you when to switch."

"Got it."

"You remember it's important to disguise the tactic, right?" Lots of nodding. "At one point, I might ask Lula and Bella to sub off, and that's a cue to go all-out defence."

"Why?" said Beth.

"Their manager can only make radical changes at half-time, right? If we park the bus before half-time, she might think that's how we're going to play, and she'll react to that instead of the false midfield."

"Right," said Freyja. "I like that. Sneaky boy."

They were all grinning at me. Why? I was sure we were going to get thrashed.

"One last thing," I said. I pointed at Jackie. "The most important thing. Which *Star Wars* character is he?"

While the ladies took up their positions, laughing and joking, I let my eyes unfocus and concentrated on the thing I had made transparent. It was two large buttons in the left-hand side of my vision. Since I'd bought the Fantasy Football perk, they always appeared in the ten minutes before kick-off of matches where I was the manager (i.e. a couple of Met Heads fixtures but not the full-sized games where I'd taken over at half-time). The first one said TRIPLE CAPTAIN, and the other one was labelled BENCH BOOST.

I waited a second, just to check that this match was definitely going ahead. I only got these perks once per season and didn't want to waste them. You might think I was wasting them on a game I knew we'd lose, but it was one of those "promise to myself" situations. I had earmarked them for this game, so that was that. Also, I wanted to see them in action.

The referee was counting the players on each team. The clock and scores had been reset. This match was on like Donkey Kong.

I smashed both buttons and glanced over at Beth. Had I been expecting her armband to start crackling with eldritch power? Well, no, of course not. But yes, a little bit.

If anything was happening, it was invisible.

The referee blew her whistle, one midget passed the ball to another, and it was on.

The big game.

Big game? Big deal.

One thing was bothering me. "Jackie," I said, "What was that?"

"What? A load of girls who don't watch sci-fi trying to say I look like Jean-Luc Picard?"

"No, the whole vibe. They were, like, confident or something."

Jackie laughed. "You're so clueless sometimes. You piss me off more than anyone I've ever met. They're confident because you are."

"Me?"

"You're so calm. I've never seen you this calm. You're always a bit manic. Today you're talking slower; you've got all the time in the world. Why are you playing dress-up with Beth? Why are you using the team talk to make fun of me? Because you're so sure of winning."

Huh. "It's kind of the opposite."

His expression lost some of its usual wryness and went to his other favourite look, calculation. "Had *me* fooled. I don't get that from you at all." His attention went back to the pitch. "It doesn't matter. They think you're confident. You infected them." He visibly swallowed a joke. Bit his lip.

City were already into their groove. Zip zip zap. Lovely, balanced techniques. Control, pass. Control, pass. 2-3-1, but the ball was never going near their striker. She was growing confused. Something was wrong. City were dominating but achieving nothing.

I was almost tempted to leave things like this.

We weren't totally passive though. We stuck to our tasks. Didn't overreach. And when someone strayed from the plan, Freyja was very talkative. During breaks in play she'd discuss what had just happened with her teammates. She had a keen tactical mind, and she was trying to implement my theories within the 2-2-2 structure.

"Do you think I should have made Freyja the captain?" I asked Jackie, worrying that I'd misused my perk.

"I don't think it makes much difference," he said, looking around the sports hall. It wasn't exactly the World Cup final.

"As manager, it's one of about four things I get to choose. Freyja's the brain on the pitch. Maybe I should have picked her."

Eva was listening. "Beth's the captain," she said. "End of."

Jackie nodded. "Some players have an aura. You can make Freyja captain if you want. The rest are still going to look to Beth when the going gets tough."

Anna glanced over at me. "What's the armband for? Really?"

I grinned at her. "Probably nothing."

I was grinning because it was, indeed, probably nothing. The Triple Captain perk had, so far, done bugger all. Maybe the curse hadn't accepted Beth as the captain, because I didn't have a match tactics screen where I could select that. Or maybe Beth's influence attribute was one, and the perk had tripled it to 3. I didn't know. The grin was me being amused at myself for believing my own wild theories. But—and I was starting to see Jackie's point—Anna took the smile to mean I had a trick up my sleeve. She grinned back at me, excited to see my scheme pay off.

At that point, I was still perfectly calm.

One of us was experiencing the exact right amount of excitement. And, spoiler alert, it wasn't me. Because six minutes into the first half, everything went nuts.

35

FREE HIT

One of the reasons I wanted to use the Bench Boost perk in this game was the fact that it was rolling subs. Normally, in professional games you could bring on three substitutes and you'd do so with twenty minutes to go. (It had been bumped up to five subs for the 2022/23 season, but I wasn't sure if that would be permanent or if it would revert to three.) In short, the Bench Boost would have a nice impact at the end of one match. Great. Good to have.

But in this game, where the players kept coming off the pitch and returning a few minutes later, this was me using the perk in cheat mode. I made Beth come off for half a minute, then sent her back on. Soon, only Jane, the goalkeeper, didn't count—in my opinion—as a substitute.

I checked the wording of the perk:

Bench Boost. Your substitutes will play better in one game of your choice per season.

And . . . it seemed to be working. Maybe it was Jackie's mid-week coaching; maybe it was my languid charisma (born of secret despair); or maybe it really was the perk. But we seemed tighter and smoother. Defending was easier. We passed the ball nicely. Normally, City had about ninety percent possession in these games. Now, it was about seventy percent. We were competing.

I checked the other perk I'd used.

Triple Captain. Your captain's influence attribute will be tripled for one game of your choice per season.

I didn't know Beth's influence score, but it was probably high. Maybe it was fifteen, which when tripled, sent it higher than Gamestop shares. To the moon! Forty-five out of twenty. Or maybe her influence was twenty, I'd tripled it to sixty, and the curse capped it at twenty.

I thought I'd never know for sure, but Beth's performance made a pretty strong case for the former.

It was sometime around the fourth minute when City's top players realised something had gone awry and, to their credit, they stepped things up. They passed faster and ran harder. They tried to play 1-2s to progress the ball. They tried zipping the ball to their striker.

And Beth fucking made mincemeat out of everything they did. Any time a City kid got anywhere near her, she was on them in a flash, taking the ball away. Not desperate blocks or had-to-be-pixel-perfect interceptions; she was purring around her side of the defence like a jaguar. Complete control. Complete domination.

It's no exaggeration to say that by the sixth minute, City had realised the folly of attacking down Beth's side. Their pattern of play, quite simply, buckled.

My pulse added ten beats per minute.

I assumed that City's manager would figure out a solution, but in the meantime, wow.

And Beth's solidity led directly to the key incident.

City's striker came back to midfield to get a touch of the ball, then sprinted forward to get the return pass. Too late, she remembered the futility of attacking Beth, and she tried to put her foot on the ball and turn backwards. Instead, the ball squirted away from her. She basically wrapped the ball in a cute little laser blue ribbon and handed it to us.

Beth played one of the long, low passes we'd been doing in training. We didn't have three in attack, but Lula took a nice first touch and cut back inside while waiting for Anna to join the forwards.

But the frazzled City defender, a little oik called Meghan, kicked out at where the ball had been and crunched Lula's ankle.

Lula collapsed into a heap. I went apeshit.

Now a normal human man doesn't react like this. I know that. But visions of the leg-break from the night before had been tormenting me for almost twenty-four hours. Lula's numbers didn't go red, thank fuck, but I saw red anyway. A red mist. I raced onto the pitch to check on her, but Ziggy had beaten me to it.

The referee suggested I might want to leave the pitch. I glared at her. "Leave the pitch will I? Or what? Meghan will cripple me too?" I turned around and raised my voice. "Hey ladies, did you bring your spare ankles? Meghan's on the warpath." I looked up into the stand. "Kisi. Have you got your phone? Will you check Wish.com and see if they've got any bionic legs in stock?"

"Okay, Max," said Jackie, pulling me away. "Okay."

Ziggy carried Lula off, and Anna replaced her. I calmed some of the way down. "I'll check on her."

Jackie's voice was soft. Soothing. "Let me. You focus. Do it for Lula."

Do it for Lula. Win for Lula. Is that what he meant? That's what I heard.

I saw the FREE HIT button in my vision. The ref had given a free kick, I guess, though I hadn't heard the whistle. Beth was holding the ball like she meant to take a shot.

"Jane!" I shouted. "Take this free kick!"

Jane, the goalkeeper, gave me a weird look—what's new?—but jogged forward. Beth handed her the ball. I wanted to tell Beth to mark Meghan, but the Butcher of Platt Lane had already scuttled off the pitch and was trying to hide behind a bag of footballs.

I sledgehammered the free hit button. With Jane taking the shot, every outfield player was around City's penalty area; the space in front of the goal was packed. A forest of legs. The ball would probably be blocked, but with the ten percent free hit bonus, maybe it would deflect towards the goal. That was fine by me. For this indirect free kick to count as a goal, we needed someone to touch the ball after Jane struck it.

I didn't have the match commentary, but there's no mystery to what it would have said:

Jane steps up to take the free kick.

She strikes it low and hard.

It takes a big deflection.

And it's in!

GOOOOOAAAAAALLLLLLL!

My fists squeezed into little balls. I've never been a punch-the-air kinda guy, but I got pretty close just then.

The Met Heads celebrated, delighted for Jane. Her first ever goal!

I didn't give a shit. I wanted them back in position, so they could get back in City's faces.

Annoyed that they were happy, I turned to check on Lula. Jackie was fussing over her ankle. He said, "She's fine. She might get a bruise. She was pretty lucky." Ziggy pulled a weird face just then, but before he could say anything, Jackie asked him to pass the magic spray. Strange.

The game restarted at a new level of intensity. City were rattled. We were cruising.

Freyja subbed off. "Max? Is it time?"

Time for what? Oh. "Don't you want to continue like this?"

"No. I want to see how it goes."

I offered her a fist bump. "False midfield."

She bumped me. "False midfield."

She subbed back on and mumbled something to Eva, who would be our third striker. Then Nobby broke up a City move, kicking the ball out of play.

Freyja took a breath and yelled, "Come on, Beth Heads!"

Over to my left, Lula jumped to her feet. It was like the scene in *Back to the Future* where one moment Marty is dying and then the next he's absolutely fine. Upright, ready to play. Lula screamed, "Come on, Beth Heads!"

I swallowed, afraid to move. My eyes rolled, guiltily, of their own accord, towards Jackie. He returned my gaze with a little smile. He knew.

City knew, too. They shrunk. Now they were three feet tall. Tiny little specks on a map seen from a great height. We were Mega Titans.

To say that Beth had reacted well to the shout of Beth Heads would be an understatement. It was one thing coming from me. It was another thing coming from the team. She crunched into a tackle and left Sarah Greene flat on her arse. The referee brought her whistle to her lips, but for what? The tackle had been perfect. The whistle retreated. Beth passed the ball back to Jane, who hit our now-trademark low, hard pass towards the two strikers, while Eva sprinted forward to support them.

Anna ran to the right of the goal, and our plan was obvious to City's keeper: Bex would touch Jane's pass to Anna, who would then have a choice of shooting or passing to Eva, whose lung-bursting run was taking her to the far post.

City's keeper dashed off towards Anna, hoping to close down the angles. It was pretty impressive anticipation, to be honest. It actually annoyed me, because her good move was ruining our great move.

But Bex didn't pass to Anna. She pretended to. As the ball came to her, she moved her entire body towards Anna. The defender marking Bex followed her. Whatever happened, Bex wouldn't get a free shot.

She didn't need to shoot.

Bex allowed the ball to run under her foot, and with the defender following her and the goalie moving towards Anna, the ball simply continued forwards into the unguarded net.

I fucking punched the air like it owed me money. I gave a particular square foot of air the beating of a lifetime.

Jane had scored two goals!

The team celebrated like maniacs, and this time I was absolutely on board with it.

As we made our post-goal subs, I signalled to Freyja.

"Wrap this half up," I said. "Park the bus."

36

THE HALF-TIME TEAM TALK

Jane was in goal, alert in the D, the white, painted curve that defined the area where she was allowed to handle the ball. Six Beth Heads on patrol. Six rumbling, trundling forts forcing City players to go sideways and around. Tower defence on easy mode. The Maginot Line. None shall pass.

Beth defaulted to the right-hand side, where she'd been playing, but I moved her into the centre so that her aura would envelop everyone.

City passed the ball around for a couple of minutes, but as the timer ticked down to zero they started taking potshots. Weak, inaccurate, easily blocked, easily saved. It stank of desperation. Their manager was getting agitated, but mostly swallowed her feelings. She'd sort this mess out at half-time.

When was the last time one of her matches had gone this badly? She'd have to give a superb half-time team talk.

And to keep things going, so would I.

As the timer ticked down into the last twenty seconds, I spoke to Jackie. "Half-time speech. What should my vibe be? Churchillian? Technocratic? Funny?"

Jackie considered these choices. "Five minute break, isn't it? Let them switch off for a minute. All nice and calm." He rubbed his mouth. "Then it depends what you want. What mental state do you want them to start the second half in? You could pump them up, but that might cost you in the last ten minutes of the match. You might try to keep them cool-headed, but if City get a couple of quick goals, you might not be able to regain the intensity they've got now. There are always trade-offs."

I hadn't heard the buzzer, but the half had ended, and the team was gathering in our area. "Good half, my dudes. Take it easy for a minute." They sat on chairs or on the floor with one leg extended. Ziggy went round making sure they all had energy drinks and stuff. Just trying to be useful. Being supportive. He was strangely unconcerned about Lula's ankle. The referee came over and checked on her, which I thought was nice until I realised it was a scam to get some half-time refreshments. She left with an energy drink, an orange, and a couple of triangular sandwiches with the crusts cut off. She put them by her holdall, then went to see what she could rustle up from City.

Soon enough, it was time for my speech. I glanced over at City's manager, and she was going bonkers, slapping her hands, pointing at certain players, doing little hand-squiggles. If she was going down the high-energy route, it felt right for me to be more theoretical. More abstract. More *intellectual*. And quite right too. This was a *university* team.

Pleased that the right answer had come to me, I sucked in a lungful of air and felt the whole lot get expelled as a powerful hand slapped me on the back.

Astonished, I turned to see Mr. Yalley in his ill-fitting, off-colour suit. My eyes were drawn to his neck. It was very sweaty. He began babbling in his language, which Wikipedia says was probably called Akan. I say babbling, but it was more like haranguing. The ladies looked a bit taken aback, and I glanced at Jackie, wondering if he'd have my back in case I needed to drag Mr. Yalley away from the scene. I suspected the older man, despite being a good Christian and all that, could have absolutely battered me.

The Ghanaian paused, and his daughter, trying to look as small as possible, squirmed out from behind him and spoke. She was the centre of attention now as we all tried to understand what was happening and why. And she really, really didn't want the job.

"Um. Sorry about this. I've never seen him like this. Um. Sorry."

"What's going on, Kisi?" said Beth. She was perfectly relaxed. I got a hint of a vibe that this kind of thing happened to her a lot, and I didn't care for that feeling.

"Um. He's complaining about the taps."

"Excuse me?" said Anna.

"The taps. In the bathrooms."

"The faucets?" asked Lula. "In this gym?"

Mr. Yalley understood English much better than he spoke. He made a kind of tsk noise and patted Kisi on the shoulder. "Speak it," he said. "Say."

Kisi looked up at the ceiling and said, "When I came to this country, this is my father's words, you understand? When I came to this country, I knew there would be things I wouldn't understand. The five o'clock tea. Cricket. The TV show with the robots who can't go up the stairs. What's scary about that? But I never expected the taps. One is for the hot water. One is for the cold water." She paused to let her father speak some more.

I looked over at Sandra, the Man City manager. She was still very animated, but was giving tactical instructions now. The City kids were rapt. Something big was going on. The contrast with our team talk was . . . hilarious. Ours was light on the motivating and the tactics and surprisingly heavy on the plumbing.

"But," said Kisi, "the water comes out of separate holes. You cannot wash your face with warm water. It must be freezing hot or, oh, I've messed that up. He's still talking. I'll skip forward. This great empire, this great nation, and *these* are the taps. Surely, I thought, it is merely an eccentric situation unique to this one house. It cannot be everywhere like this. But it is. The taps? They are *confounding*."

There were many things that were confounding about this speech. One, that it was happening at all. Two, what's wrong with our taps? I'd lived in the UK for twenty-two years and never given them a second thought. Presumably, British taps were the best in the world.

Mr. Yalley shook his head, spoke, and his daughter translated. "Many other things are strange here. My daughter would not like me to list them—too right I wouldn't!—but one of the strangest to me is sports. Life is so tough. Raising a family is such a struggle. Living as a good Christian is so hard. Who has time for frivolous hobbies? For chasing a ball? But cut this country and it bleeds sports. Mr. Best said my Kisi could be a football player. I do not wish to stand in her way. But it is such a purposeless pursuit. I told her that life is short and time is precious, and she may serve God and her community in other ways. Follow the example of her brother."

Mr. Yalley's eyes narrowed, and he swallowed. "Kisi dragged us here this evening to make us watch the sports, and I do not remember being so surprised by anything in my life. Maybe the taps. Yes, this is second to the taps. The bad kick in the beginning." He pointed to Lula. "How you rallied around her. The speed of the play. The quality. Watching you compete has given me a rainbow of emotions. I am sweating. The tension is barely tolerable. My wife cannot watch. I could not watch the last five minutes." He laughed nervously, and pulled at his collar. He put his hands on his daughter's shoulders. "How do you have the courage for it? I was wrong. You are not frivolous. You are not a hobby. You are a *team*. A tribe. A nation. Captain," he said, saying the word in English while levelling his gaze at Beth, "if you will accept my daughter into your community, into your Beth Heads, I will be most proud."

Well, that took a turn. Kisi's voice had become more and more uncertain as she had translated. There was a major, major wobble on the word proud. But I knew Beth would ruin the moment by complaining about the name and pointing out that Kisi would have to go to uni to join them, that *Mr. Best* hadn't intended Kisi for *this*.

Beth stood tall. "Kisi Yalley. If you want to join the Beth Heads, there's one thing you need to agree to."

Kisi's eyes shone. Join the Beth Heads? Really? "What is it?"

"On Wednesdays, we wear pink."

"Okay."

Beth gestured. "Hug it out."

Kisi laughed and entered the hug. When it ended, she wiped away tears.

Beth eyed Mr. Yalley. "Sir, please leave Kisi here for the second half. We will take care of her. She is one of us now."

A few words were mumbled somewhere, then they grew louder, and were taken up by more of the players.

"One of us. One of us. One of us!"

Before long, all the Beth Heads, including their new mascot, were jumping around shouting "one of us." It was electric. Forget careful calibration of their emotional state. They were pumped. A rainbow of emotions was about to be blasted out—hot and hot—from all the taps.

The referee blew her whistle, and the entire squad invaded the pitch. A couple of City kids actually fell over. The referee started counting the number of players on both teams and, overwhelmed by the noise and the fuss, deemed everything in order. Lula made her wait. Beth pushed a couple of the surplus Met Heads to the side of the pitch, and the second half could begin.

Mr. Yalley slapped my back again. I smiled at him, but could just barely make my muscles move. I was drained. I flopped onto a seat, rubbed my face, and nearly missed the most extraordinary start to a half I'd ever seen.

37

A BLUE WAVE

We hadn't talked tactics, but so hyped were the players that they'd defaulted to the false midfield formation. 3-0-3. The problem was that City thought we were going to park the bus again, and they'd come out with a ballsy 1-2-3 concept. One defender, the abominable Meghan. Two midfielders, including Sarah Greene. And three forwards, although none of them were particularly formidable in that role.

Basically, City were going for it. Hoo-rah. If *you're* going to defend, *we're* going to attack. City, fuck yeah!

But City had kicked off the first half. Which meant we started with the ball in the second half.

Lula, somehow moving just fine on her mangled ankle, passed backwards to Freyja, who touched it to Nobby. She passed to Beth.

That's how long it took for City's kids to steam forward. Like a tidal wave, if you can imagine a *blue* wave. Pretty abstract stuff, I know.

Beth hesitated for half a second. I know what she was thinking. She was thinking "what the actual . . ." Because ahead of her, she saw three Beth Heads against one defender. Surely this was a trap? Regardless, she played a simple pass forwards to Lula. Lula took a touch and passed it sideways to the advancing Eva. Eva controlled and passed it diagonally left-forwards to Bex. Bex scored. City's goalkeeper didn't even move. Once the ball had gone past her, she stood and pointed. At what? I'd never know.

I looked up at the scoreboard. The referee pressed her little button, and the scoreline changed to 3–0. The countdown read 24:49. If we continued scoring at this rate, we'd win about 135–0. How's that for defensive football?

I heard Ziggy laugh, and he started singing.

"Park the bus, park the bus, Man United!"

It was a song City fans had sung to make fun of United at a time when City were so superior to us that all we could do was defend for ninety minutes and hope not to lose. (We lost anyway.) Now the song that rejoiced in *his* team's superiority over *mine* was sung to mark *our* team's superiority over *his*.

Wait, what?

Fuck it. I joined in too, and Jackie was way ahead of me. His contribution was to change one of the words. The three of us formed a triumvirate and bounced around in a circle.

"Park the bus, park the bus, Max United!

Park the bus, park the bus, I say!

Park the bus, park the bus, Max United!

Playing football the Max Best way."

The next five minutes were intense. Forget Mr. Yalley and his sweaty neck. Every inch of me was damp. I stopped prowling the touchline in case I left a trail, like a slug.

City didn't change their approach. 1-2-3 all day long, baby!

We were three goals to the good. What did we have to fear? We stuck with the false midfield.

So it was like basketball; we get a shot then you get a shot then we get a shot. The first crack in my plan came when City realised we were playing those long, low passes out of defence. City were starting to anticipate them, to get between the defender passing and the striker receiving. That was muy muy no bueno. I pointed this out to Jackie.

"Every strength is a weakness," he said. He meant that our strength had been turned into a weakness, but I misunderstood him. I thought he was giving cryptic advice. "Freyja! Beth! Guys! Loop those long passes! Bypass!" I drew a big parabola with my finger.

That worked. It worked muy muy yes bueno.

Beth blocks the pass.

She gathers the ball and plays a short pass back to the goalkeeper.

Jane chips it high and long.

Meghan and Lula compete for the ball.

It breaks loose.

Eva is on it like a flash! She shoots low and . . . it's saved! Great reflexes from the pint-sized shot stopper.

But the ball squirts loose. Right into the path of Lula. She reacted fastest!

GOOOOOOAAAAAAAALLLLLLLLLL

It was 4–0 and I was in dreamland. Delirious. Seriously, I was on some kind of substance-free high. You could have sold me a bridge.

Freyja came running up to me, gave me a shake. "What? What?" It's my only lie-in this week! Let me enjoy it!

"She knows," said Freyja.

Huh? I lifted my eyes and saw Sandra, City's manager, thundering instructions to her team. All the bad chemicals came flooding back. "Shit," I said. I replayed the goal in my head. Eva had been too far forward. She had given the game away. Not literally, I hoped.

"3-2-1," I said. "Match them up. Man-marking all round."

Freyja nodded and zoomed off.

Jackie shook his head. "They'll have to start dribbling if you do that."

Fuck. He was right. If we blocked every pass, they would have to start running with the ball. Argh! "Give me an option," I said.

"Keep doing the false midfield. Or just say fuck it, and play 3-0-3. Fuck the disguise. Go for broke."

I bit my nails. Maybe. Maybe we'd score two for every three that City scored. It didn't feel like much of a trade. "Ziggy, what do you think?"

"Could defend. Men behind ball."

"Yeah," I said. I liked it as a way to mess up City's flow. There was only one problem. "There's almost eighteen minutes left. We can't defend nonstop for eighteen minutes. Fuck." I looked over. "Sorry, Kisi."

She nodded at me, but she had the strangest look in her eye. "Play man-to-man, Mr. Best."

"What about when they start dribbling us?"

"It's like we agreed," she said. "If they do that, then we have won."

"From four-nil up, I'd hope for more than a moral victory," I said.

"Trust in God, Mr. Best," she said. "Have faith."

So that was pretty much the least helpful thing anyone had ever said to me. With a slight groan, I watched as City's keeper got the ball.

She had no one to pass to. Every time a City player dropped towards her, one of ours was shadowing her. So City's keeper moved a little bit further forward and then a little bit more. Meghan, the hooligan, turned out to have half a brain, and she moved to the other side of the pitch. Our player followed, and so City's keeper had a free path to the halfway line. She got there and waited. We weren't stupid enough to attack her, but we couldn't track every movement every time. Sarah Greene broke free of Nobby and was passed to. She faked to lay the ball off, did a tiny move past our Japanese defender, and burst forward. Jane, though, had been on high alert. She flew out of her D and booted the ball into touch. It flew at about eight million metres per second . . . right at me. I languidly angled a shoe, tapped the ball downwards, and let it bounce up into my hand. Meghan raced towards me to get the ball and take the kick-in. I hid the ball behind my back and said, "Not you."

Meghan looked uncertain, but she was by far the closest City player to the ball.

The referee blew her whistle at me.

With a cheeky grin, I handed the ball to Kisi. I held my hands up and backed away. *All good! We're all having a lovely old time!*

Kisi was about to hand Meghan the ball, but at the last second she hesitated. With a big frown, she said, "Meghan, why doesn't your coach give you instructions? Does she not like you?" And she relinquished the ball.

Meghan—God knows what was going on in her head—placed the ball on the touchline and kicked it backwards, blindly, towards her goalkeeper. Lula was inches away from intercepting! City's keeper had better acceleration, though, and kicked it away.

Kisi smiled at me. The sweetest smile you ever did see. She turned away and clapped her hands. "Come on, girls!"

Jackie gave me one of his looks.

Freyja tweaked my tactic. Saved me from myself. She instructed Lula to goalhang, to make sure City always had someone to pass to, like we'd discussed. It slowed the tactical arms race, helped us run the clock down. Every time City passed, we got closer to victory.

But that was the high-level view. Close-up, it was wild. A complete slugfest. City got two low-quality shots at goal; we got one half-decent chance to break. Our legs were slowing. Our defenders were starting to make little mistakes. Nothing critical, but the emotional investment was taking its toll. Just as Jackie had predicted. It was my turn to give *him* an appraising stare.

Twelve minutes to go. Still winning 4–0. City were pushing, still sticking to plan A. I found the stubbornness thrilling. Their philosophy was: there's a right way to play football, and we're going to keep doing that. Insane. Insipid. Inspirational.

Pass pass pass. Zip zip zop.

Eleven minutes to go. City made a mass substitution. The same tactics with slightly worse players. Hilarious! But the new batch were fresher, ran harder, pushed us back. We didn't give them space to shoot. They had three low-quality shots, four, five. And suddenly they were out of ideas. Why wasn't it working?

We weren't very threatening when we got the ball. Our attackers had sprinted much, much more than usual and were running on fumes. But I tried to keep two players up the pitch. City had to keep at least two defenders back just in case. It helped.

Ten minutes to go. Bex and Bella combined to cut out a run-of-the-mill City attack down our left. They screamed as they high-fived each other. Total commitment.

Nine minutes to go. The first sign of real danger. Sarah Greene, City's pocket dynamo, got the ball and looked for someone to pass to. The only options were backwards, but she was done retreating. She was rebelling against her programming! Ban all robotics research immediately!

Greene switched the ball onto her right foot and danced forwards. She dropped a shoulder and took Freyja out of the game. So easy. It was beautiful. She had a shot lined up. Nobby came to block it. The shot never came. When Nobby looked up, Greene had already dribbled around her, and now she was one-on-one with Jane.

Greene is on a mazy dribble. She beats two players . . .

She shoots low and hard towards the near post.

But the goalkeeper flicks out a foot. Deflects it onto the post!

The ball rebounds to Greene . . . but she puts it over!

A lucky break for the Met Heads.

Weirdly, Beth took that as her cue to sub off.

She grabbed some water and drank deeply. Then she pulled me away from Jackie and jabbed me in the chest.

"Tell me you aren't going to quit if we win."

"What? No, I'll do the rest of the season, if you aren't sick of me. I do *actually* like you."

"I don't mean that, you cock. You said you'd quit your job if we won this game. I don't want that shit on my head. Take it back."

"Take it back?" I scoffed. Like we were ten-year-olds. Even the City girls wouldn't talk like that. But Beth was super intense. Her glare could have melted a goalpost. "You're serious."

"I *am* serious, Max. You want to become an agent? Seems like it'll suit you. But you're not there yet. You need money. How are you going to survive the winter if you need fifty quid from me? It's not even October. If you want to quit your steady job and starve to death, do it on your own time. Don't involve us in it."

Fair dos. And she was right. I still needed the income. "Okay. I hear you." She relaxed a bit. I added, "Don't think we're going to hold out, anyway."

She jabbed me in the chest again, really quite hard. "Don't you fucking talk like that, Max Best. Bella, sub!"

And she raced back onto the pitch, in midfield. When I'd met her, she was a striker. I'd moved her into defence. Midfield? What was she doing?

38

FIVE GOALS
IN SIX MINUTES

Six minutes to go. Still ahead by four. But the clock was starting to drag. Time stretching. Maybe the City manager had her own curse with her own perks. "Fergie Time," perhaps, named after the legendary Man U manager Alex Ferguson who won so, so many games with late, late goals.

And City scoring five goals in six minutes was more than possible. We were all past our limits. Lula was struggling to get a tune out of her body. Nobby's head was bobbing up and down like she'd been in a mosh pit a couple of hours too long. Freyja was trying to conduct, but she was always a beat behind.

In the blue corner, Sarah Greene was a one-man band. She was thumping a drum, crashing a cymbal, wibbling the harmonica, and noodling a keytar. She was freestyling the lyrics, rap battling against all and sundry, harmonising with herself, dedicating her EGOT to Jesus and her parents.

The rest of her team were quietly singing "bom bom biddly bom" in the background. If they'd been raptured up to heaven, the game would barely have changed.

Beth was watching Greene. Tracking her, staying five yards away. Was Beth past her limits? In a way, yes. Greene got the ball and started yet another dribble. Beth adjusted her armband.

It's Greene again. She is unstoppable today! She moves forward. Anna tries to block. Greene leaves her for dead.

Freyja comes over to make a challenge. She is looking fatigued.

Greene nutmegs her.

Freyja gains ten humiliation points. From this moment on, she will never be able to find true happiness.

Greene spins past Beth. Nobby is the last man. She does well to delay the attacker.

Greene shapes to shoot.

But she's fouled!

A really poor challenge from behind.

Greene was crumpled up on the floor, clutching her ankle. Beth was explaining to the referee that the City trickster was just too fast; it had been accidental. Hmm, I thought.

The referee, and I was really starting to like this girl, showed Beth the yellow card. One more of those, and she'd be sent off. And that would be the end of that. No way we could defend if City had an extra man. Beth couldn't commit that sort of foul again.

The City manager signalled that Greene should sub off. But she said no, she wanted to keep playing. Actually, I'm pretty sure she just wanted to take the free kick. There are some players who are like that. Their team gets a free kick or a penalty, and they are just drawn to the ball like bored shoppers to a half-decent busker.

Greene didn't leave the pitch, but she did, at least, hobble to the edge to get some magic spray. And Beth went over to apologise. Let me try that again. Beth went over "to apologise."

Beth put her arm around Greene's shoulders and leaned a bit closer.

I don't know what she said.

You don't know what she said.

But we both know what she said.

Greene turned a bit paler, and suddenly she didn't want to take the free kick. The one-man band reverted to being just another cog in the machine.

Five minutes to go. City's manager was about to make her last big change. Carmen, City's worst player, was primed and ready. A disaster waiting to happen. But Sandra had her principles, and one was that every player played every game. Admirable. But dude. Not today.

I stared at Sandra. Tried to telepathically beg her not to do it. In her current mood, Beth would chomp Carmen's head off.

Amazingly, Sandra looked over at me. I shook my head. Sandra frowned, I think, but slapped Carmen on the back, and the kid sprinted on.

Even more amazingly, when Carmen stepped onto the pitch Sophia was next to me. Just like in the first game between the sides. What were the odds? "Oh!" said Sophia, slapping her forehead. "That's why you were being so weird."

"What?" I said, fooling no one.

"Back in the first City match. I thought you were autistic. But you wanted us to press that one. Why didn't you *say*?"

"What do you mean? She's no better or worse than the rest of them."

Sophia stretched her leg behind her back. "I know you a little bit, Max. Your poker face needs work."

"What's all this?" said Jackie.

"Max wants us to attack that girl who just came on," said Sophia. She stopped stretching and looked up at me. "Don't you, Max?"

Did I? I looked around. To the right was Jane, who'd scored two goals and risked harm throwing herself at every shot. To the left was Kisi, wondering what I was going to say. Ahead was Beth, who'd brutally put paid to the Sarah Greene show. And up above, the scoreboard read 4–0. That would be a good result, wouldn't it? Hadn't I asked enough of these women?

"Sweep the leg," I said.

"Yes!" said Kisi, punching the air.

"Okay but what?" said Sophia.

She hadn't seen *The Karate Kid*. What a world. "Swipe left," I said. "Push her in a puddle, and steal her lunch money."

"Yeah, okay, okay," she said. "I'll do it."

"No," I said. "Get Beth to do it."

There isn't a lot to say about the next phase. City's goalie passed to Carmen, and Beth pounced on her like a mountain lion from a trampoline. Beth took the ball, moved closer to goal, and hit a weak shot. The goalie collected it and waved at her team to breathe, to slow down, to be calm.

"Beth," I said, subbing her off. She was knackered. They all were, but I needed Beth's aggression in reserve in case someone else started dribbling us. Nobody did.

The game slowed to a crawl. It was done. City had lost. We'd won. We had a couple of minutes to think about it. To let it sink in.

With twenty seconds left, Sarah Greene took the ball, went on a mazy dribble, and shot. It went wide, and then she subbed off for the last few seconds. Just in case.

I felt sorry for her. She just wanted to play. To pass the ball, control the game, and win, sure, but also to dribble, to do tricks, to shoot. And it wasn't just defenders kicking her that made her think twice; it was her coaching. She was being coached against her natural inclination. Would that make her a better player in the end? I mean, probably, yeah. But it would also make her a more antiseptic player. Lifeless. It was such a shame. If Beth hadn't threatened to send her home in an ambulance, would she have treated us to a wonderful display of dynamic, breezy forward play? Probably. Would we have lost? Probably.

I still would have liked to see it.

And then the buzzer went.

The Beth Heads tried to go tonto, but they were so utterly spent all they could really do was cheer and then flop to the floor. The next set of players would need to wipe the playing surface with towels or they'd slip everywhere.

Jackie gave me a little pat on the shoulder and went off to chat to Freyja. Ziggy hugged Lula. They kissed. Was that their first? It didn't look like it. Beth came and sat cross-legged in front of me.

"Well, Max. You did it."

"I couldn't have done it without your help," I said. Magnanimously.

She laughed. "You little shit." She flopped onto her back and closed her eyes. We stayed like that for a moment. The City players were quietly gathering their kit and shuffling towards the changing rooms. Their manager looked shell-shocked. Beth, eyes still closed, said, "Do you remember when I said this was impossible?"

"Yes."

"But it *was*."

Another moment. I wrung my hands. "Do you think I should apologise to their manager?"

Eyes popped open. "What the fuck for?"

"You know," I said. "The stuff." *The stuff I made you do.*

Beth narrowed her eyes at me. "You're doing it again, Max. If I had any energy left I'd beat the shit out of you." She lay back. Her breaths were slowing. "When we met, you were pretty obnoxious about women's football. But when you watched us, you really watched us. When you coached, we felt coached. I *know* you paid Jackie to come and train us. I'm one thousand percent positive you've got an ulterior motive, but I don't give a shit. I want to be treated seriously, and this is the one part of my life where you, Max Best, treat me absolutely seriously. And you treated those Man City kids like the four horsemen of the apocalypse and their manager like the devil herself. You came up with a plan and pushed us and got in our heads and we beat them. We fucking beat them. They won't be happy right now, but at some point they'll realise that the lot of us spent three fucking weeks preparing for tonight, and they'll be thankful someone took them seriously enough to do that. I know I would." She had turned away from me, and now she wiped a hand around her eyes. Suddenly, she was upright, and in my face. Jabbing a finger at me. "If you apologise for that, I'll never speak to you again."

I licked my lips. "Aye, aye, Cap'n."

That reminded her. The armband. She ripped it off and waved it in front of my face. "And this? I'm keeping this," she said, and stormed off towards the changing rooms.

As she flounced away, I saw something strange. Sandra was talking to Jane. Their manager and our keeper. A combination of people I'd never expected to see! I briefly wondered if they were related or something like that. It was possible.

Sandra walked away. I caught Jane's eye, and she came over. "What was that all about?" I said.

"Oh," Jane said, as she pressed a football between her gloved hands. "City's manager said I scored two goals and that was as good as a hat trick for a goalkeeper. So she gave me the match ball."

"You deserve it," I said. "You were fantastic. And a clean sheet too!"

"Yeah," she grinned. She wandered off, bouncing the ball a few times.

City's manager. Class act. Jesus Christ.

The Yalleys took Kisi home. Mr. Yalley wanted a big chat, but I promised to meet them after church on Sunday. Jackie, Ziggy, and I waited around the reception area. I wanted to go home and sleep—I was wrecked—but that was out of the question. It was pub or eternal social leperdom. I'd started the City mania. I had to be there.

The City kids dribbled past in ones and twos. Many had earbuds in, and some wore massive, garish headphones like the pros. I wasn't sure if they had a big team bus that drove them round, or a minivan or what. When the kids went by, I tried to blend into the wall. But when Sandra and Meghan came through at the same time, I felt myself darting forward.

"Oh, Sandra," I said.

She gave me a fairly cold look. Probably not amused that I'd been dancing around singing songs about myself. Fair comment. "Max, wasn't it?"

"Yes. Quick thing. Can I apologise to Meghan, please?" Neither of them had been expecting that. Meghan had taken out one Airpod, and now she took the other one out too. I was trying to rush through, like ripping off a plaster. Which, by the way, is stupid, and I never do. I looked at the girl. "Last night I was watching a match here and saw a really bad leg break. It put me on edge. So when you did that foul I lost my mind. But it wasn't really about you, and you don't deserve that. So I'm sorry."

Meghan didn't know what to say, so she said nothing. She did a sort of half shrug.

Sandra must have been a teacher. She just *must*. What she said next was genetically hard-coded into all teachers, everywhere. "Meghan, do you have anything to say?"

"No," she said. "I don't really believe him."

"Oh," I said. "That's fine. I wanted to apologise, and I've done it."

Sandra thought this was a teachable moment or whatever, and she dragged it out. "Max, did you really see a broken leg?"

I pulled my phone out and showed them the fourteen-minute call I'd made to 999.

"Oh," said Meghan. "Okay. Soz."

"Nah," I said. "It doesn't matter if I saw the leg break or not. I still shouldn't have lost my shit. It was bang out of order."

Sandra was very happy with how this little exchange had gone. "Wonderful," she said. "And fortunately, the girl you fouled was able to run it off. A generous helping of magic spray, yes?" She laughed and started towards the exit.

"Yeah," said Meghan. She started putting her earbuds back in and got ready to pull her hoodie up. "Also the fact that I didn't even touch her."

Her words chilled me.

I didn't even touch her. Where had I heard something almost identical to that quite recently?

I stared at Jackie and Ziggy. The tension ratcheted up to unbearable levels. My body was ready to act even if my brain needed a few more seconds to check my workings.

Those *bastards*! They'd let me believe Lula was really injured! They'd helped to wind me up so that I'd, what? Be more entertaining?

As soon as I clenched my fists, Ziggy scrambled to his feet and ran back into the main hall. Jackie zoomed towards the front door.

It didn't matter. The only question was which one I was going to murder *first*.

39

SHOCKTOBER

Saturday October 1.

I didn't murder my friends but I did murder a couple of pints. Woke up feeling really happy. At one with the universe. Not thinking about grinding and hustling, just enjoying the morning for what it was. Nice cup of tea. Toast where the butter melted perfectly. Then a short walk to the shops, not because I needed anything but just to be outside and see a couple of trees and clouds and birds.

I had new cursemail, but I didn't open it right away. It wasn't going to make me happier. Let me enjoy this one little morning. K? Thanks.

By lunchtime, I was ready. I clicked on the envelope and saw I had three messages. One was the monthly update. So far, these hadn't been interesting, but now? Now I'd beaten Manchester City Ladies Under-Sixteens. Now I was kind of a big deal.

Your Reputation in England: Unknown

Your World Reputation: Unknown

XP: 936

So obviously "unknown" was actually the highest level. Because mate. My victory over those little kids was a thousand times more impressive than Greece winning the European Championships or Leicester winning the Premier League or the UK getting a point in the Eurovision Song Contest. Come on! *Unknown?* That's taking the piss!

Jokes aside, I did wonder what the function of reputation was. Would being "renowned" help me get jobs at elite clubs? Was reputation the *only* consideration? And how granular did this go? Did I have a reputation score with FC United? Would I get reputation points that afternoon at Oldham if I was charming? Could it go negative if I was a dick? Did I have a reputation score with individuals like Jackie? If yes then surely I had a reputation score with everyone, not just football people. Because what if they *became* football people? People like Emma, for example. With her, my score was certainly sliding since I hadn't texted or called since the leg break incident.

Well, Arsenal were about to play Tottenham in today's lunchtime match, and I could message her then.

The next mail listed my recent achievements.

New Achievements: Winner Winner Chicken Dinner; Winning Streak 1; Master of the Dark Arts; Pitch Invader

Pretty basic stuff. The first was because I'd won a game. The second was for winning one game *in a row*, a concept that annoyed me even if I understood why it was needed. Master of the Dark Arts was awarded because the curse, weirdly, blamed ME for Lula's dive, for Kisi's mental disintegration tactics, and for Beth's shithousery. Mate! That claim wouldn't stand up in court. Pitch Invader was given because I'd run onto the pitch when Lula was fouled. Like the others, it came with one experience point. That made me uncomfortable. I shouldn't have done it, and I shouldn't be rewarded for it.

The last mail detailed the monthly perk special offer.

Seasonal Special Offer

New perk collection available to buy until the witching hour on All Hallow's Eve: Shocktober

Cost: 2,777 XP

Effects: Increases your chance of winning when playing a team with higher reputation in the month of October. This special offer contains three mini-packs: Expected Ghouls; The Full Protonic Reversal Pack; A Nightmare on Filbert Street.

This perk was a sort of selection box bursting with mini-perks which, cumulatively, would help me win games in October, but only in October, and only against stronger teams. It was basically a long series of ghastly Halloween puns. More on that later.

I drove to Oldham (population two hundred thousand). It was a half an hour drive, but I wanted to be mega early 1) just in case, and 2) to get a feel for the town. The latter didn't take long. Oldham was like most of Greater Manchester. Lots of red brick terraces. Lots of walls with gaps, pavements with weeds, faded signs, black wrought iron gates, the general vibe that if every human vanished, the place would be covered in damp, squidgy moss within a season.

I popped into a cafe and bought a sausage and cheese bap. That was three pounds. Tea was a pound. The cheese was smothering the sausage, drowning it, but the cheese's stickiness and viscosity meant it never left the soft bread. It was like a wizard made it. It was incredible. The tea blasted the roof of my mouth with the force of a tactical nuclear warhead. I wanted to stay and gulp the stuff down until I started getting caffeine headaches, but I restrained myself.

My phone shook. A long-distance text! All the way from the far, far, north.

Emma: I don't know what's happening but that was a great goal!

I checked. Arsenal had scored and were winning 1–0.

More interesting than the scoreline was Emma contacting me first. Could this day get any better?

Me: I'm missing it. I'm on a scouting mission in deepest, darkest Oldham. They're going to put me in the special scout seats. I'm a VIP now. No big deal.

Me: Are you joining in the conversations? Are they impressed?

Emma: No, I'm too shy. I thought I understood what you said, but it's all just a mess. They run too fast!

Me: Be brave. Ask the one with the best tats if he thinks there's going to be a St. Totteringham's Day this year.

Emma: Why do I feel like you're inviting me to a fancy dress party, but I'll be the only one dressed up?

Me: St. Totteringham's Day. I promise.

Emma: Oh God.

That was it for a while. I went looking for info about the Oldham squad. The recent history of the team was a complete mess. There was a video on YouTube called "The Worst Run Football Team in the World," all very bleak, but they had a new owner and a new start, and I was really only interested in the here and now. What players they had, what players they needed. I found a fan podcast called *The Boundary Park Alert System,* and listened to that while I worked.

Emma: The Brazilian players are kicking each other!

I laughed. I bet they were.

Me: Did you say anything?

Emma: No. I'm sure I'll say it wrong.

There wasn't a ton I could learn about Oldham online. There were websites like Transfermarkt that had good stats for famous players, but this far down the English pyramid, it was all a bit sparse. I'd learn more in the first ten seconds of the match than in ten hours of trawling the net. The podcast was good though. I quickly got a feel for the mood of the fans.

I put my phone away for a bit and concentrated on the Shocktober perk. The first batch of mini-perks had been grouped under the name Expected Ghouls. That was a pun on the new data analytics term "expected goals."

The first mini-perk was called Ghoulkeeper, which should give you a clue about the standard of pun work on display. Who was writing this stuff? Polish Nick? The guys who tossed off the scripts for season eight of *Game of Thrones* in one hungover afternoon? I felt my skull heating up, so I took a few deep breaths and let it go. In the end, it didn't matter. I'd buy the perk, or I wouldn't.

Expected Ghouls

This pack contains the following mini-perks:

Ghoulkeeper - Goalkeepers will perform better in one-on-one situations.

Grim Sweeper - Players set in the sweeper position will play better.

The Mummy - Wrap a player in bandages to give him/her +1 influence.

The Invisible Manager - Opposing players are slightly less likely to see or hear instructions from their managers.

Goblin Up Chances - Provides a random chance for a striker to gain a brief boost to finishing.

It's Not Over Yeti - Provides a slight chance that the referee will allow the game to continue up to 90 more seconds if you have a chance of scoring an equaliser or winner.

Frankenstein Is the Doctor Not the Monster - Referees will make decisions in a fussy, pedantic manner. Activation optional.

These were mostly self-explanatory, I hope. A couple of things, though. First, I didn't have access to any formations that used a sweeper. Presumably, if I kept gaining XP I would unlock more formations. But if I kept buying these perks it would be slow going. Second, the whole thing was full of terms like "slight" and "brief." Third, the Frankenstein one was very, very appealing. Why? Because it said activation *optional*. Which meant I'd get a button before kickoff in games where this perk was in effect. So if I was—and this is just an example and not something I had started to *regularly* daydream about—the manager of Manchester United, and we were about to play Man City, then if this button appeared in my vision, I'd know for sure that City were rated higher by the curse. Not only that, but I'd know that the other mini-perks were taking effect. It made me slightly more likely to buy Shocktober, because without something concrete like this, I wouldn't know if anything was happening and would always wonder if I'd wasted my XP.

Emma: Oh, God. I tried to be brave. It didn't go well.

Me: What happened?

Emma: I used the word protagonist. None of them know it. Now they think I'm pretentious.

Me: Pretentious? That's a big word. No wonder they think you're pompously grandiloquent.

Where was I? Slightly more likely to buy the perk. Yes. Increasing from about zero percent to about one percent. The simple fact was that I was still vanishingly unlikely to ever manage a pro football team. But but but. Last night's evisceration of Man City had done something to me. It wasn't quite like the scene in *The Matrix* where Morpheus says "he's beginning to BELIEVE," but it was in that direction. I could do it. I could. I'd outfoxed Neil with his own players. I'd got a tune out of Moss Side Celtic. And I'd frazzled the floating megabrain that managed Man City.

A few years as an agent. Gaining financial freedom. A few years networking. Getting to know people in the business. A few years coaching Beth's team and maybe some Sunday League. Building a reputation. Then getting a chance to manage FC United. Or Oldham.

Why not?

Still, though. Spending nearly 3,000 XP on this perk seemed mad. It was about EIGHTEEN evenings of watching Powerleague games. The effects seemed minuscule, and even if I found myself in charge of a real team, Shocktober would only be useful for ONE month a year, and only against stronger teams.

Oh. Except for the teams listed in the second collection.

The Full Protonic Reversal Pack

In addition to improving your chances against teams with higher reputation, your Shocktober mini-perks will also always work against the following teams:

AFC Bonemouth

Creepy Crawley

Dreading

Frighten and Hove Albion

Ghöstersunds FK

Ipswitch Town

Minotaurino

Plymouth Gargoyle

Rottingman Forest

Scareborough Athletic

Sheffield Wednesday

Shuddersfield Town

Werewolves

Wraith Rovers

Demented. Three of these teams didn't even play in England. What were the chances I'd manage a team that was playing a European match—in October no less—against Raith Rovers (Scotland), Torino (Italy), or Östersund (Sweden)? As for the others, they were spread out over many divisions, so the chances were slim that I'd be in the same league as a particular team and that our fixture would be scheduled in October. This section was basically worthless.

Oh, oh, oh! And what was Sheffield Wednesday doing on the list? That wasn't a pun. That was just the name of the team.

I shook my head and left the cafe. Started to head towards the stadium. It was a strange place. From outside, it didn't look like much. There was a fairly low wall, behind which some large floodlights stood. They were the only real proof that there was a stadium there. I walked around, and from the next side, with the brown brickwork and the dark blue Oldham Athletic sign, you'd have thought you were going into an old hospital.

A receptionist greeted me, and bade me sit. While I waited for Bill Brown, Oldham's hospitality guy, I looked around at the historic shirts from the club's past, and re-read the last little group of mini-perks. They dealt with more "environmental" factors and raised a LOT of questions.

A Nightmare on Filbert Street

This pack contains the following mini-perks:

Cauldron of Noise - Your stadium is turned into a theatre of

screams. The home fans will be noisier and more intimidating.

Silence of the Lahms - Your opponent's stadium is turned into a library like Highbury. The home fans will be quieter and less intimidating.

The Ken Bates Motel - Opposing teams who play at your home stadium will have a restless night, causing their players to start the match with slightly reduced fitness.

Gremlins - Provides a slight chance that when losing away from home, a brief floodlight failure will give you time to reorganise your team.

Murder on Zidane's Floor - Play a 2001 megahit from the musical temptress Sophie Ellis-Bextor to receive a team-wide morale boost.

Where to even start with *this* shit? Probably with the fact that the curse was offering to change the mood of thousands of thousands of people! And mess up the sleep patterns of various hard-working professionals. And its taste in music was . . . actually, its taste in music was impeccable. No problem with that. But I did have a problem with the other stuff. How would any of it even work?

It seemed like the curse wouldn't actually need to make one set of fans more fervent or dampen the spirits of another set. It could simply tamper with what was heard by the players on the pitch. Sort of twist the volume button. And the hotel thing might just involve slicing a couple of fitness points off the players, not *actually* sending ghosts into their bedrooms or whatever. It was just a flowery description from some hack writers. Right?

I thought about it some more, but my head didn't heat up. That was odd. It was like the curse didn't mind me speculating about this set of mini-perks the way it had minded about the first set. When I started to speculate about why my head heated up sometimes and not others, my head started to heat up.

Fortunately, Bill Brown came to reception and escorted me up into the main stand. Along the way, he got stopped by another member of staff, allowing me time to check and reply to the message I just received.

Emma: I gave it a go, but I think I still don't like football.

Me: Understandable. But one last try! Get one of your beefcakes to take you to St James' Park to watch Newcastle. Watching it live is totally different.

Bill finished giving instructions and brought me to my seat. He promised to come and check on me at half-time. I thanked him and felt another vibration.

Emma: I want you to take me.

Me: Okay.

Me: And then we'll go to the football?

Emma: *blushing girl emoji*

Emma: You're such a protagonist.

Me: Do you like Halloween?

Emma: I love it!

Ugh. Well, nobody's perfect.

40

OLDHAM ATHLETIC

My seat was a normal plastic fold-up deal, like every other one in the stadium, but there was a nice open space behind it that made it seem more premium. It made me think of those headstones that are set apart in a graveyard. *That guy*, you think, must have been a big deal. The view was great too: just to the right of the halfway line, not so low that my view was blocked, not so high that I had to walk up loads of stairs like a pleb. Bury me here, and I promise not to haunt you. Deal?

The match kicked off, and I was bombarded with information. First, the attendance. There were still people filing into the stadium and finding their seats, but it was busy! This was non-league football, so I'd expected about two thousand fans, but there seemed to be way more than that. Later, I'd find out that the official attendance was around 9,500. Wow! Oldham was a pretty big club. Or was this atypical, and there was a bumper crowd to see Wrexham? That made no sense. Wrexham? That little town in Wales? What? Anyway, the place was bursting with movement and energy. Hearty songs, lusty chanting, ear-slapping claps.

Next, the levels of CA among the players. Oldham's average was about sixty, while Wrexham's was about ninety. That meant Ziggy, if he reached his potential, could play for Oldham. Could survive in the fifth tier. That was very, very nice to know! In the "Worst Run Team in the World" video, the YouTuber said that one Oldham player had been paid twelve thousand pounds a week. That had been when they were in the fourth tier with their previous spendthrift owner, but still. That was only a couple of years ago. Some of football's riches found their way down here.

Imagining Ziggy on twelve thousand pounds a week made me hot and bothered, not in a bad curse way, but in a good Emma way. I tried to calm myself down, but just as I was getting frisky, a raven-haired girl appeared next to me, bending down solicitously. She was very pale, and her breasts were pushing hard against the black buttons of a crisp, white shirt. The effect—pale, innocent beauty keen to be ravaged by a naughty vampire—was ruined by an Oldham-branded nametag: *Caroline: Happy to Help*. She bent even further and checked a little notepad she was carrying. When she looked at it, her neck was exposed to me. That *had* to be deliberate. "Are you Max Beth?"

"Yes," I said, smouldering at her quite by accident. Honest.

Weirdly, maximum Max had zero effect. She simply put a tick next to my name. "Welcome to Boundary Park. Not a lot of agents brave enough to come here these days. Have you got any food allergies?"

"Pineapple on pizza."

She wasn't amused. "Sir, I need to tell the kitchen staff if you have allergies."

Right. Health and Safety legislation. And I'd broken one of my personal rules for life: never flirt if they're paid to talk to you. I got it together. "No allergies. But why are you asking?"

"You're getting the two-course meal. Didn't Mr. Brown tell you?"

"Jesus, really? That's awesome. Wow." Oldham Athletic! Legendary! I had a sudden dread that at some point, someone would ask me for money. For the ticket and the food. That was why I'd asked Beth to lend me fifty quid, just in case. But I was still in such a good mood that any embarrassment suffered here would have just slid off me. So I ripped the plaster, which, as a reminder, you shouldn't do unless it's a *metaphorical* plaster. "Do I have to pay something? I might need to find a cash machine or whatever."

Her eyebrows quivered. She hadn't been expecting that. "No, sir. It's all complimentary. Half-time refreshments are included, and there's a cash bar after the match."

I'd made a necessary mistake, like when a player fouls an attacker and gets a yellow card but buys his team time to regroup. "At Chelsea they gave me a prosecco, and then sent me a bill," I lied. "Twenty quid. And my player didn't even come off the bench."

She didn't react in the slightest. "Enjoy the match, Mr. Beth."

I intended to, now that I knew everything was free. Free food! Free refreshments! Free experience points! And the best news . . . drum roll, please . . . I was getting 3 XP per minute. So the system seemed pretty clear: I got one XP per minute for all matches lower than the seventh tier (FC United). It was 3 XP for the fifth tier (Oldham), and it was 7 XP for the Premier League. I mentally sketched out a table that seemed pretty solid.

Tier - XP/Min

1 - 7

2 - 6

3 - 5

4 - 4

5 - 3

6 - 2

7 - 1

Easy enough. Assuming I could get into any stadium for free, it would make sense to focus on Premier League games. I doubted it would be that simple. Anyway, I'd get at least 270 XP today. It slightly changed the calculation on whether I'd buy Shocktober or not. Instead of eighteen evenings at Powerleagues, it would cost ten National League matches.

While I was thinking all of this, I got the sense that the person in the next seat was glaring at me. I didn't want to look away from the football, but I gave him a quick glance. It was a dude, the type of ruddy-faced older guy known in England as a "gammon" (yes, named after the deep-pink slices of pork). Gammons go on a TV show in the UK called *Question Time* and turn puce and clammy, as they demand politicians promise to nuke Iran if elected. (I'm not joking. That's a thing that happened.) This Oldham guy bore all the hallmarks of the species: the complexion, the hunted look they seem to get after a lifetime of baffled privilege, the narrow eyelids, presumably caused by too much staring at long Facebook rants with no paragraph breaks. Long story short, after one second of knowing this guy, I felt pretty sure I knew who he voted for and what he thought about the death penalty and "brown people." He looked away. What was his deal? Rival agent? Big Man City Ladies Under-Sixteens fan?

The guy himself didn't worry me, but the vibe he was giving off most certainly did. It was the same vibe I'd gotten from Caroline, though she at least maintained a professional veneer. Something was amiss.

The match wasn't all that interesting, although there were *some* things that caught my eye. For example, both teams were playing 4-4-2. Wow! No Premier League team had played 4-4-2 in a decade. It was kind of prehistoric. Seeing two fairly big teams employing it was . . . well, I didn't know what it was. Unexpected. Sort of . . . amateur? I did have just a tiny tiny fleeting thought that I could do better than either of these managers . . . . But that was just some residual smugness talking.

Another thing, the best players on both teams were strikers. Fondop for Oldham (CA 82), and Mullin for Wrexham (CA 114). That was good and bad. Bad because it suggested that clubs were stocked in that position, so they wouldn't need Ziggy (although Ziggy had 4 better finishing than Fondop). But it also gave credence to my theory that clubs were prioritising strikers in their recruitment, so when a club did need Ziggy, they'd be ready to pay for Ziggy.

I sent my only client a WhatsApp asking what he was up to. He replied that he was at Broadhurst Park watching the game. I had a tiny moment of panic and looked around to see who was stealing him. Then I reread the text. Broadhurst Park was where FC United played. *Boundary* Park was Oldham. I asked if he was a United fan now. He said, no, but he was training with them, and it was only right that he went to the games to cheer them on. He said I should go with him once. Absolutely, I should. I asked him to get me a scout ticket, and he said he could do better than that. Ooh! Ziggy bringing some mystery.

Oldham played really well in the first half. A Wrexham defender made a mistake, and that allowed Fondop to score a thumping goal. The crowd went nuts. Real spine-tingling stuff. A lot of extra emotion in there. They'd had a few bad years. If I was being romantic, I would have said that the fans were trying to roar the club back to life.

As half-time approached, I started to get nervous. On the way to the stadium I'd been on a post-win high, and been distracted by Shocktober and Emma. So far inside the stadium, things had gone so smoothly I had just accepted that I was a football insider now. But I wasn't. I had one client, and he didn't have a professional contract. I was a chancer. One step above a grifter. Bill Brown said he'd come and check on me at half-time. When he'd said it, it had seemed nice. Friendly. Solicitous. Now I wondered. Check on me.

Check on me.

That could mean a lot of things.

At half-time, a lot of fans wandered into the bowels of the stadium to refuel. The gammon and everyone in my little row vanished. The waitress came back. "Sir? The meal is inside."

I looked behind me. Along this entire sweep of the Joe Royle Stand were big plates of glass enclosing the VIP boxes, the Executive Suites, and the media rooms. I had glanced at it without a second thought. I'd never been inside such a space. Now, I was being invited to cross the threshold.

I know this is weird, but I wondered if I should or not. Going through the door seemed like it would make my misdemeanour worse. It was one thing to skip school, but skiving off to go paintballing was ten times as bad.

And now that I was looking, I could see people inside. Like, duh. But I mean a group of people in a small room. An enclosed space. Out here, on this side of the glass, I felt free. I could escape in any direction. Did I want to enter the bad vibes zone? The House of Gammon?

These were fleeting thoughts. If someone was going to tell me off, it would be better to have a full stomach. I followed Caroline through the door and into my first ever VIP box.

Imagine, if you can, a five-metre-long room, white, six recessed spots giving light from above, a boardroom-style table shrunk to fit, now accommodating ten chairs, ten sets of cutlery next to ten large square plates under ten large round bowls, two TVs on the walls at either end of the room, plus one wall of glass providing a clear view of the pitch.

If you can't imagine that, just picture a room with a table. That'll do.

It smelled, deliciously, of pie.

At the table were seven gammons and two gammon wives. Most gave me the evil eye when I walked in, but a quick stare made them return to their soup.

Soup was the starter, and it was delish. Cream of mushroom. Couple of husks of white bread, spready butter. Nom nom.

Caroline asked if I wanted a beer or a glass of wine. I did, but I was driving, so I suggested tea and some mineral water. That brought a scoff from one of the Oldham fans. Or maybe they were Wrexham fans, and I'd been put in their box? Maybe that's why they were pissed at me?

It became clear from the murmur of conversation that they *were* Oldham fans and that beating Wrexham would be a very big deal. One guy called them "moneybags Wrexham." What? I'd missed some important piece of information here.

The second course arrived. It was, and this delighted me no end, a pie. Non-league football and pies go together like Halloween and bad puns. Caroline deposited the crusted delight on my plate and was about to leave without telling me what it was. I didn't need Michelin-star service here, but I like to know what I'm putting in my gob.

"Miss," I said. "What is it?"

"It's a pie."

That got a laugh from my new-found enemies. I gave her a patient smile. "May I ask what is contained within?" I did a fluttery hand gesture on the word "within." Like a magician's misdirect.

"Steak," she said and was about to scoot off when she saw my expression. "Are you vegetarian?"

That wasn't what I was worried about. "Will there be gravy?" Pie looked a bit dry. Gravy essential.

"It's steak and gravy," she said. "The gravy is . . . *within*." Yep, she did the gesture. Raucous laughter followed. Strangely, I didn't mind. Whatever their problem was, it was their problem. These guys had paid extra for their VIP experience, and they were subsidising my XP growth. If they wanted to detest me unprovoked, let 'em.

I sliced into the pie, and lordy, it was good. All fears of dryness, ironically, evaporated. Moist, juicy bits of meat. Lovely, thick, viscous gravy. Meat stewing in a meaty bath. I think Caroline was worried she'd crossed a line into actual disrespect, because she reappeared with a jar of mineral water, a tea, and a couple of tiny chocolates.

"That good?" she said.

"I think it's the best pie I've ever eaten," I said. That got me some reputation points. Presumably nudging me up from minus a thousand. The aggressive stares from my fellow diners diminished. Clearly, I had ascended to the relationship level where they aggressively ignored me. In other words, the perfect level.

I polished off the pie and sat drinking my tea and digesting. It was warm in the room. I was stuffed and content, and I really, really, wanted a nap. Bill Brown came, as promised, to check on me.

"One-nil!" he beamed. No hint of menace there. "Good start, isn't it? So what do you think?"

"Oh, it was very tender," I said. "Slow cooked? Lovely crust. Amazing gravy. Ten out of ten pie, no notes."

"I meant the game. The players. Who would you want to sign?"

"Oh! Great question. I mean, obviously Paul Mullin." As I spoke, I realised this wasn't the most diplomatic answer. I should have chosen an Oldham player.

"Oh, him," said Bill. "He's considered a bit of a mercenary. Not too popular around here."

"Why not?"

"He was at Cambridge. League Two. Scored a lot of goals for them. A lot. They got promoted to League One." So his team went from the fourth tier to the third. That explained why his CA was so high. "But he didn't sign a new contract with them. Instead, he vanishes, and turns up at Wrexham. God knows how much they're paying him. But it's all Monopoly money to them."

"Wait," I said. "Wrexham? They're rich?"

Some half-remembered fact-fractions were swimming around me, refusing to coalesce into one coherent piece.

Bill gave me a quizzical look. "You know who their owners are."

Owners. Wrexham. No. Why would I? Why would anyone have heard of the local businessman who owned Wrexham? Obviously because it wasn't a local businessman. It must have been someone more famous, like when Elton John owned Watford. Some celebrity born in Wales? "Tom Jones? David Lloyd George? I give up," I said.

"That Ryan Reynolds. And the other one."

"Oh!" I said. It all came together. "Rob thingy. From the TV show." Of course I'd known that a pair of Hollywood A-listers (or an A and a B) had bought a team. I'd probably *heard* it was Wrexham, but it hadn't stuck as useful information.

"McElhenney."

"That's why they've got such a good team," I mused.

"They aren't that good," said one of the gammons. "We're playing them off the park." All his mates went "hear hear," like in the House of Commons.

Well, in the House of Commons everyone gets a say, I guess. I don't really know, but in my world, conversations are invitation-only, and this guy was gatecrashing. I focused my attention on Bill and asked him about one of Oldham's subs. "I like the look of that kid Benny Couto. Why isn't he in the first team?"

"It's the new manager's first home game. He probably wants experience on the pitch. You've seen him before, have you, Couto?"

"No, he just stood out in the warm-ups. Some players have it, don't they? The X factor." Which was another way of saying he was young with a relatively high PA.

"I've never really seen it in him myself. Caught your eye, did he? That's interesting."

"Mr. Brown," I started, but he asked to be called by his first name. "Bill," I said, "I was listening to your podcast, and they were having a bit of an argument about whether you should consolidate this season after being relegated last time. They were getting pretty heated about it. What's your take?"

"We have a podcast, do we? I don't know how to do that."

"Hand me your phone," I said.

While I subscribed him to *The Boundary Park Alert System*, he continued. "You have to understand, Max, that Oldham was a founding member of the Premier League. That's where we were in 1992, and this is where we are now. We're the *only* team to go from the Premier League to non-league. We haven't finished in the top half of a table in fourteen years. We've had, let's say, thrifty owners. Stability. We all wanted a bit more excitement. Be careful what you wish for. We got excitement, and we didn't much care for it. The last owner, he was an agent."

All sound in the room stopped. Every head turned towards me. "Your owner was an agent?"

"That's right. You know all those older stars who go to play in the Middle East? He did a lot of those deals. Good money in that. Thought he'd spread his wings. Buy an English club, bring over some young talents, let them develop, get them a big move."

"Sounds like a win-win all round," I suggested, knowing from the vibe in the room that no one would agree with me. The players were starting to come out for the second half, but no one in this room was moving. This scene was like *Love Island* for them. Or *Murder on the Orient Express* if I said the wrong things.

"I see why you'd say that," Bill said. "But that's only going to work if you have the first clue about football. And the former guy

. . . didn't. It was a disaster from start to finish, and when fans took to complaining, he banned them from the stadium. Which, by the way, he didn't own. So the team's been decaying, the stadium's been decaying. Now, it's better. We're back on our feet. Got a proper, local businessman owning the whole bundle. He's a bit mad, but he's one of ours. Consolidation? Yes, please. But not too long. We're too big for this division. We need to get back into the Football League where we belong. And Hollywood fly-by-nights throwing money around isn't making it any easier."

I half expected the gammons to thump the table in agreement, but they just nodded along.

"So," I said, slowly, eyeing Caroline as I pieced together all the things that had happened since my arrival. "Would I be right in thinking that agents aren't too popular around here right now?"

One gammon let out an incredulous "kah!" kind of noise. Bill glanced at him with a slight forehead crease. Then he looked towards Caroline with an even deeper frown. "Well, Max, as you might have guessed I used to tread the boards. Back in my salad days, my thespian days, my days of *Waiting for Godot*. And the dream of every young actor was to get an agent. Someone to do your running for you in footballing parlance. Someone to sniff out opportunities. Someone to shake the hands you'd never want to touch yourself, to shamelessly put your name forward for every part, to bear the burden of rejection on your behalf. I never got one, more's the pity. I didn't have what it took. Maybe I was too handsome for the 1990s . . . . Anyway, I'm sure most people see agents as grease in the wheel. Blood for the soil. Part of the ecosystem. But when a simple agent gets too big for his boots, wants to own a hundred-year-old club, wants to start picking the team . . ."

Bill had done a good job of contrasting the role of agents in general with the role of this one individual who had overreached. As he spoke, I could see the distaste fading away from the faces of the gammons. They started to look like normal people. Decent people. Caroline looked a bit pale. I mean, even paler. She probably thought, and she was probably correct, that Bill's speech had been a bit of a telling-off aimed at her.

But while he'd masterfully dissolved the tension in this particular room, he'd also given me something to think about. My trajectory of becoming an agent, and using that as a springboard into the manager's dugout, might come with a great deal of resistance from agent-hating fans. Sure, Oldham was an extreme example where an agent had trashed the club, but agents weren't popular anywhere. We were seen as leeches, sucking the blood out of clubs.

It was tricky. There were many pathways into the football industry, but every door was locked and barred, all except one. And taking the door marked "agent" was like accepting a brand onto my forehead. One that read "vampire." Tricky, tricky, tricky.

Bill said he had to rush off, and the Oldham VIPs started shuffling back through the glass door and onto the terraces. I called out to Bill. "Tell him I said thanks."

"Who?" he called back at me.

"Whoever gave up this ticket," I said.

He looked a bit confused and just sort of vanished with a wave/ thumbs up hybrid.

I was alone in the room with the gammon who'd given me the first evil eye and Caroline, who was loading our empty plates onto a trolley.

The gammon got into my face. "He didn't give up his ticket," he hissed at me. His cheeks flushed a darker shade of pink. Guys like this spent their whole lives angry. I wished I could get XP for every ulcer this guy developed; a few questions about Brexit and I'd be able to buy everything in the curse shop.

"Gosh," I said, absolutely emotionless.

"He didn't give up his ticket," repeated Peptic Guardiola. The guy was both angry and delighted. "He died. You just ate a dead man's meal. You're a parasite. You're a vampire."

"No, no, no," I said, in a soothing voice. "I might be a parasite, but I'm not a vampire." I looked over at Caroline. "Vampires get the girl."

And with a stomach-perforating grin, I slapped the guy on the shoulder and went to leech maximum XP from the second half.

41

THE MANCHESTER DERBY

The ulcer dude was so furious with me, he didn't retake his seat. He must have fucked off somewhere else and watched from there, quietly fuming. I'd be lying if I said that brought me no joy.

The second half was more of the same: Oldham playing out of their skin, Wrexham struggling. But then the defender who'd made the mistake for Oldham's goal scored the equaliser. This happened so often in football. Redemption. Zero to hero. The Shakespeare bit.

Then Wrexham got a penalty in the ninety-sixth minute. The ninety-sixth minute! Six minutes, 18 XP after the match was due to end. Mullin, the guy who should have been playing three divisions higher, stepped up and there was never any doubt about the outcome.

Oldham one, Moneybags Wrexham two.

Heartbreaking for the Oldham fans. I found myself imagining what would be discussed on their podcast: the gap between where they yearned to be and where they were. I was getting sucked into their story now, a downward spiral, a life of quiet desperation, one false dawn after another. Oldham was me. I was Oldham. Well, there was one difference between us. I found the idea of Ryan Reynolds putting his *Deadpool* money into non-league football exciting.

On Sunday, I woke up in a foul mood. It hadn't bothered me much at the time, but the hostility from Oldham's gammons and the waitress had gotten under my skin and festered. Prejudice was one thing coming from a group whose default position was ruddy-cheeked, spluttering outrage, but quite another coming from a pretty young woman.

Still stewing, I went to Wythenshawe again. I popped into the refugee shelter place I'd tried previously. That first time it had been empty, deserted. This time, there were a few people milling about. A few women sitting around a desk, writing. It seemed like one was helping the others to fill in forms. Over in another corner, there was a rotating pamphlet rack and a few harshly upright wooden chairs. One was occupied by a woman who was just staring straight ahead. I found myself watching for ages. Normally, when you stare at someone, e.g. the person next to you in a football stadium, that person feels it. This woman didn't. She was just sitting there. Staring. I left feeling uneasy.

To cheer myself up, I watched some abysmal football in the nearest park. An hour thereof. Sixty XP. I was starting to get itchy about my bulging wallet.

XP balance: 1,284

If I wasn't going to buy the Shocktober perk, I had to make a choice. Wait to see what November's was, or spend my capital soon and then buy God Save the King. Or, and this was tempting, buy something cheap, and see if that unlocked any cool new options. For 100 XP I could buy Match Stats 1 (but I didn't have any eleven-a-side matches on the horizon); 4-4-2 diamond (ditto); or Player Profile 2. The last one would unlock the History tab on a player's profile, so that had potential scouting benefits.

I decided I'd almost certainly treat myself to Player Profile 2 the next time I was at a pro game, and the others, the next time I was about to take charge of a full-sized game.

I normally walk pretty fast—I want to get where I'm going—but as I headed towards the church, I unconsciously slowed down. It was a quiet autumn morning. Wythenshawe isn't a place I'd like to live, but it's surprisingly leafy. Lots of parks, lots of trees. They were yellow and red and various stages of naked. Really nice. Soothing. Nice, long, empty pavements. Just me and the fallen leaves. No, the problem with living here wasn't the foliage, but the people.

I stopped walking and looked around. Being an agent or a manager would mean dealing with people. Lots of people. That was unappealing. The pandemic had done something to me, or accelerated a process that had already begun. Whatever the cause, I had woken up one day and realised I had become an extremely judgmental person. And not wanting to deal with modern life—the daily hate, the culture wars, the weapons-grade stupidity, the grifters, the populists, the psychopaths, the "influencers," the hot takes, all of it—I had withdrawn. I had gone internal.

Now, I was on a path back towards normalcy. Towards being social. Towards putting myself in a position where my income depended on what other people were feeling and thinking.

The call centre? That was fine. I talked to people for three minutes. It was transactional. Even if I might have disliked the bank's customers if I'd met them, they still deserved to have the service they paid for. Plus, I controlled how long the conversations lasted.

Ziggy and the Met Heads? We were fairly alike. Had a lot in common. Easy chats. Good laughs. Jackie, too, though he was quite political and had some hidden agenda. All in all, they were a great bunch. Spending time with them cost no energy.

Raffi Brown? I'd never spoken to him. What was his family like? Probably rough. Definitely not going to be nicknaming me Max Beth and quoting Shakespeare. I'd have to sit in a room with them. Smile. Listen to whatever bigoted views they had without losing my temper. Shit, I'd have to take them to Raffi's first game as a pro. Sit with them for ninety minutes. Charm them. I was already thinking of ways to rush away at full-time. Fake emergencies. Shit, gotta run, just got a call that Mum has had a fall. We hadn't even met, and I was trying to spend less time with them! That wasn't a good sign.

The gammons? I imagined being the Oldham manager and masterminding a 3–0 win. How would it feel to know I was bringing joy to people I detested?

The Yalleys? They were nice, but this meeting was going to be hard work. I felt fatigued just thinking about it. There were big communication gaps between us. With Mr. Yalley, language. With his wife and son, their faith. With Kisi, well, she was cool, but she was a teenage girl. Bit of a nightmare tbh.

A leaf fell from a tree, and I watched it float down. It seemed pretty content. It had done its job, and now it was getting its eternal rest. Maybe, if it was lucky, it'd be picked up by a toddler and used in an artwork that would live on someone's fridge until Christmas.

I started walking again. If I signed Youngster as a client, I wouldn't need to deal with other people for very long. One big transfer. That's all it would take to free me from society's shackles. Then I could hang out with the Met Heads and spend time with clients I really liked. Or go internal again, but in a bigger house. One with a tree in the garden. Sit in its shade and devour the classics: *Moby Dick*; *Bleak House*; *Shopaholic*.

I snuck into the back of the church. Let's be honest: I was trying to give the impression I'd been there for the whole service (without actually lying about it). But I'd misjudged the timing, and I had to sit through almost half an hour of church stuff. The end of the sermon, which was very odd to my ears, and then the concluding songs and—incredibly— more songs after those songs.

The boredom was spectacular. I learned one thing, at least: I still had it in me to grind. To put myself in places and positions I didn't really want to be.

The pastor had annoyed me by dragging the service out, but at the end he did me a favour and raced across, drawing everyone's attention to my presence. I think he was excited to see me again, since I'd made such an impression the last time.

"We were not introduced," he said, giving me a hearty handshake. "But I believe you are Mr. Best."

"Max. You're Pastor Yaw."

"Just so. It is good to see you again in the House of God."

"I'm here to talk to the Yalleys," I said, in case he wanted me to write out my sins or whatever.

"For a particular purpose, I have no doubt."

"I want to sign James as a client and guide him to the Premier League."

Confusion. "The Premier League of what?"

"Football. I see him playing for West Ham. Maybe Ghana, too. Not sure how stocked they are in that position."

"Which position do you mean?"

"Defensive midfielder."

The calculations came thick and fast. If this was a joke, I was very seriously committed to it. He seemed to dismiss the idea. Then what? I was a lunatic? Perhaps. I had, after all, sprinted into his church mid-service. "What makes you think . . ."

I put my hand on his arm. "You don't need to have faith." I took my hand away. "It would all happen very quickly. I would find a club where he could train. They'd offer him a professional contract within weeks. His talent is obvious. James is a glistening jewel."

This brought a tiny smile to Yaw's mouth. "It is strange no one else has ever seen what you discovered so readily." He turned. "And odd that the Yalleys have not discussed this wonderful news with everyone. It would bring hope and joy to the community."

Good to know. Pop that factoid in my jacket pocket. "He's uncertain if he wants to become a footballer. We're going to discuss it today. I think he will refuse."

"Oh. Indeed?" He looked thoughtful. "Perhaps you should not have told me."

"I don't lie in churches. I've seen too many movies."

"In which movies do people lie in churches and get struck down? No, really. I would love to watch them!"

I laughed. My first laugh of the day. "I don't know. Maybe it doesn't happen. But still. No lying."

"An honest man, at long last. Tell me, what did you think of my sermon?"

"Oh, walked straight into that one. You want honesty? If I did a sermon, it'd be about five minutes. Ten, tops. Quote from the Bible, put it in a modern perspective, end with a call to action."

Now it was his turn to laugh. "I should like to experience your ten-minute sermon, Max Best. Good luck with your quest."

He walked off, and I was left there, alone for a second, absolutely buzzing. Almost all the negativity of the morning was washed away. Cleansed in a holy river. And all it took was one laugh and one smile. I felt rejuvenated, and I realised I wasn't misanthropic, I didn't hate the general public, I did like talking to people. I just needed to ration my energy expenditure so I didn't burn out. And, of course, I needed to give negative people the exact amount of attention they deserved: zero.

And how interesting that he used the word quest. Trying to convince Youngster was a bit like a quest, wasn't it? A quest in a video game. But was this a main quest or a side quest? I supposed it didn't matter. I tended to complete all the side quests first anyway, to level up before the boss battles.

In a much more upbeat, positive frame of mind, I went to find the Yalleys and walked with them from the church to their home.

They had prepared a big lunch. The only thing I knew the name of was plantain, but it smelled great. Very colourful. While they prepared everything, and I hovered around, Kisi asked me if I was nervous about the match. The Manchester Derby, which was due to kick off in about an hour.

"Not really," I said. "The gap between the teams is huge. There's virtually no chance United can win."

"They would if you were in charge," said Kisi.

"You think I'd cook up some scam and have three goalkeepers or something?" I laughed. "No, United's new manager is said to be a tactical genius. He's probably close to the level of City's manager. But he doesn't have the raw materials to work with. City are a machine, and they have Haaland playing like The Terminator. City's win today is one of the most inevitable events in the history of human civilisation."

"How could the gap between the teams be closed?" asked Mrs. Yalley.

"I'm not sure it can be," I said. City were too far ahead, had too many resources, and didn't make mistakes.

"There has to be a way," said Kisi. "That's sport, isn't it? Jackie told me you always say a strength becomes a weakness."

That was confusing. "No, *he* said that to *me*."

"He learned it from you." Kisi's eyes widened. "He told me!"

"Huh. I don't remember that. But okay. Maybe there's a way a team could get closer to City's level. A few good deals in the transfer market, a bit of luck . . . ." I glanced at James, who was laying the table. "And some divine intervention." James looked up at me, and unexpectedly, smiled. "Let's not talk about football during the meal though. Is that okay with you?"

While we ate, we chatted about life in Wythenshawe, about trees, about birds, about side quests, and, after we'd cleared away the plates and dishes, about how I liked my tea. I demonstrated the *proper* way to make tea. Mrs. Yalley was fascinated. Mr. Yalley shook his head, said things that Kisi refused to translate, and wandered out to his shed.

Mrs. Yalley sat at the head of the table, to my left, as some sort of chairperson. Or a judge. Kisi sat to my right, planting her flag as part of Team Max. Max United. She spent most of the time on her phone. James sat opposite me, the little stretch of table acting like a vast chasm. A gap that couldn't be crossed. After a few more pleasantries, battle commenced.

42

MIND THE GAP

"So, James. Youngster." I felt one side of my mouth lifting up. I didn't have high hopes for this contest, but I wanted to enjoy it at least. "You have decided to sign the contract and want to discuss which team you'll start at."

James looked a bit panicked. "Ah, no, Mr. Best." His mother made a noise inside her throat, and James switched his attention to her. His anxiety became a smile. "Oh. You're teasing me. You're teasing me because . . ." He peered at me, trying to read my face. He wasn't very good at that sort of thing. He was too serious. His own face barely ever twitched. "Because you already know my decision?"

"Decision?" I said, startled. "I hoped we'd discuss your objections, and *then* you'd decide."

"Oh, certainly," he said.

I didn't like this one little bit. He wasn't lying to me, but he was so close to having made up his mind that it was a foregone conclusion. I glanced across at Kisi's phone. It was the score from the derby. City 3, United 0, and there had only *been* about half an hour. A vast, uncrossable gap. "Why don't you tell me your concerns? Football is a troubled industry, you said."

He turned over a ream of paper on the table. It'd been there the whole time, but I hadn't noticed. They were pages and pages of notes in untidy, teenage boy handwriting. I know what boy handwriting looks like, because I've never grown out of mine. I instinctively sensed that this had taken him ages. He had high pace and acceleration, but at school he was a slowpoke. How did I know? He must have reminded me of someone from my class, though I doubted anyone from my school had enough talent to play in the Premier League. I wondered if I'd ever met *anyone* as talented as James. "By my reckoning, football players routinely break eight of the ten commandments and five of the seven deadly sins. In many cases, these sins are hard-wired into the nature of the game itself. It seems unChristian to list the ones I saw you break on Wednesday, and the ones Kisi told me about from Friday."

"Yeah, that does sound unChristian," I agreed. "Isn't my sin between me and God?"

"It is," said James. "Which is why I stopped making the list."

"Oh, but you started?" I was torn between curiosity and the fear of losing my cool.

"Do not misunderstand me, Mr. Best. I think you try to be a good man, and you have some Christian virtues. I merely sought to understand my revulsion at the idea of becoming a footballer." Revulsion. Ugh. The gap widened. "I have distilled my thoughts into three thesis statements. They are thus: The football pitch is a sinful, wicked place. The football stadium is a sinful, wicked place. The football industry is sinful and wicked."

I felt like he was cheating, in that sinful and wicked were synonyms. He made it sound twice as bad as it was! Good scam. I made a mental note of the technique. Not wanting to go through every line of his dissertation, I waved some of it through. No defence, your honour. "The last one is probably going to be hard to disagree with. You mean gambling and fake crypto tokens and money laundering and things like that?" He did, and there was a lot more. "Got it. But I'm not asking you to own a club. I'm offering you a job. It's like being a doctor or a nurse. You don't have to share an office with the Minister for Health; you have to give some guy two white pills and one green one. It's a job. It's really that simple. This is so interesting though. Let's move on to the stadium stuff. Don't tell me. Let me guess. Ah . . . alcohol and . . . cocaine in the toilets."

James blinked at me. "I did not know about that. I shall write it down." He did so while I exchanged exasperated glances with his sister. She was quite stressed for some reason. Even more than me. Was it because Man City were winning? James laid down his pen, perpendicular to the paper. "Racism. Homophobia. Anti-semitism. Disgusting chants. Cruel taunts. Violence, implied and real. May I read you a short passage from the Bible? I suspect you don't like this sort of thing." I nodded at him. Go for it. "*The fruit of the Spirit is love, joy, peace, patience, kindness, goodness, faithfulness, gentleness, self-control.* These are Christian virtues, Mr. Best. *If we live by the Spirit, let us also walk by the Spirit. Let us not become conceited, provoking one another, envying one another.* Conceit, provocation, and envy. Can you imagine a football crowd which did not display these feelings?"

"Of course not. They're the best bits." Today, the City fans would be very conceited, very provocative. The United fans would be very envious. What's wrong with that?

To my surprise, he grinned at me. "I understand it, Mr. Best. I really do." He had bravery 16. It wasn't that he was afraid of a hostile crowd, and he had a sense of humour. A microscopic one, but it existed. "But it is not Christian. Love, joy, peace, patience, kindness." He sighed. "Perhaps I have wasted your time. It seems my path is clear."

I thought back to my first meeting with Emma. The structure of that conversation had been similar, but with me painting a breezy, optimistic view of the sport. Funny how two people could look at the same thing and see the exact opposite. "Before you commit to a lifetime of regret, tell me the other section. *The football pitch is a wicked and sinful place.* What do you mean by that?"

By mentioning regret, I'd put him off his stride, which wasn't exactly my intention. Or maybe it was. He picked up the relevant piece of paper. "Deception. I do not mean your clever false midfield idea. Tricking the opposing coach is perfectly ethical. There are many biblical precedents. David and Goliath. Joshua's fake retreat. No, I refer to deceiving the referee. Players appeal for every decision: they put their hands up to claim a throw-in even though they know they touched the ball last. They pretend to have been fouled, and they simulate injury." He looked at me, wondering how I'd react. "They even kick their feet into an opponent, so that the referee will see there was contact between them. Furthermore, when decisions go against them, the players surround and intimidate the referee. The levels of disrespect are appalling." This was true. At the Sunday League level there was a growing crisis because no one wanted to become a referee anymore. I hadn't seen any outrageous behaviour myself, but some of the stories of players—entire teams—violently attacking referees were absolutely sickening. With fewer and fewer referees, the base of the football pyramid was crumbling.

"If you're on the pitch you can defend the ref. Stop it happening."

He shook his head. "If I am on the pitch, it will be my job to join in. I know that."

And that was that. I'd shot myself in the foot. I'd demonstrated how to con the referee and encouraged the Met Heads to threaten violence against their opponents. And I'd done that within twenty minutes, really, of meeting James. A PA 181 cash machine, and I'd shown him that my wallet was full of skimmed credit cards. But that had probably merely widened the gap by a few metres. There had never been any way of bridging it. Not really.

I stretched, preparing to leave. "Absolutely fascinating. Thanks, James."

"Ugh," said Kisi. "Aren't you going to tell him he's wrong?"

"He's not wrong."

Mrs. Yalley spoke. "Tell us what you really think, please, Mr. Best."

I shrugged and pushed my hands forward on the table to stretch my lower back. "I know there are lots of Christian footballers. Good Muslims, too. Really good people. Pious and all that. I've never heard anyone say 'oh he's a bad player because he doesn't cheat hard enough.' There's a video on YouTube called 'Messi Never Dives,' and it's just Messi being hacked down like he was a rainforest. He always stays on his feet, always tries to keep going. He's probably the best player of all time. I can't think of a single thing he ever did to cheat." That blew my mind as I said it. "Literally can't think of anything. I'd be very interested for you to watch that video and then tell me that cheating is hardwired into the game. But that's just Messi, you might say. What about the rubbish players? Well, personally, I don't see claiming a throw-in as any worse than being a salesman and knowing your product isn't quite the best, or some other job you'd ideally not do. Where there *is* a difference is in terms of scale. The salesman might make a couple of thousand a month. The rewards for football are unthinkable. Fifty thousand a week buys a lot of cornflakes for the food bank." I picked up the top sheet of paper. A lot of words were underlined. Words like patience and kindness. Bible verses. "But James has thought about it a lot more than I have. I respect his decision. It just seems—"

"What?" said James.

"Nothing," I said. What I was thinking was: why had this happened? If James didn't want to play football, why had the curse set this up? "I think I'll head back to my car. Maybe go via the field and see if anyone's playing."

"Don't you want to watch the rest of the derby?" asked James.

"Absolutely not. It's already three nil, and it'll only get worse." I tapped his papers. "Cowardice. Add that to your list."

"You are not a coward, Mr. Best," said James. "I admire the way you fought against a superior foe."

I rapped the table twice with a knuckle and started to rise. Kisi nearly had a fit. "Mum!"

"One moment please, Mr. Best."

Mrs. Yalley left and came back with one of my contracts. The Kisi one. Oh! That's right. I had *two* potential clients here. She passed it over to me. It was signed. "You're sure?" I said.

"I'm sure," said Mrs. Yalley.

"You don't think it's sinful?"

"Kisi is free to make her own choices. And, for what it is worth, seeing her accepted by Beth and the others warmed my heart."

"Kisi? Not worried about any of that?" I pointed at James's stack of objections.

"I want to be a Beth Head."

I took a pen out of my inner jacket pocket and clicked the top. I looked at the last, empty line. It just needed my name to be scrawled on. I looked at Kisi. I'd never make money from this. I doubted it would lead to any opportunities. But the curse told me she was a highly talented player, a flair player, a thrill player. PA 143, fast dribbler, could add goals to her game as she matured. I wanted to see her grow and develop, and I'd learn a lot from it too. Best of all, watching her dribble past a couple of defenders and nutmeg the goalie would bring a smile to my face. Having her as a client would lead to a permanent plus one to my joy attribute. An exuberant antidote to this grim, gammony country. What if she got an England cap? That would be a red letter day for me as much as her.

Still, though. It would increase my workload. Could I afford to invest my precious time in a girl who would probably have to train and play for *four years* before signing a contract so slim that ten percent wouldn't even buy me a new biro?

I brought the pen away from the page. Kisi's eyes tracked it. I moved it back towards the contract; her eyes widened. I moved it away; they narrowed. Kisi wanted to play football! She was the opposite of her brother; she wanted to get started right away, no hesitation, just eagerness.

Fuck it. This would be fun.

I put the pen on the line and . . . and paused. I leaned back. "You know," I said. "Maybe I should talk to Pastor Yaw about this."

Kisi looked distraught. Her mother cleared her throat and said, "Mr. Best."

When Kisi realised I was teasing her, all the latent excitement burst out of her. She gave my arm a feeble double-slap. "Max!" she said.

I laughed. "No violence, remember! Now, normally I'd take potential clients to be inspected by a psychic dog. But I'll take your word for this." I thought about how to explain what I wanted. "You know I'm not against a bit of light skullduggery. But James is right about one thing. The abuse of match officials is out of control. I want you to promise to respect the referees." I thought about all the times I'd lost my shit at some grotesque miscarriage of justice. "As much as possible."

"Okay," she said. It came out weird; I think she was holding her breath.

"And you won't be a Beth Head."

She deflated. "Oh."

"Sorry, but you're much too good for that." I signed the last page. "You are going to play in blue."

She grimaced and looked at her phone. She held it up. The score was City 4, United 0. "You don't mean . . . ?"

"I do."

"But you hate them."

"Nah," I said, standing up, clutching my unexpected windfall. "Someone needs to knock them off their perch. Me, if it comes to it," I added, with a laugh. "But when it comes to being an agent," I smiled at Kisi, my second ever client, "my prejudices don't matter. City are the best, and you'll fit right in." I thought back to Friday's game. "And you're already best buds with that Meghan girl." Kisi blushed. I got serious. "One more thing. You know how they operate. Pass, pass, control the ball. All that stuff. You'll learn how to do it. You'll have to fit in with the team, please your coaches. Now I'm just talking as a football fan. *Don't* lose your flair and your dribbling. Keep improving your flicks and tricks even if you can't use them in every game. Fit in, be a team player, but stay true to yourself and your talent."

"She is a flair player?" said James.

"Haven't you been watching her?" I said. If he wasn't going to join my illustrious client pool, he could at least support his sister's journey. "How about you watch her doing some tricks, and I'll watch that boat movie you mentioned. Deal?"

"Deal," he said, after mumbling the word "ship." It was the only deal I was ever likely to get from him. As I shook his hand, I considered his player profile. Such a waste. But I had to respect his decision. Chapter closed.

I realised I'd missed something. "Oh! We need to do the contract signing photo. Kisi, come and pretend to sign this, and I'll stand here. Mrs. Yalley, do you want to be in the picture?"

She didn't; it was her daughter's special moment. So James took the photo. Kisi, absurdly happy, pretended to sign a document she wasn't old enough to have a say in. Me, pretending to be coolly professional. But actually, Kisi's enthusiasm was overwhelming. In the picture, you can see me burning with excitement. Client and agent very much on the same page. Overlapping wavelengths. No gap.

I wanted to say goodbye to Mr. Yalley, but he was in his shed, and that meant he wasn't to be disturbed. For someone bemused by British habits, he'd certainly picked up one of the main ones: the man of the house retreating to his little man cave in the garden.

I was smiling to myself as I arrived in the park. There weren't any games going on. I sighed and wondered what to do with the rest of the day.

I had an incoming call from Ziggy. Before answering, I checked the latest score. City were winning 6–1. He was calling to gloat. I declined the call and turned my phone off. The day had started badly but gotten better, and even though James had turned me down, it had been interesting getting to know him. Spending time with the Yalleys hadn't taken energy. So I didn't want Ziggy spoiling the mood.

That was a mistake. I'm sure he would have gloated, at least a little bit. But in fact, he was calling with good news. Exciting news. News that would bring me three months closer to being a football insider.

43

MAKING HISTORY

After a little stroll where I rehearsed the Kisi sales pitch—She's fast! She's dynamic! She's motivated!—I went back to my car and turned my phone on. Ziggy had sent a few texts that I didn't understand. They didn't *seem* to be taunts. I called him.

"Max! Where've you been?" He was hyper. It sounded like he was bouncing around some enclosed space. For a second I worried he'd been arrested and was hoping I'd bail him out.

"I was with my new client," I said.

Whatever movement he was doing, he stopped doing. "Oh. Who?"

"Kisi Yalley."

"Huh." He tried to process the news but couldn't. He resumed his restless movements. I could hear every swish of his clothes. "Listen, Max, listen. Did you see what happened in the game?"

"Yeah, yeah, 6–1. Good job."

"What? No. Anyway, it was 6–3. I'll mock you later. No, I mean FC United. I was there yesterday and Sandro got injured in the first half. It didn't look that bad. Then Max got sent off. Ugh, not you. Max *McCartney.*"

"Okay."

"And today it seems Sandro's injury is worse than they thought. I got a text from Jackie asking me not to play with my mates this week!"

Why would Jackie ask Ziggy not to play his weekly five-a-side?

Oh my God.

Oh my Godohmygod.

Full. Body. Tingles.

"Max, you there?"

"Ziggy, are you thinking what I'm thinking?"

"Yes!" He was doing little hops. He wasn't the only one.

"Who have they got fit who can play striker?"

"Not many! Will. Dontai. They've been playing Ribbit up front, since they saw you do it. But they're short. One more injury or suspension, and they're toast."

"And they can't sign anyone until January," I said. "Unless they happen to find a talented striker who doesn't have a club."

"Maybe someone who's already been training with them!"

"Ziggy," I said.

"Max," he said.

And we both sort of made weird noises into the phone.

After ending the call, I did an impromptu sprint around the car park. I dribbled a pebble. *Here comes Ziggy. He's through on goal. He shoots, he scores!*

Ziggy, mate!

Later, he called me again. A lot more subdued. The self-loathing after the sugar rush. "Max. I can't not play on Thursday. I thought I should tell you. I'll stick on the sides, try not to get involved. But I can't let my mates down."

"Getting injured ten minutes before you sign a pro contract, Ziggy, is the very fucking definition of letting your mates down."

"I'm sorry, Max. It's too short notice. I'll play. If I get injured, that's on me."

"I forbid it."

"Good luck with that," he said. Secret reserves of self-belief coming back to bite me in the arse!

I gnashed my teeth for a bit. Fantasised about encasing him in carbonite until the signing ceremony. "This is demented, Barrett."

"I know."

He was not for moving. Down in London, the Prime Minister kept announcing new policies, defending them for two days, then doing a u-turn. I knew Ziggy wouldn't back down from this. How did this random guy have more backbone than the British government? I couldn't sit by while he put his career on the line out of some misplaced loyalty to his friends and their shitty five-a-side league. I sighed. "Fine. I'll do it."

"What?" he said.

"I'll play."

"You?"

That annoyed me. "You don't think I can hack it in a Stockport Powerleague?"

"I didn't mean that. I meant . . . the other way. You're too good."

"Jesus, don't start talking like Jackie. Just text me the details."

Speak of the devil, and he will appear. Kind of. I decided to call Jackie. He picked up right away.

"Jackie, if you want to scout me, I'll be playing instead of Ziggy in his five-a-side league on Thursday."

"Five-a-side?"

"Yep. My first game in three years. Can't touch the ball inside the goalie's D. Play off the sides. No head height." That last rule stopped you kicking the ball too high, tried to keep the ball on the ground. Encouraged passing and skill. Optimistic with a lot of overweight CA 1 blokes. "You can get the details from Ziggy."

"Why would I want to watch that, Maxy boy?"

"I don't know, Jackie. Because you're weird?"

"It's good you called. I'm calling in the favour you owe me. Don't plan anything for Saturday."

"Are you taking me to a theme park?"

"Better."

He clicked off.

After work on Monday, I went home to do some online grinding. Since I'd been checking out videos about Oldham, YouTube was recommending all kinds of content about non-league football and "day in the life of a pro" type stuff. Slice of life stories. Some people enjoy that, I guess.

There was one that I watched right away about which training drills were good and which weren't. That made me get on the phone to Beth and ask if I could take training on my own this Wednesday. Without Jackie.

"I never knew you'd invite Jackie, Max. You did that on your own, remember? Of course you can take the session."

"Can I invite Kisi? She's my client now."

"She's an honorary Beth Head, so yes. You don't need to ask."

"An honorary what?"

"Met Head," she said and hung up.

Another video was about an amateur player trying to take on a half-decent pro. That was fascinating. The amateur guy was pretty good. At the Powerleagues he'd catch the eye. He was well-balanced, quite nippy, good technique. But the pro just made mincemeat out of him. It wasn't even close. Fascinating.

But the most interesting video was about a club called AFC Fylde. The video sought to answer the question: Why is AFC Fylde the most hated non-league team in England? In brief, they had a gammony owner who every decent person hated. Fun football-as-a-soap-opera fare, but the important thing was one particular detail. The owner had advertised a job, and the text of that advert had gone viral. It was really bizarre, cringeworthy stuff. But the advert was posted on a site called Jobsinfootball.com. A whole website about jobs in the football industry! I have never typed anything so fast.

Latest Jobs:

Lead Female Community Football Coach, Bromley UK

Sessional Community Football Coach, Cheadle UK

Matchday Safety Steward, Bournemouth UK

Channel Manager, Chelsea FC, London UK

Holy fucking shit!

I spent half an hour on the site, basically just verifying that it was a real thing and allowing myself to imagine these jobs and whether I'd like them. I called it research. You might call it daydreaming. Eggplant, aubergine.

Most were badly paid—coaching kids for fifteen pounds an hour, for example—but they encompassed everything in the world of football except being the manager of a men's team. And maybe those would be listed too, when there were vacancies. The General Manager of the Blackburn Ladies team was on there. Could I work my way up from a groundsman in Southport to being the manager of Man United?

Astonishingly quickly, this website had become a kind of security blanket. A safety net. There was nothing I could mess up so badly that I wouldn't be able to apply for a position in the Bromley Community Sports Trust or writing copy for the Crystal Palace website. So I called Newcastle United, trying to get two tickets in the scouting section.

It . . . didn't go well. Long story short, given a choice between reserving those seats for some of the richest men in the world, the England manager, various super-agents, or Max Best, a twenty-two-year-old with two clients who had played zero minutes . . . yeah, yeah. You get the picture.

"I understand," I said. "And it's even worse. I need *two* tickets. I met a Newcastle girl and want to take her to St. James's to let her experience the atmosphere. Last throw of the dice to get her into footy."

"Oh, so you want to use us for your dating?"

"Absolutely."

There was a stony silence, but then a cackle of laughter. "I like you, Max. Call us back when you're . . . you know."

"Not a nobody."

"Yeah. Where's your lass from?"

"Newcastle," I said.

"Which part!" the guy laughed.

"Oh. Does it have parts?"

"Man. These tickets are like gold dust. Don't waste them on a first date."

That was wise. I texted Emma telling her that I'd been shot down by her local team, so she was free to keep hating football. But I invited her to join my Culture Club.

Emma: What's that?

Me: We watch a movie, read a book, or listen to a song, and discuss it.

Emma: I knew it. That's why you seem so sophisticated. You just parrot the opinions of everyone else in your little gang. How many are in it?

Me: If you join, two.

Emma: Oh, exclusive. I like that. What's next on the to-do list?

Me: Can you choose? My life is getting frantic. If it has Ryan Reynolds in it, that's probably a bonus.

Emma: Sure. I nominate *The Proposal.* **Sandra Bullock/RR romcom.**

Me: Okay.

Emma: No complaints?

Me: No. Why? Were you joking?

Emma: I was. I didn't think you'd agree. But all right! *Proposal* **it is! When do we discuss it?**

Me: How about Saturday evening?

Emma: I'm probably going clubbing.

Clubbing. Weirdest thing. If I wanted to be pumped full of drugs and be hot, sweaty, and cramped, I'd become a factory farm chicken.

Me: Okay. Sunday then? Sunday evening.

Emma: It's a date.

So I had to watch a romantic comedy before Sunday. I added it to a post-it note where I'd been tracking all the things I wanted to watch. There were three seasons of the documentary *All or Nothing* (Tottenham/Man City/Arsenal). There was *Sunderland 'Til I Die.* And, maybe most urgently, *Welcome to Wrexham,* made by Ryan Reynolds and the other one. And the algorithm was throwing up all kinds of interesting things on YouTube. Plus, there were tons of books I would have to find time to read: *Inverting the Pyramid. Moneyball. The Damned United.*

I'd certainly be stress-testing the adage that busy people are happy people.

On Tuesday, October 4, I went to Ardwick Powerleague to see Raffi Brown. While I waited for his team to turn up, I collected fifty XP.

There was a lot going on in my life: new clients, new failures, a website jam packed with football careers. Something occurred to me. As soon as I'd stopped trying to land James Yalley in my big net, I'd been on the move again. It was like he'd been anchoring me, tying me to a particular vision of the future. Now that I'd cut that cord, there was a palpable feeling of forward momentum. It was intoxicating. Just like that, I decided to buy the Player Profile 2 upgrade.

Boom! Big moment. One hundred XP. One hundred minutes of watching awful sports . . . poof! Used up in a flash.

Was it worth it?

The first thing to say is that it unlocked a new option, Player Profile 3: Nerdlonger. This would cost 500 XP and offered "more history." Bit underwhelming.

I turned to the nearest pitch, and now, when I looked at someone's player profile, there were those little tabs you get on computer windows to indicate that there is something behind. I tapped on it and saw the History screen. I wondered if I had to concentrate on that little tab thing when I wanted to switch back and forth or if I could swipe left and right to move between the screens. My in-vision interface sort of went squiggly for a minute—bit scary—but then came back. and I could swipe left and right through the tabs.

Had I just reprogrammed the curse?

Anyway. History. This was . . . useless. Useless in the Powerleagues anyway.

In the focal point of this new screen were eleven new columns, and after a bit of guesswork and testing, I discovered what they meant: on the left was the season for this string of data (I only had access to 2021/22), which team the player played for, how many appearances they'd made, goals, assists, man of the match awards, pass completion, tackles made, dribbles per game, shots on target per game, and average rating.

Enough to satisfy any football hipster! But there was more!

There was a little arrow, and clicking on it changed some of the columns:

Now I also saw goals conceded (for goalies), penalties scored, yellow and red cards earned, games won, games lost, team goals scored, team goals conceded. This lot was a bit less useful; it was good design to tuck this stuff away.

No player in the Powerleague had a professional club in the previous season, so every data point for the players I was currently watching was blank. But for players I'd already scouted, like Ronaldo and Salah, I could see half their stats. I cross-checked them, and the data seemed reliable. But even for the superstars, many of the fields were populated by question marks, indicating that I'd have to buy a perk to unlock that data.

Of the missing data, one field stood out. Average rating. That was tantalising. It almost seemed as useful as knowing someone's PA. Unlocking that would certainly be a big step forward in player analysis. I checked the curse shop and couldn't see anything that would unlock the ratings.

Anyway, what I'd just gotten was great but only for some very specific scenarios. For example, when talking to Bill Brown about the young left-back I liked, I could have mentioned how many games he'd played the year before, or commented on how frequently he picked up yellow cards. Made it seem like I'd done my homework.

It was definitely worth 100 XP. Would I spend 500 XP to unlock more years in this tab? Sure. Eventually. When I was able to watch tier one and two games every night of the week. I'd want to investigate some of the other basics first though. See how this knowledge helped or hindered me.

I played with my new toy for a while.

Then Raffi and his team turned up, and I gave him my full attention. It was First Contact day.

I was completely calm about it. If Raffi started quoting Bible verses at me, no problem. I could always become a goalkeeper coach in Yorkshire or a nutritionist at Leeds United's academy. The footballing world was my oyster!

44

LANDING ON GREEN

Raffi Brown. A few weeks before, he had been my dream client, and, to some extent, my dream footballer. I loved how he played. Now, he was PG Tips, my favourite brand of tea, until someone gave me a cup of Yorkshire Gold. Seeing James with his high PA and perfect position/skillset match had led to a big recalibration of Raffi's value.

But still, Raffi could become a good Championship (tier two) player, and maybe his team would get promoted and he would play some minutes in the Premier League. That'd be fun. And lucrative. Financially, Raffi would probably be worth four Ziggys in the short term, with the potential for much, much more in future. So I wanted him as a client. Very much so. But at the same time, I was relaxed about meeting him; it had been a good idea to wait.

Seeing him play again, though, rekindled some of the old affection. Stirred up the old loins. The guy—footballistically—was sexy. So powerful; so smooth. Put him on Netflix with the tag *Swoonworthy*. Oh, matron! Pass the smelling salts.

"Excuse me, Raffi? My name's Max. Have you got a minute?"
"Sure."
"You've probably seen me around."
Raffi squinted at me. "Yeah. Watching the games and that. Do you work here?" His voice was rough and aggressive, but his manner was polite.
"No. I'm an agent. I've been scouting you. I'm on the lookout for a powerful, quick-witted midfielder who can take care of himself on the pitch. That's you. Would you like to be a professional footballer?" I'd decided to ask that question early on with all potential clients. I

thought ninety-nine percent of people would say yes, but James had taught me not to make assumptions.

"What's the upfront?"

I laughed. He thought I was a con artist. I took my phone out and showed him the folder I'd created with the contract signing photos. "I've got two clients so far. This guy, Ziggy, he does construction. Helps on sites, does odd jobs, electrics. This girl, she's fourteen. Her dad is a baggage handler at the airport. She doesn't get pocket money. If I was going to become a scammer, I wouldn't start with *you* three."

"That's your whole client list, is it?"

"Jesus, Raffi! I'm a scammer or I'm incompetent. Make up your mind!" I laughed. "I've only been doing this gig for ten minutes. The first guy is close to getting a pro deal. We just need one more injury in the first team. Not that we're hoping and praying for that, you understand. And the girl. I'm going to meet someone from Man City about her on Friday. And you. If you're interested, I could introduce you to a top coach *this Thursday*. Get him intrigued. Get you a trial. And we'll see what happens. Look, I get you're suspicious. I would be too. But there's a difference between a player like me and a player like you. You boss every fucking game you play in. You're top. You're *mint*! You must know you're good enough to play at a good level. It can't be *that* incredible that someone would think you've got a shot."

Raffi looked down. "I've been scouted. I've had trials."

"Oh."

"Yeah. I was in an academy for a bit. They liked me. It was going well. But I was in with a bad crowd. Things happened." He straightened up. "So that was that. I had my chance."

"Fuck that. Do you want to be a footballer, yes or no?"

He shrugged. "It won't happen."

I frowned. "Did you murder someone?"

"No."

"So what's the problem?" I put my fingers to my temples. I was rushing again; I needed to slow things all the way down. I'd been boning up on Shakespeare quotes in case I had to deal with more people like Bill Brown. "What's past is prologue. It's over. Yeah? Raffi. Go grab your shower. I'll wait in the bar. Come and talk to me. Let's be honest with each other, and we'll see where we get. How does that sound?"

He thought about it. "Show me the photo again."

"Ziggy?"

"No, the girl." I showed him Kisi pretending to sign her contract. He broke out into a lopsided grin. "You're so proud, and she's so happy. Look at that smile. I've got a daughter, you know."

"Mate. You're twenty . . . you're in your early twenties." Way too young to be a dad. Why wasn't he a constant, gibbering wreck? I know I would have been.

"Yeah. Life comes *at* you." He looked at the photo again. Finally, he took out his own phone and showed me a really cute baby doing one of those totally liberated baby gurgle-laughs. I'm not big on babies, but my mirror neurons went nuts. Raffi liked that.

"What's her name?"

"Leavsa," he said, waiting for my reaction. It was unusual, sure, but I'd heard weirder names. I'd been reading up on players with Ghanaian roots and found one called Nortei Nortey. (Don't believe in nominative determinism? He had eight yellow cards in his last twenty-eight games.) "Leavsa Brown," he said, nodding significantly. I still didn't react, so he started singing, "All the leaves are brown . . ."

I groaned, which made him laugh. "Leaves are brown? That doesn't even make sense. It's not funny. Why is it funny?"

He finished his little joke and said, "Her name's Serina. Serina Julia Brown. All right, Max. I'll be there. Ten minutes."

"One thing," I said. "Do you have any *moral* objections to becoming a pro footballer?"

"Like what?"

"Religious. Don't want to play in a kit with a gambling sponsor, stuff like that."

"No mate," he said, walking off. "I work in a casino."

He worked in the casino in Didsbury, cajoling customers to fill the gaming tables, solving problems, keeping the pit floor running smoothly. He liked the work, liked the people. The customers got a bit rowdy sometimes, but he could handle it. I told him that didn't surprise me, considering how he never reacted to the many times he got fouled.

He told me about his own, ah, rowdy past. He'd been one of the feral kids, the kind that infested my local park. Basically got up to a lot of weapons-grade mischief. Think joyriding (stealing a car, driving it around fast, then dumping it), shoplifting, thievery, vandalism.

Ironically, the crime that ended his football career was one he hadn't committed. One of the other lads had passed a certain door code to a local gang, and they'd burgled the changing rooms while a session was going on. Fled with a lot of watches and phones, emptied a few wallets.

"It wasn't me, but I could hardly plead my innocence, could I? I'd done worse than that."

I wanted to keep talking about him, keep digging, but he was just as interested in me. Especially about being an agent. So I told him my war stories (without mentioning the curse), how I got my break because the Queen died; how I gatecrashed the FC United training session; how I'd unscrupulously beaten Man City's Under-Sixteens and now had to go cap in hand, asking them to give my client a trial.

"And that doesn't bother you? Humbling yourself?"

The way he asked it irritated me, even though he didn't mean anything by it. I thought about the question. "If it was for me, yeah, I'd die of cringe. But it's for Kisi. She put her trust in me, and my role is to make things happen. They might shoot me down, but nothing's going to stop me from trying."

He was thoughtful for a while. "And what about me? What do you see for me?"

"I think you can play in the Championship. The path to getting there will be smooth sailing. Seriously. As long as you don't nick Ronaldo's car or some mad shit, you'll fly up the leagues. This season, FC United. They'll teach you the ropes, get you fit. Next season, Oldham. Wrexham. Someone like that. League Two, League One, Championship. A couple of years there, and we'll have a problem."

"What?"

"Like, do you want to play every week for . . . Preston or Birmingham. Big, big clubs, those! Be their first-choice midfielder, be one of the best players in the division. Or do you want a big move to . . ."

"Chelsea. My dad's a Chelsea fan."

"In Manchester? Weird. But Chelsea's a perfect example. They're always buying players they never use. So do you want to double your money and never play, or take less money but play every week? That's going to be the hardest choice in your life from now on."

He raised an eyebrow at me, which, ironically, made his face more symmetrical. "You're an agent. You'd push me to take the money."

I scoffed. "I'll do no such thing. When it comes to playing versus paying, your decision is final. Plus, by then, I'll be set for life. But generally, I want to see you play, not rot in the reserves keeping the bench warm."

"For Premier League money," he said, "I'll be the best bench warmer in the world. I'll pre-warm my arse before I sit down."

We didn't click. It wasn't easy. Being honest, I thought he was the kind of guy who starts fights in pubs. And he probably thought I was a smug twat. A showoff like the ones who kept leaving his casino with empty pockets. But we were both willing to take a step out of our comfort zones. We were both willing to work at it.

We came to a verbal agreement. We'd go for it. He was due to work this Thursday, but he'd try to swap shifts with someone. He thought it would be easy, because Thursday was a busy night in the casino, which meant good tips. People liked taking those shifts. We exchanged contact details.

I asked him to bring his best astroturf trainers and a white top. (I'd have to inform/sweet-talk Ziggy; I'd learned *one* lesson from bringing randos to the Beth Heads masterclass.)

Raffi wasn't on my hook, but he was sniffing the bait and was giving serious consideration to taking a bite.

Wednesday, October 5.

I took training with the Met Heads. Anna and Eva were there, as was Kisi. Her mother watched from the sidelines. She tried to be supportive, but soon boredom took over, and she whipped out a book.

Beth or someone had thought to bring a pair of shorts and a shirt for Kisi. See? People are great. I'm always saying that.

The coaching women's football story had sort of ended with the City game, but I wanted to see out the season. There were only a few games left; it wasn't that much of a commitment. We actually had the same number of points as City, and they were only top because of their vastly superior goal difference. If they somehow dropped a point somewhere, we'd win the league. But it was so improbable that I barely gave it any thought. If anything, they'd win their last games by even more goals than usual.

I wanted to see if I could improve players on my own without Jackie. Looking around at the ladies, I could see there had been a couple of drops in passing and technique, which was perfect for me. I only needed to improve them a fraction of a fraction of a point to see those attributes turn green.

So I copied Jackie's methods as exactly as possible. The Met Heads didn't mind, which is a testament to how interesting and useful the drills were. We did the basic passing drill, the sprint-and-pass drill, and the standing in a circle control drill (with imaginary circles, since I didn't have access to endless lengths of string).

Absolutely nothing happened.

Okay, I thought, no need to start crying just yet. Maybe it was because I was using Jackie's methods, and I needed my own. Well, thanks to a very tanned, very shiny-toothed footballer who had his own YouTube channel, I had some drills of my own. I didn't have any little plastic cones, but I did have a crate of beer that I'd bought from a discount shop during one of the lockdowns. The beer was completely undrinkable, which is to be expected when each can costs about forty-five pence, but the cans were luminous green.

Beth was unimpressed. "Max, you nutjob. Are you using shit beer as cones?"

"The beer is a metaphor," I said. "Also, whoever does the drill best gets to keep some cans. Terms and conditions apply." I finished laying out the cones. Yeah, let's call them cones. The players had to do little sidesteps for about a metre, then sprint forward, sprint left, gather a ball and dribble it forwards, cut back inside, and shoot. Then they'd walk to the back of the line and be ready to do it again. It was a lot more demanding than it sounds.

I realised Kisi hadn't joined in; she had vanished. Not for long though. She came out of the storage room with hundreds of little plastic cones. Right. The storage room. See, a proper coach would have remembered about that.

I thanked her and suggested she might want to stop *lollygagging* and start *drilling*. Soon she was as wobbly-legged as everyone else. I let this go on for a couple of minutes longer than I'd planned. The ladies were enjoying it, by which I mean they were complaining about it and calling me a sadist.

Finally, I blew my whistle. Twenty minutes into the session and no one had improved in anything. No green anywhere, except where someone had hit a beer can and it had started to spill. Why was it green on the *inside*? Jesus. Even Kisi, who should have been the one heading to the moon, was stuck on the launch pad.

I let everyone catch their breath while I considered this. I wasn't a coach. I wasn't improving these players. From a curse point of view, this session was useless. What else could we do? When I'd asked Jackie to change the drills, he'd done so instantly. He had years of experience and a solution to every coaching problem. I had zip.

We *could* work on some tactics, but we didn't need tactics for the remaining fixtures. We didn't have enough players for a full match. I felt a bit lost.

In lieu of preparing the ladies for a boss battle, I got them doing attack versus defence drills, keeping it interesting by changing the number of players. Four attackers versus two defenders, three on three, four versus three, but the attackers could only score from the right hand side. Stuff like that.

It was enjoyable, but in the overall scheme of my progression, pointless.

I needed a project. Something to work towards. A target. A mission. A quest!

45

THE HOSPITAL PASS

Football glossary: Hospital Pass. When a teammate passes the ball to you in such a way that you are likely to be clobbered by someone on the other team.

On Thursday, when I went to pick Raffi up, he had a surprise for me.

"This is Shona," he said, as I fist-bumped his wife. "And you know Serina." His little girl, all wrapped up like a Stay Puft Marshmallow Man in the crook of his arm. Shona wasn't what I would have expected. She was plus-sized, had a big, round face, and her hair tied back into a serious little bun. At first glance, she seemed like the brains of the couple. A smart cookie, weighing me up. I'd have to be careful with her.

It was clear Raffi wanted them to come along. I didn't mind, but had practical considerations. "I don't have a baby seat."

"I know the way to Stockport. We'll take our car and meet you there."

"We're not going to Stockport. I mean, we are, but we're stopping off somewhere first."

Raffi and his wife exchanged a glance. They'd expected some shenanigans. I didn't speak. They had to decide to trust me or not. Raffi had rearranged his shift; there was no point backing out over something so trivial. "Fine. I'll drive. You can leave your car here. Good?"

"Good," I said. I grabbed my sports bag and sports briefcase and gave Raffi directions to the care home.

I popped in to see Mum. Just for a minute. Raffi was uncomfortable. He told me he didn't like hospitals. Shona was fantastic. She offered to keep my mum company while I did whatever I was doing. I grinned and said she should come too, since she was part of this.

She wanted to ask what "this" was, but by now she was more curious than suspicious. We went in next door, and I introduced everybody to everybody.

Anna was looking much better. She was up and moving, leaning on a walking stick with oversized ferrules. "Max!" she barked. Her voice didn't have the power it had when I met her, but she was clearly on the mend. "Solly misses his walks."

"Max has been grinding," I said.

"I'm sure I don't want to know what that means," she sniffed.

Shona stepped in. "It means he's been working hard. Scouting football players." She gave Raffi a sideways hug.

"Oh. Is that what he does? We were wondering." Anna looked from Raffi to me. "Oh, I see. You want an assessment?"

"Yes, please."

Raffi shrank back. "Whoa whoa whoa."

I grinned at him. "We can discuss your phobias later. Come and stand here."

He didn't want to, but Shona pushed him.

"Solly," I said. "Should I take this guy on as a client?"

Solly had been waiting to get this moment over with, so he could return to his nap. He pottered over and sniffed Raffi. He looked up and started panting, a big dopey look on his face.

"Strong pass," said Anna.

"Pass like skip this one?" said Shona.

"Pass like he passed the test."

"Oh, good." Shona beamed. A sort of amused, joking pride. She didn't mind taking part in my charade.

"Shona. You're up."

"Me?" She was astonished.

"I told you. You're part of this."

She gave me an odd look, then stepped forward and bent down towards the dog. She put her hand out, and he sniffed it and rubbed his cheek against her. I waited for him to give the signal, but apparently that *was* the signal.

Anna said, "Top marks!"

"What about the baby?" I asked.

"No point," said Anna. "Solomon loves all babies. They're his weak spot."

Raffi looked quite bemused by the whole situation, but his relief that there was no medical stuff about to happen was obvious. I tapped him on the arm. "Let's roll. Anna, I'll be round to walk Solly one day soon. Promise."

Because we were about to meet a football insider, we had a quick discussion about signing a contract. *I* wanted it done before they met Jackie. *They* wanted to do it after.

"It makes no sense to introduce you to a guy who you can run off with and live happily ever after," I said.

"We're not signing anything until there's proof you know what you're doing," countered Shona.

"I'm about to burn a lot of networking capital if this goes wrong," I said. "This is a big risk for me."

"You'll survive," she said. "If there's something in this, we'll sign your contract, Max. Until then, put your seatbelt on."

I had to trust them. I had no choice.

We drove to Stockport. I got more and more stressed that Jackie wouldn't be there, but I had a strong suspicion that he would be. Surely, the thought of seeing me play would be absolute catnip to him? Still, I practically sagged with relief when I saw him, Ziggy, and Lula hanging around the entrance.

I did some quick introductions, and while Ziggy and Raffi went ahead into the changing rooms, Jackie held me back. "Ey up, Maxy Boy. If Raffi plays for this team, and Ziggy plays for this team, then why do they need to be introduced to each other? Why do I get the feeling you're going to play for two minutes and make me watch this Raffi guy the rest of the match?"

His doubts brought out a big smile. For once, I'd be able to keep everybody happy. "Jackie, I'll show you my best weaksauce moves; don't worry about that. But when you see this guy play, you're going to be begging me to get off the pitch and out of his way. Begging me."

He gave me one of his flat looks, those ones that are so out of character they practically hum with meaning.

I went into the changing room, whistling all the way.

Ziggy's team was called Cheshire Jokes, a pun on the local shopping centre, Cheshire Oaks. The Jokers played in white. The team was: Deck in goal; and outfield they had Graham, the frustrated plasterer; Hugh, who had told Ziggy to give me a chance; plus Musa, who had some Malian background. I was replacing Ziggy, and Raffi would be our sub. It was annoying that Jackie wouldn't get to see the star attraction for the whole game, but we weren't there to do a hostile takeover of the team. Anyway, even ten minutes would be enough. Raffi's talent had to be evident to the curse-free eye. It had to be.

I'd insisted on wearing shirt number seven. It was the shirt number of the player I always dreamed of being, a fast, tricky flair player. A show-off. From George Best to Eric Cantona to Ronaldo, the number seven is part of Manchester United folklore. If you see a United fan wearing seven, it's a fair guess they have the same delusions of grandeur that I had.

And now there I was, on the pitch, under the floodlights, kicking a ball around. It was very, very strange. Almost an out-of-body experience. I'd see the ball move away from my foot and feel the impact a second later. Huh?

I'd kicked a ball during the FC United training session. I'd joined in a Beth Head masterclass to check my false midfield tactic from the inside, but this was completely different. This was a real game against a real team: Viaduct Vikings, wearing blue. They seemed overly tall and fit for a game at this level. Like someone had stretched them out, or fed them wagyu beef every meal since they were toddlers.

I hadn't given this match much thought. I would turn up and run around. No big deal. The goal was noble, to protect Ziggy from himself. But now that I was there, everything was twisted and rotten. The artificial grass seemed unusually fake, a lurid green. When I moved, my feet were far too heavy, sort of like I was running in those Acme weights from a Bugs Bunny cartoon. I felt like I was wading through treacle underwater, like every blade of plastic was covered in thousands of little velcro hooks, and so was I.

I tried doing a couple of sprints but had to slow down, because I genuinely feared I'd topple forward and slam, head-first, into the wooden sidings. And worse, I felt my chest was zipped up. My lungs weren't there. I was sucking in air, trying to breathe, but there was nothing. The light was so harsh I was having trouble making my passes. I took a couple of shots, and they blooped feebly to the right. I had no sense of depth perception. Everything was too close and too far.

My body just wasn't working.

I started to panic. My team was so small and feeble. Our opponents were enormous. The referee was pressed against the side, a sinister, recessed, ghostly presence. Behind him were the faces of my friends and acquaintances. Ziggy, hoping I'd hold up my end of the bargain. Lula, interested. Shona and Raffi, carefully neutral. And Jackie, blank-faced.

If Jackie didn't think I was trying, he'd get pissed and leave. If I tried to sub off before the game had even started, he'd think I'd lured him here under false pretences. And leave.

I felt my brow. I was sweating profusely. What the fuck was happening?

The referee blew his whistle to start the game, and I drifted towards the defence. But I remembered I was replacing Ziggy, and he had been playing striker, as per my request. The ball bounced around a bit. I made some little runs away from the ball. Making space for other players? No, just cowardice. I didn't want to be involved. The way I was feeling, I'd probably try to play a pass and shatter into a thousand pieces.

This made no sense.

This made no sense.

While my brain was melting down into a kind of soupy mush, something happened. Musa got the ball and passed it forwards to a scampering Graham. I knew he'd try to do some trick way beyond his skill level. I had a premonition of where the ball would go, and suddenly I was moving. It felt like watching a point-of-view video with the sound off as I sprinted, gathered Graham's mis-kick, dashed towards goal, and slid the ball into the bottom left-hand corner. No one on the blue team got anywhere near me.

One-nil.

The game restarted. I still couldn't breathe. Just one big, satisfying breath. Please!

I watched as the blues knocked the ball around. I spotted an overload about to happen on the right. I ran back and intercepted the ball. Passed it back to Deck. Jogged back up the pitch, away from the action. I felt close to tears. Maybe I'd finally caught Covid. Maybe I was having hundreds of tiny heart attacks, like you read about sometimes. I had to get off the pitch. I had to go and beg someone to take me to the hospital.

I was just standing there, trying to be anonymous, when the defender I was using as cover ran forward to join an attack. I remained rooted to the spot, horrified. Now everyone could see me. There was no one near me. I was goalhanging.

Worse was to come. The defence held firm and recovered the ball. Hugh played a long pass out to me. I was one-on-one with the goalie, and I had all the time in the world.

I dribbled towards him, quite slowly, then turned to the right and ran along the curve of the goalkeeper's area, "the D." In this league, he wasn't allowed to leave it, so all he could do was shuffle sideways, inside the white line, like a crab, itty-bitty sideways steps, his arms as low as he could get them, waiting for me to shoot. The rest of the blues were thundering back towards me. With an insouciant look over my right shoulder, I booped a soft, back-heeled shot through the goalkeeper's legs.

I didn't even check to see if it had gone in.

Two-nil.

There was a lot of noise, but it all landed strangely on my ears. It was like listening to someone wiggling a large, flexible piece of plastic, strangely opposite waveforms. A soft cacophony.

On autopilot, I trudged back to our half. I should have taken that chance to leave the pitch.

Instead, the Jokers had decided I was George Best reincarnated and began passing to me at every chance. The last thing I wanted. I tried to play simple one-touch passes back to them. I really did. But a couple of minutes later there developed a particular pattern to how everyone was moving that triggered something in me. I zipped past one player and tapped the ball to Musa. All he had to do was knock it forward, anywhere really, and I'd latch onto it and be through on goal.

Musa did. He put it on a plate for me.

But I wasn't there.

As I played the pass with my left foot, one of the blues lunged at me, putting the full force of his fifteen stones (ninety-five kg) onto my vulnerable right ankle. Nowhere *near* the ball. I tumbled and howled with agony. I grabbed my foot like a baby grabs a nipple. It was still there, thank fuck! I tried to lift it, and another huge grunt of pain escaped me. I slapped the astroturf in a torrent of pain-fuelled rage and frustration. The guy had tried to cripple me!

Jackie and Ziggy came to lift me off the pitch. Raffi turned the baby away, protecting her from the horror. Shona had her hands covering her cheeks. Lula was torn—I thought—between worry and suspicion. "That one was real," I told her.

"I know," she said, in little more than a whisper.

Raffi asked if I was all right.

"It hurts like fuck," I said, looking up at them from my new home, the ground, where I was stuck on my back like an upturned beetle.

Raffi looked at Jackie. The guy who could help him become a pro footballer. It was conceivable Raffi might never get a chance like this again. With me off the pitch, Raffi would go on. Go on and show what he was made of. The first step in his new destiny. I saw the exact moment he made a decision. He handed his daughter to his wife, knelt, and tapped me on the chest. "Where's your locker key? I'll get your stuff, then take you to the hospital."

Something clicked inside me then. All negative thoughts of the guy just slipped away. Vanished into some other dimension. Gone. The pain in my ankle eased a little. "Hospital?" He wanted me to leave? What about the twat who'd attacked me? He was still ready to play. Satisfied with himself. Job done. Oh, job done, was it? I gritted my teeth. I had a vague memory of having felt weird. But now I simply felt cold. "Raffi?"

"Yeah?"

"Sub on."

"Be serious."

I grabbed him. "Get on the fff . . . ." I grinned. I'm guessing the least attractive grin of my life. "Get on the pitch, *please*." He didn't want to. He had, like, perspective or whatever. "Shona. Tell him."

She nodded at her husband, but Jackie reached out and held him back. "Raffi, yeah? I'm supposed to be taking a look at you, I guess?"

Raffi didn't know how to take this. "Yeah? I guess?"

Jackie gave him a friendly slap on the arm. "You just relax and play your natural game. But if that involves no-look backheel nutmegs . . . maybe keep 'em saved up fer a rainy day." Raffi vanished from my line of sight. Jackie looked down at me and shook his head. "Fucking hell, Max." He laughed. "You're such a prick."

"Is he on the pitch?" I said. "Is he playing?"

"Yes," said Shona, bouncing her daughter up and down. "There's daddy! Impressing the scout!"

"Has anyone got any cash?"

"I do," said Lula.

"Will you buy me a drink?"

"Of course. What do you want? Powerade?"

I tried to wiggle my foot around. It hurt. "Needs to be a bit stronger," I said. "Get me a brandy."

46

SOULMATES

Brandy is borderline disgusting, but it's what heroes drink in action movies when they've taken damage and want to keep fighting. My situation was more complicated; I wanted to get on my feet and watch the rest of the first half, but I needed to keep my foot elevated. So I lay there, head on the disgusting passageway, listening to the match, smelling the scene. Down at foot level it was all artificial smells: container ship plastic and deodorant spray and spilled Powerade.

One oddity: I'd picked up 1 XP per minute for the time I'd played. I suppose playing counted as watching.

XP balance: 1,299

But the real point of today was hoping my client would impress Jackie. "How's he doing?" I asked.

Ziggy replied. "Raffi? He's really good. But we're struggling. The Vikings are all over us." He was itching to get on the pitch and help his mates. No way I was going to allow that. There are times in life you have to put your foot down.

I heard two cheers, and both times the mood in our little camp cooled. Two-all.

The alcohol warmed me up though. I slipped into my brain pool, swam around, pushed myself back into memories of the first half. That first goal. The anticipation, the dribble, the shot. There was nothing particularly hard about any of it. I'd scored a lot of goals like that growing up. Perhaps this time it was a little sharper, a little more angular, a little . . . faster. I rewound the memory and pressed play. I found no emotion. *There* was the goalie, *there* were the defenders, *there's* the ball, so I take it, move *that* way, shoot. It was all inevitable.

The next goal was similar, but with added pizzazz. It looked like I was taking the piss, but it was simply the most efficient way to score from that particular scenario. I tried to replay the injury scene, but it was unavailable. Blocked.

I wouldn't let myself watch.

The pain and the boredom equalised. I spaced out.

The lads came off for half-time. They saw me lying there and discussed abandoning the game. "Don't talk shit," I said. "How long's the half-time break?"

I'd been to tons of these matches in recent weeks, but I'd also been to tons of others, all with slightly different timings and rules. "Five minutes."

"Great," I said. "Eat your bananas or whatever. Wake me up thirty seconds before the second half, and we'll talk strategy."

I closed my eyes and was immediately startled to feel someone shaking my left knee. "What?"

"It's time."

"Pull me up." I held my hand out and waited for it to be gripped. Someone pulled me upright, and I latched onto the nearest wooden perimeter board while standing on one leg. The Jokers gathered round to hear my thoughts. I suppose Ziggy had told them I was Tommy Tactics. Raffi was right in front of me, looking worried and interested. Maybe that's why he looked lopsided, because each half of his face showed a different emotion. "Lads. Here's the plan. Deck in goal. Hugh, Graham, Musa, two of you will be in defence at all times. Run hard, sub often. Pass to Raffi. Raffi. You're my omni-half. That's a new position I've just invented. I need you to do everything, be everywhere."

I brought my right foot down onto the floor with all the care of someone sliding nuclear rods into a new power plant. It hurt. Raffi spoke in his usual abrasive style. "That's only four. Who's up front?"

I pushed the gate open and stepped onto the pitch. *Hobbled* onto the pitch.

"Oh, no fucking way," cried Jackie. "Get back out here."

"Maaaax," whinged Ziggy. "Come onnnnnnn."

The second half kicked off, and I just pottered around for a minute. Every step was painful. Shooting with my right was out of the question. I could maybe use it to pass if I sort of locked my ankle and hit the ball close to the heel. As long as it didn't twist the foot, it should be all right.

Then I saw the guy who'd attacked me go into a challenge with Raffi. Raffi turned sideways, let the guy bounce into him. No big deal for a specimen like Raffi. But seeing it got my blood pumping. Big adrenaline spike. As Raffi stepped away with the ball, I found myself dashing towards him. He passed to me. I stopped the ball with my left foot, stopped it dead, left it there for Raffi to come on to, sprinted off towards the right of the goal. Two defenders tracked me. Four metres away from the goalie's D, I veered left, and found that Raffi had passed it exactly into my path. I struck the ball left-footed into the near post.

Three-two.

My momentum took me to the side boards in the corner of the goal. I held onto one. Something was happening to me.

It wasn't the surreal waking nightmare of the first twenty minutes. That was all long gone. No, this was something else. I looked at Raffi. He was grinning at me. I grinned back. I hobbled back to my own half so that the game could restart.

It went about the same. The blues attacked, tried to get into position to shoot. The whites closed down the spaces until Raffi got the ball. But when he got it, I'd already moved and was ready to collect his pass. I shaped my body as though I'd pass it back to the keeper but instead did a little backheel flick, spin, and sprint forwards. The ball rolled perfectly into Raffi's path, and he pushed it hard, diagonally, to where I met it and smashed it with extreme prejudice at the top-right of the goal. The goalie spread his arms out like a starfish, and actually got a good chunk of his upper arm onto the ball, but it barely changed the direction.

Four-two.

The contact I'd made with the ball was so perfect that it didn't hurt in the slightest. I barely felt it.

And again, there was that feeling. While the blues bickered with each other, I tried to identify what was going on. It was something barely within the realms of my comprehension.

Football is a team game, but it's one that I've always played solo. It's normally easy to spot an egotistical player. They are the ones who always shoot and never pass. They are total dicks. Me? I like passing and making assists. You'd need a very, very specific curse to notice that I, the great provider, the ultimate team player, was, in fact, utterly disconnected from the other guys. But that's how I'd felt my whole life. Pass me the ball, and I start making calculations. There's a guy running on *that* path, so if I pass the ball *there* he'll have a chance to shoot. Football as mathematics. One guy called me out on it once at school. Accused me of turning the sport into an exercise in trigonometry. I'd given him a harsh look, because I was astonished that he'd discovered my secret; he apologised and took it back.

What was happening here with Raffi was nothing like maths. It was . . . it was a true synergy. My movements, Raffi's movements, my vision, his vision. Intertwined. As one. I dropped deeper. Desperate to get more connection with him. We passed to each other a couple of times. Each pass was an affirmation of my existence, my place in the world. Our vectors, the only vectors.

Disgusted by our unity, sickened by the beauty of our process, one of the players darted towards me. Furious that the spell had been broken, I faked that I would sprint down the line, while Raffi made the same movement on the other side of the pitch, but for real. The assailant adjusted his line of attack to account for my new trajectory. I nutmegged him. Oops. And before I'd even looked up, I was playing a dream-swept left-footed pass that arced around and in front of Raffi, so that at the last moment he could clip the ball with his right foot, *doop!*, low into the net. Absolute perfection from start to finish.

Five-two.

The warmth was incredible now, and it wasn't the brandy. Raffi turned and beamed at me. Jogged back, smiling broadly, gave me a fist bump.

Graham came over, laughing, smiling, frowning. This was sport on a level he'd never seen so close at hand. "Bloody hell! How long have you two been playing together?"

"First time," said Raffi.

"Maybe in a past life," I said.

"Matthews and Mortensen," he said, and that pushed me so far past smitten, my knees nearly buckled.

1953.

The FA Cup Final, when that was the biggest game in world football. One hundred thousand in Wembley Stadium. The first game watched live by a huge television audience. Millions of people up and down the UK had bought TVs to watch the Coronation of Queen Elizabeth. Now they were using those TVs to watch one of the most incredible sporting events in history.

Bolton Wanderers are leading 3–1 against Blackpool. Their first goal was scored by Nat Lofthouse. Calling him a giant of the game reduces the word "giant" to pathetic, meaningless proportions. In some sports, the jersey numbers of famous players are retired. In a just universe, the very *name* Lofthouse would be retired. There is nowhere else for it to go.

Nat Lofthouse.

Type his name and choose any font size you want, the bigger the better. But leave yourself somewhere to go. Because there were two better players in that cup final.

Stan Mortensen scored a hat trick. The only player to score a cup final hat trick at the old Wembley. (He also scored four goals on his debut for England, amongst countless other achievements.) You'd think the game would be known as the "Mortensen Match." Not so. To find this match report, you need to type "the Matthews Final."

Remember Bolton were winning 3–1?

Enter Stanley Matthews. He'd been on the losing team in the two previous finals, and he was in no mood for the hat trick. He put in a personal performance so monumental that Mortensen's three goals faded into the background. It finished 4–3 with ten million watching, including millions of kids who would run outside and try to dribble like Stan. The year 1953 was the Matthews Final. End of.

Matthews kept playing at the top of English football until he was fifty years old. The first winner of the Ballon d'Or. The best player in Europe. Despite being hacked to pieces, he was never booked or sent off.

If Raffi and I were Matthews and Mortensen, I wanted to be Matthews. But I was Mortensen.

The real joy was knowing that Raffi was a student of the game. Interested in its history. Normally, the only people who cared about the OGs of the sport were octogenarians. Dudes who'd been around at the time or heard their dads going on about them. Hearing a guy younger than me say those names made me dizzy. I felt drunk; it wasn't the brandy.

47

PAINKILLERS

Watching me and Raffi did something to Graham. Instead of trying to do insane video game tricks every time he got the ball, he got simple. Simple pass, move into space, track back. Don't overcomplicate things. Yes, mate! Yes!

I walked past Raffi and murmured, "Let's see if we can get these guys on the scoresheet, yeah?"

"Aight."

And that's how we played the next five minutes. There was a lot of dribbling towards the sides of the pitch to attract defenders, a lot of fake shots to draw the goalie to one side of his goal, followed by switches of play to where Graham, Hugh, or Musa had a chance to score. The pressure of being on the end of such beautiful moves got to them, though, and they kept missing or hitting the crossbar. Not their fault, none of them had high finishing. Ziggy would have scored tons.

By now I was moving freely, while really pushing my luck in a way that infuriated me when I saw other people doing it.

I took a loose ball, burst into the corner, and waited for a defender to come and challenge me. It was Public Enemy Number One. The guy who'd tried to do me. Well, I was way past caring about that little shit but thought I'd give him a bit of a razzle-dazzle, just out of princi-ple, before setting up one of the others. When he came towards me—a lot more cautiously than before—I did some little pump-fakes with my right foot. I'm going left! I'm going left! But then I really did dab the ball to the left, and instantly flicked it back to where it had started.

As I accelerated past him, pushing the ball away with my left foot, he lowered his head to see where the ball had gone. His forehead crashed into the bone around my left eye. I fell to the ground. Half of my face felt numb. I tried to move, but I was simply stunned. After a few seconds I felt my face, and it seemed enormous. But it couldn't have swelled up that much in such a short time; it must have been some trick of the nerves.

I saw Raffi appear over me. He was pushing the other player away. The push contained a warning.

"That was an accident! That was an accident!" he was saying.

After cooling whatever the sitch was, Raffi bent to check on me. "How you doing?"

"Fine," I said. "Lift me up. I'll drop to the halfway line. You take the free kick, play it back to me on my left foot." I'd power home a low, curving thunderbolt. I could already hear the sound of it bursting through the net and hitting the board behind. *Swish! Thunk!* Matthews takes the free kick . . . and Mortensen has won it!

Raffi tsked at me. "Mate. You're done for the day." He turned and called "sub."

"No fucking way, man. We're just getting started." I tried to pull myself up. It's 1953, bro. There are no subs.

He put a hand on my chest and pushed me down. "You get off the pitch right now, or you can kiss your contract bye bye."

That's when reality bit. Stan Mortensen wasn't the agent for Stanley Matthews. I had to get back in my lane. And fast.

XP balance: 1,313

Someone, Jackie, I think, organised an ice pack and a pair of crutches. I was able to get home and pour painkillers down my throat.

Next morning, I could think, but I couldn't drive, so I took the bus to the call centre.

No one at work mentioned the crutches.

No one mentioned the enormous black-and-blue bulge around my eye.

Thank heavens for small mercies.

Manchester City Under-Sixteens were playing before the Met Heads. I went an hour early to watch them. Did I get 25 extra XP for paying close attention to the first half? Did I fuck. I was off my tits on painkillers. I got about six.

As the ref blew for half-time, I shuffled across the pitch at what I thought was ramming speed, but I was overtaken by two City girls, one walking backwards to face her friend. Well, the turtle beats the hare, doesn't he?

Sandra, City's manager, was looking at her notes. She was about to give her half-time team talk. I wiped away the drool that had built up over the last fifteen yards. "Hi, Sandra! Can I have a quick word?"

"I'm doing the half-time team talk."

"It won't take long. Anyway, you always overdo it. Thirty seconds is enough."

"Oh, is that right?"

"Yeah! You want me to demonstrate?"

"Be my guest. Ladies, meet your new coach, Captain Blackbeard."

"Huh?"

"The fierce pirate. I'm suggesting you're a brute. Not only because of your fresh new look."

"Wasn't he from hundreds of years ago? You need to update your references." I looked at all the tiny little faces peering back at me. The pain vanished. Absolute clarity. Just then, I *was* City's manager. My only defence is that I really *was* in agony. "All right, ladies, listen up. My name's Jake Paul." A chorus of complaints. "What? Not up to date enough? Jesus. Forget that. I'm some foetus who's got a TikTok. Fuck."

"What happened to you?" It wasn't Sarah Greene. It was the other midfielder. That didn't narrow it down. They were all midfielders.

"I was playing five-a-side last night and I got Meghaned," I said.

There was a huge uproar; they loved it. Meghan gave me a double-barreled middle finger.

"Here's my thirty second team talk. You ready?" I took a breath, nearly wobbled over. "We're going to play 1-3-2." I pointed to the midfielder that had been playing as City's main striker and used my fingers to demonstrate positions on the pitch. It was hard because taking my hands off the crutches meant risking a fall. "You. You and Carmen, you're the strikers. Play wide of the D. Don't track back. I know you want to come back and get involved, but you can't. Every time you do that, that's bringing the Beth Heads closer to winning. Yeah?" They weren't playing the Beth Heads. That was the pills talking. "Stay up there. Meghan, you're the one in the 1-3-2. The defender. Everyone else, you're the three in midfield. But you know what? It's more like 1-3-0-2. Those strikers need to be waaaay up there." Big wobble on the word "way." I steadied myself. "Midfield, do your Man City thing. But the strikers will be occupying two or more defenders, so you'll get loads of shots off. Wait for good chances, and hit low into the corners. Piece of piss. And, get this, Sarah, where's Sarah? You and that one. Sorry, I don't know your name," I lied. "You two can dribble sometimes. What you're doing wrong is dribbling and taking a shot. Taking the mick. That's why you're getting kicked by brutes like me. So dribble with the aim of pulling one of the last defenders out of their pockets, then pass to a striker. Carmen's got good finishing. She'll have an open net. Don't overdo it, and you're golden. Any questions? No? Good. One last thing, if you're through on goal, don't score a no-look backheel nutmeg."

I let that hang. Meghan put her hand up. "Why?"

I used my nose to point at my foot. "Coz this is what you get."

That unleashed a tirade of disbelieving taunts and mockery. Sandra, smiling, moved next to me. "Thanks to Loki over here. Okay, here's the real team talk." She waited until her squad was paying full attention. Then she grinned and jabbed her thumb at me. "What he said."

"Are you okay? Does it hurt?"

"What?" The City kids had run onto the pitch to experiment with their new formation. Carmen, their only true striker, looked terrified. I was wondering if I'd just dropped one of my trademark tactical nukes. The ones that tended to explode in my own face. But I'd achieved my main goal of ending the team talk early, so I could chat with Sandra.

Sandra was looking at my leg as though she might be able to X-ray it. "You winced or something. Are you in pain?"

I sighed. "No, that was social pain. I didn't mean to . . . show you up or be a dick or anything."

She reassessed me. "Your idea is weird. I love it. Teaching me isn't showing me up."

"Yeah, but," I started. I stopped myself and took some of the heat out of my voice. "But I didn't come over to teach you or anything of the sort. You're miles ahead of me. Look, I . . . Thing is, I've got a player for you."

Some kind of barrier came up. Fuck! I'd done it all wrong. *Quelle surprise.* But I had to get through this before the second half started.

And before I collapsed from ingesting more painkillers than calories. "Thing is, I'm not a manager. I'm not a tactical thinker. There's one thing I know I'm good at, and that's spotting talent. I've found a girl, and she's amazing. Almost as good as Sarah Greene. Attacking midfielder. Everything I've seen tells me this City team, under you, is the right place for her. I'd love you to give her a chance. You might not see it right away, but after like three weeks you'll be the one harassing me."

"Harassing? Why?"

"I'm her agent. I'm saying she might not blow your mind on day one. She'll be nervous and stuff. I don't know how much attention you give newbies. Not much, probably. I get it. But she's different. She's a top prospect. She just needs a start." I shook my head. "She's going to end up at City. She might as well start here." Sandra gave me a look. I knew that look. It was the face of a woman about to refuse to give me her phone number. So I dove in. "Wait wait wait." I took a deep breath. Wobbled. "If the problem is me, which is legit, that's fine. I'll cut myself out. You can deal with her mum instead. Just let her train with you for a month. You'll see. Really. You'll see."

"If I say yes, will you go to the hospital?"

"Yes," I lied.

"Fine."

"Wait." I said. "Get Meghan."

"According to you, she's our entire defence."

"Get Meghan."

Sandra whistled, and Meghan jogged over.

I squinted at where she seemed to be. "Meghan. Sorry again for the thing."

She shrugged. "We checked. Someone did get their leg broke."

"Yeah. But the other thing. Remember when we played you? I told this girl to say something mean to you. So we could win. But . . . that's on me, yeah? Don't blame her."

"I don't. It's all right. It wound me up, but I need to get used to that sort of bottom feeder mentality."

Ouch. "Right. Well, she's going to try out with you lot. I'd love it if you showed her the ropes."

"Why me?"

I rolled my eyes. "Because you're class?"

She tutted, but she seemed to like what I said and how I'd said it.

"I mean, I'll show her around, but I doubt we'll ever be soulmates."

And again, just for a moment, the pain cleared. I pointed at her. "You don't know that. You really don't know that. I thought I met mine. Gorgeous blonde from Newcastle." Meghan and Sandra looked at each other while rolling their eyes, which is literally impossible to do at the same time. I continued. "Turns out my *real* soulmate is a two-footed box-to-box midfielder from Longsight."

And while I stared into the distance like Ryan Reynolds in the six-out-of-ten movie *The Proposal*, Meghan mimed that she wanted to vomit.

I smiled at her. I hoped she'd find one someday.

48

PASSENGER

Football glossary: *Passenger. A player who sits back while his teammates do all the work. Used unfairly to describe Mesut Özil from 2016 to 2017. Used fairly to describe Mesut Özil from 2018 to 2022.*

Saturday, October 8.

Heavy knocks on the front door. I was ready, sort of. I'd woken up early, gotten dressed, prepared a little go-bag, then popped some pills and crashed back onto the bed.

More knocks.

"I'm coming, you dick. Kin 'ell." If I'd known this was going to be one of the most important journeys of my entire life, I might have been a little more reverential.

The letterbox built into the front door flapped open, and I saw someone trying to bend down to look through. No mean feat! The slot was only just above ground level, approximately ankle height. "Come on, Maxy boy! Big day ahead." Jackie, in the best mood of any person since humans developed happy hormones.

"Get fucked," I suggested.

I finally pirate-shipped my way to the door and opened it. "Rise and shine!" he cried, barging past me. "Did you eat brek? I brought you a roast beef butty. Your favourite."

"That's not my favourite," I said.

"Oh, that's right. It's *my* favourite. So if you don't want it, I'll have it. That was clever of me. Now then. You ready? Where's all your stuff? I'll grab it for you."

"There," I said, pointing to my little bag. It contained a thermos, an apple, and some Penguin chocolate bars.

Jackie, invading my privacy as well as my home, opened it. "Fuck! Are you a toddler or what? What's in the thermos? Lemon cordial? Where's your favourite Action Man for when you get disruptive?" Done taunting me, he looked up at the unusually high ceiling and decided to treat himself to a tour of my house. He zoomed around, flew up the stairs in three bounds. Just showing off because he had a functioning pair of legs. Prick. "Well, this place is grim. No wonder you never take girls back here."

I raised an eyebrow at him. How had he worked that out? "You think I'd bring a girl back to *Moss Side*?"

"I don't know *what* you'd do, Maxy boy." He grinned at me as he pushed past. "That's what today's all about."

Although he was being brash and annoying, he was pretty careful about helping me into his car. He'd already put the front passenger seat back as far as it'd go, he just generally let me take as much time as I wanted to slide-fall into it, and he supported my arm and whatnot.

He even ran in to get my baseball cap and sunglasses that I'd forgotten on the kitchen table. It didn't occur to me for days after that I'd left my "Queen's funeral notes" there by the toaster. He could have read it and discovered all my secrets! But he didn't, *I think* . . .

Once I was settled, he got in the driver's seat and turned the engine on.

"What are we—" I started.

He raised a finger. "Ah ah! We must respect the traditions."

He pressed play on his stereo, and we drove off. He turned onto Princess Parkway, heading south. And for three minutes there was no sound in the universe except the aggravatingly tedious strains of "You'll Never Walk Alone" by Gerry and the Pacemakers, the anthem of Liverpool FC.

Jackie was delighted with himself. "Did you enjoy that?"

"Did I endure that? Yes, I did. Very much."

He smiled. Good comeback. It was one-all. "How did you get on last night?"

I rubbed my nose. "Yeah, it went well. The kids loved my formation, and she's going to give Kisi a go. Fuck, I didn't even tell her!" I got my phone out.

"I meant the Met Heads, not . . . whatever the fuck you're talking about."

"Oh. Won 7–0. Five up at the break and they agreed to take it easy in the second half. They only really scored those last two goals out of boredom. Give me one second?" I'd also got a "win two in a row" achievement. Woop. The phone had connected to my client. "Kisi? Are you awake? Well, how am I supposed to know what time you wake up? Just shush your mouth a minute. You ready? I got you a trial at City." The scream filled the car and brought a big smile to Jackie's face. "Yeah, yeah," I said, trying to pretend to be serious. "Ho Chi Minh City," I said. She replied. I laughed and passed her response on to Jackie. "She says: when's the flight? This girl, seriously." Back to Kisi. "All right, listen. The coach is called Sandra. She's got your mum's number. They can work everything out. When you get there, ask yourself: what would Max do?" Jackie mumbled something. I laughed. "Jackie says: *and do the opposite.* If you have any problems, let me know." Jackie mumbled something else. "Right. Don't sign any papers if I'm not there. Got that? Good. Right, go and celebrate. Bye."

I relaxed back into the seat. With my frequent lapses in concentration, I'd only earned 96 XP the night before even though I had my eyes pointed at one full game and coaching the second gave me double XP. But it had been a big day. Maybe wearing a suit wasn't my ticket to becoming a successful agent. Maybe hopping around on crutches with a smashed-to-bits face was the thing.

XP balance: 1,409

"So it was Kisi," he mused.

"What?"

"When you were dancing around kissing Beth and generally acting the maggot, I thought it was because James was a prospect. But it was Kisi. And you think she's good enough for City?"

"Yeah," I said.

"And you've got the Met Heads crushing their league."

"The Met Heads are crushing their league. My input was minimal."

He laughed, but with almost no humour. "Ah, it's going to be one of those days, is it?"

"What do you mean?"

"There *are* times when you tell the truth. We've got a long ride ahead. I was hoping to hear from the real Max today."

We lapsed into silence.

Around Northenden, the meds started to kick in, and the pain became a little bit less overwhelming. After the golf course there would be some red lights, a bit of traffic, and at some point we'd hit the ring road and head . . . where? A long ride ahead, he said. How did I want to spend that time? In surly silence?

"Go on, then."

He glanced at me. "What?"

"What do you want to know?" I said. A peace offering.

That got his attention. He shifted in his seat like an F1 race was about to start. His excitement exhausted me. "I looked at the Met Heads results. This season and last. That game last night, it's always been close in the past. Now they're walking it. I want you to admit that's because of you."

I shook my head. "I put the ladies in the right positions. Beth and Nobby in defence. You've seen it. Left-foot, right-foot. Hard to beat. It's solid. Great base."

"So if you managed a struggling team, you'd start by fixing the defence?"

"What?"

"FC United, for example. You're the new manager. You start by making sure the defence is watertight?"

"No, I'd get the best striker I could."

He rolled his eyes. "You don't need to give me the Ziggy sales pitch," he said, driving absurdly close to the car in front.

Beyond annoying! "You wanted honesty! I'd start at the top. Goals. I want a dominant goal-scorer."

"Why? Coz goals win games? The striker's hat trick is no good if you lose 4–3."

Jackie tapped the brakes, and I grabbed the handle above my head. While I let out thousands of miniature swear words, Jackie let a little distance build up between the cars. I relaxed an equivalent amount. "I want a star striker . . . to sell. Guy's scoring thirty goals a season. Sell him for five hundred grand. Buy a new striker for two fifty. New striker's just as good as the last one. Scores thirty goals. Sell him for double what we paid. Rinse and repeat. Soon, you've got an entire team of players who are the best in their positions in the league."

"Squad building," he said. "You're into that."

"I love a bargain," I said.

"Squad building is a big process. Need to scout a lot of players," he said. "It's a lot of resources. And how can you be sure the new striker will be as good as the one you've sold?" He shook his head. "It's not easy. Every transfer is a risk."

"So don't pay. Get them in on a free. Like Ziggy. Like Raffi."

He tapped the steering wheel. Tapped the beat to some tune only he could hear. "Yeah. Like Ziggy." He was thoughtful for a moment. "Raffi I get. It's not hard to imagine him taking what he did on Thursday and doing it on a bigger pitch. A player like that, you'd want to test."

He was practically offering me a trial for Raffi! Now I was the one squirming like the race was about to start. "Are we going to talk about that?"

"All in good time, Maxy boy. We're still talking about Ziggy."

"We weren't, but okay."

Jackie glanced at me. I pointed straight ahead. Where his eyes should have been pointing. He tutted and pulled a face but turned to keep his gaze on the road. "Early September. Broadhurst Park. You turned up that day with the worst player ever to grace the pitch of FC United. The guy had none of the qualities of a good player. None. He was slow, physically and mentally. He looked like Bambi on ice, in headlights, except Bambi would have a better first touch. When you said he was a striker my appendix nearly exploded; I was trying that hard not to laugh. Well, I'm not laughing now."

The road in front of us was suddenly clear. "He's doing well in training, is he?"

Jackie nodded. "He's coming along. See, football isn't just about no-look backheel nutmegs and rainbow passes with a pot of gold at the end. It's about professionalism. Conscious living, conscious eating, conscious practising. Doing things to help the team win, whether that's chatting to an injured goalie to keep his mood up or making sure your absent-minded buddy gets to training on time. Or yeah, winding up an opponent or playing hurt. It's thousands of little things that separate football as fun from football as a profession. Hence, professional. Now, turns out Ziggy's got that mentality. He's learning, and he's willing to learn. No one is asking why he's still turning up to training. Some of the strikers are starting to look over their shoulders at him. In the words of one Max Best: *it's happening.*"

I felt a little surge of pride. "Ziggy, mate." We were still heading south. Towards the airport. Towards Birmingham. London?

"Yeah, yeah. But listen. Day one Ziggy, what've we got? We've got a guy with no visible skills. Nothing technical, nothing physical. And day one Ziggy is not a dominant personality. He's a nice lad, trying to fit in, a bit overawed, doing things he can't do because he's been asked. He doesn't have that Max Best *fuck you I'm not doing that* attitude. He's a puppy dog. So there's an obvious question, isn't there?"

"No."

"Question is, what did you see in him?"

I turned my head and stared at Jackie. He wanted me to confess to having Super Scout or what? The road surface was suddenly that bumpy one they use near the airport to give drivers a sympathetic dose of turbulence. "I'll tell you if you tell me what you're plotting."

"Plotting?"

"With Ziggy. There's something going on there. You've had chats with him about contracts."

"You're paranoid."

"So you haven't spoken to him about contracts?"

Jackie smiled. "I have. But you're still paranoid."

"It's not paranoia if it's really going on! Tell me what you discussed."

"That's between me and the lad. It doesn't go against your interests, I can tell you that much."

I was fuming. "You're not planning to ease me out of the way and become his agent?"

Jackie laughed. He lost his shit. He hadn't been expecting that. "What!" He laughed some more. "Ahhh, Max, I can't think of anyone less suited to being an agent than me."

The most absurd aspect of the situation was that because I was mad at him I had to praise him. How did *that* happen? "You'd be good at it. You've got contacts. You're good with people. You could even train clients up in your spare time before trials. What's the problem?"

"The problem is that if I dicked Man City 4–0, I wouldn't have the fucking nerve to say, by the way have you met my client. I wouldn't walk into a full church on a Sunday morning and come out with—what did you say?—an *ebullient* attacking midfielder. Jesus, Max, if I listed all the mad shit I've seen you do and asked a hundred people how many'd be willing to do that for their clients . . . fuck that. Big fat zero. Including me."

Well, he wasn't planning to steal Ziggy. That much was certain. Or he was the best actor ever.

So now it was time to explain how I could see potential in players. I'd been mentally workshopping this for quite a while. Ideally, it would have been delivered alongside stirring Hollywood music.

"Right," I said. "You're not going to steal my clients. Fine. I believe you. But you're up to something, and I don't like it." The road was smooth again, and we'd passed a long haul truck to find it was the last one for ages. Plain sailing. A good omen for the test drive of my big lie. One based on a foundation of truth. "When it comes to how I find a player, do you want the long version or the short version?"

"Short."

"I watch them and see who they remind me of."

He chewed his lip for a while. He wasn't convinced. "Give me the long version."

I sighed. "I bet you were always first pick in school. I was always last." The daily playground ritual, carried out tens of thousands of times a day all across the nation. Two captains choosing teammates one by one. The last choices in my playground? Paul, a chubby goalhanger wearing glasses. Max Best, a footballing void. "I'll take Paul," was something I heard hundreds of times.

"You?" he said, incredulous.

"Yes."

"Most lads who make it as a pro were first picks. It's hard to think that a pro player was ever last pick."

"Yes!" I exclaimed. "I agree!" Anything that would shut him up about me having potential was most welcome. It was a pointless distraction from the real prospects: my clients. "Anyway, I liked footy but only as a thing to do instead of Maths. Cricket was just as good."

"Tennis ball cricket in the playground?"

"Yep. Hand for a bat. Or Tickey-It. What Time Is It Mr. Wolf? Obstacle courses. I suppose I just liked running around, and if there were rules, so much the better. So then came the 2006 World Cup."

"That was your first, was it?"

"Yep. Italy won. Do you remember who their best player was?"

"I do. Cannavaro. Centre back. Like me."

"Everyone was raving about him, but I couldn't see the difference between him and the next guy. How long's a World Cup? Five weeks? I thought about it all the time for five weeks. And I didn't think of it in those terms then, but I started to suspect the difference between him and another defender was their *quality of movement*. His general balance, his control over his body, the self-control to only do the things he's mastered."

Jackie looked doubtful. "Okay."

"I'm not saying I was good at it when I was six. I'm just saying I started to watch sport with that thought in the front of my head. I built a mental image of Cannavaro and every centre back I saw got compared to him. And Vidic. And van Dijk. I'm really interested in Lisandro Martinez now, because if he can succeed as a short centre back, then he opens the door to thousands more players. I found that because I was studying players so intently, it made me a better player. I could copy some of their moves. My problem was putting it all together; in the exact right conditions I might be able to flick a looping header into the corner of the goal, but then I'd miss the thirteen other headers in the game. So it's not just the movements but the consistency of it. I wasn't the worst player anymore, but I was still picked last. Isn't that crazy? People are shit at spotting talent. Me being me, I decided I wanted to be good at it. I never thought, *oh I should be a scout*. I just wanted to be able to pick a player. Comparison. That's the key to it all." I tapped the dashboard. "When I saw Ziggy, I instantly thought: oh! He's Chicharito."

"Chicharito!" This blew Jackie's tiny little mind. Chicharito was a Mexican striker who played for Man United for a while. He didn't do much for the team. He couldn't dribble, tackle, cross, or hold the ball up. All he could do was score goals. Jackie's amused contempt for the idea pushed his face out in all directions, but it soon started to settle back. There was even a tiny frown developing. "Chicharito . . . Oh my God . . . I think you're right. I see it!" He went silent and moved into the slow lane, so he could concentrate more. "If Ziggy keeps developing the way he is, he could end up as a sort of Chicharito comp. Sure. But you didn't see that the first time you scouted him."

"I did," I said. "Not consciously maybe. But the patterns. The movements. The way he addresses the ball. The way he hides then pops up. His scampering little run. A thousand tiny factors. I've been training myself to compare players against each other since I was little."

Jackie took ten seconds to chew this over. I saw him swallow some question, then he indicated, accelerated, and brought us back into the fast lane.

We must have swung to the west, because the motorway signs suggested destinations like Warrington (why?), Wrexham (maybe I'd meet Ryan Reynolds!), or . . . and it seemed inevitable . . . Liverpool.

49

DETOURS

One does not simply walk into Mordor. And one does not simply drive into Liverpool.

"I need a break," I said.

"What?"

"My leg hurts. I need to potter around a bit. Stretch." The truth: I wanted to mentally prepare for the ordeal. What was the population of Liverpool? Eight hundred thousand? Eight million? All sounding like Jackie. All with knowing smiles. All bringing every conversation round to The Beatles. "What's your favourite band, Jackie?"

"Arcade Fire."

Okay so they didn't talk about them *all* the time. Still. I needed to get ready.

"What's yours?" he asked.

"Coldplay."

"That's what people say when they want the conversation to be over."

"Yep," I said.

"You started it."

I checked my phone for new messages. "I don't listen to loads of music. I like songs that go *wooh*."

Jackie scoffed and frowned and, after a while, turned into one of those motorway cafe places. We topped up on petrol first, then drove on to the mini mart slash restaurant car park. "Walk around the shop or just stay here?"

"Stay here," I said. He helped me out. It was nice to stretch my legs, but the area was an echoey concrete horror show with cars and trucks whizzing past fifty yards away. What had I been expecting? The Hanging Gardens of Babylon? "Changed my mind. How about a cup of tea?"

Inside, I settled at a table while he went to grab some drinks. He poured sugar into his tea—of course, despicable—while staring at me. "You're a nervous passenger."

"If you say so. I just hate when people watch films with Al Pacino 'driving' for eight minutes looking sideways and think they can do the same."

Jackie rubbed his temples. I was exasperating him as much as he was annoying me. "Max, what do you want?"

Big question. "In terms of . . . ?"

He sighed. "Can I ask you a question without you bursting a blood vessel?"

I sipped my tea. I felt quite chill. Not completely centred, because I didn't know what was going on. Maybe we were just going to watch Liverpool or Everton. Whatever the plan was, I wasn't exactly excited, but I wasn't exactly apprehensive either. I suppose what it boiled down to was that I trusted Jackie. "Ask away. I'll show you a zen master at work."

"Have you really never played Champion Manager?"

My eyes widened. We were back to that! I didn't need to count to ten before answering. "I'd never heard of it." I scratched the back of my neck. "I suppose it made me look a bit of a dick that day. Mum must have mixed me up with some TV show or something. That's what was so stressful. Seeing her have these false memories. That's not good. You get that, right?"

"Oh, yeah. Like I said, I know it must be hard." He looked around the cafe. There were all kinds of people there. All kinds except the rich. "What's your plan right now? Your plan for life. You don't want to stay in that call centre."

"No. You guys are going to give Ziggy a contract. You're going to sign Raffi. Thousand pounds a week between them, hundred for me. If I can find seven players like that by January, get them all signed before the end of the transfer window . . . I can quit my job."

"What about Kisi?"

"A fourteen-year-old in the women's game? There's no money in that. Is there?"

He thought about it. "Not for years, no. So you've quit your job. Then what?"

"Get more clients. Go to games. Do football things full-time until one of my guys gets a big move. Then . . . see how I feel."

"What about Beth?"

"What?"

He did something with his mouth. Uprooted some expression before it could flower. "What about coaching the Met Heads?"

"There's nowhere to go with that."

"You like it though."

"Yeah. But it's not going to lead anywhere. If I was in charge next season we'd have to beat City twice to win the league. Okay. I don't think they'd let us do that. And it's two interesting games out of ten. Last night wasn't really fun. There's nothing for me to do." Just clicking Free Hit and shouting "Yes, Nobby." Even Frank Lampard could do that. "I'd like to do eleven-a-side."

He looked up sharply. "Playing?"

"Managing. Like Sunday League or something. But . . . ideally with less shit players. I really loved doing FC United reserves. If . . ." I stopped. Felt guilty. But fuck it, he wanted honesty. "If I got rich enough to buy a little team, I'd be the manager. Bring in new players, do the tactics and that. Make money wheeler dealing. That's pretty much my ultimate dream right now."

He stared at some point on the ceiling before fixing his gaze on me once more. "And what about playing, Maxy boy?"

I groaned, but we'd discussed that hideous computer game thing plus my current wildest dream. Why not get this out of the way too? Maybe there would be a normal, healthy relationship on the other side. "What the fuck is your obsession with me as a player? I am dogshit. I've told you several hundred times."

His face had lost all expression. That thing he did. What did it mean? That he was angry?

"Dogshit?"

"I am no good. All flash, no cash. I have a couple of party pieces. Decent five-a-side player. I'm virtually *useless* on a full-size pitch. Trust me! I've been me for twenty-two years! I'm flattered you think I'm talented, some kind of throwback number seven, but you're way off." I couldn't see my own player profile, but I was definitely CA 1 and maybe, maybe had a slightly higher PA. Like 7. Ten at the outside. And that was extremely wishful thinking. I'd seen thousands of players, and almost all had CA 1 PA 1. Why would I be different?

Jackie smiled, entirely without mirth. "Decent player, are you? Decent." He clicked his neck left and right the way action movie stars do before they start throwing wall-smashing haymakers. "You wanted me to watch Raffi on Thursday. And I agree with you, he's got something. He's decent. More than decent. Would I give him a trial? Absolutely. But he looked like a two-legged dog strapped into a roller skate compared to you. Before you got injured, you looked like peak Messi. Absolute, stripped-down efficiency. Didn't waste a single movement. That's not possible to coach. Believe me, I've tried. Anticipation. Imagination. Execution. Then you get kicked, justifiably so, some might say. And in the second half we get phase two of the Max Best Cinematic Universe. The Drunken Master. Nimble. Crafty. Elusive. And you and Raffi. Mate. I've seen some good connections between players in my life. McManaman and Fowler. Salah and Mane. Messi and Alves. And yeah, even your own Cole and Yorke. But I've never seen actual fucking telepathy on a football pitch before!" He was turning red. He seemed genuinely furious. He pushed his palm down onto the table. The gesture helped to calm him. "You might be the best judge of a player in the *history* of football. That remains to be seen. I'll grant you've got a good eye. But you can't scout yourself. You just can't. And I'm saying: I *wouldn't* give you a *trial*. I'd hand you a professional contract right now. Right now!"

His anger had wound me up. "In what position?"

"Striker. Playmaker. Right-midfield, number seven, yeah. The new Beckham. Except you're not right-footed. You're ambipedal. So you can be Beckham one match, Robertson the next. Who knows? I don't know. And you certainly don't fucking know. We won't know until you *try*. I don't know why you're so resistant to it. Why you're so belligerent about it."

"Because I know exactly how good I am."

"I don't think you do."

"What you saw on Thursday says more about Raffi than me."

"Fucking endless sales crap. Will you cut it out for one minute? Please? For *Christ's* sake. I saw it *before* Thursday. I saw it the first time you came down to Broadhurst. The first time you kicked a ball. I called you a silky-smooth playmaker, remember? Why do you think I agreed to train the Met Heads? It wasn't to spend more time with Ziggy. That's when I caught your next performance. Perfect technique, perfect control. And the week after, nutmegging me to prove a point. After you *said* you wanted to meg me. After you narrowed the space so the only way round me was *through* me. And you did it anyway." He shook his head with a wry smile. "I used to be a pretty good defender, you know." He unwrapped the little biscuit he'd gotten with his tea. I chucked mine across to his side of the table. He devoured that too. In a more normal tone of voice, he said, "I'd like to set up a trial for Raffi *and* you. We'll all learn something about Raffi, and we'll all learn something about Max Best. Unless you want to climb the Empire State Building and thump your chest at the very *temerity* of the proposal."

I thought about how it would be to turn up for a trial alongside a group of actual professionals. It would be humiliating in a potentially psyche-crushing way. But maybe I could style it out. *Yeah, I know I'm shit. I'm an agent. I just wanted to know what my clients have to go through. Trying to become a better agent, you know? Yeah, it* is *a good idea.* "If I go to a trial, will you shut up about it forever?"

"Yes."

I looked down at my ankle. "I'll do my best for fifteen or twenty minutes, I promise, just so you can see that I'm abysmal. But I'm done getting crippled one body part at a time. I'm not going into fifty-fifty challenges. I won't challenge for headers against hardened defenders."

He considered that. He wasn't completely happy about it. "Fine. You can take the corners."

"Take the corners," I muttered, "Jesus. And my 'trial' will have to wait till I can move more freely. Raffi can't wait. He's got a glittering career ahead. If he's not at the casino, can you take Met Head training again next Wednesday? We can get him working on his skills, get him thinking like a pro. If I can book you for private sessions with him, let's talk about that. Actually, let's bring Ziggy and Kisi too." This was an exciting idea. If it cost me a hundred pounds to improve all my clients' CA by 1, once per week, that would quickly prove to be a bargain. By January, that alone would bring Ziggy to about CA 20 and Raffi and Kisi to CA 10, quite apart from whatever other training they were getting. And maybe I could get the same results even cheaper! I was paying Jackie a premium because I was desperate. "Actually, do you know any other good coaches I could try? You know I'd prefer you but you're not available Tuesdays and Saturdays." A thought occurred to me for the first time: FC United had a match today. Why wasn't Jackie there? I expected the answer would present itself. "Maybe I can use someone cheaper until my boat comes in. What's the minimum number you need for a training session? I reckon I could convince some Beth Heads to make up the numbers. Or Ziggy's mates." But maybe my clients would improve faster if there weren't rubbish players in the way . . . I bit my nails. I'd have to do some tests. This theoretical second coach might be cheaper, but they'd want the cash up front. Maybe it'd be better to keep using Jackie, since he was curiously laid back about working today for payment tomorrow. "I wonder if Beth's lot have that sports hall the whole year or just during their season. I'll have to ask."

Jackie rubbed his shiny head, two-handed. Then he flopped his arm on the table and looked to the left. It was a gesture halfway between relaxed and defeated. He groaned and sat back. "I try to talk about *you,* and you always bring it back to your clients. I mean," he scoffed, "fair play. I've met a lot of agents and a lot are parasites who don't give a shit about their clients, but you really fucking put the work in." He rubbed his head some more, then slapped himself on the cheeks. He held his hands there for a second. "I could do a session with four," he mused. He went internal for a minute, obviously thinking of some drills and challenges suitable for a small group. With an annoyed shake of his head, he finished his tea and stood up. "How's your ankle?"

"Mashed."

"Did you get it checked out?"

"I didn't have a thirty-six-hour gap in my schedule to wait in ER."

He tutted and wandered off. I saw him dial someone, but then I had to focus on trying to stand up. The process was like assembling an IKEA bed, but with even more swearing.

Back in the car, there was a bit of residual temper in the air. Jackie seemed to be deep in thought. Infinite monkeys with infinite type-writers wouldn't have produced his next question. "Who'd win: a team of Messis or a team of Ronaldos?"

I blinked. "Are we done with the heavy stuff?"

Jackie laughed. "For now, yeah."

As we approached an enormous motorway sign saying, "Next exit: Liverpool," Jackie moved into the closest lane and slowed down. Exit: four hundred yards. Three hundred. One hundred. And then we were past it. In disbelief, I turned my head as far as I could. We really had missed the turn! Jackie accelerated and moved back into the fast lane.

I glanced at him; he was grinning.

He'd been fucking with me this whole time.

So where were we going? For the first time I was curious.

I took my phone out and went to the maps app. On this road, the only destination that made sense was Wrexham. Unless he wanted to drive to the coast and fling us both off a cliff, Thelma and Louise style.

Fishing for clues as to our destination, I said, "So what do you think about Wrexham being bought by Ryan Reynolds and Rob Macinally?"

"Mac-ul-henny," he said. "Rhymes with penny. Like the song. Haven't you seen the documentary?"

He meant *Welcome to Wrexham*. "I've started but I've got lots to get through. *All or Nothing*. *The Sunderland* one. There's even one about Southampton's academy."

"Huh. I've never heard of that."

"It's on CBBC." The children's wing of the BBC. No surprise Jackie hadn't come across it.

"Why you watching *that*?"

"I feel a lot of this football stuff is sanitised. Clubs don't want their secrets getting out; they don't want you to know what football really looks like from the inside. But there's so much content now. If you keep your eyes peeled, you might be able to piece it all together. From the fragments."

"You make it sound like a murder mystery."

"You've got the right name for a Scandi noir," I said. "Jackie Reaper. You could be the killer or the detective."

"It's just a name," he said. He didn't like talking about his surname. Didn't think the jokes were funny. "So you want to see football from the inside? How about we take a little detour to one of my old clubs? I'll show you around the dressing rooms and stuff."

I stared at him for a while. He was doing to me what I should have done with James Yalley, slowly get him interested in the idea of playing football. Take him to the inner sanctums. Meet a few pro players. Smell the changing rooms. "This *detour*," I said. "Are we going to get into the dressing room and find there's a shirt hanging up with my name on the back?"

He went blank-faced again. "Why would we see that, Maxy boy?" He scoffed. "I work for FC United, remember? Christ. You should write detective books. Your imagination is vivid as fuck."

50

CHESTER ZOO

On the way to Wrexham, we stopped off in Chester. I'd never been there before. Pretty much the only things I knew about it were that Jackie had played for Chester FC a few years before and that it had a big zoo. When we left the motorway, and it became clear we were going into the city itself, I looked it up on Wikipedia. Population eighty thousand. Cathedral, castle, city walls. One of *those* places.

The outskirts were very green. Large, empty fields, big, lush trees. We drove through the centre, where there was a lot of traffic. Jackie knew every turn and didn't once consult his phone's navigation. I got the sense that we were taking a slower route so that I could have a look around.

From the car, the city was unremarkable. Very much like Wythenshawe or much of Manchester. Not as obviously poor as Moss Side, not as obviously affluent as Didsbury. Just an average kind of place but with the occasional bit of preserved wall or an olde time shoppe that explained why it was considered a tourist destination.

We left the tourist stuff behind and entered a light industrial zone. I was looking at a huge car showroom when suddenly we were pulling into the car park of a small football stadium. Was this where the youth team played?

White text on a blue background: Deva Stadium. And on a new line: Home of Chester FC.

That was written on a sort of office building attached to the stadium. On the actual main stand were the words "Our City, Our Community, Our Club." To me, it seemed that those words were in the wrong order. Surely they should have been reversed?

The car park was far from full, but it was obvious that today was a match day. There were stewards and attendants and people in high-vis jackets. There were vans selling jacket potatoes, burgers, or smoothies (ooh posh!). There were stalls selling blue-and-white scarves and unofficial merch.

Jackie parked, got out, and waved at someone. It was a cute woman in a ponytail. Oh! A bit of excitement at last. She moved with the grace of a swan. She was pushing a wheelchair. Maybe she was one of those volunteers who helped disabled fans.

Nope. She pushed the chair right over to my side of the car. When he wasn't trying to get me to become a pro player, Jackie was busy trying to have a laugh at my expense. He opened my door. "Your carriage awaits, Mister Best." He beamed at me. Delighted with himself.

Fortunately, I was still wearing my baseball cap and sunglasses, so the cutie wouldn't remember who I was.

Strangely, I already knew who *she* was.

Her name was hovering over her head, along with a lot of question marks. Livia Strandon. She was twenty-five and, presumably, part of the coaching staff. "Aren't you going to introduce me?" I said.

"Livia, this is Max. Max, Livia."

They both sort of stared at me expectantly. I think—scratch that—I'm *one hundred percent sure* Jackie had told her I'd start flirting with her hard from minute one, and they were both waiting for the show to begin. I tried to think of something mundane to say. "Before I forget," I said, "Do either of you have Disney Plus?"

Jackie wheeled me into the office building, through a lot of doors, past a lot of people saying, "Oh hi Jackie!" and "Jackie! Great to see you!" and so on. He was king of the jungle around here! The insane level of social proof was doing something to Livia. She looked at Jackie with big doe eyes; she was into him in a big way. I briefly wondered if I could put on a show so dazzling that her eyes would wander, but the thought didn't last long. Impressing Jackie's lady by accident was one thing. Consciously doing it was . . . unthinkable.

The lovebirds eased me onto a treatment table. Wait, what? We'd just been walking through some bog-standard office corridors.

I looked around and found I was in a medical space. It was all very confusing at first, but obviously there were always breaks and strains in matches, and injured players needed a place to get treatment. It was busy before the games too, it seemed. Players were coming in to get massages and to discuss little bumps and scrapes with the medical staff.

The curse was giving me tons of data. There must have been, like, ten coaches at this club.

Ow!

Livia was trying to take my right trainer (sneaker) off. "Sorry," she said. "No, it's okay. I just didn't expect it. Are you a coach?"

She laughed. "Physio."

Of course! Physios! The curse was showing me *their* profiles, too. So I could get the profiles for players, managers, coaches, and physios, except that in the last three categories I could mostly see only question marks. Something to unlock later in my career.

But—and here was another mystery—there was one physio who had side-arrows on his profile screen. I did that thing where I reprogrammed the curse to let me swipe instead of having to tap the arrows. I got a short, sharp pang of headache, but then I was able to swipe. And on the next screen was . . . drum roll . . . a player profile. So this guy was a player slash physio! I'd never heard of that.

His name was Magnus Evergreen.

Seeing his profile briefly made all the pain vanish from my body. I was there, floating in space like a second moon, but the heavenly body I orbited wasn't the delectable Livia. It was Magnus. I checked and double-checked his profile. It was beyond baffling.

First, it listed him as competent in every position except goalkeeper and striker. This guy could play virtually anywhere.

He was below average on the technical attributes that I could see and above average on the physical ones.

He had CA 23.

He had played a few games last season, if I was interpreting the history screen right, all as a substitute.

But his PA . . .

I wish I knew a way to tell you this next bit really slowly so that your eyes would double in size like mine did.

His potential ability was . . . minus two.

I called out to him. "Excuse me, sir?"

The guy was bending some player's leg backwards in a way that reminded me of a flamingo. I say "some player" like I didn't know who it was. I think it was because I was in the bowels of the stadium or being treated as a football insider instead of a scout, but I was seeing all the profile data from everyone. More on the players later.

Magnus Evergreen looked over at me. He was white but not necessarily Swedish white. Do you know what I mean? He had super overgrown arms, think Vin Diesel. But then he had thin, spindly calves. Talk about skipping leg day! I would have called him handsome if his biceps didn't make his head look about four times too small for his body. His nationality said English slash question mark. I'd never seen anything like that on the nationality section before. It seemed the curse didn't know! He pointed to himself as if to say: *who, me?*

"Yes, you. Is your name . . . Marcus?" I was trying to be better at the whole knowing people's names thing. This seemed like a good workaround.

"Magnus," he said. He asked his patient to wait and then came over to me. I was still wearing my cap and sunglasses, indoors on an overcast day, but somehow I wasn't the weird one.

"Right!" I said. "Magnus Evergreen. I remember now. And you're a player-physio?"

"Player-coach," he said. "But just coach, really."

"You played three games last season," I said.

Jackie had been typing on his phone, but now he was looking at me like a mobster who's just found out the guy sitting next to him at the bar has got a winning lottery ticket in his pocket and hasn't told anyone he's won. Why did me knowing this guy's history make him suspicious? Maybe because Evergreen was one of the most obscure players in world football. I *had* to be careful with this curse, or it was going to bite me in the behind!

"Just to make up the numbers when there was Covid or injuries," said Magnus. "I'm really just a coach."

"Magnus specialises in fitness training," said Livia. "That's why he helps us out. He knows more about anatomy and biomechanics than any of us have forgotten. Except Dean. Wait, did I say that wrong?"

"Who's Dean?"

"Head Physio. He'll be here in a minute wondering why you're taking up a bed on a matchday." Livia looked at Jackie, who was still staring at me in that uncanny way. Seeing that Jackie wasn't bothered by her words, she turned her focus back to me. She'd gotten my trainer and sock off and was examining my foot.

"Magnus," I said, fascinated by his negative PA. "There's something about you I can't put my finger on. What would that be?"

"Oh," he said, daring to smile. "Perhaps you're reading my aura. I have the cleanest aura of anyone in the staff."

"It could be that," I admitted. "Are you a rower?" I wanted to find out why he had massive arms without asking if he had gorilla DNA.

"A rower?" He held up his thunderguns. "Oh, these? No. I was a world champion bodybuilder. But once I'd mastered that, I put it behind me and sought a new challenge. My goal now is . . ." He looked down, then up at Livia. "Is not interesting."

She nodded at him. They'd discussed this before. Potentially many times before. So he was into auras, was a fitness genius, and had an ambition so weird he'd been told never to mention it.

"Well, I don't mean to pry," I said, but it was hard to wrench my attention away from him.

The next intensely weird moment was when the Head Physio, Dean, came in. Fairly short, fit, looked like he did half marathons for fun, and talked about anti-inflammatories with waiters. He scanned the room like a true master of the universe. He saw Livia gently rotating and palpating my ankle and sidled close to her. He watched her for a moment; she turned red. His entire being screamed that he didn't want me there, and her entire being screamed that she knew that. I wondered why Jackie had set things up like this. It was *his* girl in the firing line.

Dean took in a deep breath, an angry dog about to bark, when a whooshing noise came from Jackie's phone. He'd sent a message.

"Ah, Dean," he said. "Glad you could make it to work today." Jackie checked his watch. "Let's have a tiny chat in the gym."

"Oh," said Dean. "Jackie. Yes, of course."

They left together through a pair of double doors. Livia stared in their direction, my injury forgotten.

"Sorry to be a bother," I said.

She re-engaged with me. "Oh," she said, her professional mask reassembling with every breath. "No bother. Any friend of Jackie's is . . . How long have you been friends?"

"Since we met. I liked him right away."

"How did you meet?"

"I was climbing a tree and couldn't get down. Jackie rescued me."

"Oh, interesting," she said, proving that she hadn't been listening. Then it clicked. "You're from Manchester, right? I spent a weekend there once. Never got a straight answer from anyone. I don't know how Jackie stands it."

"Oh, Manchester!" I said. Well . . . sung. Everyone in the room turned to watch. "Is wonderful! Oh, Manchester is wonderful! We've got chips, pie, and United! Oh, Manchester is wonderful!" I gave myself a little clap at the end, as the chant demands.

"Boo!" booed the three Chester players who were in the room. "Hiss!"

I treated them all to a middle finger. They loved it. People are weird.

Now, in retrospect, it was only the idea that this was a detour on the way to Wrexham that had me so relaxed and willing to be myself. The truth was, even though this was a small club, it was a proper club on a proper match day. Real inner sanctum stuff. Jackie hadn't been joking when he said he'd show me the inside. If I'd had time to think about it, I might have been more timid.

The double doors burst open, and Dean came striding towards my table. He looked at Livia. "Well? What do you think?"

"Really bad sprain," she said. "Could be worse, but we'd need an X-ray to know."

"So?" said Dean. His entire aspect had flipped. "Book it. Emergency!" She was dialling before her eyebrows had finished shooting up. Dean spoke to me for the first time. "Max, isn't it? In the early hours of an injury like this, it's good to keep the joint elevated and iced. Did you do that?"

"No."

"I see. Magnus?"

The world's only non-Swedish Magnus abandoned his patient, dashed to a fridge, and emerged with two huge ice packs. He gently extended my leg, raised it, and brought the ice close on either side.

"Thank you. Max, we're going to take you to a local clinic to get you X-rayed. In the meantime, I need to check your eye socket. Ah, your sunglasses?"

I whipped them off, along with my baseball cap.

"Ah," said Dean. "That's rather . . ." He looked for a synonym for "horrific" that matched his new "kind-hearted bedside manner" persona and couldn't think of one. He pulled on a pair of blue medical gloves. "Please let me know if there's pain." He started exploring the mass around my eye. "Tricky," he said. "I think we should let the swelling diminish before deciding on a course of action. I'm not keen

355

on orbital X-rays, unless there might be a foreign object involved. That isn't the case here. Hmm. No strenuous activity for a month. I must put my foot down about that, and Jackie can shout at me all he wants. Do you follow me? No strenuous activity."

"I have a date tomorrow," I said.

"Oh dear," said Dean.

"She's from Newcastle."

"Oh dear!"

"It's a virtual date. We're going to talk about a movie. That's why I need someone to give me their Disney Plus password. Just for one night. The film's not on any other platform." I tried to make eye contact with someone in a significant manner, but the doc was gripping my forehead; I could only move my eyeballs.

Dean smiled for the first time. "A virtual date should be all right. If you're going to do video sex, don't let it involve sneezing or blowing your nose."

I wasn't allowed to sneeze for a month. Had I just heard that right? "What? Why?"

Dean's smile froze. "It would be bad." He unfroze, but his expression had returned to a sort of irritated one. I got the impression that he didn't let the Chester players negotiate their injuries with him. *Stubborn as a mule*, I thought. "So, no visits to Newcastle for a month. Doctor's orders. No football either, obviously. Come for a reassessment. We might have to fit you a mask before you get back on a pitch."

"Like Aubameyang? Like Rudiger?"

"In your case, more like *Phantom of the Opera*," he said, and made the most *extraordinary* sniffing noise that I later realised was him laughing. It sounded like a guinea pig eating a watermelon. Once finished, he gave the double doors a guilty look. "Right. How about that X-ray?"

51

MEDICAL DEVICES

What do I have in common with Lionel Messi (Seven time Ballon D'Or winner)?

What do I have in common with Ryan Giggs (Thirteen time Premier League winner)?

What do I have in common with the American striker Jozy Altidore (Two goals in seventy Premier League games)?

We've all had a football medical.

That's right, kids. I had a medical. I *underwent* a medical.

Medicals are the tests clubs do with players before they sign them. You've seen the photos. You've seen Richarlison relaxing on a bed. He's covered in sensors, and he's giving the camera a thumbs up. You've seen Lukaku on a treadmill, and he's giving the camera a thumbs up. You've seen Neymar at his sister's birthday party, and he's flicking Vs at the camera because he's a twat. That last one is nothing to do with medicals. Not sure why I even mentioned it.

(Random thought: whenever a player "fails a medical" I always wonder if that's true or if the buying club has got cold feet and is using that as an excuse to cancel the deal.)

While Livia drove me to the small private clinic that Chester FC used to carry out their medicals, she asked if I was a player Jackie had recommended to Chester. "No," I said.

"It's just that for insurance purposes you need to be a prospective employee," she said. She left that hanging. I thought through the implications. If I lied about potentially signing for Chester, that would get me some top-notch healthcare for free. Chester's insurance would cover the costs, so the club weren't losing out. "It's all fun and games until someone discovers the fraud," I mused.

"Why would they?" she said. "You're the right age, the right athletic profile. Anyway," she went on. "You might join us one day."

"Sure," I said, "as a scout." That caught her interest, which I'm afraid to say filled me with a childlike urge to interest her *more*. She wanted to know who I was and why Jackie had brought me, but despite my burgeoning intoxication with her, I was fixated on the upcoming scenario. It seemed like I'd have to sign some documents implying that Chester wanted to sign me as a player. And what would that do? Register me with FIFA? Stop me from signing with another team for six months? What was Jackie's *game*?

I voiced my doubts, and Livia was utterly bewildered. Why would Jackie trick me into signing for Chester, she said, when he worked for FC United?

"Well," I said, "Jackie is always cooking up a scheme."

And she said, "like what? What's the scheme? What other schemes have you found him doing?"

"Trying to get me to become a footballer," I said. She laughed and asked if that wasn't every boy's fantasy. I nearly replied with something flirtatious, but it would have been too crude.

"Where's Jackie disappeared to, anyway?"

"He's just taking care of some things, and he had to re-park his car away from the stadium. Sometimes he forgets he doesn't work here anymore."

Doesn't work here anymore. Yeah. Maybe someone should tell the Head Physio that. Dean had behaved like Jackie was Stalin, but Jackie didn't even have his own parking space. I stared out of the window and pulled at my lip. Curiouser and curiouser.

The next quarter hour was coldly professional. At the clinic, I signed some boilerplate documents. They seemed harmless. I couldn't imagine a world where they could be used to prevent me doing whatever the fuck I wanted in life. As usual, I'd worried for nothing. A doctor took a look at my eye, then X-rayed my ankle.

"No fractures," said the doc. She was middle-aged. Brown hair, brown eyes. She had been injected with a healthy dose of the X-factor. If she'd been behind you in the queue at ASDA, you might not have thought to look twice. But in the doctor's coat you really, really got full exposure. Megabonus: slight Eastern European accent. Call me Marie Curious!

"Will I ever walk again?" I said, sort of breaking my rule on flirting with women at work. But I was actually using her to score social proof points with Livia, so I felt it didn't really count as proper flirting.

She smirked at me. "If you sign for *us* instead of Chester, you'll never walk alone."

"What?" That phrase! I couldn't believe my ears. Surely she should have supported FC Krakow or whatever. "You're a *Liverpool* fan?"

"Yeah, why not?"

"Because I've never been attracted to a Liverpool fan before."

Her mouth sort of medically flatlined—superb self-control!—but her smile shone out of her eyes even more. "Do you have any questions for me?"

Well, I still didn't know her name, which was dumb. But it was sort of too late to ask for it. And she'd obviously asked this question thousands of times before and knew when to expect some lame quip in reply. She was steeling herself for it.

Which made forming my next question even harder. This woman dealt with more footballers than most doctors in the world, so her opinion was really fascinating to me.

"I've been called a narcissist and an egomaniac many times. Can't really argue with that. If I was good at some sport, I'd never shut up about it. But I do think I have a pretty clear-eyed picture of my physical gifts. Not average, but . . . average for a twenty-two-year-old who doesn't binge drink or do drugs and that sort of thing. Do you know what I mean?"

She did, but couldn't predict where I was going with this. "I know what you mean."

"Livia here—a professional physiotherapist at a historic club—described me as having the *right athletic profile* for a footballer."

The doctor was veering towards being annoyed now. "Yes." That was all she said.

"What do you mean, yes? Do you mean, yes, I'm listening?"

"I mean, yes you do."

I looked from woman to woman. "This is . . . this is confusing. What are you basing that on? It's not possible."

"Why not?" said Livia.

"How about because I haven't done any serious training for three years?"

The doctor's growing annoyance vanished. "Impossible."

"What?"

She grabbed a stethoscope and placed it on my chest. "Breathe normally," she said. She palpated bits of my body. Especially my calves. She stared at my torso. After a while, she checked her watch. She looked at Livia. "Kick off's at three, is it? Won't be much action until then. We could do a medical. As much as his injury allows. Pretty much the same cost to the club."

"Max?" said Livia. "What do you say? Want to let two nice Liverpool fans run tests on you?"

Oh. My. God.

Did she say what I thought she said?

Talk about heartbreak.

I recovered like a champion. It helped that all the machines looked really complicated and cool. And if you think failing a medical is ever going to hurt my chances of getting a phone number, you haven't been paying attention.

"Let's do it."

"We'd normally get you warmed up on an exercise bike," said the doctor.

"No probs," I said. "I can do that."

"The role of a doctor is to heal, not make things worse."

"I'll pedal one-footed."

"Don't be stupid." She had just eased my right foot into a fancy ankle stabiliser.

"Just help me on the bike." I actually would have loved to get a sweat on; the crutches had started doing my head in. But I didn't have a change of clothes or anywhere to shower, so anything strenuous was out of the question.

I pedalled one-legged for a while, resting my mangled foot on the middle of the bike. It was just to get my blood pumping a bit.

The ladies then helped me into a Biodex machine. It's a chair with a computer attached and loads of wires and levers and shit. I love things like this! They always look like they can boil an egg, make your tea, and update you on your bond holdings. (Scottish woman's voice: Currently your portfolio is valued at . . . Robot voice: Zero. Dollaaaars.) In reality, they seem super complicated but only do one specific thing.

The Biodex measures muscle group strength in a way that is somehow useful for sportspeople.

The ladies helped me into the chair. There were no fewer than four different seatbelts, which just added to the drama. And, to be honest, added to the sexual tension I was feeling.

Once I was strapped in, the ladies kind of ignored me and turned to look at the screen. Which was probably helpful in terms of my blood flow. I had to kick out my (healthy) leg then pull it back, repeat, repeat with more resistance, and so on. Something beeped. The doctor pressed buttons on the screen, stared at Livia, then back at the screen. Their postures seemed pretty conclusive. You don't stare at a screen like that unless you're trying to work out how to deliver bad news.

"I'm still not quite sure what this thing does or how I failed," I said.

The doctor was the alpha, so it fell to her to deliver the bad news. "Typically with an isokinetic dynamometer you might find that a patient's joint torque favours eccentric or concentric muscle action. Or put *even* more simply, their hamstrings are weaker than their quads. Your numbers . . . are not only sky high but in perfect balance." She stared at the screen like the data was a male stripper wearing . . . I don't know . . . nothing but a cowboy hat and crotchless chaps. "Let me take a photo of this."

I reached out to grab her arm. She turned to stare at me. "Please don't," I said. I was starting to have a very bad feeling about this whole adventure. Jackie thought I could be a good footballer. He would skip the trial and go straight to the contract signing if it was up to him. And these medical professionals were talking like I was ready for the Olympics. What . . . just what. I mean, there was one very obvious explanation, and it wasn't two years of watching classic Hong Kong kung fu movies on a sofa, sideways.

Doc slid her phone back into her pocket.

"We'll have to skip the VO2 Max test. Let's go to the orthopaedic and movement screen. What we're looking for here, Max, is the quality of your joint mobility. Obviously, your right ankle is out of action, but if we're careful we'll get a good sense of your other one, plus your knees and hips. Have you ever had any injuries there?"

I closed my eyes and thought about it. "Not that I can remember."

"We grade your joints from one to seven. One would be something like occlusive effusion in the knee joint. Seven is perfect musculoskeletal capacity."

"And what would your score be?"

"Mine?" exclaimed the doctor. I must have been the first person ever to ask that. "Six, I suppose. What do you think, Livvy?"

Livia looked sheepish. "Sorry but six is a stretch. You can't be more than a five."

"Oh? Be like that. *You* can do this."

"This" involved Livia twisting my legs, palpating me, and generally touching me in a way that should have been extremely erotic but was way, way on the other end of the spectrum.

The women looked at each other again.

"Let me guess," I said. "Seven."

While Doc and Livia purred over my test results, I felt a growing unease. In their view, I was, essentially, a perfect specimen of a man. Perfect specimen of a footballer anyway. My thoughts turned to a small park in a rough part of Manchester.

I tried to remember what I'd said when I'd been talking to Old Nick, the Polish guy who'd gotten into my head and messed up my tidy, orderly, boring life. Hadn't I said something about wanting to understand football the way Klopp and Guardiola did? When I'd started getting all these powers and perks, it had been scary and even annoying, but it had at least been consistent. They were all geared towards making me a good football manager.

Nick, it seemed, had gone above and beyond.

But wait, hadn't I also specifically said I didn't want to be a player?

Maybe he'd played fair with me. Maybe Jackie, a good player and top coach, was wrong. Maybe Doc and Livia, trained professionals who'd tested hundreds of footballers . . . were wrong. Even in my mind, the thought trailed off.

I blinked and realised the women were staring at me. They had baffled looks on their faces. Maybe that's because they'd given me what they thought was incredible news, and I was biting my nails.

They say you are born with a certain number of heartbeats and when you hit that number, boom, game over. And if you ask me, it's the same with the extremely beautiful women of the world. You get four billion heartbeats. You get four questions with a woman like Livia.

She drove me back to the stadium. It was quarter to three, and the match was about to start. My head was swimming with all the new images and information. There was much I'd like to have discussed with her.

I stayed internal.

I tried not to look as terrified as I felt.

She helped me into the wheelchair and pushed me into the stadium.

"Livia," I said. "Sorry if I haven't been sparkling company."

"That's all right," she said, accidentally confirming that I'd been weird.

"Do we have doctor patient confidentiality?"

"I mean . . . Not the way you think. But if you're going to ask me to keep certain things private, yeah, absolutely."

"Could you . . . Could you come with me into a small, windowless room?"

She stopped, and I turned to check her face. After a mild panic, a tiny smile appeared. "Yes, I think we can do that."

I was on my back, looking up at her. She brought her face close to mine. God, she was beautiful.

"How hard do you want it?" she said.

"What can other players do?" I said. "What can Jackie take?"

"How would I know?" she said, with a half-flirty, half-pissed expression.

"Approx."

She looked to the right. Her hair bounced, and I briefly forgot my mission. "I don't know. I'm more on the therapeutic side. I think they expect you to do ninety kilos as a sort of base line."

I scoffed. "Ninety kilos? Are you insane?" I shook my head. I'd never lifted a weight in my life. Never saw the attraction of it. "Can you put, like, forty kilos on there, and I'll see if I can even budge that?"

Livia fitted two twenty-kg weights to my long hard rod, secured the ends, and gave me the go ahead. I gripped the metal bar and pushed. Even though I couldn't use my right foot as leverage, it was piss easy.

"Good?" she said.

"Yeah." I looked around the tiny gym. The bench press was the only thing I could really do with a dodgy ankle. I wondered what this room smelled like after a few players had spent a few hours in there. "Can you bring it up to sixty?"

"Sixty in weights, yeah?"

"Yeah."

Reader, bench pressing sixty kilos (plus whatever the bar weighed) was as easy as flipping a pillow on a Sunday morning.

"More?" she said. She seemed keen to see what I could achieve, and more keen for me to show off for her.

"Think I'll stop there. Don't want to aggravate my injury. Thanks a lot."

She wheeled me through the double doors and back into the physio room.

Still no sign of Jackie, and the sounds of the match were really picking up. It was a small stadium, but they made a good bit of noise. Fair play to them.

Through all the walls between me and the pitch, I heard the referee blow his whistle, and the crowd give a throaty roar. "I guess I'm not going to Wrexham," I mumbled.

"Why would you want to go there?" she said. "Haven't we made you feel welcome?" Very flirty vibe to this. What the eff? That had come out of nowhere.

I was about to push myself along in the wheelchair, but I realised in time how stupid that would be. If I could propel myself, Livia would leave me to do her actual job. I put my hands on my lap, and she grabbed the handles. "I just have a big crush on . . ."

"Ryan Reynolds," she said.

"No. Tom Jones."

"The singer? He's not from Wrexham."

"Oh. Then I'll stay here."

"Good choice. Jackie texted. He wants me to take you upstairs and make sure you get a good view."

Oh, God . . .

We went into a lift and, after a short but slow ride, emerged into a corridor. She helped me into a media box—like the one at Oldham but designed for scouts or media types instead of affluent fans—and said she'd have to get back to her post in case there were injuries in the game.

"Wait," I said. "What's this?"

I'd found something on a desk. It was a piece of paper with a printed template on. In the top right was the badge of Southport FC. There was a place to fill in a team's formation, plus slots where you could fill in details of the starting eleven. Under each slot were six boxes. Three had plus signs, three had minus signs. My galaxy-sized brain speculated this was where you noted a player's strengths and weaknesses. Then there was another section containing three sub-columns: Fit, re$, and Score. I had ideas of what these would mean, but they were fairly ambiguous and could have meant many things.

"I have no idea," said Livia. "I'm not sure anyone's been in here for a while. Southport, that was ages ago."

"Was it your last home match?"

She looked up and to the left. "No, but it was the last home *league* match. We played Hanley in the FA Cup. And Pontefract. I think that was after Southport."

"They're teeny tiny clubs, right? They don't have scouts. So Southport was the last team that sent a scout to a match."

She thought about it. "Possibly. Is everything okay?"

"Everything is amazing! Can you get me a pen? I want to have a go at filling this in."

She ran off and came back with one a couple of minutes after the game had kicked off. "Thanks!" I said and started scribbling furiously.

She said something, but when the sound made it deep enough into my consciousness to warrant a reaction, she'd already gone.

Old Nick might have changed my body against my will, citation needed. But when it came to scouting, the whole curse thing felt *clean*. It didn't involve me asking grown women to kick fourteen-year-olds. It didn't involve dampening the ardour of thirty thousand fans just so I could engineer a shock October victory. So far scouting had involved finding crouching tigers and hidden dragons, and there were no moral grey areas to bringing joy and hope to Ziggy, Raffi, and Kisi.

I watched the match for a couple of minutes then continued filling in the scouting report.

52

SEXY BEAST

It was a relief having some time alone, and deciphering and filling in the match report was a fun challenge. But my mind kept wandering. Kept returning to the same, distressing revelation.

Whether overnight or slowly over time, the curse had turned me into a footballer. I hadn't woken up with an eight-pack. I didn't suddenly have giant Magnus Evergreen-style arms or Roberto Carlos thunder thighs. But I was faster and stronger than I'd ever been. Plus, based on the match with Ziggy's team, I now had the skill and technique to rival my imagination.

If that sounds exciting to you . . . I get it. So why wasn't it exciting to me?

Because if the curse really had made me into a player, it was affecting more than just what happened when I stepped onto a pitch. Remember that I spent the pandemic more isolated than most. Two years of being internal. Two years of growing weird. Beth was the first woman I'd met in a long, long time, and in that first meeting I was ignorant and borderline offensive. Despite that, she'd chased me after the match and demanded my phone number. The Met Heads—a group of twenty-two-year-old women, mostly single—instantly accepted me as their coach and dragged me to the pub whenever possible. All the women I'd met when walking Solly, I thought he was the secret weapon to getting into their beds. But Solly had nothing to do with it. Those women were responding to the new me. The footballer me.

I thought back to how Gemma's mild interest in Ziggy had tripled in intensity when she discovered he was a star striker . . . . Footballers are as attractive to women as yoga teachers are to men. Gary Bailey had below average luck with women until he became Manchester United's goalkeeper, and now he's married to a Miss Universe.

I chewed the end of the ballpoint pen.

What did that mean about Emma? Did she even like *me*? Or was she just responding to what the curse had turned me into?

I felt like a vampire or a werewolf.

A sexy monster.

But a monster.

Over the course of about ten minutes, I was able to park those misgivings and focus on the match. Chester were playing 4-4-2 in their blue and white vertical stripes. The other team were employing a modified 4-4-2 and playing in red. I realised I had absolutely no clue who they were! No one had mentioned it. But looking at the player histories, half the team had spent last season at Darlington. So the reds were—probably!—Darlington. Elementary, my dear Watson.

I was earning 2 XP per minute, which according to my theory meant this was the sixth tier, the National League North. Christ! I knew even less about Chester FC than I did about the city.

I whipped my phone out and confirmed all of the above.

The phone also told me that Darlington were in the top six and Chester in the bottom six. Probably a tough match ahead for the home team!

And Super Scout hinted as much. Chester's average CA was 40, and Darlington's was 50.

Chester had a few interesting players. In defence, a half-American called Carl Carlile caught my eye. He had the potential to improve a lot, while Diarmuid Dubhlainn was a speedy Irish winger who had good defensive attributes too. Say what you want about Man United fans, but we love a fast winger. I just didn't want to have to pronounce his name.

Darlington's best player was a substitute wrapped up in a scarf and gloves, Henri Lyons. A French striker with higher CA and PA than the rest of his teammates. So why was he on the bench? For hundreds of potential reasons. Maybe Jackie would know.

Filling in the scouting report started easy: name the players, and draw their position on the pitch. But then came the real challenge. How would I fill in the pros and cons in a way that was useful to whoever read the report while not giving away the secret of the curse? For example, it would be ludicrous to suggest that Carlile had good finishing for a defender when I hadn't even seen him in the Darlington half!

Tricky.

But even worse was the goalkeepers. I could see their CA/PA, of course, and presumably jumping was a relevant attribute. Plus passing and bravery. But surely there were more goalkeeper-specific attributes that I didn't have access to? Could I be a scout who specialised in strikers? Was that a thing?

I tried to sort of float away from my current mood and look down on myself from a great height. If I had the skills to be a professional player, was I still interested in doing the whole scouting/agent thing? It wasn't too late to tie a knot in that thread. My clients would be thrilled if I got them contracts with pro clubs and could easily find a new agent once their feet were in the door.

But the thought of Ziggy calling his new agent to discuss a potential move to a bigger club made me feel queasy.

No, I still wanted to oversee their careers. It was fun and, presumably, would start helping out with the bills soon . . . . Pro players only trained a couple of hours a day, didn't they? What did they do with the rest of their time? Design clothes? Dick around on Instagram? I'd be happier going to a Powerleague and finding the next Raffi.

But what I really wanted was to be a manager. That was the biggest thrill, the biggest challenge. Even with the Match Overview and tactics screens, even with everything the curse gave me, it would still be a monumental achievement if I could become a successful manager. Managing was chess with living pieces. Command and Conquer with territory instead of Tiberium. High stakes poker crossed with heavyweight boxing. Once I was financially stable, everything I did had to be done with one goal in mind: getting into the big chair.

I made a decision. Shocktober was consigned to the dustbin of history. It was time to improve my skills. It was time to splash the cash.

I had 1,409 XP in my stash and decided to buy Attributes 2 (for 630 XP) and Match Stats 1 (100 XP). When I bought Attributes 2, it unlocked the ability to buy Attributes 3. I had assumed the price would double again, to 1,260. But I was wrong. Attributes 3 was available for just 850 XP. It was bundled with the Match Report perk, which would normally cost 100 XP.

The price made no mathematical sense. But it made a certain kind of narrative sense, because if I concentrated, I'd be able to buy it by the end of *this match.*

I threw the pen at the window, and it bounced behind me. It'd be a hassle picking it up, so I left it.

Why was I chucking stationery around? Because the curse wasn't offering me perks at preset prices. It was adjusting the costs based on some kind of supply and demand. Or to be blunt, it was directing me. Forcing me down a certain path. If we want to be charitable, we could say the curse was *making sure I had the skills needed to overcome oncoming obstacles*. Like the old Greek gods, it had its finger on the scales. I didn't have long to stew on it, because suddenly my vision was overtaken by the animation that told me which attribute I had unlocked.

A generic player profile popped up, and a yellow block bounced around the locked cells; they changed colour until the yellow block came to rest on one particular cell.

And the unlocked attribute was . . .

Handling.

My first reaction was to groan. Handling? How well a player could catch the ball? Who gave a shit? I'd gone from the best one (finishing) to the worst.

But I'd been wrong about a lot of things recently.

So I scanned the pitch with a mind as open as possible. A mind *slightly* ajar. Every single outfield player had handling one. Chester's goalie had handling twelve, while Darlington's was fourteen.

The only slightly interesting thing to come from this was that Chester's reserve keeper (Ben Cavanagh) had higher handling than the one starting for the first team. And the same was true for Darlington's young reserve goalie.

Like I said, slightly interesting.

But that disappointment soon faded, because buying Match Stats 1 was transformative.

Remember Super Scout? The curse told me that would normally cost 10,000 XP but that I could have it at a big discount. From what I'd learned since buying it, there was no doubt it was worth ten thousand. Would you pay for fifteen Premier League tickets to gain the chance to discover a one hundred million pound player? Of course you would. Even if you had to watch ten thousand minutes of shitty Sunday League games, you'd do it if you knew what you were getting.

But Match Stats 1 only cost 100 XP. How good could it be?

Good. Very good.

Annoyingly good.

What have I been doing with my life all this time good.

Now, when I opened my curse screens, there was an option in the top-left to access the Match Overview area. That had previously only been available when I was managing a team. I clicked on it and was gobsmacked.

I actually experienced an enormous, splitting headache at the exact same moment, but I'm choosing to gloss over that. It didn't last long, and I decided to chalk it up to unlocking too many perks too fast.

Once my head had cooled a bit, I tried to leave the overview area and get back to the top menu. When I was managing a game, that wasn't possible. But now it was. Perhaps I wasn't locked in because I wasn't the manager.

So I went back to the Match Overview and saw:

Chester FC	0	Darlington	0
	First	Half	

That was revolutionary in its own right. For example, if this had been available to me fifteen minutes earlier, I'd have known which teams were playing! And I didn't need to stare at the pitch for thirty seconds trying to map where all the players were. I had access to the tactics screens for both teams.

But the best, best, *best* thing was that a new tab had been unlocked. Yes, the one called Match Stats! The other two, Action Zones and Match Report, were both still locked. But who cared? Not me. Not much.

Because Match Stats was the bee's knees. The cat's whiskers. The dog's bollocks. The pig's tits.

And it was so simple!

On the left, a list of the Chester players and their subs. On the right, Darlington.

But everyone who was on the pitch was given a rating. Out of ten. Simple, right?

No! This was extraordinary information.

For example, after a quarter of an hour, Carl Carlile was rated six out of ten. And so was thingy. The Irish one. There was only one Chester player who had a seven. The rest were on fives or sixes. Darlington were sixes and sevens with one eight.

So already it seemed pretty obvious who was likely to win this match!

I watched the match with this screen sort of overlaid full screen, until I discovered I could have it as a partially transparent window wherever I wanted. When players missed tackles and passes, their match rating tended to decrease. When they made interceptions or set up shots on goal, their rating increased.

Pretty clear! Pretty vivid!

With a start, I remembered where I'd seen the word "rating" recently. The history tab! I looked up Carl Carlile and now his previous seasons' data included an average rating.

Season: 2021. Team: Chester. Appearances eleven as a starter, six as a sub. Goals: zero. Assists: zero. Question mark, question mark, question mark. Average Rating: 6.13.

It already seemed obvious to me that 6.13 was a very low average rating, and a quick look at some other players confirmed it. Based on that number, it was surprising that Carlile was even playing today. If I had a guy giving me six out of ten every week, I'd want to replace him with someone a lot better.

It was very possible that there were mitigating circumstances. Maybe he'd come back from a big injury. Maybe he'd been played out of position. Maybe those six substitute appearances dragged his average down, but in the eleven games he started he was really good. Something like that.

But overall, if the numbers were reliable, this was an incredible boon when it came to scouting.

And, I thought bouncing in my chair excitedly, an incredible boon for managing games. If I had a right-winger giving me eight out of ten while the left-winger was giving me four out of ten, then my tactical plan had gone wrong, and I'd need to rebalance the side or find a way to get the left guy playing well without disrupting what the right one was up to.

Yes yes yes!

This beast had claws!

53

TALENTED
YOUNGSTERS

Jackie and another dude came into my little room. Jackie took the swivel chair to my left while the other guy flipped down a little seat built into the wall and sat there. Obviously not planning to stay for long.

"How you getting on, Max?"

"Great," I said. "I love being abandoned in other countries when I haven't brought my passport."

"This is Mike," said Jackie.

I shook hands with Mike. If I had to guess I would have said he was forty-two years and 122 days old. But I didn't have to guess, because he had a profile hovering over his head. Name, age, question marks. But question marks in a different pattern to the coaches or physios. Had I just unlocked something that showed me profiles for every fan in the stadium? He was wearing a casual suit, so he looked business-like but approachable.

Jackie glanced at the pitch and at the scouting report. He turned his attention back to me. "Why would you need your passport?"

I pointed to my phone. Jackie had seen me using Google Maps, so it wasn't as ludicrous as it seems in retrospect. "Isn't this Wales?"

Mike awarded me an amused look, even though he must have had this conversation hundreds of times. "The pitch and most of the stadium are in Wales, but you're in England right now."

"The border goes right across like this?" I made a chopping gesture with my hand.

"More like this," he said. You can imagine whatever direction you want. "It was a big problem during the pandemic. We couldn't have fans in matches because the lockdown restrictions barred people going from England to Wales."

"No way! That's mad. Wait, you had fans during lockdown?"

"Non-league was less restricted, yeah."

"So," said Jackie, nodding towards my ankle. "They took a look at you?"

"Yep," I said. "They were great. Nothing broken. It feels less painful already, just knowing that. Do you know what I mean?"

"Yeah," he said, leaning forward. "Listen, I was telling Mike that you've got a good eye for a player."

"Okay," I said. This might be a good time to say that during this whole conversation I was staring at the pitch, only tearing my eyes away very quickly to check for reactions. But my demeanour probably contributed to a vibe where I seemed somewhat disinterested.

Jackie was confused by my lack of . . . what did he expect? Excitement? "Right. What do you think of the match so far?"

"Well, it's only been fifteen minutes," I said. "I've seen some guys I like the look of. But I need a bit more time to form any real conclusions."

"You've never seen any of them before, I take it?" said Mike.

"No. I've never even seen a game in this *division*. Listen, this is Chester FC. But I always want to say Chester City. Is that a different team?"

"No, that's us. We're a Phoenix club. City went bust. The fans brought it back to life. Now we're Chester FC."

"Oh, cool," I said. "Another fan-owned club. Like FC United. Big fan of that."

"You are?" said Jackie. "I didn't think you were political."

"I'm not. I'm a single-issue voter."

"What issue is that?" asked Mike.

"Healthcare," guessed Jackie. Probably thinking about my mum.

"Wave machines in the English Channel," I said.

Mike laughed.

Jackie shook his head. "He's not joking." He sighed. "Max, you're really fucking weird sometimes." He shook his head again. "Why don't you tell us which players you like," said Jackie.

"No rush," said Mike. "We can have a chat at half-time if you like."

Hmm. My plan for half-time was to see if Livia had an Instagram account. One hint of a bikini pic, and I'd be rejoining the world of social media faster than Usain Bolt RSVPed to that party invitation from the Swedish women's handball team.

Jackie was weirdly keen to get me to show off my skills though. Before I could mumble something about half-time being great, he said, "Have you been filling in this scouting report? Why is it from Southport?"

"Yeah it was just lying here. Can you grab that pen? Thanks. What does Fit, re$, and Score mean?"

Mike glanced at the document. "Fitness. That's like, based on our current playing style, how well would this player fit?"

"Ah. Not the other fitness, then. So if I worked for a team that played fast counterattacks, Marcus Rashford would get a ten. But for slow, possession-based teams I'd give him a four or five."

"That's it. And re$ is resale value. If we pay money for this player, are we going to get it back?"

I nodded. Made sense. "Like you can buy a player and, if it doesn't work out for some reason, you can sell him and not lose your whole shirt. So what do I put here? A tick or a number or what?"

"I don't know how Southport does it. Our scouting reports are different. A lot more detailed . . . in theory. But yeah, a tick. Why not? And then Score is just an overall number to show how keen the scout is on that player. It's like at school you get an overall A or an F, and, if you're bothered, you can look into the sub-scores that explain the total grade. If you give a player a six, the manager probably isn't going to read the whole report, but if you give him a ten, he is."

"Top. Thanks." I was warming up to Mike now. He was easy to be around. "I do have a couple of thoughts if you really want to know. Couple of clarifying questions first."

"Go for it."

"How do you pronounce the Irish winger's name?"

He did it by syllable. "Deer-mid dove-lin. But we all call him Aff."

"Aff?"

"Aff."

"He's good. I like him. Not playing well today. Next question. Carl Carlile. What's his story?"

Mike looked out onto the pitch. "He's from a weird family. They all left England and went to America in the olden days. Then there were family feuds, so half of them came back to get away from the other half. The way Carl tells it, the family keeps splitting in half and one lot fucks off to America while one of the American factions fucks off back here."

"People. I get the sense," I said, carefully, "from the crowd reaction when he's on the ball and stuff, that he's not been playing very well."

"You do? Huh. I didn't notice that. Yeah, his form's not been good. He's had back trouble and got things going on in his private life. He's only playing today because of injuries."

"Okay. The reserve goalie seems better than the first team one. You know, from what I saw in the warm up. Small sample size."

I was worried I'd gotten too specific. There was only a two-point difference in handling between the players. Surely you'd need to watch them at least ten times to see that? But Mike was impressed. "Ah, yes. Well, a lot of people agree with you. But Ben is young. Too young for Ian."

"Who's Ian?"

"Ian Evans. Our manager."

"Oh, right. He doesn't trust young players?"

"He's old school." I pulled a face. In this context, old school was code for gammon. Mike noted my reaction. "He's not what you think. He was progressive in his day."

"But his day was years ago," added Jackie.

"Jack," complained Mike. "He's come out of retirement to help us out. He's what we need this season. We can't have another relegation battle."

"I know, I know. I'm with Max, though. I want to see young players in the team." I'd gone internal, comparing the formations used by the two managers. "What's on your mind, lad?"

"It makes sense now. I was wondering about the formations. Chester are at home but they're set up so defensively."

Mike's head snapped towards the big window. He pointed. "We've got two wingers," he said.

Wingers are normally fast and/or skillful players who run up and down the sides of the pitch. They start in the same place as a right or left midfielder, but the *winger* has more licence to get forward and attack, and the *midfielder* has to be more defensively aware. "No," I said. "It's a straight 4-4-2. Those wingers are midfielders. They're getting forward a lot but that's coincidental. And you'll note that—here, now, look!—when Aff dribbles forward, the other guy stays back, and the two central midfielders aren't keen to bomb forward either. There's never more than three Chester players in the penalty box. I don't see how you're going to score."

"Corners," said Jackie. "Set pieces."

I shook my head. "You're the home team. You've got to be more progressive. And the Darlington guy's no better. He's got the better team, but he's so cautious."

"It's 4-4-2, isn't it?" said Jackie, peering out at the pitch.

"Yes," I said, "but heavily modified." I flipped the scouting report over and drew on the back. The tactics screen displayed these little dotted arrows that showed where the players were supposed to run to, so I copied them along with the basic formation.

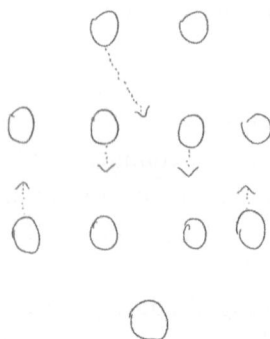

I explained what we were looking at. "It's 4-4-2 but with the full-backs pushing up. And the central midfielders are both *coming back*. They're almost like defensive midfielders. And the second striker is dropping deep."

"What's the aim?" said Mike.

I asked if anyone had a different colour pen, and Mike found a red one on a shelf at the back of the room. I drew the formation with the players moved to the ends of their arrows and highlighted three boxes.

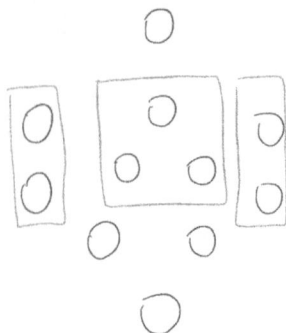

"Pushing the full-back close to the midfielder creates a blockage on either wing. This square in the centre has three guys in it. They're absolutely flooding the midfield. It's just a swamp now. They're making it a stodgy game. They should win but Christ, it's boring."

"Huh," said Mike, looking at my drawing with a healthy dose of polite scepticism. "Flooding the midfield. I'll have to watch out for that." He stood, and his seat flipped back into the wall. "I've got to see a man about a bog."

"Before you go, what can you tell me about Henri Lyons?"

"He's a nutjob," said Mike. "Talk to you later, Max Best."

I glanced over and saw that Jackie was slumped forwards, head in hands. Probably going over all the things he wanted to say to Livia but was too chickenshit.

At a certain point he slouched back in his chair and divided his attention between the pitch and his phone. I kept staring at the pitch, picking up XP.

After a while, he said, "How is it that you don't know anything about Chester, but you know Magnus Evergreen played three games last season?"

"I must have seen him on some Reddit post. Some feature on one of those banter websites. Article called 'Freaks of Football' or whatever."

"He's not a freak. He's a great guy."

"I didn't say otherwise. I'm just saying where I might have seen him." Jackie shook his head. He was mad at me again and not only because I'd used the F word. I didn't really care about Jackie's moods. I wanted to understand how Magnus had defied what I'd come to think of as a law of football, that one couldn't have a CA higher than one's PA. "Jackie, mate. How do players improve?"

He slumped again, head back in his hands. "Are you fucking kidding me right now?"

"What?" I said.

He threw his hand towards the door that Mike had left via. "I just tried to . . . Ugh!" He rubbed his bald head again. Loads. Then he crossed his arms and stared at a ceiling strip light. "How do *you* think players improve?"

I'd been thinking about this a ton, but without access to daily CA/ PA data, and without much on the time axis, I could only speculate.

But it's not like I was thrown into some parallel dimension where everyone played a trampoline-based martial art called Kosho and I had to learn everything from scratch. "I think players have an innate ceiling. They move towards that ceiling based on the quality of their coaches. The intensity of their team's training. How much they play in games. The quality of the competition or opponents."

"Why can't you talk like that when other people are in the room, you twat?"

"My question, Jackie mate, is, what are the rules of how much someone needs to play? You know Garnacho at United?"

"Yes." His tone suggested he didn't want to talk about a young talent from a rival club.

"I saw him earlier this season, and I thought he had something. They moved him into the United first team setup, and he got called up by the national team. Now he's with the Argentina squad. So he's training with Messi one day and Ronaldo the next. The two best players ever!"

Jackie grinned. This was a unique footballing happenstance that the romantic in him could appreciate. "It's mad, isn't it? Good for him."

"But . . . okay. I can't quite work out how much playing time you need to reach your potential. If you were the manager of United, how much would you play him?"

Jackie let out a breath like it was a tough question. "I haven't seen much of him to be honest, so I don't really know, you know? But my dad always compared what happened to Michael Owen and Ryan Giggs." I knew the names, of course. Which football fan didn't? Owen, the phenomenal young England (yay!) and Liverpool (hiss) talent. Giggs, the sensational Man United (yay!) and Wales (shrug) winger who is the most decorated player in British history but may or may not be legally problematic, so shhh, end of biography. "Sir Alex Ferguson took over at Man United. Had a team of hard-drinking hard men. Bought a team of slightly more talented hard men who didn't get blottoed after every game. Great. But they lacked the X-factor. Enter Giggs. Do you know his story?"

"Some of it. Which bit do you mean?"

"Ferguson started in Scotland. Turned the league there into a three-horse race. He was the manager of *Aberdeen* and they beat Real fucking Madrid. He was the real deal. Intimidating, but charming when he wanted. When Fergie took over at United, Ryan Giggs was a Man City player."

"What?"

"Seriously. Thirteen-year-old Ryan Giggs played for City. I don't know if it was midnight or 9 a.m. or whatever, but as soon as Giggs turns fourteen, when he could sign a senior contract, Ferguson was on his doorstep. Knock knock! Fergie charms the fuck out of Giggs's mum, little Ryan signs for United. Three years later Giggs scores the winning goal against Man City. Giggs and United win the league, again and again."

"I love hearing you say that."

"What people don't remember is in the early days, Giggs only played like one game in three. If anyone complained, Fergie would go mental at them. People learned to stop asking. Young Giggs was a sexy beast. A heart-throb winger who played for Man United. Who does that remind you of? The media wanted to turn him into the new George Best. The Fifth Beatle." Finally, Jackie was talking about The Beatles, but in praise of a Manchester legend! He continued, "If any journalists came asking to talk to Giggs, Fergie would hear about it and fucking explode out of his office window, appear in a pool of shattered glass next to the journo, and give him the hairdryer."

"Hairdryer?"

"That's when Ferguson, this angry Scottish man, would put his mouth next to your face and shout at you so violently and so consistently that it was like having a hairdryer an inch from your nose. But do you get the point?"

"Not really."

"Fergie was obsessed with protecting Giggs. Aged seventeen, no media, played a little bit, a little bit, a little bit. Slowly adding more minutes a game. He was very, very careful. If it cost United a win here or there, Fergie was man enough to take it. He wasn't going to ruin Giggs whatever anyone threw at him. That's why he's in the top five British managers of all time, just below four Liverpool ones."

"Huh."

"Michael Owen. Broke every goalscoring record there was in Liverpool's youth system. As good as Giggs? Sure. Liverpool were trying to catch United then. So Owen played every game. Every game, every game. And for a couple of years it was great. Owen was the star of the World Cup. Was named the best player in Europe. Then, pop! His hamstrings went. And he was never the same again. If you ask me, that's why Ferguson's the . . . ." Jackie glanced at me, and away. He almost mumbled the next part. "The GOAT. He knew exactly how much his young players needed, and he gave it to them, and not a second more. Giggs. Rooney. Ronaldo. With any other manager, they might not have had the careers they had."

I let this digest. I hadn't really learned about Magnus Evergreen, but it was valuable stuff regardless. "So," I said, carefully. "Ziggy, Raffi, Kisi . . . me." Jackie looked over at me, eyes wide. Well, fuck it. If he could acknowledge that Ferguson was the greatest manager of all time, even over Bill Shankly or Bob Paisley, then I could admit that maybe I might have some small talent for playing. "We should play, like, three minutes. Then five. Then ten."

"No," he said. "Three minutes. Then zero. Then five. Then zero."

"Wow," I said. "That slow."

He gave me a long stare, which ended with him frowning at my ankle. "There are exceptions," he said.

54

BIZARRE RANTS

As we neared half-time, Jackie was suddenly talking into his phone. He'd had it on vibrate instead of being obnoxious. Plus ten relationship points!

His tone was hard to read, but he kept glancing at me as he said things like "oh?" and "how long?" I knew instantly what was up. Someone at FC United had picked up an injury, and now they needed Ziggy!

It wasn't long until he pressed a button on his screen and placed the phone down. He cleared his throat.

"Ahem. Max. You with me? I've got my FC United hat on now."

"Right."

"Would you and your client be available to come to Broadhurst on Monday evening?"

"Gosh," I said. "Whatever for?"

"You know what for."

"I should like to hear you say it."

He grimaced. "Owing to injuries and suspensions in the forward areas, we would like to offer your client a short-term contract."

My gut went:

Hurrrrrrrh! Come onnnn! Whoop there it is! Whoop there it is! U-N-I . . . T-E-D . . . United are the team for me!

My face went: Politely blank.

"Short-term? Do you mean eighteen months?"

Jackie grinned on one side of his face. "Until January, Max."

Basically a two-month deal. My joy completely vanished.

My face went: Thunderous.

"I see. You want Ziggy to help you out of a jam until you can sign someone better in the January window." I pointed to his phone. "Call your minion there, and tell them they can go fuck themselves." Minus a billion relationship points!

"Max," said Jackie, unusually calm and reasonable. "You're new to this, but even you must know there's a thing called negotiation. You can't just fly off the handle at every little thing."

"I fucking can and I fucking will. Ziggy is going to be a club legend for someone. I wanted it to be FC United, but if you're going to play silly buggers I'll get motoring in my shitty car and get networking again." I pressed my knuckles into my forehead. Why was everything so hard? "You need him more than he needs you. Offering terms till January is sick. It's a joke. He's supposed to quit his job for the privilege of being shafted by you clowns two months from now?"

"We've been training him. Developing him into an asset you can monetise. You owe us."

"Agreed. So when he scores the goal that relegates you, he won't celebrate. Call me a taxi to Manchester. And pay for it."

"Max!" said Jackie, still absurdly calm given that I was blasting him with both barrels. "Don't you think you should talk to your client before you make these decisions? Maybe he'd be fine with playing till January. It's a foot in the door. Way easier to find a new club. He might even grab a goal or two. Earn an extension."

"Sure," I said. "I'll talk to him." I picked up my phone and pretended to dial Ziggy. Pretended to get huffy waiting for him to pick up. This is what Jackie heard: "Ziggers. Bad news. FCU want to take you on, but only till Jan. Yeah, it's a piss-take. I know. I know! Well, I know this guy at Oldham. We'll get you in there. It's a higher level, yeah, bit less playing time, but I'll tell you one thing, when they see how good you are, they won't offer you a zero-hours contract like some poor shelf-stacker in a trainer shop."

"Max," said Jackie.

"No, yeah," I ranted. "Jackie knows about it. He's here. Yeah, he acts like some sort of high priest of socialism, but he's not above a bit of casual exploitation when it suits him. I know. But goalscorers own the means of production, mate. That's you. He's going to wake up tomorrow and realise he's let a twenty-goal a season striker slip through his grubby little hands."

"Max," said Ziggy.

I blinked.

My client's voice had come out of Jackie's phone. I thought he'd hung up, but he'd actually put the call on speaker. Ziggy had heard everything. They both burst out laughing. Jackie had completely outplayed me.

Good joke.

Funny.

I'd have a permanent plus one to my blood pressure, but there are times you have to admit you are beaten.

While Jackie continued pissing himself laughing, Ziggy clarified that there *had* been an injury and that there really *was* going to be a contract discussion.

We agreed to meet on Monday at the stadium. My temper was still up, and Jackie was still sniggering. But Ziggy would enjoy the rest of his weekend. Potentially his last weekend as an amateur player!

At half-time, Mike Dean returned. Now that there was no XP on offer, I could give him my full attention. Realising I'd been a bit rude earlier, I stood and turned the charm up. That was hard with my massive bruise making me look grotesque. But I tried.

After a quick burst of SmoothMax™, a visibly more relaxed Mike returned to his mission. "So, Max. I've been watching the game trying to see what you were talking about. I'm not a tactician, but yeah, I started to get it. Very impressive. I talked to the coaching staff, and they're in a huddle now trying to counter it. We could use a lot more of that kind of insight around here."

I did a little frown and looked at Jackie. When he wasn't trying to humiliate me, he was trying to help me with my career. Why? "Sorry, Mike. I don't mean to be rude, but . . . who are you?"

He laughed. "Left you to figure it out for himself, did he? He's like that. Socratic Method or some bollocks. I'm the Managing Director here."

"We call him MD MD," said Jackie.

"Sort of the CEO. Now, we don't have a lot of money like those kleptoclubs in the Premier League. We're a community outfit. But we still need to win football games. I'd be interested in hiring you as a scouting specialist."

"Excuse me?"

"Go to scout our opponents." He tapped my piece of paper. "Give us this kind of tactical insight. And tell us which players to look out for. Who are their dangermen? Are they strong on set pieces? That sort of thing."

My mind was completely blown. Was I being offered a real job in the football industry? "And which to sign. That's my superpower."

Mike's eyebrows rose. "You're pretty confident in your abilities."

Jackie stepped in. "Max, who'd get into a combined team?"

He was asking me to pick players from Chester and Darlington and make a sort of all-star team. "Ben Cavanagh, Carl Carlile, Aff, Henri Lyons. The rest would be the Darlington team that's on the pitch."

Jackie was nodding. He liked what I'd said. Agreed with me.

Mike was perplexed, but shrugged it off. "What we can do is, you make recommendations on players, and we'll track them over time and see how often you're right."

"There's an easier way," said Jackie. "He's found a player. Free agent. Top midfield prospect. I've scouted him, briefly. Ian and the coaches will lose their minds when they see him." Now here was Jackie doing my pitching for me. I wasn't sure how I felt about that. It felt like part of his wider plot. "Let him come and train. Get his fitness up. Max found him playing five-a-side. We're about to sign a striker he found. He found a girl who's been signed by Man City. If the midfielder makes it, that's three for three. You'd be mad not to take whoever else he recommends."

Mike scratched his face. "There's no harm in looking at the guy."

"What about Henri Lyons?" I said.

Jackie was exasperated. "Max! He isn't even your client!"

"If you can get him, you should! If I'm going to recommend players I'd like to think someone is listening."

"He's difficult," said Mike. "There's more to football than talent."

"That's fair," I said. "Yeah. That's fair." That was one weakness I had. The CA/PA numbers didn't tell me anything about someone's character. Although in some cases I could get a reference from Solly the dog.

Mike sort of blew a raspberry. "Well. Looks like I just offered you a trial as a scout and your . . . client? . . . a trial as a player."

"How much do I get paid? For the scouting."

Mike calculated. "Fifty quid."

Fifty quid to travel the country watching sixth tier games in the cold and the rain? I kept my shit together. "Jackie. Is this one of your wind-ups?"

Mike grinned. He was no stranger to the world of negotiation. He didn't mind a bit of pushback.

Jackie acted as my agent. "A hundred a match, plus you pay his expenses. Petrol, parking. Tenner for a pie and a programme. The office sorts out his tickets."

Mike picked up the scouting report. Looked at the formations I'd drawn. He was thinking, is this worth a hundred quid? I wished I'd had more colours. He looked at Jackie in a slightly strange way. "Deal. Tuesdays and Saturdays till the end of the year. Sound good?"

I grinned. Free XP! Free money! "Deal. One more thing. Have you got any teams I can manage? Just for one-off games or whatever. Just for the practice."

Mike laughed. "You can manage the Knights!"

I did a tiny head wiggle and said, "Fine. Love to. When do they play?"

His face dropped. "I wasn't serious. They're . . . well, they're sweet kids but they never win."

"They'll be happy I turned up then."

Mike's demeanour radically changed. He did something like the thing that Jackie did, sort of went internal and blank-faced. But coming from an older guy, a more mature guy, a managing director guy, it was even more impressive. He turned his new face on Jackie, but the scouser was unmoved. "Don't underestimate him. I watched him turn some no-hopers into a team that thrashed Man City."

"Jackie loves to exaggerate that story," I said. "But if they always lose, what have you got to . . . ah . . . lose?"

He shrugged. "Nothing, I suppose."

"It's a youth team is it? Is it eleven-a-side?"

"They're nine to fifteen years old. Seven-a-side is the ideal. Sometimes they play five or six, depending on how many turn up."

Confusing. "Aren't they affiliated with Chester FC?"

"Yes. But . . ."

Obviously whatever this was, it wasn't my dream team. But I'd pretty much take anything on offer. "Ah, well. I've said I'll do it, and I'll do it with a smile. But I really wanted to do some eleven-a-side matches. I've done a lot of small-sided games recently. I need something more serious."

Mike appraised me. "Tell you what. You win with the Knights, I'll put you in charge of the boys under-fourteens for a game."

"Top," I said, rubbing my hands. "When's the next Knights fixture?"

"Tomorrow morning," he said. "You aren't thinking . . ."

"Yeah. Let's get on with it. I'll drive back here in the morning. Just tell me what time."

"Max, you prick," said Jackie. "You're on crutches. You aren't driving like that. I'll call the police and dob you in myself if you try."

I glared at him. "Fine. Buy me a sleeping bag, and I'll kip in a bus stop. I'll pay you back with my scouting money. Then, after the match I'll find her and see if she'll give me a lift home." I didn't explain who "she" was. Jackie's reaction showed he knew exactly who I meant.

Mike put a hand on my arm. "Are you seriously going to stay the night in Chester just so you can manage the Knights in the morning?"

I stared at him like he was the stupidest man in the world, which, to be fair, he might have been, though there was no evidence to suggest that. "Yes. Managing a team from a proper club is a big step up for me. Honestly, I've had a lot of good news today, but if you tell me that's definitely going to happen I'll be proper buzzing."

Mike looked from me to Jackie. Out of the corner of my eye, I felt like Jackie gave him a tiny little nod, but I can't be sure that *actually* happened. "All right," Mike said. "I'll get that arranged. And I'll find you somewhere to stay tonight. Not sure about how you'll get home tomorrow."

"I'll take him," said Jackie. So he had a place to stay in Chester? With Livia, maybe? I hoped so. "Make sure he doesn't get up to any more mischief."

MD left to do MD things.

As I caught myself in the reflection of the door as it closed, I reflected on how strange life is. After months of grinding, everything was falling into place.

In the last hour, Ziggy had moved within touching distance of becoming a pro. Raffi was about to get a second chance at a first impression. I had—and this was bizarre—landed a job. At a professional football club! For good money! Wasn't that . . . two games a week, a hundred pounds a pop . . . eight hundred pounds a month for Tuesday evenings and Saturdays? I was going to say that coaching the Knights in the morning was the most exciting thing of all, but eight hundred pounds a month blew it out of the water.

Life was . . . amazing.

But also . . . lacking.

"Jackie. Thanks for everything. I mean it. But I'm desperate for a tea. My mouth is the most arid surface on earth."

"I'll get you one. And I'll get someone to bring you another during the second half. You read this article I'm about to send you about Henri Lyons. Then I'll go and sort some personal stuff out, and I'll come and find you after the game. All right?"

"All right. Jackie?"

"Yeah?"

"Were we ever going to Wrexham?"

He grinned at me and left.

The link Jackie sent me took me to an article in *The Durham Evening News*. That was the moment I learned that Darlington was in Durham. I would have guessed Yorkshire.

Frenchman DROPPED by Quakers After Bizarre Rant

[The Quakers are the nickname for Darlington FC. All British clubs have nicknames like that. Man United are The Red Devils, which is cool. Liverpool are The Reds, which is abysmal. Man City are The Cthulhu Anthropoids. Chester are The Seals, named after their old stadium. You might be thinking that seals aren't especially intimidating. It's rare but not unknown for teams to change their nicknames. Benin (the country) used to be The Squirrels, but they decided it wasn't fierce enough and are now The Cheetahs, which, you know, is sort of a poor choice of name in a sport that has fussy referees.
All right, on with the article.]

Quaker fans are reeling after star striker Henri Lyons blasted the club and its manager in a surreal interview last week in the French magazine *Scrogneugneu*. In the interview, Lyons appeared to BLAST experienced Quakers manager David Cutter, his fellow players, and the club and CITY itself. The 27-year-old French import, signed with great fanfare from Corsican outfit FC Borgo, has scored 30 goals in 60 first-team appearances. But now, with his contract in its last season, there are questions as to whether he will ever make the starting line-up again.

"It's horrible," said Quaker Supporter's Trust spokesman Roy Macateer. "He's gone in two-footed. He's bitten the hand that feeds him. I'm happy to see the club taking action against him." Other fans on social media shared the sentiments:

[Here there were a few embedded tweets, but my browser blocks all that shit. We don't need a sentiment tracker to guess what they said.]

The club declined to comment, citing British employment laws, but leaks from the dressing room indicate Lyons has been told he will not be considered available for the first team until further notice.

What Was Said?
On playing in England:

"Football is not played. Football is created. Therefore, if you are merely playing, it is not football. In England, effort is rewarded. By the manager, by the fans. Creation is not. That is why Banksy remains anonymous."

On his relationship with his manager:

"The constraints of some coaches are liberating; the liberations of others are a straitjacket."

On his teammates:

"In France a dressing room is full of sound and fury. Players argue bitterly with their coaches. Thesis. Antithesis. And in the winning teams, synthesis.

In England you have authoritarianism. Dissent is stifled. Diversity of opinion exists on your phone. Not in the dressing room. Not in the town. Am I a philosopher? Of course not. I work in England. If I were a philosopher I would postulate that there could be the green shoots of valid ideas forming within the minds of the players, who have trained from a young age to find solutions; if we find one solution we might consider that other solutions could exist. I would postulate that debate is not terrible, to be feared, but is the fertiliser that solutions consume to grow."

On his future:

"The act of touching a ball is the act of adding to a poem. One day I am E.E. Cummings. The next perhaps I am T.S. Eliot. There is only one constant; I never rhyme."

The referee blew his whistle, and the second half kicked off. I watched the game as best I could, but it was pretty drab. My eye kept rolling towards the dugouts. In the away section sat a guy so French that everything he said was like nails on a chalkboard to the average Englishman.

I felt slightly light-headed, and it wasn't just that I had barely eaten anything all day. The air was heavy with the smell of opportunity.

I checked the text again. Yep, there it was. Contract running out.

Henri Lyons. A poet-philosopher with great heading and finishing. I had to meet him.

But first I had to grind for XP and unlock another attribute.

With a sigh, I shifted my attention back to the game.

With an even bigger sigh, I checked the tactics screens and both were the same. Chester's manager had been told what was happening and had done fuck all about it. It was going to be a long forty-five minutes.

55

CHESTER NIGHTS

The game ended Chester 0 Darlington 1.

Darlington had the better players but ensured the match stayed as a boring war of attrition. The one moment of quality in the game came from their CA 50 striker, who bullied a Chester defender and gave himself the chance to dribble forward and smash the ball into the net.

In my opinion, the whole second half was utterly tedious. And, since I'd diagnosed Darlington's plan after fifteen minutes, utterly preventable.

I just couldn't understand it. Even within the confines of 4-4-2, I could think of ways to combat Darlington's strategy. MD had given Ian Evans my report. Plus Ian Evans had the evidence of his own eyes. Yet he hadn't made a single tactical change in the entire match. Why?

But whatever. If Chester's manager didn't care, why should I?

It was in injury time that I finally got the XP needed to buy Attributes 3. The stupid animation did its stupid little animation dance, and the attribute it unlocked was . . .

Teamwork.

Teamwork. Huh.

I would have thought that all professional players scored twenty in that. Otherwise, how had they progressed so far?

But in the last, dying moments of the match after I'd unlocked it, I saw a huge range of scores. Carl Carlile had teamwork twenty, which I supposed made him the ultimate team player unless one of his family members was on the pitch. Henri Lyons had seventeen, which was unexpectedly high for a guy who seemed like a selfish French prick. Aff had fifteen, which was still quite high. It made sense that a winger wouldn't be maxed in teamwork. They had to be a bit selfish to try to dribble sometimes. (This thought started to mess with my head. The team needed people to be selfish for the benefit of the team. *What?* So if a winger was selfish, did that mean he'd have a high teamwork score? I let it go. I chose to allow my brain to merely absorb the info. Let it marinate. And eventually I'd come to a conclusion I could verbalise.)

Okay, so I'd unlocked Handling and Teamwork. Good! I was getting there. And the Match Report section was available. It was simply a record of all the in-curse commentary that had happened in the match. Handy to check some incident that had happened earlier in the game. Good good good.

One slightly odd thing was that Attributes 4 was priced at 1,567 XP. Such a specific number! There had to be a reason behind that, surely?

But that was a long grind in the future. I had under 10 XP and would soon buy God Save the King, going 3,000 XP into debt. Soon? Maybe as soon as Monday evening. If Ziggy got a contract, I'd push him closer to Denis Law's finishing.

After the final whistle, I hobbled as fast as I could down to where the changing rooms were. Through the physio room, through the teeny tiny gym, out into the corridor, and towards the noisiest room. The Quakers were blasting aggressive "winning" music which, honestly, I found a bit classless. The vibration of their dressing room wall did at least fit their team's nickname.

"Hey," I said to some rando who tried to stop me from going in. "I need to talk to Henri."

"Why dat?" said this prick.

My blood roiled! Roiling is like boiling but more literary, which means it's scarier. I gave this guy the staredown of a lifetime and said, "Henri Lyons. Get him or get bent."

Henri eased out of the changing room a few moments later. I dragged him away, because the insistent bass was giving me a headache. "Henri?" I said. "My name's Max Best."

Henri was pretty much the most French person who ever lived. And I include Napoleon, Emile Zola, and William Gallas in that. He had that big, shaped, fluffy hair that dreamy pop idols have until they rebrand with a hard-edged image. Henri had completed the Five Pillars of Frenchness: the scarf, the disjointed nose, the accent, the permanent shrug, and the insouciant air. The scarf! Jesus Christ! The match had only finished about four minutes ago, and he was already wearing highly-textured, perfectly-fitted clothes topped off by a jaunty scarf which had a different but complementary pattern to his jacket. Sacre bleu! "Oui?"

I showed him the newspaper link on my phone; he rolled his eyes. "I've just read this article about you. You said you think the players should be able to share their insights with the manager?"

"Oh?" he said. "You are the first Englishman to actually read it."

I wasn't going to engage his self-pity. I wasn't sure how long I'd be allowed to roam the corridors. "Is that what you meant or not?"

He considered the question. "It is. Every team is one insight away from utopia. Or dystopia." He grinned, Frenchly. "With a match-day squad of twenty, ideas may grow in a cornucopia."

"I thought you said you never rhymed. But God, that's what I want. I've never heard it verbalised like that. I want a team where everyone's thinking about the game the way I do," I said. "Bicker, fight, marketplace of ideas, Darwin. But then once the manager has listened and chosen, full commitment to the plan." I put my hand on his arm. "Holy fuck," I said, suddenly wide-eyed. "I think that might be my ultimate fantasy."

Henri Lyons smiled at me. "Max Best, I like you. What do you want of me?"

Good question. "Well, I'm an agent. I could be an English to English translator for you. If you want to pay someone ten percent of your salary to say you're at the wrong club, I volunteer. But mostly I'm a football fan, and I'd like to see you in a team that appreciates your gifts. Watching you rot on the bench today was torture. You'd have electrified this game."

His chin shot up. "Your taste is incredible. Are you sure you are English?"

"English," I said. "French. Eritrean. Who gives a shit? You're meant to play football, and if you're not doing that, there's an inefficiency. Inefficiency means profit for the guy who fixes that. Me. Someone else. I don't care. But I tell you what: two thousand people paid good money to come to this game today, and the best player wasn't playing. That's abysmal. I can't fix global warming or disinformation or any of that. But I can fix your career."

Henri, chin still high, tried to look down on me. Haughty. Confident. "You have the advantage of me. You can read about *me* online. Watch clips of my best moments. Yes, there are so many, but it is theoretically possible. Where would I find out more about *you*?"

I signalled that he should whip out his phone and started to share contact details with him. "Tomorrow I'll be coaching a youth team here in Chester. Check into a hotel. Come and watch. They never win; tomorrow they will. Football reveals personality. Mine will be on display."

"You want me to come to a youth team game . . . in Chester?" His tone suggested he had dismissed the idea, like, ten years ago.

"A great deal of football will be created," I said. "If you are happy to stay on the bench, then it was great meeting you. If you want to see something you've never seen before . . . the Max Best Show has come to town. One morning only."

And I strode off like an absolute boss.

Except . . . I was still on the crutches so it took me approximately six minutes to clunk along the corridor.

Still. Good speech.

Jackie dropped me off at a grey-brick, terraced house. It belonged to a family of die-hard Chester FC fans that MD MD knew well. Dad was out having some pints with his mates. Mum was perfectly pleasant. A bit flustered that I'd been foisted on her, but she soon settled into the mother hen role and got me fed and watered. They had a kid. I was to sleep in his room. Jackie had suggested I should keep up the pretence of being a possible future signing for Chester. The kid was all over the idea of being the first to meet Chester's new player, big bragging rights at school, I reckoned. He showed me around his room: his posters (Messi, Neymar, Marcus Rashford, the Chester squad), his football books, his copy of Champion Manager 2023. I put my hands in my pockets, so I wouldn't slap the box out of his hands.

"Are you in the game?" he asked me.

"I can't talk about it until I sign for a club," I said. "Top secret."

"But what would your stats be? Are you fast?"

I sat on the bed and tested the mattress. All I really cared about was the bed. It had a headboard but, thank God, no leg board. Otherwise I would have had to sleep scrunched up like a prawn. "Fast asleep," I said. "Soon enough."

Mum and kid (named Chester, seriously wtf is wrong with people?) watched me eat a bland curry and peppered me with questions about football. I told them about my recent adventures. Chesterkid listened with eyes bulging. He had a strange way of looking at me but not quite at me. There was something off about him, but whatever it was, he was enthralled by me, which I found gratifying. Mum was not so gullible. Most of what I told them seemed to her to be obvious bullshit. She was in for a shock if she ever fact-checked my tales; they were all true.

When I told them I was going to be managing the Chester Knights in the morning, they were both equally astonished.

"But that's Terry's job."

Right. I'd have to manage their normal coach. That would probably be harder than managing the kids. "I'm not taking Terry's job. I'm just doing one game. I'm sure Terry is a prince among men. I hope there's enough players. Apparently, there's low turnout."

"Some people get dispirited, because we lose every week."

"The more kids who turn up, the better the chance of winning. But what was it King Henry said? *The fewer men, the greater share of honour!* Give me a midfield pivot and a fox-in-the-box, and I shall move the world! Oh, and a goalkeeper, I suppose. Personally I'd be happy to just put a Henry Hoover in goal and have done with it. But it's against the rules. Bloody FIFA!"

That went down like a lead statue of Neymar in a slight gust of wind, so I announced that I'd had a long day, needed to go to bed soon, and would like a couple of extra pillows to put my leg up. And also, could we take the Neymar poster down, just for tonight, so I wouldn't have nightmares?

The mum told me that Neymar was misunderstood and did a lot of charity work, especially with disabled kids. Great, I said. But I don't like him. Yes, she said, but he's great with disabled kids. Clearly, the conversation had the potential to subsume the rest of my days on earth. Its circularity could compete with the CERN collider. So as a compromise I suggested we leave the poster up but cover Neymar's face with post-it notes. I was joking. But actually not. There was a stack of post-it notes that I put in my pocket. Cue nervous laughter. Surely I was joking . . . Right? Right?

"Oh," I said, as an afterthought pointing to their TV and Playstation 3 combo, "I don't suppose you have Disney Plus?"

They did.

So I popped a bunch of extra-strength painkillers and lay in bed with my foot raised, watching *The Proposal* on the family's insanely slow Android tablet. I made notes but fell asleep halfway through.

I woke, wiped away quite a lot of drool, and grabbed my phone, which was vibrating like a dressing room full of twats. It was my soulmate.

"Raffi?"

"How's my agent doing?"

"Ugh . . . mixed. What year is it?"

He laughed. I heard him knocking on a door. "Come and open your door, man."

"What?"

"We're here! Open your door."

"No, wait, what? No, I'm in Chester. I'm not there, I'm in Chester."

"He's in Chester!" said Raffi. Presumably to his wife. "Why you in Chester?" I heard his wife say something like "he got on the wrong train," which they both thought was hilarious.

"Getting you a trial."

"You serious?"

"Yeah. Details to be confirmed. Chester is the National League North. Sixth tier. Ideal starting block. It's happening."

There was a lot of shouting and hugging and that. Finally, it subsided, and Raffi returned to the call. "Man! You're not fracking with me now?"

"No. I would never frack you. Not without a lengthy consultation process. Wait wait wait. Why are you at my house?"

"We came to pick you up, so we could take your dog for a walk." His wife shouted something that I couldn't catch. Raffi passed it on. "Like you promised! Yeah. Well, never mind. How about we go and do it anyway?"

"Why would you do that?"

"Someone has to, right? I'll talk to you." And he hung up.

I woke up again. Someone was knocking on my door.

"Raffi?" I said.

The door opened. Chesterkid came in. "Max? We have to go now, or we'll be late." His eyes drifted to the Neymar poster. He couldn't believe I'd actually put the post-it notes up.

"Why didn't you wake me up earlier?"

"Jackie Reaper said you needed your beauty sleep." The eyes again.
"What does that mean?"

"Give me two minutes, bro."

He scarpered, and I got dressed and slapped myself in the face a few times.

As I put my hand on the doorknob, I froze. Had I been dreaming, or had Raffi Brown, the world's most beautiful man, called me his agent?

When had he decided *that*?

I shook it off. Next stop: Chester Knights.

56

CHESTER KNIGHTS

Football glossary: The Treble. In most European countries, the best thing a team can do is win the Treble. This involves winning the three most important trophies: the National League, the Major Domestic Cup, and the Champions League. Manchester United won the Treble in 1999. Liverpool say they won the Treble in 1984, but historians are baffled by the claim, because Everton won the FA Cup that year.

I was not at my mental sharpest when I arrived at the pitch. The meds, the foreign locale, the speed at which events were eventuating. But what did it matter? I'd use the curse to rearrange the team, they'd win comfortably, and I'd earn the chance to manage a full-size under-fourteens game. Progression. Love it. If I kept this up, I'd be managing Chester by the end of the season.

There wasn't time to get to know the team or do anything tactical. We arrived a full minute before kickoff. Just enough time to shake hands with Terry, the team's coach, apologise for barging into his domain (which he took with good grace), and give my drink order to a teenager, who sprinted off to get it. The VIP treatment for Max! At last!

The match kicked off.

Almost instantly, a Knight crashed into an opponent. A full speed collision! Instead of rolling around, begging for a foul, they helped each other up and sprinted towards the ball, where they collided again.

This was not what I'd expected, not in the slightest. But my heart pumped just a little bit faster. This had the potential to be fun!

It was Para football. Both teams comprised partially sighted players, ones with hearing impairments, ones with cerebral palsy, and some with Down's Syndrome. This was baffling. I clarified it with Terry. "Is this normal? They've got such different strengths and weaknesses."

"Yeah," he said. "It's called pan-disability footy. It's big and it's growing. Think how many competitive games you'd get if you only played with people with the exact same disability you had. The biggest benefit is getting games scheduled. Games are the pathway to growth. The kids who excel here can get taken up by disability-specific teams."

"Huh. But isn't it unfair?"

"A lot of things are unfair." Well, true. I took in a drag of crisp, cool air. It was a sunny morning. Cold but bright. The pitch was small, but the grass was green and the lines were white. A level playing field. A prerequisite condition for sport. He saw that I was still stressed about the mixed abilities and gave me a little smile. "Max, relax. We know what we're doing!" He tapped my crutches. "You should try frame football. You'd be good at it. And when everyone's in the same boat, everyone's in the same boat."

I smiled back. "Who are the other team?"

"Ellesmere Eleven. They're decent. They have a big CP centre there."

"Oh," I said, trying to understand. "The more cerebral palsy players, the better?"

"We try not to think like that," he said. "We're the top destination for Para players in the region, so we get first dibs. Not to be too harsh, but we've looked at all the Ellesmere kids, and if we wanted to sign one, they'd be here."

"But you always lose, I was told."

Terry gave me a look. "There's more important things than winning. Our kids are two years younger than theirs. Our goal is to develop players. We've had kids go on to play for Wales. For Team GB at the Olympics. For the big Para teams."

"Great," I said. "But I was told people drop out of the programme because you always lose."

"That's just mad parents who want to live out their childhood fantasies through their kids. If they stop coming, it's a shame for those kids, but honestly, we're all better off without them. Without the parents, I mean."

"Huh."

My tea arrived, and I took stock of the picture in front of me.

The Chester Knights were in jerseys very much like the blue-and-white Chester FC home kit. The sponsor was different, even more local sounding. And if my eyes weren't deceiving me, the names on the shirts weren't in quite the same font as the first team. But that didn't matter. The kids were *resplendent*.

I clarified the rules. Rolling subs, no offsides, and when the ball went out of bounds, the players could do a kick-in, throw-in, or roll-in depending on what they preferred. There were several other minor tweaks, and the goalposts were made of rope surrounded by white tape, so the partially-sighted players could crash into them and not get hurt.

Now that I felt I had a sort of global overview of Para football, I zoomed in to the pitch itself. Watching the match was like watching two swarms of bees buzz around. It was like primary school playground football but without the goalhangers. Just loads of kids running towards the ball, wherever the ball was. Mayhem. And "my" swarm had bees that were smaller and slower than the other swarm. If I couldn't change anything, then defeat was inevitable.

Fine. So what about the players? We had seven on the pitch, plus three subs. Chester's mum must have spread the word that something interesting was happening. She'd ensured a bumper turnout. So in principle, the Knights were more talented than their opponents, but so much younger they were unlikely to win. Okay. On my left, Chester himself was in goal. After I'd made jokes about how goalkeepers could be replaced by home appliances! Ah, well. He was wearing absolutely mad steampunk-style goggles. No wonder he never looked me in the eyes. Without his goggles he probably couldn't see me! "How far can Chester see?" I asked Terry.

"Not far," he said. "Like five, ten metres."

"Shit," I said. "And how far with the goggles on?"

"That's with the goggles on."

"Shit! Is he waiting for a cornea transplant or something like that?"

Terry squirmed. "It's probably best if you don't think about it," he said.

Fuck.

We had another partially sighted girl. She was wearing very thick, round-framed glasses. She was playing as a sort of attacking mid-swarmer. The ball bobbled towards her, and she hit a fierce shot that went just wide. "Who's that?"

"We call her Scrappy. She's a real terrier. Gets stuck in. And she's got fantastic ball striking."

Ball striking. Interesting way to put it. I thought through the ramifications of what that meant and why he'd said it. I imagined having poor vision and finding the ball at my feet. How well would I be able to kick it? Probably quite well, to be honest, because I had years of experience to fall back on. What if I'd been born differently? What if I'd been born blind? Could I score a penalty with my eyes closed? Only through luck. If I blindfolded myself and just left a couple of little holes to look through, how good would my technique be? Probably awful. So Terry saying that Scrappy had good technique meant a lot. "Have you tried her in defence?"

He gave me a sour look. "Mike Dean said to let you do what you want, so if that's what you're recommending . . ."

I gave him a reassuring smile. "I'm not changing anything until I understand what I'm seeing. I'm not a complete nutjob, whatever you've heard." The game continued, the players moving seemingly at random, like Brownian motion. I wished I had a tactics screen, but that was only available for eleven-a-side matches. I noticed that Terry had a little whiteboard among all the bags of balls and equipment behind him. It seemed to suggest a 2-2-2 formation. A reliable classic! "Er . . . the kids aren't really following your plan. Are they able . . . ? Are they . . . ?" I wasn't sure how to word the question without seeming like a total gammon.

"Are they capable of understanding tactics?" He gave me a withering look. "Yes, Max."

I understood that he'd want to defend his players. He worked with them up to four times a week. "But I mean," I said, pointing to the mayhem.

"But what?"

"But they aren't doing it."

"They are." He picked up the whiteboard and pointed to the two centre-backs, then pointed to the pitch. "Clogger and Wilson." He pointed to the midfield duo on the board and on the pitch. "Zoe and Scrappy." The strikers. "Beans and John."

I watched the boy called Clogger and the girl called Zoe for a while. And, indeed, their average position was as they'd been coached. It was just that they spent a lot of time running *around* that area.

"Okay, that's good," I said. "I can work with that." There was another thumping collision in the midfield. "Shit!" I said.

Terry laughed. "Yeah. They're absolutely fearless. It takes some getting used to."

I shook my head in wonderment.

Fearless was a great way to describe it. Another way was brave. What was that kid's bravery score?

And that thought was the catalyst for the crisis that followed.

There were no player profiles. I hadn't noticed at first, because I'd been busy trying to get up to speed with Para football. Also, I hadn't been offered the chance to play a Free Hit when we got free kicks or corners. I was definitely in charge, though. Terry had said as much.

I did a little test and threw on one of our subs. Terry was surprised by the change but didn't say anything. The referee accepted my authority, as did my players. Okay.

Next, I tried asking Clogger to drop back a few yards. He nodded and did it. I gave him a big thumbs up.

Right. I was in charge. So why wasn't I getting the Free Hit button?

I thought that maybe I wasn't seeing it because I'd arrived late. But I'd always seen player profiles no matter when I turned up. As long as there were people playing football and the football was considered serious, I saw the profiles. Five-a-side always triggered it, and this was *sevens*.

"Terry, can I ask you some questions? They might be annoying."

"I'm used to it," he said. Did he mean he was used to *me* asking annoying questions? Cheeky!

"Do you work for Chester FC? Like, are you an employee of the club?"

"Yep. Full-time. I do bits and bobs of coaching. Some admin. The hours are long, but at least the pay is bad."

"The Chester Knights are affiliated with Chester FC? Like, if one of these kids attacks the referee, it'll be Chester City's name in the newspaper?"

He narrowed his eyes at me. "Chester FC. But yes."

I nodded. This game was more embedded into and higher up the English footballing ecosystem than almost all the ones I'd been to since getting the curse. With a jolt, I checked and realised I wasn't even getting XP from it! What the actual! "And you said about pathways. Kids go from here to bigger teams. To the Wales team."

"Yes."

"Wait, wait!" I said, excited to have solved the problem. "Is this game technically in a Welsh league or something like that?" Maybe the curse only worked in England! That would be insane, but at least it would explain what was happening.

"No, it's England."

Well, fuck.

Ellesmere darted through and hit a low shot that Chester saved, but he could do nothing about the rebound. One-nil. Not the best of starts to my twelve-month plan to take over as first-team manager here.

Terry clapped and gave a little shout of encouragement to his wards. "Come on, Chester! Champion mentality!"

The Knights pulled themselves taller and spent the next twenty seconds zipping around with even more intensity than before.

I glanced at Terry. He seemed like a super guy. There was no curse data over his head, so maybe he wasn't a proper coach. He was coaching the hell out of these kids, though. "Terry, you don't seem to mind me coming here and disrupting your day."

He looked a bit shifty. "I do mind," he admitted. "Only a bit, though. I don't know who you are, but suddenly we've got a lot of bigwigs showing an interest. I've been on the phone all morning." I glanced over my shoulder to see who he was talking about. He helped me out. "There's MD. A couple of the first team coaches. And Jackie Reaper."

An opportunity to get some hot goss! I played it cool. "Oh?" I said. "Who's that?"

"Used to play for Chester. Big talent. Got injured, started coaching. I think he's in Manchester now."

"Huh. I've seen him. The way he swaggers around you'd think he owns the place."

Terry shrugged. "I think CFU trusts him. That's City Fans United. The group that owns the club. Reaper helped the club get back on its feet in the early days. He's a bit of a ledge."

Ledge was footy shorthand for legend. "So you don't mind getting some senior eyeballs on the Knights even if it means letting me make weird substitutions."

He bit his lip, then looked sheepish. "Yeah. Could say it like that. And," he added, "it's something different for the kids. Learning opportunity." He took in my ankle and black eye. "Maybe."

"One last question. And I'm not trying to be offensive. I'm not saying it's what I believe. But if someone said to you that this wasn't real football, what would you say?"

"I wouldn't want to have too many conversations with people like that. Life's too short. But I'd just say look at the players. They think it's real football."

And yeah, they did. They were going through all the emotions. Putting in the effort. Getting stuck into tackles and trying to move up the pitch.

So why wasn't the curse treating it like football?

As if to hammer home the point, Ellesmere scored a second goal, caused by a mistake from our partially deaf midfielder, Zoe. She had this large, flat hearing aid sort of running up her skull giving her huge cyberpunk vibes. After hitting a loose pass that led to the goal, she fell on all fours, and pounded the turf in frustration.

I'd seen that before.

Flashback!

The year: 1999. Manchester United are playing Bayern Munich. United have an amazing team, but half the midfield is suspended and can't play because of a moronic rule that was later changed. The ninetieth and last minute. Munich are 1–0 up, and they take off their star defender so he can get a round of applause. The match officials tie Munich colours to the trophy. The English commentator says, "Can United score? They always score!" He's right. Ninety-first minute. United get a corner. The ball bounces around. Goal! Munich are stunned. Ninety-second minute. United get another corner. They fucking score again! It's insane. The United fans go bonkers except for one twat who is looking the wrong way so he can take a photo. I hate that prick. Watch the game! Anyway. That's how United won the Treble. Sport is joy! A Munich defender called Samuel Kuffour falls on all fours and slaps the turf in frustration and disbelief. It's an iconic image. Sport is pain.

I've never had that emotion. To me, sport is process. I've never cared that much.

But our cyberpunk girl cared that much. That's why she was slapping the turf. Conceding that goal meant more to her than any goal ever has to me. A Down's kid had his head in his hands. Chester was lying prone on the pitch, hoping it would swallow him whole.

Okay, 2–0 down and I wasn't getting any help from the curse. I kind of needed this match to go well. This was something of an audition.

I took a step away from the pitch and tried to think clearly.

The first time I'd gone to a five-a-side game, I'd briefly wondered if the curse would give me XP for it, but it had never really been in doubt. Five-a-side football was football. The clue was in the name.

Before I watched Beth's team play I'd wondered if women's football would give me XP. But again, I hadn't ever *really* thought it wouldn't. At school there were a few girls who would join in our lunchtime games, they'd sometimes do skills as well as any boy, and they'd defend and tackle and get scraped knees and all the rest. Even the kinds of people who would complain about women's football being slow and boring would still admit it was football.

So what kind of twat would look at this Para football match and decide it didn't count as real football? Some of the gammons from Oldham, maybe? No . . . that didn't feel right. They were annoying, but they weren't actual monsters. Not when it came to kids, anyway. Not when it came to English kids anyway.

So, who was the villain here?

I swallowed. "Terry," I said. "What's frame football?"

"It's indoor football, but everyone uses a special rollator." He whipped his phone out and brought up a video. It was loads of kids milling around a blue-floored sports hall in walking frames, kicking a ball. With all the human legs and metal legs, it looked even more chaotic and congested than the pan-disability match.

I instantly felt sick. My neck was hot.

"Got it," I said, trying to smile. "Thanks."

I took a couple of steps away and drank the last of my VIP tea.

I had a bad, bad feeling about this.

Seeing the frame football clip brought back a memory. Some school friends and I had seen such a match going on in a local sports hall, and we'd stayed for a while to watch it and laugh our heads off.

We didn't know what it was, but we all agreed on two things. One, that it was hilarious. Two, that it wasn't football.

I leant onto my crutches while I felt my face turn red. Imagine being disabled and trying to play the sport you loved and having some fucking brats mock you for it. The heat had spread up my skull. But the worst was to come.

I finally put two and two together.

Since I'd been hijacked by the curse, something had been bothering me. Little details. God Save the King featuring players I'd read about in old comics and football annuals. Why not some obscure guy who was a genius but didn't have a Wikipedia page? The renaming of the Tommy Tactics achievement. Why would the curse rename *anything* except to use a new phrase I'd only just heard? And most of all, the fact that the perks didn't have fixed prices but changed according to my mood/needs/motivation.

What it all boiled down to was that I influenced the curse as much as it influenced me. It was very, very definitely taking my personal footballing opinions and making them into some sort of foundation for how it interacted with me.

And when the curse said it didn't give a shit about disabled football, that it wasn't real football, that meant that I, Max Best, agreed with it.

I'd invited Henri Lyons to watch this game, because football showed character. And that's exactly what was happening. Come on, everybody. Come on down and see Max's character. Okay! So where is it? That's the joke. He doesn't have one!

I dared to look up. Our short little CP player, John, got the ball and went on a mazy dribble. He beat one, he beat another, but was finally crowded out. There were just too many players in his way. Including his teammates sometimes. John looked towards me, wondering if I would approve or tell him off.

I gave him a thumbs up.

This prompted a brief but monumental surge of disgust and self-recrimination.

I looked at the sky and sucked in a deep breath.

So I was a twat. What was I going to do about it?

Option one. Complain to the curse's management. If that meant Old Polish Nick, well, he was elusive. I got the feeling he'd be in the crowd somewhere, watching, mocking me, but I was even less able to chase him than before. And how could you chase someone who could teleport?

Option two. Admit defeat. Walk away from my commitment to these kids. Try to explain to MD and Jackie that they'd backed the wrong horse, that this was out of my skill set. Flee to Manchester. Try to sleep it off. Feel like shit forever.

Option three? There was no option three.

Oh, but . . .

Option four. Blow it up. Press the retire button.

As soon as I thought that, my vision went bonkers.

There was the grass, the players, the sky. But it was all sort of jagging sideways like an old TV where the signal wasn't quite working. I wasn't quite attuned to the frequency of the universe.

The pain in my head was briefly extraordinary.

The pain ebbed, my vision settled back, and now all the players had profiles, but every single cell was plastered with question marks.

Then there was another jab of pain, and the profiles disappeared.

Huh. I'd almost changed something there. Maybe if I kept threatening to retire the curse, it would sort this shit out?

But hitting retire wasn't really an option yet. If I nuked my footballing skills, almost nobody in the universe would notice. Life would get no better for these disabled footballers, that was for sure. I shook my head. No rash decisions. I took a couple of steps forward, back in line with Terry.

The curse's shitty designers, including me, could go fuck themselves. I'd spent weeks and weeks thinking about seven-a-side football, about formations, about skills. I'd seen enough to affect this game.

I glanced from player to player.

We *had* a goalie. *That guy* could tackle, *she* could pass, *he* could dribble, *she* could run box-to-box, and *he* could score. The last kid didn't have obvious skills, but we could use him by not using him.

"It's game on, Terry." He gave me a weird look. I wondered how long I'd been internal. "I've cracked the case. It's game on."

Game on, and the treble was on:

Sort out this formation, win the game, convince people I had character.

I hesitated and changed my goals. Increased the degree of difficulty.

Sort out this formation, win the game, convince *myself* I had character.

57

JOHNNY WINGER

With five minutes to go till half-time, I threw on the remaining substitutes, bringing off John, the skilful striker; Zoe, the hearing-impaired cyberpunk midfielder; and Scrappy, the other midfielder whose ball striking had drawn a compliment.

Terry took me a little bit away from where the subs were recovering. "Max, you've brought off our three best players."

"Yep."

He wanted to say something, but whatever it was, he swallowed it. "Are you trying to make a point or something?"

"Huh? No."

He let out a tiny grunt of frustration. "Then why?"

"Every player plays every game," I said.

He bit his tongue, then sucked in a breath.

Before he could speak, I said, "Every player plays every game. I learned that from the best. Now, relax," I said, repeating his words back to him with a smile: "We know what we're doing."

Just then, Ellesmere scored again, and Terry's head dropped. He didn't mind losing, but the self-sabotage of taking the best players off the pitch was more than he could stomach.

But I needed to see what the subs had to offer, and I needed my stars fresh for the second half. They would be doing a lot of work.

Half-time. The kids had battled to keep the score at "only" 3–0. Now they were arrayed in front of me, waiting to receive my tactical insights.

I checked over my shoulder to see if Mr. Yalley was about to barge in. Fortunately, he was in church thirty miles away. This wasn't a time for motivation. The kids were motivated all right. This was a time for Tommy Tactics.

"Good effort, team," I said. "Love it. Now listen up. I came here to win a match and chew bubble gum, and I'm all out of bubble gum."

Zoe raised her hand. "What?"

"I'm saying we're going to win this match."

"Oh. Okay."

Half the kids started rummaging in their kit. I needed to be a lot more lucid here.

"Forget the gum," I said. I held up Terry's whiteboard and drew on it. I started by drawing two horizontal lines and two vertical ones, splitting the pitch into boxes. "There are nine zones here. Yes? I'm going to write one name in one box, and that's your zone. Try to stay there unless it's an emergency. Let's put some names into boxes. Most important, the goalkeeper. Chester, you're in zone two. You're a goalkeeper and that's where the goal is, so it makes sense. Happy? Next, we need goals. Beans, you're in box eight. What's the most you've ever scored in a game? Next, back in zone two we've got our classy centre-back Scrappy."

Scrappy complained. "I normally play as a CAM." That's what the young people call a central attacking midfielder.

I did an exaggerated look at the whiteboard. "Huh. That's not what it says. It says you're in defence. Wow. Then in zone five we've got Zoe. So that's Chester, Scrappy, Zoe, Beans. That's called a spine. Strong spine!" I had a brief moment of doubt. Did some of these kids have bad spines? I shot a semi-panicked look at Terry, but he was just looking at my sketch with furrowed brows. I pressed on. "Zoe, you're going to be my brain. You're in the middle, and you can move around based on where we need you. Join attacks or help the defence. But remember, only cross into another box if it's an emergency."

Chester had come forward to examine the whiteboard. "There are two people in my zone."

"Yes, Chester. That's right. Your name is written in green, do you see? So that's okay." He seemed to accept that logic. I should have created a special box just for the goalkeeper, but it was too late now. "All righty, then. Next, we need support for Scrappy, so Clogger, you're in zone one. Anything that comes down the left, that's your job. Clog it! Now, John. Where's John? John. I've got a new nickname for you to help you remember your new position." In box three, I wrote *Johnny Winger*. "Remember when they renamed Marathon to Snickers? Remember when they renamed Opal Fruits to Starburst? Remember when they renamed One Direction to Harry Styles? No? Don't worry. For the rest of the match, I'll be calling you Johnny Winger. Why? Because you're a winger now. Look at zones two and three. Two Scrappy, three Johnny. This is the key to the whole team. Scrappy, you've got the best passing. So when you get the ball, you're going to pass to Johnny Winger. Every time. Okay? Then Johnny, you're going to run . . . ." I drew a dotted line. "Run like the wind! All the way to the byline. Then you'll pass to Beans and he'll score. In the second half I'd like you to do this ten times, okay? You wait in zone three till we get the ball. Wait for Scrappy to pass to you. Then boom! Ten times. Thank you very much."

I took a sip of water to let the kids digest this information. Zoe put her hand up. "That's only six players."

"Yeah, well, we only need six to win. But if you want to make it really, really easy . . ." I wrote Wilson in box seven.

"Wilson. What I need from you is . . ." I wanted him to run around like a maniac, but I didn't know how to explain it to him.

What was the simplest way to say it? The easiest word? Terms like "distraction" and "decoy" seemed overly complicated and joyless. "Stay in zone seven, and shout and make a nuisance of yourself . . . ." I paused. I'd lost him on the word nuisance. I looked to see if Terry would help me, but he was still frowning at the whiteboard.

"Wilson," came a voice from over my shoulder. Henri Lyons stepped forward! He was dressed, preposterously, in a totally different outfit than the day before. How many changes of clothes did this guy pack for a two-hour away trip? "Coach Max would like you to be a magnet." He plucked a little magnet from the side of the whiteboard, and knelt in front of Wilson. "You are the magnet, and the opposition are the pieces of metal. Move around your zone, and attract the other team to you." He took another magnet, and they stuck together. He pushed it away to the side of the pitch. "Every player you lead away from zone eight, you make it easier for Mister Beans to score."

Wilson nodded. "Okay!"

The referee blew his whistle and the kids ran onto the pitch for the second half.

"Terry," I said. "This is Henri Lyons."

"I know," said Terry, stepping closer to exchange fist bumps. "I've seen you play."

"Lucky you," said Henri. He hesitated. "Your voice is familiar. Is it possible you were the gentleman who during last season's Chester match shouted at me to, quote, fuck off back to France?"

Terry turned pale. "No."

"Indeed?" said Henri. Terry hastily turned away to shout encouragement to the kids. Henri leaned closer to me and spoke softly. "I love doing that." At normal volume, he looked around and said, "Para football. Not what I expected from you, Max." That was a dagger to the heart. "Bien. I enjoyed hearing your team talk. It was worth the hardship."

"The hardship of staying overnight in scenic Chester?"

"Oui."

"What do you think of my strategy?"

"I like it. I play chess, too."

"Chess?"

Henri's eyebrows did a Mexican wave. "Your plan is pure chess. Johnny Winger is the rook."

"This is Chester," said Terry. "We call it a castle."

"Bien sur," agreed Henri. "The castle. You cleared his path to attack his zones. The girl in the middle is the Chevalier."

"The knight," said Terry. "But they're all Knights."

"That's the name of the team," I said. "Chester Knights."

Our conversation was interrupted when Ellesmere attacked down their right. Clogger got in the way of the ball and gave it to Scrappy. She looked up and sent a hard, low pass towards Johnny Winger. It took him a few touches to get control, but with no one near him, he had time. Then he set off, zoomed down the wing, and fired the ball square. Beans challenged a defender for it, and, for a moment, the chance appeared to have gone. But Beans kept scrapping, and with his long leg, reached to nab the ball. He fired it into the bottom corner. Goal!

"Yes, Scrappy!" I said, clapping her. "Passing machine! Love it!"

They didn't mess about in this league. Ellesmere brought the ball to the centre-spot and kicked off right away. My players followed their instructions and spread out. Ellesmere attacked with all their players through the middle. Zoe tackled, the ball broke to Scrappy, and she fired it blind—no pun intended—to the right. Johnny Winger latched onto it, sprinted forward, completely unopposed, and suddenly we were two-on-one. JW shaped to pass to Beans, and the defender moved to intercept. So JW took the ball even closer to the goal and passed it into the net. Easy as you like.

Three-two, and we'd only played a minute of the second half.

"Two down, eight to go, Johnny Winger!" I said.

"What?"

"I asked for ten dribbles, remember."

"Oh, okay!"

Terry tapped me on the elbow. "Max, Wilson is struggling."

I looked over at the kid. He looked pretty emotional, in a bad way. "What's happening?"

"He doesn't understand his role. He needs a refresher."

I cursed my crutches, but then again, I had two assistants now. "Terry, can you sprint round, and support him for a bit?"

"Sure," he said.

"Wait," said Henri. "You could start him in zone nine, and tell him to run across to seven."

"Max?" said Terry. Asking my permission!

"What he said."

With a nod, he scampered off.

Henri sighed and glanced back towards the throng of spectators. He kept watching them while he spoke. "Johan Cruyff achieved such mastery of the game that he would sometimes hit the post instead of scoring, because he said the near-miss was more entertaining for the fans than the goal. Is that what you were doing here? Increasing the entertainment in the second half by making the first so miserable?"

"No," I said. "I had to learn about the players. I didn't know it was Para football. It was all new to me."

"Is that so? You have taken to it like a Frenchman to smoking."

"What? Nah. It's not complicated. Make space for the better players. Put people where they can be useful."

"I think maybe we could get along. Would you like to talk about how you might help my career?"

"No. I'd like you to help Johnny Winger with his starting position. Right now, he's blocked by that player, and he isn't doing anything about it. I want a clear line between Scrappy and him."

"When did I become your assistant?"

"When you started assisting me."

He scowled at me, but he took off his scarf, folded it, placed it on a little chair, patted it a couple of times, then ambled over to JW and started giving him advice.

After a few more minutes of scrappy football, we got a chance to break down the right again. JW played a pass to Beans, who blazed it over the bar. "Seven more!" I said.

Ellesmere, for once, attacked down our left-hand side. That's where we were weakest. An overload developed, they had a spare man, and they scored.

Four–two.

All the Knights looked at me. I stretched my arms wide. "What?" I said. "Nothing changed. I want seven more attacks! Come on! Zoe," I said, waving her over. She subbed off for a couple of minutes, and I discussed her role. I said she was most useful at the top or bottom of her zone, that I didn't mind which one she was in, and I trusted her judgement. But I wanted her to choose one depending on the game state. She said she understood, and she went back on.

And that was pretty much all I had to offer this team. I'd sub players off to have little chats with them. Henri had expanded his coaching role to encompass the entire defence. Wilson got into the game, so Terry came back asking what else he wanted me to do. I didn't have anything. Maybe if I'd had the player profiles I could have tweaked things a bit more. Maybe someone else had the same passing skill as Scrappy. Maybe we had a secret dribbler who I could have used to mirror Johnny Winger on the left.

But I felt pretty good about what I'd done. Possibly my best contribution was to demand ten dribbles from JW. Every time he did one, I called out how many more he had to do. It was also a message to Scrappy, since she was the one who had to pass to him. And it was a message to Beans that he needed to be in position for when JW went on his run.

Ellesmere moved a defender over to try to counter JW, but it wasn't enough. His fourth dribble led to a shot, which the keeper saved. A second guy came over, messing up my plan, and blocked JW's fifth run. I sent Henri over to the far side of the pitch and switched JW to the left. That got us a free attack! JW zoomed forwards, and the only danger came from the enthusiastic Wilson whose decoy run ended up with him, JW, and a defender colliding into each other. The ball, though, rolled through to Beans, and he slotted it home.

Four–three.

Ellesmere reshuffled again, so I brought JW (and a grumpy Henri) back to the right. On our next attack, Scrappy passed to JW, who paused. I was about to yell at him to run, because two defenders were racing towards him. But he launched a long pass straight down the line. Straight to Wilson, who hadn't made his usual decoy run. Wilson, shocked to finally have the ball at his feet, pottered towards the goalkeeper, waited for him to get close, then passed to Beans. Open net! Easy!

Four all.

The crowd was into it now. There were a few minutes left, and anything was possible. Parents were shrieking when the ball got to their children. There were gasps as shots went just wide, groans as passes went just too far in front of their targets. Wilson was very affected by the mood, and I had to sub him off. The Knights in general were losing their positions, getting sucked into their old habits. I was about to shout their names one by one and remind them of what I wanted when I had the thought, "I wish I had a Freyja." But I did: Zoe. She was supposed to be my brain on the pitch. I wanted to win, but there was a bigger picture here, the development of the players. "Zoe," I shouted. She ran towards me. "Zoe, I need you to get everyone back in their positions."

"Me?" she said, astonished.

"Yes, you!" I called. "You're the captain!"

She sort of reacted like she'd been jabbed, and her cheeks flushed red. But she started to run around giving instructions. Getting a grip. Gelling the team.

I didn't notice. When I'd proclaimed her the captain, an invisible ninja had sliced my head in half with one of those razor-sharp swords. Or in other words, I had a mega pang of headache, one so bad my knees buckled. I got myself over to a little canvas caravan chair and leaned forward with my hands over my face. I closed my eyes, just for a second. When I opened them, Henri, Terry, and Wilson were looking at me, worried.

"Sorry," I said. "Bit of gip from the old leg."

All eyes travelled towards my ankle. "I had no idea it was so bad," said Henri.

"It's not," I said. Why were they both checking on me? At least one of them should have been watching the match! "I'm fine. Really. Stop fussing. Check they're not doubling-up on JW."

"They're not," said Terry. "Game's over."

"What?"

"We won. Five–four. Last second Zoe screamer."

A thrilling victory! I saw I had cursemail, no doubt rewarding me with 1 XP for continuing my winning streak. But something even better had happened. Terry was giving me coach data. I looked down to where Wilson's name was hovering over his head. His age and nationality were stated, but the rest of his attributes were question marks. Good enough for now! I threw my crutches down, picked him up, and held him aloft like he was three trophies in one.

Yes, mate!

It got better. Mike Dean came over, along with Jackie and some similar-looking men. The first-team coaches I'd heard about, I supposed. They were all smiling.

"Never a dull moment Max," said Jackie.

"It's a shame you're not feeling well," said MD. "I promised you could take the boys under-fourteens if you won."

"I'm feeling great," I said. "I'm ready when you are."

He looked at his watch. "They're kicking off in two minutes."

"Perfect," I said.

"But," he said. "You're not well."

"I've never felt better. Seriously. Plus I've got an assistant now. Henri, pop over here a second. We're going to manage the under-fourteens. Are you up for it?"

Henri shrugged. "Pourquoi pas?"

I smiled at MD, and I saw the exact moment he decided to put me in charge. In my vision, two options appeared. Bench Boost and Triple Captain. Why? That was a question for later. I smashed them both. I went to the Match Overview screen and saw that Chester FC Under-fourteens were set up in a 3-5-2 formation.

I'd get to try a new formation! Without having to buy it first. Bonus!

Grinning like a madman, I started hopping away. Then I stopped. Henri ran up to me with my crutches. I called out to MD. "Which way is the pitch?"

He pointed, and my French assistant and I hopped (me) and jogged (him) in that direction. A few strides away, Henri started chuckling. I joined in. We looked at each other, and the chuckles soon turned to belly laughs. Jackie later told me we looked more like kids than the teenagers we were about to manage.

58

BROUGHTON UNDER-FOURTEENS

We got there shortly after kickoff. A guy was expecting us. He was in a Chester tracksuit, was very young for a coach (twenty-five years, thirty-nine days, according to the curse, which was back in full operation), and wore glasses, which was quite unusual in the world of professional football.

"Hi," he said, holding out a hand. "You must be Max. And er . . . aren't you *Henri Lyons*? What the . . . ? Er . . . Anyway, I'm Spectrum."

"That's your nickname, is it?"

"Yes."

"Is it so people can call you Speccy?" Speccy four-eyes. The taunt for kids with glasses.

"A bit. Also because I'm into data analysis."

I didn't quite make the connection, but it wasn't what I wanted to talk about. "Is data why you've gone 3-5-2 today?" His mouth dropped open. I'd only been there for a few seconds. How could I have known? There's a fine line between looking like a genius and looking like a weird freak that needed to be locked up and studied. "Have you got a team sheet?"

"Oh, yes. Here."

It was labelled: Chester Under-Fourteens versus Broughton Under-Fourteens.

This was a perfect scam. With the team sheet I'd be able to explain how I knew everyone's names. I pretended to study it while I actually did my customary summing up of the situation.

First, the pitch and environment. The weather was still cold and sunny with no wind. Really superb conditions for football. I cursed my stupid ankle. The pitch itself was not quite full-sized. Some special dimensions for youth-team games. Seventy percent, I reckoned. With the players being seventy percent the size of Premier League players, the playing area looked big enough. A fast kid would be able to run from halfway to the goal in two seconds flat, though.

The grass was beautifully cut, full marks to the groundsmen, and there were only a few worn patches in the penalty areas. The Chester players were rolling passes to each other, and it was like watching snooker. Smooth as you like. Gorgeous. Around the sides of the pitch, about three metres back, stood a railing. It didn't seem close enough so that kids would ever crash into it, and it gave the spectators something to lean against. There were quite a few of those. Maybe a hundred, probably mostly relatives of the players. But I noticed a few people who might have been around to see the Max Best Show. MD and Jackie had made their way from the other pitch, as had the first-team coaches. Magnus Evergreen was loitering near the back. Chester and his parents had come. Chester waved at me with a colossal smile on his face. And, best of all, Livia.

It was good that she was there. Her presence probably helped save me from having a complete meltdown, but I'm getting ahead of myself.

"Mon dieu," said Henri. "It *is* 3-5-2! How did you see that in nought point nought seconds Max?"

But I was too internal to reply. I'd been there about thirty seconds and already picked up 1 XP, so we were back to the usual amount, doubled for being the manager. Great. And one of the players was the kid who'd brought me my tea. Nice to see them being made to do odd jobs. I hoped they had to clean the boots of the first team too. Traditions matter.

The next thing to note was that for the first time since being cursed, I was managing the better team. Chester's kids ranged from CA 2 to CA 4. Still very early in their careers. The PA was a wide range. Some had 6 or 7; they wouldn't make it as professionals and were only there because they were currently bigger, stronger, or faster than their peers. But a few had 25 to 30, meaning they were maybe good enough to play in the seventh tier. A couple were between thirty and forty, giving them a shot at playing for the Chester first team one day. One, Tyson, had PA fifty-eight, the same as Ziggy. And he was skillful! He had great technical attributes and was very direct. He loved storming towards the other team's goal. Exciting. His only problem was his teamwork attribute: one. One. One less than two. I supposed that at this level it didn't matter.

The most talented player was our only substitute. He was twelve years old, really tiny, and had the profile of a ball-playing defender. His PA was ninety-nine. Could a short defender have a career in the brutal world of professional football? Maybe! Remember that Manchester United had bought a short centre-back for sixty million pounds.

"Spectrum," I said, tapping the dates of birth on the team sheet. "I notice that all the starters are fourteen. Isn't that a bit weird?"

"It's the under-fourteens," he said.

"Right. But isn't it normal that the better the youth system, the younger the players?" I looked to Henri for confirmation, and he nodded.

Spectrum pushed his glasses up his nose and moved closer to us. He spoke quietly. "Normally, there's a pathway from the under-eighteens into the first-team squad. And so some under-sixteens get moved up to the eighteens. And some fourteens get moved up to the sixteens. See what I mean?"

"Yeah. The best kids get moved up. Play against older boys. Get pushed to be better. Totally."

Henri spoke, his voice uncomfortably loud given the topic. "The Chester squad is one of the oldest in the division."

Ian Evans doesn't trust young players.

I exchanged a look with Spectrum. "Got it."

Well, I'd pretended to study the situation for long enough. I started reorganising the team on the tactics screen. Every time I did so, I called out some near-gibberish that made me sound like a Wall Street trader in the 1980s. "Boyce go C! Nuge, Clive, give me a swap please. Benny! I'll take striker, thank you."

My changes swung the pendulum even further in our favour. We were camped in Broughton's half, putting pressure on. They didn't have the technique to pass their way out, so they hoofed long balls towards the centre circle, where our tall midfielders and centre backs headed the ball to one of their teammates, and we swept forwards again. Relentless.

Once my changes were in place, I kept an eye on the match ratings.

Oh, the match ratings. Going from managing the Knights, with just the dubious evidence of my eyes, to this game, where I had the full powers of the curse behind me, was like jumping off an e-scooter into an Aston Martin DB5. Seeing the match ratings was like finding out that the Aston had an ejector seat and twin machine guns.

Broughton, a team of CA 1 PA 1 no-hopers, were playing 4-4-2, and even this early in the match were all getting fives and sixes. Chester's kids were getting sixes, sevens, and eights. And one of the sixes was the goalkeeper, who had nothing to do. If he wasn't involved in the game, he couldn't improve his score! Seemed a bit unfair, but as a wise man once told me, lots of things are unfair.

I grinned. This was going to be nice and easy. The only issue would be getting the boys to stop scoring after six or seven goals. I didn't want to humiliate the other team. They didn't deserve that, and winning 12–0 would probably make me look a bit of a dick.

Something struck me. "Spectrum, what's this league called?"

"Chester and District Junior Football League."

Ah. That might explain why I'd been able to use Triple Captain and Bench Boost. It was a different league, which meant a different season! In theory, if I kept managing one game per team in random leagues all around the world, I'd be able to use my once-per-season perks hundreds of times a year.

Looooophole!

I sighed. I was pretty happy with life, and it wasn't just the ongoing buzz from winning with the Knights. It was everything about Chester. There was the two hundred pounds a week boost to my income. There was Raffi's trial. There was the fact that they stretched their tiny budget to include a disabled team. And, perhaps above all, there was the opportunity MD MD had given me to waggle my enormous . . . er . . . talent in front of the delightful Livia.

Relaxed as a cat in a beam of sunshine, I had a lovely old chat with my assistants. I asked Spectrum why he'd chosen 3-5-2 for the game, since Ian Evans played a bog-standard 4-4-2. "I thought the youth teams were supposed to play the same way as the first team."

He looked a bit shifty. "Er . . . we're encouraged to play a mid-field-based system. Progressive but possession-based. And to mix it up so the kids learn to be tactically flexible. We've been doing a lot of 4-3-3 variations."

"You're encouraged to be tactically flexible?" I said. "That doesn't sound like the Ian Evans I've come to . . ." I nearly said *despise*. "Come to know."

"Yeah, well. He's only going to be here for this season. Just so we're not in another dogfight at the bottom of the table. But next season we're hoping to, you know."

"Play some actual football."

"It's not that bad," he lied.

I looked over at the first-team coaches. One of those guys was in line to take over from Ian Evans. And one of them had asked Spectrum to prepare tactically-flexible youth team players. Interesting. So the best thing I could do now would be to use several different formations over the course of the match. Show my stuff. But I didn't have stuff. I had 4-4-2. The only reason I could use 3-5-2 today was that Spectrum had set it up. If I changed the formation, I wouldn't be able to change it back.

Ah, well.

"Henri, do you like playing in a 3-5-2?"

"Sometimes it's wonderful. We control the midfield, control the ball. If you have goalscoring midfielders, it's superb." I loved the way he said "superb." It was like "sup-herb." "There are always lots of passing options. Players need to be adept at multiple skills. Which is why Spectrum is correct to keep changing the formation. Keep the kids learning. Of course, you create points of weakness elsewhere. The sides of the pitch. I don't want to play 3-5-2 against Liverpool. And you need athletic centre-backs and at least two need to be able to pass."

Spectrum was falling in love with Henri. "Are you doing your coaching badges?" he mooned.

"No, I am not doing my coaching badges. I am a professional football player. It is my job to understand the game I play, no?"

Spectrum nodded, but it was obvious that it was rare to find a player who thought like a coach. Why?

The conversation turned to me. Henri wanted to know more about why I was being allowed to manage these games. I told them I was a scout and an agent, but what I loved most was being a manager so I'd offered my services slash begged for a chance.

"And this game is a reward for winning with the Knights? And what do you get if you win this one?"

I shrugged. "It's just an honour to participate in the development of these kids," I said.

And Henri Lyons—correctly—laughed.

That was the last moment of levity. The last upbeat moment of the match.

About fifteen minutes through the thirty-five-minute half, it was still 0–0 and I was getting a weird vibe.

I checked the match ratings, and while Broughton's were still low, ours had dropped by one point more or less across the board. My changes had initially given a boost to the performance, which made sense because more players were in their best positions. But it seemed that after the initial improvement, things had turned sour.

"What the . . ." I said, holding up the team-sheet again. That was a snapshot of where the players had started. My solution was definitely, objectively better.

So how had I made things worse?

I dipped into Broughton's tactics page to see if they'd tweaked anything. No. Identical to the start.

Huh.

"What troubles you, Max?" said Henri.

"Why are we suddenly dogshit?" I said.

"We are?" Henri hadn't been closely tracking the game. He'd been enjoying the conversation more. His eyes swept the field.

Just then, Tyson, the fifty-eight PA kid, got the ball on the edge of the penalty area and went on a dribble. I switched to the match commentary:

Tyson moves past one player. The angle is too tight for a shot.

He switches the ball to his left foot, moves inside, and shapes to shoot. A defender throws himself at the ball.

Tyson pushes the ball back onto his right. He has defenders all around him.

Mitchell is calling for the ball on the left. He's unmarked!

Tyson slaps the ball towards the goal. It's blocked, and Broughton clear the danger.

"It seems all right to me," said Henri.

"It's not," I said. "But I can't quite . . ." For some reason, I glanced at Spectrum. He saw me looking, blushed, and turned away. If I had more confidence in my ability to read faces, I would have said he was scared.

Thirty seconds later, we were attacking again. The ball was played to the left-midfielder. He had a fairly easy option to get the ball forward, but he turned back and played it safe. Back to the nearest centre-back. His match rating dropped to five out of ten. After a successful pass!

The ball was recycled out to the right. We had a good prospect there, a lad called Sevenoaks, who everyone called Seven. (Nominative determinism? He played in position number seven, the right of midfield. The position I used to play.) He was one whose rating had dropped, but now he went on a nice dribble. Parents were screaming and shouting as he swept by them. He played a gorgeous ball to the near post, a really nice attacking opportunity. One of our strikers was there, perfect movement! But so was Tyson. They got in each other's way, and the ball went straight through them both.

Tyson wheeled away, throwing his arms into the air in disgust.

"Ugh," said Henri.

I had my hands on my head, the crutches dangling stupidly. This match was spiralling out of control, and I couldn't work out why. But I could start by instructing Tyson to stop making forward runs for now.

I opened our tactics screen and nearly fell backwards.

"Jesus fucking Christ!" I said. I couldn't believe my eyes.

"What? What happened?" said Henri.

"That's what I want to know!"

59

ONE FOR THE FUTURE

Most football formations are symmetrical. Some are quite pleasant to look at. For instance, 3-4-3 is more aesthetic than 5-3-2. Even just visually, 4-2-4 is as thrilling as 4-5-1 is depressing.

And 3-5-2 is what you'd get if you bought a formation in IKEA. It's a solid, functional classic with instructions that seem clear.

3. Three narrow centre-backs. The other team might get crosses in, but their strikers will always be outnumbered.

5. Five players spread across the midfield. You can reasonably expect to dominate the centre of the pitch.

2. Two strikers. Ideally good at pressing.

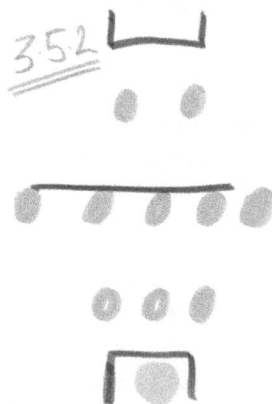

Isn't it compelling? If it was a chair, wouldn't you want to sit in it? If it was a bed, wouldn't you want to take a nap?

Sigh.

Now consider what I had to deal with. Let me describe what I saw when I went to my tactics screen.

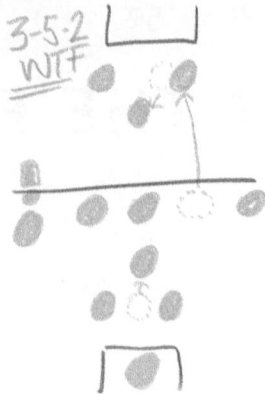

Let's go through the problems one-by-one, starting at the base of the team. Henk, one of the three centre backs, was playing between defence and midfield, a defensive midfielder. Despite being a disobedient little S.O.B, his match rating had actually gone up, a fact that I squirrelled away in my little box of footballing trivia.

Moving into the midfield, there were two issues. The guy on the left, Sullivan, the guy who kept playing safe passes, was in the correct position, but his icon was surrounded by a thick line (instead of the usual thin one). I took it to mean that his role had changed in some way that I couldn't see just from the simplistic formation graphic.

Then Tyson, who should have been playing on the right of the three central midfielders, was playing as a striker. And Benny, who I'd set as striker, had dropped into an attacking midfielder slot.

I stood there, biting my fingernails, trying to puzzle it out.

I thought back to my previous experiences with eleven-a-side matches. The first had been when I'd taken control of FC United Reserves. And "taken control" was really the right term! They did whatever I wanted, including smacking the ball miles into the sky for my amusement. Next, I'd been in charge of Moss Side Celtic. Again, there had been no hint whatsoever that it was possible for players to drift out of position. And this wasn't a guy joining an attack and being a bit slow to get back. Tyson was playing as a striker. He had no intention of going back into midfield.

It was so, so strange.

What could explain it? The most obvious solution was that it was happening because I hadn't bought 3-5-2. Maybe the players were sort of torn in some way between the 3-5-2 and the only formation I did own: 4-4-2.

Or perhaps sometimes some players would be drawn towards positions that would suit their skills or the game state. If Broughton weren't attacking, then we didn't need three centre-backs. And so Henk would automatically move forward.

If that was true, that was muy muy no bueno. As a manager, I wanted players to do what I told them and not deviate from my plan in any way. This was a centrally-planned economy! If I sent you to the bed factory, you'd better make beds. Players could choose if the legs would be square or round, if there would be headboards or not. But beds means beds.

I didn't feel like I was going to get any answers being internal, so I turned to the twelve-year-old who was my only sub for this game. "Are you warmed up? Can you go on for a couple of minutes?" His eyes widened. "What?" I laughed. "You didn't think you'd play?"

Spectrum coughed. "Er . . . Max. He's really only here for emergencies. Getting a taste of the atmosphere and that. He's not really meant to come on. He's one for the future."

I smiled at the kid. "Future. How do you like that for a nickname?" He tilted his head. "I don't mind it!"

"Positive attitude. Love it. Go and run my defence please." I mentally replaced Benny with Future and, for the benefit of Henri and Spectrum, shouted, "Benny sub!"

The rejigged team had Future in the centre of the back three, with Henk in Tyson's midfield position, and Tyson in Benny's striker slot.

I let that play out for a minute, and things seemed to stabilise. There was still the issue with Sullivan on the left, but at least it looked like a 3-5-2 again. To be honest. I got a tiny thrill from solving three problems in one move. After patting myself on the back, I turned to Benny. "Hey. I'm Max. This is Henri Lyons, my assistant. Thirty goals in his last sixty games." My tone changed from jocular to questioning. "What happened out there, Benny mate?"

"Nuffin." He looked . . . depressed? Had he forgotten it was rolling subs? He'd be back on the pitch in two minutes.

I rubbed my chin. I was getting some stubble. "Do you remember I asked you to play striker?"

"Uh," he said. It was just some kind of vaguely positive grunt. Fucking teenagers, man!

"Henri was telling me how impressed he was with your movement," I lied.

That perked him up. "Really?"

"Yeah," I said. "So I don't want you dropping back. When I tell you to be a striker, be a striker. All right? Is that fair enough?"

"But," he said. Some expression crossed his face, but then it was gone. And he simply nodded.

"Get ready to go back on." I turned away, ready to call out the change I wanted to make. But when I dipped into the tactics screen, fucking Henk had dropped into the DM slot again! "Jesus wept!" I said. So I subbed him off, moved Tyson back into the midfield where he should have been the whole match, and put Benny back up front. "This is like a Whitehall farce," I complained. "Henk," I said, as he drank his Powerade. "I'm Max. This is the legendary striker Henri Lyons. We can't help but notice you keep trying to play as a DM. Is there any particular reason for that?"

He looked left and right, then shrugged. "Just where the ball was and that."

Well, that was a blatant lie. But I couldn't think *why* he'd lie about it. He could have just said it was his best position or something. I spoke flatly; I didn't want to be too harsh on the kid because I wasn't sure why he was always out of position. The first time something like this had happened, when Ziggy started as a left-back, it had been my fault. Quite possibly this was too. "When you're a CB, you're a CB. When you're a DM, you're a DM. Is that clear?"

He nodded, but I knew his look. He was assessing me like I was a substitute teacher. *Could he take the piss or was I one of the scary ones?*

I jerked my thumb toward the pitch. "Sub for Future."

He knew who I meant. They swapped. Now everything was set up in a perfect 3-5-2 (except for the thick line around Sullivan). I watched for a few more minutes. And sure enough, it happened again. Henk became a DM. Tyson became a third striker. Benny stayed where he was on the formation screen, but on the pitch he simply walked around, standing near a defender so it looked like he was doing something. In fact, he was moping. Sulking.

You know that expression: *"I was tearing my hair out?"*

Mate.

The worst thing was that while most of the team was quietly imploding, the only players with good ratings were Tyson and Henk. Two of the out-of-position ones. Tyson was really pissing me off. He never passed to anyone. He'd dribble and shoot no matter the situation.

If someone didn't pass to him, he'd throw his arms up in a theatrical show of annoyance. If someone tried to pass to him but the pass didn't arrive, he'd throw his arms up. If someone passed to him and he tried to dribble and fell over, he'd throw his arms up at the referee.

He was a prick and a half.

But mostly I was annoyed at myself for failing to diagnose the problem. "Can someone tell me what is going on, please?" Beside me, Henri laughed. "What's funny?"

He adjusted his cuffs in a very self-satisfied way. "I worried you were a footballing savant. I'm delighted to discover you are mortal after all."

I pinched my nose. It was that or violence. After counting to five, I said, "Have you ever been in a team where players actively disobeyed their manager's instructions? Because I've seen a lot of conflict at clubs with players asked to do things they didn't want to. And they did it. They might have whinged to the papers, asked for a transfer, or faked injury to get out of it. But when they got on the pitch, they did what they were told."

"Are you sure? Maybe they disobeyed, and the manager pretended that had been his plan."

"Really? Is that how it goes?"

"No. Never." He grinned at me, which was a bad idea seeing as I had two long bashing sticks attached to my arms.

"Mate," I said, with the patience of several saints. "Do you know why they're out of position or do you not know?"

"Max," he said, suddenly realising that I was genuinely asking for help. "Didn't you go to an academy yourself?"

"Me? No. What's that got to do with it?"

Henri shook his head at me. "Stop looking at the problem." He placed his hands on my shoulders and gave me a little twist. Away from the pitch. "And start listening."

At first, I didn't understand. I was too busy gritting my teeth and thinking things that included phrases like "pseudo-intellectual claptrap" and "skull crushed like a boiled egg." Then, as I closed my eyes and opened my ears, I suddenly heard it. But it was insane. It couldn't be real.

I hobbled down the line, double-quick, and parked a few metres away from an enormous man whose wrists were thicker than my calves. He was covered in tats, had a squashed face, and had somehow managed to clone himself almost to scale. Bulldog One, Bulldog Two. The Bulldog Brothers. Something told me the bigger one was Tyson's father.

"Pass to Tyson! Tyson's open! Good lad! Man on, T! Set up on your left. On your left! Fucking hell, T! Hit with your left for once in your fucking life!"

He paused his tirade, because I was staring at him. He wasn't quite sure how to react, so he just gripped the railing, showing that he had huge rings on almost every finger.

From behind me, like a ghost's whisper, came a soft voice. "Can I help you?"

It was Broughton's coach. I'd wandered right into his technical area. "Oh. I'm Max. Hi. Am I in your way? I was just wondering why my team weren't following instructions. I guess I found out."

The guy laughed. He had small ears and a big belly. "Notice we've got five subs and you've got one? The kids prefer playing away, and so do I. Fewer parents." He turned towards the spectators who were, presumably, mostly parents of the Chester kids.

I nodded. Things were—thank fuck—starting to make sense. "Most parents don't travel to the away games?"

"We get a van and squash all the kids in the back. Sensible parents take the chance to have a lie-in. Your guy here. He's not one of them. Goes to every match. You've got a bunch of hard cases." He shook his head. "I do hate playing Chester. Sorry to say."

I sighed. By taking this gig, I'd walked into a quagmire, and it would take some delicate manoeuvring to get out. "Thanks."

I hobbled back to my spot and fumed.

Parents! Messing up my tactics!

My thoughts looped around in a cycle.

Just let it go, Max. Look at the bigger picture.

But then I looked at the tactics screen.

And I saw Tyson swanning around, flapping his arms like Icarus.

One word kept bouncing around my head: Unacceptable.

Two hundred quid a week. Just let it go.

And the loop would repeat.

Henri heard me muttering under my breath and tried to talk me down from the ledge. "Max. A quick primer on football academies. It is like McKinsey. You know McKinsey?"

"The consultants?"

"The same. Their motto is "up or out." If you don't get promoted, they fire you. Up or out. It's the same with football. These fourteens.

Half are promoted to the next age group. The rest are kicked, and that's the end of their careers. It's understandable that parents push their kids. It's a brutal business. Darwin didn't need to go to Galapagos to see survival of the fittest. He could have observed it at his local football club. Had one existed."

"Henri," I said. "They're sabotaging the team. This should have been a cakewalk. Nice little session learning a new formation. Instead, half the players are ruining their careers by being dicks. The other half are demotivated. I can't stand here and do nothing."

"Indeed? But you can, though."

"Can I?"

"Oui. Easily. Tyson will score eventually, Chester will win, and your career can continue. These issues are not your problem. You don't even work for Chester. You have no responsibility to the kids."

Was that true? I tried to believe it. I mean, it was obviously true in a wider sense. I didn't work for Chester. I wasn't a parent. But the curse had given me the tools to see objectively what these parents were doing to the team. If I didn't do anything, would Spectrum? No chance. He knew what was up. That's why he was acting so shifty.

I heard the bark of the Bulldog Brothers, and my heart hardened. I could do something about this situation without ruining my reputation. I just had to be smart. Cool, calm, and collected. "P.G. Wodehouse used to drop letters onto the street and see if people picked them up to post them. When they arrived at their destination, he knew society was functioning well."

"Max Best," said Henri. "Wherever there is unjustice, there he'll be."

"*In*justice."

"Oh? But situations are *unjust*. What a language."

I turned to the only Chester employee in the area. "Spectrum. Don't parents have to agree not to scream at their kids?"

He squirmed. He'd been listening to our conversation, vacillating between fear and hope, depending on what we were saying. Now, the fear was back. "Er . . . you mean the code of conduct."

"I'd like to read it."

"I'll drop a copy and someone will post it to you." I suppose it was a jokey reference to P.G. Wodehouse, but it made me start seething again. And I'd been doing so well keeping my temper under wraps!

"I'd like to read it now."

He sort of giggled, but me stepping towards him put an end to that. He gulped and tapped at his phone. He quickly found a PDF. I skimmed it, and sure enough, the parents had agreed not to give tactical instruction during games, not to harangue referees, and not to criticise their children.

"I'll keep this for a few minutes, if you don't mind." I slipped his phone into my pocket. The subtitles on this scene will read: [*Max's seething intensifies.*] I knew there was a slight chance I was about to steer my career straight towards the iceberg of "doing the right thing." No one else needed to go down with the ship. "Henri, this is your captain speaking. Mayday. Mayday. We're going down. I suggest you head towards the emergency exits."

"I could walk away," he said, gesturing away from the technical area. "And cross the railing. A rat leaving the sinking ship, yes?"

Good idea. "Go on, then."

He didn't move. "Max, I take it you mean to blow yourself up with some gesture . . . aimed at what? Stopping overbearing parents from shouting at their children? Stopping parents from living out their dreams through their kids? Putting an end to a tradition as old as football itself?"

"No. Nothing so extreme. I'll do everything you said, but only with four parents. And I don't intend to blow myself up." Not with Livia watching. "I will be calm personified."

"Merde," he said. He sat on the bench next to Future and crossed his leg over his knee. "I never wanted to play for Chester anyway." He sighed. "God, I need a cigarette."

"Spectrum. You ready for this?"

"Please don't."

"It's already done. Future, your debut continues." I turned to the pitch and shouted, "Sullivan, Henk, Benny, Tyson: sub!"

At the next break, the four players trudged off. Future went on. We would finish the half with eight players on the pitch.

There was subdued pandemonium. The spectators couldn't believe what they'd just seen. My rival manager gave me a long, hard look. The referee started to walk towards me, his face a question: *Did I really want to play three players short?* I gave him a nod and a double thumbs up; he shrugged and blew his whistle.

The last word fell to Henri.

"Magnifique, Max." He pretended to exhale from an imaginary cigarette. "Fucking magnifique."

60

BROS BEFORE PROS

In the seconds after I hauled off the four rebel players, a lot of thoughts went through my head:

- The Bench Boost perk would be nerfed in this match, since the only substitute on the pitch was Future.
- I didn't know who the captain was, so I didn't know if Triple Captain was helping.
- While Tyson was clearly an awful human being, he was fourteen years old. When I was that age, I was making fun of disabled kids. So I needed to be extra careful in laying the blame for this debacle at his door. The other kids even less so. The parents were to blame.
- But then again, Henri had told me this pushy, overbearing parenting was normal. And even Terry, the coach of the Knights, had said something about parents living through their kids. Obviously they should do that by driving them to training and buying them new boots and so on, not by screaming at them and/or giving them extra in-match coaching. Although what I'd witnessed was over the top, it was just parents being parents.
- So, in fact, the blame lay with Spectrum. I liked the guy, but he really should have put a stop to this garbage a long time ago.

And THEN! Spectrum was just one guy. I knew two things about him. One, he loved coaching. Two, he shied away from confrontation. The positions were contradictory, in my opinion, because Two was stopping him from doing One. But that's why he should have gone to his superiors to get help. If he didn't feel comfortable doing that, it raised suspicions about the culture of the club. Maybe MD MD wasn't the chill guy he seemed.

While those thoughts were germinating, I tinkered with my tactics. I had eight players.

One goalkeeper.

Three centre-backs.

Two central midfielders.

One right-midfielder/winger.

One striker.

The more I looked at it, the more nightmarish it became. We had literally nobody who could play on the left-hand side of the pitch! The only left-midfielder was Sullivan, and he was sitting behind me looking shell-shocked.

My solution was pretty lame: micromanagement. At dead balls—goal kicks, throw-ins, etc—I had the striker drop into midfield and one of the CMs take a position on the left. Then as soon as the ball was in play, I let them move to their more natural positions. I hoped the other team wouldn't notice the lack of a permanent left-sided player. It helped that the Broughton coach was on the far side of the pitch from our weak point. Another advantage of the tactics screen was that I saw the entire pitch wherever my body was.

In a hushed whisper, Henri and I discussed my "false entire left-side of the pitch" problem/solution. We discussed the strengths and weaknesses of various players, did a lot of pointing, and generally looked very much like a war council. Henri wanted me to station a permanent left-sided player, but I worried that would stop us from ever scoring. Tricky.

For all the chaos in our formation, Broughton weren't able to string too many passes together, and our two fourteen-year-old centre-backs were seriously dominant. Future scampered about between them, cleaning things up, and playing short, simple passes to the midfielders.

We entered a new phase in play, a sort of stasis. Broughton lacked the ability to hurt us, and we lacked the numbers to hurt them. I still had the free hit perk if we could get a free kick near the other team's goal. Winning 1–0 sounded like a wonderful dream. Nil–nil seemed the most likely outcome. A defeat would have been a real punch to the gut.

"Henri. Plan. Get to half-time and cook up some wheeze?" I said.

Henri put his scarf back on. "I don't know what those words mean, but yes. My worry is that we can't keep up this intensity. I foresee some exhausted players in the second half of the second half." He glanced behind us at the rebels. "What of those?"

"Who gives a shit?" I said. Within a minute of them leaving the pitch, the rest of the team's match ratings had started to creep up. The two centre-backs were on seven out of ten and heading to eights. Future was on a solid seven. Sevenoaks in the number seven slot (the right of midfield) was back up to seven, which I found oddly satisfying.

"Max," whined Spectrum. He'd inched closer to hear what we were saying. I'd mentally discarded him as an ally since realising he was more to blame than the kids. "They got the message. Let them play."

"Fuck 'em," I said. "Don't want, don't need."

"Max." From behind the railing came a new voice. Henri responded to it like Pavlov's dog, which was absurd because he couldn't have heard it before.

"Hi Livia," I said. "Enjoying your Sunday?"

"Sure," she smiled. She turned to look at the sub's bench, and her ponytail swished around. I think I heard Henri make a tiny little noise. "We're just worried about the kids. You've taken . . . four? . . . off. Do they need medical attention?"

"No," I said. "They're grand."

She looked confused. "So . . . er . . . why?"

I looked at Spectrum. "What's the right word? Disciplinary?" The young coach shook his head. Hard disagreement. "That's right," I said. "A disciplinary issue. No big deal."

"No big deal," she repeated, eyeing the four boys who were undergoing emotions ranging from "teenage angst" to "intense teenage angst."

"Has Jackie spoken to you today?"

That flummoxed her. "Jackie? No. Why?"

"Just wondering. Talk to you later!"

It had the tone of a dismissal, and Livia pottered off.

Henri gave me a vicious thwack in the upper arm. "Why did you do that?"

"What?" I said, rubbing the area.

"You made her leave. Leave. Leave-ia. That's her name, right? Keep subbing players off until she returns."

His being attracted to Livia was totally normal and natural, but it triggered something in me. A reaction even stronger than seeing the parents mess up my tactics screen. For a moment, football was totally forgotten, and I was back in secondary school. "Don't get any ideas. My friend has first dibs on her."

"Excuse me? Do I understand you correctly? You want me, your possible future client, to wait for another man to make his move? Wait to make beautiful memories with a rare beauty? Wait my *turn* like a pensioner in one of your *cheese* shops?"

I felt my neck get hot and got ready to drop my crutches. "Yes, Henri. That's right. I'm going to give him a deadline to make a move. And if he doesn't, it's every man for himself. You, me, and all comers. And may the Best man win."

"Ho, ho. I see what you did there. Well, at least you also place yourself in the queue." After his initial flare-up, he had calmed a little. "It hirks me that you place a friend over a possible client. I do not feel seduced Max."

"Bros before pros, Henri. Bros before pros."

He sort of snarled at me, showing his gums, but the rictus grin turned into a real laugh. "Max! You are extraordinary. I was lying just now. I do feel seduced. Bros before pros . . . friends first, football second? Is that one of your principles?"

While I reacquired a firm grip on my crutches, I thought about it. "I don't have principles. I'm not a deep thinker like you. But sometimes I see something wrong, and I act. Like with these kids and their shitty parents. The principle was there all along, and it just bubbled out of me. It happens sometimes; I can't do anything about it."

"Yes! Yes, Max! This is how I feel! You think I came to England ignorant? No. I knew it would be culture shock. Hard professionally. I am willing to knuckle down, as you say. Sacrifice for the collective. But yes. Sometimes the inner truth bubbles out. Oh, Max. Let us go for the same woman. It will be a romance for the ages."

"Sure. But not that one. Not yet."

"And if I refuse? If I jump the gun?" He arched an eyebrow at me. Very dashing.

I gave him a pleasant smile, and, in the tone of one passing over a cucumber sandwich, said, "Then I will punch you so hard in the dick you'll spend the rest of your life pissing out of your tail."

His eyebrow dropped, and his face hardened. "Fine." He let out a stream of invective in his native tongue. "Fine. Max, I don't want you as my agent. Les dés sont jetés."

"Livia is a physio for Chester FC, and if I get you a move here, you'll see her every day."

A pause. "Max, you may consider yourself engaged. My preference is for a move to the northwest. Preferably a scenic town. The more castles, the better." He was joking. Mostly.

"Consider it done," I said. "Subject to conditions."

"No, Max. I hold the power. I set the conditions."

I rolled my neck. "Nope. There's only one person in this entire country who has ever tried to understand you. Good luck finding another version of me outside the changing rooms in Hereford or Kidderminster."

"Mon dieu. You're actually crazy." He laughed. "Very well. Win this match, and I will give you a trial period as my agent."

I narrowed my eyes at him. For all his bluster and talking like a poet and all that, he was unhappy at Darlington and wanted a move. If I had a good relationship with Chester, such a move could happen quickly. We could theoretically have things in place so that he could sign at 8 a.m. on January first. If I went full "Will Smith at the Oscars," then Chester would be out of the question. Telling me to win was a subtle way of giving me permission to douse the fire I'd lit.

Or maybe he was just testing me. Seeing how deep my so-called principles ran. Maybe the only way to get him as a client was to push back against these bad parents no matter the personal cost.

Either way, there was a clear next step. I went to the bench and talked to the rebels.

"Sullivan. I'm Max. I subbed you off because I noticed you not doing what you were told on the pitch. Obviously, we expect you to carry out your instructions to the best of your ability."

He looked scared. Hunted. "But I did! I did!"

"Nope. Anyway, just thought I'd let you know why you won't be playing the rest of the game." Spectrum let out a kind of hiss, and Henri sort of stiffened. I moved on to the next one. "Henk, we already talked about this, and you did it again. Two strikes, bro! Not sure the rules of baseball, but in this game it's two strikes and *you're outta here!*" I swung a crutch like a baseball bat. Henk sagged. What was happening was not what had been promised. "Tyson. You've got some nice moves. I'm sure you'll have a great career . . ." I left the teeniest-tiniest pause, just for my own satisfaction, ". . . in the junior leagues. I prefer players who can follow instructions, though." I *didn't* add about eight minutes of complaints about his playing style, character, and haircut, which I felt was a sign of tremendous personal growth on my part. "So I won't be using you again. Thanks for coming. Benny. What can I say? I guess you're not feeling it today. It's probably my inexperience that's demotivating you. Consider yourself unburdened. No need for any of you to hang around. Spectrum can unlock the changing rooms if that's what's keeping you here."

"Wait," said Tyson. He had a surprisingly middle-class voice. "You're sending us home? Are you saying you'd rather play with eight than with me? That's mental. I'm your best player. And the captain!"

Instead of laughing in his face (my first impulse), I checked the match ratings. They were looking good! I got the strangest feeling. An absolute conviction that I was doing the right thing. And it wasn't just that these rebels and their parents needed to be taught a lesson or get shown up or whatever. It was that the kids on the pitch were playing so much better without them. I'd cut off some dead branches, and now the tree could bloom (or whatever trees did). I forgot about Tyson, scampered over to the side of the pitch, and started shouting out nonsense phrases while tweaking the individual instructions on the tactics screen. I yelled to one of the centre-backs that he was the captain, and a C appeared next to his name on the tactics screen. I adjusted the roles of the two central midfielders so that they could make forward runs and run with the ball. This would give us the chance to get three guys in the other team's penalty box: those two plus the striker. Once I'd done that, I remembered Henri's warning that if I asked too much of the players, they'd run out of steam. So I switched the "go forward" option off every time they made a lung-bursting run. Gave them a chance to recover. Maybe later in the game I could give them one minute on and two or three minutes off. I wished I had a way to monitor an individual player's current stamina reserves.

I was really getting into the weeds of the options, really getting sucked into the game, and I felt like the players and the match were starting to bend to my will. The only real cloud on the horizon was that . . .

"Max," said Henri. I got the impression he'd been calling me for a while.

"What?"

"This gentleman would like to talk to you."

It was Mike Dean. I swung myself closer to the railing. "Hi!" I said, in a cheerful tone.

"Hi Max," he said, with little warmth. "Everything okay?"

"Yep!" I said. "The boys are battling hard, showing their quality. Very pleased with them. You've got a good bunch there."

He hadn't been expecting praise. "Ah . . . I thought you wanted to practice your *eleven*-a-side skills." His line of sight moved from me to the subs bench.

I ignored the implicit question. *Why are you doing this?* "I know. Ironic isn't it? I also wanted to try different tactics, but it looks like I might end up playing 4-4-2 again!" That was true. I was doing everything in my power to stick with 3-5-2.

"Do you mean 4-3-0?"

I laughed as though he was making a funny joke. "No, I'd go 3-3-1, I think. One guy at left-back, one right-mid." I nodded a few times. "Yep. That would do it, I think."

He very nearly exploded, but too many years in boardrooms had smoothed his edges. "Livia said you removed these boys because of disciplinary reasons. Would you please enlighten me as to what they are?"

"Sure," I said, projecting a sort of breezy helpfulness. "The code of conduct was breached."

"The code . . . was breached. Breached by the players?"

"No."

"Max, I'm not enjoying this conversation."

"Okay," I said. I noticed Henri amble closer to me. I presumed he wanted to be on hand to unplug me if I got too hot. "The main breach is that these players are receiving instructions from parents and or guardians. Those instructions contradict the team's tactics and, along with the streams of verbals, are having knock-on effects on the rest of the team. For example, team morale is shot. I'm hoping a barnstorming half-time team talk will perk the other lads up a bit!"

Mike gave me a long, displeased look, then glanced up and down the line of parents. "Max," he said carefully. "These families are part of the community. We're a community club. You understand that, right? We can't just . . . bench players like this. We have to sit down and talk it through."

"Oh, I agree," I said. "Quite a lot of sitting down and talking on the horizon for somebody."

"So will you let them go back on?"

"Mike," I said, no longer bothering to be jovial. "It's *your* code of conduct. There have to be sanctions. Putting them back on wouldn't be fair on the kids and parents who *haven't* broken the rules. I want to win, and trust me, there's a better chance without these guys. And I never thought I'd say this, but it's not all about me. Every one of these kids is learning a lesson about teamwork. I thought I'd roll up and practise my tactics, but it's all got a bit serious. Some of those kids can make the first team, and I have a chance to be part of that. But maybe letting parents rage against their kids is more community-minded."

He slammed his palms into the railing. Then he took a deep breath. "You know what? You're right. About the sanctions. But don't take it out on the kids!"

We turned to look at the little brats.

Henri mumbled, "Max." Was it a warning? Until the second half kicked off, Mike had the power to unseat me. He could still do it during the second half, but that would be as humiliating for him as for me. I was worried about losing my prospects here, but I had one hundred other clubs I could deal with. He was worried about losing face. If he was sacked, that could be the end of his career in football.

Looking at Mike, I said, "What do you propose?"

"Let me bring the parents over. We'll have a little chat at half-time. Try to sort things out." He held his hands up. "We'll still have the sit-downs. I promise. But right now, let's compromise. For the sake of the kids."

I thought about it. Being the vehicle the universe used to put some shitty parents in their place? Er, yes please. "Love to," I said. "But first I've got a speech to give. And it's going to be a belter."

61

TWELVE ANGRY MEN

The referee blew for half-time with the score still 0–0.

Seeing all the kids walk towards our technical area raised my pulse a few bpm. I had to give a team talk that not only motivated them but used as much time as possible. Ideally, I didn't want to start talking to the rebel parents until the second half had kicked off.

"Future," I said, pulling him aside. "Can you run and get your dad?"

His face fell. "I'm with my nana."

Some story there. Shit. "Even better! I'd love to talk to her."

"Am I in trouble?"

"No, you're my hero today. But hurry up please."

He zoomed off. The gran was part of my Maxterplan for the second half, a plan that would take effect if I could make sure the kids trusted me. She came, and I begged her to hang around the technical area, because I'd need her at the start of the second half. She was pretty taken aback, and it didn't help that I was talking fast and being mysterious like a true Manc pixie dream boy. (That's a pixie dream boy from Manchester.) But she agreed to help me. I got the sense she'd do anything for that little kid. I would put that to the test soon enough.

Future joined the rest of the team in a semicircle. The lads were drinking, eating some kind of paste, or munching on bananas, depending on how much spare cash their families had.

Before I could dive in, the referee came over and took me aside. He was a young guy, about my own age. He wanted to check everything was all right. I hinted at what the problem was, without being too indiscreet, and his entire demeanour changed. He even gave me a raised-eyebrows nod and wished me luck. I warned him that the second half was likely to be quite weird and apologised in advance. Basically tried to make sure he knew my upcoming weirdness was aimed at the parents, not at him. That intrigued him, but I saw that Mike Dean had already gathered the Bulldog Brothers and some other adults and was trying to catch my attention; he wouldn't accept me chatting to the ref as cause for delaying our Code of Conduct Tribunal.

What he *would* accept as a suitable delay was the half-time team talk. I looked around the semicircle. Eight kids in front of me. The current first team. The four rebels were over on the subs bench. Of the twelve, none looked feral, none seemed to glow with intelligence. They were normal kids. A jury of my peers. The overall vibe was two parts wary to one part skeptical.

As well as the twelve kids, Henri, and Spectrum, there were a fair few parents within earshot. That was unfortunate, because it meant I needed to retain some measure of self-control. I couldn't just let rip. No hairdryers. I had to be calm and rational but highly persuasive, like a courtroom lawyer.

A flash of ponytail, and the way Henri started volumising his hair suggested that Livia was part of my audience, just out of my line of sight. Fine. To increase the sex appeal, I mentally changed my role model from Perry Mason to Tom Cruise in That Movie. I wiped the whiteboard and turned the markers upside down. Ready.

"Hi guys. I'm Max. This is Henri. Bit of a wild half, that. I'm very impressed with the eight of you. You've ended the half strong, and throughout the whole mess you've not let Broughton have a sniff of goal." I clicked my fingers like I'd just had a great idea. "Goalie, can you play left-midfield?"

He scoffed in a good-natured way. "No!"

"Ah, well. We're going to take more risks in the second half, so they'll get some shots eventually."

The goalie seemed pleased. He was vaguely on my side, but that wasn't saying much. Goalkeepers are weird. Future was mooning at me. State of affairs: two votes for Max. Six abstainers. Four against. I didn't care much about the latter group. I wanted a majority of the first eight to buy into my plan.

The guy I'd set as captain spoke up, and I started to wonder if I'd chosen the wrong dude. Maybe there were more *against* than I thought. "Take more risks? You mean attack more? When we're three players short?"

"Yes," I said. "We're the better team. We're the home team. We're the protagonists. We *will* attack."

I left a space for that to sink in, but it didn't really work. "But who *are* you?"

"I'm Max Best."

I left a space for *that* to sink in, and weirdly, it sort of worked. They'd never heard of me, but being teenagers, they assumed that was their ignorance, not the fact that I was a nobody. "And why's *he* here?"

"Henri Lyons? Clairefontaine graduate Henri Lyons? Darlington's record signing Henri Lyons?" I let one crutch drop while I used the other one to stretch my arms behind my head like bad boy Americans do with a baseball bat. "He's come to learn how it's done." I dared to glance at him, and he was fuming at me so hard I burst out laughing. I relented. "He's come to help me out, and I'm very grateful." Henri pursed his lips, paused, then nodded once.

The kids weren't very invested in this particular aspect of the scene. "Why did you take those four off?"

"Why do you think?" Nobody wanted to be the first to talk. "It's like that, is it? Fine. I'll lay it all out."

"Without swearing please," said Spectrum, who had visibly shrunk and was all too aware of the audience.

Some of the boys turned to look at him, then turned back to me. His intervention had raised my status. Good. That'd make it easier to win hearts and minds. "I don't swear *that* much, do I?" Henri shrugged. I dropped the other crutch. If I didn't move too much, my ankle didn't hurt. "Okay. Why did I sub off four players? Without swearing . . . Tricky . . ." Some of the smarter boys were already wide-eyed. They understood what I was doing, slagging off the four kids without even verbalising it. They couldn't believe it. For the slow-on-the-uptake ones I said, "What's another way to say they were playing like fucking clowns, but you know, without swearing?"

"They were not following instructions," said Henri.

"Thanks, mate!" By now the entire first eight were staring at me as though I was their headmaster filming himself doing viral dances during school assembly. Whoever I was, whatever I was about to say, this wasn't your bog-standard team talk. "Yeah," I said. "That's better. Not following fucking instructions. Argh, I swore. Shit. I mean, shoot. Not following instructions. Now, we all know *why*. Maybe on another day it would have been *your* dad and it would have been *you.* Maybe if I was in your shoes it would have been me. So in at least seventy-five percent of cases, this isn't personal." Every single pair of eyebrows shot to the moon. They knew exactly what *that* meant! "And Henri did it all the time at Clairefontaine. He was always meant to be a striker, but his dad wanted him to play as a CAM." Henri responded to my invention with a tiny moment of surprise, but then did three large, slow nods. "But now Henri is a professional player, and the idea that he'd disobey instructions is long in his past. So from where you are," I pointed to them, "to where you want to be," I pointed to Henri, "there's a moment where you stop doing your own thing. You stop being selfish and you start putting the team first." I paused. That hit home. Won me a couple of votes. "I know it's a tough environment. Up or out. But some of you have learned the wrong fucking lessons. It's not every man for himself. If you think you're going to make the first team because you did the most dribbles, had the most shots, made the most tackles against Broughton Under-Fourteens, you're delusional. The absolute fucking simple starting point is: are you a team player? If the answer is no, then Do Not Pass Go. Do not collect two hundred pounds."

I really wanted to pace around at this moment. The spirit was in me!

"I'm a Manchester United fan. I've said that many times but no one's ever asked me why. It's self-explanatory, innit? But let me answer it anyway. One, I'm from Manchester. Two, they play in red. Three, they've got the biggest stadium. Four, they've won the most trophies. Five, great history. Six, famous players."

I lowered the volume and turned up the emotion slider. Made strong eye contact with as many abstainers as poss. "Seven. They're called United. Think about it. *United.* When I was a kid, I literally couldn't understand why every team wasn't called United. It was a name that made me think of the whole city coming together as one. A community united. A city united. Then I grew up and realised some pricks in blue had ruined that fantasy for me, but never mind. When you go to Old Trafford and the away team score, the home fans will start chanting *United! United!* They're behind their team whatever happens. It's goosebumps every time, guys. Every time."

I picked up the whiteboard and a marker. I drew circles for the three defenders, and, as an afterthought, added the goalie too. "United.

U-N-I-T. Unit. Today you're a back three. Lads, you're like a fucking brick wall out there. Winning every header, getting good tackles in. It's impressive. But I haven't seen you work as a unit. I haven't seen one of you drop back a few yards in case the other guy misses the header. I don't see you talking to each other. I don't see you checking how Future's doing. I don't see you giving the goalie a touch of the ball every few minutes. I don't see teamwork. You need to be a fucking UNIT." Boom. That hit Captain right in the solar plexus. His eyes dropped. It was fifty-fifty if he'd respond well.

I wiped the defensive lines away and drew a striker, the right midfielder, and a central midfielder. "Let's talk attack. We're short-staffed, now, but you're still attacking as *individuals*. How's that going to work? You three, you've got to attack as one. The Three Musketeers, yeah? The striker has to hold the ball up so these two can come and help. If the RM dribbles but the CM stays, nothing's going to happen. All of you move, or none of you move. If you three start talking to each other, helping each other, we'll score. We'll score loads. I fucking guarantee it. *Unit*." I didn't bother looking at the guys. I didn't want to interrupt myself. They'd respond or they wouldn't.

I wiped the board clean again and drew a single, isolated circle. "We're fucked on the left. Someone's going to have to play out of position. That's going to be a shitty thirty-five minutes for one of you. Boyce, probably. Yeah? Think about it. The people looking at you for the sixteens next year. What are they going to be thinking? Oh, Boyce had a shit game? No way. They'll blame me for playing him out of position. But what about you? Did you do anything to support your mate? Or did you leave him out to dry?" I put on a voice. "*Hey, do you remember when fucking Mitchell sprinted thirty yards to cover Boyce when Broughton had that overload? Do you remember when Seven let him take the corners so he'd get to do some of the fun stuff? Yeah, that's the kind of lad I want to work with.*"

I wiped it clean and drew the full formation with the player's names. It was a shambolic 3-3-1. More holes than in the goal nets. "Here's the team. Nothing matters except the person playing next to you. You defend together, you attack together, you win together. Unit, unit, team. Defend, attack, win."

I left another pause then returned with another change in emotional energy. I was almost wistful as I said, "My dad always said football shows character. One guy's a coward, one's got the weight of the world on his shoulders, one's a show pony, one's a prick. But he was talking about the pros. You're fourteen. You're not set in stone. It must be fucking grim playing in this team week after week. So yeah, now there are less of you, but you get one chance—maybe your only chance—to play as a *team*. Do you understand what I'm saying? Next week's business as usual. I'm only here today. One chance. Unit, unit, team. I'd fucking love to see it, lads. I'd fucking love to see it."

The defence rests, your honour.

The captain jutted his chin at the whiteboard. "Will that work?"

"Yes," I said. I tossed it away. "But I don't care. It doesn't matter if the plan works. It matters that you try to *make* it work. It matters that you show some fucking character. Help Future. Be there for Boyce. Hunt in pairs. Work on your units." I looked around. Playing as a team wasn't such a revolutionary idea. Most seemed willing to give it a go. They were leaving a space for me to say or do the last, hugely inspirational thing that would pump them up and get them going. Perversely, I didn't want to do that. I wanted it to come from them. It *had* to come from them. "Enough talk. Do it or don't. Captain, take them out."

Has the jury reached a verdict?

The tall centre-back stood, waved at his mates to do the same, and shouted, "Come on!"

With a roar, they stormed onto the pitch. Some of the nearby parents clapped.

Seeing the charge of our kids, Broughton's coach sent his back on. Seeing all the players ready, the referee cut short his break and brought his whistle to his mouth, ready to signal the restart.

With the players standing in their formation, our captain yelled, "United!" and I got fucking goosebumps.

I shouted, "Come on, Chester!"

Somehow I'd gone above and beyond what I'd expected. The eight on the pitch were all in. All the way in! Boyce was on the side of the pitch closest to me, and he was striding around with his fists balled up. Ready for war. He wasn't alone.

I was extremely pleased with myself. Trust a Frenchman to ruin the mood.

"A bit heavy-handed," said Henri. "A bit overwrought. I rate it seven out of ten. Make that six. I'm withdrawing a point for inaccuracy."

"Huh?"

"Liverpool have won more trophies than Manchester United."

"Don't talk shit," I said, but our bickering was cut short. Mike Dean was calling me. He was more than ready to get on with the Tribunal, to get the rebels back in the game ASAP. I held up a finger—one moment, please!—and went to Future's grandmother. I told her what I'd like her to do, and she said that if it was a joke, it was in poor taste. "Trust me," I said. She walked off, down the side of the pitch towards the corner flags. Away from the main throng of parents.

So having done all I could to sort out this shitty team, now I had to deal with four shitty parents.

"Hi again, Mike. It's all go today, isn't it?"

He had warmed up a bit since our last conversation. I think he liked my team talk. Well, maybe not all of it. "I didn't know you'd be using this match to spread your Man United propaganda."

"Oh," I said, with a superficial chuckle. "Doesn't quite work with city though, does it?"

"The kids responded well. You've challenged them. I like that."

I quarter-turned, so I could be in the conversation while keeping half an eye on the match. I also kept dipping into the match commentary. When I had a moment, I needed to find a way to take elements out of their tabs and add them to my vision. For example, having the commentary semi-transparent would let me "see" what was going on even when my head was turned away.

With that thought came a pang of headache. The curse trying to reprogramme itself again?

It wasn't the right time. I focused on Mike. "How do you want to do this?"

"One at a time."

I looked at the parents and tried to match them to the kids. It was easy. Except . . . "Where's Benny's whoever?"

"They're not here."

That was one of the most shocking things yet. "What? Seriously? No parent, no guardian? Not even a gran? Okay, let's do him first." I felt a thrill of anticipation. I'd gone from being a courtroom lawyer to being a detective.

If Benny's parents weren't guilty, then who was?

62

FIRED UP

Mike Dean, Benny, Henri, Spectrum, and I moved to a sparsely populated area. "Benny," I said. "I don't get it. The others are being led astray by their parents. Yours aren't even here. What the . . ." Four men surrounding one little kid. Swearing at him would be too much. "What the *what?*"

He looked . . . defensive. "Dunno."

"Do you want to play?"

"Yeah."

"Then articulate yourself." He sucked in a breath but got stuck. He wasn't someone who spent a lot of time talking about his feelings. In case he didn't want to talk in front of his coach, I shooed the Chester guys away, keeping Henri as my youth football expert. "Benny, I'm not a counsellor or whatever. I want to get back to the game. So talk fast or get out of Dodge."

His eyes flashed with anger briefly, but then he shook his head in a kind of sad way. Speaking quietly, and waving his hands away in tiny but highly expressive gestures, he said, "Tyson always plays striker, wherever you put him. You moved him to midfield, and I knew his dad would tell him to go up top, and he did, and he *did*. So I tried to go CAM. To get some space. I wasn't trying to . . . show you up."

"All right," I said. "I get that. But then I talked to you and told you to stay as a striker, and you were moping around like a little bitch."

"Because he moved himself to striker again!"

"But then I got rid of him, didn't I?"

"I didn't know you'd do that! No one's ever done it before."

"If you'd played with a bit of fire, you'd still be on the pitch."

"Max," said Henri. "That is unfair. Be calm. It's not his fault. I would do what he did, and so would you. He *has* been completely rational. You can't blame him for not playing for the team when you rightly say there *is* no team."

I pulled at my earlobe for a bit. "Fuck it, you're right. Benny, you've been hard done by. But I'm still not sure I can trust you on the pitch. You changed your role and sulked around. You get that, right?"

He looked at the ground. "Suppose."

"You heard the tactics. Are you willing to play left-midfield?"

He looked up at me. "Yeah!"

"It's a shit job."

"I'll do it. Then you can put Boyce back in the centre."

"No. We're playing with eight until I get what I want."

A tut from beside me. "Fucking hell, Max."

"Get warmed up, Benny. And stop smiling. You've got thirty minutes to give me an hour's worth of sprints."

I checked the tactics screen and smiled. Future's nan had pulled through. Before going back to the Rebel Alliance, I went to the side of the pitch and yelled, "Boyce, sub! Future DM PM." Benny sprinted into the left-midfield spot while Boyce walked off, wondering if he'd done bad.

"Good job, buddy. Take a drink. You'll be back on in no time."

In case continuing to play with eight seems unusually demented, I was actually planning to cycle through the entire outfield team, so they'd all count as subs. Bench boost, remember? Once I was happy they were trying to play as a team, they could play with nine.

Or ten, depending on how the next chat went.

Sullivan's dad was Irish, or of Irish stock. He was pretty good looking, in good trim for his age, and was wearing a black puffy coat with a fake fur hood lining that looked good behind his white hair. His son had black hair and similar features.

"Right," I said, trying to rush through this process. "What's the deal?"

"What exactly do you mean?" said the dad. His accent was local. He must've been born in the area.

I pointed at his kid. "He's not doing his role. It's because of you. That's all I know."

"Chris," he said, and it took me a second to realise who he was talking to. "What's the story?"

"With respect," I said. "I asked *you*."

"Well, now how should I know? All I know is you turn up, and suddenly everything goes to hell in a handbasket." His expression hadn't changed much, but it had changed. I couldn't quite put my finger on it.

I watched as the boys passed the ball in a lovely zig-zag across the pitch: from Sevenoaks on the right, through the CM, back to Future, who played it to the left-sided CB, who sent it out to Benny. Benny checked his options, dribbled into space, and tried to slide a pass to the striker's feet. He got it all wrong, but there was a fucking BURST of support from half the team. "That's it, Benny!" "Head up, B!" "Yes, Chester that's what I like!"

I snorted. "Yeah. Looks like fucking Vietnam out there. Absolute carnage. Your boy was doing the exact opposite of that. I can't work out why. So why don't you tell me?"

Strangely, Henri spoke next. "Stay onside. How'd you miss that? Make the run, make the run now. Too far out, get in the box. Stop coming back, go forward."

My mouth dropped. I pointed at the dad. "Is that *him*?" Henri nodded.

Spectrum finally got involved. "He considers himself a second manager. Sort of an unofficial coach."

I stepped towards the dad. "Do you *coach* the other players, too?"

"No!" he said.

"He does," said Henri.

"We're done here," I said and hobbled off to the next dad.

The next "dad" was Henk's mum, a blonde woman with a long pony-tail. My first encounter with a soccer mom! Henri found her quite pleasing. She *was* attractive but not to me. Not if she was ruining my team. Also she did something weird with eyeliner, but that's not important.

She was smart as a whip. She'd seen that Benny had been redeemed somehow and that Sullivan hadn't. So she got straight to the point. "I've been telling Henk to play DM."

I nodded. "Why?"

"There's more demand for DMs. And today there isn't enough work for three centre-backs. So I told him to go to DM where he could get involved in the game more and catch the eye."

She knows all about catching the eye, thought Henri to himself (in my imagination), before adding the French version of *hubba hubba*.

"Thanks for your honesty. Let me be honest in return. Henk can be a professional centre-back but not a DM. Also, the point of today was to give him practice in a back three. You've denied him that opportunity. And you've made a lot of people think he's not a team player. That's why Chester asked you to promise not to coach from the touchline. You're smart, but you can't know more than his coaches."

"*You* seem to think you can."

Just then, Broughton launched a long ball that our captain jumped to head away. It glanced off his head and bounced towards our goal: danger! The other centre-back had anticipated the possibility and got there in a flash. He passed back to our goalie and we started to build another attack. The CBs gave each other a little nod. It's hard to describe how it made me feel. Just . . . big. Henri gave me a slap on the back, and that doubled the dose.

Mike Dean had sort of tolerated my stance with Sullivan, but now he was impatient. "So, Max, we've cleared this up. Some future discussions needed, obviously. Are you going to let Henk back on?"

"There's still the issue of why they want to develop a DM when no Chester age group uses a DM. I'd say they're using Chester as a platform to move to another club when the time suits. I'd say you're investing a lot of time and money trying to develop a player who will leave as soon as the chance arises." Henk's mum dropped her pleasant facade and gave me some serious evil eye. But I continued. "But that's not really my business. This match is, and I'm happy with my back three right now."

"But that little one is playing as a DM!" she said to my back as I walked away. "Why don't you take him off too?"

She was vindictive, but she was right. We had a back two and Future ahead of them. She really knew football!

Seeing Henk get a good match rating in the DM slot had been fascinating to me. His profile said he was strictly a CB. A lot of centre-backs could also play as a full-back (i.e., they could play centre-back and right-back and, less commonly, centre-back and left-back). Henk? No. He was a one-position guy. Which wasn't necessarily bad for his career, by the way. But he wasn't supposed to be good anywhere except centre-back. Certainly not as a DM. So why was he getting a solid eight out of ten for this match?

Well, Future's profile had him as a centre-back who could play defensive midfield too. I was desperate to put him as a DM and see what happened.

The problem? I, Max Best, couldn't set him as a DM. I could only use the positions given by the curse, and neither 4-4-2 nor 3-5-2 used a defensive midfielder.

The solution? Begging his gran to stand on the sidelines and yell at him to disobey me.

I was using the "shitty parent" tactic to hack the curse! Our 3-3-1 was now a 2-1-3-1. Ooh! Look at all the numbers!

With Future settling nicely into the strategic DM position, I'd also set him as our team's playmaker. Our attacks were supposed to develop through him. Playmakers normally play in attacking positions, but this made sense to me. It felt right.

And it was paying off. Future was on eight out of ten. In the time he'd played as a centre-back, before his gran had got in his ear, he was getting six out of ten. Which you'd expect from a very young kid making his debut against some older boys. Moving him slightly up the pitch had added two to his match rating.

Long story short, the DM slot seemed powerful. Even just visually, its advantages were clear. It gave the midfield and defence a safe passing option. The DM patrolled the space between the two lines making interceptions and tackles. He added his strength to two different units.

I once again had a wistful moment thinking about James Yalley and his wasted gifts.

But here in front of me was a talented kid getting his chance to shine and making it happen. It brought a smile to my face.

That didn't last long. Next were the Bulldog Brothers.

I'd spent an eternity dealing with these parents when all I wanted was to focus on the match. I did spare a few seconds to scan the pitch and absorb the shape of the game. It was going amazingly well. The boys were running hard and playing with real intensity in defence, and being super cool and calm when we had the ball. It was possible Broughton would run out of steam before we did!

One last tweak: I released the CM and RM to "make forward runs," and I allowed Future to "play through balls." The idea was that the midfielders—sadly not the guy on the left—would run forward to join attacks, and Future would try to pass the ball to someone in a dangerous position behind the defence's offside trap. His passing skill seemed good enough for the task. My only worry was that he literally wouldn't be able to kick the ball hard enough . . . he was so tiny!

"Hi guys," I said to the Bulldogs. "I'm Max. You know why I took Tyson off. Choosing his own position, not passing to anyone, flapping his arms around like a goose. You shouting at him, giving him instructions is bad for Tyson, bad for the team. You know that. Any questions?"

"Yeah," said Bulldog Two, the lesser clone. "Who the fuck are you?"

A week before, he might have intimidated me just through his massive bulk. Now, his size plus his tats, rings, and air of menace . . . had no effect on me. I took in his appearance and his tone then half-turned back to the match. "I'm Max Best."

"But who *are* you?"

I watched as the lads passed the ball around, probing, looking for a chance to move forward. "What's that got to do with you breaking the code of conduct? That you signed? I'm the guy picking the team is all you need to know. What you do is you apologise, and say you won't do it again. What you do is set up a meeting with Spectrum or Mike or whoever, and explain the steps you're going to take to change your behaviour. What you do is work with Tyson to stop him flapping his arms around. All right? See you." I took a step away.

Bulldog One turned puce. "Do you know who I am?" I had a LOT of jokes to choose from, and it was hard to bite my tongue. Frustrated, he continued. "I'm going to find out what happened here today and make sure whoever's responsible pays. No one talks to me like that, specially not some rando. Mike, put a stop to this. Right now."

I hobbled away, finally in my rightful place. Finally able to concentrate on the game. We got a free kick on the right, perfect for Seven to whip in a cross. Send up the tall centre-backs to attack the ball. The free hit perk came up, and I chose not to hit it. As far as possible, I wanted the kids to work for their win. To suffer for it. At some point, it had become vital to me that these kids learn the lesson I wanted them to learn. Nothing else mattered.

"Max," said Mike.

The cross came in, and Broughton headed it away. They attacked on our left, our weak side. Boyce was back in that slot. He had the choice between trying to win the ball in a tackle or slowing down the attack and waiting for support. He chose the latter.

"Yes Boycey!" I roared. His teammates were storming over to help him. "Nuge, stay! Future, no thanks! Keep the structure. Wait for it. That's it boys! Love it."

"Max," said Mike.

I'd forgotten he was there. The match was sucking me in, but I needed to spare some mental energy for this man. He held the keys to one of the doors I could escape through. "Mike."

"This isn't working out," he said. He was about to fire me. Sacking managers was something of a hobby for guys like him. Maybe I should have gone for the free hit.

"Just one second, Mike. Sorry. One second."

The ball had been cycled around to Future, and now he was in a pretty nice position. He strolled forward—he really had a lot of style, that kid—and shaped to play a pass to Seven. Too early!

"No," said Henri. It was almost a cry of despair.

"Wait," I said, eyes wide. "It's happening."

Future went through his passing motion, and three defenders moved accordingly. But the pass never came. He'd faked it! Seven sprinted forwards; Future passed the ball in front of him; Seven ran onto it, took a touch, and while our striker burst to the front post, taking the goalkeeper and two defenders with him; our central midfielder appeared out of nowhere at the edge of the box. Seven cut the ball back towards him, he ran onto it, and passed it into the unguarded left-hand side of the goal.

One-nil!

"Bloody hell," said Mike, stunned by the goal's beautiful simplicity.

"Max," said Henri, "you're a wizard. *Formidable.* Mwah!" He did a chef's kiss.

A delirious Benny had run a few yards onto the pitch to celebrate. Some of the players ran towards him.

Then I realised, they weren't running towards him. They were running towards me.

Future was first. He threw himself at me, tried to wrap me in a hug. His arms weren't long enough; I hugged him instead.

The others joined in too. Group hug! *Team* hug. It was a throbbing maelstrom of joy, pride, disbelief, relief. I wondered if they'd remember the moment for as long as I would. If they did, they might reach their potential.

I stood tall and looked down at the kids. There was such a fire burning inside me. They gawped at me, expectant.

"What are you standing *there* for?" I said, with a fierce scowl. I felt my face soften, and I grinned on one side of my mouth. "Go and do it again."

With a lot of smiles and shouts of "come on!" they jogged back to their positions.

I went to the tactics screen to stop the midfield running forward; they needed a rest. There was no such screen.

Mike had already fired me.

63

RYAN REYNOLDS

Once the kids had turned away, I picked up my crutches and checked my pockets for my phone and keys.

"Henri, we're leaving."

"*Excuse-moi*? Why that?"

"I've been sacked."

"Sacked? When?"

"Just now." If you want to get specific, it must have been the moment Mike said, "*This isn't working*." "Can you get the gate for me?" Ahead on the railing there was a little gate with a fiddly handle. You notice such things when you're on crutches.

Mike looked startled. "Max, wait." I gave him a sort of polite nod but kept going. "Max! Maaax. Shit."

Henri jogged ahead and cleared my path. A bunch of confused people parted, and I made my way towards the car park. Jackie was already moving to intercept. He had been watching from near the corner flag, and his footballing sixth sense must have kicked in. I wondered how much he'd guessed just from me making such wild subs and the subsequent kerfuffles with MD and the parents. Probably ninety-seven percent of it.

Jackie nodded at me. "You okay?"

"Yes. Can we go please? This is Henri."

Jackie knew. "We've met."

Henri remembered too. "Your friend was a good defender."

"How good?" I said.

"Very good."

They shook hands like they were trying to wring the testosterone out of each other.

"Cut that shit out," I said, setting off towards the cars again. Macho handshakes do my head in.

"Is this our . . . mutual friend?" said Henri. *Is this the guy I'm supposed to wait for?*

"Maybe," I confirmed.

Jackie shook his head. He was used to weird conversations happening around me. He was about to speak when Livia turned up. "Max," she said, breathless, falling in with us. "What is going on?"

"I got fired," I said with a smile, still swinging myself back towards Manchester.

"Why?"

"Well, that's a good question," I said. "I think the managing director didn't like my attitude. And to be fair, he probably has a point."

Henri stepped in. "That's not what it was. Max put the needs of the kids above his own. He stepped on the wrong toes along the way."

Well, that put me in a very heroic light. I gave the Frenchman a look, but he didn't seem to be playing a game. I mean, obviously he *was*, but he didn't *seem* to be. Very impressive skullduggery. I presumed the plan was to make *me* look good so that Livia would end her interest in *Jackie,* which would make *her* fair game, leading to an invite down to Henri's chateau or his flat on the Seine or whatever his usual move was.

Livia reacted as Henri had intended. "No! That's awful. That's not fair. I saw the way the kids celebrated the goal. Whatever you were doing, they were really invested."

I put my hand on Henri's shoulder and gave it a little shake. "I couldn't have done it without Henri. He was fantastic. A real sharp mind in there, a great listener, and a dab hand when it comes to kids."

"What Henri is trying to say," said Jackie, somehow picking up the rules of the game and joining in, "is that Max put his future on the line out there today. When I saw him take those kids off the pitch, I felt something about him I've never felt before."

"What's that?" I said. "Lust?"

"Admiration," he said.

"Aww," said Livia, sort of rubbing his back.

And that put Jackie back in pole position. Which was great! But I couldn't help myself. I just couldn't. She was so beautiful, and I knew the exact right thing to say. "Well, Jackie mate. In the words of Kevin

James in *Paul Blart: Mall Cop 2* . . . if you believe the purpose of life is to only serve yourself then you *have* no purpose."

Livia stared at me, unblinking, eyes glistening, before moving away and vanishing into a little white Fiat.

Henri punched me in the arm. "Max. Did you just quote *Paul Blart: Mall Cop 2* to flirt with that *goddess*?"

"Yes."

He exhaled. "I can't compete with that." He slapped me on the back and ambled over to a dark green Lotus Super 7. He started the engine, gave us a 1920s kind of wave, and zoomed off. His licence plate read H3NR1.

Livia came back and shyly handed me a piece of paper. "See you soon," she said, before adding, in what I chose to believe was a flirty tone, "I hope!"

I slipped the paper into a pocket and followed Jackie to his car.

We got in. Jackie didn't help me, but simply sat with his hands on the wheel, his knuckles white.

After about fifteen seconds, I took out Livia's note and began to read it aloud. "Dear Max, you are . . . oh, dear. She spelled it "u r." The letter U and the letter R." I pretended to skim the text. "It's all like that. What a shame. Dear Max, u r so good with kids. I hope you—the letter U—come to Chester. We would—spelled W-U-D—have beautiful babies. Why—the letter Y—don't 'U' call me and 'U' can put a little baby inside me. No question mark even though it's a question. Then there's a phone number. I don't think she'd give me a fake one. Do you?"

Jackie's death grip weakened. He took a quiet, shuddering breath that I only heard, because there was no other sound in the universe. Slowly, he turned to me. "That's her Disney Plus password, isn't it?"

I showed it to him. "Yep."

"Please don't do that to me, Max."

I did the world's tiniest dance. "If you want it better put a ring on it." Repeat times three.

"It's not that easy."

"It is. Drop me off, then call her. Or next time . . ." I flicked my index finger against the paper like a doctor flicks a syringe.

He shook his head. "It's not that easy. And by the way, she can spell."

We drove off.

We didn't talk much at first, but I did tell him most of what happened with the parents. He seemed very interested in why I did what I did, but I was more interested in why the parents did what they did. He made me describe Sullivan's dad, asked a few follow-up questions, then said, "He does it because he's insecure. It's a constant stream of instruction and correction that's like a sonar. Pinging himself in the world of football. If he is heard, he exists. He's always trying to reassure himself that he has a place in our little ecosystem. And he's desperate for his son to progress. If he doesn't, it's his failure. He couldn't afford the extra coaching. He didn't push his kid enough. His genes are defective. He'll find *something* and torment himself with it forever."

"You've seen it all before?"

"Not everything. Just a lot. Looking back, my dad wasn't ideal. I think I made it despite him."

"What about Henk's mum? You think she's just using Chester as a springboard to something better?"

"Based on what you said, probably. That's not necessarily bad for Chester, by the way. Developing a talented youngster who goes to a bigger club can bring in some cash. There's transfer fees for the obvious stars and, if a fee can't be agreed, there's a tribunal to decide a fair price. But sometimes a big club will just give a small one a few hundred grand to avoid all the mess. Anyway, parents like those, they'll hate what you did today. One of them told me once: 'It isn't about the team winning, it's about my son progressing to the best of his ability.'"

"How do you feel about what I did? Really?"

He dipped his head while he considered the question. "It was so obviously in the best interests of those kids, and so obviously against your own interests, that I can't really understand it. So I don't have an opinion on it."

Hearing him say the "against my interests" bit was something of a dagger to the heart. I'd sort of hoped that maybe I could have my cake and eat it: be the hero to the kids, and still scout for Chester. But I'd made my choice.

"I'd do it again, Jackie. Exactly the same. I loved managing them. The Knights, too. Thanks for this weekend. Really."

But the weekend wasn't quite over.

I popped a few pills to deaden the pain and lay on my lumpy but familiar bed with my phone fully charged and my laptop logged in to Livia's Disney Plus and tuned to *The Proposal*. At exactly six o'clock, I video called Emma. She picked up instantly. She was made up, but not like she was going to the Oscars. And I'm pretty sure she was wearing a soft tracksuit kind of thing. Hot but chill. My kind of woman!

We did some small talk, but before she could really get going, I said I had an idea. We could press play on *The Proposal* and watch it together.

"Didn't you have time to watch it yet?" she said. Not judgmental. More . . . supportive. Understanding that I was a busy person. Which I wasn't. Usually.

"I did the first hour and made notes, but I fell asleep."

"Wow. I quite enjoyed it."

"It wasn't *fall asleep* bad. There were also the meds and the match and the drive."

"Meds? Drive?"

I had a lot to tell her. "Just get ready to press play, and I'll tell you everything." Everything except that a curse lived rent-free in my head and that I'd briefly checked OnlyFans for women called Livia. "Three, two, one, play!"

I told her some of my recent highs and lows. New clients, new injuries, new opportunities. I tried to explain about the under-fourteens and the bad parents, but she didn't really get it. She didn't get why I'd risk the two hundred pounds a week I so desperately needed. She didn't get why it was such a big deal to me that these random kids tried to play football the way I wanted it to be played. She didn't get why Jackie would take me to Chester for medical care and to watch a match, why I'd be allowed to coach their youth teams, and why Henri Lyons would want to be my assistant.

Eventually, I just laughed. "It's weird, isn't it? It's a weird world, or it's weird when I'm around. I know I'm supposed to ease my way in and learn the ropes, but I'm finding I'm not good at that. I've apparent-ly only got one setting: bull in a china shop. But listen, let's talk about Ryan Reynolds, okay? No more football for tonight."

"Sure, but why did you want to watch a *Ryan Reynolds* movie, specifically?"

I shook my head. "Because he bought a football club. But *that's* the end of the football. Okay? Let me read some of my notes. Number One: Max Best Pet Peeve. People in movies carrying or drinking out of visibly empty cups. Number Two: Hilarious 2009 reference to 'that little internet site' which turns out to be YouTube. Number Three: The plot of the movie is that she's being deported because she's Canadian, which is a meta joke because, famously, *he* is. Number Four is coming up soon, if I remember: There's a room with those huge glass doors that you can't see. That's scary to me. If we ever buy a house, we're not doing that. Ever. No glass doors. Veto."

"Okay. Then I want my own sink."

"Deal."

"And a walk-in closet."

"Maybe. You know what? This Reynolds guy. He's got a super shredded man body and a tiny little baby face. Is he handsome? Really?"

"Er . . . yes."

"You like baby-faced men. Got it. No black eyes from now on. Now this bit here is good. He's been her dogsbody this whole time, and he's finally standing up for himself. That's better. They're more equal now."

"You like being in charge?"

"It's not about that. It's more about not being a doormat. I think we're coming up to a pretty long, boring stretch where virtually nothing happens. So let me read the rest of my notes and get your thoughts."

"Okay, but first, did you like the movie?"

"I like the concept. They have to get to know each other fast so that's juicy chum for the writers. And I suppose it starts well enough. But there's not enough there to sustain the story, I don't think. Some of it's actively annoying. Ryan Reynolds is handsome and capable, and *then* we find out he's rich too! His family owns half of Alaska. So where's the romance? From what I read, this is a rip-off of a similar movie where the dude is a struggling musician, and his *rival* is rich. That's a better dynamic, right? It's not romantic if the guy is perfect in every way. He's got to be flawed. Don't you think?"

"What are your flaws?"

"Jesus. Loads. I'm all flaws held together with blu-tack and sel-lotape."

"So you'd be a good lead in a rom-com?"

"I don't think so. I wouldn't pay to watch me. All right, we can skip some of these notes. My main problem with this movie is there are loads of scenes that they should have cut. This could have been a charming one-hour streaming special."

"They didn't have Netflix then. But I know what you mean. What scenes would you cut?"

"There's one around where I dozed off. Sandra Bullock is in bed and Ryan is in a sleeping bag on the floor. And they just chat about nothing, and then the scene ends. It's hilarious how pointless it is!"

"Oh."

"What?"

"That's my favourite scene."

Wow. That blew my mind. Her comment made me remember why I'd set this "date" up in the first place—to get to know her. "Hey, Emma."

"What?"

"What part of Newcastle are you from?"

I woke up covered in drool. Confused. I picked up my phone to continue chatting to Emma, but she was gone. I stared at the time for *ages,* before it finally clicked that it was 4 a.m., and I'd slept through the whole end of the movie and beyond. I couldn't remember anything past one of the "Reynolds shows off his abs" scenes from about fifty minutes in. I checked the phone log, and the call had lasted one hour fifty-two minutes. Some impulse made me look up the length of the movie, and it was one hour forty-eight minutes. Emma had stayed watching it with me even though I'd fallen asleep. And she'd stayed through the credits and a little extra.

Water. So thirsty. I hobbled to the bathroom and drank deeply. When I got back to bed, I saw I had an email from just after she'd hung up.

From: Emma

The bit you wanted to cut is my fave scene because until then they've been fighting the whole time. Their relationship is all about status. Who's got the upper hand. It's all transactional, you know? That is the first time they really talk. Just talk together. It's their first real connection.

Had a great time.

Let's do it again. You choose the next one :) x

First real connection? They'd been talking to each other since minute one of the film. I think her opinion would have been gibberish to me only a day earlier. But after the drive home with Jackie, it made sense.

After I'd told Jackie I'd do it all again, he started to talk. To really talk. He told me about the knee injuries that had ended his career. About the despair and desperation of those dark days. That the message he'd been getting from the club and fans had *finally* sunk in, they'd be there for him come what may. And when he'd belatedly, fully committed to rehab, Livia had been his physio, his nurse, his therapist, his sole point of connection to the rest of the world. There were stretches of days where she was the only person he'd speak to.

And for him, according to his principles, asking her out would be gross. A cliché. A poor reward for everything she'd done for him.

I'd sighed at his stupidity and started telling him some of my "secrets." Just random things that came into my head. That I'd been the number one guy in the entire call centre and was now trying to finish every day as number three in my team. All because my boss had annoyed me in some minor way I barely remembered. That I was an expert in *Love Island* even though I'd never watched more than thirty seconds of it. And that the moment during the FC United versus AFC Phoenix game where Jackie had given Ziggy some direct instructions was indelibly imprinted on my mind. "That's when I knew you were a great coach," I said.

Chester, then. I'd ended my trip with Attributes 3 in the bag, and 95 XP in the bank. Henri Lyons was a new ally when it came to football and a rival when it came to women. Livia knew I existed. I'd been in the bowels of a stadium on match day and learned what scouts do.

I'd had a crash course in disabled and youth football. Mike Dean had dangled two hundred pounds a week in my face and then snatched it away, but at least I knew how much to charge for my services. I'd learned a lot.

Most of all, though, I'd made a deeper connection with Emma and Jackie. Deep, meaningful, human connection wasn't something I knew I needed. It wasn't something I would have thought about grinding towards. It wasn't something that could be expressed in a number. It wasn't something that would make me richer or stronger.

But it was progress.

64

BOSTON UNITED

Back to life. Back to reality. Back to the daily grind at the call centre. Another day, another dollar. All my illusions of progress were shattered by my first inbound call of the day. Another hundred to go. The ego-smashing mundanity of it all.

But I *had* made progress. Around ten o'clock, I got a call from an 01244 number. Chester! I couldn't pick up when I was plugged in, but I took a break and called back. It was a woman called Inga, and she claimed to be from Chester FC's admin team. She was calling to say she'd arranged tickets for me to attend Boston United versus Alfreton Town the following night.

I'll spare you the back and forth of me saying things like "What?" and "Are you sure?" and "But *when* did Mike Dean ask you to do this?"

Long story short, it seemed legit. Mike might have fired me from the under-fourteens, but he still wanted my scouting reports. Wow. That was . . . unexpected. And potentially exciting.

On the other hand, Boston was in Lincolnshire and a quick search suggested it would be almost a three-hour drive to the stadium. And a three-hour drive back. Pretty much the ideal choice if someone was feeling vindictive.

I spent the rest of my shift ploughing through calls in case I needed to leave early the next day. Grabbing relationship points in case I needed a favour. By 5 p.m., I was miles ahead on the stats, and I even gave my boss a tiny smile and a nod.

Then I went to Broadhurst Park and was led into the manager's office; FC United wanted to sign Ziggy on a short-term contract to cover their injuries.

On one side of the manager's desk was the grey-haired man I'd met the first time I'd gone to FC United. The one who thought I was a top monarchist. The one who thought I was distraught that the Queen had died. Turns out, he was the big boss! The managing director. He asked me to call him Steve. Next to him were Neil, the first-team manager, and Jackie. There was also an admin guy loitering at the back, struggling to get comfortable leaning against a filing cabinet. They called him Statto.

Ziggy and I sat next to each other in separate chairs. Ziggy's right leg was bouncing.

"Thanks for coming Max," said Neil. "This shouldn't take long. It's all pretty straightforward, yeah? We're short up front and Ziggy's been doing well. We'd like to give him a short-term deal until . . ." He glanced at Jackie, who held up two fingers. Two months? We'd HAD this discussion! But he was pranking me again, and I'd fallen for it. Again! Jackie suppressed a grin. Neil continued. "Until the end of the season. So you'll be helping us out short-term, and we'll be continuing Ziggy's training until the summer. It seems a fair deal. The only thing is, we need to get the paperwork done by the end of today, so he's available for Saturday."

Ziggy was nodding like one of those puppy toys you stick on your car's dashboard.

"All sounds very smooth," I agreed. "There's just the question of his salary." I'd read that in a negotiation it was good to start with a high number. "I was thinking six hundred thousand pounds a week. Same as Cristiano Ronaldo."

Steve, the guy whose grey hair made him seem like an eighteenth-century Prime Minister, put his palm up. "Max, you're very charming and everything. But I've got to get to a family dinner. The deal is pretty much take it or leave it and no hard feelings either way. We're offering three hundred and fifty quid a week."

That meant thirty-five a week for me. Which was, frankly, awful. But it was just the start. Next season, we'd get a proper salary. I eyed Ziggy, and he widened his eyes at me. I think he'd have signed if it had *cost* him money.

"Fine. We want shirt number thirty-three and a five hundred pound goal bonus."

Steve's eyebrows shot up. But he smiled. "Maaaax."

"If it's like you say and he's just helping out and won't play most of the season, what's the problem? What's he going to do? Score fifteen goals?"

Jackie shifted uneasily and shook his head at Steve. I didn't mind. He *was* working for FC United, after all. But I shouldn't have mentioned the fifteen goals. Me saying it had made Jackie think it was possible.

Steve said, "Two hundred a goal. Come on now. Let's get this puppy signed."

"Fine."

"Okay, Mr. Best," said Statto. "I just need the FA Number attached to your agent licence. Then I can add the goal bonus clause and print out the contracts. It won't take two minutes."

There was dead silence.

Everyone stared at me.

I realised I'd gotten ahead of myself. I didn't have a Football Association Number. I didn't have my licence.

"I don't have it yet," I said. "Should come soon. Can we add that in later?"

Statto shook his head. "No, sorry. We need it now, or the FA will come down on us like a ton of pricks."

My first contract talks were going to shit. Why was everything so hard?

I said, "Can I have a word with you outside for a second?" Ziggy started to get up, but I clarified. "I mean Jackie."

More weird looks, but Jackie came out, and I closed the door behind him. I took a few shuffles away and said, "Did you plan this somehow?"

"Plan what, mate?"

"You knew I didn't have that number so you," I waved my hands around, "did this."

He was still except for his eyebrows, which didn't know what to do. "Are you okay, Max? Because it sounds like you're accusing me of injuring all our strikers to clear a path for Ziggy to sign a contract. And how should I know you're not a real agent? You've been saying you're an agent since I met you. I kind of thought maybe you were one."

I rubbed my face hard. "Fuck. Sorry. You're right. I just wanted to blame someone else. It's my fault."

"Why don't you have your licence?"

"It's five hundred pounds. I thought I had until the next transfer window to get it. I can save five hundred quid by then. I didn't think anything would happen till January, and the last week's been so frantic it slipped my mind."

"Well, anyway, that's Ziggy fucked." He shook his head. "Poor kid."

I opened the door and swapped Jackie for Ziggy. Closed the door again.

"Ziggy, mate. I won't have that licence till January, probably."

His face fell, but not all the way. There was a kind of steel there. "So what are you saying? I can't sign?"

I blew air through my lips. Was my poverty going to be the reason this guy couldn't achieve his dreams? "No. I would never stand in your way like that. You'll have to sign without me. Neil's right; you'll get some minutes in the next few games, and when the stars are back you'll know what it's going to take to compete with them. And you'll be a real pro with real stats. You'll be on Wikipedia maybe." I beamed at the thought.

"What about you?" he said, not returning my smile.

I shrugged. "Maybe now you're a big shot you can lend me five hundred quid, so I can get registered. Make sure it doesn't happen like this with Raffi."

He shook his head. The steel was back. "We made a deal. I'll sign without you and pay you in cash. You're my agent, Max, whatever we tell the authorities. You believed in me." His eyes softened, and he gave me a microscopic smile. "Do you remember in your car before my trial? You made me promise to sign a contract with you. Everyone thought I was shit that day, but you believed even harder." He shook his head. "I know what you've done. I won't ever forget it. So in the summer when we sign the next one, you'll be there, and you'll bring your agent badge and your agent gun. All right?"

"You're going to pay me even though you don't have to?"

"I do have to."

"Without telling the FA." I looked up and to the right. "That makes me a secret agent. Jackie was right all along! All right. Let's do it."

He held his arm up like a barrier. "Before we go back in," he said, all serious-faced. "Will you do me one favour?"

"What's that?"

"Will you enjoy it?"

The phrasing seemed familiar. Something cool from a movie? I mimed adjusting a bow tie and said, "Hell, yeah!"

Ziggy signed a professional contract.

I'm in the photo, and so is my black eye.

Ziggy is radiant.

Mike Dean had wanted me to scout on Tuesdays and Saturdays. Well, not *this* Saturday. Ziggy was going to make his debut. I had to be there. Steve told Statto to sort me a ticket. Ziggy mumbled that he thought I might sit in the coach's area behind the dugout.

Neil said that was okay. Just this once. "But maybe keep your tactical ideas to yourself, hey?" Oh. What was that a reference to?

We moved into another room where there was a mini-fridge with some cans of beer. Said beer was distributed, and we all toasted Ziggy's new life.

Ziggy took a swig, and Jackie swiped the can from his hand. "Did you enjoy that? Good. Because that's the last alcohol you'll drink until you retire. Welcome to your new life. Welcome to hell! Now drop, and give me twenty." Ziggy's big eyes shone. He was fairly sure Jackie was teasing him. About the push-ups anyway. But he wasn't one hundred percent sure.

I asked Steve if he wasn't going to be late for his dinner, and he said he'd made that up to pressure me into signing the contract fast. While I gaped at him, he laughed, took a big swig of beer, and said he really did have to leave. He picked up one of those suit containers you get from a dry cleaner and said he was off.

"What's the occasion?" I said.

"It's my wife's wedding anniversary," he said, and then he was gone.

I lay in bed that night wondering why I wasn't happier than I was. I'd finally turned the curse into cash, it seemed. But Ziggy was planning to pay me under the table and could change his mind whenever he wanted. And Chester . . . who knew if that was real or not? I'd believe it when I saw the money in my bank account.

I tried to sleep early to be ready for a very, very long day, but I couldn't. I needed to pick up some XP before Saturday so that I could finally buy 4-4-2 diamond. There were no eleven-a-side matches on the horizon, but I wanted the option. Tweaking formations, individual instructions, and watching the match rating change, that's where my thoughts went. And why the deadline? Because I was going to buy God Save the King and give Ziggy another point in finishing before his big game. That would plunge me three thousand XP into debt, and it would be a long slog getting back to zero.

So that was the shopping plan for the week. Buy a formation, and improve Ziggy. Maybe I'd place a twenty pound bet on him to score. As a complete unknown, his odds would be long, at least ten to one, so I could make a quick two hundred quid from it. Plus, I'd get my twenty quid share of his goal bonus. Three thousand XP suddenly didn't seem so expensive.

I ran through the pros and cons and decided that if I had inside information that he'd start the game, I'd have a cheeky little flutter, but if he was going to be a sub, I'd keep my money in my pocket. I loved Ziggy, but he didn't seem like the kind of player who'd excel coming off the bench.

I drove to work. My ankle had improved, but it was still sore. Just on the border of being insane to start a six-hour round trip after a hard day taking calls.

But that's exactly what I did. Fortunately, the traffic wasn't too bad, and I got to Boston United's ground with plenty of time to spare. I'd decided there should be at least one club in the country where everybody liked me, so I vowed to be nice to every gammon, every bulldog, and every soccer mom I met.

Boston were playing 5-3-2 and Alfreton 4-5-1. Formations don't tell the whole story. It's possible to play a very attacking version of either formation. But nah. This was a defensive borefest. Two old managers trying to make sure their lads didn't lose and hoping to nick a winner from a corner or free kick. Pretty grim.

But I wasn't complaining. I was—hopefully—being paid. And even if I wasn't, I was picking up 2 XP per minute. Even better, I could see the match ratings and match commentary, even though I was just a spectator, which made scouting even easier.

Inga hadn't given me any forms to fill in. Mike Dean had said that Chester had their own version of the scouting reports, but I hadn't ever seen one. Which, yeah, made me uneasy about the whole "this was a revenge prank" thought that had been nagging me. Anyway, I made up my own method based on what I'd want to know if I were managing Chester. I drew the formations for both teams with shirt numbers in the circles and a legend with the player names. I noted their main strengths and weaknesses, according to what the curse told me, but also added a little bit from my own observations.

On an inexplicable impulse, I put stars next to the three best players in each team, chosen by who had the highest CA.

There was no one like Henri Lyons where I thought "that guy would massively improve Chester," but I noted a few dudes who were solid in their positions in case they were ever out of contract.

This, since I was alone in my little scouting area, took me all of ten minutes, and I spent the next ten wondering what else I could do. Someone like Chester's manager, Ian Evans, wasn't going to read a detailed scouting report, so I didn't feel that I had to plot things to the nth degree. The opposition's basic tactical principles would be enough for him. Which side do they attack down? Where are they weak? Who gets sucked out of position? Basic stuff.

I bit my nails and tried to get in the mindset of someone like Evans. An old-school manager. Fundamentals. Mostly interested in keeping a good defensive shape and hoping to get something from a . . . corner. That was it. Corners and set pieces.

I went to the Match Overview screen and stared at the Match Report tab. I scrolled it all the way to the start of the match. Then, as I was scrolling back down looking for the word "corner," I thought, *what I need here is a control-F function.* One mega pang of headache later, and the curse had reprogrammed the interface. Now I could search for keywords OR filter by incident type. I selected "corners" and voila, only the text related to corner kicks was visible. I looked for patterns and didn't find one, but the match had only been going for twenty minutes.

So that was productive. While I waited for some dead balls (corners and free kicks) I tried reformatting something else. I was successful in getting the match clock to appear in my vision without having to go into the Match Overview screen, and I left it at that. I didn't want a massive headache driving back on the M62. I'd change things one bit at a time, thank you very much. Lesson learned from unlocking two perks in one day.

At half-time, I had a dubious pie and an ill-advised beer and chatted with some locals. Friendly bunch.

By the seventieth minute, I thought I'd done enough. My report said Boston were stronger on the right than the left and liked to hit the far post from corners and free kicks. Alfreton aimed their set pieces more centrally, and because the player they left in defence in those situations was slow and had bad technique, they'd be vulnerable to a fast break. So playing Chester's fastest striker against them would be advisable.

I took photos of my notes and sent them to the email address Inga had given me. Then I hobbled out into the car park. Of course it was suboptimal to miss out on the rest of the XP, but this way I'd beat the traffic leaving the stadium. The alternative was to delay my return home by ages. I needed to experience sleep more than I needed the experience.

When I was just getting out into the car park, my phone rang. Weirdly, it was Inga. I thought it was odd that she was working late, but obviously she'd got an unexpected notification on her phone, and on later reflection, she probably worked during Chester's matches.

"Mr. Best, I got your report. But the match isn't finished, is it?"

"No, there's about ten minutes left. But I have a three-hour drive and need to get out before two thousand people all rush to their cars." There was an unpleasant silence. "I mean, I could go back in if you really insist."

"What? Oh, no. I was just looking at these scans. The pages seem quite thorough and well thought out. Will Wainwright: pros, heading, strength; cons, technique. Stars to show the best players on each team. Yes, I can almost understand this myself!"

It wasn't that complicated, especially for someone who worked for a football club. "You don't know football?"

"No, I hate it. Just a lot of grown men chasing a little ball. Pointless. But my grandkids love it, and they're proud I work for Chester. I'll send these scans on to everybody. You have a safe drive home."

"Er . . . could you pay me sort of . . . soonish? I could really use the money, to be honest. I had to fill my tank on the way here, and that was financially catastrophic."

"I've got down that we're to pay your petrol and add ten pounds for food and drink. So don't worry about that. But I understand. I'll get this paid ASAP. Just this once though. Normally, we do everything monthly. We don't have a big enough admin team to be making exceptions all the time."

"Understood. Oh, and I can't work this Saturday. My friend is making his debut, and I need to be there to watch him. Unless you want a scouting report for FC United."

"I don't know a lot about football, but I know they're not in the same division as us. So no. But no problem. We'll send you somewhere again next Tuesday. I'll be in touch."

Once I was close-ish to my house, I bought 4-4-2 diamond. At last I had more than one formation! Thankfully this didn't come with a headache, but I suspected I'd get one the first time I actually used it.

Buying that one unlocked another. I'd hoped the curse would offer me a sort of tree of formation options, for example, all the ones with a back four in one branch and all the ones with three at the back in another. But it seemed like I'd have to buy one at a time. Next up was 4-3-3, available for two hundred XP. Double what I'd just paid, but very affordable.

I'd be able to buy it during the Beth Heads match on Friday, but I'd have to be careful about using it for the first time. Using two new formations in one match seemed like a recipe for a very bad night. But that match was way off in the distance.

In fact, I couldn't quite tell where my next management gig was going to come from. There were a hundred professional clubs in the English pyramid . . . seemingly endless possibilities. But Neil had told me to keep my tactics to myself. Maybe he felt I'd shown him up when I'd threatened to lead the reserves to victory over the first team? He was still happy to deal with me, at arm's length. So there was one club unlikely to give me a reserve or youth team to experiment with.

And yeah, similar story at Chester. Similar but worse! I thought about the daydreams I'd had of being Chester's manager. How did it go? I'd be their manager by the end of the season?

It was like Jackie said.

I had a vivid imagination.

65

DUELS

Tuesday night, home late, few hours sleep, up bright and early for work on Wednesday. Or since this was England in the autumn, up dark and early. Around lunch I got a text from my former assistant.

Henri Lyons: Max! Three days with no communication. I do not feel seduced. I expect you to chase me like you'd chase a lover.

Me: I always wait six days before texting. But hey, if I drive to Darlington, will you take me up to Newcastle to meet a girl? I could ask her to bring a friend for you.

Henri: Duel date? It sounds awful. No chance.

Two minutes later.

Henri: Send me a picture of the girls.

Me: No. One is out of your league and the other is tbc.

Henri: Blind date too? It sounds awful.

Me: And it'll have to be a Sunday afternoon. Just a brunch and a chat, and then we all go home. Literally no possibility of action.

Henri: It sounds worse than awful. I'm in. Set it up.

I arrived very early at the sports hall, and the team before us were training, not playing, so there was no XP available. I bought a tea and sat in the reception area, just decompressing. It was good for me. I needed it. My life had been go-go-go for ages.

Jackie was the next to arrive.

"Oh Max, you're here. Great. We need to talk."

That put me on edge. Nothing good ever happened after those words. "Oh. Okay."

He settled into the chair opposite me and put his hands on the table that separated us. "I've been thinking. It's been fun doing all this stuff with you. The training, Ziggy, Chester." He smiled. "Beating Man City. But I need my Wednesdays back. And Ziggy's a pro now. Your client will get his trial at Chester. You too, if you want. I've connected you with some insiders. You know what to do now. You can make it on your own. You *will* make it on your own. So this will be the last training session. And the last . . ." He pushed his index fingers towards me and away from me and towards and away. "The last whatever this is."

Lump, meet throat. "Are you breaking up with me?"

He laughed. "Yes. Kicking you out of the nest. You'll either splat on the ground or start flying. Both sound entertaining."

"But why did you do any of it?"

He shook his head. "None of your business, Maxy boy. Now, did you have anything specific you wanted to do in the session?"

Session? Session? Who gave a shit about that? My mentor had just taken me behind the bike shed and kicked me in the balls. "Just stuff," I said. "Skills."

"I thought you might say that," he said, rising to his feet. "So I've prepared accordingly. One thing though. Why did you want shirt number thirty-three for Ziggy?"

I told him.

He sighed. "Absolutely insane, as always. Well. I'd better get started." He slapped the table and hoisted his big bag of cones and discs and hula hoops and left me alone.

So alone.

I hadn't realised how much of a safety net Jackie had become. In Chester, for example, I'd been intense, laser-focused on the football and Doing The Right Thing. But I should have been managing Mike Dean, not some brats. I *knew*, though, that Jackie would introduce me to someone else. In the back of my mind, there was no downside to taking the nuclear option.

And maybe Jackie sensed that, and that's why he'd left all my stuff in a box outside the front door and changed all the locks. Yes, I could become someone in the football industry on my own. But only on my own. Only if I had a fear of falling.

Or maybe he was protecting himself. Maybe I was so toxic and abrasive that it was damaging his reputation.

I sat there deep in thought, wallowing in misery, until Kisi arrived. It's hard to be grumpy when she's in the area and certainly not when she's chatting at a thousand miles a minute about what she's learned at Man City, how much fun she's having, how excited she is to wake up every day.

I interrupted to explain to her mother that I'd made a mistake in signing the contract with them. It was actually illegal to have a client under the age of sixteen. (I'd re-read the rules and regulations of being a football agent since Monday.) If Kisi still wanted me as an agent when she turned sixteen, we could redo it. And in the meantime, I'd still check on her and help her out and whatnot.

"Max you dummy," said Kisi, which got her a bit of a telling-off from her mother. Once that was over, Kisi resumed. "Do not worry, Mr. Best. I will want to sign it. Actually, this makes sense. Some of the girls gave me funny looks when I talked about how you're my agent. I thought they were confused because you coached the Beth Heads. But it's because I'm not allowed one. Oh! I'll be a big star in two years. We'll have to renegotiate! Since you broke the law, Mr. Best, I'm only going to give you nine percent!"

I smiled. "Deal."

So it was the last training session with the Met Heads and the last with Jackie. I'd invited my whole gang, so that made it even more poignant: Raffi (plus Shona and baby), Ziggy (wrapped in cotton wool, but there was very little risk of injury if we stuck to passing drills), and Kisi. Plus, almost all of the Met Heads were there. Beth looked really tired; she said she'd been working on a big project for her course.

Kisi had helped Jackie lay out some yellow discs. I couldn't work out what the drill would be. It kind of made the hall look like a swimming pool with two wide lanes.

"Ladies and gentlemen," said Jackie. "Gather round. Everybody here? Good. This is your last session of the season, I understand, and Friday's your last game. You've already won your big match, and if you win this week, you'll finish level on points with City. That's incredible, right? Well done. I don't *really* know why Max asked me to come and train you this time, with the job *done*. So I had a think about doing a session that was really for Max's benefit. Are there any objections to that?"

One hand went up. Mine. I was ignored.

Jackie, grinning, continued. "Perfect. I've seen Max manage a few games now and heard him talk about football a lot. He's great on the strategy and the plans and the schemes. In a war you'd want him to be the general. But if you're down in the trenches, you want the guy next to you to know all about storing matchsticks so they don't get wet. How to tell if a bomb's dropping on your section or if it's going to pass overhead. When to wash your socks. All that sort of stuff you learned about trenches in school. Er . . . Kisi. You look blank."

Kisi said, "We didn't do World War I. We did the Suffragettes."

"I . . . I have mixed feelings about that," said Jackie. "It shouldn't be one or the other. What I'm trying to say is that I think Max thinks footy is all about systems and passing routines and opening space that can be attacked. But sometimes a war isn't about feints and pincer movements, it's about stabbing a dude in the neck." He pointed to the swimming pool thing. "Duels. Winning your duels. Striker versus defender. Winger versus full-back." I understood the layout now. He would get someone to dribble the ball from left to right, while a defender tried to stop them. Then presumably the same from right to left. Possibly, once you finished, you'd slot into the queue at the other lane, and it would be a constant whirlwind of dribbles and lost balls. Jackie continued. "Max had two defenders in the last game who were winning all their duels. They were crushing it. He *still* tweaked them so they'd support each other more. Yeah, good, I get it. It's not wrong. There was a wider point to be made about teamwork. But I would have left them alone. You don't need fancy tactics if all your players are winning all their duels. Ziggy, go on the left. Kisi, go on the right. Ziggy, you know what to do. Go."

In the two weeks since I'd seen him play, Ziggy had only added a point in acceleration and his CA had edged up to eleven. His improvement was slowing. Still, he was my only pro client.

"Stay away from his ankles!" I called out. Kisi nodded without taking her eyes off the ball. Now that she was playing, I saw her profile too. After a few sessions at City, her CA had increased to 3. Still a lot of catching up to do, but I had no doubt she'd do it.

Ziggy ran towards her, dropped his shoulder one way and tried to dribble the other. Kisi kicked the ball away then retracted her foot so she wouldn't touch him. Pretty good defence for an attacking player!

Jackie clapped. "Great, Kisi! That's good. Right. Everyone else. Take a side." The players got in position. Jackie tweaked the numbers so that the duels would never be against the same person twice in a row.

The drill went on for five minutes before Jackie blew his whistle. While everyone watched, he turned to me. "What do you think, Max?"

I shrugged. No attribute was turning green, though it made sense that this drill could improve someone's dribbling and maybe the defender's tackling. Overall, it did seem like . . . not a waste of time exactly. But something I'd want my players to do once a month or something like that. The daily focus should be on formations, passing, technique. Tactics and skills. That was the way. "Honestly?"

"Honestly."

"I'm not a big fan. If I was fit, I'd be shit at this. In a match situation, I'd have passing options to the left and right, and the goal would be behind the defender. So I could fake a pass or fake a shot and do a nutmeg or a flick. Or I could actually pass. Do a 1-2 and get past the defender with no risk."

Jackie nodded. "Max, you're unusually aware of what's around you. You're unusually good at feints and dummies. You're unusually likely to make the right decision."

I stole a line. "I do not feel seduced Jackie. If you want to flirt with me, stop calling me unusual."

"If you're going to manage a team, you have to understand that most players can't do what you can. Can't see what you see. And for us plebs, Max, most of the game is about duels. Rolling your sleeves up, fixing bayonets, gritting your teeth. Yeah? You don't like Ian Evans and managers like him. But what they're good at is getting the team worked up before the game so they come out and win their duels. Same at half-time. Bit of praise, bit of hairdryer. Yeah? Come out strong in the second half. Beth, Raffi, go there." The two moved to the spot indicated, and Jackie threw the ball up between them. Raffi jumped and headed it away. "Compete Beth!" Jackie called, and threw it again. Raffi won again. "Duels. If your tactic is to hit long balls to

Beth, Raffi's going to piss on your chips." He looked at the ball. "We're doing less drills like that because of the new head impact guidelines. And we can't do some of the tackling drills on this hard surface. But if I was the manager of the Met Heads, I'd want to train skills fifty percent and duels fifty percent. So Max. Shall we continue with this? Or do you want to switch to skills?"

I bit my thumbnail. I wasn't sure I shared Jackie's gritty vision of football—being honest, I didn't *want* to believe he was right—but it would have been moronic to assume I knew better than an actual ex-pro. I jabbed my thumb towards the cones. "More duels, please. But guys. You can't just amble up to the defender and then decide what to do. Decide what you're going to do, then DO it. Be decisive."

Jackie grinned. "So he's been paying attention after all."

I swung myself closer, suddenly excited. "But I don't like this drill. This scenario barely happens in a game. Have the attacker and defender stand close to each other, facing the same way. Someone pass to the attacker, and see if they can get round the defender. Like receiving the ball from a throw-in. Yeah?"

Jackie gave me one of those looks. "Yes, Max. That's coming. We don't start with the hardest drill, do we? We work up to it."

It wasn't a contest between Jackie and I to see who was the better coach; I knew the answer to that one. I took a step back and spread my crutches. "Yes, coach." I looked at the players. The level of motivation seemed pretty high. There didn't seem to be a reason not to increase it though. "Anyone who beats Raffi in a duel gets to slap me in the face." Beth swapped places so that she'd be in the same line as him. Who said I don't know how to talk to women?

Jackie blew his whistle and the duelling resumed.

When I was no longer the centre of attention, my smile faded into nothingness. I stared from the side of the hall, absentmindedly noting a couple of attributes turning green, and wondered why Jackie had done everything that he had done, and why he had chosen to end with this.

Most of the adults planned a quick visit to the pub. You know, to support the local economy. I wondered what Ziggy would order and who'd be the person plying me with drinks to get me to stay. Not Beth. She said she had to rush home and finish her coursework.

Kisi and her mother came to say goodbye.

"Mr. Best," said Kisi. "Thanks for this. It was fun. Mr. Reaper is excellent. One principle but lots of variety. It truly is a masterclass. And of course we get to watch you duel with him, so that's even more fun."

What did she mean by that? "You're welcome."

"Yes. Well. Er . . ." She scratched her elbow. "I wanted to say one other thing. Mum says it isn't my place but . . ." Kisi looked up at her mother, "But also she agrees with me." She took a deep breath. "Don't give up on James."

"What do you mean?"

"I was telling him about my first training sesh with City."

"Session," said her mother.

"And his eyes were big as saucers. And the next one, he found some excuse to take me, and he watched. He doesn't experience human emotions like envy, as you know, but . . ."

"Do not tease your brother," said Mrs. Yalley.

"I get it," I said. I'd only seen the City campus in photos, but I could imagine how overwhelmingly cool it would be in person.

"And it wasn't just the facilities," said Kisi. "Everyone was so friendly. Of course, it's competitive and no one wants me to take their spot in the team. But they're nice too and peppered James with questions. What position do you play? Have you had a trial? Are you better than your sister? Coach Sandra offered him a Man City hoodie, and he was quite startled and said 'no thanks,' but I know he regrets it." She took another breath. "I think if you asked him again he would at least . . . try. Do you know what I mean?"

Of course I did. She was describing what I knew I should have done. Take him to a stadium, bring him onto the pitch, let him meet a sexy physio if the club had one, then enter the home team's dressing room where a shirt would be hanging up with his name on it. He might have ummed and aaahed, but once he started daydreaming about it, he would have been helpless to resist.

"All right," I said slowly. "Let me think about what to do. In the meantime, can you get him to take you to City a few more times?"

Her eyes shone. "I'll try!" Then doubt set in. "Like how?"

"Say you don't always understand the tactical instructions, and can he come to explain them to you. Say there's one girl you can't beat in the duels, and can he help you find her weakness. Say you're comfortable playing seven-a-side because of Mr. Best and Mr. Reaper, but you are a bit lost when it comes to eleven-a-side, and can he maybe stand by the pitch and give you some extra help."

Kisi smiled. "Max, you're evil!" She looked at her mother. "In a good way."

Mrs. Yalley looked worried. "I do not know about this. We can discuss it on the bus. Mr. Best, please do not lead my daughter astray."

"Okay," I said. "I promise. Starting . . . now."

66

CELEBRATIONS

Thursday was fine. My ankle was much better, and the black eye was no longer sore when I touched it. I celebrated by eating my last Hobnobs. There would be no more treats until I had sent my five hundred pounds off to the FA. Strict frugality.

I went to work and in the gaps between calls thought about my options. Earning money via scouting was a useful side hustle, but there were only twenty-four clubs in Chester's division so, if Inga was clever and optimised my schedule, potentially only twelve matches I'd be paid to attend. Twelve matches could cover every team in the league. Of course, if one of the other team's managers was sacked, Chester might want me to go again and see what the new guy's default tactic was. And maybe they'd want me to do it all again next season. But still, this was not life-changing money we were talking about.

Then there was the loss of Jackie. The loss of my career's easy mode. There was always that football jobs website, I supposed, but I was coming round to the idea that my real backup plan was becoming a player. Jackie thought I was good enough to be a pro, so I guessed a lot of other football insiders would too. When I was healed, I could do a trial and maybe get a basic contract like Ziggy's. Three fifty a week would let me quit my job and give me tons of time off to do scouting and agenting and whatnot. And, of course, once I had my feet in some club's door, I'd be able to sniff out all kinds of opportunities to guest manage a youth team or the reserves or whatever. The problem would be finding a lower division team that didn't play in a defensive style that would bore me to death. The only thing worse than watching a defensive team, for me, would be playing in one. On that note, playing for Chester was out of the question, not only because I'd pissed off half the people I'd met there, but also because Ian Evans was a tactical dinosaur who seemed to think football was frozen in 1988.

And then there was James Yalley. Youngster. The walking lottery ticket. I wasn't sure how to approach him. And that's what I was thinking about when I took my last call of the day. It was from a lovely older guy called Asuquo Uche. Based on the names of footballers, I could guess his background. I fixed his problem in about eight seconds and then said, "Is your name Nigerian?" It was. "This might sound crazy, but are you a Christian?" He was. "What do you think about sportspeople who don't compete on Sundays?"

"Ah!" he said, in that deep, resonant voice a lot of African guys have. "That is a tremendous question! As it happens, I have given the matter a lot of thought. You see, back when I was young . . ."

Then it was off to Platt Lane for some low-level grinding and one more kebab to put on my tab at Emre's. I warned him there might be a few more before I paid him back, but I theoretically had some new income streams going. He was fascinated to hear about my latest adventures but skeptical that he'd see my money in the timeframes I was suggesting. Then he switched into complaints mode, directing his ire towards some council official who kept asking for the same paperwork again and again. I let it wash over me; it was always nice to have conversations that weren't about football. To hear about the real world. In small doses anyway.

As for the actual grinding, it only took forty-five minutes to get up to 200 XP. I instantly bought 4-3-3, knowing it would likely be the last formation I would buy for a long time. I now had 4-4-2, 4-4-2 diamond, and 4-3-3. Nice! Next in the shop was 4-5-1, retailing for 400 XP.

But it was time now to buy God Save the King. I re-read the sales blurb:

Effects: Nominate a "King" and channel one of his notable attributes into a player of your choosing. One use per season.

Kings: John Charles (STR; HD). Carlos Valderrama (FL; CRE). Michel Platini (PAS; SET). Denis Law (OFF; FIN).

I took a few minutes to think through what I was doing. To be honest, I'd been a bit shocked to see Ziggy still on such a low current ability. With CA 11, he'd be by far the worst player on the pitch this Saturday, and having an extra point in finishing seemed unlikely to make any difference. Giving the same point to a premium player, like, just hypothetically you understand, James Yalley, would be much more impactful. Like, *adding a million pounds to his future transfer value* kind of impactful.

But I decided to stick to the plan. I bought the God Save the King perk and heard a little celebratory blast of trumpets. The curse had gone multimedia! Nothing seemed to change in my interface. My XP balance was plus three. If it hadn't been for the sound effect, I would have assumed the purchase had failed. Wrong PIN number! Try again later!

It took me a minute, but I found that something *had* changed. I opened Ziggy's player profile and there was a little up arrow button there. I went into Cristiano Ronaldo's profile, and the button was also there. It seemed I'd be able to give the improvement point to any player I'd ever scouted! Incredible and sort of useless. I was only ever going to use it on my personal clients. So I went back to Ziggy, clicked the icon, and chose FIN from the list. And that was it. His finishing turned green and now read: seventeen.

There wasn't even another trumpet sound effect.

So it was sort of underwhelming but also sort of . . . incredibly thrilling? Whether it was a good decision or not, I'd reshaped the universe with the power of a single thought. Roar!

But why wasn't I on minus 2997 XP?

I decided to stay and watch the last half an hour of this game and then go home and rest. But when the final whistle went, and I should have had about 30 more XP, I found that I'd only picked up twenty-five. It was always hard to tell exactly how many minutes I'd really paid attention to. To try to get some clarity, I watched the first half of the next match. It was quite good in terms of being end-to-end, lots of shots, some good goals and good saves. At half-time, which meant forty minutes, I'd earned 36 XP.

So that cleared that up. God Save the King was docking my pay to the tune of ten percent. Much better than having to work off the entire debt just to get to zero. It meant I could keep grinding and keep improving myself. A very motivational discovery!

XP balance: 64

On Friday evening, I managed the Met Heads for the last time, picking up ninety XP. The atmosphere was a bit flat. No one celebrated their goals. The scorers just walked back to our half so the game could continue. We were winning 7–0 until the last minute, when Beth made a mistake. Jackie might say she lost a duel. The other team scored, and there was a strange, subdued kind of atmosphere. One you don't normally get after a 7–1 victory that takes you three points clear at the top of the table. I couldn't explain it then, and I still can't.

I had stopped getting "games won in a row" achievements when I was sacked by Mike Dean. I supposed this victory would reset the counter back to one. The achievements side of the curse still didn't motivate me. I was just curious how it worked. There usually seemed to be a methodology behind everything it did, but sometimes I wondered if it didn't simply make things up as it went.

Anyway, the Met Heads went to have their showers, and I stayed in the hall watching the next match. It was quite boring and I got distracted, but I picked up 30 XP. It was odd. I'd expected the ladies to come and say goodbye or stay with me to watch Man City later. The Met Heads still had a chance to win the league after all. But no. They all left through the other door without saying goodbye. Maybe they thought that because I wasn't in the reception, I'd already gone. Crossed wires. Or maybe they'd all thought Wednesday night's pub had been the end-of-season party.

But it was just . . . not a very satisfying way for that chapter of my life to end. This is why we have weddings and funerals. People need rituals. Even antisocial people.

But then City arrived, and my mood lifted all the way up. (Wow. Never thought I'd say *that*.) There was Kisi! Decked out in that sickening laser blue. Some of her teammates waved at me too. I suppose I was a minor celebrity in their world. I was the mad scientist who concocted strategies and bashed his head against the sink while daydreaming about a time-travelling goalkeeper. I stayed on the far side, away from Coach Sandra. I needed to practise shutting my gob. Staying in my lane. Being a well-behaved boy. Keeping my thoughts inside my skull for more than three minutes at a time.

To my surprise, James turned up and came to sit next to me. He wanted to talk about football, but every time, I changed the subject. My reasoning is hard to put into words. It was a bit like flirting. One way to build sexual tension is by not talking about sex. Some comedians build tension by not delivering the punchline. Anyway, I had this instinct that if I refused to talk about football with James, he'd only become more interested in it. He'd have to find that release somewhere else. For example, by becoming a player. Far-fetched? Maybe. But going head-on hadn't worked.

We spent most of the match talking about movies until Kisi—the team's worst player by CA—came on for ten minutes at the end. Every player plays every game! I celebrated this milestone by putting two hands on James's arm and shaking him like he was a coconut tree. He seemed to enjoy it.

City won the league on goal difference. Sandra did a little presentation ceremony, which was incredibly poorly attended. I counted two spectators. That said, if Jackie was right about me, and I was right about James, then 100% of the people applauding Meghan as she lifted the trophy were fantastic footballers.

Kisi got a little medal for her part in winning the league. She was a bit embarrassed by it, since she'd only played ten minutes of the campaign. If it had been me, I would have played it cool too but then secretly looked at it every day.

I noticed that half of the girls didn't collect their medals. Kisi noticed too and asked Meghan if she'd made a mistake in taking hers. Meghan looked confused, but then said, "Oh, I don't bother taking them anymore. I've got hundreds."

"Oh," said Kisi. "This is my first."

So Meghan made *everyone* get their medals, and they held them up for a team photo, and something about Kisi's joy infected the others. They were no longer playing it cool but smiling like it was the first medal *they'd* ever won, too.

I only said one thing to Coach Sandra that day. "Meghan," I said, "is pure fucking class."

On Saturday morning, I popped into the care home to see my mum and take Solly for a quick walk. Very quick—with the crutches it was awful, and I didn't want to ruin my recovery by ditching them. I like to think it's the thought that counts, but Solly showed a rare flash of bad temper when I announced that we had to turn back before we'd even made it to the park.

Then there were a few hours of absolute torture: waiting for the big game with no way to influence it. As a manager, even as a player, you have the chance to sort it out. Turn the tide. Sure, be the hero, if that's your bag. As a guy's unofficial agent, you're no more involved than a passing stork looking down on the stadium.

Eventually, I made my way to Broadhurst Park and pottered around outside for a while. I saw a betting shop (known as a "bookie" in the UK) and called Ziggy. He didn't pick up. I called Jackie. He did.

"Jackie. Is Ziggy starting?"

"You'll find out soon enough, Maxy boy."

"Is Ziggy starting, yes or no?"

He sighed. "Yes. Sandro isn't quite fit. We're hoping he can do the second half. The last thirty minutes. So your boy's going to get an hour under his belt. Happy now?"

"Delirious."

There were all sorts of rules for players and managers regarding betting, but I wasn't either. I didn't even have an FA Number. I went in and tried to place a bet on Ziggy to score against Marske United. This turned into quite the sitcom moment, as the lady at the counter had to get the manager, and I had to explain that Ziggy was Barrett Graves, and he was a rando who'd been given a short-term contract, and he was shit but I still wanted to place a bet on him. I also had to explain that Marske United was a real football team, and this wasn't a prank.

The manager made me repeat things a million times while he typed, one-fingered, on his stupid 1983 Amstrad all-in-one computer-and-greenscreen-monitor. At one point he asked me what squad number Ziggy was, and I was getting annoyed and said, "how should I know?" and then he said, "oh never mind I've got him." Because that was the moment the team sheets had been uploaded to his system, and Ziggy was there. Barrett 'Ziggy' Graves, it said. Shirt number thirty-three.

Well, that put me in an amazing mood, I can tell you.

The guy offered me odds of fifteen to one, which I thought was pretty feeble given that Ziggy had CA 11. But I couldn't exactly say that to the dude. So I put twenty quid on, then got a bit carried away and changed it to thirty. If Ziggy scored, I'd get four hundred and fifty pounds in winnings, plus my thirty quid back. Almost enough to pay for my agent licence!

I had to be realistic though and assume he wouldn't score. He was, for now, still pretty awful.

Betting slip safely tucked away, I announced myself at reception and was ushered into the place behind the dugout. I don't think there's a proper name for it. I mean the dugout overspill where the physios and doctors and some of the injured players hang out.

Some of the FC United players recognised my face, but there were still a lot of odd looks sent my way as they filled the dugout and the spillover. There was an empty seat next to me. I spent a couple of minutes wondering who in the world I'd want to be there. Livia? Emma? Kylie Minogue? I settled on Henri Lyons; he'd be able to analyse Ziggy's performance in minute detail. Then I decided I was happier alone. I could go internal. Let my mind wander around all aspects of the experience. The fans, the coaches, the players, whatever.

Once again, I was on my best behaviour. Maybe Jackie breaking up with me had been a good thing after all. I felt a lot less powerful without him in my corner. A lot more like a normal person. So although I had a LOT of thoughts when I saw how the two teams were lining up, I kept my gob shut, once again, like a champion.

Marske United were a team of very physical, strong lads, set up in a very central 5-3-2 formation. Neil had FC United playing an expansive 4-3-3 with a short passing mentality. They got bullied up and down the pitch and couldn't get a foothold in the game. Neil didn't change things even after the team's disastrous start; Marske were 2–0 up after twenty minutes. Ziggy had barely had a kick. His match rating was four out of ten.

He looked lost, dwarfed by three huge, hulking centre-backs.

BARRETT GRAVES		
Born 13.1.1999	(Age 23)	English
Acceleration 4		
		Stamina 4
	Heading 6	Strength 6
		Tackling 3
	Jumping 6	
Bravery 4		Technique 6

	Pace 3	preferred foot R
	Passing 5	
Dribbling 3		
Finishing 17		
CA 11	PA 58	
Striker		

The only positive was that FC United had taken my idea on board. Ziggy was wearing shirt number thirty-three, but the number wasn't in the normal font; it was custom-made, based on a sketch I'd sent to the kit man. The lines of the threes were straight and broken, like zigzags. Ziggy! It was a bit twee, a bit whimsical, but it was unique.

As an agent, I was supposed to do more than put players in the right clubs. I was also supposed to get them boot deals and sponsorships. That was way in the future for Ziggy, but why not get started now? Hashtag building the brand, or whatever.

Of course, if he continued to stink the place up, he wouldn't need a marketing gimmick. He'd need a new club.

I sighed and settled back into my seat. Patience, Max. This was going to happen with every client I found on the street. Raffi was CA 3. James Yalley was CA 2. It'd be months of training merely to get them up to tier seven standards. There would be a lot of frustrating days like these. A lot.

The ball was booted forwards and Ziggy had the chance to chase it. The defender was much faster though, and Ziggy was left with his hands behind his head, gasping for air.

Okay, so maybe this was going to be especially frustrating . . .

At half-time I bought a pie with mushy peas, but I wasn't allowed to bring it back into the spillover. So I ate in the concourse, listening to the fans grumble about the performance and the rando playing as striker. Mancunians are pretty creative when it comes to insults, and I heard at least ten I'd never heard before, mostly aimed at Ziggy.

There was one dissenting voice. "He fucking tries, at least, though. Dunee?" (That last word is "doesn't he," by the way.)

"That's true. Shame he's shit."

In the fifty-fifth minute, Marske scored again. United were losing 3–0. At home. To a team I'd never heard of before. I thought about the corkboard in my kitchen. It had out-of-date league tables from every division. I must have seen the name Marske hundreds of times. But it had just never clicked. Marske Marske Marske. It just didn't sound like *anything*, except maybe a Norwegian shipping company. And to think that this unknown team was crushing FC United, and my client was taking the brunt of the blame. I was powerless to do anything about it.

After sixty minutes, I felt eyes on me, and noticed that Neil, Jackie, and the gang were giving me looks. Were they blaming me for this? Ziggy was better than *nothing*, wasn't he? Jackie had told me that Sandro was going to play for the last half hour. Maybe they'd decided not to rush him back from his injury since the game was already lost.

At sixty-five minutes, when United still hadn't had a shot or even a meaningful attack, the home fans started to leave. And there was another flurry of looks in my direction. A reluctant Jackie was sent to talk to me.

Now what the fuck was this all about? I'd been on my best behaviour! I hadn't spoken out loud since the bookies! Except to order a pie. I tensed.

"Max," said Jackie, leaning close.

"Awight?"

"Do you er . . . do you have any ideas? Of what we could do?"

I blinked. "Tommy Tactics stuff?"

"Yes."

"Well, yeah, sure, but why? I thought Neil didn't . . ."

"Not now, Max. Just tell me."

I was a bit annoyed, to be honest. Neil had been all "stick your tactics up your arse," and now he wanted help getting out of this jam.

I'd like to say I did it for Ziggy. But I did it for me. I loved showing off. "Play 4-5-1. Attacking full-backs. Get overloads on both flanks. Wingers to the bylines, do cut backs for Ziggy. Anyone attacks down the middle, you fine them a week's wages. Except Gribbin. Put him in the centre of the five let him do what he wants."

Jackie did a weird thing with his lips. A sort of exaggerated show of patience. "We don't train 4-5-1, Max."

"Fine. 4-4-2 with Gribbin as second striker. But give him a free role. Playmaker."

"That's your plan is it? 4-4-2?" He seemed close to laughing at me.

Which yeah, wound me up. My neck started to burn. "Yes, mate. It is." He turned. I added, "And maybe some of your lads could try winning some duels. Yeah?"

His grin turned into a snarl, and he crashed back into his seat and began gesticulating wildly, telling Neil what a twat I was etc., etc.

United kept doing what they were doing. Marske stopped an attack like they were stubbing out a cigarette, then broke through the middle of the pitch and ended up hitting the crossbar. The United fans started booing.

A flurry of activity from the United bench, and I dipped into the tactics screen. They'd switched to 4-4-2 (with attacking full-backs), and Gribbin was set to playmaker. Finally!

The pattern of the match changed so quickly, it was almost hilarious. United began storming up both sides of the pitch and had overloads on every attack. Instead of booting high balls for Ziggy to compete for, they started getting to the goal line and cutting the ball back for him to try to redirect into the net. The first time this happened, Ziggy couldn't get a shot away, so he turned back and laid it off for the oncoming Gribbin. His shot smacked into the post.

United! United!

Finally, something for the fans to respond to.

Marske's manager was pretty bright. He tweaked his tactics, switching from 5-3-2 to 5-4-1. Very defensive! I called out to Jackie, who came over. A bit faster this time. Strange. I wonder why? (LOL.) "They've switched to 5-4-1. Just trying to hold out. No risks. He got lucky his plan paid off so well, but he knows you've got the better players."

Jackie checked what I was saying. It was pretty obvious; there was only one Marske guy within a billion miles of the United half. "So we don't need four at the back. What do you suggest?"

I shrugged. "You don't practise 4-5-1. Do you practise 1-4-5?" I was telling him to throw men forward. Go for it. Kamikaze.

"That one didn't come up when I did my coaching badges, no Max." He went back to the dugout.

Over the next ten minutes, Neil tweaked his formation one player at a time. It was like he couldn't believe the evidence of his own eyes and that Marske really had turtled up. By the end of the match, United were attacking nonstop, and what remained of the crowd were appreciative of their effort. But there were only a few minutes left. Even if United scored a goal, it would be too late to launch a recovery. And once Marske launched a counterattack, Neil's conservatism kicked in. Losing 3-0 was better than losing 4-0. He dragged a couple of players back to more defensive positions, and the match slowly petered out.

By the ninety-second minute, about seventy percent of the home fans had left. So they missed the big moment.

Gribbin was still set as playmaker, and his match rating had increased by two points. He was now United's outstanding player on the day with seven out of ten. With nothing to lose, and with plenty of defenders behind him, he went on a mazy dribble that caused chaos in Marske's back lines. And then . . .

Gribbin passes it out to Wooley.

Wooley takes a touch and looks up. He fires a low cross towards the near post.

The goalkeeper throws himself at the ball.

It rebounds into the path of Ziggy.

And it's in!

GOOOOOOAAAAAAAALLLLLLLLLLL!!!!!

I couldn't believe what I'd just seen. Ziggy, mate! He'd done it! There was some applause from the dugout and a half-hearted cheer from the few hundred United fans who were left. The overall mood in the stadium can be summed up by the ironic, taunting "aaaah!" noise made by the away fans. Their team conceding a goal somehow *added* to their joy, because the home fans couldn't celebrate it without seeming like even bigger losers.

Then came the most cringeworthy thing I've ever seen.

Ziggy went nuts.

There's a famous goal celebration from the 1982 World Cup. Marco Tardelli scored for Italy, and I'll let sports writer Doug McIntyre describe what happened next:

With tears of joy rolling down his cheeks, Tardelli ran across the field shaking his head from side to side in disbelief, repeatedly yelling "goal" as if to convince himself that the feat he had just accomplished actually happened. The raw emotion of the moment was visceral, and it resonated with fans across the globe—which is why it remains the most unforgettable World Cup goal celebration of all time.

Ziggy did pretty much the same, but instead of scoring the winner in the World Cup final, he had scored a meaningless consolation goal in a crushing defeat. Also, instead of tears streaming down his face, he did a sort of tumbling roll as his legs gave way underneath him. Part of the celebration involved him pushing himself forwards on his knees for five yards until he remembered how to walk, and he ended the celebration by showing his bicep to the main stand and shouting "come on!" on repeat.

The guy who did the PA announcements said, in a flat voice, "FC United's goal scored by number thirty-three, Ziggy."

There were peals of laughter from the away end.

Before Marske could restart the match, the referee blew the whistle for full-time. Ziggy had scored with the last kick of the game. I prayed to God that no one had filmed his celebration. He left the pitch happier than any player from the winning team. Possibly happier than Marco Tardelli.

Oh, Ziggy. Mate. You're not Italian. You can't act like that.

I wondered what would hurt his career more: his four out of ten performance or his celebration.

67

NEXT STOP VEGAS

I wasn't allowed into the changing rooms after the match and wouldn't have wanted to be there. So I texted Ziggy a string of ball emojis followed by a string of goal! emojis.

Then I went to the bookies to collect my winnings.

While I was in the queue, I saw that Chester had drawn 1–1. Against Oldham, weirdly. The club with the agent-hating gammons. Small world! Chester hadn't won in a while. It seemed that hiring the safe, experienced manager wasn't really working for them. Part of me was happy they were doing badly. Fuck 'em.

I showed the lady my betting slip: Ziggy to score, fifteen to one. She instantly called for the manager who told me I wasn't going to get my *moneh*. While I grew increasingly apoplectic, he explained that the goal *had* initially been awarded to Ziggy but had since been reviewed and changed to an own goal (one scored by a player against his own team).

I was about to launch into a rant about the betting industry being corrupt and evil and predatory and that I would make sure the world knew they were ripping me off, but the guy was clearly just a harmless dude doing his job to the best of his ability. With a monumental effort, I bottled my fury and calmly explained that I had SEEN the goal with my very eyes.

As the manager repeated everything he'd already said with equal patience (*I could learn a few lessons from this guy*, the rational part of my brain said), I reviewed my own words. I'd SEEN the goal with my eyes . . . but that was the whole point of the curse, wasn't it? It wasn't about what I saw and what I thought I saw. It was about what was REAL. What was TRUE.

So I opened Ziggy's player profile and, of course, I had the data from his previous years (blank, in his case), but not *this* year. I'd have to buy a perk for that. I also didn't seem to have a way to see the match stats and read the commentaries once a game was over. Again, I was sure that would be available to buy eventually.

I hadn't checked the match overview screen in the seconds between the goal and the final whistle. It would have said "Ziggy 90+3" or "OG 90+3." But I *had* seen the match commentary. What had it said? Something like: "Ziggy shoots. And it's in." That seemed conclusive. But . . . *and it's in* could mean a lot of things. There was a potential gap there. Ziggy shoots, it hits the defender, and it bounces in. If Ziggy's shot was going wide and only went in because of the deflection, that would count as an own goal.

Going through that thought process calmed me.

I said, "Who decides if it's Ziggy's goal or an own goal?"

"An independent panel," said the bookie. "Not connected to any betting firm, mind you. Clubs use the same data source. Otherwise, every club would have its own records, and it would be chaos. No sir, I assure you. The experts are quite fastidious. You'll see when you see the replays."

"Can I have the slip back, please?" He gave it to me. "If I find a clip that proves my dude scored that goal, can I come back and discuss it with you?"

"Of course sir!"

I was totally chill now. The thought that the guy was trying to rip me off was gone. He was just following a process. I smiled at him. "I'm going to find it was an own goal, aren't I?"

He nodded. Pleased that I'd calmed so quickly. "The panel don't make mistakes. I understand that it's frustrating, but . . ." He spread his arms as if to say, "what can you do?"

Well, shit. I really thought I'd be walking out of there with 480 pounds, cash.

Instead, I was down thirty.

Next stop: Vegas.

Not.

By the time I got home, I had reframed my loss. If I considered that I'd gotten a free ticket to watch the game and picked up 82 XP, then the bet had been made with house money. Hadn't *really* cost me anything.

Not really. But I wouldn't gamble again until I had money to spare, by which time gambling would be pointless.

I drank a cup of tea while going through all the other 3 p.m. results. Darlington had won. Henri was an unused sub. Alfreton, who I'd just scouted for Chester, lost 2–1 at home. I checked the Premier League scores and found I couldn't give two shits about any of it. There were a couple of interesting top-flight games scheduled for the following day (Man United versus Newcastle; Liverpool versus Man City), but again, I wasn't really too bothered about the megaclubs. I was in the world of Chester, FC United, Oldham, and Darlington these days.

While I waited for someone to upload the video mocking Ziggy's celebration—which hopefully would include footage of his goal—I caught up on some of the football documentaries and YouTube videos I'd started.

As far as I could tell, by the time I fell asleep no one had posted the Ziggy incident to Reddit or Twitter. Maybe it wasn't as cringeworthy as I'd thought.

On Sunday morning, I felt nostalgic for the Hough End playing fields, and went to watch some games. I picked up 60 XP and then went to take Solly for a walk. If I went slowly, I could manage without the crutches.

I took a picture of me keeping my promise and sent it to Raffi. "Promise kept, green tick emoji. Next: your trial. Working on it!"

His reply was a thumbs up. Not big on typing complete sentences that guy.

While Solly scampered around the park, I thought about my next steps. How to get replacement income so I could quit my job. I told myself that whichever aspect of football got me out of the call centre first would become my focus, whether that meant scouting, being an agent, playing, or managing.

So what could I do to accelerate that program?

Scouting.

I could show my scouting reports to my contact at Oldham and ask if they'd hire me to do the same. Then keep trying other clubs until I found a taker. If I found another tier six club, I could sell them the reports I made for Chester. Double dip! In theory I could sell all my reports to every team in that division, but that seemed unrealistic to say the least.

Agenting.

I hadn't discovered any new players recently, but I hadn't really been going to new places. If I "seduced" Henri Lyons and got Raffi a contract—after getting my licence, of course—I could replace maybe half of my current income. (I assumed Henri was on good money. Maybe a thousand a week?) So a big push to find some new talent, while also grinding for XP? Sure. That'd work. James Yalley? I didn't want to think about it. If anything ever happened with him, that would be a bonus. I would never again let him become the basis for any planning.

Ziggy's debut was a shot in the arm for my career as an agent, both for convincing players to trust me and for clubs hoping to get free players that could end up in their first team. His wild celebration . . . *probably* helped me out here. Yes, it was funny, but which guy playing amateur five-a-side wouldn't go weak at the knees at the thought that it could be *him* in the next video?

Playing.

Becoming a player would mean networking. Introducing myself to some clubs other than Chester and FC United. Somehow, it felt harder to pick up the phone and get a trial for myself than for a client. Probably because I didn't really believe in Max Best the player the way I did with Ziggy or Raffi. Still, it was an option. A club could sign me right away, whereas for most players they'd have to wait till January, so if I found a team like FC United who had a lot of injuries, I could get going pretty fast. I'd just have to work my notice period at the call centre. Was it one month or two? I'd have to check. There were ways to get fired fast, if it came to it.

There was just this nagging doubt. Did I *want* to be a player? With my unique way of Pissing Everyone Off I felt like I'd spend most of my playing career being kicked to bits. Did I really want to spend the rest of my life taking cortisone injections just to be able to limp to my car? Was it *that* unbearable to work in a call centre for a few more months? The phrase "if you can't beat them, join them" sprung to mind. I could be the flair player for an aggressive team. Be their set piece taker. Their tricky number seven. Having ten beefy boys as my bouncers would insulate me from the real rough stuff. You kick me in the shin, my mate will knock two of your teeth out. Yeah, not bad. But I tried to imagine myself playing in midfield for Marske United. It didn't really resonate my crystals, if you know what I mean.

Managing.

Er . . . no. For money? No. *Your reputation in the entire universe: unknown.* I'd have to do one of the other things for a while first. Reputation first, manager second. How could it be different?

So that was my outlook and it was sort of . . . not bleak, exactly, but not fun and exciting either. The next few months would be a slog. What I wanted was a sort of catalyst, a way to roll a double six and skip half the steps. I only needed three hundred and fifty pounds a week, for Christ's sake! I wasn't asking for the moon on a stick.

Back in the real world, the leash was being yanked pretty hard. Solly was straining at it so he could go and sniff some other dog. A little white one with black patches and pointy ears. I wandered in that direction and glanced at the other dog's owner. Surprise, surprise, it was a foxy woman who was absolutely delighted that her dog had brought me into her life. We had eye sex, made small talk, and the contrast between spending time with this woman and thinking about the upcoming months of grinding was so extreme that I felt about seventy-five percent of my brain being activated. The part that dealt with flirting.

Just as I was getting cheeky, my phone rang, which was probably fortunate because Chester's head physio had told me not to have sex for a month. The call stopped me feeling downbeat, that's for sure.

It was Mike Dean. He wanted to meet as soon as poss. Could I get to Chester right away?

I couldn't believe my ears. Meet? Why? Stupidly, I didn't even think to ask. "I'm still on crutches," I lied. "You'll have to come here."

"I can't today," he said, and I wondered if maybe I should have been a bit more eager. But he continued. "Tomorrow? What time?"

"You're going to come to Manchester?" I said, dumbstruck.

"It's not that far, Max!" he laughed. He was in a great mood for someone whose team was dropping into the relegation zone.

"I have to work all day," I said. "Any time after five. We can meet in town."

"What's town? Town? What's town?"

"Manchester city centre. We can have a meal. Or we can go and watch some five-a-side. It depends what you want."

"A meal? Oh. Yes, let's do that. Curry! What's that place with the famous curries?"

"The curry mile? Yeah, if you want a curry that's the spot. So then I'll go home and get changed. How about 7 p.m.? I'll text you a place with good parking."

"Great. Bye."

Weird. I took the foxy woman's number because why not. I sat with my mum and Anna in the care home, just the three of us (plus a psychic dog) in one room doing different things. Anna said I should turn up the sound on my laptop, because it was something different, and they listened to me watch Liverpool beat Man City 1–0. It was a game of incredibly high quality and fine margins, but I felt totally disembodied. The Liverpool fans have a slightly undeserved reputation for being noisy and intense, but fuck, they were noisy and intense. It just didn't press any of my buttons.

Instead, I thought about Mike Dean. Chester Zoo. Future, Sevenoaks, teamwork. The fourteen-year-old whose player profile I had renamed "Flappy Bird." The Bulldog Brothers, Soccer Milf, Spectrum, and the Chester Knights. Johnny Winger! Oh, Johnny Winger. Thinking about him made me annoyed at myself for being glad Chester's first team were struggling. And yeah, I thought about Livia a bit. So sue me. Okay, I thought about Livia more than a bit, and only stopped when Solly looked up at me and went "huh?" Stay out of my daydreams, you psychic mutt!

Mike Dean, then.

What could he want?

68

MAXY NO-THUMBS

I was early. I'd brought the crutches, because I'd told Mike Dean that I was still using them. And I was, sometimes. But at about 10 a.m. I'd gotten a notification that Chester FC had sent me one hundred and seventy pounds: sixty for the petrol, ten for a pie, and one hundred for my scouting report. And that had reduced what remained of my pain by approximately eighty percent.

Alchemy! For the first time, I'd turned football into CASH.

I could have danced, yo!

Fine. I danced *a bit*. Relax. No one was watching.

MD MD arrived, parked, and we did some small talk and whatnot. The curry place wasn't busy, but we weren't alone. Next to us was a group of three older women. Older than me, you understand. Younger than MD. A blonde, a brunette, and a ginge (AKA a ginger). He seemed very happy to see them, but they barely looked at us.

Okay, fine. Jesus. They barely looked at *him*. With me, they came for the crutches and stayed for the fireplace snuggles in an Irish cottage, or whatever they thought my default move was. I tried to snub them, but they kept shooting hopeful glances my way.

Our waiter was wearing a crisp white shirt and was polite and professional but had the air of someone who didn't want to be helping out in the family business. Mike ordered chilli chicken and I had chicken korma. Pretty basic, but that's what I like.

Did I mention the small talk? There was a bit more of that. Let's skip to the important bits. Which was, ah, most of it.

Mike. Serious face. Dabbing a napkin against his lips. "Max, I just wanted to clear up any misunderstanding about last weekend."

I held up a hand. "Mike. Let me stop you right there. I'm here and you're here, so neither of us is particularly grumpy about it. Right? But let's not call it a misunderstanding. We both know what happened. You didn't like what I was doing, and you fired me. No hard feelings. I wasn't blameless, but I don't think this conversation is going to go well if we start pretending it was something it wasn't."

He tapped his fork against a blob of chicken. "Yeah. Good. Even better. But let's talk about it. No, hold on. Let me think." He speared a chunk and munched on it while he deliberated. Finally, he put his cutlery down and folded his arms. "History. Chester City. Proud old club. Older than most American cities. Run into the ground by its owners. Club folded. Kicked out of the league. Big trauma. Still hurts. We formed a new club. Chester FC. Community owned, community run. I wanted to get involved. I've got experience running pretty big businesses, Max. I ran a division of a pharma company. Huge turnover. Running a football club? It's peanuts, financially. Tiny. But it's such a part of the community. Outsized. Nothing compares. It's a heavy burden. The stress is suffocating. I'm from a business background, Max. And I'm from Chester. My priority, my absolute priority, is that the club survives. Has enough money to survive. Anything else is secondary. You get that, right? You're a United fan, so maybe you don't. But that's what gets me out of bed every morning. Shitty, unglamorous work. Begging for sponsorships. Staring at a balance sheet like it's an oncoming truck. Cold, hard numbers. What I don't know, if I'm being honest, is football. There are times I think I'm learning, but then something will happen and I realise I know bugger all. Times like last weekend when you rolled up. So that's some background. Some context. I was hoping maybe you'd tell me the story from your side?"

"Which bit?"

He shook his head. "Why you took those four players off? Just explain that to me."

I shoved a spoonful of curry in my gob, chewed, swallowed, then told him the whole thing. Without mentioning curses and all that jazz, obvs. It didn't take that long, maybe two minutes. In those two minutes, he chewed twice.

"Okay," he said, when I indicated I was finished. "Okay. So that was the under-fourteens. I saw the Chester Knights. And you're a scout, too. Is this the player you found at five-a-side?" He tapped his phone and showed me footage of Ziggy's wild celebration. Sound blaring, the jeers from the away fans only slightly louder than Ziggy's shouts of "come on!" I glanced at the women at the next table, and they didn't seem too bothered by Mike's rudeness. I confirmed that it was my client in the video, which felt like confessing to a crime. Mike did a cheeky kind of grin that suited him but was all too rare. "Amazing." He took his phone back. I wanted to ask to see the whole clip, but it didn't seem the right moment. Something more important was happening than me winning my bet. "Jackie told me all about it. Jackie told me a lot about you. He said we should sign you before someone else did, and I asked if he'd seen you play, and he said only for ten seconds, and that was enough. Then he called me again and said he'd seen you *really* play, and I should get the red carpet ready. And then he said you were injured, and he wanted to get you checked out, but also he wanted to show you around, and I said sure, my casa is your casa."

"You really trust him, don't you?"

"This is what I'm trying to say, Max. I know fuck all about football. I know a thousand times more than the man on the street, but he knows the square root of fuck all. Someone like me needs someone like Jackie."

"You've got Ian Evans."

"Well," he said, and that signalled a break in the chat.

I got the sense that MD had gotten carried away, and now he was trying to get his thoughts into order. I ate and drank and tried not to be sexy.

"Max. You sent that scouting report in."

"Boston versus Alfreton," I said.

"Yeah. I loved it. I read it three times. Tactical diagrams, player strengths, great. But there was a kind of assumption in your thinking that the reader would be . . . well, would be Ian Evans."

"Yes," I said, with a little frown. Who else?

"A couple of times you added notes, almost like an afterthought. This player makes mistakes, press him. This guy tires—if they have used all their subs, attack down his side. Just offhand recommendations like it was nothing."

I'd almost not included any of that stuff, because it seemed so remedial. It was just to flesh out the word count. Make sure I got a second gig. "Yeah."

"And I got excited. This is what I wanted! And I sent the email round to all the staff. And do you know who was in my office five minutes later wanting to talk about it?"

"Ian Evans, who it was written for," I said, deadpan.

"Terry. The coach of the Knights." The disabled team I'd managed. "He's a huge fan of yours. The kids never shut up about you apparently, and he loves it. He came in, and we had a big chat about it all. I had it out with him. Because I couldn't make head nor tail of what you did that day. The Knights. One minute it was pure chaos and we were losing, the next it was pure chaos and we were winning. So he talked me through it, step by step. And I have to say . . . I don't know, Max. I was pretty skeptical. It seemed impossible. But then he told me he'd gone to watch the under-fourteens, and what you did there was even harder. He said I should talk to Spectrum and find out what steps you'd taken." He sipped his beer as his mood darkened. "Well, I'm sorry to say that Spectrum wasn't as complimentary. He portrayed you as erratic and capricious. And based on what I'd seen myself, it was easy to agree with him. After you left, Tyson went back on the pitch and scored two goals. So . . . that showed you up, right? I asked one of the first-team coaches what he thought of you, and he said the guys had nicknamed you 'Maxy No-Thumbs.'"

I looked at my hands. What was wrong with them?

Mike held his hands up, but pushed his thumbs into his palms. "Because you can only count to eight."

"Oh," I said. "Good gag."

"Yeah," he said, picking up his fork and tapping his meal again. "But this is what I'm trying to get at. Obliquely, I know. Just bear with me. If a load of football people tell me something, I have to listen. The beginning of the end for Chester City was when our old owner installed himself as manager. That was when we started laying the foundations for the Phoenix club. Everyone's got an opinion about football, but there are experts and dilettantes, like with everything. So when five people tell me Max Best is an idiot, I have to pay attention. Sorry to say. But I wasn't born yesterday either. I know there are cliques, and I know people will look after their own fiefdoms and feel threatened by change. In my old company, I had a VP once who came to me and told me he thought his department was obsolete, and I should look into scrapping it. Can you imagine that? The guy was amazing. Not great for his career though, is it? Most people cling onto power for as long as possible." His face lit up, and he picked up his phone again. "Which brings me to this."

He handed me the phone, and I watched a clip from whatever website had all these football snippets. One team had a corner, and they fired it into the penalty area. It was cleared as far as the halfway line. Some clumsy defender was on his own—no one within twenty yards of him—but he took a bad touch, and suddenly he was in full panic mode. He turned to pass the ball back to the goalkeeper, but this blisteringly fast guy on the other team swooped in, took the ball from him, ran the rest of the pitch, and scored.

"Sorry ladies," I said to the table next to us. "He's so excited, he forgot to turn the sound off."

"What's he excited about?" asked the blonde.

"Oh, he's the managing director of a football club," I said, like that explained anything. It got the desired effect, though. They thought that was tremendous, but Mike Dean was stupefied by the attention. Surely he was one of the biggest alphas in Chester?

"And who are *you*?" said the brunette.

"You know after a match, the guy who goes round the stadium picking up crisp packets?" She said yeah. "I'm his assistant."

They laughed. I tried to kick MD but missed. "Buy them a drink," I said from the corner of my mouth.

He took slightly too long, but finally unfroze, smiled at the ladies, apologised for being uncouth, and offered to buy the table a bottle of wine. They said they'd prefer beer, and that particular chapter ended with all the middle-aged people being a little bit giddy. Jesus. Was it *so* boring being old that a spot of light flirting made everyone blush?

I clicked the sound off and watched the clip again. A goal scored from a counterattack. It was something that happens hundreds of times a year. *Thousands* of times a year. "Mike, mate, I have no idea what I'm looking at."

"Don't you recognise the teams?"

"No."

"The one conceding from the corner . . . that's Alfreton Town." I still didn't get it. "Max! That's exactly what you predicted!" He pulled out a piece of paper. "I have it here. When taking corners, Alfreton leave Garry Osgood as their covering player. He is slow, with poor technique, so Alfreton are vulnerable to a break. Chester should play their fastest strikers to take advantage of this weakness. Kin hell, Max! This is Nostradamus stuff!"

I shook my head. "It's trivial. Anyone could see that."

"No!" He very nearly slammed his fist into the table but controlled himself. "No, Max. It's trivial to you. It's trivial to Jackie. Yes! It's trivial to Henri Lyons, and holy shit was it weird to see him being your assistant. I have to apologise for calling him a nutjob. Shows what I know. Do you know he did more for our disabled programme in one morning than any of Chester's first team have ever done? Yeah, anyway. Let's put everything together. You can scout. You know tactics. You take one look at a seemingly healthy youth team and say it's got six months to live." He looked around furtively and spoke in a whisper. "And the people who hate you are the ones I've always thought were total shits." Delighted with his indiscretion, he was about to take a big swig of beer, when he remembered something else. Much too loud, he said, "And you can get bloody Jackie Reaper to sing your praises and fucking Henri Lyons to be your *youth team assistant!*" He beamed at me like I was a table full of horny Mancunian women he could choose from. "You've got a bleeding *enormous* football brain in there. Enormous. I shouldn't say this, but when I saw that corner routine and the goal I got really excited. You may be the answer to all my problems, Max! I need someone with a football brain. Someone who can spot talent, see points of failure in our culture, help on the tactical side. Imagine it! Someone who could help me find good players for free. Stop me wasting money on shitheads. Improve the youth setup. Help us win games! Help us get promoted! Get back into the football league. Where we belong." The guy couldn't hold his drink, so I was alarmed to see him take another massive swig of beer. "Max. I need someone who can help me on football matters and won't take shit from anyone."

This was too much to take in. I hadn't really been expecting anything in particular, and I thought I was ready for anything Mike Dean could throw at me. But it sounded like . . . player recruitment, player development, tactical input, the conduit between the money people and the football people . . . . Yes, it really sounded like . . . "Mike, are you saying you want me to be Chester's Director of Football?"

69

THE PROMISED LAND

What's the busiest train station in the world? I'm not sure what Trivial Pursuit would say, but the real answer is: my head: hundreds of trains of thought departing in all directions.

Director of Football! I'd be in charge of most of the football stuff. Contracts. Buying and selling players. Improving the squad. Making sales, reinvesting in better players while improving the facilities. That shitty little gym had to go. How much did a cryotherapy chamber cost? The youth facilities needed *millions* to get up to par. (Southampton's academy looked like a UFO. Man City's covered about four postcodes.) Tactical unity. Every age group should play the way the first team did. I wouldn't get to choose *that*, the manager would, but I'd be able to discuss it with him. Maybe there'd be two main formations that could cover most game states. We'd have a Chester style of play, and every kid that came through would be taught it. Every new signing would fit the profile. The club would become my personal little progression fantasy, constant, incremental improvement.

Constant? Hmm. There was, presumably, a limit to how far good management could take Chester. Even if we got to the Championship (tier two), our attendance would be quite low just because of geography and population. We were stuck next to Liverpool *and* Manchester! So even if I traded well and got the entire club aligned to my way of doing things, there would be a ceiling.

I instantly rejected the notion. Or to put it in other words: fuck that.

We would hit the ceiling . . . and smash it to bits. *No one* had my advantages. As Director of Football I could relentlessly hammer them.

I'd find the hottest talents in the region; we'd develop them and sell them for millions. We'd keep doing it, year after year. Meanwhile,

I'd bring in a mix of undervalued free transfers (players whose contracts at other clubs had come to an end), veterans who'd take a low wage just to stave off retirement for another year, and whatever ragtag band of misfits I found here, there, and everywhere. And while other teams laughed at us, I'd know that we had assembled the best team in our division.

We'd win relentlessly and make money every step of the way.

And yeah . . . maybe we'd have to sack a manager every now and then. And I'd step into the hot seat. Just for a few games, you understand. Reluctantly, you understand. Except, weirdly, we'd win every game I managed. And Mike Dean would say, "Max, I've just had a crazy idea," and I'd say, "Gosh, pray tell."

As my brain drowned in happy chemicals, I heard the voice of the football commentator Clive Tyldesley: *"And Max Best has reached the promised land!"*

The crowd roared!

Which is to say: the blonde, the brunette, and the ginger laughed at some joke.

Back in a quite-good curry house in Manchester, I looked at Mike Dean. The happy chemicals hopped onto the nearest train, the trains zoomed through portals, and the train station vanished. Mike Dean was . . . well, frankly, he was sniggering. And not at the joke.

"Sorry," he said, and tried to control himself. "It's just . . ." and he was away again.

So he didn't want me to be Chester's DoF. Well, *duh*. Vivid imagination strikes again! "I see." I picked up my fork. Food was getting cold! "Yes, I see. You don't want to work alongside me. You want me to *replace* you."

That stopped the worst of the sniggering, at least. He let out one last contented sigh, then said, "Max, you haven't been listening."

"I have."

"You haven't. I'll try again. Chester are a *community club*. For the community, owned by the community. We don't have fifty thousand pounds a year to hire a Director of Football, and if we did there would be a big, public process, and I can tell you one thing. The role would not go to a twenty-five-year-old with almost no experience in the game."

"I'm twenty-two."

"You are? Shit." He shook his head. "Now if I sent out an email right this minute announcing that I'd hired a nobody to advise me on football matters, I'd be out of a job by kickoff tomorrow. And as I said, my absolute priority is to make sure Chester has enough income to survive. Last Sunday you caused havoc with our youth team, and one of the parents of one of the kids is a sponsor. That's eight thousand pounds a year, Max, that you put at risk. I see from your face that eight thousand doesn't sound like a lot. It's a lot to Chester. That's what I'm trying to say. And by the way, it's not just the money. That boy you took against, he's a Chester lad and a Chester fan. All his mates wear Liverpool tops. Man City tops. He's in our colours, and he's proud. Even if you don't rate him, you can't shoot him. Because murdering our fans is suicide. Is that clear? If you want to work with us and live out your football fantasies, you're going to have to be more diplomatic. A *lot* more diplomatic. Show me and everyone else that you can put the needs of the club before your own brand of football fascism. Do you get what I'm saying?" He'd gotten a bit worked up, and him telling me off got him a bit more attention from the ladies. "You being rough around the edges is fine. It means I get you cheap. Because look, you're right. I need a Director of Football-type person, don't I? Like you say, it should be Ian Evans, but the plan is for him to see out his contract. That's until the summer. Then we'll, you know."

I did know. Spectrum had told me. "Bring in one of the first-team coaches who has more progressive ideas."

He narrowed his eyes. How had I heard *that*? "Something of the sort. Point is, Ian isn't really a patient man. Doesn't think there's any point explaining things to dullards like me."

"You're his boss," I said.

"Try telling him that," he said. "And the trust agrees with him."

"The trust?"

"City Fans United. They own the club. They. We. I'm in it. Take it from me, if I sell a player that Ian wants to keep, I'm going to have a very bad day. If I suggest he switches to 3-5-2, he's going to laugh in my face. I'm his boss literally twice. Once when I hire him, once when I fire him. In the meantime, he's the captain of the ship. So let's talk about you. I can't hire you in any meaningful role until you've got some experience."

"I can't get experience until someone hires me."

"Yep! It's like that story. A Gordian knot. But I wanted to meet today and tell you what I want. I want you to help me. There has to be a way. Start small. Grow the role over time. Do you see what I mean? And that'll be a kind of trial period, anyway." He tapped his phone. The video of the goal. Both videos of goals. "In case this was dumb luck."

"Mike, I don't get what you're saying. What role are you offering me?"

"I don't have anything specific. Imagine a big circle that describes your skills and a big circle that describes what I need. There's a ton of overlap. We just have to push the circles closer together in a way that the trust can understand. What role? I was hoping we could create one. Work something out, somehow. Salami tactics. I can't appoint you Director of Football, but I can expand your scouting duties. Then I can say you're going to help with youth recruitment. And then. And then. Are you with me?"

"Yes," I said. I did understand what he was saying. I did. And there *was* a lot of overlap between what he needed and what I could do. More than he knew. "There's a few issues, though."

He stopped me. "I know, Max."

He didn't want to talk about the issues, but I did. "Apart from Terry, how many people read the scouting report I gave you?"

"I don't know."

"How many do you *think* read it?"

"I don't know, Max. Maybe not that many."

I really, really wanted to work in football. But I'd rather write bland copy for a club website than be ignored by the "real football people." I wasn't the best driver in the world, but I knew a dead end when I saw one. "Mike, if I say to you that Tyson Bulldog should be cut, what are you going to do about it?"

He sighed. "Nothing. The youth team coaches decide those things. And it's better that way. Otherwise, the teams would be full of players with rich dads."

"I need a role where I can make decisions. Where people will take me seriously."

"You're going to have to earn that. Yes, it'll take years. But it's better than being in a call centre, right?"

I shook my head. "No. In the call centre, if there's an unhappy customer I'm allowed to upgrade their service for a while. I'm nobody, but even the lunatics who run the place trust me to do what's needed. Mike, I could *transform* the youth setup. Chester could have the most talented bunch of players in the country. Within a year. What you're saying, I think, is that you want me to write more reports that Ian Evans won't read and have an office and a computer inside a failing setup that I can't change." I was suddenly quite unhappy. "It'd be worse than the call centre. Emotionally. I think I'd rather stick to being an agent."

Mike kind of scowled at me. "So you're saying you aren't willing to work in a team? Discuss your ideas? You're right, and that's it?"

Yes. "If I recommend ten teenagers and you sign two, that's tragic. That's huge money you've thrown away. If those two players end up being blocked because Tyson is in their way, that's maddening. If those players end up in the same team as Tyson, and they start flapping their arms around too, then we've killed two more careers. I just . . ." I patted the table, emphasising certain words. "If I'm an agent then I get *paid*. I'm an outsider and things might not go as I'd want, but I get *paid*. If I worked for Chester, I'd want to *work* for Chester. That means doing what's best for the *squad*. Minmax. Minimum wages, maximum talent. I can't be an *outsider* on the *inside*. That's pointless! Do you . . . do you get what I'm saying?"

He dabbed his lips with his napkin. "I do. But I'm saying you can start as an insider on the outside." He did a funny cross-eyed gesture and laughed. "Max. Tomorrow night I'd like you to scout a very special game. Chester versus Oldham."

He'd lost his mind. "No, that was Saturday's game."

He smiled again. "So you don't know everything. That's good to know! Max, it's the FA Cup. The last qualifying round for the FA Cup. We drew in Oldham, and tomorrow's the replay."

"I thought there weren't any replays anymore because of Covid and the World Cup."

"That's for the big boys. Down here we do things the old way. Extra time and penalties, Max. One team goes through, and if they win another couple of games, they'll play the third round. You know what the third round is? It's when the big dogs are let loose. Imagine being drawn away to Man United! United's games are always on TV. In the cup, the money gets split. That one match could secure our future for two years! The magic of the FA Cup, Max! Come and watch it with me. We'll pay you. Same conditions, but you won't need a pie. You'll be in the Directors' Box. You can tell me what you see. And we can brainstorm."

A job in football . . . it was so close. So very close. But just out of reach. "Brainstorm how to be inside and outside at the same time?"

"Yes! Schrödinger's Director of Football!"

There was a lot to think about, but I didn't really want to think about it just then. MD MD was paying for the meal, and I was proving to be a cheap date. I thought it would be fun to see him flirting. I got the impression he hadn't done much recently. And yeah, pushing him out of his comfort zone might have been a bit of a punishment for him laughing at my daydream. So I turned to the ladies at the table next to us. "We've finished our big, important chat, and we're ready to be flirted with. I'm Max. This is Mike."

Mike, to my everlasting astonishment, spoke up. "And we know who you are."

The blonde said, "Who?"

"Charlie's Angels!"

There was a long but not unfriendly silence. I filled it. "Who's that?"

"Er . . ." Mike had lost confidence. "It's three women who are spies and have adventures."

"Oh!" said the ginger one. "That's a movie with Lucy Liu. Which one of us is her?"

"I didn't see that," said Mike. "I meant the old TV show. I think they had the same hair colour as you three. I only said you were Charlie's Angels because you're . . . pretty." His voice tapered off again. He was absolutely abysmal! Talk about having a last-minute penalty and hitting it miles over the bar.

So what happened next was, Mike turned red in the silence, and the contrast between him being all *top international businessman telling me off* and *awkward middle-aged man who got tongue-tied around women* was like fucking catnip to Charlie's Angels! They loved it! They were willing to give him a chance anyway.

All right, the universe was saying to me. Look. You don't have to get everything right the first time. You're allowed to make mistakes.

After a little bit of semi-playful chat—it would have been easier if more than twenty percent of the group had ever seen Charlie's Angels—I clapped my hands and rubbed them. "Are we staying here, or shall we go somewhere less classy?"

70

PLANTING SEEDS

Mike Dean had a good time, by his standards a legendary night on the tiles, until it was home o'clock, at which point he realised he'd have to spend the night in Moss Side. You'd think that would sober him up, but no. Even though *I* had the dodgy ankle, it fell to *me* to help *him* back to my place. When he found out there was only one bed, I worried he'd burst into tears, so I let him take it.

Down in my living room, I took the two cushions from my sofa and tried to create a sort of mattress from them. That didn't go well, and I ended up lying on my back with my right leg resting on the sofa, eyes closed but wide awake, until 5 a.m. when MD woke up and got dressed. He left, groggy, to find his car, and I thought I'd slip into the bed and get a few hours kip. It was a bit moist from Mike's beer sweats, so I threw all the bedding into the machine and abandoned all hope of sleep.

Fortunately, I had a lot to think about. In a way, the calculation was simple. Mike would give me a job at Chester if he could, and I'd take it if people would listen to me.

I'd take it if . . . where had that *if* come from?

I should take any job they'd give me and bide my time until a better opportunity came my way. So what if parts of the job would be frustrating? If I worked for Chester for a year, that would make me much more attractive to some other club. I'd have a year of experience! And Jesus Christ, Max. Being frustrated by your job *in a football club* was a million times better than being frustrated working in a bank. Get a grip!

So yeah. I'd go and watch Chester versus Oldham, and I'd be open-minded about what Mike was proposing. Barriers, obstacles, potential problems, so what? Being ignored by Ian Evans? Being laughed at by the coaches? Being the loser in the battle with the Bulldog Brothers? Lying there on my pitch-black living room floor, waiting for the day to start, wishing I owned a hundred pound IKEA sofa bed or even just a sleeping bag, yeah, I could take whatever shit the footballing world had to throw at me.

Absolutely I could.

By the way, Mike Dean snores.

Before work, I spent a while sending out texts. Better late than never!

I started with Jackie, thanking him for giving Ziggy a chance. I asked Ziggy how he was feeling. I sent Kisi, Raffi, and Emma a still image of Ziggy going wild. I sent Henri Lyons a string of heart emojis. I messaged Bill Brown, my contact at Oldham, saying I'd be seeing his team play again, and if he was going to Chester would he join me for a quick pint? I texted the ginger one from Charlie's Angels asking her to let me know if either of her friends wanted to see Mike Dean again. (She never replied.)

At lunch, I asked Raffi to call me. We talked about the ideal day for him to pop down to Chester and show his stuff. I told him that he should work on his fitness as though he'd signed a pre-contract because one way or another, it was going to happen. He said he'd been doing his old boxing routines and was already feeling a lot trimmer. I mentioned that I'd asked Ziggy to jump on his bed to improve his jumping skill, and there was a long silence. "I'm not joking," I said. And he said, "I know. That's what worries me."

I finished my shift with a few lovely chats with African customers and one surprisingly fascinating chat with an elderly English lady who had been raised as a strict Anglican but now, as she aged, wondered if it had all been worth it.

In the context of me trying to get James Yalley to play football, these chats were fascinating. Absolutely riveting. But had I sat in a church on a Sunday morning and had the same conversations, I would have been bored to bits.

I logged off and drove straight to Chester. I got to the stadium before Mike Dean and parked in his spot.

If he complained, our deal was off.

The dude owed me.

Chester FC. The Deva Stadium. Capacity: sixty-five hundred. Attendance on the night: just under four thousand. The competition? The FA Cup Fourth Qualifying Round. The prize for winning? Progress through to the FA Cup First Round. The third round came with the potential for a match against one of the biggest teams in the world. Huge prestige, huge excitement, and a huge influx of cash.

The Directors' Box. The best seats in the entire stadium, except (in my opinion) for the manager's dugout. The best view, the best grub: Belgian beer on tap, British cheese by the wheel, French wine by the jeroboam. Plus, American cinema-style comfy chairs, Austrian sound-proofed windows for those more serious chats, Italian three-ply toilet rolls. It was very nice.

Annoyingly, I wasn't alone with MD. There was space for about twenty in there, and the place was packed with people who had their own Wikipedia pages. But I eventually realised this was MD's plan. A chance for me to meet some movers and shakers, some of the big names in Chester and the trust that owned the club. I experienced a flash of annoyance. Why couldn't MD have told me? I might have rented a suit, or at least worn my work clothes instead of a Sports Direct hoodie. But then again, I was hardly blameless on the "not telling people my plans" score. And maybe him dropping me into this unexpected social situation was his revenge for me merging our duo with Charlie's Angels, which was my revenge for him laughing when I thought I was getting the Director of Football job.

Truly, if you go looking for revenge you should dig two graves, I thought to myself as I sipped from a bottle of wine that cost more than all the clothes I was wearing.

Anyhow, I turned up the charm with most of the bigwigs. There were a few business type dudes: sponsors or potential sponsors, I guess. With them I achieved "charm" by flirting with their wives. Not even flirting, really. Just saying things like, "If I move to Chester, promise you'll tell me where you get your hair done." Just inane shit like that. Bit of attention. They love it.

The guests of honour were a couple of former players wearing retro kits. They called themselves Smasho and Nice One, and that's what it said on the backs of their shirts. Consistent branding! The three of us really got into the weeds, discussing tactics; the recent changes in the offside and handball rules; Messi versus Ronaldo; and VAR, the video assistant referee that was saving football/destroying football, delete as appropriate. Great fun! I guess they were normally bored to tears in this type of gathering and were ecstatic to find someone who spoke their language. When Mike came to join the group, they took the piss out of him for having an opinion. Well, I put a stop to that sharpish. Stern face. No messing. "I'd rather talk to Mike about footy than ninety-nine percent of the people in this country. Most pricks think they know everything. Mike knows he doesn't. So when he *does* have an opinion, I find it's worth listening to." And I stared them out. Well, it killed the mood for about five seconds, but they relented. One agreed with me, and the other said he'd never thought about it like that. And I wasn't just blowing smoke up MD's arse either. I really meant it. If I went round pretending to be an expert in the pharma industry, I'd expect to be mocked by the actual experts, too.

Mike was pleased, I think, but forced me to mingle.

One of the guys was the mayor, but his job was to be in the photos. No one wanted to actually talk to him.

There were five or six people from City Fans United. Basically normal people chosen at random to be in the big box for Chester's biggest game of the year. They kept themselves to themselves, as we say in Britain. I guess they felt a bit out of place. I tried to talk to them but Mike kept steering me away. Probably some internal politics.

Speaking of . . .

Mike introduced me to this guy. Let's call him "Politician 1." If you held a gun to my head and said "tell me his name," I wouldn't. It'd be like naming a tumour. The guy gave me very sinister vibes right from the start, before I even knew he was the local MP. He was the person in the room most attuned to status, I think, and he was fascinated by me. Everyone else was, apart from the trustees, the cream of the crop. Chester's economic, cultural, or football elite. So who the fuck was I? The mystery fascinated him, and he rightly assumed that I was a coming power that he should get to know. But my hairs stood on end as soon as I saw him, and when he tried to talk to me I just felt . . . I just felt urgh.

[The previous sentence has been nominated for Sentence of the Year. Please vote.]

"Hi, I'm Politician 1," he said, holding out his hand.

I shook it because there are norms in society, but holy fuck I'd have sawn my hand off instead had there been a suitable tool. "Max Best," I said.

"I'm the MP for the City of Chester," he said. "I haven't seen you around before?"

It was a transparent attempt to make me defend my presence and thus reveal who I was. Did that work on people? I stared into his soul and saw he didn't have one. "What's your stance on wave machines in the English Channel?" I said.

He reacted like I'd announced my intention to shoot his kneecaps off. "Er . . . I'm against it. I'm in the *Labour* Party."

"Right," I said. Bland. Unsmiling.

The interaction unnerved him. "That's the other lot," he said, and he scuttled away.

The ex-pros, if they'd been put out by my defence of Mike Dean, were all the way back on my side. "Well played, Max!" said Nice One. "Good riddance," said Smasho. "That guy creeps me out."

And now that I'd mingled and exorcised our demon, we could start talking shit again. "Who'd win," I pondered, "the Chester team that you played in, or this one?"

Fun fun fun.

Cheese, wine, kittensoft toilet roll.

It was like a Christmas party . . . until the match kicked off.

The jolly, upbeat, hopeful mood didn't survive a quarter of an hour. By the time of the first goal, I'd already told MD and the ex-pros about the formations (4-4-2 on both teams), the mentality (defensive on both teams), the likely winner (Oldham), the most likely goalscorer (Fondop), and more importantly, the likely entertainment value (close to nil). Smasho and Nice One had a much higher opinion of Ian Evans, and we had a bit of a bicker about it.

Oldham's Ben Tollitt scored an unreal goal after ten minutes, and that seemed to confirm what I knew and the others feared: the away team was superior and Chester's FA Cup dreams were over before they even really began. Smasho and Nice One weren't so keen to defend Evans after that. Reader, I felt like a smug twat. Sorry not sorry. But actually, sorry a little bit.

Twenty minutes in, MD took me to the side and asked if I'd thought about what he'd said about being an outside insider. I said I had, nonstop, but that nights like this were so frustrating. Ian Evans could tweak sooo many little things but he *didn't*. If the manager never changed anything, what did that say about the culture of the club? How would I fit in? And he said he knew, he knew, and pottered over to schmooze some rich people.

Half an hour in, MD came back. I softened my stance. "Me as DoF is a long way off, sure, but there are seeds we can plant. But I don't want to plant them if you-know-who is going to be in charge of the tractor." He said my metaphor was confusing him, and he reminded me that he hadn't had much sleep. So I clarified. "Hire me as a full-time scout. I'll find you loads of good players. Cheshire and North Wales must be full of hidden gems. We can bring in a *shitload* of quality prospects. It won't cost much, but they won't be ready until next season or the one after that. So the next manager needs to be one who'll *use* them. Yeah?" MD said great, sure, but what about *this* season? And I suggested Chester sign Henri Lyons, and he tutted like I was teasing him and went to make sure everyone had enough booze. I noted that he wasn't drinking himself. Sensible.

Forty minutes in, he was muttering in my ear again. Was I serious about Henri Lyons? Was he good enough to make a difference? "Yes," I said. "He's way better than what you've got. The only question is, if you sign him, will Evans pick him?" It wasn't the *only* question. There were millions of other questions. But that was a good one to start with. "We'll have to introduce them," mused MD. "See how they get on." Fair enough.

At half-time, I left the box to find Bill, the hospitality guy from Oldham. We had a five-minute chat. That was enough to delight him. Plus, he was disposed to be delighted because his team were playing well. He was happy to see I was "finding my feet." He was referencing the progression from the tiny VIP box he'd sat me in, to an actual Directors' Box. Yeah. It *was* progress, wasn't it?

"What ah . . ." He was trying to frame the question in a discreet way. "What are you in there for? I mean, if it's not too personal."

"Career opportunities," I said, with a smile that meant the conversation was not necessarily over.

He grinned. "What do you hope to get out of this evening? A job offer?"

"Honestly, Bill, I'd be happy with a job *description*."

He did an intelligent sort of frown, trying to assemble an entire backstory based on the little info I'd given him. The buzz of the crowd increased. The players were coming back out.

I wished him luck for the second half.

Before going back into the box, I found a quiet corner to hide in. I needed to collect my thoughts.

Seeing Ian Evans and his absolute refusal to make the smallest tactical changes was really hard to stomach. Could I deal with that twice a week until the summer of 2023? Of course I could. Every time I had doubts, I recalled the discomfort and boredom of the night before.

I took some deep breaths and steeled myself. I wanted a job.

Steeled as I was, I don't think anything could have prepared me for what came next.

71

HOME TO ROOST

When I say "next" I don't mean the next ten minutes of the match, because they were fairly mediocre. I was concentrating, gathering XP, checking the match ratings and the commentary and all the other things. By the way, I'd reprogrammed the curse to show me the match ratings in my normal vision even if I was looking away from the pitch. So I could *seem* to be giving a vice president of a biotech company my full attention while also keeping track of what was happening behind me. For now, I had that plus the match clock. Next, I'd add the commentary, then the match overview. I could make the "widgets" more opaque or more transparent with barely a thought. It was getting to be a pretty slick user interface.

What I started to notice in those ten minutes was that none of the people in the Directors' Box wanted to talk to me. It was quite a big change from the first half, when I'd appeared as fresh and exotic.

And in most cases, I didn't really care, but I was a bit surprised that Smasho and Nice One were snubbing me. They were over at the back of the box in deep discussion with each other and what looked like WhatsApp. But whatever. I focused on the match.

At a certain point I went to get a refill on wine, then thought better of it. I had to drive home and didn't want to crash on the motorway *or* crash on MD's sofa. So I grabbed a big bottle of Evian and took it back to the corner.

"Gizzasip," said Nice One, settling into the chair next to me. That's "give me a sip," in case your English to English translator doesn't know that one. He held out a glass, and I filled it with water. "Cheers."

"Cheers," I said, drinking from the bottle.

"Ahem," he said. That is, he made a weird noise that signalled he had something awkward to say.

"Sup?"

"Max. We were saying how you really knew your onions. Really impressed." Oh! My heart jumped a bit. This was good. Smasho and Nice One were Chester FC royalty. Everyone here looked up to them, even the multi-millionaires. But then the overall vibe hit me, and my heart sank. "And at half-time we mentioned you to one of the coaches down in the dressing room. We just popped round to have a decko, yeah? Not sticking our noses in or anything. But me and Smasho, we made it to the fifth round so it's not like we're lepers, know what I mean? Anyhoo," he sipped his water. "We mentioned we'd met this smart young man in the box and . . ."

Smasho arrived with a big glass of wine. Hopefully, he wasn't driving. "And they said you're a prick," he said, laughing.

Nice One gave his mate an irritated glance. "They didn't say *that*. But yeah. They said there was . . . an incident. At a youth team game. Under-sixteens, was it? And we'd like to hear your side of the story. Give you a fair hearing and that."

Well, this was a tester. In theory, if I handled this right, I could get two legendary players onto Team Best. Handy. But honestly, as soon as he said the word "incident," I just crumpled. All the energy seeped out of me. I'd have to start again at some other club. Clean slate. Don't stir up a hornet's nest on day one. I half wanted to lash out and defend myself. It would be futile, but it would be immensely satisfying. Instead, I said, "Whatever they said, they were right."

Nice One wasn't buying it. "Come on, Max."

I shook my head. "I'm not here to rock the boat. In the end, everyone's doing their best and trying their hardest, and all I want is for Chester to do well. Do you know what I mean? I'm not . . . I'm not . . ." I couldn't really think how to end the sentence. So I just took a breath, and said the first thing that came into my head. "What happened is on me."

There was a little raised platform that the big sheet of glass in front of us was set into, and Smasho sat down on it. "I hear you. We're not asking you to dob anyone in." Not asking me to become an informant. "We've heard one side of the story. We just want to hear yours." He jabbed his thumb behind him. "It'll be more interesting than the game at least."

I put the water down and rubbed my temples. "Fine. Quick version. MD let me coach the under-fourteens. Just getting some practice in.

They were doing 3-5-2, and that was great for me because I hadn't done that before. Ten minutes, everything's peachy. Suddenly things are going haywire, four kids out of position, and, let's be honest, anyone with a bit of experience would instantly know what was wrong. But because it was me, I was clueless. So someone explains it's the parents. Midfielders being told to play striker. Shit like that. I mean, I'm not a parent. I can't know what it's like. Maybe I'd be the same. Probably I'd be worse! But I took it personally, which was dumb, and I subbed off the four players and put on my only reserve. Yes, I played with eight. That's pretty much the whole story. I just lost my mind for a minute."

Smasho was grinning like I'd told him how I'd injured one thumb demonstrating how I'd injured the other thumb. "You played with eight? Against eleven?"

"Yep."

Nice One rolled his hand in front of me. "Go on."

"That's it."

"That's not it. Surely someone tried to talk some sense into you."

"Well, yeah. Mike Dean. He made me talk to the parents and sort things out. But they weren't really into it. To be honest, I was happier playing with eight. I did a big half-time speech about teamwork and shit."

"I heard," said Nice One, with extreme care, "that you actually had nine players to choose from."

"Oh yeah," I said, remembering. "The first kid wasn't being misled by a parent. He'd been sort of displaced, and then he sulked a bit."

"What was his name?" said Smasho.

"Benny."

"What do you think about him as a player? As a kid?"

"Yeah, good. Annoyed me at first but turned it round. Got potential." Something occurred to me. "You know, whoever you've been talking to, they've got their own agenda. And obviously I've got mine. If you really want the hot goss on that day, you should go to the four-teens, and talk to Benny."

"Why him?"

"He was one of the ones subbed off, so it'd be fair if he had an axe to grind. But he was the only one I let back on. Who knows what he thinks about it, but he'd be your best bet for an unbiased view of the day. His version would be colourful at least."

Nice One rubbed his eyebrow. "I still don't get why you played with eight when you had nine available. That's cutting off your nose to spite your face, isn't it?"

No, I thought. "Yes," I said.

"Max," said Smasho.

I flapped my arms around. "Look, I'd made a big half-time speech about teamwork and how if they started fucking trying it, they could win with eight! Playing with nine would have defeated the point! Anyway," I sighed. "With a sub I could keep giving tactical advice. Tips. Praise." I was annoyed that I'd been sucked back into this conversation. It was worthless. My head rocked back, and I looked at the ceiling. When I looked back down, Smasho and Nice One were grinning at me. "What?"

Nice One said, "Is your name Max . . . Best?"

"Yes."

He nodded at Smasho, who pressed a button on the wall. All the sound from the stadium . . . ceased. The rest of the bigwigs turned to give the perpetrator the evil eye, but when they saw it was their former star, they simply shrugged and got on with their conversations.

Nice One was tapping on his phone. Soon he was doing a video call.

"Hey, Benny." Uh-oh.

"Dad!" Uh-oh! "What's the score?"

"One-nil down," said Nice One.

"Aww."

Well, wasn't this dreamy? One of the kids I'd hauled off the pitch was the son of a former player. At least I hadn't slagged the kid off. But this was not good. How do you say muy muy no bueno in Spanish?

"You remember that game against Broughton? You had that special coach?"

"Yeah. Mr. Best."

"We were just talking about him here. I'm trying to remember what happened, so I can tell everyone. So you had to play with eight, didn't you? Eight against eleven. How did you feel about that?"

"Not good."

I slumped forwards, head in hands. I turned the match ratings off. This evening didn't matter. After today, I'd be back to square one. I'd be lucky if Chester paid for my petrol. Chickens were coming home to roost.

"And then after the game, what did you tell me?"

Benny sighed. He was bored of this story. I couldn't blame him. "I said I didn't want to play for Chester anymore."

Jesus fucking Christ. No! No! No, Benny, no!

"Why not?"

"Dad, you know this."

"Just tell me. It's important."

Benny sighed. "Because I want to play for a proper team like Mr. Best said."

Stop the presses! Breaking news! I perked up, I can tell you.

Nice One continued. "And there's been a bit of a rumpus, hasn't there? Because some people are sick of some people's attitude. And it's all a bit dramatic. Isn't it?"

"*You* love the drama. I just want to play football."

"What would you say to Mr. Best if he was here?"

"Dunno. Just when's he coming back."

"Well, he's here right now."

Nice One handed me the phone, and in those few seconds, Benny had moved from where he was lying prone on his bed NOT doing his homework to sitting bolt upright on a hard-backed chair. It was that gesture that got me.

"Hello Benny," I said. Keeping it together. Face and tone bordering on stern.

"Mr. Best!"

"Do you really want to leave Chester?"

"No, but . . . but . . ."

"How about you stay for now while I try to help sort things out?"

"Okay! Will you be our new manager?"

Careful, Max. "You just focus on what you need to do."

His dad leaned into frame. "Benny's been training like a demon," he said.

"I do a hundred kick-ups a day!" said Benny.

I frowned at him. "Kick-ups?" Kicking the ball so that it doesn't touch the floor. I was always terrible at it.

"Yeah!"

"Why? Do you do kick-ups in games?"

"Er . . . no."

"So what sport are you training for? Benny, you need to train skills you do *in the game.* You're in your back garden, yeah? In trainers? You don't play in trainers, you play in boots. When you want to drag the ball back in a game, suddenly you've got studs in your way." Studs. Cleats. You're smart. You get it. "Train skills you can use in matches. Roll the ball around in a figure eight. Get used to the feel of the studs on the ball. Shoulder drops. Drop and burst left. Drop and burst right. Can you make the movement look the same?"

He was absolutely rapt. But he snapped out of it. "Dad won't let me wear boots on the lawn."

I gave Nice One a withering look before I knew what I was doing. I shook it off my face. "I'm going to have a little chat with him now about getting a bit of astroturf put down so you can train in your boots. All right?"

"Yes, Mr. Best!"

"I'll see you around, Benny."

I hit the red button on the phone and stared at the silent pitch.

Oldham attacked, lost the ball, and Chester broke quickly. On the left, Aff burst forward at great speed. Smasho pressed the button that let the sound back in. Everyone in the box who wasn't paying attention turned, shocked by the sudden increase in decibels. Aff got to the edge of the penalty area, far on the left, and crossed the ball. A Chester striker had made a great run, and headed the ball downwards. It bounced where the goalie had no chance to get it, then up into the roof of the net.

The stadium went wild. *Wild.* It was pandemonium.

The noise hit me and deflected away. I was in a kind of trance, like my brain was trying to protect me from an overwhelming surge. Benny, mate.

Benny. *Mate.*

After hugging Smasho and jumping round a bit, Nice One went "whoo!" and turned to get his phone. He saw me in a bit of a state and gave me a hug too. He kept one arm round my shoulder, and he punched me in the ribs with the other. "Max," he said, as I tried to clean my face up. "Everyone knows who Benny is. It's hard being a famous kid in the youth teams. People don't want to tell him off because he's got a famous dad. Yeah? You've come in, bull in a china shop, this is shit, that's shit, and everything you've said is everything the kids already know but they've never heard from anyone. Are you with me? Maybe it was stupid, maybe it was fearless. I couldn't give two flying figs. You got through to my son and, oh my days, many have tried and failed." He gave me one last dig. "I'm going to have to get a quote for astroturf now, aren't I? No wonder everyone says you're a prick." He grinned. "Next time, tell him to tidy his room."

You know that thing in movies where people are crying, and they do one single ugly laugh? It's so unrealistic. I hate that I did it.

I was in a bit of emotional turmoil. The doubts and the fears passing through and competing with the hopes and the pride. So what I needed was a nice, calm end to the match. Oldham to score, Chester's subdued fans to leave the stadium. All nice and soothing.

The universe said: nah.

Chester's equaliser provoked a fucking maelstrom, on and off the pitch.

Whatever Ian Evans had said to his players at half-time, he'd transformed them. Where the left-midfielder, Aff, had been manic in the first half, now he was playing with a kind of controlled fury. Sam Topps, an aggressive pitbull guy whose usual job was fouling opponents, was suddenly playing like Roy Keane, moving the ball around, dictating the tempo of the game, tackling with such purity fouls didn't come into it. A velvet fist in an iron glove.

But Oldham reacted, and all their match ratings went up, too. So these twenty-two guys were just smashing each other, again and again. Attack, chance! Attack, chance! Like basketball. End to end. Utterly unbelievable passages of play, and with every near-miss the noise increased by one decibel.

In extra time, Chester scored, and the crowd were in an absolute frenzy. The Deva Stadium was as deafening as any Turkish cauldron. Nice One and Smasho hugged each other, and, in delirium, I threw myself into the mix and bounced around with these local superstars.

Ian Evans Blue and White Army!
Ian Evans Blue and White Army!

Mate. I was along for the ride. Yeah, I joined in the chant. Why the fuck not? The man was a titan. A legend.

And then.

One minute of extra time left. Oldham's dangerman, Fondop, scored. Holy shit, I've never been more unhappy to be proven right.

Fucking no, mate! Fondop my dude. Not now!

The match went to penalties. The VIPs weren't chatting about fucking trade deals or pharma conferences or whatever. They'd gone feral. Me too. Mike Dean looked like a caricature of a villain: massive, bulging eyes; throbbing veins. We were all holding each other, jumping around, a riotous mass, reacting with ecstasy to every scored penalty, wailing and gnashing our teeth at every missed one.

It played out so that Oldham had two chances to win. They missed the first one—pandemonium—and Chester's next penalty went in. Still in the game! Still in with a shot! But the away team scored the second. For the home fans, motionless despair.

The Oldham players ran around, hugging, falling into little groups. They were going into the FA Cup. Chester's lads fell to the floor, head in hands, spent.

I nearly joined them. I was shattered.

Football. Bloody hell.

I waited in the Directors' Box. There was no point trying to leave until the traffic cleared. The bigwigs whizzed away in their private monorails or whatever, and in the end it was just me and Mike Dean watching the ground-staff poke the grass with long forks.

"Mike," I said. "I've made a decision."

"Yeah?"

"There's an easy way to become an insider. There's a job where people will listen to what I say. Where I can turn up to youth matches and no one will bat an eyelid. Where the sponsors will be happy to see me. You won't even have to change the org chart."

He frowned. "Max, I'm on no sleep. It's been a long day. We're out of the Cup. Can you just . . ."

I pointed to one of the framed Chester FC shirts that was hanging on a wall, signed by two former players. Legends. Allies.

Mike raised his eyebrows. "Do you mean . . . ?"

I leaned against the glass and stared onto the pitch. A place where all my dreams could come true. "I want my own parking space. I want a goal bonus. And I want shirt number seven."

ABOUT THE AUTHOR

Ted Steel is the author of the Player Manager series, which features a charming but secretive main character. He also wrote *Nerves of Steel*, a LitRPG featuring a charming but secretive main character. When asked to provide a bit of colour for his biography, Steel was charming but . . . secretive. Learn more at www.ted-steel.com.

Podium

DISCOVER
STORIES UNBOUND

PodiumAudio.com

Milton Keynes UK
Ingram Content Group UK Ltd.
UKHW011430140724
445326UK00001B/91

9 781039 438392